THE OX STUNNER

"Thick enough to stun an ox"

Comprises the Triangle trilogy
The Triangle
The Square
The Circle

Ed Adams

a firstelement production

Ed Adams

IT HAD TO BE DONE

There's individual 'Thanks' pages for each of the three novels that follow in this 'Ox Stunner' edition. The Triangle was always envisaged as a trilogy and this is the first attempt to publish the three books together.

I've always wanted to have a book that I could call an 'Ox Stunner'.

Thank you, Laurie Anderson:

You know, I could write a book
And this book would be thick enough to stun an ox
Cause I can see the future and it's a place
About 70 miles east of here
Where it's lighter
Linger on over here
Got the time?

Let X = X

And thank you, dear reader, for at least 'giving it a go'.
Published in Great Britain in 2020 by first element
Directed by the six twenty

10 9 8 7 6 5 4 3 2 1   All rights reserved.

ISBN : 978-1-8380146-0-5
Ebook ISBN : 978-1-8380146-1-2

Printed and bound in Great Britain by Ingram Spark

Ed Adams
an imprint of first element rashbre@mac.com

Mailing list: https://mailchi.mp/9f0b30712620/ed_adams

The Triangle

Ed Adams

a firstelement production

Ed Adams

Ed Adams

First published in Great Britain in 2009 by bubbleandsqueek
Published in Great Britain in 2020 by first element
Directed by the six twenty

A CIP catalogue record for this book is available from the British Library.

ISBN : 978-1-9163383-2-6

Ebook ISBN : 978-1-9163383-3-3

Printed and bound in Great Britain by
Ingram Spark

Ed Adams
an imprint of first element
rashbre@mac.com

Mailing list: https://mailchi.mp/9f0b30712620/ed_adams

The Triangle

For Mum

Ed Adams

THANKS

Thanks to first (partial) reviewer Melanie, full reviewer Debra and then expert proofer Chris.

Big thanks for the tolerance and bemused support from all of those around me.

Additional thanks to the NaNoWriMo gang for the inspiration to have a go at this.

And, of course, thanks to the extensive support for the random scribbles of rashbre via http://rashbre2.blogspot.com and its cast of amazing and varied readers whether human, twittery, smoky, London, Mediterranean, cool kats, Hollywood, photographic, musical, anagrammed, globalized or simply maxed-out.

We all know how mixed up the world ~~of blogging~~ can be and long may it continue.

Not forgetting the cast of characters involved in producing this, from Christina, Bigsy, Clare and Jake, right through to the made-up ones.

Oh, and to you, dear reader, for at least 'giving it a go'.

Contents

Book 1: The Triangle

PART ONE	**16**
Don't let it get to you	**17**
Art for art's sake?	18
Walking through walls	24
The Interview	30
Nothing leads South	40
Broken in	44
Delays and findings	48
Safety First	52
Sunshine and shades	**57**
Cannes	58
A business transaction	61
A matter of procedure	65
PART TWO	**70**
Puzzle Palaces	**71**
Langley	72
Sound reasoning	75
For the record	80
Crazy	**84**
An apple a day	85
Canned Heat	88
Dare	**94**
Meet the Russians	95
Sushi	102
Being elsewhere	116
Bigsy's	119
Bad	121

Any place in the world   **127**

    Brophy visits London   128
    Eurostar   132
    It gives you wings   135
    To the dance?   141
    Bouquet in Zurich   142
    Please identify yourself   148
    A hands-off approach   159
    Manners on a mission   163
    Fabric   165

PART THREE   **168**

Killer instincts   **169**

    Amelia gets personal   170
    Dillon, sounds a bit like Collins?   173
    Sand and vodka storm   176
    Secure grip   182

Inspiration   **185**

    Brophy considers a new name   186
    Manners makes a new friend   189
    Hammered out   192
    ZRH -> LHR (J Class)   194
    Faux synchronisation   196
    Run with it   198
    Clothes Match   202

Universal   **205**

    Staged   206
    The right kind of bill   215
    Serious Crimes Unit   219

Party Time   **225**

    Quiet evening in Kensington   226
    Endings or beginnings?   233
    Chapter Forty-five: Post   241

Book 2: The Square

PART ONE   249

NOW   251
Sand   **252**
  Cairo   253
London   **265**
  SI6   266
  Gerald   271
  Muhammad   279
  Lambeth Walk   290

TWO WEEKS EARLIER   295
The Pentagon   **296**
  Washington Alert   297
  Hoxton   305
Politician   **308**
  Defence Secretary   309
  Westminster Bridge   315
  Thames House   321
Walk like an Egyptian   **326**
  Coded binary   327
  Firepower   330
  Driscoll   335

NOW   339
Park Lane   **340**
  Car chase victims   341
  Mossad   348

New York bed 351
Unwind 363
Chuck goes to MI6 366

Manhattan **374**

Molly's 375
Léa 378
Anonymity 382
Take the AirTrain 384
Sleek brown tee shirt 386
Calling Chuck 388

La Côte d'Azur **390**

Croisette 391
Trip to London 399
Huxley's 401
Diversion 413
Truck One 420

PART TWO 423

THREE WEEKS AGO 424
Kent **425**

Ashford 426
Back to the lock-up 430
Containment 435

RIGHT NOW 442
Strong women **443**

Elisa Solomons 444
Mesopotamian Heritage? 468
Chuck's involvement 474

Planning a gig **479**

Birmingham Mailbox District 480
The Market Porter 486

Fake News   **491**

   Carson's meetings   492
   Weight throwing   498
   Tracker lock   502
   Bad America   505
   Brief Ramirez   508

Unstoppable   **512**

   Al Aktar   513
   Unstable   520
   Truck Two   523

PART THREE   529

Event Management   **530**

   The gig   531
   Listening in   537
   The crunch   541

Under Pressure   **546**

   Ramirez thoughts   547
   Unexpected guest   549
   Unbelievable   556
   Carson and Ramirez   562

Triangulation stations   **564**

   Showdown mechanics   565
   Bank   572
   The Anchor   576

Contents   **583**

Book 3: The Circle

PART ONE	**587**
Starting Out	**588**
Arizona	589
London	592
Sedona	596
How did we get away?	602
Sleepers and Ties	607
Campfire	611
Crossed Arrows	615
Esther	618
The Desert	**631**
Scottsdale, AZ	632
Mount Ord Trailhead	635
Elemental	638
Gas station	643
Missed calls	647
The I-17	651
Phoenix Airport	654
Navajo Nation	**659**
Dangerous bends	660
Saddle up	668
Esther's end	671
Homing in on the range	677
Starting a fire	685
How the people caught the sun	688
As above, so below.	694
Albuquerque	698
Hotel Parq Central	700
Legal document	711
Chucking it down	714
Ministry Moments	**718**
Penny for the Guy	719
The four winds	724

War Chalk 728
Vauxhall Cross 731
Amanda Miller 733
Route SI6 737
Cold Stone Creamery Jelly Belly jelly beans [TM] 741
Los Alamos 748
Tonto (Jay Silverheels) 753

PART TWO 759

Route 66 760

La Fonda 761
Cache 765
Loreto Chapel 769
Breakfast in Santa Fe 772
Quickcode 776
Shortcut to the museum 779
Galaxy Defenders 782
Leaving 788
Delta Seven loses it 791

Wagons roll 793

Interstate 794
Private Security 797
Frosting 799
Get your kicks on Route 66. 808
Taxi swap 812
Quesadilla and meatloaf 814
Durango 817
Kirtland 820

Bagels, Guns, Shacks and Oilfields 824

Einstein bagels for breakfast 825
Tonto One 830
Jake sifts 836
Safe shack 840
Second Amendment, 1789 845
Texan oilfields 849
Two hours west 854

Mormons came thru' a hole in the rocks　857

Bluff, Utah　858
Leaving, on a prop plan　863
Regular Jeeps from the carpool　871
Footsteps　875
The Groove　877
On the radio　880
Jake update　883
Predator　885
ScanEagle　893

PART THREE　896

Don't Mess with Texas　897

Houston　898
Refundable　903
Cowboy boots from Sheplers　906
SI6　923
Liaison　925
Joint Terrorism Task Force　933

You can't touch this　946

Trap　947
Conference Call　950
Tony Capaldi　958
AVGAS 110LL (blue)　963
All together now　965
International call　967
EnergyChina　970

Pressing the wrong buttons　972

Bunker　973
DEFCON　976
Amber Alert　979
Tom　982
Monumental　984
A quicker scramble　987

Know a pistol shot's effective range　989

The Triangle

UAV 990
DFW 994
Free to go 997

Let X = X
You know, it could be you
It's a sky-blue sky
The satellites are out tonight
Let X = X

Hug and kisses XXXX0000

Ed Adams

16

THE TRIANGLE
PART ONE

17

Don't let it get to you

A wise person should have money in their head,
but not in their heart. –
Jonathan Swift

Art for art's sake?

The white cube's sterile tranquillity gave no clue of the impending violence. Lucien took the programme for this Sloane Square gallery to orient himself. The white rooms serially displayed cutting edge art. Very different from the place he'd visited the last time he'd received private tickets. That had been a rather grim gallery the size and appearance of a newsagent's, somewhere out west — Graffiti art, decomposing artefacts on the floor and rats running free as part of the installation.

Not this time. It was clean pictures on clean walls in a gallery which Lucien had pretty much to himself. He looked towards the white space between the hanging pictures.

Pristine.

Then he noticed it from the corner of his eye. A fragile red line was arcing across the wall. A second line appeared as he looked at it. Then he felt it. The knife had done serious damage.

Then he felt nothing.

Outside, November graphite skies, gentle rain. A quiet, smartly dressed woman slowly left the gallery, flicked her umbrella up and walked across to a modern metallic BMW. The driver clicked the locks, she climbed into the back seat, and the vehicle slipped into the heavy traffic.

Hours later, across town, Jake Lambers was walking to the pub. He'd had a tough day. The boss had torn him off a strip about the expenses from his recent trip to Liverpool. He'd been trying to get "an exclusive" with a singer who was supposed to be "seeing" a footballer. It would have made an excellent insider piece, but the trip was doomed because he'd received incorrect information. Instead, he'd made the best of a lousy job in a lively city with a great nightlife. The expenses had only just arrived and, upon reflection, seemed excessive, mainly because there was no story. So now he was going to meet Bigsy and Clare to drown his sorrows.

The pub in Westminster was buzzing. There were no tables and pretty much a mob standing by the bar. It was early evening, and the local offices had tipped out into the neighbourhood, and the inevitable 'one before the train' ritual was in full flood.

"Jake, Jake – here!" called Bigsy – whose real name was Dave but had adopted Bigsy on account of his size and didn't mind this affectionate but somewhat politically incorrect nickname.

Bigsy had commandeered a prime corner spot at the bar and standing with him was Clare. They were well into their second drinks of the early evening. Bigsy had spotted Jake the moment he'd entered the bar in customary journalist semi-smart clothing, dark jacket and an open-necked white shirt.

"Can dress it up or dress it down", Jake had once explained. Bigsy was pleased to see Jake; he, Clare and Jake were the nuclei of a gang of friends who often met and attended many social functions together.

"Let's go to the Crown," said Bigsy, "this place is heaving!" As he spoke, Jake's phone rang – he knew it rang because it vibrated – you couldn't hear the phone above the pub noise.

"Just a minute," called Jake as he reversed out of the side door of the pub, back onto the busy street near Westminster tube. Only then did he notice the number – Mark, one of his other drinking buddies.

"Jake, it's Mark. Have you heard already? We've just been called about Lucien. He's been killed, at an art gallery."

Heavy traffic was passing, mainly a stream of buses and taxis. Jake couldn't take in this conversation. Was he hearing it badly because of the traffic or was it a wind up?

"Mark – are you pissed? This doesn't make sense!"

Mark repeated what he had said previously. To Jake, it felt like one of those occasions where he'd had to sober up suddenly when something big was about to go down after chucking-out time, except this time he wasn't drunk.

Jake started to take in that what he was hearing was true. Lucien had been murdered. Lucien, who he'd been with a few days previously. Jake watched as Clare backed out of the pub, pushing the door slowly with her hip, whilst still holding a glass of something. She caught Jake's eye and waited a few steps away from him.

"Jake – what is it? You look in shock!" she said in a teasing voice wagging a finger of her spare hand towards him because he'd only just arrived and then left them for his cell-phone. Jake noticed her expression change as she became aware that Jake was looking unusually grave.

Jake continued the conversation with Mark for a few moments longer and could see Clare listening and piecing together the fragments she could hear of the conversation. As he hung up, he looked towards Clare to begin to tell her.

"I think I heard most of it," she started to say. Jake knew Clare was smart and that she would very likely have figured out what had happened even from only hearing part of one side of the conversation.

"I'll get Bigsy," she continued, "you can tell us both together." Clare strode back into the pub and a few moments later the three of them were standing together on the pavement as Jake relayed the news from Mark about Lucien's murder. Jake said he'd agreed to go to visit Mark to get further information.

"Let's go," said Bigsy.

By this time, at the gallery, a full crime scene had been established. The detective in charge, Detective Inspector Trueman, had walked into what he knew was a professional hit. This crime scene wasn't casual violence; it was a clinically executed assassination. There was no weapon to see, but the precision of the knife was medical. To his surprise, Trueman had found himself thinking that the red arcs across the wall almost looked like part of the art exhibition.

Radios crackled, police forensics operated, cameras whined (they used to click, he thought, but now they've gone digital you hear the flash recharging more than the whirring sounds from the old motor drives). There was blue and white police tape — a lot of it. The white cube now looked messy, distorted and unclean.

"What is the story?" asked Trueman of the medical examiner checking the sprawled body.

"Quick version", replied the medic, "This was professional; fast, but with a lot of deliberate blood spill. Someone wanted this to get someone else very annoyed. I can tell you the usual things about the height and weight of assassin – probably a woman, by the way, but this looks like something from martial arts."

Trueman's assistant was Sergeant Andy Green. They had worked together for around three years and knew how each other operated. Trueman gestured to Green, "And what do we know about the victim?"

Green began to search the body, "er...Recent suit from Marks and Spencer; M&S tie too; this could all be a matching set." From one bloodied pocket he pulled out a driving license. "Lucien Deschamps - lives in Hampstead," he read from the card. "Normal bank cards, nothing special. There's an oyster card in here too, so he's probably a regular commuter. Seems to work in a corporate travel group according to this business card. Quite honestly, there's nothing out of the ordinary."

The processing continued, and Trueman called his station.

"We're coming in", he said, "We need to get some sense around this situation. A lot of people know about this already, what with this being a Press day at the gallery. It is impossible to stop the general news getting out, but I want us to keep anything else we find under wraps for a few more hours. If this is a serious crime, we need to decide how we want to release any findings."

Trueman looked across to Green and gestured with his eyes, "let's go", he called, and Green nodded back in agreement. Green was a modern law enforcer, DNA, CCTV, profiling, all part of the contemporary way. Trueman was more traditional, though respectful of modern techniques; he'd been through the various modernisation courses along the way but still had a strong belief in basic policing methods. They made a good team, because they complemented one another in the way they thought about cases.

By the time they reached the nearby Chelsea police station, Trueman had already called to obtain a search of police files for anything on Deschamps as well as basic enquiries with his employer and some general bank statements and phone bills. Nothing showed circumstances out of the ordinary. There didn't appear to be anything special about the victim.

"So, was the assassin clever at covering tracks?" queried Green, "or did the professional get the wrong person?" he suggested.

The Triangle

"I think we can rule out random violence," responded Trueman, "This was done by a cold-blooded professional killer, almost certainly a hit for someone."

"Maybe there was someone else in the gallery who was the real target? Or perhaps it is linked with the exhibition or owners?" ventured Green.

Trueman knew these were a long shots or mere guesses because most times a professional hitman would stake a victim for some time before making their move unless this was a request for sudden and violent action by someone, as yet, unknown. Trueman's time in the force meant he had come across some strange and twisted behaviours and much violence, but this one was giving him a powerful sensation which almost felt like personal danger.

Trueman and Green had looked through the records for who had appeared for this private viewing. The irony was that it was not even the main private viewing. The day was to get the artwork arranged and to invite the press to preview before the main event started. It meant there was hardly anyone at the gallery. Attendees were spinning through fast for impressions to write in their chosen media. The exhibiting artist was tucked away in a suite at the Dorchester like a film star handling successive repetitive interviews.

The razzmatazz of the exhibition was planned to start on Wednesday, some two days after the bloody incident.

Except now there had been a block put on the start by the police. A gallery filled with blue and white tape, police officers and the aftermath of serious crime didn't make for a good show unless it was some sort of warped installation piece.

Walking through walls

Late afternoon near Deauville, Northern France and a little Cessna plane landed smoothly. It taxied towards an edge of the small but rather exclusive airport. A dark Mercedes saloon waited while a woman climbed out of the flight. The driver shook hands with the woman who got into the back of the car which edged quietly away. The pilot busied himself with plane checking procedures in the closing light of a surprisingly pleasant November evening.

A little later, the same car pulled up at a distinguished hotel, which looked like a Norman manor. The passenger left the vehicle and, carrying no luggage, walked directly to the elevators and towards a room in the hotel.

In London, Jake, Bigsy and Clare had grabbed a cab to Mark's. Of them all, Mark was probably the staunchest friend of Lucien, and they had known one another for many years. Jake, Bigsy and Clare decided it was respectful to let Jake relay the news in more detail to Mark, alone. Bigsy knew a nearby pub, so he and Clare left Jake at Mark's door and walked the few yards to the pub.

Bigsy quickly scoped the room and selected a corner table. He and Clare made to claim it by depositing coats and then Bigsy approached the bar to order the drinks. Clare sat waiting, noting a strong slightly sweet-smelling aroma from the immediate surroundings. Bigsy returned, and they looked at one another.

"I know," said Clare, "I think its jasmine." They looked around, and then Clare pointed to a small white box at the same height as the music speakers. "There it is," she pointed.

"How American", said Bigsy "We can't go to a bar now without having perfume squirted at us; now if it was chips and whisky..." Bigsy trailed off. They sat in silence for a few seconds, except for the noise of Bigsy opening some 'flamed steak' potato crisps and spreading the opened packet on the dark oak table between them.

"...That news about Lucien was terrible," Bigsy eventually continued. Bigsy and Clare's eyes locked in agreement. They both had similar views about Lucien.

Bigsy tested the way he could say it, "He was a nice enough guy, but, er, quite quiet. I always found him pretty intense, and this could make him hard work for a whole evening".

Clare nodded agreement. "I think he was a little bit afraid of me or something. Not just shy. He didn't seem to find it very easy to talk to me and always looked as if he was getting ready to make apologies to move on."

They both knew that Lucien usually looked a little reserved and formal in his choice of clothes and general style. He always wore a suit to work, and when they'd been out with him, it had usually been with him along as an accessory to an event selected by Jake or Mark. Lucien had nearly always come along alone and often still in his' work clothes'.

Bigsy and Clare thought of Lucien mainly as Jake's friend. In the chain of social friendships, Lucien knew Mark well. Jake also knew Mark well, and Lucien would sometimes show up at Jake's social occasions. They'd all been for drinks together occasionally although Jake, Clare and Bigsy had regarded Lucien as something of an outsider at social events. Lucien was pleasant but didn't enter the spirit of their 'in-jokes' nor take the lead in the conversation. Lucien did seem to have done well for himself, living in Hampstead, which pretty much guaranteed him a smart address, but in reality, he was in a house converted from a larger house into a number of expensively priced little boxes.

Bigsy continued, "I can't really see why anyone would do that to Lucien. He's got to be a victim of some kind of accident or mistake. Lucien's not exactly a risk taker."

Clare nodded. "Yes, Lucien's highlights seemed to involve stories about things that happened on his bus ride to work."

Both Bigsy and Clare thought Lucien completely under exploited where he lived, both in terms of the immediate environment and also the lack of use he made of his easy access to all of central London.

If he'd been alive, Clare and Bigsy would have privately labelled Lucien a loser, but because he was a friend of Jake and he was now dead, they owed the loyalty of support to Jake.

"So, will we stick around here tonight?" asked Bigsy, "or head back North" – It was only to Finsbury Park in North London, but they were near to Gloucester Road, on the edges of fashionable Kensington in west London at the moment. Clare shrugged her answer, "Whatever – I think we're all going to be calling in sick tomorrow at this rate."

Clare's job was expendable. She'd been seeing a different friend of Jake's for a long time, got to know a lot of Jake's crowd and then when she'd had a major break up had decided to stay around Jake, who always seemed to have good things happening. She was between men right now and hung out with Bigsy (purely platonic) and Jake (why spoil a good thing?).

The Triangle

Clare's real interest was to get into TV or radio, and the other jobs she had were really time markers until she could crack the media formula. She was quite a good actress and had been in some lesser roles in stage productions and her other day work was really what she considered to be "between roles", but one up from bar-work or waitressing. Clare was also very interested in 'backstage' roles and production and in her heart she knew she'd probably wind up there rather than on stage or in front of the cameras, but that would still do nicely.

Jake's crowd had been a real find because Jake worked for a magazine and seemed to interview all kinds of interesting people, admittedly usually C-list types, but C-list with access, nonetheless. This gave her more of the ever-essential 'contacts' as she sought ways to further herself in 'show-biz'.

Clare's original slightly mercenary interest in Jake's friends had flipped into a true friendship with the group when she'd broken up with her last boyfriend. When she first lived in London, she'd been in a nasty flat around Elephant and Castle. Then she'd moved in with Steve until he drove her nuts and then she didn't have anywhere to stay. Using the Evening Standard to find a new flat was ridiculous; they walked off the page as fast as they were advertised. Word of mouth was the only answer.

Jake and his friends had rallied round, found her a temporary room in Bigsy's place (which he shared with two other fellas) and then moved her into a new nearby flat that a friend was leaving somewhat better than the place she'd left in the Elephant and Castle. They'd bailed her out on rent for a couple of weeks and then she'd got the new job – which paid well but was mind-numbingly boring creating photographic images for corporate leaflets. The joke was that the fees she could charge for taking a photograph, tweaking the colours and then merging it into a document with some text was obscene and Clare thought this was a quick way to pay off some debts and get solvent again.

Bigsy's job was semi-manual. He repaired company computer networks as a 'geek in a van' – except he used his cherished, though slightly scruffy, Rover car. Mainly he was a freelance addition to various large companies who needed something repaired at a diverse location. Half the time this meant driving somewhere, pulling the plug out of the back, counting to ten, plugging it back in and everything worked. Sometimes it was more complicated and Bigsy really did know how computers worked, so he could fix most things. Tomorrow, if he didn't go to his client in 'out west' in Andover, he might just have to phone them and tell them the unplugging trick, although once he'd done that, his supply of repeat business may tail off from that particular organization.

Jake was the common link that had introduced Bigsy, Lucien, Clare and Mark. Jake was a pretty well-established journalist and had his own by-line in the monthly magazine that was his main source of income. In addition, he did freelance work for other publications and this veered from the Guardian through to the advertising flyers handed out free on the Heathrow Express.

Jake had been writing in newspapers and magazines pretty much since school. He'd edited a school broadsheet, then at University ran a music magazine (which also let him get into many gigs without paying) and then after a rather odd dalliance with a fishing magazine, he'd moved into more cutting edge urban style magazines, which was where he worked now.

'Street' was the current magazine. Strong readership, internet profile, good advertising and viewed as a foreteller of the next big thing. That's how the graffiti artist show with the rats had first appeared, after Jake saw the early signs of the admittedly classy graffiti around the streets of east London. Bizarrely, Lucien had accompanied Jake to the show a few weeks earlier and appeared very interested, which is the reason Jake passed the free tickets from the private viewing to Lucien a week or so ago.

There was a buzzing sound from the table in the pub. Both Bigsy and Clare looked down to where their drinks were stood. It was Bigsy's phone that was buzzing and ever so slightly moving across the table. Grim faced, Bigsy lifted it to his ear.

"Come over," said the voice, "Mark's given me the low-down – I think there may be more to this than it seems. Let's leave for tonight but I think I may need some help tomorrow." Bigsy nodded to Clare. She already knew they'd all be spending time on this tomorrow.

"Okay," replied Bigsy, downing the remains of his beer and delicately picking up the last two crisps, "but let's go back to my place so that we are all ready for an early start tomorrow."

At the same moment, in Deauville, France, the well-dressed woman slid her key into the electronic lock of her hotel room. She walked in, closed the door quietly and flicked the deadlock. She crossed the room past the bed and stood near to the balcony, which looked out to the sea.

Near to the side of the bed, there was another door, the type that is used to make two adjacent rooms in a hotel link together. She twisted the door lock and opened her door, revealing another door belonging to the adjoining room. She pushed on the second door, which opened immediately. She softly closed both doors, locking the one for the new room she had entered.

Inside the room she looked towards the bed and then picked up the nearest pillow. She felt inside it and retrieved a large envelope. Without further examination, in one movement she stepped towards the door of the new room, quietly opened it and after checking both ways, made her way back into the hotel corridor. If she was stopped, she could say that she had been asked to carry the unopened envelope by someone else.

A few minutes later she stepped into an Italian registered Alfa Romeo. She flicked on the headlights, briefly revved the engine and then pulled out of the hotel and headed for the Autoroute.

Ed Adams

The Interview

A noisy kitchen scene, Capital Radio burbling, coffee machine fizzing and an occasional bang from some bacon fried on too high heat. Bigsy, with a cooking spatula in one hand, was already on the telephone. "Thanks, mate- I owe you for this one".

Bigsy had been on the phone to James, a friend and fellow computer geek who had a well-paid job in a city Bank. Bigsy had just persuaded James to take a day off from work and to make the journey to Andover to look at whatever it was that was broken.

James would need to say he was from Bigsy's outfit and was more than happy to help Bigsy. A month earlier, Bigsy had helped James out on a personal matter that called for a man with some bulk, following a problem with a motor car purchase by James. That very vehicle could now be used by James to help dig Bigsy out of an inconvenient appointment.

The previous night, when they had returned to Bigsy's, Jake had relayed the story of Lucien to Bigsy and Clare over a couple of bottles of wine. Bigsy and Clare had decided to help out in what seemed to be a scary and somewhat complicated situation. Jake and Clare had both decided it was easiest to simply stay at Bigsy's overnight, especially after two bottles of red wine, on top of the earlier evening's consumption.

The hissing and popping sound from the bacon and scrambled eggs reminded Bigsy of the breakfast, which he was assembling in the kitchen. "If we're going to be wandering around all day, we'll need something inside us," he mused to no-one in particular.

Clare had scrunched her hair and was still wearing the same clothes, which she somehow had made look different for what was a continuation of the previous day.

Bigsy, by comparison, appeared to be demonstrating the art of deterioration, with new grease spatters from the cooking on what was once a white tee-shirt emblazoned with "iBurn" and a picture of a smoking computer.

"Let's get Jake; we need to get started," he commented to Clare.

"Jake!" he shouted, "C'mon! It's going to be a busy one". He flipped the first portion of the intriguing-looking breakfast into a plate and handed it to Clare.

Clare slightly wrinkled her nose but remembered from her previous stint staying at Bigsy's that whatever it looked like, it usually tasted pretty good.

Jake's story from last night set anticipation with both Clare and Bigsy. Clare always thought Lucien had lived on a different planet from Jake and the rest of Jake's clan, but at a time like this would hold these thoughts private. The part Jake told them the previous evening meant they would expect today to be pretty eventful.

The door clicked open, and Jake walked into the kitchen. Wet hair from a shower, a new, oversized tee-shirt emblazoned with 'Siouxsie' from Bigsy's wardrobe and dark rings under his eyes which indicated he'd not slept much.

"Sorry about the shirt - but it will look great under your jacket," said Bigsy, "Here's some Maison Bigsy breakfast, now let's go over your story again!"

Jake scraped a wooden chair and sat, beginning to explain the last few days and the part that Lucien had inadvertently played.

He began, "I was supposed to report on the art show for the magazine but passed them to Lucien when we were out at the Builder's Arms a few days ago. Lucien had been to that graffiti show with me and seemed to enjoy it, so I thought this could be a 'win-win'."

Jake took a piece of the bacon from his plate by two fingers and placed it between a slice of unbuttered bread. Then he flipped the lid on some brown sauce and dribbled a small amount over the improvised sandwich.

"I figured that if Lucien could get me a catalogue and maybe describe a few of the things he spotted in the visit over a quick beer, then I could write the review 'blind'. That way I could scoot over to the Dorchester, get ten minutes with the artist and 'bing'!"

Bigsy was eyeing the remnants of Jake's plate after the sandwich-making operation. Ever so delicately, he slid the plate to one side, as if clearing it away.

"I don't think I'd told anyone else about what I'd done," continued Jake, "It was supposed to give Lucien a preview of the show and me a chance to get the story without quite as much running around."

"So whatever happened to Lucien could have been aimed at you?" questioned Clare. Jake had hinted at this last night, but Clare had been slow to accept this somewhat paranoid theory. It all seemed too implausible, except that Lucien was dead, but that also seemed unbelievable.

The Triangle

"Nice egg, is it?" questioned Jake to Bigsy, who was just finishing the remnants of Jake's plate.

"Mmm", said Bigsy, "...But I thought with murders and mysteries there was supposed to be a motive? You are not exactly Mr Big League gangster!" he smiled towards Jake.

Jake had stayed awake pretty much all of the previous night. He'd been a journalist long enough to know that a good article needed an angle, a motivation. When he interviewed someone, and it didn't stack up, he had acquired a good sense that something was missing. He called it 'evidence' which was not supposed to sound like a criminal investigation but had some of the same techniques.

Jake continued "I've been thinking about Lucien and the killing a lot. I really do think it must be something to do with me. I promise you both that I'm not involved with anything truly dodgy and I'd tell you both if there was something bad that I'd done, especially when it's something like this."

Bigsy and Clare both nodded. They knew Jake well and could read him if he lied, like the time he'd borrowed Clare's leather jacket and then somehow lost it in a club. Jake was professional for his work but transparent to both Bigsy and Clare.

"So here's my partial theory", said Jake as he sipped the freshly brewed coffee. "I've been working on a lifestyle piece called 'fast boys' about twenty-somethings who drove exotic fast supercars. The interviewees were mainly pop stars, footballers and the occasional mobile phone salesman with his own business. I had interviewed several Ferrari and Lamborghini owners and then gone to see a guy named Darren Collins, who owned a particularly expensive McLaren supercar which was apparently one of only several in the world. It's amazing how many of these guys there are in central London alone. See how some of the underground car parks are crammed full of Porsche, Astons these supercars."

"I had to go to an office in South London, just over Tower Bridge. You know the area before you get to Southwark and Borough Market. It's all recently renovated area with old warehouses made good. Bermondsey, I guess you'd call it."

Bigsy and Clare nodded. They'd both been to parties in the area.

"The neighbourhood was well-heeled and had fashion house headquarters in the nearby streets. Typical 'American film about London Town territory' but still only a few streets away from the rough scenes in 'Lock, Stock and Two Smoking Barrels'."

"Sounds like a walk-fast area", interrupted Bigsy.

"More or less", continued Jake, "At least a 'be careful at night' zone. Anyway, I'd been waiting in the office for Darren, who was late for our meeting. I was sitting in a ground floor meeting room with a glass wall and slatted blinds. They had good coffee, and I'd already finished the first cup while waiting for Darren. I was about to grab another cup when there was a noise outside the room, several people, softly spoken English but with a foreign accent."

"The accents sounded middle eastern. I wasn't paying a lot of attention to begin with, just waiting for a chance to refill my coffee without disturbing anyone. But then, call it my journalistic instincts rather than nosey parker; I decided to see what was happening just in case it would add some depth to the interview."

Jake explained he had left the door of the meeting room open so that he could get a warning of Darren Collin's approach, and this had helped him hear what was happening.

"The conversation was something to do with international trade and payments. I switched on my little old-school Olympus recorder when I started to pay attention to the conversation. The talking actually went on for quite a long time, maybe fifteen minutes. It had started softly but got louder and louder and then suddenly stopped. I decided to grab another coffee to give me a glimpse of what was happening."

Jake looked at Clare and Bigsy who were taking in the whole of his story.

"As I walked from the meeting room, I startled the people who had been talking and were now getting ready to leave. To be honest, they startled me, too, because I thought they were sitting in an adjacent room. There were five men in total. Three Arabic looking people in dark suits, a very tall guy with cropped hair, dark tan and what seemed to be a dark green suit and a fifth person who turned out to be Darren Collins."

"We were together in the entrance area to the office suite. Their group carried on making its way towards the door and I made a beeline for the coffee. Out of the corner of my eye, I saw the tall person with the unusual suit peel off from the group and come towards me."

"Mr Collins will be with you in a few minutes", the green suit said with a strong southern American accent. "We have just finished – Do you mind if I have one of your business cards", he asked, "I know that Mr Collins would want to recommend you to my colleagues", he continued.

Jake had been surprised by this, he'd never met this group before, had no idea why Darren Collins would have recommended him to anyone, but hey, maybe there was some freelance business available. He'd swapped cards with the American.

Jake continued the story to Clare and Bigsy, "A few moments later, Darren returned, and we returned to the meeting room where I'd been sitting to start the lifestyle interview. Darren appeared smartly dressed; suit, no tie, crisp white shirt. Sort of expensive city trader look with some discreet bling, if you know what I mean. I'd normally have a picture, but no photographer for this trip because as the article was about the fast car, the photoshoot was handled separately."

Jake looked briefly at Clare and Bigsy. Clare had finished the breakfast provided by Bigsy and was now scribbling a few notes based upon what Jake was saying. It appeared to be on the inside of a cereal packet.

Jake continued, "Collins seemed preoccupied during the interview, which was also quite obvious. He didn't seem to be very interested in talking about the car, which is unusual; normally, someone with a super special car wants to flaunt it to show how great they think they are. Although Collins didn't seem to care about most of the interview, there was just one area where he emphasized what he was saying."

Jake explained that he thought maybe Darren Collins was trying to project a version of 'cool', but it seemed the previous meeting rattled him.

"I'll come back to the moment in the interview, but the next part is why I think everything may be linked. A week or so after the interview, well before the story was due, my editor called me. He told me that Darren Collins had been killed in a road accident. The section of the story covering Darren Collins was being replaced with a twenty-something golfer with a Dodge Viper. 'Street' wouldn't still write about 'fast boys' if one of them had just died. There wasn't going to be an alternative story about Collins, so in 'Street' terms, the interview was no longer relevant."

Clare commented, "This does all seem to link together with what's happened to Lucien. How come you didn't think of this earlier?"

Jake replied, "There's always something happening when involved in this type of journalism. The nature of celebrity and wannabe means people are getting arrested for airline tantrums, too much booze and pills and the occasional car crash or similar.

The Triangle

"It's like the wallpaper of the B-listers. So Collins' tragic accident was more of an inconvenience in the newsgathering world. It affected my quota more than anything else. I'll admit it knocked me back when I first heard, but I hardly warmed to the guy, and he seemed to be off in his own world anyway."

Clare and Bigsy nodded as Jake continued, "I suppose if I'd paid more attention, then I might have connected the dots.

"I sort of regarded this as a dead story, and to be honest, I was also in some trouble from that trip I made to Liverpool."

Bigsy laughed, "...that trip. I'm not surprised- I think we all thought you'd get the boot after that example of expense account creativity!"

Jake had found several clubs and expensive hotels on his otherwise wasted visit. He'd decided to take 'wasted' in an altogether different direction.

"So when I got back to London, I was told by the office that someone had made several calls to the main switchboard and visited a couple of times looking for me. The description was of a tall American, short hair and suntan, looked vaguely military. It could only be the guy I'd met at Darren Collins' office, although the business card left with the office was for a different company. Eventually, I checked the names, and in both cases, it was Chuck Manners."

Clare stifled a laugh. "No, that's not a real name. It can't be. Chuck Manners."

"He looked as if he could 'chuck' me across a room," responded Jake.

Bigsy was fussing around with the remaining bacon, which had somehow congealed in the frying pan. He looked over and said,

"So if we add it all together, there is a story. The meeting with Darren Collins, the overheard conversation. The strange behaviour of Chuck the green-suited American. The death of Collins and the visits of the American to your office.

"Plus the different business cards and now the murder of Lucien, who was standing in for you at the art show. These things can't all be a coincidence!"

"I agree," said Clare,

"I was also thinking about this last night. To begin with I just thought you were in shock about Lucien and some of your journalistic imagination was coming through in the way you looked at the situation.

"But now I've had a chance to take it in, and I think you may have a point."

Clare scraped the kitchen chair across the floor and sat closer to Jake. "Look, I've listed some of the points". She scanned the list she'd made on the cereal box. The list comprised:

Visit Collins
Overhear Arabs
Get American business card
Meet Collins
Collins dies in a car crash
American shows up at Jake's office
Lucien takes your tickets to the art show
Lucien murdered

Clare had now retrieved some paper from a drawer in Bigsy's kitchen. She knew her way around the flat from the time she'd spent crashed there when Jake and Bigsy had helped her out earlier in the year.

"Okay, Jake, you'll need to take this to the police, but you still haven't told us about the thing that Collins emphasized during the interview. What can you remember?"

Jake went on to explain. "When I went to interview Collins, I'd also noticed the general look of the office. It was modern, clean-lined, stylish and minimalist. A designer had created it with taste, and budget limits didn't seem to have been any concern. Trust me, I know cutting edge cool, and Darren's office was a pretty good approximation.

"But the other thing that struck me was the complete lack of industriousness in what seemed to be a high-worth empire. For Darren to be turning the kind of money he appeared to be, there had to be some kind of activity to support it. I visit plenty of offices for interviews and client shoots and this was by far the most impressive looking, but the least busy. Something looked wrong, and the phrase 'shell company' was flickering through my mind while I sipped the coffee."

"Also, as the conversation with the middle eastern gentlemen became noisier I'd heard them talk about some kind of problem with the way Collins had been operating 'the clearances'. The quietly spoken Arab gentleman was politely advising him that the contract would close if he was unable to regain sufficient control. The American had emphasized this point as the group were about to break up. That was about the time when I pretended to wander out to get the coffee refill."

At the time Jake had just regarded this argument as the hustle-bustle of busy commerce. Still, he also thought (maybe politically incorrectly) that there may be some carpet bazaar bargaining going on as well.

"...and guys," continued Jake, "...there is another reason I think this may be more complicated, and that I may be in some danger."

Ed Adams

Nothing leads South

At the Chelsea Police station, Trueman had been going through standard police procedures for this case. A cold-blooded killing, more like an execution than any random violence. No sign of theft and no real crime scene evidence leading towards the killer.

They had started using routine procedures to look at records for any similar crimes seeking advice from police army forensics about the style and precision of the wound that had been the inflicted.

There was nothing obvious, except the view that this was a professional hit.

Furthermore, there was no discernible motive and no witnesses. There was camera footage from the gallery, but the room where the crime took place had suffered a defective camera for the last day. The gallery owner had said they'd never had any trouble previously at the gallery and the cameras in the entrance were the most useful for general surveillance. There was a call out to get the broken camera fixed, but the outfit repairing it had said it would be better to replace the unit, which appeared to have shattered inside. The repair was scheduled in time for the public opening, but not for the press preview. As a result, there was nothing captured of the crime although they did have clear footage of everyone visiting the gallery on the day of the incident.

They'd already combed the video for the entire day as well as the nearby street surveillance from a bus lane, a jeweller's and a couple of fashion stores. Many of the people entering and leaving the gallery were recognized, were employees or members of the trade press. After Lucien's entry, there had been a couple of further visitors, and shortly after the incident a couple of people managed to leave before the arrival of police, ambulance and others associated by the crime investigators.

Everyone leaving tallied except for one man picked up on the bus lane camera getting into a BMW. They had a number plate for the car, but it was a fake, cloned from a Vauxhall Astra still on a dealer forecourt in South London.

They were trying to trace the car's route, picking it up on other cameras, but even with Congestion Charge and traffic management cameras, it was long, laborious and painstaking work. Coupled with the other aspects of the killer's professionalism, they expected the car would have disappeared somewhere not far from the original scene.

The passenger of that BMW was by now a long way from London. Driving from Deauville to the Cote d'Azur was a long journey, across the whole landmass of France. The driver followed her sat-nav but had pre-planned to use Autoroutes for almost the entire journey, taking a reasonably direct autoroute bypassing Paris, Lyon, Valance and Aix which was many hundreds of kilometres of driving.

She briefly looked down at her Irish passport, which she would be using for this journey. Brophy. Amelia Brophy.

After Paris, the road had cleared, and she was making good time, staying within the speed limits to avoid being timed by police on long section between the tolls.

Sometimes a route on normal roads ran parallel to the Autoroutes. Still, she maintained her speed and focus on the journey, eventually pulling off at services ostensibly to refuel, but first parking in a row of mixed registration cars from Great Britain, France, Germany and Holland. She was looking for a blue Peugeot saloon and parked a couple of rows from it but with a direct view to it. She blipped another key on her keyring, seeing the locks in the Peugeot's car door rise and then fall again as she re-locked the car.

The next services, with its adjacent hotel, would be fine for the overnight stop, except she'd be in the blue car instead of the red one.

Picking up just the hotel envelope from the car, she walked across to the services shop, bought an apple and some bottled water and after a few minutes pause made her way back to the parking lot and into the Peugeot. It was a diesel and had enough range to get the rest of the way to Cannes, without stopping.

She sat in the car and looked at the envelope she'd picked up back in Deauville. Now she was far enough away to open it. To her surprise, there were two items inside instead of the one she had expected. The first a photocopy of a banker's draft in Swiss francs for a considerable sum of money, made out to her, with her real name. The second was a photocopied sheet of A4, with a selection of photographs of Jake, a series of addresses and phone numbers.

She realized the message she was seeing. She was not getting paid. Her target was still active, and the person she had killed in the gallery must have been someone else. This situation was extremely irregular and increased her risks considerably. The only option was to finish the job. She would have to go back to London and repeat the mission, albeit with different arrangements.

The risk increased because there would now be a degree of

alarm and suspicion raised, and the approach to the second assignment would need to be very different to avoid creating a visible crime footprint.

She also realized that any failure to comply placed her in immediate danger, whereas completing the assignment would yield the large sum shown on the copied Banker's draft.

She weighed her options and decided to continue. She thought briefly about the choice of vehicles for the rest of the journey. No-one knew she had left this car in these services; no-one knew she had planned this vehicle swap. It was safest to stay with the Peugeot and to continue the journey.

She picked up the cheap, garish Nokia phone from under the passenger seat of the Peugeot, held down the 2, which power dialled a number beginning +31. After six rings a phone operator style voicemail cut in. She listened to the standard greeting and said "Yes, one week." and then hung up.

Then she flipped the battery from the back of the cell-phone, prized out the SIM card and walked to a nearby refuse bin. She deposited the remnants of her apple and then walking back to the car dropped the SIM into a nearby kerb-side storm drain. As she approached the Peugeot, she stooped to look at the tyres, as if checking pressures. She was checking underneath for any signs of interference.

She re-entered the car, flicked the ignition and smiled to herself as the car started. A few moments of fiddling with the new sat-nav and she was ready to leave.

She pushed the defunct phone into the glove box and manoeuvred the car back onto the Autoroute, still heading South-East.

Broken in

"So, Jake, what other things and why do you think there's still danger?" asked Bigsy, "I think we, no you, should take all of this to the cops and get the professionals on to this. If you are really in danger, then they should have the best ways to help."

"Let me finish. I didn't think any of this was that important until right now," said Jake. "There's a difference between getting some sections together for a piece of low-key investigative journalism, compared with having one accidental death followed by a murder of a friend right on the doorstep."

Clare had finished transferring her list from the cereal packaging to a sheet to paper. It was the same list as the original scribble, but now, neatened and written starkly, it did seem to point towards a story.

Jake continued to explain the Collins interview to Clare and Bigsy.

"So the interview with Darren was supposed to be routine," he continued, "Successful fly-boy poser with big shiny wheels – except we are talking almost Formula One prices for this car –

it does over 240 miles per hour, and there are only a few dozen variants in the world."

"But as the interview started, I could see that Collins looked rattled. It wasn't my questions or anything to do with the interview, but here we have a Mr Successful who had asked to be in our 'Flaunt' section now stuttering over his words and seeming to be very disengaged."

Clare and Bigsy exchanged a glance, "So you knew he was freaked about something; did you ask him about it?" asked Bigsy.

"Yes, I tried to," continued Jake, "but initially Collins dismissed it saying he'd got a big deal going down. Of course, I needed to ask him some background questions about his company and how he had made his money because it's not so apparent as a footballer hero or popstar. He gave me a "bit o' this and a bit o' that" type of line. My original assessment seemed right that he was a fly-boy."

Jake recounted this section of the interview. Collins had started in trading with perfumes and other market barrow-boy items. He'd moved into a small and legitimate import/export business and then seemed to strike it rich with a few large deals where he appeared as the middleman in large transactions. Jake wondered whether there was anything dubious, like drugs, along the way, but the basics seemed to be much more to do with conventional commercial intermediation.

"Yeah, he seemed to have a knack of making a turn on big trade deals between countries," continued Jake, "but I couldn't see anything illegal in the basic story.

"Apart from the dodgy perfumes when he started out. Hey, even the most august of today's rich and famous may have started pushing bootleg records or car aerials."

Bigsy nodded and thought of a couple of well-known British millionaires.

Jake continued, "But partway through the interview, Collins said something very unusual. I can't remember it exactly, but it was along the lines that with him being successful and all, he had to take certain precautions."

"That was the only part of the interview where he seemed fully engaged. I took this to be posturing like a lot of popstars have 'security' and bouncers and so-on. He said 'no' that there was more to it than that. He said that if ever anything were to happen to him, there was more than just financial insurance for him. That there was a special process - I took it to mean like a legal process - to handle his affairs. That's when he said something odd. He knew my machine was running and he said, "Yes I have a special code which can stop the process", and then he gave me a number- which at the time sounded like a phone number."

"I looked at him surprised that he had done this. He said it didn't mean anything to me anyway, so what was the harm in telling me. He did look, pointedly, at my machine when he said this though."

"I decided at this time to lighten up the conversation before we closed (tricks of the trade, always leave them feeling good), so I asked him some more questions about his car. It's a nutter, by the way, goes so fast that it is practically unusable on British roads. The acceleration is like a fast motorbike. It has these really cool doors, though, they sort of swing upwards."

Jake paused. He could see that Clare and Bigsy were taking in the main story and the piece about the car was an incidental distraction.

"And you know," said Jake, "I've got the recording of pretty much all of this - the Arabs, the argument, the American, and the interview with Darren Collins. It's back at my place - and not bad quality. My little gadget boosts the volume during the quiet pieces, you know.

The Triangle

"I didn't even get to listen to it again because the story got cut and then I had to go on that wild goose chase to Liverpool for the footballer story."

"So the next thing we need is the recording from Jake's," said Bigsy.

"Okay," said Clare, "but we need to think first – and that includes thinking about getting the police involved and also about safety".

"I agree, although at the moment, by pure chance, no one knows I'm here at Bigsy's," said Jake, "whereas they may expect me to show up at my flat, the Police station or my office. Call me a chicken, but it might be better for me to lay low until we've heard that tape again and then maybe to call the police when we have all of the evidence. I will want to be taken somewhere out of the way if things are as bad as they seem."

"I also think the only person who would know about me making the recording would be Collins – and I suppose other journos could work it out, but it's pretty unlikely that anyone is thinking about it."

"Yeah," said Bigsy, "And it's funny that we still all call it 'tape' when we all know its digital!" Clare and Jake both simultaneously turned as if to hit Bigsy, who was ready to defend himself with the frying pan.

Delays and findings

A few streets away, Jake's apartment had been watched for around two hours. Two local petty criminals sourced by a mysterious American were looking for the best way into the flat. The two burglars had seen a few people leave during early morning and then and some routine delivery of milk and mail, but the property looked easy enough to enter.

It was easy. A communal door to the stairwell. No special locks, no alarm, not even an entry camera.

Jake's door was easy to open. Inside it was easy to see why. There were not a lot of valuable items. There were books, CDs, a few magazines, a fancy plasma TV and a sleek MacBook laptop. The two intruders opened a large blue IKEA bag they had brought with them and dropped the MacBook into it. They riffled through the CDs, picking up a large pile of hand-labelled ones and added those to the collection.

Then they started a long and mainly silent and thorough search of the apartment, picking a few further items to add to their collection in the bag. They seized paper notepads, a few electronic gadgets, a couple of memory sticks, a digital camera and a music player. By now, they were using a second IKEA bag. Their search lasted less than ten minutes, and then they looked at one another, then at the rooms they had searched which still looked much as when they entered. They re-opened the door, left and one of them reset the lock such that their entry would not be obvious.

Struggling downstairs with the two bright blue bags, they slipped around the nearby street corner into a parked and slightly dented white van. Then a short drive of no more than a few hundred yards to meet the American again who had been patiently waiting for them in a nearby coffee shop. In a few moments the three of them were in the van and mingling with the London traffic.

On the French Autoroute, things had slowed to a standstill. There had been an accident ahead, and both lanes seemed blocked. Amelia looked into the air and saw a helicopter. Air ambulance. There was going to be a significant delay. She switched on the radio and tuned to a classics channel.

This gave her some time to reflect. Her best option was to get back to Cannes and then complete the alibi from the first assignment. She could also review the ease of access to the target, based upon the information and addresses given. Most of that could be done by the internet, but she would not use any communications until she returned to Cannes. She did not want any signals which could pinpoint her until she was good and ready.

She drank from the bottled water. It said 'sport water' on the side. She wondered what the difference was.

The delay outside Lyon became excruciating. The accident had pretty much closed the Autoroute. By the time Amelia was moving again, nearly two hours had passed. The French emergency services had been driving along the hard shoulder. By the position of the helicopter, it looked as if the accident was at least a couple of kilometres ahead. As she edged forward, most of whatever had happened had been cleared.

Off to the side of the road, like some felled dinosaur, was an articulated truck, on its side. As she drove past it, she knew the rules about not slowing to look, but it was almost unavoidable after two hours of boredom and then a chance to see the source of the inflicted pain.

As she started to pick up speed again, Amelia noticed that she had consumed more fuel than expected as a consequence of the holdup and would now need to stop somewhere again to fill up for the last part of the journey.

The American was in a Lebanese restaurant in London. He sat in a private room with the two men who had visited Jake's flat. Together they had been sifting through the contents of the blue bags, looking for something very specific.

The American picked up the digital recorder. "We need to check this," he said, "and also the computers." He flicked quickly through the menu on the Olympus. It showed dates and durations of recordings.

He scrolled the dates and located an entry around two weeks earlier when Jake had visited Darren Collins. The recorder showed a note "Uploaded Oct, 27". So, Jake had moved the recording to his PC.

They opened the Macbook; the screen had a big diagonal crack, but still immediately sprang to life and displayed a blue background with a small number of icons, including, to their surprise, a small picture of the digital recorder. A click later and they were in a folder full of voice recordings. A few moments later they were scrolling to the date of Jake's visit and a click later they listened to the recording, which began with a lengthy, if muffled conversation by the Arabs, followed by the interview with Darren Collins.

The whole recording was stuttery, which seemed to be a factor of the damage suffered to the computer, as if the disk was having trouble reading the file.

The American shook his head and thought, "I hate these Brit criminal low lives. They can wreck anything."

He weighed up the odds of finding anything else useful from

the two criminals and then reached in his pocket to produce an envelope counting a large number of banknotes. "It's all here", he said, "you can count it later, but at the moment I need you out of here. If you stay, you will be in danger and remember, if you meet or see me again, you will also be in danger. Goodbye"

He dismissed the two burglars, and they left the restaurant. The American remained in the room for another hour. He had loaded his own computer and linked it to the damaged one stolen from Jake. He selected some specialised software, copied the stuttering sound recording across to his computer, spent some time editing it and then cut a copy of the modified recording to a USB stick in his own PC.

Next, the American made a phone call, "I have something I think you should hear," he said.

After a few minutes of discussion, the American assembled Jake's belongings back into one of the blue bags. He placed his own PC into a backpack and then, carrying both bags, he left the room.

Safety First

"I agree with Bigsy," said Clare. "We need to think about safety – one of us needs to go back to Jake's, but," looking at Bigsy, "...it will better for it to be one of us two, Bigsy."

"...or both of us," answered Bigsy, "that way, we can look out for one another."

Clare shot a glance to Bigsy and then to Jake, "...or we could just call the police right now?" said Clare.

"The thing is...", said Jake, "... there's a little bit more".

They looked back at Jake. He looked sheepish.

"Well, after the calls from the American, I did call him back", said Jake,

"He asked to meet me and to explain a few things about the meeting with Darren. I asked him why, and he said there was a good story for me as well as some information for him. He said that I might be in some danger, but that I should not call the police. Also that all was not what it seemed when I saw him with the Arabs at Collin's office. I agreed on a date to meet him at 'Yo Sushi's' for lunch, - you know - the one across the bridge from Westminster. I thought he might have been a possible client, and that is why I let it run".

"Jake", sighed Clare, "Is there anything else you haven't told us?" she asked, "we can't help you if you don't tell us everything."

"Clare's right", said Bigsy, "This is looking quite dangerous, and I don't want to be finding out extra facts when it's just too late!"

"Okay," said Jake, "the only other thing is my meeting with the American is tomorrow!"

Clare looked at Jake and Bigsy," We can get a lot done today", she said.

"We can get the recording from Jake's, try to find out some more about Lucien's murder, make a list of everything we know and then decide whether we should take it to the police, even despite the American's warning to Jake."

"I also think Jake should stay here", said Clare, "If someone is looking for him, it would be stupid to return to his flat. Also, no-one will be able to connect the three of us. Jake, take my phone, switch yours off and don't answer any calls, except Bigsy's number. Once this is clearer, we can re-evaluate."

All three thought this sounded very melodramatic, although Lucien's murder meant they knew they were getting into something perilous.

Bigsy suggested that he and Clare travel over to Jake's. Bigsy already had a key to Jake's flat, which had sometimes been useful if they were meeting there in an evening and Jake was late - which was often the case. They decided to use taxis to get around. It wasn't far from Bigsy's to Jake's, but they could be invisible for longer in taxis.

"Jake," said Clare, "This is important. If you don't hear from us by phone in two hours, you must call the police anyway."

Jake nodded his acceptance and looked at his watch. By now, it was ten-thirty in the morning.

In France, the Peugeot was just pulling into the diesel line in the service station. Amelia driver got out and quickly filled the tank of the car. She paid with Euros and was back on the road inside ten minutes. Another three hundred kilometres to Cannes, mainly Autoroute.

Clare had a good idea on the way to Jake's. They would stop off at the nearby Tesco metro supermarket and buy a small quantity of groceries. Bigsy liked this because it could be a new supply of junk food.

Clare's point was to make it look as if they were routinely shopping and then carrying something into Jake's. If no-one was watching, it didn't matter if they were, it would look as if they were doing something normal. The carrier also gave them a container for their return journey. They splashed out on a £3.00 recyclable bag, which had robust handles and looked as if it could take some weight.

Getting into Jake's was easy enough, although they had both wanted to look around the area first. In reality, with no-one watching, the visit looked as if it would be uneventful.

Bigsy went straight to the kitchen and switched on the kettle while Clare looked around the fairly neat room for the recorder and Jake's MacBook. To begin with, neither of them considered anything abnormal in the flat. Then Clare noticed that Jake's computer was missing. And there were none of Jake's computer disks either.

"It looks as if Jake's computer has gone!" called Clare to Bigsy. He walked in and surveyed the room.

"Definitely," he said, looking at where the laptop was normally situated. Then he looked under the desk, "The Wi-Fi connection is still here," he said, dropping into his professional techno-babble. He traced wires to another box, "and here's Jake's backup drive," he proclaimed, pulling a small dusty box from the floor behind the desk. "I installed this myself," he said," I knew Jake would be hopeless at this type of thing, so I set him up a little box to do the backups automatically overnight, as long as he left the computer switched on".

He carefully unplugged the box, which was about the size of a large novel and put it, with its connecting wires, into the Tesco's bag. Then he looked through a couple of other shelves and asked whether Clare had found the digital recorder. Clare shook her head. They continued to search through drawers. Bigsy found a stash of Mars chocolate bars and added them to the Tesco bag.

"Okay," said Bigsy, "Let's get out of here, we have everything useful". As they left, Bigsy texted to Jake that everything was okay.

Around a mile away, Trueman and Green were leaving the police station. They had spent most of last night and the morning together continuing the investigation. They were pretty sure that the identity information for Lucien Deschamps was accurate. They were also surmising that his background was legitimate, and they could not find links of him to anything even slightly off colour. No parking tickets, nothing.

"C'mon," said Trueman, realising they had worked a solid twenty hours, "a swift pint is in order."

They trooped over the road to the nearby pub. Inside were a brown bar and several roughly placed brown tables, with four chairs around each table. There were three men, each alone, sitting in the bar. A fruit machine twinkled lights in the corner and television without sound was running an old soccer match on a Sky TV channel.

They picked a corner table, and Andy Green ordered two pints of beer from the bar. "What do you make of it?" he asked as he sat down, balancing the beers on slightly curled beer mats on the dark brown table.

"It's all dead ends," answered Trueman, "A blame-free victim, no enemies, no suspicion of crime connections, yet a clinically executed assassination.

"The only woman suspect is captured on TV inside the gallery and across the road, yet the car with false plates she is being driven in seems to disappear without a trace in London's traffic. There are no traceable cell phones to give whereabouts, and no-one else has come forward with any comments. We can up the stakes with a poster appeal, but I wonder what this was all about."

Green nodded his agreement.

"It's as if this was the wrong victim, but there was hardly anyone else in the gallery. Those present have all got strong stories and nothing to create any reason for anything like this."

"So maybe it was the wrong victim..." ventured Green, "...I know we still need to run lots of checks, but the victim's basic story seems legitimate."

"Yeah, I was wondering too," responded Trueman.

"The gallery was open for Press viewings when this happened, not for the general public. Yet Deschamps was an office worker. I think this may be the lead - perhaps the murderer thought Deschamps was someone else."

They looked at one another. "So how did Spurs get on?" continued Green, sipping at his pint.

Sunshine and shades

" The French Riviera;
a sunny place for shady people"

Postcard from Cannes

Cannes

Cannes was crowded with a trade event. The city famous for the film festival was used for much of the year for other less well-known events and had many ingredients for a good week away from the office for various types of commercial visitors. Whether it was TV soaps, physiology, retail technology or yachts, there was some show or convention and Cannes could provide lavish hotels and a great backdrop.

It was November, but the splendour of the Mediterranean resort was undiluted. Sun bleached, supersaturated colours and the unmistakable allure of a chic resort, even if it was only a week or so before it would plunge into Winter. The sky was bright blue, cloudless and a big contrast to a few days earlier when Amelia had left, and there had been a steady rain against a darkened sky. The elements were feeling playful in the last moments of the transition to the darker seasons.

She drove slowly along the Croisette, past the Palais de Congress where the film festival and many of the trade shows were held. She was heading back to the Carlton but had to lose the Peugeot first.

The Carlton was one of the most splendid hotels along the Croisette. A gaggle of valets and doormen stood outside. Amelia drove slowly past, then turned into a side street and sought a parking spot for the car close to the hotel.

For Amelia Brophy, this town was a perfect place to create an alibi. She could arrive, book into the trade conference in an obvious way and then use Nice airport as a hub during the week to move around to follow her instructions. She could easily disappear into the conference of several thousand people and at the end of the week would have perfect evidence of her whereabouts from badges, booking-in materials and the general paraphernalia of the conference.

She drove the Peugeot to a parking lot near to the train station and then walked back to the Carlton hotel, a few blocks away. By her planning, she had now ostensibly been in Cannes for three days. The conference was soon coming to its close. Her documentation and travel would be consistent with spending the week in Cannes.

There was no link with the events at the gallery or with the unusual route she had taken from the UK back to the conference. The change of orders had interfered with her original plan, but as a professional, she knew she needed to reach her anonymous bolthole in the Carlton and then to take stock of what to do next.

Her room at the Carlton was luxurious. She had not chosen a suite, which would be easier to notice if unused, but a room of the type that many conferences booked in large quantities. Unoccupied rooms overnight at a large conference were nothing unusual to the hotel staff, who had seen everything. As she walked back into her sea-facing room, she saw the jacket she had hung outside of the wardrobe, a PC laptop switched on with a screen saver and the bed already showing turn down service, complete with a little chocolate confection on both of the pillows. The whole room told a short story to any staff that happened to drop by.

She threw the envelope onto the bed and headed directly to the shower. Two days of travelling after an arduous job in London gave her a great sense of need to freshen up. She also transformed herself from businesswoman to a somewhat more sophisticated and continental look, wearing a casual blouse and a light-coloured jacket over black trousers and some sharply-pointed high-heeled shoes. If before she had looked the archetypal travelling businessman, she now looked far more 'Continental-European' and casual.

Then she sat down with her computer to start to consider her next actions. She began to look up information about Jake and the 'Street' magazine.

A business transaction

Bigsy and Clare travelled in a second taxi back to Bigsy's place. As they arrived, they noticed that one of Bigsy's flatmate's cars had managed to park close to the house, a rare feat in this part of Central London.

Rick worked for a well-known estate agents' chain, and they had given many of their mobile employees' cars that were all almost identical Minis. The vehicles were tricked out with a unique green, black and yellow camouflage paint job which also advertised the estate agency firm. They had become a frequent and commonplace sight on the streets of London. Inside, Rick was chatting affably to Jake, and they turned as Clare and Bigsy walked in.

"I was telling Rick about our plan to take a couple of days to photograph London for your project Clare," he lied, and both Bigsy and Clare picked up from this that Jake was saying nothing about what had been happening, to Rick.

"I told Rick we might need to do some detailed planning this evening". Rick smiled, "Yeah, that's great, I'm out tonight seeing a gig over in Camden. I may stay out over there".

The four continued to chat and then Rick made some excuses and prepared to leave for his evening.

"Okay, so what did you find?" asked Jake, in hushed tones. The others explained; Jake's flat looked superficially normal, but there had been a break-in, and the laptop, digital recorder and many CDs had gone.

"But look," Bigsy exclaimed, "this is your backup unit, and they didn't take it. Please tell me you are backing up your computers the way I told you?"

Jake smiled, he was known to be somewhat lackadaisical on most things related to technology, but because of his work, the one thing he was good at was backups. The infamous 'missing Royal College Report" had led to this fastidiousness for backup because he'd nearly lost his job when he deleted an important story, which had been partly written by somebody else from the office. He'd had to spend four or five days, including midnight hours, to get the work done again so that his colleague didn't suffer, although it also taught Jake to play it safe when using computers.

Half a world away, in Riyadh, Saudi Arabia, another scene was unfolding in this capital city grown from the desert. Riyadh's skyline is dominated by two enormous towers, one featuring a pointed building and the other taking the appearance of a crown. They are known as Al Faisaliah and the Kingdom Tower. The Faisaliah building's top area features a revolving restaurant, from where it is possible to look out from the capital to the city and the desert. The restaurant is shaped like a ball and has a distinctive and more private area for smoking exquisite cigars. The meeting was taking place in this restaurant.

In keeping with the dress code of Saudi Arabia, five of the six men seated around the table were wearing conventional Arab clothing, three with the traditional red and white chequered headdresses and the other two with the less common white. The sixth man was wearing a western suit, elegant but quite understated. White shirt and red tie of similar hue to the colours in the headscarves.

The Triangle

They had been drinking fruit drinks and eating from a light tabbouleh and meze. Then one of the men spoke to the group, in English, of the situation they had convened to discuss.

"We will need to re-examine our trade clearance processes," he stated, "The route we have been using has been compromised - we will need to find another way. Mr Fredriksson here is to help us create the next route for our shipments. Mr Fredriksson, can you explain how this will work?"

Fredriksson was the suited westerner in this group. From Sweden, slim, blond hair, spectacles and a light tan suggesting someone well-travelled, he started his explanation. It was filled with business jargon but essentially said that he could facilitate the creation of some new trading processes which could help certain transfers of large sums of money on a global scale. These needed to go through 'special' procedures before the money was available for use.

To do what he intended, he needed some substantial down-payments from the assembled group. This was his fee for the work and separate from the further great operating expenses he expected to incur in creating the new environment.

The five Arabs switched into Arabic conversation for around ten minutes, and Fredriksson waited patiently. It was the second meeting; in the first one, there had been much bargaining to reach a position. He knew that when working with this group, he would need to build in some points which could be conceded as well as some individual handling fees payable to each of the people around the table.

"We will need to negotiate the detail of your terms, but we accept the general approach." The five Arabs nodded their acceptance and then continued to speak to one another in Arabic.

Fredriksson said, "In that case, gentlemen, I will bid you all good evening. I can catch the next flight to London at 0200 and this will mean I can start making the arrangements. Overall this is going to take around three weeks to set up. My colleague will be in contact to finalize the payment terms. Please understand this agreement is irreversible, and once we start, there will be no going back."

The five Arabs nodded "Shukran," said their leader "Ma'assalama!" Fredriksson stood, bowed his head slightly, made eye contact with each of the Arabs and then left the table and walked back towards the staircase from the cigar room, back to the express elevator and the ground floor.

Then a detour to his room on the 40th floor using a separate elevator where he collected an already packed slim traveller bag and then made his way again to the ground floor.

He walked across the front lobby where a combination of Arabs sipped tea in a conventional Arabic way, from tiny cups and Western-looking businesspeople sat in huddles talking about deals and business in the Kingdom. He noted the absence of women in this strict Islamic country.

The lobby entrance was vast sweeps of breath-taking glass, and as he approached, he signalled to the doorman, and within a few seconds, a sleek black Lincoln Town car had pulled up outside the lobby. He could head straight for the airport, out through the suburbs and across the desert to the vast Khalid International Airport, with its massive underground car park, huge mosque and misleading architectural design like a major American hub. Deceptive because the airport lacked shops or other conventional Western trappings. He steeled himself for what he knew would not be a particularly pleasant wait for his plane.

A matter of procedure

Trueman and Green had no idea of the magnitude of the situation they were entering. They knew the killing of Deschamps was professional, had worked out that it was probably mistaken identity, had seen a woman on camera leaving the crime scene but had no further idea about who could have been involved.

As procedure, they were following up on the invitations to the gallery show and discovered that the invitation list for the preview day was short and included mainly trade and some magazine and news journalists.

The trail had led them to the Street magazine and Jake's editor, Robert Davis. He was not particularly phased to have a couple of policemen invite themselves to his offices, as from time to time the magazine got itself caught up in the periphery of other investigations. The nature of their journalism meant they would stumble into mostly petty matters and so there would be an occasional visit as part of routine procedures.

This time, the discussion was about the new showing by a subversive and controversial artist who had been exhibiting near Sloane Square. The show start was delayed because of a murder, played down in most press coverage.

"Mr Davis," began Trueman, "We have a few questions about one of your journalists."

"Fire away," answered Davis, "But remember I may have to take advice on certain questions". Robert Davis was slightly intrigued by the turn of events and realized that Jake had been at the show. Trueman explained the background and Davis responded.

"Well, the whole story was put on hold after the death and the delay to the opening. We keep our stories upbeat unless we are targeting a celebrity, but this situation of a 'murder in the gallery' didn't fit with the monthly flow of the magazine.

"We can't beat the newspapers to the punch on topicality and, frankly, the delayed show pushes it further back in the magazine. We may do a more general piece later, but at the moment there's a couple of other stories we pushed up as we bumped this one down."

As he said it, Davis realized that there were now three stories by Jake which hadn't been delivered over the last few weeks; moreover, Jake was now sick from work.

In a light-hearted way, Davis recounted to the police, firstly Jake's Liverpool fiasco with the substantial expenses but no story, then the current art exhibition and finally the collapse of part of the "fast boys" story because of the accidental death of Darren Collins.

Green and Trueman looked at one another. This was a

promising lead. Here was someone supposed to be at the art show, someone with a recent track record of absences and on the periphery of two recent deaths.

Davis went on to point out that Jake may be erratic but was a good writer and had been with the magazine for at least eighteen months. These situations were close together, but frankly, in the business of 'Street', errant journalists were not a particularly unusual occurrence.

They walked back into the busy bus-filled street by the magazine's offices. "We're on to something," said Trueman, "Mr Jake Lambers is about to get a visit."

Back at Bigsy's flat, Bigsy was now intent on fiddling with computers, wires and the backup unit from Jake's place, Clare and Jake chatted idly, but waited expectantly for the little box to burst into life.

"Eureka!" called Bigsy, "we have contact! Houston, the lights are now flashing!" and sure enough Bigsy had connected the backup box to one of his computers and now had access to the folder structure to read the files.

He browsed through the files, "Well done, mate - you followed the backup routine!" he said absently, to Jake as he looked at what was on the disk.

"We seem to have a good backup of your laptop." He scrolled along until he found the digital recorder directory and there inside it was a large selection of files containing recordings from various interviews conducted by Jake. And amongst them, was a recording from the date of Jake's meeting with Collins.

Bigsy clicked it. iTunes popped up on the computer, the software usually used to play music tracks, and then almost immediately, the sounds of the muffled meeting with the Arabs, interspersed with louder sounds of Jake drinking coffee.

"We can improve the sound quality a bit," said Bigsy, "But let's just listen to it through once". He fiddled around in his pocket whilst he said this and withdrew his keyring. "I'm also making another copy," he announced, showing a small electronic gizmo on his keyring, with a plug on its end to connect into the side of the computer.

He plugged the memory stick into the side of the computer and copied the still playing file into his storage device.

The recording ran for about five minutes with the muffled conversation, which was about something about trade routes and seemed to be quite agitated by the end.

There was then the distant conversation where Jake had met the group outside the room and then the click as the session finished, almost immediately running into a new session comprising Jake and Darren Collins sitting together in the place where the recorder was situated.

What followed was the interview Jake had described. There was nothing particularly interesting beyond the points which Jake had accurately recounted to Bigsy and Clare, but both Bigsy and Clare picked up on the agitation in the tone of Collin's replies.

It was as if Collins didn't want to be there doing the interview but was still trying to give polite replies to the questions he was being asked. As Jake had said, there was also the section where he talked about the secure code and gave a number which all three of them wrote down. It was "Blue Flame mph 7539".

After twenty-five minutes or so, the interview concluded, and then the recording stopped abruptly. There was a moment of silence in the room.

"See..." said Jake, "...I was pretty accurate with what I told you." The others nodded agreement.

The Triangle

"We need to get a better version of the first section," said Bigsy, "I'm sure I'll have something to help this."

He fiddled around with the computer again for another ten minutes.

"OK," he said, "I've added some sound mixing software to this PC. It's only a trial edition from a download, but we get to use it for thirty days!"

Clare and Jake looked at one another; they were hardly leading-edge counter-espionage agents if they were using free trial software to crack hidden messages. To their joint amazement, the program started up, and after a few screens of text imploring them to buy the full version, it eventually led them to a complicated control panel.

"Drag and drop," said Bugsy, by this time in full geek-ville. He found the folder with Jake's recording and dropped the little file icon into the new program. Some wiggly lines appeared which looked like the sound wave of the recording. Bigsy pressed 'play', and the same bad recording started again; only now he could change the sound quality. To begin with, he was playing with controls akin to the tone controls on a hi-fi, but then he started clicking other buttons, and to the surprise of Jake and Clare, the sound started to get clearer and the background hum and other interference sounds seemed to melt into the background.

"I'm using a multi compressor to sweep for the best frequencies," mumbled Bigsy, "and set a shelf for the low end to cut out that low rumble".

"Whatever it is, it's a bloody genius," chuckled Jake, amused at Bigsy's intensity in this exercise. Bigsy saved the settings and rewound the recording to the start.

"Let's listen," he said.

Ed Adams

PART TWO

Puzzle Palaces

"The best secrets are the most twisted"
— Sara Shepard, Twisted

Langley

The National Security Administration in Langley, Virginia, USA is set inside a complex often referred to as Fort Meade.

To locals, there is another nickname, "the Puzzle Palace" because it is used as the most extensive electronic surveillance and counter-espionage environment on the planet.

This means that Langley eavesdrops. It has giant computers able to monitor millions of phone calls and e-mails each day. Most items tracked are innocent. Langley has to be good at spotting the few that are not.

At that moment, a particular chain of events was beginning to raise a few alerts in their systems. There was activity in Saudi Arabia as several seriously wealthy Arabian businessmen were clustered together with a person who the NSA had been monitoring for some time.

They had been particularly clever at triangulating the

individual under surveillance. He was skilled at counter-espionage technique and often used multiple cellular phones in a way that made him difficult to track. His smart part was that he also kept a routine phone which he regularly used, which could create a decoy usage print of normal behaviour. The not so smart part was that he used different phones but often first enabled them from either his home or his office. This gave a useful signal to the monitoring authorities, who could then pick up the cell phone number and the handset serial number, by noting its first activation from a known location. After that, it was easy enough to switch on tracker software to record any use of the phone.

So the person being tracked, JA/RU/059 was easy to follow, and the monitoring of his meeting with the Arabs in Riyadh had been a matter of identifying his cell phone and noting five other long usage cell phones all in the same location.

Langley had noted another 657 phones in the same location as the person they were monitoring. They had quickly reduced it to 47 phones with similar arrival and departure times. The monitoring picked up usage consistent with a meeting. The group all arrived within a few minutes of one another, they all left and split up at roughly the same time. The central mark had left around 35 minutes earlier and next been stationary at Riyadh's airport, before the signal had de-activated. Since that time there was no signal anywhere.

NSA removed several people from their remaining list as highly improbable, but finally identified a small group within the cell phones left, that were high profile individuals.

NSA also cross-checked their findings with their "Five Eyes" allies. This included the UK's GCHQ, although the British did not have the same level of monitoring capability as the Americans.

The theory was that their suspect had met around five senior Arabian businessmen in Riyadh. They had been in a high-profile location, spent an hour together, and then dispersed.

Their suspect had travelled to Riyadh's airport, de-activated his phone and was now no-longer visible, The NSA were now tracking the routine phone of the suspect, for its re-activation, but so far there had been no signal.

The request for information from the Americans to GCHQ had also created an alert which had routinely also been passed to the UK's National Crime Squad, who normally worked in areas related to organized crime.

On this occasion, the alert was considered to be civil and consequently more relevant to the police forces than the counter-espionage units, with whom GCHQ regularly operated.

GCHQ passed the report to the National Crime Squad, who triaged the reported incident to decide whether to take action. Frugality ruled, and an economical low-key monitoring option was selected, partly as a consequence of the lowered terror threat level in the UK.

Sound reasoning

Fredriksson's plane from Riyadh was on time. The journey was about five and a half hours according to the schedule, but he also knew that early morning landings at London's Heathrow could be delayed. In the event, his arrival was punctual, and because he had been seated at the front of the plane, he'd taken full advantage of the available bed. He would also freshen up in the arrivals lounge allocated for the more privileged passengers of British Airways.

His objective now was to get into central London and to meet the American who had some interesting news. The American's name was Chuck Manners, which sounded part British and was a rather apt name for someone in his line of business. Chuck didn't seem to see the irony of his name, and it wasn't something to make a direct joke about. But Fredriksson normally thought of him as 'The American' in any case.

From Heathrow, he picked a taxi from the line and asked for Edgware Road, on the western outskirts of central London. Every taxi driver would know this location and the ride was around fifty minutes. Sure enough, the taxi pulled up at the appropriate office block, in an area which seemed to have a fair smattering of Arabic shops in the neighbourhood. He stepped out of the cab, walked the few steps to the office block, pressed a buzzer and was admitted to the lobby area and the elevators where the American had his office.

A few miles away, in Bigsy's flat, Bigsy's technical attempts to adjust the sound from the recording were surprisingly successful. The first part of the recording comprised the majority of the conversation which had taken place in the next room, interspersed with some loud sounds of Jake stirring and sipping coffee.

The dialogue started without much by way of introductions. This could be simply that the recording started a little way into the conversation. A softly spoken Arab with a definite edge to his accent, particularly on words with 'R' in them, had been describing the current transfer arrangements of some funds.

He explained the purpose of the arrangement with Collins to move funds efficiently and with the minimum of interest from other organizations. The recent development seemed to be that since 'they' (he did not say who) had become interested, it was slowing down the process to an unacceptable degree.

Bigsy, Clare and Jake assumed 'They' referred to the authorities in some form, whether police or some kind of regulatory organization.

The softly spoken Arab had continued explaining that the consortium that he represented was most displeased at the recent delays and irregularities in handling payments and that they were reviewing their options.

A second and gruff-sounding Arab took over, saying that the agreement between Collins and the consortium was ended because of recent developments. He wanted to know from Collins whether the current funds in transit would be rapidly processed. Then, the entire consortium may wish to seek a new business partner. The first Arab had continued saying that they needed to see an up-to-date list of the transactions still in progress and their anticipated completion dates.

Collins had blustered at this point. He had sounded

uncomfortable throughout the entire conversation and now was trying to explain the current position. The funds still involved seemed high, but Collins did not seem to have a clear idea of when the payments would all be complete. There was a pause, the gruff Arab then continued stating, in a very firm voice, that because of that uncertainty, the consortium would be invoking a clause in their original agreement to take back control of the remaining transactions.

The fees due to Collins would be revoked, and Collins would need to sign over control of the remaining processes to another one of their business associates. There was a noise of clicking and sounds of paper rustling. Collins was saying over the top of this that he was sure the situation could be fixed and that any action on the part of the consortium was premature.

"I disagree," said a new voice, well educated and to an English ear, it sounded rounded in a public-school kind of way. It must have been the third Arabian looking gentleman because the American had a clear southern state drawl when Jake had spoken to him later.

The voice continued, "We have followed the procedure in the original agreement. The basis of the agreement was clear when we started. You have given your word that you would handle this impeccably. We now have a difficult situation for the consortium and need your full co-operation. I strongly advise you to listen to my business associates and to follow their advice".

There was a long silence.

The first Arab, with a quiet voice, spoke again. "It will be much easier for all of us if we simply follow the original agreement. We need you to sign the document in the places indicated. We can take over from there and leave any finalization details to our other colleague, Mr. Manners."

The American spoke, for the first time since the recording had started, "Mr. Collins, I strongly urge you to take the advice of your business partners. I believe their legal agreement is binding and that they also have a solid point about the current status of our business transactions. Please do not make things more difficult through senseless obstinacy."

There was another pause. Collins asked if there was an opportunity for him to seek legal advice. He was told that the agreement was signed with full knowledge of what would happen in a situation of dispute. They reiterated that this situation was beyond contradiction.

There were a few more pauses and then Collins could be heard rather unenthusiastically agreeing to the demands of the group. Some rustling and scraping sounds, presumably of the paperwork being signed and then within a few moments, the sound of chairs moved around.

"A good decision," said the original softly spoken Arabic voice as the sounds turned to those of opening the office door and of people moving into the lobby area. Jake could then hear himself first making contact with the group and the clumsy exchange followed by the more strident exchange from the American asking to swap business cards.

The next section transitioned into the arrival of Collins in Jake's meeting room and the clear transcript, including the little sequence with the exchange of the number, but nothing else particularly noteworthy to the listeners.

There was a pause as Bigsy, Jake and Clare looked at one another at the end of the recording. They were all caught in thought and in particular of the tense discussion between the Arabs and Collins, which Jake was hearing for the first time.

Jake spoke first. "Well that puts a lot more of what has been happening into perspective," he commented, and the others nodded. "We still don't know exactly what the business is about, but it's clear that Collins has delayed some payments and the Arabs were not very happy. It sounds as if he has signed some rights over to the Arabs as part of this transaction."

Clare commented next, "It looks as if the Arabs were threatening him as well – we can't tell what the body language of the session was like, but the words certainly sounded menacing."

"And that is consistent with the look as they all left and with the way that Collins seemed shaken up when I was interviewing him," said Jake.

"And what about the American?" asked Bigsy. "He seemed to be there as some sort of heavy artillery if Collins got out of order!" he suggested.

"Okay," said Clare. "What about the code that Collins gave you. Was it a pass-code, an email login, a combination or what?"

They all stared at the code individually.

"Okay," said Bigsy, "but let's think about this first. If it is a password or code, we don't want it to be traced back to here that we are so that we are accessing from a place that someone could locate. And maybe we should try some internet searches first, in any case?"

"Good point!" echoed Clare, "We need to find a place with lots of people if we are going to try that."

Once again, they decided that Clare and Bigsy would make the journey, but before that, they decided to write out as many options for the code that they could invent, to try out which would work. They all felt they were getting somewhat paranoid but didn't want to take any chances after what had happened to Lucien and Collins.

For the record

In Edgware Road, Fredriksson had found the American's office quickly and approached the person seated at a solitary desk. It was Mr Manners, with his Southern drawl.

"Thank you for seeing me here," began Manners.
"Let's keep this to the point," responded Fredriksson.

"I've got the recording," Manners began, "and there is an important part for you. I've edited the important piece onto a short extract, which is on this memory stick."

He flipped the stick into a small player on the desk in front of him. There was a part of the conversation between Jake and Collins. They were talking about car prices and the McLaren supercar. Then Collins started to talk about the code and sure enough, gave information which seemed to confuse Jake.

Then the conversation moved on to a few other points finishing with the section about the arrangements for the photography session.

At the end, the American handed the stick to Fredriksson.

The Triangle

"Here you are," he said, "I think you can understand why I have kept the original version as a type of insurance. You will do whatever you need to with this recording; yes, all of it is here, but I will be keeping the original and a paper transcript in a safe place."

Fredriksson nodded. The two men professionally understood one another. Each needed some leverage to be sure that there could be some trust and security between one another.

"There may be some sudden endings, but I doubt that you and I will ever meet again," said Fredriksson. They nodded to one another and Fredriksson left the office with the CD.

A few moments later, the American picked up the CD player and walked out of the office. He didn't look back. He would never need to see this office again. Its use for 48 hours had been all he needed.

Bigsy and Clare were also working on the meaning of the recording. They had heard the whole scene involving the Arabs and had a pretty clear idea that it was a threat and that Collins was coerced into something before his death. They also had the code number and suspected it to be a telephone number.

"Okay," said Jake as Clare and Bigsy made their way to the door. Outside they hailed another taxi for the short ride to Regent's Street.

In Cannes, France, the phone rang in the Amelia's hotel room. She paused. No-one knew she was here. She answered it cautiously. "Hello?" she said, giving away as little information as possible.

"Ms Brophy, I trust you are refreshed from the conference?" came a clear voice, "We have some interesting opportunities to discuss; I believe you saw the paperwork earlier? It would be advantageous for us both to meet at, let's say, 4 p.m. at the Martinez. I am in room 731. Please do come straight to the room. This is quite important."

The phone clicked off.

Amelia Brophy scribbled down the room number 731. He knew the Martinez, which was another famous hotel along the Croisette. She looked at her watch. It was already three twenty-five in the afternoon. A ten-minute walk to the other hotel. Was this a trap?

Lots of people knew she was in Cannes from the perspective of her alibi. She had been careful to separate her undercover role from the obvious story she had been creating. She was sure that the call was from the clandestine side of what she had been doing, and it was from someone very close. It had to be related to the people who had given her the envelope with the unexpected contents.

She ran some scenarios in her head. Meet, Fight, Flight. She decided that she should visit but would take some defensive precautions. Still logged on to her computer, she loaded her email software, selected scheduled email, created a short message and pressed enter. The email would not leave her system immediately. It was held in a 'pending' file until 17:30.

If she returned, she would cancel the message.

If there were a problem, the message would go to an interesting area in eBay, where it would form part of an auction. The auction was somewhat specialized and should not attract unwanted attention. This process had become a way to build insurance for some rather unconventional associates to operate together anonymously.

Placing advertisements for an obscure category of heavy equipment, they were able to post contracts about people they wanted removed. It allowed bidders to use the site anonymously to publish contracts and then bid to complete them.

The Triangle

The only use was for professional assassin contractors who considered themselves in danger. Respondents were also in the same line of business and operating on a strict bounty basis.

She left the computer switched on but emptied everything else from the room into a small holdall.

She placed the holdall in a cupboard in the room, which now looked unoccupied, except for the small laptop connected to the internet and a mains supply.

"Primed," she thought as she closed the door on her way out of the room.

Crazy

Here's to the crazy ones.
The misfits. The rebels. The troublemakers.
The round pegs in the square holes.
The ones who see things differently.
They're not fond of rules.
And they have no respect for the status quo.
You can quote them, disagree with them, glorify or vilify them.
About the only thing you can't do is ignore them.
Because they change things.
They push the human race forward.
And while some may see them as the crazy ones, we see genius.
Because the people who are crazy enough to think they can change the world, are the ones who do.

--Steve Jobs

An apple a day

The main reason that Bigsy and Clare had selected to go to the Apple Store in Regent's Street was for anonymity. It was close by, had plenty of computers connected to the internet and a very fast-changing series of customers. By selecting a random computer (after some wait to be able to obtain one from the many students reading and sending emails) and then by using Google, they could quickly find out whether Bigsy's idea was correct.

Once more, they typed in the internet web search for the 'Blue Flame mph 7539' passcode sequence. They soon found a few Blue Flame websites and even several where the code number was also used. Bigsy flicked through the sites. One looked promising with 'Blue Flame' across the top and then a series of pictures of various engineering elements.

Bigsy clicked a few of the photographs and many words on the page, but nothing happened. "This doesn't lead anywhere," he said, "It's a dead-end - there has to be more," he continued. He flicked back to a couple of other sites. There has to be more than this list of gas fitters.

Clare looked the screen, "Wait," she said, "Blue Flame – a very fast car! – miles per hour!" She pointed to a Wikipedia entry.

Bigsy nodded, "Yes, good idea, there's a tie-in to Darren's interest in cars."

"Let's try it," said Clare, "and we should also write it down."

She reached into her jacket and found a flyer handed to her in the street.

Bigsy was looking through the entry. "Here we are," he said, "Blue Flame, a rocket car. Check this; It's the speed of the car. It is written to look like the start of a phone number. 622.407 – let's add the 7539 to the end."

Clare wrote the "phone number" on her paper and Bigsy clicked another search term. The screen flicked to another web page very different from the first one.

A picture of an apartment block, in Switzerland, with an address. It looked like an advertisement for rental, but also included a caption, which said "Suite 009 available for rental, reference Blue/FLA/me"

Clare and Bigsy re-read this. It was a reasonably unambiguous instruction to visit a specific town and a particular room.

"No way," said Clare, "This is too crazy." Bigsy nodded and continued to click on the keyboard. He was running a search for the city and apartments, to validate that this was a real address.

Sure enough, a Google map blinked back at them, and then a satellite image of the street, close to the lake.

He found that there were 89 rooms in the development, including nine suites. Clare continued to take notes as they flicked through the various websites. Bigsy looked to see if there was a way to find out about the specific suite referred to on the other web page. There was nothing.

For another 45 minutes, Bigsy ran other searches in an attempt to find a way to make useful contact with the apartments without a visit. There was nothing. They would need to visit in person to follow the instructions.

"Yay!" said Clare, "but this is starting to get expensive".

Canned Heat

The frontage of the Martinez was more understated than some of the other grand hotels along the front in Cannes. An original art deco confection, it had been substantially modernised over the last years, which meant it was well-equipped with the latest high-speed internet connections and extensive access to most of the world's cable TV.

Amelia walked across the sleek lobby, requesting a room and stipulating the sixth floor. As it was the last day of the conference, she knew there would be likely spare capacity, and she was rewarded with a room immediately.

She looked around for the elevators. She was used to looking as if she knew where she was going in hotels, while simultaneously scoping them out.

She noted the offices behind the reception area and that the reception was in a type of cul-de-sac area in the hotel. In a shootout, the area would be difficult to manage unless using the back exit by the side of the administration offices.

The elevator was also small inside, and as she pressed the button for the seventh floor, she noted that it didn't light, although the elevator did start to move. "Security," she thought, "someone going to floor seven isn't going to be noticed by travellers to other floors."

She wondered if this was accidental but recognised it as a typical security trick used by several Agencies as well as the Russian mafia. It also gave a signal to those in the know about the way a floor may not be quite what it seemed.

She glanced around the elevator for a camera, but there was nothing visible. Given the unlit button, she assumed that the elevator was wired, but that it would be exceptionally discreet.

Then to the floor. She exited the elevator and looked immediately to the rather grandiose and sweeping stairway. She looked over the edge making quick mental calculations about angles of view. She then walked down a floor to check the positions of exits and routes.

She sought her sixth-floor room and entered it using the swipe key. A good room, looking better than the standard room she had at the Carlton. A view of the sparkling sea. She walked to the bed, not turned down. She pulled down the bedcovers and pushed the courtesy cushions into the bed, making a form which looked like a sleeping body. She added the courtesy bathrobe to the ensemble and found the pillows (no doubt to be used by the turndown service) in a wardrobe. Now she drew the curtains, so the room was now dark. Going back to the door, she looked towards the bed. From the door, it gave every impression of a sleeping person, facing away from the door on the far side of the bed.

These preparations completed, she flipped the room card into her jacket pocket and made her way back to the stairway.

Now it was around ten minutes to four o'clock. She ascended to the seventh floor. "Givenchy Spa" said the signage.

The floor had almost no room markings. It was a well-thought-out plan for the most exclusive part of the hotel. If you didn't know where you were going, it was hard to find anything. Amelia followed the signs towards the spa and along the way were several doors on the right-hand side. Each led to an entrance lobby. She looked in the first. Then she spotted the small door numbers discreetly placed by the bell push. She needed to go further to the end of the corridor.

At around five minutes to four, she was outside the requisite room, which had a public space lobby almost the size of the room she had left at the Carlton.

Amelia looked back along the corridor. Then she walked to the door, which had a small spy hole. It was blanked from inside. There was another adjacent door, which looked like service cupboards. If anything bad was going to happen, this was a tight spot to handle, and her best space management techniques didn't give her a good feeling. She thought back to the PC with its primed death contract in the other hotel.

Then she rang the bell of room 731.

Leaving the Apple Store and feeling triumphant, Bigsy and Clare used another black cab to get back to Bigsy's place. They had found the essential information they needed and had done it in an almost untraceable way.

Someone would need to visit the Apple store and get the security footage even to be able to spot them. Bigsy has also deleted the 'History' from the browsing they had just completed. It would not fool an expert but would at least slow someone down. They had also moved three times to different computers during their investigation, which also covered their tracks, along with the substantial other traffic of random shoppers, students and tourists into the store.

Back at Bigsy's, they told Jake what they had discovered and the linkage across to Zurich.

"So, Jake, what are we going to do next?" asked Clare "If we continue to look into this ourselves, then it is dangerous AND expensive!"

"I agree," replied Jake, "We're onto something, that's for sure. I think I'm in danger anyway, and I doubt the police will be able to stop that, short of hiding me somewhere. At the moment, this is a good place, because no one expects me to be here and we arrived here in a random way. I want us to try to link with the American, who has told me that I need to contact him. In any case. I know I'm asking you two to do a lot of this, but how about we make contact with the American tomorrow and then decide what to do next?"

"How much danger is there to meet the American?" queried Bigsy, "by your own account, he looked like a military-grade person."

"We need to think this through," replied Jake. Clare nodded.

Jake explained the arrangements for the next day. He was supposed to meet the American in 'Yo, Sushi,' a busy lunchtime restaurant chain just over the River Thames from Westminster. The location was also very close to Waterloo train station. They started to assemble a plan.

Bigsy would meet the American. Jake would be in the vicinity, in case it was essential, but they would keep him away from the American if practical.

Clare would control events by cell phone. They also needed an extra phone because they could not use Jake's. Clare must buy a cheap 'pay as you go' phone from a local store.

It would be suitably anonymous and meant that the three of them could communicate during the meeting. Jake knew the restaurant's location well and also that there was plenty of good viewpoints nearby all within a short walk of the famous landmark of the London Eye.

They contrived a plan. Privately, each realised they were dealing with professionals, and just hoped that their amateur efforts would be so far outside the way a professional would think that they would be able to make it work.

In Chelsea Police Station, Detective Inspector Trueman was still engrossed in the case. Although his other workload was heavy, this case had created some interesting developments.

He received information via a regular bulletin that a serious crime suspect with international connections had recently been tracked via the US National Security Administration. This person of interest had shown up first in Riyadh and then in London. They were now staying close to the area of the gallery and the murder.

Whilst this was probably co-incidence, the appearance of a serious 'player' on his patch was an interesting development. However, the timings of his arrival did not match the murder and Trueman viewed it as 'one to watch' rather than for direct enquiry.

Trueman was, however, interested in what had happened to Jake Lambers, the person who appeared to have given the tickets to Lucien Deschamps. After trying to contact Jake, at home, at his office and by phone, they were drawing a blank.

Jake's employers had admitted that Jake was something of a free spirit, but it was interesting that he didn't seem to have any visibility at all at the moment.

Trueman had some theories; maybe Jake was 'loose' somewhere; perhaps Jake was hiding for a reason yet to be determined or perhaps Jake was in trouble or worse.

Trueman had discussed this with Green, and they were examining places where Jake could have gone, including the pursuit of other stories. Green had obtained his cellular phone number from 'Street' and had contacted Vodafone to check for recent calls. There had been none since shortly after the murder of Lucien, and this was very much at odds with Jake's usually frequent usage pattern.

The Triangle

So, although it was not a very strong lead, Trueman and Green were trying to find Jake Lambers.

Dare

Fortune sides with they who dare.

–Virgil

Meet the Russians

At the Martinez, Amelia waited for the doorbell of room 731 to be answered. Apart from the entrance lobby, there was no particular clue to the type of place she was about to enter. As the door opened, she walked into a huge apartment. This may be a hotel room, but it was achingly expensive. The person opening the door was a tall, dark-suited blond-haired woman. "Please stand here, Ms Brophy," she said gesturing to a large area just inside the room.

The area contained a conference table for around six people and a set of doors leading out onto a sun-lit balcony. The curtains in the window fluttered lightly indicating the doors were already open. The room was chilled from an air conditioning set low. Two men stood up from their comfortable chairs further into the room. One wore a dark suit, white shirt and dark tie, the other a black leather three quarter length jacket.

"We need to ensure you are not carrying any form of weapon, or any form of listening device," said the woman. Her accent was strong, and her voice quite low. It reminded Amelia of a Russian accent, but she could not be sure.

The leather-jacketed man spoke. "I will be using an electronic sweeper to check you," he said. He reached to an aluminium case and retrieved a large electrically operated device with a large flat surface about half the size of a sheet of A4 paper. He clicked the device on saying, "If you are not carrying weapons or surveillance, then you have nothing to fear."

Amelia was used to this type of reception and knew they would not find anything because she had considered it too dangerous to carry anything to this group. He also noted the Russian's technique for searching and sweeping her and realised that this was effective looking but ultimately unsophisticated security. She mentally scored the man's technique and considered him to have professional training for his role, but not to a very high standard.

"Well, Ms Brophy," said the second man, wearing the elegant suit. He had a stronger Russian accent, typical of the inhabitants of Moscow, "we have someone you should meet."

The woman opened another door at the far end of the long apartment. The room was in three major sections. They comprised a meeting area, a sitting area and then an office area.

Alone, this was three or four times the size of the room Amelia had used in the Carlton. A flat screen television was switched on with no sound in the comfortable seating area. A program in Russian was playing, which looked like a news report. At the far end of the room another set of curtains billowed. There was another set of doors onto a balcony. The woman gestured to him to go on to the balcony. It was a large decked area, easily big enough for a reasonable sized party. A large oval wooden table was in front of him, big enough to seat six or eight people.

At the table sat a deeply tanned man in his mid-forties. He was wearing an open-necked shirt, and Amelia could see the glint of a heavy golden chain around his neck.

"Ah, Ms Brophy," he started, "It is very unusual to meet employees of your type. But then, it is unusual for these employees to need to do the same job twice. I think we both understand one another?"

The Triangle

Amelia nodded. She didn't want to get more drawn into the discussion than necessary. There were sometimes reasons to remain ignorant of certain situations. She knew the balcony was exposed. She was seven floors above ground, in a corner of the hotel. From the corner of her eye he could see the large white roof lettering spelling 'Martinez'. The penthouse complex she was in was under the last few letters of the huge sign.

"So, Ms Brophy, we have decided to give you the chance to complete the original job. I believe you will have seen the papers, which give more comprehensive information about our target. Please make sure you complete the assignment this time. And now look up behind you..."

Amelia looked up in the air again, back towards the sign. She noticed something on the 'Z'. it was a point of red light. The tanned man raised an arm. The red dot of light started to move slowly along the outline of the 'Z' and then down the building. It then traced a path towards her and finished on the middle of her chest. She knew it was a laser sight and she recognised it was on a high-performance weapon a long way away. She realised it was on a yacht either in the expanse of Mediterranean bay before him, or else in the harbour across to the left looking out from the hotel balcony. It appeared to be stabilised too, so from expensive kit, or with a cool hired hand.

"I see you have noticed my little exhibition," said the tanned man. "I know you know what this is. Today I am simply making a point. In a week, if I don't see the conclusion of our project, then the point I make may be somewhat sharper. We do understand one another?"

Amelia understood only too well. She had walked into a Russian crime syndicate, and they were now asking her to complete her assignment to kill Jake Lambers, or else she would be killed after a further week. The fact that the Russians has found her so easily suggested that even with her skill at becoming invisible, it was implausible to believe that she could stay hidden from this Russian group.

"I understand, and already have researched a repeat visit," she replied.

"Well then, let me bid you a good evening.," responded the Russian. "Cannes is remarkably pretty for this time of year; the sunset will be very soon, across behind those hills. In the last few moments as the light turns to evening, it is something spectacular to see," continued the Russian.

"I shall look at the sun setting on my way back to my hotel," responded Amelia, as she made her way towards the door to the penthouse. As she stepped back from the balcony decking, she noticed the way through to yet another area of the apartment and via a gate to a balcony garden where two tanned, streamlined women were sitting in what appeared to be a hot tub. This was certainly opulent and costing thousands of dollars per evening.

She nodded to the two men and then briefly met the eyes of the woman as she walked back to the exit from the room. She pointedly walked back to the stairs and then down the single flight back to the sixth floor, directly to her room. She opened the door theatrically and closed it again, still outside of the room, then slipping quickly around a corner and on towards another set of service elevators.

She had no idea whether anyone would be fooled that she had gone into the room, but he thought it would add some confusion if she was being followed. In addition, she now found a back way out of the hotel via the service elevator. She had noted that the penthouse gave a perfect view of the hotel entrance, filled with expensive cars. By not visibly leaving, it would give the Russians something to think about and for them to inevitably investigate her apparent lodging at this hotel.

She removed the jacket she had been wearing as she walked and dropped it into a roadside bin. She made her way back to the Rue d'Antibes, which is the main shopping thoroughfare in Cannes. As she approached the first Department store, she selected a new mountain gear style outer coat and an oversized check shirt. She also picked some miniature binoculars and a few other camping accessories, along with a black backpack. Ten minutes later, she was back on the Rue d'Antibes, walking towards the Carlton, wearing the new outer garment and carrying the backpack.

As with the Martinez, she was able to find a non-public way back into the Carlton, this time through a side door which led towards the kitchens. The door was propped open and looked as if it was a way for hotel employees to get outside to smoke during working hours. She followed the corridor inside, which had rubber bumpers along it, presumably because it was used to take large containers out to be picked up by trucks.

She gently clicked through a sprung door and found himself back in an area of high decoration and with ornate pictures on the wall. It was clearly part of a conference and meeting area of the hotel. She traced through this area and found herself back in the main bar area, then through a lobby to the main elevator and back to her room.

The diversion, shopping expedition and unorthodox re-entry to the hotel had cost her time and she realised he only had around ten minutes to disarm her computer and prevent it sending her violent request to eBay.

As Amelia arrived at her room, she searched for her room key, suddenly worrying that she may have left it in the discarded jacket. After a few moments of misgivings, she remembered he had transferred it to the backpack. She opened the door, crossed the room to the laptop computer, pressed cancel, then sleep. She gently unplugged the computer's connections and placed it, along with the mains adapter into the rucksack. Amelia briefly flicked through the other bag she had left in the room earlier, selected a few small items and then, carrying the old holdall in one hand and with the new rucksack on her back, she left the room.

Back at the Martinez, the Russian with the leather jacket had been watching from the rooftop. After ten minutes of looking, Amelia Brophy had not emerged. "There's something wrong," he said, "Amelia Brophy is still in the hotel." His colleague in the suit made his way, via the stairs to the ground floor. He looked around the lobby, restaurant and bar and then approached the reception. "Excuse me, my colleague was to call me, but I have forgotten his room." I am in room 729, with my other associate is in room 731. The person I am trying to contact is Ms Brophy."

The receptionist looked down. They would not typically give out room numbers, but the special guests in Rooms 729 and 731 had met a wide range of visitors over the last few days. "Room 610," the receptionist replied, "shall I connect you?"

"No that's fine, I will visit her instead". He walked back towards the elevators and called on his mobile. "Brophy is still in the hotel. She has a room."

There was a pause. "This is wrong. Finish it" said the voice. The neatly dressed man walked into the elevator, selected six and started the ascent. He walked to the room and then past it. He quietly pulled a sleek pistol from underneath his jacket. He quietly added the screw-in silencer and removed the safety catch.

Now he retrieved a golden coloured key from his wallet and inserted it into the lock. A small green light flashed; the door was opened. He slipped through the door into the dark room. He let the door close but had already flipped the deadlock, so that the door stayed ajar, but ostensibly closed.

He allowed a few seconds for his eyes to adjust to the low lighting, because the room was in darkness with the curtains drawn. He could see that Brophy was in the bed, an easy shot. Without waiting, he fired four rounds, three to the body and one to the head. The shots were almost silent, but the smoke and feathers created a cloud in the room. He quickly retreated,

The Triangle

fearful that the smoke alarm would be activated and even worse the sprinklers.

A few steps later and he was back at the stairwell. The room's door was closed, a 'do not disturb' sign hanging outside. It should give until the next day before discovery.

He returned briefly to Room 731. "It's done," he said, "Do you want me to make the arrangements for Lambers, as well?".

Ten minutes later, he along with his colleague in the leather jacket, they were in a chauffeured S Class Mercedes on their way to Nice airport. They both held Belgian passports for this part of their work.

Sushi

Jake, Bigsy and Clare took the taxi to Waterloo and walked back to the venue for the rendezvous with the American. They had devised a relatively simple plan designed to keep some initiative with themselves during the meeting. They had arrived two hours early and were looking around the location of the restaurant.

The lunchtime rush was in full swing. They had taken up a position across the busy road from the restaurant. At 12:30, some thirty minutes before the arranged meeting time, Bigsy had crossed the road into the restaurant and taken up a corner position facing towards the door. As a sushi bar, it worked on a kind of 'as much as you can eat' principle, with little trays of food of varying types passing on a conveyor belt in front of the clientele. For Bigsy this was the ideal way to be involved in a stake-out, with continuing replenishment of food, "at elbow". He was most impressed.

The first part of the plan was simple. When the American approached the restaurant, Jake would recognise him. They had Clare's best camera with a long telephoto zoom lens and would also photograph him. Jake would do this while Clare walked into the restaurant to ensure that Bigsy knew what was

The Triangle

happening.

During the period leading up to 13:00, several people entered and left the restaurant, some singularly and others in groups. Jake said to Clare that he found it challenging to be sure that the American was not in one of the groups.

Then suddenly at about one minute to one o'clock, he saw someone he recognised. Unmistakable. It was the American. tall, tanned, short hair, even wearing the slightly green looking suit. "That's him," exclaimed Jake.

Clare stood up and started to walk to the restaurant, not in a straight line from where they were sitting, but in a 'U' shape crossing the road at a pedestrian crossing. She strolled towards the restaurant, looking as if she was looking around for a friend.

Inside the restaurant, Clare looked around the table. She saw where the American was sitting and sat in the adjacent position. She looked as if checking whether her friend was in the restaurant. She blanked Bigsy, and he carried on eating some kind of rice and salmon dish, with chopsticks.

Clare selected a small passing portion of sushi and fiddled with a tiny clasp bag. The American watched out of the corner of his eye, while looking towards the door.

Clare pulled a paper from her bag and placed it on the table, as if about to take notes. Then she turned it over.

In bold print it said, "READ THIS". She gestured slightly towards the American who looked down momentarily and saw the paper.

It read as follows:

```
READ THIS.

FOLLOW THESE INSTRUCTIONS PRECISELY:

WE KNOW YOU ARE LOOKING FOR JAKE LAMBERS.

WE ASSUME YOU HAVE OTHER SUPPORT HERE. YOU MUST STAND IT DOWN.

WE WILL LEAVE THIS PREMISES AND GO TO ANOTHER LOCATION.

DO WHAT IT TAKES TO STAND DOWN YOUR TEAM.

WE WILL THEN LEAVE TOGETHER.

IF WE ARE FOLLOWED, THEN YOU WILL NOT MAKE CONTACT WITH JAKE.

WILL YOU CO OPERATE?
YES            NO
```

Clare pointed to the question. The American pointed to 'Yes.'

He stood up and coughed loudly three times. There was no sign of activity from anywhere else in the restaurant and the other diners, including Bigsy, kept eating.

As they made their way towards the door, they paid their bills, in fact, the American paid for everything, which Clare thought was something of a minor result. Bigsy noticed this too, and privately wondered how he could have got in on the act. He then snapped back into thinking about Clare's safety and started to prepare to leave the restaurant.

As he did this, the American said something to Clare, "He is NOT anything to do with me." Clare kept a straight face as they walked outside.

"Okay," said the American immediately they were outside. "My name is Chuck Manners, and I need to speak to Jake Lambers. He is in immense danger, and I think I can help. He also knows something which is of great significance."

Clare looked at the American, "Look we need your total co-operation," she said, "I am keeping you somewhere public. You are observed and being filmed right now. If you don't co-operate we will not allow you to contact Jake and we do need to know what you are doing. I am taking you to another location."

They walked, crossed a road and headed back towards Westminster. Jake took a steady stream of pictures from across the road but also noticed that there were no obvious signs of them being followed.

Bigsy left the restaurant about 100 yards behind Clare and the American and followed slowly. All three of them crossed towards Westminster Bridge and then made their way to the nearby County Hall complex, once the seat of Greater London's council and nowadays a Marriott Hotel. The long corridor walkway on the entrance was useful because it gave a view backward, which meant anyone following would be exposed.

Of course, this gave the American a chance to notice Bigsy. They walked into the hotel and found a seat in the bar. "Right," said Clare, "what is all of this about?" the American started again.

"As I said, I'm Chuck Manners, and I want to make contact with Jake Lambers, who I assume is your friend? I am here alone, although I believe that large guy over there eating the peanuts is following us. I also suspect he is linked to you in some way?"

Clare looked towards Bigsy and did her best to pretend not to recognise him. She thought that she was probably not convincing but kept up the facade in any case.

"My full title is Colonel Chuck Manners, and I am a fully serving member of the American military. I work for American Intelligence at present, although my prior time has been with the Marines. I am going to remove a document from my inside jacket pocket which confirms this. I will do this with my left hand and will move very slowly".

Clare was not ready for this development and a little stunned as he put his hand into his pocket and pulled out what looked like an American passport. Still using his left hand he opened it and inside the front cover was an individual declaration describing that Colonel Charles Jackson Manners was provided with diplomatic status and operated on behalf of the Government of the United States of America.

"I doubt if you will be convinced, even after this," continued the American, "I am involved in a major international investigation and the group of Arabs that Jake observed, along with the recently deceased Darren Collins are all integral parts. Jake is in great danger, and I think I have ways to be able to help him, but I do need to discuss this with him. I am not part of the recent killing of Darren Collins or Lucien Deschamps."

Clare was deciding the next action. "Okay," she uttered, "tell me what you think is happening."

"I will, but I need something in return," said Manners.

Clare asked, "and what is that?"

"I need you to get Jake to provide me with a copy of the digital transcript," replied Manners, "The version I have was damaged - but I know there is another copy."

"When we looked at the material on Jake's laptop, we saw that it had been backed up. Unfortunately, in the transfer from Jake's to our premises, the laptop had been left switched on and the disk drive had sustained some damage."

A waiter appeared, and they ordered two diet cokes.

Manners continued, "We were able to reconstruct most of the recording, but there are some significant gaps, including the section about the exchange of the code. We have created a replica of the section, which will keep our contacts busy for a few days, but we do need to give them a proper version."

The Triangle

Clare was looking carefully at Manners' face, for any sign of lying. She wasn't quite sure how she would know, but to her, it looked as if Manners was telling the truth.

"My role has been to infiltrate the group involved in the business of Darren Collins, the Arab team and others. It is critical to me that I remain undetected because we are on to a major international form of corruption."

Clare was also aware as these words came from Manners that she was sitting within short range of someone mixed up in some form of international crime and closely linked with extreme violence.

"We visited Jake's flat a second time to try to find the missing section, but when we looked around, we realised that Jake had created a backup system, but that the system had now been removed. It looked as if the removal was recent, particularly as there was a nice oblong break in the dust where the unit had been standing."

Clare listened as the story was unfolding. She was deciding whether to bring Bigsy into the picture.

"The point is," continued Manners, "that people involved in this via Darren Collins, or now via Jake, could all be in danger. The associates of the Arabs will stop at nothing to obtain that code.

"Until I met you today, I doubt whether anyone knows of your involvement. Now you and presumably that peanut eating friend of yours are also involved and become potential targets. Don't rely on the British Police to help you with this; they are as vulnerable as anyone else."

"But why?" asked Clare, "What is this about?"

"Look - I'll tell you some more, but if that guy is with you, then bring him over here, and I'll tell you both together."

Clare paused, and as she did so, she realised that the very act of thinking about it had told Manners what he wanted. He now knew Bigsy was part of it. She signalled to Bigsy. He approached, not sure what was happening. Clare briefly introduced them. Bigsy and Manners shook hands, and Bigsy sat down at the same table. The waiter appeared with two drinks for Manners and Clare.

"Here's the situation," said Manners, "The case we are involved with here is about international crime and money. There's a set of processes between organised crime and the way that the proceeds are made available."

"Laundering?" queried Bigsy, "we all know about that."

"This is more than laundering," replied Manners, "it's known as the triangle, and this is how it works..."

Manners continued to explain, "In normal society, there are many restrictions on money processing. For example, there is Sarbanes-Oxley, the Fed, the Bank of England, anti-laundering legislation in most countries and many cross border agreements and legislations. That keeps things under control but is not 'convenient' for two types of organisation. There are the very big legitimate organisations processing huge quantities of global transactions daily, and then there's organised crime."

"They both want roughly the same thing. A green lane. A lane, like on a toll road, that if you're pre-authorized, you can go through fast, without stopping, without excess paperwork, without having to get out the small change."

Manners sipped his coke, "So what happens? In an organised and commercial world, extra operational structures are created to help speed the transactions for global world trade. Big organisations get special authorisations, special dispensations and pre-clearances from government, national banks and other organisations to keep the wheels turning. For the right reasons this literally helps make the world go around. And of course, access to these processes is worth a lot of money. An absolutely huge amount of money."

Manners continued, "The other group with high interest in this are organised crime. At a global level, there are some organisations who want to do exactly the same thing as big business, but their motives are somewhat different. They start from a position where they have created a traffic in something which needs to be reprocessed. The simplest example is drugs, but there are many. The drug sales create money, we'll call it 'dirty' money. It can't be banked or used, but it accumulates at a tremendous rate. The second part of the process is to use 'green lane' style processes to convert the money from illegal businesses through institutions that look legitimate and onward into proper businesses. A part of the money stays 'dirty' and feeds back around the illegal system, and the rest flows on into surprisingly well-funded legitimate businesses."

Clare and Bigsy nodded. They had both seen movies about Las Vegas and using the Casinos to convert stolen money into clean money.

Manners smiled as he saw their look of recognition, "This isn't like the old Mafia days. The system nowadays is called 'the triangle' because of the way the money flows. At one point are the illegal organisations, at the second point the pseudo trustworthy organisations and at the third point the legitimate businesses."

"The people involved in this are huge consortia. We are talking about drug barons in South America, The '-istan' countries smuggling drugs and guns and anything else they can get their hands on, the Russian Mafia and some less scrupulous parts of the Gulf states, mixing oil skimming and other criminal acts together."

He looked at both Clare and Bigsy again; they certainly seemed to be taking in what he was describing.

"Yeah, this is huge," responded Bigsy. "How is it we don't hear more of this in the media?"

Manners continued, "The scale of this type of financial crime is huge, but it still only represents a small part of the total world economy. Increasing general knowledge of it only serves to further undermine other confidence in banks, governments and similar institutions."

"The NSA - that's the National Security Agency - in North America has been examining the parts of this which can be dismantled and the recent situation with Darren Collins was part of that. Collins had created an empire which was being used mainly by Arab interests who were taking money out of oil transactions and converting it into a mixture of legitimate and some illegal activities."

"Collins would never have been able to fund nor to establish his businesses without major help from people with a large bankroll but his recent situation was a consequence of his own greed and attempt to outwit the people controlling him. He already had a huge personal cash-flow and great margin on the business he was conducting but had tried to intervene in his own way to make more money for himself. It was stupid and was wrecking his empire and as a side effect drawing lots of undue attention to it."

Manners explained, "From an investigatory perspective, I was asked to get involved and to find out what was happening. It has been easier for me to align with the Arab interests and to treat the Collins situation as a way to get involved."

Clare summarised," So we've got a global ring of people laundering illegally gained money into normal money by passing it through fake institutions?" she queried, "and Collins was involved?"

"Yes, and already by now someone else will be setting up a new business empire to replace the one that has been destroyed by Collins," continued Manners.

The Triangle

"So how do you think Jake is involved?" questioned Bigsy.

Manners smiled, "Jake met Collins a few days before Collins was killed and just after Collins had been threatened by the Arabs. There's a high chance that Collins had passed something to Jake. Look, I know he did because I've got the recording from their conversation together. I don't believe Jake was involved before this. Also, the focus moves away from Jake as soon as the information is available. No-one is really interested in Jake; he is just a means to an end. Get him out of play. Provide the information."

Manners looked at them both. "I know you have the information. Or I know Jake has the information. Once I have possession everything can go back to normal. There's no point in further violence. We all just want to move along."

"Further violence..." was this a veiled threat from Manners?

Bigsy raised his eyebrows and looked carefully at Manners. "So why are you alone if this is so important? Where's your backup? Why haven't you just arrested us or something? You could take us to the police?"

Manners nodded, "You've worked it out already. I'm not exactly on the payroll of Uncle Sam nowadays. I'm acting freelance and working for the Arabs."

"They pay well and need someone like me who can 'get things done' with minimum fuss. You two, and Jake, are all in danger because of what they think you know about this.

"But I'm reviewing my options to get out of this. It's a treadmill, and I simply want a means to exit and disappear. Help me, and I help you."

"Give us a contact number for you," said Clare, "we will not give you the equivalent about us, though. We need to think about this and what we can best do. I can't say that we have the code you referred to, but if something comes to light, we will want to be able to find you," she added.

"I travel a lot," said Manners, "but here is a way to find me." He handed over a business card with his civilian name and a cellular number. The card looked like one that could be made in blocks of twenty in a stationery store.

"Trust me," commented Manners, "You are better to have a card like this, innocent and innocuous, rather than something which has 'Colonel Manners, Spy" written on it." Bigsy and Clare nodded.

"Time for you to leave," said Bigsy, "You go first; we will follow later." This made sense from a tactical standpoint. It gave Clare and Bigsy a chance to confer, but there was also a completely different exit available from the bar in the hotel, leading directly back onto the River Thames.

Manners paid the bill as he left the bar and as soon as Manners had walked to the end of the long walkway back to the street, Bigsy and Clare took the alternate route from the hotel and then melted into the many tourists walking along by the London Eye.

They walked further along the river past the street performers and crossed the river on the pedestrian bridge adjacent to the rail bridge leading to Charing Cross train station.

The bridge finished by the Embankment Tube train station which was also bustling with both tourists and working Londoners. They located a small Starbucks, situated or a corner and with a clear view of most of the area. Clare bought a tall skinny latte for herself and a grande cappuccino for Bigsy. They sat outside the cafe, in a cool early evening and waited for Jake to arrive through the exit from the station.

Chuck Manners had taken a cab to a small office behind Grosvenor Square, a part of London housing many embassies and with strong American connections. The office was behind an expensive but unprepossessing entrance in a block of similar residences. There was nothing obvious to announce the state-of-the-art technological interior. This was a monitoring station and had listening posts for several embassies, nearby cafes, clubs and coffee bars. If anyone in the intelligence or diplomacy world was indiscrete with information in the area around the prime embassies, there was a good chance that this would be monitored.

Manners wanted to be back to the tracking facility quickly. The meeting had taken nearly two hours, but he had achieved his objective, and interestingly he had also created an insurance policy.

He had considered it very unlikely that Jake would have appeared in person - he had been prepared for that, but anyway was less interested in Jake than in the whereabouts of the recording. During the first few minutes of meeting Clare, whilst still in the sushi bar, he had been able to place two miniature transmitters on Clare's clothing. They looked like tiny seed pods from a roadside weed each around the size of a grain of rice, rather than something high-tech and if Clare spotted them, she would be much more likely to brush them off, rather than to wonder what they were. And even better, the second one had been placed into the pocket of her jacket, a much harder place to find it.

And then when Bigsy had joined them at the table he had casually placed his jacket on the seat next to them making it easy for Manners to add a further two transmitters to the pockets of the jacket. He now had four available transmitters to give a signal and hopefully lead back to the site of the recording.

Jake was now approaching the Starbucks and spotted Bigsy and Clare sitting outside. He pulled up another metal chair to the shiny round table. Bigsy had just finished a slice of carrot cake and pulled the plate out of Jake's way. He carefully placed Clare's camera onto the table in front of them.

"I got some good photos," Jake said, "but when you all left for the hotel I had no idea what was happening. After Bigsy left, a couple of others left the restaurant within a few minutes, but they said goodbye outside and then walked away in different directions. The people after that caught a cab. I couldn't see any signs that you were followed. I really think Manners was on his own."

Bigsy and Clare concurred. They also had looked around for signs of others following them and also considered that Manners was alone. They explained to Jake what had occurred and about the idea that they were getting involved with something international and probably global.

"I don't know what to make of Manners though," said Clare, "He could be working for the Arabs, the US government or just for himself. It was impossible to tell. I would not want to have to guess whether he was telling the truth." Bigsy nodded agreement, although Jake thought Bigsy's face showed a different story. It looked as if Bigsy had believed every word of what Manners had said.

Jake's view was that they had stumbled into something big. That Darren Collin's death, Lucien's murder, the theft from his flat of his computer and the link of the Arabs and the American named Manners were all part of the same situation. The piece about 'the triangle' of illegal trade and money laundering was new information but was also highly consistent. So was the thought that he now possessed a key to another part of the puzzle.

Clare continued with her thoughts, "Manners just said that police help and protection was not viable and that all three of us are now implicated. I think we have been pretty careful up to now and only Manners knows we three are all involved."

"Yeah, Manners and whose army!" added Bigsy, "If he really works for the Marines or the US Government, then we are probably all over their system by now".

"And if he works alone then we are probably not," added Clare.

"If he works for law enforcement then I can't see why he would stop us from going to the police?"

"So, what next?" asked Jake.

"I have a suggestion," answered Clare, "How about this?"

Clare outlined a plan that they would visit the Zurich location from the internet web description, find out what was involved and then take it to the police as proof that something big was happening.

Jake would need to stay undercover. With only Manners knowing about Clare and Bigsy, they could move relatively freely, in the knowledge that if Manners had wanted to do something bad, he would already have done so.

They agreed their preparations over another coffee at the Starbucks and then headed back to Bigsy's flat, again by taxi. A short journey, they travelled together picking up a taxi from the cab rank outside Charing Cross station.

Manners watched their progress from the tracking room, his high clearance status with the Americans meant he could easily insert himself into one of the surveillance stations in central London. He had avoided the main embassy where the security was extra tight. A nearby facility was perfect.

The dots he was monitoring were travelling together and had paused in two locations. One was close to where the meeting had taken place, by Embankment Tube and the second was in a residential area. The dots were paused here for over two hours. Then they started to move again, this time, towards the Eurostar train station.

Being elsewhere

Amelia Brophy had decided to 'get the hell out of Dodge'. She was not sure how the Russians would react to her subterfuge at the Martinez, but she had a pretty good idea.

As she had met them but not shown them anything to trade, then there was a high probability that they would be on her tail. She decided to avoid the obvious route to London via Nice airport, but instead to work another route. She had to decide whether to simply finish the job with Jake Lambers, or whether she should first try to extract more information.

Amelia assessed that there was danger in either route, but that simply executing Jake would provide her with the Banker's draft she was expecting.

This would be a routine response from her current employer, and if she did this, took the money and then efficiently disappeared, it would be regarded by all as the end of her commitment.

On the other hand, if she started to dig into whatever secrets Jake held, then she was also sentencing himself to further pursuit and maybe elimination.

Amelia surveyed the local map to look for another suitable route back to the UK, other than via Nice airport. She did not want to use the roads back across France, which would take a long time, and there was a chance that she would be intercepted.

She decided to use Genoa instead, which was across the border into Italy. The drive from Cannes could be Autoroute for almost the whole journey, and she could do the drive in around an hour and a half. She would head for the Christopher Columbus airport in Genoa and then take a direct flight to the UK, or if there were any sign of delays, she would split the journey in either Frankfurt or Paris and then head back.

Her top priority was to get out of Cannes fast now, and she was keen to do this in a way that meant if he was followed that she had a chance to defend herself. Cannes is a prestige resort and getting a chauffeured car to Genoa would be easy and allowed her to break away from the Peugeot still parked by the Cannes train station. But she had also seen the selection of vehicles available to the rich and famous who stayed in the area.

There were small fast sports cars, expensive Mercedes and - her vehicle of choice - a Hummer.

The black Hummer was parked on the Croisette, with metallic detachable signage saying 'One Limo rental - A louer'.

This was an ideal vehicle for her journey. She could drive herself, had maximum protection should she need it and if she hired it for a week, there would be a long gap before the vehicle was detected as missing. Twenty minutes of paperwork, a false passport and driving license and a large credit card bill later, she had control of the vehicle. She had told the rental company of her plans to head along the coast. They had charged her extra for crossing the border into Italy, but were used to 'high rollers' who wanted to use flashy vehicles to smooth their way around the Cote D'Azur.

She fired the engine, confidently flipped the automatic transmission and moved off along the Croisette, turning right first into side roads and then nosing her way towards the Autoroute. She would be in Genoa within two hours, at the airport and seeking a flight towards London.

As she drove, she watched the sides and rear-view mirror; As she approached toll-booths, he looked around for cars idling to follow her. She was good at this. She was sure she was not being tailed.

The precautions of the huge black Hummer H2 were probably an over-reaction but, "Only the paranoid survive," she mused.

Bigsy's

Clare, Bigsy and Jake had returned to Bigsy's flat. They had decided that Clare and Bigsy would visit Zurich and check the apartment featured in the website. They suspected that a significant key to what was happening would be found if they did this. They were worried about Jake and decided that it was too dangerous for him to accompany them. Jake would continue to stay in Bigsy's apartment.

Clare left Jake and Bigsy for a short time while she ventured to her own flat to pick up some clothes and her passport. She collected a small backpack and a much smaller camera than the one she had used with Jake. She also dropped her own slim MacBook laptop into the rucksack and a selection of plugs and wires.

A short cab ride to Bigsy's and they made preparations for their hasty journey to Zurich. They were using the Eurostar train from London to Paris and then changing to a TGV Express train for the second section to Zurich. They considered the route to be fast to Paris and then after a change of stations in Paris; they would be on a fast train to Zurich. The route was direct but not particularly obvious, and they relied upon this to reduce the chance of being followed and certainly to reduce the possibility of being monitored, which would have been much easier if they had travelled by plane.

They checked their various phones, realizing that they only had two which would function internationally. Jake's could not be used; Jake continued to keep Clare's and Clare and Bigsy would share Bigsy's. The recently acquired "pay as you go" phone could only be used in UK and would also stay with Jake, but Bigsy insisted on taking Jake's phone, with the battery disconnected, in case they really needed a further international phone whilst they were in Europe. At least they could cross communicate, both by text and person to person.

"See you soon," said Clare to Jake. Bigsy winked, and Jake attempted to look amused back. All three of them were thinking that this could be a tough and uncertain few days. Bigsy and Clare, both carrying backpacks, then started their adventure on the way to the terminal for the next Eurostar express train to Paris.

Bad

From Cannes, the two Russians had soon reached Nice airport and, travelling on their Belgian passports, had caught the last flight back to London's Heathrow airport. They had arrived at around nine p.m. and decided to stay in a hotel close to the airport. They had the address of Jake's flat and would prepare to handle the situation with Jake in the morning. They used a shuttle bus to get to the Radisson Edwardian at Heathrow, which was close to the airport and also close to the main route running east from the airport into London, along the A4 trunk road and M4 motorway. From the hotel's concierge, they ordered a hire car to be available from the next morning, which they could use to get into central London.

By ten o'clock, they were in the hotel's brasserie, ordering a late meal and arranging to meet an associate for breakfast in a nearby venue.

Detective Inspector Trueman and Sergeant Green had decided to use the same morning to visit Jake's flat. They had already made several calls to his cellular phone as well as contacting his office. They had asked for an alert if Jake tried to call his office. They had also made a prior visit to his flat, and if they were unable to make contact on this occasion, then they would be taking a search warrant.

The Russians had started their own preparations to visit Jake's. They had started extremely early, picked up the hire car and driven from the hotel to an adjacent McDonald's burger restaurant.

Their plan was simple. If Jake didn't know anything about the plan on his life, then it would be easy to visit him while he was indoors and to finish the job. They knew that both Jake and also access to the information stored in his flat were important, with the trade-off that the information was paramount, and Jake was expendable.

In the neon-lit early-morning darkness adjacent to the McDonald's car park, they met their associate and transferred two aluminium cases from one car to the other. The exchange took a few seconds and both cars were back into the busy London traffic, the Russians heading towards London and the other car heading in the opposite direction, towards the West.

The Russians intended to execute their plan quickly. Visit Jake's flat; silently terminate Jake and then search the flat for the missing information. They knew that if Amelia Brophy had found the information, she would have used it to bargain during their meeting in France.

Without that, she had no leverage, she had failed a mission, not got paid and then faced her own execution. The two Russians would not make the same mistake. They had clear instructions with regard to Jake and also to the information that they required.

They would ask Jake for information first, rough him up second and if he was unwilling to divulge, then they would kill him anyway. If he told them the information, they would briefly verify it and then kill him. If he didn't appear to know anything, they would kill him and then tear the place apart. It was a simple plan, and the two end objectives were the termination of Jake and the retrieval of the missing information. They had planned the approach to Jake's to be early enough for him to be indoors and probably still in bed.

As they approached the area of Jake's flat, they surveyed the parking options. Central London, very early morning, residents still at home, so limited parking. They found a residents' spot and parked anyway. They realized the car may be clamped or worse towed away, but they knew that they could find an alternative escape route if needed.

From the back of the car, they opened the aluminium cases. Each contained a Pernach OT33 automatic pistol capable of firing eighteen rounds and the second case also included an army green holdall and a small bag of specialized tools. They took the tools, the two weapons and loaded them into the holdall. None of this was particularly heavy and the end result was easy enough to carry.

As they approached the house, they surveyed the parked cars in the vicinity. They were looking for something more than five years old. A red Vauxhall Carlton. This was easy. They quietly broke into the car, disabled the steering lock and ensured that they could start the engine. They now had two options for a getaway vehicle, as well as taxis and public transport.

They climbed the steps at the front of the house within which was Jake's flat, unaware that they were the third group to visit in this way. It was still early in the morning, and they made their way directly to his room. The Yale lock on the door was easy to disable. One of the tools in the smaller bag was designed to cut through the barrels in a household lock and to insert a new blank blade which could be used to turn the lock.

This made a small amount of noise, like a skipping power screwdriver, but within ten seconds the door was open. They both stepped in with their guns held alert, safety catches off. They could scare Jake witless before they started to question him. Like professionals, they moved swiftly from room to room, covering each other as they swiftly searched for Jake.

Nothing. No one present.

They both relaxed slightly and brought their guns down. Maybe they could find the information now and if necessary, wait for Jake to return later. The way they had disabled the lock was going to leave a tell-tale reminder that something had happened, so they realized at this stage that they were getting in deep.

One spoke, "Let's search for the recorder, or any computers which could store the information".

They started to search. It became quickly apparent that they were not the first people to work through the flat. There were enough mains leads and cables, spare keyboards and computer mice on the desktop to show that there had been one and possibly two computers there until a short time ago. There were dust marks from a fan inlet and some disconnected network cables, some of which ran to a junction box on the floor. Someone had been here and disconnected whatever technology had been present.

Trueman and Green were on their way to Jake's flat. This was their second visit. It was early morning, and if Jake was still living in his flat, he should still be there at the time they would arrive.

They had the same problem parking as the Russians. In their case, they parked in the same resident's area, but by flipping a small document onto the front dashboard, they had a different expectation from the Russians. They would not be towed away; their little card indicated they were from the local constabulary.

Together they climbed the steps to the main entrance to the house, which was already open. They knew the way to the flat, having visited previously. As they got to the door, they rang the bell but immediately noticed that the door was ajar and the lock looked damaged.

"Radio for some cover," whispered Trueman as Green pulled

his communicator from his suit. Trueman gently pushed the door open. He immediately saw the two men, who were both looking towards him. There was a staccato puff as the first bullet hit him, followed by two others. Before he fell, he saw Green walking backwards and then also falling to the ground. Two more bullets were fired and the room again became quiet.

The Russians looked at one another. "Whatever was here has been taken already - we should go." The second Russian nodded, picking up the walkie-talkie from Trueman's body.

"They were Police," he said, "We need to go right now".

They quickly gathered the tools and holdall and placed the pistols inside. The first Russian opened the door to the kitchen.

He turned on the four hobs and the oven and opened the oven door. Back in the area where the two police bodies lay, he lit a candle which was perched on a windowsill. He moved the candle further into the room and placed it on the floor.

"We have about five minutes," he said. They walked out of the room, closing the door. Then across the hallway and out of the front door, descending the three steps and back to their hire car, still parked in the residents' bay. The first Russian sat in the driver's seat, turned the ignition, and the two of them drove slowly away.

Seven minutes later, the police arrived, quietly, without use of sirens. The nature of the call from Green had suggested stealth and discretion. Two cars arrived, one ordinary police car and the other a more specialized armed response unit.

There were a few moments of radio exchange and then the men of the armed unit started to climb the stairs towards Jake's flat.

As they were preparing to go inside, there was a muffled sound like an explosion. It was the gas from the hob being ignited. The small blue-yellow fireball tore through the building. Immediate effects were the ignition of curtains and then cushions, the speed of the explosion was sucking the available air from the room. Blackened papers and other materials fluttered to the ground.

A steady blaze ensued as other items in the room also caught fire, more like a bonfire blaze now than the explosive nature of the first few seconds.

The armed police crouched and watched for respite from the fire, and then, as one, they noticed the prone bodies of Trueman and Green, just outside the entrance to what was rapidly becoming a blackened and smoke-filled room.

Any place in the world

"It's a little monster."
Hummer advert, Super Bowl XL, 2006

Brophy visits London

Amelia Brophy had arrived in London the previous evening. The trip from Cannes, across the border into Italy, had been uneventful. The Hummer had been an exciting driving experience and Brophy, while keeping professional had been amused at this civilian version of what was an all-American military machine.

Amelia had used Hummers in the past (Hum-Vees in military slang), but this version was quite different with its plush seating and a 12 channel Bose stereo system. She knew it could still drive over another car if things got tough, or maybe push down a wall without losing its stride, but she had just used it as an expensive and very robust taxi to get to Genoa.

She driven it to the long stay car park, noted the bay number and would inform the company a day before the rental ran out. Her main objective in the short term was to escape general detection from the Russians as he made his way back to the United Kingdom.

In the event, he was able to walk from the car park to the small airport at Christofero Columbus airport and select a direct flight with a lesser-known carrier back to London's Gatwick airport.

By evening, she had arrived, travelling light. She booked a room at the Gatwick Hilton, which was built right on the airport campus. From here, using the internet, she was able to accurately identify the location of Jake's flat and map out the surrounding area. Like the last victim at the gallery, this would be silent fast knife-work and she would be in position from early morning in two days' time to do this. Tomorrow was stake-out and the next day was execution.

In the morning, she had caught the Gatwick Express to Victoria and then caught a taxi to the general area of Jake's flat. Amelia had decided that if a direct opportunity appeared during the day, she would end it immediately, otherwise she would plan for a two or three a.m. entry to Jake's flat.

She rounded the corner into Jake's road. Immediately she noticed a police car, then a second, a police van, a fire engine and an ambulance. They were spread all over the road and there was a crackle from police radios.

Amelia looked along the road; certain this was related to her mission but convinced that no-one would know of her current plans. She started walking along the road, already creating her excuse to need to be at the shopping centre at the far end. A policeman walked slowly towards her.
"I'm sorry, Madam, I need to ask you to use another road this morning; this way is blocked. You don't know the people in the three houses over there on the left, do you?"

Amelia shook her head, "I'm just trying to get to the shops," he replied.

"You'd better go back to the corner and take the next road then," the policeman replied, "we will be here a while".

"What happened?" she asked.

"You know I can't answer that," replied the policeman, "please just take another route this morning."

Amelia looked towards the central house, taped by the police. She noted the coroner, the fireman, the large number of police and that several had bullet proof jackets. She couldn't see any police weapons but knew there must be plenty in the close vicinity.

"Okay," she responded and started to turn. Then she noticed the red Vauxhall. Unlocked, wires exposed by the steering wheel. Wired as a precaution, a safety car.

"Not cool," she mused.

He turned back to the corner of the street and into another road leading towards the shopping centre. As she walked, she processed the information. A messy hit on Jake's flat, the very place he was targeting and less than two days after his discussions with the Russians. A botched and messy hit. A broken in and wired escape vehicle.

Professional attention to detail, but badly executed hit, drawing a lot of attention. This could only be the Russians. Unsophisticated but very pragmatic. She decided it was the Russians, probably the same ones she had met in Cannes, taking the short route to Jake. But why? It was her job.

This could only mean one thing. The thing Amelia expected had happened. They'd monitored for her to leave the hotel and when she didn't, they'd tried to locate her, found her room and tried to kill her. The way she had rigged the bed and the feathers had created enough confusion to mean the assassins had not checked but now believed her dead and the need to finish the job with Jake themselves.

She wondered if Jake had been killed. She had seen the coroner and the ambulance, but it was too risky to go back to check any further. Amelia was about to disappear and adopt a new name. This had got very personal with the Russians.

Ed Adams

Eurostar

Clare and Bigsy were enjoying the train experience. There was something 'important' about travelling to Paris on the Eurostar. Many of the passengers looked like suited businesspeople on their way to meetings, flashing laptops, mobiles phones and all types of communication device.

Bigsy and Clare looked more like backpackers on the first stage of a long journey. They had been using their credit cards for ticketing and hotel bookings, and the ever-practical Clare had even told the credit card company she would be abroad to prevent the card from being stopped unexpectedly.

The miles and then kilometres sped by in a blur. Soon they were in Paris. Gare-du-Nord, and they now needed to cross Paris to the train station for Zurich. They used a taxi for speed and were soon in the new station.

A fleeting glimpse of the romantic city and they were again in the slight grime of a major train station, walking towards a sleek TGV which would take them to Zurich. In fact, the train looked more like an aeroplane and as they stepped into their second piece of luxury transportation, they both had to remind themselves that this was a mission, not a vacation.

The Triangle

Manners had been watching the cluster of dots on his surveillance system. The grain-sized transmitters were low power, and while ideally suited to monitoring movements around London, they limited traceability to within the Greater London area, bordered by the ellipse of London's peripheral M25 motorway. Bigsy and Clare slid out of London on the Eurostar. Other than the knowledge that they were on this train, Manners had no other way to track them across into Paris.

Manners could pinpoint a location when the transmitter dots had all paused at an address in Finsbury Park. With four transmitters, there was an accurate fix: Stapleton Hall Road, and an actual street number. From Google maps, it was a large house, converted into flats. Manners was getting organised to pay a visit. This time he would take a professional team, rather than the burglars he had used the first time to approach Jake's flat.

Manners was convinced that this address held the clue to the whereabouts of Jake and probably to the information he required. The travel of the two he had met in the Marriott was less impressive than getting to the coded data that was the basis for the reconstruction of the triangle network.

From his hotel near Park Lane, Fredriksson was also considering how to derive the code. He had the recording on memory stick from Manners and sure enough within this was an interview exchange which seemed to describe a code. Fredriksson knew that the code was supposed to lead first to 'the Blue Flame' but that the code number in the version supplied by Manners had an error. Fredriksson's attempts to second guess the missing code number was too difficult. All he had found was a long list of addresses, which looked like a range of churches in the North East of London.

Fredriksson paused to consider this; there was something wrong. Perhaps the recording had been manipulated? He switched to a sound analyser on his computer. He scrolled through the recording. The wave patterns showed some sudden changes as if they had been cut. This recording was a fake. Manners had doctored it. Fredriksson had no idea that this manipulation was done out of necessity, rather than as malice. Fredriksson made a mental note from this related to Manner's future.

He reached into his hand luggage and pulled out a pair of headphones. He plugged them in and re-listened to the last part of the recording. He could hear the almost imperceptible clicks as the sound had been cut and restarted. Fredriksson now decided to listen to the full recording on headphones to check for any other useful information or clues. For the first time, he listened to the first part, when Jake had been waiting for Darren Collins. Fredriksson used software like that which Bigsy had used, to boost the quality of the recording between Collins, the Arabs and Manners.

It gives you wings

Zurich, Switzerland. A pretty 10th-century town with a picturesque centre and beautiful views of the adjacent lake. Bigsy and Clare looked at the evidence of its origins. Of the wooden bridges decorated with flowers spanning parts of the central area with a history going back to the middle ages.

In the distance, they could see the outline of mountains, and they knew definitively that they were in a foreign country. For now, they needed accommodation and quickly found a Sofitel hotel close to the centre. They awkwardly discussed sharing a room but then decided to give one another space. Their credit cards were already quite dented, so decisions now would hardly make a profound difference.

In the event, the Sofitel was inexpensive, and they were both tired from the stress and travel of the day. After a brief meal in a nearby chain restaurant, they both collapsed for the night, ready to start fresh the following day in pursuit of the apartments listed on the website.

While Clare and Bigsy settled for the night, back in London Fredriksson was deep in the analysis of the original recording provided by Manners. He filtered and boosted the audio in the same way that Bigsy had achieved this a day or so earlier. Now

Manners could hear most of the conversation between the Arabs and Darren Collins, although it dawned upon him that sections were skipping which now sounded as if it was from a hardware fault. He also knew that Collins had continued the follow-up conversation with Jake Lambers, so if Jake Lambers could be found it provided the best chance to locate the missing information.

Fredriksson had no sophistication at his disposal to find Jake Lambers. Instead he looked for London phone directory enquiries on the internet and typed in "Lambers, J". There was just one. He could not believe his luck. He wrote down the address.

Manners was already planning his move on the located flat - he didn't know it was Bigsy's flat. Manners suspected that Jake and the needed information would be together at this address. He knew that the sleek woman and the large messy looking guy had moved away and that he would now have access to the flat and maybe Jake.

He was using a professional outfit for this entry. The two guys he had used at short notice for the previous break-in had damaged the stolen laptop even when stealing it from empty premises. This time he had personally selected a team. Americans, ex-military, used to working together, fast, professional and silent. Manners was in the right communities for this and could get people who would work for cash and not ask questions. Afterwards they would melt away and could be relied upon for their discretion.

The team he assembled for this was probably over-powered for the situation. He was using three men and himself as control. Four military onto one unarmed surprised civilian should be simple. They actually wanted the information, not Jake, so the objective had to be carefully proscribed to the team.

They planned an early morning entry to the flat, probably three in the morning when the occupants would be sleeping. They were going to use a surround pattern. Two through front access, one was covering back and a control across the road. This provided fast access, minimised escape routes and provided consolidation when they needed to search.

Two of the men would carry tasers. All three would have smoke canisters, and one would also carry a semi-automatic weapon. They would all wear daytime clothing with layers, so that if they needed to change identity it would be easy to discard a layer.

With their basic preparation, they collected the statutory white van which would form their primary transport. They also had another bland looking Ford hatchback which they pre-parked in the area. This was a 'B' car, to only be used in an emergency. It had been put in position the day before the operation. Two streets away were three pedal cycles, chained to railings as a third backup.

At one o'clock in the morning, the group of four were in the van. Manners and two of the men sat in the back. The fourth man drove. As they parked by Bigsy's flat, they pulled on balaclava hats. These were less to act as a disguise, but rather more to intimidate.

They synchronised watches, waited until seven minutes to two and then left the van to take up positions. Manners, acting as control, moved to the van's driving seat.

Inside Bigsy's flat, Jake was not asleep. Earlier in the evening, he had found a spare box of Red Bull caffeinated drinks, which Bigsy had stored on top of a cupboard. He vaguely recollected the poker evening about two weeks ago when they'd slightly overbought all of the drink and despite the attempts to finish everything, by the next morning they had all been sprawled around Bigsy's flat.

Jake had been trying to work out the possibilities of how the money laundering process operated. He supposed that the illicit activities could be from drugs, people trafficking, illegal gambling and other large-scale vices. The money could be flushed through casinos (simply lose it all and let the casino clean it up) but if there were significant enough quantities, even the casino route could become labour intensive. Having a process where the money was laundered through legitimate shell companies would make sense.

He found a large pack of flip chart paper and some big marker pens and started to draw the routing of the money. It did, indeed, look like a triangle of corruption.

It was around two a.m., but Jake didn't feel tired - in fact, the drinks had been giving him a real buzz to stay active. He decided to create a 'war room' about what had been happening, as he'd seen in the movies. It was this or to go stir-crazy. Wired with the excess caffeine, he decided that the sticky chewing-gum-like material known as 'Blu-tack' was needed to stick the papers onto the wall.

He flicked through Bigsy's kitchen drawers and the place where Bigsy's computers were stacked, but there was nothing suitable.

"Rick," thought Jake. "Rick the estate agent; estate agents are organised; he will have Blu-tack!"

Jake subconsciously recognised that this was a bizarre and somewhat illogical quest at two in the morning, he wondered if the drink was bringing out a latent obsessive-compulsive disorder. He wandered to the kitchen drawer and fiddled about at the back.

A key ring said "Foxtons"; it was Rick's spare keyring. Rick and Bigsy had swapped spare keyrings so that if either was locked out, they could borrow their spare sets to get back into their respective flats.

The Triangle

Jake remembered that Rick was away partying because the idea of paying a call at two o clock in the morning was beyond the normal description of neighbourly.

He opened Bigsy's door, leaving it ajar as he went into Rick's. The key worked first time.

He called "Rick?" just in case but there was no reply. He switched on the light and immediately switched it off again. He realised he had been working in semi-darkness for the last hour and that was about all his eyes could take. The light from the hallway was plenty enough. He looked around. He had visited Rick's before, a remarkably neat and well organised flat. In the general dimness, he walked to Rick's small office area and there, in a small box, was a selection of office supplies. Stapler, marker pens, erasers, computer CDs and, sure enough, a pack of Blu-tack. More than that, it was a pack of unused Blu-tack.

At that precise moment, he heard a huge bang. This was from the outside door and made him wonder what was happening.

The sound was the entry of the two intruders to the front of the house. He could see they were going directly towards Bigsy's room.

Jake kept a low profile. The noise he heard sounded as if it came from people who meant business. It could be that someone had now located him and was getting tough. He could see enough through the small gap in Jake's door.

The intruders had noticed Bigsy's open door and moved straight in. As they had walked into the entrance of Bigsy's, he could see they had noticed the spread of IT equipment on Bigsy's desktop. He noticed the third intruder making his way to Bigsy's room. They looked as if they were quickly checking throughout the flat, but there was no one present, just piles of paper and general mess.

The intruders would have their work cut out. Compared with

an average person's flat, Bigsy's had an exceptional amount of equipment. There were several PC towers, two laptops, spare disk drives and CD burners.

Jake decided his best option was to leave quietly whilst the Americans were in the flat. He slipped quietly from Rick's room, carrying Rick's spare Foxton key. Next to the flat key he noticed another one. It said 'mini' on it.

"Thank you," he thought, it was the key to Rick's estate agent's Mini, the one with the fancy paint job and the racing number on the side. As he left the flat, hecrept quietly down the steps, then he plinked the key on the fob, and a re-assuring double blip sound came from his left. It was the Mini, which now showed its taillights flashing and he sighed as he walked quickly towards it without looking back. He opened the driver's door, put the key into the ignition, turned it and then in a few seconds was manoeuvring the car out of the parked row of vehicles and past a double-parked white van.

Manners saw the car drive past, noted the registration number and waited calmly as the three Americans continued to search through the equipment in Bigsy's flat. A few minutes later, the first emerged. "There is a lot of equipment," he called, "Well, we have a lot of van," responded Manners. He knew that the equipment would be a faster way to the information and therefore more valuable than Jake. If he needed to do something further with Jake, this could be saved for another day.

Twenty minutes later, the equipment was on the van, and they moved away, driving through London to a small lock-up railway arch just south of the River Thames and near to Blackfriars. They would need to sift a lot of data now, to find the missing recording. Manners also knew the likelihood was that the recording would be easy to locate, simply by date added.

141

To the dance?

*"Dance as if you got lost
in the mystery and beauty of life."*

— Debasish Mridha

Bouquet in Zurich

Bigsy and Clare had obtained a basic map of Zurich from the hotel concierge. They had found out where the apartment block was located and decided it was near enough to Central Zurich to take a taxi. The Zurich morning was crisply cold, but the sun shone. There was white frost in the shadows, but where the sun reached, it had melted and dried already. They had decided to keep the hotel rooms for two days so that they could use them as a base camp while they were on the trail of the Apartment.

Bigsy's phone rang.

"Clare" said the writing on the screen. It was Jake using Clare's borrowed phone.

"I'm in a jam," called Jake. "We've been rumbled at your place Bigsy," he continued and then began to explain the recent developments. "So where are you right now?" asked Bigsy, and Jake explained that he had borrowed Rick's car as an escape vehicle and driven out of London to the West.

He was parked in the Heston Services on the Westbound part of the M4 motorway.

"We'd better tell Rick about his car," continued Bigsy, "We don't want him blowing the whistle." Bigsy had the phone number of Rick on his cell phone and could call him after their conversation was over. He knew that Rick would be irritated rather than annoyed once he knew the car was not exactly stolen but rather that it was borrowed. He also knew that once Rick was in on part of the story, there would be total forgiveness.

Jake explained the situation to Clare, and they decided that it was best if Jake carried on along the motorway further out of London, and then found a cheap Travelodge for a couple of nights, until they got back and could rally their thoughts.

They agreed to keep in contact by cell phone and text message and then Bigsy rang off. Jake walked to the entrance of the Heston services building and saw a large road map of the UK, with Travelodges marked. There was actually one right here at Heston. This would do fine.

He walked back towards his car, and then drove the short distance within the services complex to the overnight Travelodge facility and requested a room for the next three nights.

Back in Zurich, Bigsy and Clare hailed a taxi, and made their early way to the apartment block that they had first seen on the internet site. Clare had a print of the details from the web-site and as they travelled she unwrapped it from her pocket.

"So how will we handle it when we get there?" she asked Bigsy. They had already talked about this. They would first simply visit the concierge if there was one and ask about the flat.

They would claim to have something to deliver. Clare thought flowers was the most straightforward. She could visit the desk and look like a florist doing a delivery.

Clare did speak some basic German, and in this area of Switzerland, a foreigner doing the delivery would not seem too out of place.

They had decided that even without a concierge, the flowers story would still be a good cover. They could then directly ring the bell to see if anyone was in. The apartments were big enough to mean there was reasonable traffic of people in and out, so getting into the lobby would be easy enough.

In the event, while they discussed these options in the back of their taxi, they soon found themselves at the apartments. There was the main entrance, with ground floor letterboxes and buttons to announce arrival.

This would make access to the building easy, but access to the specific Apartment quite difficult. They walked from the entrance back onto the main street. It was a fairly busy road with a nearby roundabout and a selection of shops, plus a bar and a separate cafe quite close.

Down a small hill was a further run of shops and close to the end of the row was a beautiful and decidedly high-end florist. Clare and Bigsy looked at one another and nodded. "This'll do fine," said Bigsy, "You choose the flowers, Clare!"

Clare selected a medium sized a which seemed to be partly wrapped in some 'manly black' paper and without too many frills and bows. She then paid using some of the funny Swiss Francs, a mix of high tech bank notes and a type of coinage which nowadays seemed surprisingly large and heavy.

They walked back to the apartment block, entered the lobby, pressed the button to the apartment and waited to see what would happen.

"Bonjour," said a voice.

"Hello," said Clare, "Sprechen Sie Englisch?" - do you speak English?

"Yes," came the reply, "I prefer to speak English rather than German," the voice continued.

"Great!" she continued, "I have a delivery of flowers for you." She was pleasantly surprised how easily this was going.

"Flowers?" enquired the voice. "Who are they from?"

"I don't know," answered Clare, realising they had not worked out this part of the plan, "It says they are from 'J'," she lied, thinking quickly.

"OK," said the voice. "You can bring them up". Clare looked at Bigsy, who had remained silent. This was going too well. Was this the right apartment? Was there something else in play?

There was a buzz from an inner door, which now opened, leading to small elevator. Clare went inside, signalling to Bigsy to wait in the lobby. She ascended to the top floor and looked for the Apartment. There was another bell push on the door. She pushed it and waited for a response. Nothing. After a delay, she tried again. Still no response. At that moment, a different visitor appeared from around a corner at the end of the corridor and was making his way towards the elevator.

"Entschuldigen Sie mir," she asked, and continuing in German, "Do you know the person who lives here?"

"Nein," replied the man, who continued towards the elevator. She noticed he was wearing flip flop sandals and no socks. He also looked unshaven and unkempt. In her best German she continued and asked him if he knew any of the other people who lived on the floor. He briefly looked at her, looking up and down and at the flowers. "Es tut mir leid," he answered, "I'm sorry" and then continued in bad German to say, "I don't really understand German very well". As he said this, Clare realised that this was the same person she had spoken to on the apartment buzzer a few moments earlier.

"Look," she said, "I have come a long way to find you - I know about you and just want to talk." His posture softened, he looked as if he had received some sort of body blow. She realised it was an emotional response of relief, and she asked him if she could talk.

"Alright," he said, "You'd better come inside," now speaking English. Clare had a sense that she knew the voice from somewhere. They walked back towards the Apartment. "Wait," said Clare, "I must let my friend know what is happening". She pressed the fast dial on her phone and after around twenty seconds was connected to Bigsy, waiting downstairs.

"We are going to talk," she said, "I am also to ask him whether you can join us."

She asked the man, and he agreed to let Bigsy join them. He opened his Apartment door, pressed a buzzer and around a minute later, Bigsy stepped from the elevator.

"This is my friend Bigsy" introduced Clare, "and my name is Clare," she continued. "And my name is Darren Collins," came the reply.

In South London, Manners had already dropped off his three American assistants a short distance from their completed operation. They had then split up and made their separate travel arrangements. Each had been paid by Manners and knew that further questions would just increase risk.

Manners had now unloaded the computer equipment from the van. It was much quicker to unload with the van parked tailgate to the arch.

In around ten minutes, the equipment was spread in a row, while Manners decided how to proceed to interrogate it. He looked at what they had acquired. A few PC tower units, no doubt with large hard drives full of data; a couple of laptops, one quite old and the other very modern, some communication devices, a CD cutter and a small networked disk drive.

He looked at the disk drive again. It said 'Apple' on the top and someone had written 'Jake's Backup' in felt tip on the top cover. There was a good chance that this was the unit he needed. He started the modern laptop. It refused to co-operate. "Enter password," it blinked. This could take ages.

He looked again at the other equipment. He connected the various wires to assemble one of the tower units and switched it on. The screen was black and then some white writing flashed across. It was starting up. Around a minute later a blue screen winked 'welcome'. He pressed enter and it said, "Enter password". He tried the usual tricks, resets, special key combinations, passwords such as 'password, admin, secret, jake'. Nothing worked.

He decided he would need another approach. Picking up the small disk drive and its connector cables, he walked out of the lockup, and jumped back into the van. He was going shopping.

Ed Adams

Please identify yourself

The news that Bigsy and Clare were talking to the previously assumed dead Darren Collins was a complete shock. The three of them hurried into the apartment, which was sleek and stylish. Clare remembered Jake's words about Darren's office. How elegant and cutting-edge it had been.

This description also fitted the apartment here in Zurich although the current version of Darren standing in front of them didn't. They had never seen Darren before, and so they only had his word that he was who he said he was.

Clare realised that he and Bigsy were accidental experts on a small slice of Darren's life. His car. They had both listened to Jake's interview two or three times, looking for clues. If this was Darren, he should be able to give the same answers about his pride and joy motor vehicle.

"So, before we start," quizzed Clare, "we need to ask you some basic questions. They may seem strange at first."

"Go ahead," said Darren, "I could predict this".

Clare started to ask questions about the McLaren car. Starting with simple ones about what type of car was it, and then progressively getting more specialised, based on what she could remember from the interview. Maximum speed, number of cylinders, the way the doors opened, and Darren was getting them all right.

Bigsy realised what Clare was doing and also nodded as he heard a series of right answers. Then Darren asked a question, "So what colour was the car?" he asked the two of them. Neither knew. It was not in the interview. They hesitated. Darren said, "I thought so - you are working from the interview transcript - Is that where you got this apartment? - and what has happened to Jake...er...Lambers?" he quizzed.

"Jake is fine," answered Bigsy, "and we needed to know you were who you said you were before we went any further. How on earth did you get here, and what is the story about you being dead? - This is all very weird..."

"Weird, dangerous and complicated," responded Darren. "I will explain, but I need to know I can trust you first" - he walked to a wardrobe in the room and returned with a small metal box. Inside the box was a passport, a badge and a cell phone.

"I was recruited to a special unit within HMRC - Her Majesty's Revenue and Customs. Because of my tax status, they made me an offer I couldn't refuse. HMRC has a special operations unit, involved with international crime and international fraud. I was working on a highly sophisticated crime involving drugs, vice, major currency movements and money laundering."

"We had worked out it was something illegal," replied Clare, "We have been putting together our theories," she continued.

"Let me try to explain," responded Collins, "There's a lot to tell - I'm trusting you two; if you'd wanted to harm me, you'd have already done it by now. The story stacks up that you are friends of Jake Lambers. But understand me; the more I tell you, the more dangerous it gets for all of us."

Collins moved across the room to a bright area with two colourful yellow leather sofas facing one another and separated by a table made from some kind of grey stone. The table looked immensely heavy and probably cost as much as Bigsy's car. On the wall between the sofas hung a huge sleek plasma television.

"I was part of an undercover investigation. UK Government asked me to embed myself in the unit under investigation. The powers of the Customs and Excise in the UK are some of the most powerful in the British justice system, so I could operate in ways which were well outside the powers of the police force, for example. That's not to say I was going out of my way to break the law, let's just say that it became a necessary extension to find out the scale of what was happening. I had to get sign off from the Home Office, although even that creates problems for me now."

Clare and Bigsy looked at one another. Either they were being told the truth, or this was a wildly elaborate lie, for reasons they couldn't fathom.

Darren continued, "I've been tracking a massive money-laundering operation. I had to set up a new 'node' in their network and become part of the process. Their name for the network - alshuelat alzirqa' - the blue flame.

Bigsy interrupted, "As in the Blue Flame code word?"

"Exactly," continued Darren, "Using the Blue Flame as a code was a way to tell people involved with following up what I'd been doing that they were on the right track.

"Except no-one could say the Arabic. We decided to simplify, and it became Almathlath, which most people could spell well enough in reports. It means "The triangle," in Arabic.

Everyone I was working with knew about Almathlath as a code word, so when I used the Blue Flame and a code number, it gave a way to confirm that it was linked."

"Isn't it all a bit 'over the top'?" asked Clare.

"Trust me," continued Darren, not realising the irony, "We are dealing with some heavy people here, and they don't mess about. If they take a dislike, then someone is going to get killed."

"Yes, we've seen that already," continued Clare.

"So, Blue Flame is an organisation making money on an industrial scale from the illegal export of petrochemicals from Saudi Arabia," explained Darren. "There are several aspects, and the processes for each of them are pretty much the same. I'll explain it with oil, but it applies to other commodities too."

"It can be deceptively simple. Oil products are drilled, pumped and processed in the normal way in the eastern part of Saudi Arabia, but the supplies are then split in their transit towards the port for onward transmission."

"The legitimate part went through the normal port side and customs clearance, but the illegal part was simply split off and continued in different pipelines until they reached another sea-based destination. There are underground pipelines from two large Saudi ports at Al Jubayl and Ras al Khafji. One simply goes to an obvious offshore fuelling point but the other snakes across the border into neighbouring Iran."

Bigsy and Clare's geography was not up to the level of the description from Collins, and they stopped him to ask some questions.

"Just a minute," answered Collins and he flipped a remote control laying on the stone table. The plasma screen flickered into life. "It's an internet terminal as well as a television," commented Collins, "let me show you." He flipped a couple more buttons and reached down by the side of the table.

There was a sliding drawer, and he pulled out of it a slim white keyboard and a small white mouse. He placed both items on the table and started to type. The screen now showed a conventional-looking computer display and then up popped an internet browser display. He tapped "CIA Worldbook" into the keyboard, and sure enough, up popped a screen saying "CIA World Fact Book".

"This is a CIA website," he explained, "but anyone can use it. For field operatives, it is easy to flaunt some of the access to systems rather than hide them. If an agent in the field needs access and doesn't have specialised equipment, then the Criminal Intelligence Agency has made it easy to get basic information."

He continued and tapped in "Saudi Arabia", and within a few seconds, he was on a screen showing basics facts and figures about Saudi Arabia. A few more taps and he was looking at a map of the region.

"Look, here," he continued and gestured to the western side of Saudi Arabia on the map and then to an area around the Persian Gulf.

Here, they could see the towns Darren had referenced. Bigsy and Clare could see that they were well-positioned for access to the sea and near enough to the borders of surrounding countries.

"The investigation I was involved with started by looking at these very spots," he gestured to Al Jubayl and Ras al Khafji.

"The basics were that fuel oils were coming into the UK illegally, often from Southampton and Liverpool. There was a trail that led back to the Gulf, and the good customs people were investigating the basis of the route. At the time it started, they had no idea of the scale or reach of what we had discovered."

"Our unit asked me to get involved as a way to gain

intelligence about the scale of the operation. My trading operation at the time was iffy, and so I was given a front as a trader susceptible to corruption. Someone then introduced me to the Blue Flame crowd, and I was later approached to extend their operation."

"By whom?" asked Clare, "Surely you are provoking the illegal traffic rather than stopping it? Isn't that 'entrapment' or something?"

"You have a point, but at this stage, I didn't have a clue about the eventual process I would discover and though it would be more like a simple sting - you know, they hand me some money, I call in backup, and everyone gets arrested!" continued Darren.

"Except it wasn't like that. They approached me via an intermediary representing offshore interests and created a complete legal framework from a company based in Belgium. I was asked to participate by a Swedish businessman who was fronting a consortium of Arabs from Saudi and the other Gulf States."

" I think the people I met believed I was already involved with some other financial crimes. We used that to provide me with a stronger background story, and corroboration, both in police files and with other places we expected would get an investigation."

"The Swedish businessman was named Fredriksson. He made me the offer that became the basis of the operation that I was running when Jake met and interviewed me. I had to opt-in as a way to follow the trail and frankly was not sure about what would happen to me if I declined."

Bigsy and Clare both considered the implications of what they were hearing and tried to work out whether it was all true. A lot of it tied up with what they had heard from Jake, and with theories they had been working out between themselves.

"So how did you get the money to create the office and business that you were running?" asked Bigsy.

Darren replied, "It was amazingly easy once they had decided they wanted me to do this. I don't think I can easily describe how much money is involved in this process. Imagine an oil field which is permanently pumping its product into an illegal operation. The operation of the oil field is part of a legitimate operation which passes all the normal tests and inspections. The only difference is that the declared capacity of the oil field is only half of its true output. The rest disappears into the illegal process. Now multiply that by many fields. You should be starting to get an idea of the volume of money in this process."

"Using me and asking me to create a shell organisation to start the laundering process just created more and more cash. To begin with, I couldn't believe how much money was created, although my main interest was to follow the chain back so that we could round up the people responsible. I had to make the operation I was running look suitably big and stylish to convince them of my character as we had to create the right sort of attention."

Clare and Bigsy looked confused by the last remark.

"We needed to attract a particular type of attention so that if there were other equivalent organisations, there would be a reasonable chance to flush them out. The car article was more than just self-promotion - it was also planned as a commercial about what we were doing, to people in the know.

"Journalists like Jake may not realise it, but some of those glossy magazines are also recruitment and advertising spaces for organised crime. Spot the bling. We all know what a Rolex means, but there are other subtle signs as well. Vacheron Constantin could indicate Mafia connections. Pobeda watch, a Russian patriot - possibly connections to FSB. Do you get my drift?

"We'd realised that this particular organisation was like the tip of an iceberg. We found out that there were other organisations also operating in an interconnected way, using similar processes to launder their own money. Organised crime needs a way to re-introduce its money to the economy, and this approach seems to be a widespread thing." He paused.

"So, from starting to track down some oil tanker mischief in Liverpool for HMRC, I became more involved with it as I got deeper into their crime syndicate. I was beginning to see the scope and breadth, but I also realised that I was also becoming more and more of a target if I attempted to report back my involvement. The session with the Arab heavies that Jake Lambers spotted was a turning point for me."

"That's when I decided that I needed to get out or be in fear of my life. My way out needed to be via a plausible exit of some kind, but in a way that escaped complete detection. I had to do two different things. One was to create my separate fund so that I would be able to create a new and utterly independent life for myself. With the access to money that I had, a small adjustment to a couple of the dials would very rapidly create a fund for me to use in a way that was pretty much undetectable. The second thing I needed was to create a plausible reason for people to stop looking for me - hence the car crash story".

"But the way you describe this it makes it sound as if you've turned from 'one of the good guys' into 'one of the bad guys'," questioned Clare.

"It has become a matter of survival for me," replied Darren, "If I blew the whistle on what was happening, I doubted whether I'd make it to the next weekend," he said.

"The people involved with this have an exceptional reach, and with such funding, any minor hindrances are ruthlessly dealt with."

Collins went on to describe the complicated way he had engineered his disappearance. He had manipulated some failures the business and simultaneously been moving money away in preparation for his demise. Collins had also used his background to get himself interviewed. He wanted someone random to meet him and to use this to pass on some details. He was going to use this random factor to create a way to complete the chain of feedback without traceability back to himself.

"So, we are the chain?" stuttered Clare

"Correct," replied Collins, "there was supposed to be no link between Jake and me. Now you've come along it adds even a further stage as you are not the person who interviewed me about my car. And when you pass the information on to the people I tell you, you will need to think yourselves about how to add another link".

Collins continued, "There is a considerable amount of data to describe the network of links; it is similar to the internet, in that if one part breaks, another route is used as a diversion until the original link heals in some way.

"The size of the network means there are ways to cross-check things. That is one of the reasons it had to look like a road accident."

"Well, you certainly fooled most people," said Bigsy.

"Yes, and we didn't even know it was you when we figured out the co-ordinates from our code-word," said Clare.

"I had to use a substantial sum of money to create what is essentially an alibi based on my faked death.

"Anyone from the dark side of this network would take no chances after such a fabrication."

"Meaning what, exactly?" asked Clare.

"They would also kill the people involved in the cover-up so that there was at least one further layer of insulation to get to the truth. I didn't do that, so there is always a chance that I will be discovered as still alive by someone from inside Blue Flame."

"Now I'll have to make the best of things. I'll pass you some information which together will allow the network to be detected and attempts made to start to dismantle it.

"The reason I can do this is that I was operating on such a large scale that I started to find out about more than one operation of the system. By the time I had access to three routes, I could start to piece together how the whole environment has been created."

"You mean like triangulation?" asked Bigsy.

"In a manner of speaking," responded Collins, "if you start to assemble the network, particularly in the European and North West Asian area, then it is possible to start to see where the trunk routes of the money flow. I said it's about more than oil and it does seem to be much broader."

"Everyone expects that the Russian mafia is also involved and that there is influence from the drug traffic from Pakistan and Afghanistan's Helmand Province which flows across to Turkish connections."

"The Arabian part links with the illicit oil shipments and that is the area where I was first involved. Of course, this only represents one-eighth of the planet and doesn't even touch the United States, or South America, so I expect there are other large zones which are not even visible at present."

"The data I collected from the inside is stored on a hard drive. If I deliver it in its current form, I am certain that many people I know will be killed as retribution. We need to find a way to achieve the delivery of the data without making it so obvious about the source."

Clare asked, "So you will give the information to us? - won't it have the same effect when we try to pass it on? We may deliver it, but it will look the same and therefore link back to you?

"Precisely," said Collins, "That is why you must change the information first".

"The most straightforward way will be to use the information I have provided to pass to another new organisation. It can be done in a way that ensures interception by a government agency and becomes the plausible way for Blue Flame to be discovered.

"The trick is to do this very early in the start-up of a new organisation. The recipient won't understand the information they are getting, but the authorities will. We can add a few keywords to prove authenticity, without it being obvious that I've been involved, or that any of you are either."

"That way, the authorities get what they need, but none of us is implicated".

Clare and Bigsy remained silent as Collins stopped his description; in their wildest imagination, they could not have foreseen the events or stories of the last couple of hours, even on top of the events of the previous couple of days.

"So you are telling us that you are sitting on the key to breaking the organisation, but can't use it directly?" asked Clare, "If you do, they'll work out the source and then everyone linked will be in trouble."

"Correct," said Collins, "But using my plan means that the source is completely concealed, via the new organisation acting as the unsuspecting deliverer of the information. And it moves the trail away from all of us, completely."

A hands-off approach

Fredriksson had slept until late the next morning. Although only a few hours hop from Riyadh to London and with the time zone working in his favour, it was still disorienting. He had left Riyadh on a plane at around 0200. Then, arriving in London's early morning after not much sleep, on top of his already hectic schedule meant that he decided to take some downtime.

He had located the address for Jake's flat, but obtaining Jake's information was of secondary importance to him. He would be starting the process to build a new node relevant to the business, to replace the area taken down by Collins. He knew that Collins would have a safety net of some description and he considered that he also had factored similar things into his own plans.

Right now he had the commission to activate some of his own existing trading entities to provide the new transfer medium for the money in line with the need of the Arab consortia.

Fredriksson did most of his work through others and had many operating guises through the companies he ran. There was a degree of legitimate business included, and the diversity meant that he had easy access to a wide range of employees, from top-quality legal and financial advisors through to manual labourers.

Fredriksson was used to getting what he wanted and could use a discreet viewing of Jake's flat and maybe Jake himself, to determine the options available. This could veer from gentle persuasion, through a job offer to violence or even worse, depending on the circumstances that Fredriksson detected.

Fredriksson also considered the visit to determine Jake's whereabouts as something of a scoping exercise. He thought that probably Jake was harmless and maybe an innocent bystander. Within a couple of days, the remnants of Darren Collin's empire would no longer be relevant. Although there would be vestigial companies and paper trails, most of what was important would have disappeared. His people were good at that and would speedily create a substitute 'node' to continue the job where Darren Collins had left off.

Fredriksson was one of the people least concerned about any aftermath from Collins. The effects of Collin's companies did not touch him directly, and there were no links back to him, although he had previously taken a direct hand in their creation.

Fredriksson would financially back the start-up costs of the replacement but would take a similarly 'hands-off' approach. In all ways, that is, except he would get new creation fees for setting up the replacement routes, and that he would continue to get a modest small proportion of all of the money that transacted every day.

And that was millions for him just through the part of the network which had been operated by Collins.

Fredriksson enjoyed a brief breakfast in his hotel room; yoghurt, brown bread and a small slice of cheese, washed down with two cups of strong coffee. He was in the business part of the hotel, with a medium-sized room with some in-room office facilities. Fredriksson's black suit bag and minimal luggage hung directly in the open plan wardrobe. He could be in this location for two or three days. It had some anonymity, was not overly flashy and helped him to blend in when he needed to.

His next route was to take a taxi to the area of Jake's flat. He left the hotel and picked a cab waiting outside. The black cab took him to the area of Jake's flat, but he had asked to be dropped a couple of roads away. Like Amelia Brophy before him, he then discovered the still unfolding aftermath of the Police visit to the flat.

He was several hours later than Manners and decided not to make direct contact. It was obvious something unpleasant and violent had happened, and whether or not Jake was still alive and whoever else had been involved, Fredriksson simply registered that there was ongoing interest in Jake and that he, Fredriksson, needed to move quickly to take down the old network and to establish the new one.

He flipped open a slim black cell-phone, pressed a power-dial number and waited. A few seconds later, there was a click, and the number was answered.

"It's Fredriksson," he declared, "I have the go-ahead, and we will need to move fast. We need to meet somewhere neutral, in central London."

A few minutes later, they had agreed to meet in the Foreign and Commonwealth club, located centrally, a few minutes' walk from Trafalgar Square, in Central London.

Manners on a mission

Manners was used to working in counter espionage. He knew the moves. He could tell now that he was working with a combination of technique, but right now it was mainly 'luck' that was winning.

The disk drive he had picked up from the collection of electronics at the flat was different from the other equipment. Most of the stuff was PC related. This single item had an apple logo and also had a label saying 'Jake' on it. Manners was confident that this would contain a backup of the broken Apple MacBook which had been delivered to him by the clumsy burglars.

He had tried to read it with all of the available PCs at his disposal but would now need to get an Apple computer to try the drive. He was on his way to a nearby PC superstore. He would buy an Apple laptop and then connect the drive. He was sure this would work.

Two hours later, he was sitting in a small hotel room close to Oxford Street, with the new cardboard packaging from a small slim silver laptop computer scattered on the floor. The machine was switched on and powered up. It displayed a blue background with four simple icons and a narrow strip with further images running along the bottom of the screen.

He connected power to the disk drive from Bigsy's, he pulled a cable from some bubble packaging and plugged one end into the disk drive and the other end into a socket on the side of the slim computer. There was a moment's pause, and then a new icon joined those already displayed. It was a small picture of the disk drive,

The laptop had found the disk drive and connected to it. He clicked on it and found Jake's backup file structure, from Jake's laptop computer. Manners clicked a couple more times and found the folder containing the list of digital recordings. He located the correct file for the data he wanted and then clicked again.

The sound of the recording stated to come from Manner's laptop. It was the recording, this time it was undamaged and pristine. He listened to all of it and made a few notes along the way.

"Computers for the rest of us," he mused thinking of the simplicity with which he had fired up the Apple laptop to achieve this.

The most important note he wrote down was the reference to the secret code. This was the one that he had been unable to hear in the earlier recording because of the damage. This time the code was clear. He listened, wrote it down, rewound that section, listened again and cross-checked with the earlier recording.

Manners knew he had the right code. He then dragged the picture of the folder containing the digital recordings to the desktop of the laptop computer. He now had the files on his laptop, where he could inspect them at leisure.

Manners was now ready to hunt down the source of the number. He was on the trail of whatever Darren Collins was hiding.

Fabric

Jake was beginning to go a little crazy. He had been locked up in Bigsy's flat for two days and had then nearly been caught by some people who were looking for either him or the equipment and files he had been holding.

He had managed a lucky escape using Rick's car and was now in hiding somewhat anonymously in the Travelodge along the M4. He had called Rick to explain what had happened, using Clare's phone and as he had started to explain, he decided to let Rick in on more of the recent events.

Rick was not very phased by what he heard. An estate agent by day, Rick spent the evenings enjoying the single life in London and was often out clubbing. He met many people in his varied exploits and there were always Londoners with stories to tell.

On the club scene, or particularly on his club scene, there were always people showing that they were connected to big things in some way or other, so Jake's story sounded like other ones he had heard. Except, as Rick put it, there was a first-hand experience of people getting killed in Jake's story. And Rick also knew Lucien a little bit, so this had an extra edge compared with the stories of his clubber friends.

Jake asked Rick if they could meet somewhere so that they

could discuss this in more detail. It needed to be somewhere secure and preferably somewhere that Jake could visit without too much chance of getting followed.

"We'll meet tonight," said Rick, "Fabric, in Farringdon. No one will get in there without an invitation. Take my car to Heathrow Airport, park it in T5 car parking and then come in by train tonight."

Jake was pleased to receive this direction and plan from Rick. He had felt somewhat out of the action over the last couple of days, stuck at a motorway service while Bigsy and Clare were in Zurich. His action had been limited because he was the one under threat. Not being able to do much, not being able to communicate quickly and being the potential target of a threat did not leave him feeling particularly safe.

He was aware of the possibility of paranoia, but decided nonetheless, to visit a local shopping centre on the way to the airport parking zone. He visited a department store, bought a complete change of clothing and then, after paying, slipped into a nearby McDonald's where he changed from his existing clothes into an all new set.

His new clothes (black jeans, black tee shirt, and dark hooded jacket) were deliberately commonplace and anonymous and included a new backpack with a couple of further items so that he could change his appearance quickly if the need arose.

As he did this, he was thinking that he might be going mad, but on the other hand, it was better to be safe than sorry.

Next stop, Terminal 5 Heathrow, where he could park for a huge daily amount, and he left the car in the middle row of a busy section.

The vehicle was distinctive, but you couldn't easily see it where he had parked it unless you were already inside the parking lot. He realised that there would be number plate recognition at the airport so the car had limited time before it would be discovered if it was on a watch list. He wrote down the zone but left the ticket in the glovebox and walked through the vast car park and across the concourses into Terminal Five.

Then a Heathrow Express to Paddington and Circle Line to Farringdon, where he would meet Rick. As Jake stood on the tube, he looked at the mass of Londoners and thought how good it was to be anonymous.

Ed Adams

PART THREE

Killer instincts

Jimmy was the kind of guy that
rooted for bad guys in the movies

— Henry Hill (Ray Liotta), GoodFellas

Amelia gets personal

Amelia Brophy was still in London. She had decided that the chaos around Jake's flat was Russian inspired. Amelia knew the modus-operandi of the Russians and their more basic level of training. She was normally very dispassionate about her work, but she knew for sure that the only reason the Russians would be handling the situation with Jake Lambers was because they thought they had killed him back in France.

Amelia had been careful with his hotel room preparations back in Cannes. She had set a trap, based upon what he knew would be a lot of smoke and feathers following any attempt to 'assassinate' whatever lay under the bedclothes in the room. She had set up the bed carefully, so that anything fired into the simulated mass of his sleeping body, would cause the assailant to leave hurriedly.

She therefore knew that the Russians would have thought they had killed her and were now attempting to finish off Jake.

The Triangle

Amelia decided she would now create some disruption on the way to capturing the ringleaders of the attempt on her life. She considered it very uncivil to one minute be offered drinks and the next for the same people to be regarding her as target practice.

Amelia needed to set a trap if she was to capture the Russians.

She started by phoning a number in Saudi Arabia. Someone he knew who would be looking for large amounts of extra cash.

She was going to create a scene in London designed to jeopardize the very operation at the heart of her contract.

They were playing rough with her; she would do the same back to them.

She was going to create a situation where two parties both thought the other had the data that Jake had acquired.

Amelia didn't need the information any longer; she was going to create some havoc to send a signal that she didn't want to be messed with.

Amelia knew her actions would be seriously irritating two major international players, and she needed to be careful how he handled the situation.

Her move would be to pretend to each group that she was working for the other side.

By calling the Saudi Arabian contact, she was telling them that she had information about the whereabouts of the coded data which Darren Collins had produced, and which Jake had subsequently recorded.

She then did a similar call, but this time to the Russians. She explained that she had the disk and the data which they needed.

Aware of the fireworks it could create, she invited both groups to meet her in London.

Dillon, sounds a bit like Collins?

Fredriksson made his way to the Foreign and Commonwealth Club near to the Embankment in central London. He would be meeting a new associate there, one who came highly recommended and for whom Fredriksson had already run comprehensive checks to validate.

He knew there were a couple of suspended meeting rooms in the Club, on the first floor accessed via a walkway. They added a sense of drama to the meeting he was about to conduct. He had selected one of these rooms for the meeting and deliberately arrived early to take a seated position facing towards the door of the meeting room.

At the appointed time, his guest arrived.

Fredriksson knew that his guest would be accompanied, but that courtesy and protocol would mean that whoever else he had brought would be waiting downstairs.

"Mr Dillon," he said as he greeted his guest, "so good of you to come."

Dillon was a well-known man-about-town. His profile was a little flashy, and he featured frequently in the tabloids and weekly magazines.

He had made money from music and fashion and had a whole string of companies and miscellaneous interests.

Fredriksson had met Dillon before on two occasions and had been weighing up the possibilities of using him as a new part of the laundering operation.

Fredriksson had decided to split the previous 'node' operated by Darren Collins into two pieces. He was using upscale interests for one part and needed someone else who could front the more ragged elements of the Collins empire. That is where Dillon came in.

Fredriksson spent the next forty-five minutes speaking to Dillon. He explained that there was a large sum of money to be made, that the income was regular and that the nature of the business transactions was mainly virtual.

Dillon did not need to hold stock, and Fredriksson's associates would supply the necessary processes for the transacting of business.

There would be a need for some specific undertakings from Dillon, including a clause that permitted rapid revocation of the whole deal in the case of anything untoward. This had to be pre-signed and was an unconditional aspect of the negotiation.

Dillon listened intently to the offer. He was very interested and had been hoping that something like this was possible, based upon the previous discussions with Fredriksson.

He knew that there were probably shady aspects to the deal, but many of his other agreements were also border-line, so this was no significant exception.

The Triangle

He explained that he would need to consider and to check with his legal people and that he needed a small amount of time for this. Fundamentally Dillon believed that he was asked to be a clearinghouse for someone else's money and that he could take a percentage of the money.

The offer was highly attractive to Dillon, but he realised that there would also be some downside and that that this probably relates to personal risk.

"Do this well, keep a low profile in these transactions, and you will have nothing to worry about," came Fredriksson's reply.

Dillon and Fredriksson agreed to meet again two days later to finalise the arrangements. Fredriksson was close to restarting the entire Darren Collins organisation under its new management.

Sand and vodka storm

Amelia Brophy had decided to create a big storm in London. Always professional, she had taken the recent attempt to kill her as both a personal situation, but also a professional one which required deflection.

Creating an incident where two sets of oppositional people were "accidentally" introduced to one another would create a distraction, and she could also usefully study the aftermath.

She had already called both groups. The point was to get them to the same location in the knowledge that each group would not want to see the other one.

Brophy knew that the Russians were using the Blue Flame network to launder their money. The sources of their funds were various types of organised crime and the money that needed re-processing was of a semi-industrial proportion.

In the case of the Saudis, the money was genuinely industrial, but the source was more straightforward. Oil. And the motive was pure greed rather than a broad study of vice in the way of the Russians.

The Triangle

Amelia had selected an upmarket location in Kensington for the forthcoming event. She knew that she would need careful orchestration because the two groups would need to see one another, think one another had the information and then watch as sparks flew. Probably quite literally.

There would be a couple of days delay before the players were in place and Amelia would also need some helpful support of her own for the situation she was about to contrive.

Chuck Manners had decided to move back to the surveillance station near the American Embassy. His position in the overall situation was improving.

He had met two of Jake's associates, had tagged them both with tracker chips and had followed them to a London location. One of them had moved on to a second location and then returned, and then both of them had headed away the Eurostar to probably Paris.

The long pause at one of the locations had allowed Manners to track down the disk drive from Jake's MacBook and he now had the code. He also had the addresses of both of the individuals based upon their movements around London. Next, he would identify their cell phones, and these would give him a better beacon on where they had gone to next.

Chuck Manners started with Bigsy and quickly found the cell phone information. It would take a while to trace it via telephone billing records to see where the most recent calls originated.

For the second cell phone, he had to trace firstly the address where the tracker had visited, then the electoral role, which gave three different names, and then the cross-check of the cell phones. Three different names, one female and two males. He now had a name - Clare Crafts. He would check this as well as David Jenkins, which he assumed was the real name of Clare's accomplice at the sushi bar.

The next stage took two hours to track down the recent telephone records. He had access to the telephone billing systems, but as he suspected the calls were now emanating from abroad, at least for one of the phones. Strangely, though, the second phone was generating calls from the London area, most recently on the M4 motorway and then back in central London.

By returning to Bigsy's flat, Manners was now able to try phoning the convergent numbers in Clare's recent cell phone call list.

Manners called the cell phone number he had tracked, and was answered by Rick. Salesman Rick wasn't interested at all in Manner's attempt at accident re-insurance and soon hung up.

Now Manners just had to watch for Rick's departure from the flat. He now had someone who was communicating with Clare Craft's phone. Sure enough, Rick was heading out for the evening.

Manners followed, principally to get a sense of the individual's area of operation. Following him led to a club in Farringdon. The club was lively and loud, with two friendly-looking security standing outside. The person he was following was waved straight inside but as Manners approached, he was stopped. "This is a private party," said one of the overcoated men. "Do you have an invitation?"

Manners didn't and realised his chance to get inside was limited. "I'm here to see Jake Lambers," he hazarded.

"Well, please wait here," said the first man in an overcoat, "while we check this out."

Manners knew he could barge past these individuals but judged it unwise to create attention at this point. This line of enquiry was secondary to his main plan, which would be to follow the trail overseas and to locate whatever Collins was hiding.

Rick had turned around when he heard Jake's name but decided that it was better to keep going. Jake had been concerned about something. The last thing needed now was to find someone tailing him to the club.

Inside Fabric, there was a loud club track playing; Rick smiled when he recognised it as Clare's good friend Christina Nott with her distinctive vocals, but a mix of the song he had never heard before. Rick looked out for Jake and found that he was already seated at a small table in a rather comfortable part of the club. Fabric played loud music in the main bar area, but had a separate chill zone close to a restaurant, where Jake was seated.

Rick moved to Jake in the quieter area and immediately explained about the person who had been following him to the club.

"Hey Jake, I do get it about the car, the smashed up flat, and the danger and all. You'll have to explain it all to me some other time. Right now, I think you'd better go," said Rick.

"I don't think you'll be safe here and the longer you stay, the greater the chance that the person following me will get inside here."

Rick's choice of an exclusive club night had introduced a delay to Manners. Jake examined escape routes and worked out that the kitchens offered the best route.

"Hey, I owe you, big time," Jake quietly slipped away, leaving Rick in the club.

Manners had worked out that the club was exclusive, but the restaurant was less so. By agreeing to book an immediate meal, he was able to get inside without further scuffle. Within five minutes, he was inside and looking for the person he had been following. He spotted him sitting alone, apparently reading a drinks menu. At that exact moment, Rick looked up and stared directly at Manners, then gestured to him to come over. Manners was slightly taken aback by this but walked across.

"Hi," said Rick, "I think I saw you outside a few minutes ago? You were asking about Jake Lambers? He is a friend of mine, or was."

"That's right," said Manners, "I was hoping to say hello to him."

Rick smiled, "I don't know how well you know Jake, but he has left the country now. He moved to Canada. I think he has a job over there - Toronto, I think."

Rick made as if to get up. If he had managed to sound convincing, he knew he would not be able to stand up to any form of cross-examination.

"Thanks," replied Manners. He didn't believe what he was being told but decided he would be better to simply disengage from this line of enquiry and instead to start the tracing of Darren Collin's secret.

Manners decided to leave the club. As he walked away, Rick let out a sigh of relief. He would stay for at least another half hour and then tomorrow phone in sick to his office, thereby giving Jake a longer period with his car.

Manners had decided to follow the trail now – Jake Lambers was no longer relevant to him, but the address in Zurich was now critical. He would be moving his centre of operations to the location identified by the information on the hard drive. It was Zurich. The main thing he would need to do would be to ensure that whatever was stored in Zurich would get destroyed. The trail to the old empire required to go cold. Anything to do with Jake and his accomplices could be handled as an afterthought.

Manners still had the backpack containing the new laptop on which he had copied the data from the hard drive. He had already copied the content of the hard drive to a backup and then stored it in a locker for safekeeping. The laptop was a useful asset for the next stage of his job, which he would take as carry-on luggage for his flight to Zurich. He headed for Heathrow airport and stopped overnight in a nearby hotel, prepared for the first Zurich flight early in the morning.

Secure grip

As Clare and Bigsy left Darren Collin's Zurich apartment, they said to him that they thought he might not be safe staying there. If they could find the location, then so could others.

Collins said that he had been very meticulous with his camouflage plans and that he had spent a great deal of money setting up his identity in Switzerland. No-one could find him, and it was because he had given the information to Jake that had made his location traceable.

Clare and Bigsy didn't look all that convinced about Darren's cover story, as they left the apartment. They had enough information now to go to the UK Police and to start getting some protection set up for Jake as well as the pair of them.

They also had information about a serious money laundering ring, which they were confident would create interest from the UK police. They decided it was time to make their way back to the United Kingdom, but now they were reasonably sure they had not been followed, they would speed their return by catching a flight from Zurich's airport.

They left the apartment, hailed a taxi and climbed in. Another taxi one pulled up outside the apartment. Bigsy and Clare did not notice Manners getting out, and Manners did not see either of them. Their own taxi moved away as Manners walked towards the apartment block.

Manners quickly located the apartment from the website address and first pressed the buzzer for Suite 9.

"Is that you again?" Came a voice and the buzzer clicked as the door opened.

It was too easy.

Manners was now on his way to the apartment, which he would see if he could enter undetected.

As Manners approached the landing, he saw someone looking out of the door of a room, which he realized was the apartment he was tracing.

"Hello," he said, "I'm looking…," then he realized the person he was talking to was Darren Collins.

At the same moment, Darren recognized Manners. It was too late. Manners had Darren in a secure grip. He pushed him into the apartment and, holding his head down to the floor with one hand; Manners glanced around the apartment.

"Right," he said sharply," Do as I say, or I will start by breaking both your arms."

Darren agreed to comply, not sure at this point whether he had any options. "I am going to ask you a few questions," continued Manners, "I need the truth."

Manners released his grip on Darren, but stayed alert. Darren saw his angle.

"Okay," agreed Darren, "But consider this, I have a substantial amount of money hidden away in computerized systems. I don't know who you work for or how much they pay you, but I promise you, I can beat just about any offer.

"In return, I need to know that you will work exclusively for me and act as my protector. I don't need you to be around full-time; I need to know that I am safe."

Manners was astonished by this situation. Here he was, grappling with someone he thought was already dead. He was there to find out whatever secrets had been hidden and to take the information to his masters, who were themselves part of the underworld.

The person he was threatening was trying to bargain with him. Bizarre, but on the other hand, the emotional response of the person he threatened seemed real.

Manners was going to take some minutes to decide the course of action.

In the taxi, Clare and Bigsy were commenting to each other at how good they were getting at problem-solving. Darren Collins had told them overtly about how the money laundering worked but also how the cells were linked together only as needed. This gave a remarkable resilience to surveillance, hacking and other criminal pursuits.

Because Darren had identified two of the business cells operating adjacent to his own cells, he could perform cross-checks of who owned what.

At Zurich airport, Bigsy and Clare waited for the plane and talked about the whole situation.

They needed leverage to try to build a position protected from threats to themselves or Jake. The information about other Blue Flame nodes could be the basis of their protection. They needed to get a situation where they could declare their hand and not be derailed by other possible assailants.

Inspiration

There's more to life than being a passenger

– Amelia Earhart

Brophy considers a new name

Amelia Brophy had chosen a small and rather exclusive hotel, for the roundup of the Russians and Saudi Arabians. She wanted the event to create damage and some casualties and she was going to arrange that she was apparently included in the ensuing carnage.

The Russians already thought she was dead, and the Saudis would soon do so soon as well. But her actions would also eliminate some of the people who had been aiming their bullets at her.

This situation had become personal.

She had checked the venue, which had several important features. There was only one primary forward way in. There was a short glass tunnel canopy leading to some manned double doors. Inside, there was a small and discreet lobby, and the other side of the lobby was first a bar and then a restaurant.

The Triangle

The whole place was dimly lit and the focal area was a large cocktail bar area. At maximum, the bar would hold twelve tables worth of sofa sitting groups and the restaurant around fifty, with an area near to the back which could be screened off.

Her plan was simple. She would invite both groups to the restaurant on the same pretext that she had the data that they required. She would find a way to introduce them to one another, which would be like lighting the touch paper on a giant firework.

She could not predict whether there would be an immediate violent interchange between the two groups or whether they would discreetly leave and avoid confrontation.

She needed confrontation and was arranging her luggage to be in the lobby at the time of the meeting.

This luggage would be slightly heavier than usual, because it would contain 4 kilos of K-PEX high energy plastic explosive, which she could detonate with a mobile phone.

Her plan involved leaving the place around the time that the two groups discovered one another. If they fought directly in the hotel, it was a result, if they tried to leave, it was also a result, because she would, in both cases, be detonating the K-PEX and creating a crater the size of the restaurant cocktail bar.

The ensuing devastation would have taken out most of the Arabs and Russians, along with a number of innocent bystanders.

Included in this group would be a Ms Amelia Brophy, complete with passport and other identification. She would then be able to resume one of her other guises away from the mess of this situation. She decided that she quite fancied a poetic sounding name.

The plan was pretty simple, something she preferred. The Russians and the Saudis were already on the move, from

Riyadh and from Cannes.

High above this scene twinkled a low earth orbit satellite. It had been monotonously tracking five Saudi Arabian mobile phones for several weeks.

A trigger alarm now created an email in Langley, Virginia. Four of the Saudis were on the move, together, to Riyadh's airport and then after going off the air for six hours, the signals had re-appeared in London.

Another email flicked across to GCHQ, Cheltenham, UK.

The monitoring post for UK counterespionage and terrorism was about to activate some special forces.

Manners makes a new friend

Manners had wondered for several years about what would happen if ever anyone made him the offer he could not refuse.

An offer to insulate him from the complicated life he had led since he left the army as a hero. He had not intended to get involved in semi-military protection of high-end criminals. But there was a buzz related to the activities unlike anything he could get in civvy street.

He had been through typical jobs after his honourable discharge from active service. He had asked directly about working through further special services, but there had been budget cutbacks that meant the best he was able to do was get outplacement which led to a mid-ranking job in a bank. This role had been madly inappropriate, and through an ex-contact he had ultimately fallen into his current line of work.

It had a lot going for it; travel, excitement, use of his skills, reasonably good money.

But Manners knew that he was reaching the end. He had plenty of experience, but there were other Armani suited professionals now on the market. There were slim-waisted girls with high calibre protection skills and large calibre guns.

He needed to move to a new plan and Darren Collins could be it.

"Let's talk," he said, putting Collins into a chair, showing him a large knife which he slid from behind his jacket and then saying, "do you have some coffee?"

For an hour, over two cups of coffee, Manners and Collins discussed a new business arrangement.

Collins had money stashed away from the business he had been running. It was mainly the money that had caused the Arabs to challenge him when they had visited his office. Collins had not been losing money; he had been swindling extra funds, which now formed the basis of his escape parachute.

"There is so much money, I have a problem hiding it," said Collins, "Yet it is only a small proportion of the money which the operation has been trafficking.

You can almost name your price," said Collins, " I need to be invisible, I need someone who keeps an eye on whether anyone is showing interest in what I do, and maybe some invisible protection."

Manners understood. It was the type of silent protection offered to ex-Presidents and senior politicians.

Not flashy like pop stars or menacing like gangsters, but just quietly efficient. He could do this and do it well. He would enjoy doing it, and because Collins wanted to keep an international lifestyle, it would still give travel.

Besides, Manners knew enough of the 'community' to be able to re-construct a past for Collins and himself and make them blend unobtrusively into whatever background he chose.

"Five million dollars and a regular monthly paycheque," said Manners. Collins laughed, "I think we have a deal."

The Triangle

They shook hands and Manners relaxed slightly, but still kept a grip on the handle of the hunting knife.

191

They shook hands and Manners relaxed slightly, but still kept a grip on the handle of the hunting knife.

Hammered out

In London, Fredriksson had been patient with Dillon. There had been legal matters to resolve, and Dillon's lawyers were good. He had expected fly-by-night legal support, but Dillon had chosen wisely.

The main terms of the deal were hammered out, without significant changes and they were at the point of signing, along with an individual schedule to handle the first few days of the process during which the new systems and legal entities would ramp into production, along with initial transactions flowing through the system.

They had arranged to meet again, this time in a secluded office in the city of London, close behind the Law Courts.

Fredriksson was amused to consummate their deal so close to the traditional legal powers of the United Kingdom.

The deal was far from conventional. Fredriksson was ostensibly alone for this meeting also, but had nearby backup, in case anything untoward was suggested.

Dillon had arrived with legal brief in tow and probably also had further people out of sight. For the central part of the meeting, it was Dillon and Fredriksson. For the signatures, additional legal support attended for both parties.

The papers were signed, and a new node, covering around half of the old Collin's empire, was created. It would take another three days for the system to reach capacity.

Dillon left, instantly a multi-millionaire and with a rate of personal growth of wealth outstripping most people on the planet. Fredriksson smiled; another cog replaced in the broken machine.

ZRH -> LHR (J Class)

Trying to get from Zurich to Heathrow on the first available flight in the morning meant that Bigsy and Clare had to travel Business Class. It was nearly ten times the amount they would normally pay for the same journey with their own money. Nonetheless, they were pleased to get the seats and pleased to be able to spend a few minutes in the British Airways lounge at the airport.

In hardly any time, they were back over London, a bright early morning giving a view of the one-time London Millennium Dome, now sponsored by a mobile phone company and a clear landmark of London from the air.

As the wheels finally touched down with a skid and a screech, Bigsy and Clare looked at one another. They had another busy day ahead of them vastly away from anything they knew from a week ago.

As a priority, they were going to link back up with Jake. They needed to communicate and to find out what had been happening. After the seatbelt lights binged out on the ground, Bigsy flipped his phone on and called Jake. A few rings and Jake answered.

"Where are you?" enquired Bigsy.

The Triangle

"At Clare's," came the reply. Jake had used his own instincts to stay hidden. As his own place had been turned over, in a way he didn't fully understand, and then Bigsy's had been broken into, Jake was running out of places to hide. Clare was away, and as Jake had helped her move in, he remembered a key on his key ring; something he'd always meant to return but never got around to doing. Strangely, he'd got an almost sentimental attachment to it, something he'd never mentioned to Clare.

"I hope you don't mind," he continued.

"It's fine," came Clare's response.

Bigsy and Clare headed for Clare's place. They used the underground and mused that the journey from Zurich was only about twice as long as the journey from Heathrow to Central London.

As Clare opened the front door of the flat, Jake came towards them, and they all found themselves hugging one another, which was not their normal behaviour at all.

"OK, so what next?" questioned Bigsy.

They needed to find a way to bring this runaway situation to a sensible and safe conclusion.

"...but, can we make any money from it?" questioned Bigsy, "We have spent rather a lot". They all looked at one another.

Faux synchronisation

The security services message passed to GCHQ triggered some other events. As well as the four Arabs travelling to London, it also logged Fredriksson's move to London. This created some serious speculation that something would be happening.

The Serious Crime Unit had been notified, because of the suspected links of the four Arabs with oil shipment related crime and the separate investigations about Fredriksson related to his relationships with suspicious business practices.

Fredriksson was, himself, open in his movements, and the SCU had never been able to directly link him with any of the situations that had occurred in the past.

It now looked, however, as if there was a synchronized approach of both groups to London.

Of course, the real reasons for the link was not related to Fredriksson and had been the effect of Amelia Brophy's phone calls, but this had heightened the sense that there was something about to happen.

In a separate investigation, UK Customs had picked up a key Russian entering the UK and seen that two others accompanied him. The whole entourage from the Cannes meeting with Amelia Brophy were in London because two of them had flown from Cannes earlier in the week to attempt to eliminate Jake Lambers.

Converging on London were now both the Saudi Arabians and the Russians. They were known by the UK authorities and both planning to meet Brophy separately in the same restaurant in Kensington.

The authorities considered that there might be a meeting between the Arabs and Fredriksson and were going to take no chances in case of foul play during the session.

A separate trace was in progress towards the two Russian assassins who had killed the police officers Trueman and Green. Death of a cop was particularly bad in the eyes of the London Police, and so the heat had been turned up.

The Vauxhall car damaged at the crime scene by the Russians had been discovered and because the Russians were expecting a more straightforward get-away they had been much less careful than they should have been about breaking into the car. They had made the most basic of mistakes by leaving clumsy fingerprints on the vehicle.

These had meant the Russians could be identified. Both already had diplomatic status in the UK. Their biometric scanning was on file, and so the police had been able to identify them both.

Because of the level of suspicion and linkage to the murder of two police officers, special powers were granted to set up a five-person tracking operation on the two Russians. The botched-job Russians had not suspected the hunt which was in progress.

Run with it

Bigsy and Clare were starting to explain to Jake some of the information they had obtained from Darren Collins.

Jake told them that once he had realised how deeply he had become involved with the money laundering process; he had also identified that UK authorities would be severely challenged. Challenged to either round-up the ring or to offer him protection in the aftermath of any investigations and trials.

Therefore, Darren had decided to break away from HMRC for his own safety and to use the money he was processing to set up some separate funds so that he would have enough money to be able to disappear at some point. He needed to withdraw from his employers in Her Majesty's Government and the various shades of criminal that he was investigating.

That was when he started to devise his three-stage plan. He wanted a) a lot of funds b) someone entirely anonymous for be able to report the situation independently and c) identification of his successors in the laundering business in case of his replacement.

Bigsy and Clare understood this and that the meeting with

The Triangle

Jake was a way to pass the information from Darren to someone else relatively random. By not having a pre-defined chain, it reduced the chance of being traced and would have broken the link to Darren.

Darren had been stealthy but methodical about discovering the way his businesses had linked with others. The official reason he was doing this was as part of his investigations, but he had rapidly seen the information as useful bargaining collateral if things got tough. He had discovered that the operation was truly global with a blend of illicit and legitimate businesses to cover tracks.

So Darren had started to look at the companies with whom he interacted. He looked for the ones that were legal and straightforward, but also looked at companies that were similarly complex in the way that his own company operated. These were the companies most likely to be further 'nodes' in the laundering operation.

On this basis, Darren had shortlisted the three companies most likely to be close copies of his environment and then had made contact with each of them. Darren had ruled out the applicability of one, and this had left two, where, in principle, there was a good fit.

Darren had investigated the possible organisations and already knew the person running one of them. Although the companies in this organisation were somewhat dubious, there was something about their construction that made Darren think the organisation was not a convincing fit as a substitute for his own.

Someone formerly unknown to Darren operated the other organisation. His name was James Dillon, and he moved in some of the same circles that Darren frequented. Darren's position had been propelled upward by the significant injection of cash from his business, but before that, Darren and James Dillon's paths were somewhat intertwined, even if they didn't know it.

Darren had worked out that Dillon was probably a target for a similar role to the one he played. He didn't know how it would work, whether Dillon was 'in waiting', perhaps already recruited and maybe even operating on a small scale. As someone on the inside, it had been made very clear to him that he should not ask questions or try to find out who else was involved or how processes outside of his own companies would operate.

That had made Darren Collins' job much tougher, because he had needed to find out about things he had been expressly asked to avoid. His information was somewhat inconclusive, but he had told Bigsy and Clare his suspicions and supplied them with a large amount of data about the companies operated by Dillon.

In the discussion in Zurich, a simple deal had been cut. Collins had handed over the information which he had, related to what he supposed was the creation of the new node. He'd suggested two ways that this could be used back in England.

The first way was to provide the whole set of evidence to the police and let them take over.

The other option, if Clare and Bigsy preferred it, was that they could do something directly themselves with the information. In the course of this, Collins had told them about the Arabs, Manners and Fredriksson as well as the lead to Dillon.

Darren said he didn't now have a preference. The only condition from him was that whatever happened should not provide any further references to him. The faking of his death earlier had been effective, and he did not want any resurrection of old facts.

So Bigsy, Jake and Clare were now working out an angle on the best way to use the information they had.

The Triangle

They knew about Darren, the triangle of trade, the probability of Dillon as the new recruit and the great level of danger if they made wrong moves.

So they started to describe some outcomes.

"Look," said Clare, "I'm not greedy in this, but if there is a way to recoup our cost, or maybe a little bit more, then we should do it.

"We also need to stop the hunt for us by the 'blue flame' or any of the other organisations."

"We also need to keep the police out of the way while we get the basics sorted out," said Bigsy;

"They are bound to doubt some of what we tell them, in any case, and we don't want to be held up in police processes when we need the ability to move fast".

All three nodded their agreement; they were going to run with this a little bit longer.

Clothes Match

They decided they would make contact with Dillon, but they needed to do this in a way that would ensure Dillon was reasonable.

They decided they would need to do this by intimidating him in some way and that the most natural way would be to imply that they were involved in the shadowy organizations themselves.

"We need to make ourselves look legitimate, in some way," said Jake, "otherwise we will be brushed off."

"So why don't we become part of a Serious Crime undercover unit?" suggested Clare, knowing this may be a crazy idea. "We could scare Dillon and get him to co-operate in some way."

"Duh.," answered Jake, "Now you are crazy".

"But wait a minute," said Bigsy, "Look at the three of us - a computer geek, a journalist and a graphic designer. If we can't come up with a convincing cover story, then nobody can..."

Clare agreed, and they started to create the background that they would need to persuade Dillon to co-operate. Jake was to write a couple of fake news stories, which he could then get worked into a copy of a magazine mock-up. Clare was to produce a relatively wide range of identity forgeries and a couple of unique photographic mock-ups. Bigsy was asked to participate in some electronic engineering.

The plan was evolving. They decided they would visit Dillon at his offices. One of them would pose as a member of the Serious Crime Unit. This would be Jake. He could look serious but was not threatening. If more heat was needed, then Bigsy was available as a background player.

They would need to persuade Dillon that they already knew his game and at the same time stop him from either telling the police or the underworld organization of their involvement. The plan was to keep Dillon as the intermediary in all of this process, and potentially to do so in a way that meant that Bigsy, Clare and Jake did not ever have direct contact with the 'blue flame' organization with whom Dillon and previously Collins had been in discussion.

Their plan was evolving:

Jake was to impersonate a representative of Her Majesty's Government (an illegal impersonation, of course).

Jake would call Dillon and tell him that there was the need for an urgent meeting and that it had to be off-site, away from Dillon's offices. He should say that this was a matter of grave importance and Dillon should follow instructions and to not discuss this with anyone else.

In case he was challenged, he would be able to quote Fredriksson's name and could use the sad situation of Lucien's death as a way to illustrate that the situation was very real.

Clare was creating suitable identity badges and paperwork for Jake and working out with Bigsy how to make it look slightly used and battered. Clare knew how to do this by computer using Photoshop, but this needed to be real. Bigsy's solution was simple. "Give them to me- I'll put them in the back pocket of my jeans for a few hours". Clare smiled; she knew this would probably work.

Jake was working out how to look the part for when he met Dillon. He decided that one of his more sober interview get-ups would probably be best. Jake knew, as a journalist, that 'playing the part' when he met people often gave the best results. If he wanted to befriend them, he would try to match their style.

If he wanted to be a formal journalist he had different clothing to match. The problem was his current lack of wardrobe following the encounters at his flat, which he had still not re-visited. He would need to go shopping and acquire some suitable items.

Bigsy was assembling a lapel camera, like the ones used in the best spy films. He carefully sewed a small module into the lapel of Jake's jacket. The thin wires would run through the lapel and into the pocket, where they would re-connect to a recorder.

It was almost undetectable and gave them a camera and recording capability for Jake's meeting. Jake would press a button at the start of the meeting, and the camera and microphone would spring into life.

Universal

"Every instant is a new universe."

— Joan Tollifson, Nothing to Grasp

Staged

Clare had called Dillon. It was like many busy people, where a personal assistant screened him. Clare was half expecting this and made several calls within two hours.

Finally, she added the magic name Fredriksson to the conversation. As if a curtain had lifted, she was suddenly through to Dillon. This had a dual benefit. They now also knew conclusively that Darren Collin's speculation had been correct. Dillon was involved; otherwise, the reference to Fredriksson would not have worked so well.

Clare now explained the need for a meeting with Dillon away from his office. She did not expect him to agree to this automatically, but when she laid on the pressure about the grave nature of the situation and the need for special care, Dillon eventually agreed.

Clare had selected a quiet location for the meeting. It was a restaurant in Millbank, close to the river Thames and part of a recently modernised hotel.

The critical criteria were that it needed to be at ground level, that it needed to be bright (so that the hastily constructed video camera would work) and that it needed to be quiet enough to be able to record the conversation.

The respectability of the venue would also reduce the likelihood of a 'no show' by Dillon. Its convenience as a short taxi ride from his office was also in their favour. As luck would have it, there was extra melodrama because it was just around the corner from a seriously menacing government building, which had cameras around their walls and police guards and being on Millbank, it was less than ten minutes' walk to the Houses of Parliament. If anywhere was to be convincing for their story, then this was it.

They had arranged to meet at one o'clock in the afternoon, and Clare had stressed that there would only be a five-minute period during which the meeting would be 'on'. If Dillon was late, then the meeting was cancelled. This added further intrigue and a spurious air of professionalism. Clare and Jake knew this was all a bluff.

Bigsy took a room at the hotel, which was also the venue of the restaurant. They could use this as a short-term base camp. For the meeting itself, the plan was to use Jake as the member of the Serious Crime Unit and to have Bigsy on a nearby table in case anything untoward was going to happen. The preference was to keep Clare out of view and for Bigsy to only break cover in an emergency.

Jake and Bigsy had taken their positions at the table. Clare had used the name "John Hastings" for Jake, and all of the identity papers and other documents he carried used this name. The table was booked in this name. They all waited with bated breath for the due time, and Clare had been sitting in the hotel lobby keeping an eye on incoming people. There was an advantage to the front of this hotel because the big plate glass windows there gave an unrestricted view of people coming and going, and sure enough at around fifteen minutes before one o'clock, Dillon arrived.

Clare was able to take several photographs of Dillon through the window of the hotel before he walked into the lobby. Clare pulled a large winter hooded coat over her head and made as if to walk out of the hotel. She noticed that Dillon had made his way to the men's room and once the coast was clear, she slipped to the elevators and off to the room booked by Bigsy.

At around two minutes to one o'clock, Dillon approached the restaurant, spoke to the maître'd and was escorted to the table where Jake was sitting. It was right in the window of the hotel and faced out onto a side walkway, with a brick wall opposite. An occasional person was walking along the thoroughfare, mainly hotel guests cutting from the hotel's exit to the other side where there was a good view of the River Thames and the Embankment.

Jake stood as Dillon approached. "Mr Dillon," he started, "So good you could come along." He felt subconsciously as if he was speaking like a character from a John le Carre novel and hoped it was not too stilted.

"Hello, Mr Hastings," said Dillon, "This had better be good."

"Good is a matter of opinion," continued Jake. "Let me tell you what you are involved with."

Jake then proceeded with the story they had defined. Dillon listened intently whilst Jake took him through the key points. Firstly, Dillon had been under surveillance for at least six months, they knew everything about him and his operation. Jake handed over a couple of sheets of printout which were from the data provided by Darren Collins. It showed a few of Dillon's companies and some turnover data. Then he offered another sheet which showed a detailed breakdown of expenses from a 'sales visit' which Dillon had made to Paris a month earlier. The data showed the individual sales receipt, in the form usually used by an accountant.

"Suffice it to say we have this information for everything you operate," continued Jake.

"Anyone with access to our accounts system could have stolen that," responded Dillon. "It proves nothing- you'd better show me some ID before we go any further, and if I suspect anything, then I will be calling the police in moments."

As if to prove the point, he pulled out his mobile phone and placed it on the table. Across the room, Bigsy's eyes nearly popped when he saw this - the phone was an unexpected bonus. He felt in the small key pocket in his jeans and retrieved the old SIM from Jake's old phone.

Jake showed Dillon the identity papers produced by Clare. They did look good, but also a little dog-eared, which added a good sense of reality. Of course, it relied upon Dillon not knowing what a real identity document would look like.

"Okay," said Dillon, "keep talking."

Clare had been working in the hotel room. They had installed one of Bigsy's printers and Clare's laptop computer. She was downloading the photographs of Dillon's arrival. She added a few words to the image and then, still wearing the hooded coat, stepped out of the room and made her way outside the hotel. She carried her laptop bag and camera and made her way to the riverside of the hotel, pausing as she passed the window where she could see that Jake and Dillon were engrossed in conversation. She was able to do two things here, including taking a photograph of the pair of them talking, all of which went undetected.

Jake explained that Dillon was under surveillance, suspected of being already involved with the money laundering and would be tracked down if he joined the process via Fredriksson. His only chance was to co-operate with the authorities, and in return, he would be left alone. With the money he already had, and the money he could make from the down payment from Fredriksson, he should be able to disappear and reinvent himself. In return, the UK authorities would start to dismantle the money laundering operation.

Dillon would be able to stay disconnected from what

happened, and this would give him the highest chance of survival. Otherwise, he could continue with Fredriksson and know that he would be caught. He could tell Fredriksson what he knew, in which case Fredriksson would probably make him disappear, like Collins and Lucien. He could speak to the police directly, in which case Fredriksson would find out fast and then he would be in danger, and Fredriksson would disappear. Frankly, his best bet was to co-operate.

"You talk a convincing story," said Dillon, "but this could all be bluff. How do I know you really have information and access?"

"Let's think," said Jake, "Firstly, I know about your company, to maximum detail; secondly, I have shown you my identity information; thirdly, I have told you easily checkable facts about Darren Collins and Lucien Deschamps; fourth, this venue, around the corner from a few rather 'specialised' establishments is no coincidence and finally, take a look outside."

Jake gestured over his shoulder. There was no-one there, just the wall, with a few tatty posters on it for various clubs and gigs. Then Dillon noticed them.

Four yellow posters in a row. "Ministry of Death - Live on Thursday," it said, "featuring DJ Dillon". And the black graphic overlay on the yellow poster was a picture of his face, his face a few minutes ago getting out of the taxi to go to the meeting with Jake. Clare had done a good job of making the posters.

"Excuse the theatricality," said Jake, "but my point is that you are an easy target at present". We want to make the situation go away. Only with your help can we guarantee your safety.

"I need a minute to think," said Dillon, "give me a moment."

"Go ahead," bluffed Jake, "But don't try to go anywhere, rest assured we have you under surveillance. We need to finish this conversation". Jake was used to interviewees sometimes needing a minute to think about an important revelation.

The Triangle

When he had got the exclusive on pop star girl Rachitta's coming out, he had been through a situation just like this.

"Leave the phone here," he added, "and don't go making any public calls either."

Dillon walked away. He just needed a few moments to consider his options. He could run, call the police or just go back to Jake. At the moment, that did seem like the best option. He walked outside the lobby of the hotel to the foyer, where he lit a cigarette. A Camel.

Bigsy was delighted. He'd cleaned out Jake's SIM after he had removed it from the phone and would now replace the one in Dillon's phone with Jake's. The main reason was to get Dillon's SIM, so that they could check through the numbers. As Dillon walked out of the restaurant, Bigsy swung past Jake's table, lifted the phone and sat again at his own. A minute later he repeated the manoeuvre and then walked towards the exit from the restaurant, where he could see Dillon smoking. He paused and noticed Dillon finishing the cigarette and turning to come back into the hotel.

"A good sign," thought Bigsy.

Moments later, they were both seated again.

"Okay," said Dillon, "I'll co-operate. What do you want me to do?"

"It's simple," replied Jake, "You just need to do what Fredriksson asks, but at some point, you will need to supply some information to us." Jake was assuming that Fredriksson's approach to Dillon would be very similar to the way he had recruited Darren Collins. There had been a sizable down payment to Collins when he had started the operation and Jake had assumed that it would be the same for Dillon.

"What information?," asked Dillon.

"Let me advise you. When you are asked to participate in this, you should ask for two things. One is a twenty four to forty eight hour review period for the paperwork, and the other is a down payment of thirty percent of the initial fee. Fredriksson will agree to the first and may negotiate on the second. Almost certainly he will have a number of treasury bills to pay you the down payment, and he would probably be surprised if you didn't ask for something like this."

Dillon almost smiled; he had already told Fredriksson he wanted fifty per cent of the initial fees' up front' and the two of them had haggled this to thirty per cent. That was one point three million Euros, or in dollars, it was close to one and a half million.

"That is fine," said Dillon, "What else?"

"You will give both documents to us," continued Jake, "We only need them for forty-eight hours, but will need to cross-check them for DNA as well as any other clues to origination. You will get them both back. If there are any legal elements requiring amendment, we will tell you. The money represented by the Treasury bill will also remain yours."

Dillon was unhappy about parting from the contract and even more so from the money.

"Look," said Jake, "If you co-operate now, you will get all of the money and be forever de-coupled from this whole situation. Any other course of action will leave you exposed and under risk. We don't want the money; it is better for us when you disappear, and the money disappears with you. Her Majesty's government cannot be caught up in money theft."

Dillon relaxed slightly at this final point. If Jake was who he said he was then this was probably his best and safest bet. He was already in this too deep, and the credential from Jake seemed genuine.

"All right," said Dillon, "I'll go along with this; but if I suspect anything wrong, I will track you down and take you down,," he continued.

"Everything will be all right if you follow these instructions," continued Jake. They had both ordered Caesar salads, and both had pushed them around the plate during the conversation. The meal was an accessory to the main point of the meeting, but it was now clearly time to move on.

"Do you agree to do this?" asked Jake, "Because, if so, then we can use the papers to trace the route to Fredriksson and even further back. You will still have been paid the two sums for starting up in Treasury Bills and can then lose yourself."

"Our Government will be creating so much heat for Fredriksson and his accomplices that you will not need to worry about them again. And you will have four million Euros for your trouble. I think this is considerably better than being killed or put into prison, don't you?"

Dillon stood to leave. "You give me little choice in this matter, he continued. "I do agree to follow these instructions, but please understand that I have a great sense of self-preservation. Frankly, even from the start, this proposition seemed too good to be true, and so I am not surprised when it comes like this."

They looked one another in the eye and shook hands. Jake decided that Dillon seemed surprisingly likeable, and he wondered how he had first got mixed up in this situation. As Dillon left, Jake signalled to their waitress and then started to pay the bill.

Dillon was good for his word to Jake, and when he had visited Fredriksson the first time, the whole reason for the legal delays and the requirement for the down payment had gone precisely in the way that Jake and Dillon had discussed.

Less than fifteen minutes after the first meeting with Fredriksson in the Foreign and Commonwealth Club, in a nearby 'Pret a Mange' sandwich bar in Trafalgar Square, the contract and the treasury bill had been handed over to Jake.

Jake had walked out of the sandwich bar and climbed straight into a taxi. "Take me to Cannon Street," he had asked. Cannon Street on the edge of the area of Central London known as Bank. The area where all of the world's main banks had offices; Jake was about to pay one of them a visit.

The right kind of bill

Bigsy and Clare had been waiting for Jake to arrive at their meeting place. They had taken up residence in a Starbucks next door to Cannon Street railway station. It gave a good vantage across the road to McDonalds on the other side. They had decided to meet in a different venue so that if they were being followed, it would be fairly obvious. Not many people would first visit Starbucks and then cross the road to another shop selling coffee and food.

Jake's taxi arrived, and he stepped out, paying the driver from the pavement, before walking to the McDonalds. Clare and Bigsy followed across the road and looked at Jake.

"We have it," he said, pointing to the envelope already on the table in front of him. It contained the contract and also a separate sheet of paper bearing the title "treasury bill".

Jake, Bigsy and Clare had expected the Treasury bill to look something more spectacular. It was merely a series of computerised reference codes. As well as the code it also said that the bills were not matured (although they would be in two days). There were some simple instructions to 'sell direct'. It just requested the seller to log in to the account and to select the appropriate function.

It said that by providing the information, a request would transmit to the Federal Reserve Bank of Chicago which, acting on the Treasury Department's behalf, would offer the bill to different brokers and sell it to the highest bidder. The proceeds of the sale minus a seller's fee would then be deposited into a designated account.

Clare looked relieved. "It will be a lot easier for me to create the new version of the T-Bill from this information," she commented. She was firing up her laptop on the table in the McDonalds.

"We must move quickly," said Jake, "Firstly we need to make a good copy of the contract and the Treasury bill information."

Across the road was a Kwik-Call printing shop. They requested that everything they had in the envelope was copied and that Clare's additional item was printed.

Then they set off for the nearby banking streets of London and found a suitable commercial bank with a dealer desk. It was unusual to deal in person, but the bank was not phased by the request or the amount. Doing this in central London was a lot easier than in the provinces, although Jake, whose account was to be used, was asked for passport and other details. The nature of Jake's job meant that he always carried this type of information around and he easily provided the details requested.

"This will take around thirty minutes," said the bank employee handling the request.

Jake had decided it was better to visit the bank alone. If anything were to go wrong, he was the only one known at this point. He knew the bank systems would include comprehensive video surveillance.

Within twenty minutes, the bank employee came back with a serious expression on his face. Jake expected the worst, but the employee said, "The transaction is complete; the money is now in your account. Please sign this acknowledgment, which also includes details of our fees."

Jake was slightly numb as he heard this. Their plan had worked surprisingly well. They were now sitting on the best part of one point five million dollars.

In the meantime, Dillon was now without access to either the contract or to the money and was feeling somewhat exposed.

He had returned to his own office in the City because, on the advice of Jake, he had been asked to make everything look as routine as possible. Two hours later, a courier arrived at his office and left an envelope.

Dillon opened the envelope. It contained the contract, the Treasury bill codes and a typed note from Jake, which read as follows:

"You followed our instructions accurately. We have copied the documents you provided so that they are returned to you quickly for your processing.

"The legal document looks fine according to our own people. The Treasury bill has a hidden catch at present. It is highly discounted for the next two days and will only yield you ten percent of its face value.

"When it matures, it will have its full value so we do not recommend it to be sold at present.

"The attached Treasury direct information gives you further details about the options, but in our opinion, Fredriksson has been clever in giving you a guaranteed payment that you should only exercise after you have returned the signed contract."

The information about the level of discounting of the treasury bills was false, but Jake, Bigsy and Clare hoped it was plausible enough to hold Dillon from trying to cash the order for the next two days.

The attached Treasury Direct information also looked plausible, but with the minor doctoring to it performed by Clare, the description in the letter seemed to tie up with the 'facts' in the leaflet.

Clare had also used her graphics skills to make a minimal change to the coding shown on the master treasury information. It meant that if Dillon did try to access the information for a sale, then it would actually give an access security error.

This would look like a password transcription error, but would add a few hours to the discovery process by Dillon.

It was also a small enough error to make Dillon and Fredriksson hopefully think it was a coding error rather than anything suspicious.

Clare had changed a couple of Zeroes in the document into Eights. The computer coded form of a zero and an eight did look similar and this could be put forward as a plausible cause of an error.

In the event, Dillon took the letter at face value. He was more relieved to get everything back and assumed that the people he was dealing with were being demanding about releasing payment before the rest of the contract was signed.

And in any case, tomorrow he would make his second visit and get the other two point seven million Euros from Fredriksson.

Right now, he thinking about ways to stage his disappearance in the aftermath of the processes started by the gentleman he had met a couple of days earlier in the restaurant close to the River Thames.

Serious Crimes Unit

The combination of the National Security Agency in Langley, Government Communications Headquarters in Cheltenham, the London Metropolitan Police, the Criminal Intelligence Agency and the UK Serious Crimes Unit had been in liaison for the last two days. A sequence of events triggered, now causing a lot of attention to focus on London.

Unknown to Amelia Brophy, who was on her vendetta, the combination of Fredriksson's movements, the two clumsy Russians at Jake's flat and Amelia Brophy's calling to the Arabs in Saudi Arabia now created a cauldron effect in Central London.

The NSA in Langley had been able to easily track the four Arabs. Their American destination cell phones were equipped with the now legally standard issue GPS chips used in America. Fredriksson was somewhat unlucky. As a Scandinavian, he just happened to be from a culture where cellular phones are highly popular and had a modern and elegant Scandinavian model. It was a very recent design and also happened to have the American style GPS built in, officially so that new capabilities could be offered to the technologically interested Swedes, Norwegians, Danes and Finns.

Langley had been watching this group of five for some time, and the GPS had made this easy. Now they were in UK jurisdiction. They tracking passed to local authorities, who were tracking by both GPS and the local cellular network.

The American system was still superior and more selective than anything done via the phone network, which was more reactive, tracing things after an event instead of before it.

An incident room had been established in a set of offices close to Chelsea Police Station. The offices were officially overspill police offices, but because of the nature of the Chelsea area with its royal connections, these building were secured to a much higher standard than typical police stations.

They also had considerably more technology, communications and even access to heavy equipment from guns through to helicopters and armoured artillery than any normal cop shop.

There were the nearby Kensington barracks, the home of soldiers who, whilst able to ride around prettily on horses in arcane armour, also had some of the most high specification equipment of any modern army. And it was right on hand in Central London.

The incident room was now being run by a Chief Constable Dennis Wilson. Dennis had known Detective Inspector Trueman well, and in his mind he felt that the current events were linked with the recent shocking situation where Trueman and Green had been murdered. So the combination of his rank and only slightly revealed interest in the case ensured a suitably senior stakeholding in what was becoming a potentially major incident.

The visit of the four Arabs to London had been relayed at a high level after they had landed and cleared customs. They had all moved into the Dorchester Hotel in Mayfair, which was a typical haunt for such luminaries.

The Triangle

Fredriksson was also in a hotel in a similar area although since they had left Riyadh there had been no further communication between them.

The London police had separately been investigating the murders of two of their officers in a nearby part of London, and there were clues that two Russian 'heavies' were involved, which had led to their being shadowed as they moved around London.

As a consequence of Langley and GCHQ involvement, the UK authorities had arranged phone taps for the Arab mobiles, as well as for Fredriksson and the two Russian gangsters.

Now they were piecing the events together. There was to be a meeting between the Russians and an intermediary in the hotel's restaurant called Baglioni's. At the same time, a meeting between the four tracked Arabs and an intermediary in the same restaurant.

A professional operator was running the phone being used to arrange all of this. It had been used to set up the calls and meeting and then been disconnected and dropped out of the grid. Whoever was acting as co-ordinator was based in London but operating at a very professional level.

The Chief Constable selected Chief Inspector Donovan to run the processes for this situation.

Donovan was under a lot of pressure from various directions. In the Operations Centre (or War Room, as everyone was calling it), there were representatives from NSA, GCHQ, Met Police, the Army, Royal Protection Unit, Household Cavalry, and the Serious Crimes Unit. The Royal Protection Unit had already intervened, and the significant Royals were all out of town or currently being ferried by helicopter to Balmoral in Scotland.

The basic plan was to treat the possibility of something serious happening at the restaurant, but more likely the restaurant venue was being used to plan something which would then take place on another occasion.

The main possibilities under consideration were terrorism related. Either planning an attack or settling the bankrolling for something?

The direct location was an unlikely target for anything, so it was much more likely that this was a preparatory meeting. As the meeting was in London, there was also speculation that whatever was planned was more likely to be affecting New York, Paris, Frankfurt or another capital city.

If it was not terrorism, the other great prospect was financial in some way. This was Donovan's own personal favourite, and he linked it to the matters affecting the murder in the nearby Sloane Square art gallery, the killings of Trueman and Green in Kensington and now this meeting.

Donovan, along with everyone else, assumed that Fredriksson was involved in the situation and had no knowledge of the involvement of Amelia Brophy.

There were only two days from first notification to the meeting, and by the time the team had been mobilised, it was the day before.

Civilian clothed, Donovan had visited the hotel and restaurant and quietly informed the management that there was a severe problem. He had asked to see the guest list and the list for the date in question. In late November, on a Thursday, the hotel was not fully occupied, although from Friday and in the time leading to Christmas it soon became busy again. The stylish clientele was international. The hotel's room prices, to Donovan, were high even by London standards, so there was a mix of pop stars, fashionistas and 'IT' people who stayed there along with well-heeled Americans, Japanese, Russians and Arabs. An exclusive nightclub ran most evenings, and there was a very discerning admissions policy unless staying at the hotel.

The Triangle

Donovan was commandeering the whole restaurant for the evening of the meeting. He explained to the hotel management that he needed to do this but in a discreet way. He said the most straightforward way would be to say that there were two visiting people in the next few weeks and to imply that they were senior Royals. The location of the restaurant and its profile made this entirely plausible. The evening in question had several tables booked but was quite light apart from hotel guests who may book on the night.

Donovan considered this carefully; a lightly booked restaurant and last-minute restrictions may blow the secrecy with which his own people were being deployed. He decided to adopt a variation of the plan. He would book the rest of the tables and fill them with his own people. This could be a combination of police officers and military, but needed to be done in a way that didn't make it look as if "Mr Plod" was in town.

He decided to take all tables, keep a couple empty to not arouse suspicions and to arrange suitable small groups and 'boy plus girl' assignations in addition to the usual guests who would be present.

The restaurant was quite small, and the capacity of the combined restaurant and bar area was less than one hundred people. To minimise confusion and capacity within the bar, Donovan decided he would have a large section reserved for a small private party. He was sure that the Household Cavalry would be pleased to oblige for this and could easily simulate a sporting victory or something similar which would allow them to play to type without needing to bring too many outsiders along.

Donovan realised that this was a potentially career-enhancing or career-limiting situation. The sheer profile was about as high as it could be; he had required paperwork signed by the Home Secretary and the amount of select units involved was about as serious as it gets. The Chief Constable had inserted him into the process as the operation leader. All goes well, and he could soon be a Superintendent. If it went wrong, he may be worrying about whether he would have a pension.

There was also a maximum level of security imposed over this process. Those involved for the next two days were being kept away from other officers and individually briefed about security. In addition to the British involvement, there was also a veritable array of special advisors from the United States.

Another stage was some special equipment installed into the hotel. This was less problematic than they had expected. The hotel was already wired for full camera observation and there were an above average number of door and general security attendants as part of the hotel's high-quality image. The Italianate staff were particularly attentive and stylish. Adding directly to their front of house number would be difficult.

Donovan decided that changing waiters or bar staff would be too difficult and quickly detected. Instead, he would arrange for high coverage from the available tables and that their placed people would carry any necessary surveillance gear. It was also essential to only enable any special technologies after the guests had arrived; otherwise, it was very likely that they would be detected by a sweep of the room by one of the security people accompanying their prime visitors.

The preparation was intense both inside and outside of the restaurant. Across the road was the edge of Kensington Park and a nearby gate to enter the park. Just the other side of it, on the edge of the broad footpath, two large Portacabins were being moved into position. This was where the reinforcement firepower would be housed. Three Chevrolet Trucks and a Mercedes van were parked behind the Portacabins and were unloading grey gunmetal and green and brown cases into the back of the Portakabin units.

Party Time

And the whole world has to
Answer right now
Just to tell you once again
Who's bad?

Bad – Michael Jackson

Quiet evening in Kensington

Amelia Brophy had checked into the hotel linked to the restaurant. She was also checked into the other cheap hotel about one and a half miles away. At the new venue, she was Ms Foster. She was still using Brophy at the other hotel.

His initial check-in was with just a small holdall. She would be bringing the rest of his baggage by taxi later. The rest of her baggage, in the other hotel, was already wired with the K-PEX plastic explosive and a phone detonator.

She could phone her case from across the road at the point she wanted to cause the devastation. She walked from the hotel to the street and looked around.

A park and some construction work opposite. A busy street was leading to the Kensington High Street. A tube station. A side street with a National Car Park. The car park was about 5 minutes on foot. The car park would be her means of escape.

The Triangle

She would need a rental car, position it as close to the exit as possible, even if it meant re-parking.

She needed to know that both groups were in the restaurant and then to introduce them to one another. They would both suspect a trap, and this would be the point where they would start to make for the door. That would be when she would trigger the device. She would already be outside, across the road. She would then walk to the car park and make a casual escape while the confusion continued. Then head north by car and aim to finish at Manchester airport by midnight. Amelia then had most of the planet in reach for the following morning. She already had a reservation at the SAS Radisson, which was part of the airport complex.

Her hire car was delivered to her original hotel, and she drove it directly to the car park in Kensington and parked ready for the main evening events.

Everything was now prepared. Donovan had his men in place. Amelia Brophy was in the hotel. Her luggage was to be picked up by taxi and transferred to the new hotel. She would ask the concierge to leave it downstairs because she would be leaving the hotel shortly.

By seven p.m., the Russian group arrived at the hotel. They seemed in good spirits and regarding this session as a routine meeting. Although they were supposed to be collecting important data, none of them seemed particularly guarded or cautious. They took up their table and ordered some vodka immediately. It looked as if they had already been drinking earlier or at least that the security men supporting the group seemed particularly well oiled.

The Saudis arrived around forty-five minutes later. They also arrived in stages. Two suited men came first and walked around in the restaurant before the others arrived. They noticed the Russian group but did not take particular notice, other than they were particularly noisy.

Amelia Brophy had expected the Saudis to be late. Time worked differently for people from the middle-east and delay was mainly to emphasize their importance. The security men called on their mobiles and then waited by the front doors of the hotel for the Saudis to arrive. A short time later two stretched S class Mercedes arrived. They both had darkened windows, and the four Arabs emerged. They all wore western suits and moved quickly to their table in the restaurant.

Amelia was outside of the dining area in the bar during this process and across from a noisy party of sportsmen, who seemed to be celebrating a recent rugby victory. She guessed they were military, based upon their height, haircuts and ways of addressing one another.

Donovan had watched all of this. He, too, was sitting in the bar in a good control position to see what was happening. He could see the Russians, he could also see the Saudis, but more importantly, he was looking for Fredriksson or anyone else carrying out observation. This was made simpler because around half the people in the bar and restaurant were supplied by him.

There was additionally a table of six banking types in mid celebration, presumably of a big city deal. They may have been acting, but their language and interaction seemed realistic enough for them to be genuine. There were a few couples, who looked as if they were genuine, but then again, so did a couple of his own units. A group of five Japanese in the bar waiting for a taxi seemed unlikely, and a large mixed family group who had come in from the street for a drink also did not seem very plausible. He was interested to see their reaction to the bar bill for their drinks in a few minutes. This left four individuals seated alone as his main marks.

One was clearly waiting for a girlfriend or partner, one was reading a book, and the other two were looking around. Donovan had spotted Amelia in particular because of her attractiveness and an attentiveness to the goings-on in the rooms. She had also taken what Donovan regarded as a 'control' position in the room. She could see everything yet could easily blend into the surroundings. To Donovan she was the prime. He noticed that the person was also making several phone calls.

Donovan was now hyper-alert. In addition to the calls, he could see Amelia approached by one of the hotel staff. Donovan could see that there was an arrival of luggage at the front door. The person he was watching was giving instructions to the doorman about the luggage. Donovan had stood and could make out that the instructions were to leave the luggage in the lobby entrance. The intimate size of the hotel meant that the lobby faced across towards the bar and to the restaurant areas.

Donovan saw the woman making another call. He noticed one of the Saudi phones ringing, and the Saudi take the call. Something was in play.

Then Donovan saw Amelia putting down money and starting to walk out of the restaurant. One of the Russians had looked over and appeared to recognize her.

There was a shout, Amelia continued to walk as the second Russian also stood and then pulled a pistol from a holster under his jacket.

Both he and the other Russian were taking aim on the person leaving the hotel. As she left, he looked long at the luggage.

Two shots rang out, and then almost instantly another four.

The Russians had missed Amelia and were now both on the ground courtesy of the Metropolitan Police. Several people in the restaurant screamed, and a couple ducked low to the floor.

Donovan looked to the luggage. He'd seen that look from the woman. He was convinced the luggage was involved in this.

A bomb.

He ran towards it as the general commotion broke out behind him. The Russians were reeling from firstly their own group firing on someone and then their security being breached.

The Saudis took a different view. They did not break cover. Their two security men pushed them into a corner of the room and then edged them along wall to a side door marked "Fire Exit".

Donovan was running towards the cases, hoping that no-one would fire upon him. The Russians seemed to have been neutralised, the Arabs in the room were trying to leave. Everyone else was part of the operation.

If the cases were a bomb, he had limited time to get them outside.

He had luck. They were stacked in true concierge fashion on a wheeled trolley.

He ran at the cart and pushed the whole thing along the floor towards the door of the hotel.

To his surprise, the footmen at the door opened it as he approached — years of training. The trolley continued on the walkway to the street, and then out of control across into the road, where it toppled to a crashing halt as two taxis braked heavily to avoid it. Donovan waved to everyone to clear the area. "Bomb," he shouted.

Inside the restaurant, there was still chaos. The remaining Russians were attempting to make their way forcefully but without firepower to the front door of the hotel, but they found themselves faced with significant declared firepower from other guests in the restaurant.

The Saudis had done better. Their exit through the fire door had been successful, and their cars were on hand to pick them up. Unfortunately, they had not expected a battery of armed police officers to be waiting at the top of the street they were trying to leave.

Amelia had done the best. Her departure was some twenty seconds ahead of the main alert. The initial gunshots and deployment of the armed forces inside had taken a few seconds to create the external reaction. As she left the hotel, two people had been stepping into a taxi. She had joined them, demonstrating the power of showing the tourists her rather expensive pistol.

The taxi had pulled away and she had then abandoned it about three hundred yards away, by the end of the road leading to the Car Park.

She was outside the cordon that was rapidly tightening around the hotel. Her priority was the car, then the explosion. It took her another minute to get the car to the exit from the car park, then she turned right and then left as she moved rapidly away from the area. She reached in her pocket, picked her phone, selected the speed-dial and pressed. Two seconds later she heard the explosion. She was already three-quarters of a mile away.

Back at the hotel, there was complete chaos. Donovan had used his radio to issue commands.

"Bomb Alert! Bomb Alert!

"If you are inside the hotel, stay there. If you are in the street, get away from the hotel entrance. Stop the traffic for one hundred meters on either side of the hotel right now. Do not approach the cases and trolley in the street, it's a bomb."

Another forty-five seconds. The inside of the hotel was controlled, The Russians had surrendered. The Saudis were outside protesting innocence. The police had stopped the traffic. The area was cleared.

There was a sudden noise of glass, then a loud bang, then a

pressure wave and heat. The bomb had detonated.

Outside, it had done damage to the street and windows, inside it would have demolished the entire building and maybe the block. The street was fairly wide where the explosion had taken place. There was a small crater and blast damage, but altogether less damage and disruption than anyone might have expected. The blast could travel upwards without meeting resistance, and so a lot of its deadly force had been expended in creating a blast against nothing.

Everyone around the area looked at one another. They knew this had been a close shave. One of the Saudi security people immediately said, "We should leave the area. This could be one of several."

He had good terrorism training, but Donovan was sure that this was all there was. Whoever had just escaped had planted this as one chance. Two Russians had recognized him but were both dead now. It was not Fredriksson and looked like a professional freelancer - a woman. She would be hard to trace if she was outside of the hastily assembled cordon.

Indeed, Amelia Brophy, now Ms Jennings, was already approaching the coned road repairs leading to the M1 to head north to Manchester. Under the chair, nearest to where the bomb had initially been sited, was a passport and wallet with Brophy's documentation inside. If all had gone to plan, she would have been considered amongst the casualties. Now she was just disappeared, but as the two Russians who had previously tried to kill her were also dead, she had officially ceased to exist.

Donovan surveyed the scene. Two unoccupied burning cars. A crater the size of a small roadworks, but not very deep. A collection of dazed soldiers, security men and police. More mess than he had hoped but a lot less than there could have been. On balance, he would get promoted.

Endings or beginnings?

The events unfolding in Kensington were blissfully unknown to Fredriksson and Dillon, or to Jake and his companions.

In parallel, Fredriksson's second meeting with Dillon was taking place, again at the Commonwealth Club. Fredriksson knew that Dillon had cashed the first set of treasury-bills. The contract had been returned, the company processes were being established and Dillon was receiving the other three and a half million dollars starter fund.

Dillon was confused when Fredriksson mentioned that the treasury-bill had already been cashed. He knew he still had the notes and the codes ready once what he believed was a discounted time-period was finished.

Fredriksson moved the conversation along: "Here is the next three point five million dollars and these are already deposited in an account for you. We can resolve what has happened to the previous payment, but frankly, this will all seem insignificant in a few weeks when the main processes are up and running."

Dillon smiled wryly. He thought he might have been double-crossed on the recent transaction but either way, he was probably safely in pocket. If the unexpected Serious Crime Unit visitors had been genuine, then he would pocket the down payment, and maybe even the second part.

If his visitors from Serious Crime had been fraudulent, there was no way he would mention this to Fredriksson, because it would expose his complicity in the attempt to trap Fredriksson. Indeed, if they had been lying to him, then the original scheme with Fredriksson was still on, and he stood to make a lot of money from the new arrangement.

And, with the goods and services being virtual, the emphasis on proving the connection to anything illegal was still going to be a tough call.

Dillon considered the 'margin' on the transactions was as high as it ever could be - less Fredriksson's cut of course, which in any case was taken off the top of the deals as they flowed. Fredriksson also reminded Dillon this would be good business, as long as Dillon did not get careless in the way that Collins had. If he did, then retribution would be swift.

Dillon expected to be contacted again by Jake and at that time would be required to hand over the rest of the evidence so that Jake's organization could speedily take down Fredriksson's organization.

Back at the Travelodge near to Heathrow, Jake, Bigsy and Clare sat together sipping complimentary instant coffee from two cups and a tumbler. They all knew that the story to Dillon was made up, but that Dillon had almost wanted to accept it.

Jake, Bigsy and Clare had swiftly taken $1.5m dollars from Dillon and but at this point Dillon did not know this for sure. That was the attraction of bearer bonds and Treasury Bills. They were like high-value banknotes and untraceable after the transaction.

For Jake, Bigsy and Clare, they now had a rather large seed fund of money. If they never met Dillon again, there would be almost no way that Dillon could track them down. Dillon had no real background about Jake other than the fake story that Jake had given during the meeting.

The Travel-lodge was a suitably anonymous location and here they were summarizing what had transpired in the last few hours.

They had located Dillon, persuaded him to give them the deposit money from Fredriksson.

They had persuaded Dillon that Jake was from a special Government Department and that Dillon was already under surveillance. If they melted away from Dillon, they would not be traced. They didn't think Fredriksson had a lead to them either.

They knew that Manners was mainly interested in tracing Darren Collins's information and that this was part of another plan. They were still completely unaware of the existence of Amelia Brophy.

Their actions had, inadvertently, kept them away from the police. Their delays at the start of the week, when they had gone back to Bigsy's and the revelation from Jake that there were some extra aspects to all of this, had meant that they had never got as far as the police.

"What about the way that Lucien was killed, the robbery at Bigsy's and the big scene at Jake's?" started Clare; "We can't assume that the people chasing Jake have finished it," she continued.

"I will need to go to the police," said Jake, "They are bound to want to question me about Lucien. I'll need to play it very dumb. No one will believe how much has happened to us in the last couple of days, in any case, so I can just say I've been working on a story, from on the road. We also need to think about the other people that have links with us now. Some of them may be a little upset."

"Yeah, we're probably clear of Dillon and Fredriksson, but the original killer is still around, and we don't even know who he is working for.," added Bigsy, as he paced the small room in the Travel-lodge. He was looking anxious and started fiddling with the TV remote.

There was a loud bang. "Bigsy!" called Clare, "Turn it down!"

Bigsy had switched the TV on, and it was on a very loud volume setting. He fiddled the controls," Oops, sorry!"

He started noticing the programme. It was a news report, from Kensington. It was describing the events of the afternoon.

"This is Sebastian Walker, from outside of the Baglioni hotel in Kensington London."

"Today we have seen dramatic events unfold as police surrounded a suspected terrorist cell and then, in a lightning shoot-out, two of the suspects, both armed with rapid repeater pistols, shot on police and other innocent bystanders in the middle of the hotel lobby."

There was a cut to video footage of the hotel and some of the signs of devastation. There were the all-too-familiar signs of police blue and white tape in most of the camera shots.

The report continued, "In addition to shots fired inside the hotel lobby, there was an attempt to detonate a bomb.

"An unidentified onlooker pushed the bomb, contained in two suitcases, to the outside of the hotel. It blew up in the street, apparently detonated by remote control from a mobile phone. Fortunately, there was no injury but a huge crater and many broken windows."

There was a cut to a Chief Inspector," We had received information about a meeting of certain individuals connected with international crimes. The hotel had been chosen and we had already created a cordon around the location. We were not expecting anything as dramatic as the events which unfolded, but we did have a full terrorist and armed response unit on hand in case things escalated."

"Our expectation was of a simple meeting between interested parties. In the event, it seems that one group may have set a trap for another group, both of whom we have reason to believe may be involved in some form of gangland war".

"So were both groups apprehended?" asked the TV reporter.

"We were able to take a group of predominantly Russian speaking individuals for questioning following the incident," replied the Chief Inspector. He knew what was coming.

"So, the other suspected group?" asked the reporter.

"We don't think there was another group present," said the Chief Inspector, "It looks as if the sources were wrong, or that the other group were tipped off."

The Chief Inspector knew that the original reason his team were at the hotel was linked to the Arabs from Saudi Arabia. As they had left the hotel by a side entrance into a waiting car, they had presented diplomatic passports and documentation which allowed them to be whisked out of the area, even before the bomb had exploded.

Their car had been heading out of Kensington in the same direction as Amelia's even before she had managed to collect hers from the nearby car park. The Saudis had headed directly back to Heathrow. Their priority was to be out of the United Kingdom well before the main debate started in the UK media. And because they had not directly reacted to the situation, there was no proven linkage of them with anyone else in Baglioni's.

The reporter finished the interview and the TV cut back to the studio. Another TV presenter started a discussion about whether Kensington was becoming the "Wild West" of London. Then a cut to a panel debate about what needed to be done with police powers and security to prevent things of this type from occurring in the capital city.

"Wow," uttered Jake," This has got to be linked with what we have been involved with! It looks like a Russian group, presumably Russian mafia, were involved with a meeting, probably about the creation of the new routes? And then someone has tried to blow them up. This is all completely out of hand!"

They flicked around the limited channels on the Travelodge TV. There was a Sky news channel also describing the events. They had found a couple of eyewitnesses in the street. They gave a different account from the police. They described mostly the same information, but also that they had seen someone running from the hotel before a police officer ran outside with the bags on a trolley. They had also seen some Arabs leaving a side exit from the hotel and getting directly into a large black car and then heading away through a police road block.

"So, Russians, Arabs, a bomb and shooting," declared Jake. "This has to be linked to the Blue Flame and the triangle of money laundering. It looks as if someone was setting a trap."

"You know what this means," said Clare, "The stakes have moved past any of us. They wanted Jake when they thought he had information from the Darren Collins interview. The fact is, the game has moved past that now. Whoever is involved in these acts is beyond the likes of Jake and his sound recording. We know it's not Manners; he has had at least two opportunities to get Jake."

"There has to be someone else or another group. And they are moving up the food chain. As long as they are not tied to the money we have recently borrowed, then I think Jake will be all right now."

The Triangle

Jake didn't look so convinced, and neither did Bigsy. "Why would they stop chasing Jake?"

"My thoughts," said Clare, "Firstly, they'd try to kill Jake to get the recording information. They may have needed to kill Jake to get past him to the information, but in the end they could walk right into his house and simply steal everything. When they didn't get everything from Jake's, they located Bigsy's and stole the backup disk from there. So, they had the data they needed."

"Second reason," continued Clare, "As a warning. Jake could have been working for someone and that would be a reason to kill him. The Kensington incident we've just seen is a much stronger warning than trying to bump off dear Jake, here. If you think about it, Jake didn't know much either, other than the code numbers from Darren Collins, and they had a finite life-span with any value."

"Thirdly, I suppose Jake could have seen the Arabs, and he would recognize Manners. So, Manners could have killed him, but didn't. It was the data, not Jake, that Manners wanted."

Clare stopped. They all looked at one another.

"So, in risk to reward terms," said Jake, "At the moment we have one point five million pounds and the people who gave it to us don't know who we are". The others nodded.

"We think that someone has been after me, but that I'm no longer of interest because the events have moved on." They nodded again.

"And if we take this to the police, we will need to tell them everything, including about the money?"

They nodded again.

"You know," said Jake. "At the moment I honestly think we are ahead - we have some unique combined talents, have maybe worked our way through this with some luck, but could almost certainly learn a lot about running private investigations".

"We also have a good starter fund," nodded Bigsy, "If the money is right, I think we have some unique skills and experience to offer," continued Bigsy.

"One for all, all for one," added Clare.

The triangle was formed.

Post

He flipped the computer switch and typed:

"If you like reading endings first, then this section is for you.

"The triangle was initially written as part of a one-month project called NaNoWriMo, which takes place every November. London became the backdrop, and the characters became real. There's already a sequel, and a few clues about it dropped into the pages of this opening piece.

"The novel is thin, so that it can be read in a single European round trip flight, but it covers the distance of a blockbuster movie and, of course, 'The Triangle' has multiple meanings inside the storyline.

"There's more in store."

Enjoy.

x x x

Ed Adams

THE SQUARE

Ed Adams

a firstelement production

First published in Great Britain in 2020 by firstelement
Copyright © 2020 Ed Adams
Directed by thesixtwenty

10 9 8 7 6 5 4 3 2 1

ISBN: 978-1-9163383-8-8
ISBN-eBook : 978-1-9163383-9-5

Printed and bound in Great Britain by Ingram Spark

Ed Adams
an imprint of firstelement.co.uk
ed.adams@Ed-Adams.net
rashbre@mac.com

Mailing list: https://mailchi.mp/9f0b30712620/ed_adams

THANKS

A big thank you for the tolerance and bemused support from all of those around me, especially Julie who has to make up the excuses. To the readers of my prior novels and to the requests for further frolics from Bigsy, Clare and Jake.

This novel bridges the dots from The Triangle to The Circle, although the circumstances of its writing are more in keeping with Pulse.

When I started this, I didn't expect to be in lockdown with crashed money markets and a mystery virus on the loose. Stranger things can happen in fiction, I suppose.

And, of course, thanks to the extensive support via the scribbles of rashbre via http://rashbre2.blogspot.com and its cast of amazing and varied readers whether human, twittery, smoky, cool kats, photographic, dramatic, musical, anagrammed, globalized or simply maxed-out.

Time to put on a tune and enjoy the ride with the cast of characters involved in producing this, whether real or imaginary

And Thanks, of course, to you, dear reader, for at least 'giving it a go'.

PART ONE 249

NOW 251

   Sand 252

      Cairo 253

   London 265

      SI6 266
      Gerald 271
      Muhammad 279
      Lambeth Walk 290

TWO WEEKS EARLIER 295

   The Pentagon 296

      Washington Alert 297
      Hoxton 305

   Politician 308

      Defence Secretary 309
      Westminster Bridge 315
      Thames House 321

   Walk like an Egyptian 326

      Coded binary 327
      Firepower 330
      Driscoll 335

NOW 339

   Park Lane 340

      Car chase victims 341
      Mossad 348
      New York bed 351
      Unwind 363
      Chuck goes to MI6 366

   Manhattan 374

      Molly's 375

Léa 378
Anonymity 382
Take the AirTrain 384
Sleek brown tee shirt 386
Calling Chuck 388

La Côte d'Azur **390**

Croisette.. 391
Trip to London... 399
Huxley's 401
Diversion 413
Truck One.. 420

PART TWO 423

THREE WEEKS AGO.. 424

Kent.. **425**

Ashford.. 426
Back to the lock-up.. 430
Containment 435

RIGHT NOW 442

Strong women **443**

Elisa Solomons.. 444
Mesopotamian Heritage?.. 468
Chuck's involvement 474

Planning a gig... **479**

Birmingham Mailbox District..................................... 480
The Market Porter 486

Fake News **491**

Carson's meetings 492
Weight throwing 498
Tracker lock... 502
Bad America... 505
Brief Ramirez 508

Unstoppable **512**

Al Aktar 513
Unstable... 520

Truck Two 523

PART THREE **529**

Event Management **530**

The gig 531
Listening in 537
The crunch.. 541

Under Pressure **546**

Ramirez thoughts.. 547
Unexpected guest.. 549
Unbelievable 556
Carson and Ramirez 562

Triangulation stations.................................**564**

Showdown mechanics.. 565
Bank.. 572
The Anchor 576

THE SQUARE

PART ONE

Ed Adams

Sand

"in every grain of sand there is the story of the earth"

— Rachel Carson

Cairo

16:00 Eastern European Time (EET).

James expected this to be a short, sharp mission. He'd be paid and out of here in another couple of hours. He'd hand over the bag and be gone.

He sheltered on the edge of a dune. The vestigial grass had a razor-sharp edge, scratching his arm as he slithered into a comfortable position. The Subaru was parked about 200 metres further away, concealed behind another dune. A long way ahead, he could see the tiny outline of the truck, heading towards him in a shimmer from the heat. It seemed to be running above the ground becuse of the haze and he could understand how people thought they could see water in the desert.

The truck's progress was also almost silent, and then he heard a whine from what sounded like an American military diesel engine. He'd heard the sound before, in Germany, where there were many of these trucks used around the bases, but here it seemed displaced.

Through the sound he noticed a further noise, a slow throb which was getting louder. He looked around and could see a speck in the sky, not a bird. It was bigger and tracking the path of the truck. A helicopter, it looked like an Apache as it became closer. An attack helicopter, carrying a fair array of armaments. By now the truck was less than 800 metres away, still proceeding at a steady speed.

The Apache was low in the air, but then suddenly, but languorously, the helicopter let go of a missile. It didn't fly straight, but took a lazy path from the helicopter, like the casual throw of a soft toy from an adult to a small child.

But whatever it was, it would hit the truck. A second or so later, there was a flash, and it was as if time had moved from lazy to accelerated in a split second. As the missile hit the truck, a white flash exploded in a vertical line from the ground to two or three hundred metres in the air. The power of the explosion seemed out of proportion to the previous few seconds of activity, and James sheltered his face with his arm, the same one that had been cut a few moments earlier by the grass blade.

Now, he could hear a shrill electronic sound and he realised that the helicopter was locking on to his Subaru and was planning to vaporise it in the same way as the truck. He buried himself in the sand rather than attempting to run. That way, if the chopper was looking for vehicles, it may not spot a lone person hidden by the scratchy dune grass.

The Square

In the far distance he saw a momentary flash from the ground and a black line crossing the sky. Someone had launched a surface-to-air missile. The black trail slid through the air towards the helicopter. He heard the Apache's engine squeal as it banked first left and then right in an attempt at evasion. It was ejecting what looked like hot metal strips. But it was too late. It was still too low.

The SAM made contact with the helicopter and in a much yellower fireball than the truck's explosion he watched the helicopter drop to the desert floor. He lay low for longer in case there were any more surprises, but no, a few minutes later he was preparing his escape in the Subaru, alert to the thought that whoever fired the surface-to-air may head his way.

As he climbed into the car, he scratched his arm, remembering the grass, but as he looked down, he noticed that his arm was bright red as if scalded and that the hairs on his arm looked as if they had been shaved. At least one blast had been close enough to have scorched him. He felt his hair and noticed that part was matted, also from the blast. It had been a close thing. He floored the pedal, skittering back onto the road, heading away from the direction of the surface missile.

Two hundred kilometres away, in Cairo, Karen Martin was sitting in the Hilton, sipping a drink in the Belvedere. She was waiting for a call from James to confirm that the exchange had taken place. It was supposed to happen at four thirty in the afternoon, and now it was nearly five o'clock. This was not a pleasurable part of the plan. She had wanted to accompany James to the drop, but he had urged caution in case of unexpected events. Karen had access to further resources and by doing it this way there was no obvious trail to follow to link them together. Then suddenly, her cell phone started to warble.

She flipped the phone open.

"Yes?" she enquired.

"James" came the reply.

"We have a problem. I'm on my way back. Without the invoice," continued James.

Karen knew this meant something was wrong, but that James was not in immediate danger.

"Usual place," said Karen.

The place they had arranged to meet was far from 'their usual place' but was a safe and random place within the town. They had chosen it whilst James sat in a bar and pointed to a map of Cairo. Their plan was to use the meeting point on a signalled date at a predetermined time. That time was 6.30 in the evening, when there would be a good number of people around to mask their meeting. So, the meeting would be tomorrow.

Karen would move from the Hilton in the next few minutes. She had booked into two different hotels as a general precaution when she first arrived and would now move to the other hotel while remaining checked in at the first one. This was to help hide the trail. The activity would be good and take her mind off the next three hours whilst James made his way back to Cairo. She knew that his route would be slow because of the desert, but that once James was back on the main roads, he should speed up.

The Square

She would not know what had happened until the next day, but at the moment needed to keep a low profile and not attract attention. Another fifteen minutes and she was leaving the hotel, not taking bags and careful to leave her existing hotel room looking occupied. She needed to be in the new hotel, but without the discovery that she had moved.

Karen was using basic tradecraft. She knew that with an operation like the current one it was less menacing when she was the contact and ostensibly alone for the meeting with James.

She needed to know the location of the car and cases which James would provide and then hand the operation along to others to complete the exchange. Clean and clinical. She was the only one to directly meet James; James wouldn't see the rest of the team and they wouldn't see him. No direct contact and no physical contact with the goods. A cellular handover.

Karen suspected that this was a bigger situation than the exchange of the cases. Her boss, Robert Alton, had called her in for a briefing about this a few days ago, but had kept the entire mission very compartmentalised. She would know the transit team behind her, but for this one she just had another phone number.

Karen knew that the major aspects of her missions seemed to relate to the fronting role she had in this current situation. Sitting about in hotels, finding contacts and marshalling resources.

Occasionally she had to meet a target to relay a message. Nothing messy, dangerous, or difficult. And through doing this she had visited Washington, Helsinki, Toronto, Switzerland, Paris and Munich.

Unlike what she had expected, she often used her own name and passport, and appeared to have a travelling sales role for a marketing company. It was all very plausible and low key.

This was the first mission where the false identity was an absolute pre-requisite. Richard Alton had been insistent.

Karen made her phone call to the support team. "We haven't got the invoice." She hung up and removed the battery and sim card from the phone.

-.-- . ... --..-- / .. - / .. .. / -- --- .-. ... . / -.-. --- -.. .

James continued the drive. The Subaru had a four-wheel drive and dealt effortlessly with the trail leading back to normal roads. He kept within speed limits and made his way towards Cairo. His concern was that the car may have been recognised by the helicopter, but they would have needed to radio in some details before the missile had destroyed them. He considered it unlikely and that he had a very high chance to be undetected. He cast an eye over his shoulder to the machined case he had been given to exchange for the ones in the truck.

He'd known it was a special mission when he had noticed the USB operated electronic lock on the case.

As he arrived back in Cairo, he headed for the quieter back area of his hotel's parking lot. James checked the car again for transmitters using a small gadget which could detect GPS, Wi-fi, Tetra and simple beaconing and everything seemed to be passive. He had done this when he left for the mission but needed to check again because of the unexpected events in the desert.

James glanced at the space blanket in the trunk. It contained a metallised core and would have been used to envelop the two small cases he had expected to receive.

Back in his room, he swept the security detector across his own clothes. He showered and swapped to another complete set of clothes before taking his original clothes to a hotel rubbish skip. Anything to minimise detection.

James hated the delay in this assignment. Whatever he should have collected was important and wanted by others but was now also vaporised from the helicopter missile.

James resigned himself to the thought he may not get paid for this work. It suited him to be freelance, to switch the work on and off, but the payments were results driven and no bags would mean no fee. However, James knew that Karen worked for the UK Government. It boosted his chances of payment considerably. Not all the money, but two thirds. The Americans were not so helpful. They might not even come to a follow-up meeting in similar circumstances.

James had already opted out of any second stage to this mission. It would be easy enough for the people organising things to get a replacement for him, and now that there was a risk, they had spotted him, it was not sensible to continue. James was a professional and knew, unlike in the movies, that if you fail a drop or a mission, it is many times safer to walk away and let an unfamiliar person take over as a replacement.

James had his brief speech ready for this, but also knew that his controller Karen would expect this.

He checked his watch. He had a set time to meet Karen and wanted to be prepared. He would take his pistol and knife, but travel light, so that if he needed to move away from the area quickly, then he would be able to.

He positioned his car in an area close to the rendezvous point. The Subaru was noticeable now, on account of the dust and desert on the paintwork, which on such a new-looking vehicle looked somewhat out of keeping. He drove the car through the complicated streets of Cairo and found a good place to park close to the embassy district. He flipped out a French CD paper for the front windshield, which made the vehicle look suitably authorised, although by doing this he knew he also risked being on surveillance cameras.

Then James walked out into the streets of Cairo. The nearby offices in their skyscrapers gave it the looks of a modern and rapidly expanding city, but James knew that much of the centre was ancient and labyrinthine.

Without the air conditioning of the car, he noticed the thick air immediately. The effects of what was happening around choked the central area. Beset with environmental problems, there were old and highly polluting cars and taxis creating a permanent yellow and orange smog and a taste mixing dust with sand and copper.

But the main thoughts on James' mind were to get to the rendezvous. The original plan would have him hand over a small package to Karen, which was actually a decoy. He just needed to tell her the car location and registration and her accomplices would have picked it up. He would have been wired the money to a pre-designated account. Now, instead, he was using the car as part of a contingency escape plan.

The Square

At just after 6pm, he walked past the rendezvous, half an hour ahead of the meeting time. No sign of Karen, but he wondered if she was doing the same.

James scoped a couple of other roads and an alley which led down to the water's edge of the Nile. He took the alley to check its potential as another route. Sure enough, a path ran along the edge, busy with traders and tourists.

James re-checked his watch and then made his way back towards the cafe, this time expecting to see Karen in position. As he approached, he could see her sitting in the cafe's small terrace. She spotted him and started to stand.

James heard a crack and saw her move sharply to the left, as if she had been punched very hard. Then another crack and he saw her lifted into the air about two feet off the ground and propelled into the next table, causing cups and plates to fall to the ground.

He looked to his right and realised Karen's assailant was using a high velocity rifle from a nearby rooftop. He looked back towards her and saw that she was now on the ground, but that everyone around her had scattered.

James thought quickly. Karen identified him, but he had not signalled back, and at the time she stood up a professional marksman had shot her.

James knew it was better to move away, out of the kill-zone, but without drawing attention to himself. Instead of turning, he crossed the road diagonally as if in the same direction but was now under the awning of some nearby shops. The one on the corner was a food store. He walked in, feeling a blast of air-conditioned air and a carbon taste of air filters.

He walked directly to the back of the store and through two rubberised semi-transparent spring doors into what was the loading area at the back of the shop. He kept going through a concreted back yard and onto a busy street.

Several taxis parked in a row. He climbed into the first one and asked for the airport. It was an old car, no air-conditioning and wind-down windows in the back. He felt the heat from the seats and opened the windows to force in more air. Cairo blurred past. James was only thinking back to the scene at the cafe, of Karen, and whether he was now in danger.

James knew he needed to make himself invisible. He couldn't risk going back to the U.K. or even back to Paris. So much for this being a routine pickup and exchange. He should have known that there could be trouble when he was quoted the high fee for the work. He knew that he provided extra trustworthy insulation between the goods and their eventual recipient, but not that there would be determined forces in pursuit.

He quickly analysed the situation. The UK Government had requested a pickup but needed it to be anonymous. The main operation was in Egypt, so it was likely to be something with a middle eastern origin. Just pass the package to the Brits.

Except. They had intercepted the truck carrying the package. By whom? But then the helicopter had been destroyed. Another group? And then his U.K. contact had been shot in the rendezvous cafe.

The Square

He thought he had escaped detection through all of this. His best plan was now to be as far from Cairo as quickly as possible.

He fiddled with the strap on the small day sack he was carrying. Just credit cards, identities, passports, cash and a few other essentials. He could retrieve a couple of other items from the parked car. There was too much risk in returning to the hotel.

He had been careful with the car and hotel room. They were both on credit cards and there would be an automatic charge through to the end of the week. He would phone the car rental company from the airport to state its location. He would say it had broken down, and he had caught a taxi. The car firm would send someone to move the car – they would be pleased to be able to start it and its removal would reduce his probability of detection.

He decided that the United States was a good option and would allow him time to re-gain his thoughts and work out the next part of his plan. If he could get to New York, he had a superb place to stay, off of the radar.

He reminded himself of the need to stay focussed. His chief objective was to get out, and to get his identity adapted. As he turned towards the airline terminals, two local 'helpers' walked forward to assist him with his backpack, to make a few euros. A small guy to lift his bag and a big guy to enforce collection of a 'service charge'.

They backed away when they saw his eyes, "Don't even think about it."

Soon James was through the mayhem of the airport and on the plane, sitting back in a business class seat. As he eased back in the seat, he could feel the tiredness sweep over him. It was like someone was draining all the energy out at a speed he could almost feel rush through his body. He knew this was just a reaction to the events of the last few days. His brain was telling his body that it was now okay to relax, and the ten hours to fly to New York would give him a chance to plan his next moves.

In the short term, New York provided a suitable haystack for him to hide within, whilst he figured out what was happening. The plane taxied, accelerated, rotated and was airborne. James was already asleep.

London

"Being a seasoned Londoner, he gave the body the "London once-over"

- a quick glance to determine whether this was a drunk, a crazy or a human being in distress.

The fact that it was entirely possible for someone to be all three simultaneously is why good-Samaritanism in London is considered an extreme sport –

like BASE jumping or crocodile wrestling."

— Ben Aaronovitch (Midnight Riot)

SI6

Robert Alton had been reading routine information feeds from his office in SI6.

He'd just seen an unverified incident from Cairo. Some sort of shooting. He knew that SI6 had an operation in that area.

SI6 was the special operations unit dedicated to homeland security of the United Kingdom. Many people had heard of MI5, although Alton thought the real action was with SI6, who were involved in special operations when things were likely getting out of hand.

On average, there were between twenty and thirty special operations running related to terrorist related situations. A dozen years ago, it had been around ten operations and half of those involved Ireland.

Nowadays there was a full spectrum of countries involved, with Middle East, Afghanistan and Africa high on the list.

The Square

Ireland still featured but was a small percentage of where the time was spent.

Robert Alton had been with the unit for about five years and after the bewildering rush of situations when he joined, he was now good at identifying the serious situations.

He was also directly involved with complex events. Since the emergence of internet and satellite television and the increased use of digital mobile phones, most aspects of security and surveillance had actually become more straightforward. There was a lot more computer power involved, but the systems could sense and decode many more topics.

The Americans had started a couple of big data analysis projects, got legal backing, and now the U.K. could follow in their footsteps. It was high tech, although the ability to sift to find things was still often 'after the fact', unless the agencies received a direct tip-off.

A recent intelligence coming in from the security people at GCHQ Cheltenham, England was about a series of plots related to destabilising central London. There was no clear basis for the attack, but the underlying reason seemed to relate to a fanatical unit protesting about the demise of the state of Mesopotamia. It all sounded esoteric and the work of 'crazies', but there still needed to be an investigation.

Robert was to work with Karen Martin on this assignment. Karen was her field name, and they had worked together several times.

Robert Alton clicked a speakerphone, "Can someone update me on the Cairo situation? There's been a shooting?"

"We have more information, via the local police. A lone woman, sitting in a cafe, shot twice by sniper's bullets. High velocity. Fatal. The local police are on the scene. It was close to the French Embassy. Nationality unknown."

Alton flipped the phone off. He knew. He wouldn't be close to what Karen had been doing, but he was sure that it was her mission that had been terminated. His own knowledge gap would mean there was deniability. The shooting would be written up as a senseless act of violence.

He pulled up the file for Karen's mission onto his computer screen. He knew that Karen would keep things hidden.

The background showed a series of transmissions intercepted from Turkey. The Turks were still using a cryptography which GCHQ could already unscramble. Crypto sold to them by the Americans, who would have also intercepted the same messages.

The supposition was that a cell of Al Aktar had assembled in mainland Europe and were considering a key urban target. Two cities had been selected, Frankfurt and London, based on their financial significance.

There was no clarity about individuals involved, or the basis of the attack. The immediate thoughts had been related to aircraft-based attacks similar to the 9/11, but there was no actual intelligence to support this.

After a couple of days delay, the Turkish authorities had alerted the US and the UN and the information had rippled through to various security organisations.

The Square

Robert Alton had seen this situation before, where the security channels become so choked with the information that anyone with even vague access would know that they had discovered it. This would be a deterrent to whoever was planning the attack. The knowledge that half the world's security services were on specific alert.

So, at a first level, the subtext said this was not a real situation. That was when he had discussed a plan with Karen.

He remembered Karen's scepticism similar to his own initial analysis. Except Alton knew that the source prior to the Turkish intercept had been very strong. It came from a place that didn't break cover. It would mean that the particular network would need to cease business after sending this alert. A high price unless this was something solid.

Alton could also see that the source implicated other nation states and suggested that the funding for the attack was bigger than a typical terrorist cell.

Robert Alton had requested Karen to chase it down. Quietly, and undercover. Let the big position play out 'upstairs' which would result in the threat being written as a false alarm.

Karen had asked for support. Investigators to check the source and an 'unknown' to act as an insulation layer.

Karen's investigators had discovered that there was something in transit. Referred to as the packages. 60 small items to be shipped via Egypt, under cover of a goods load.

Alton would need to call in the investigators to find out more about their discovery. Karen's file didn't have detail of what was in the packages.

Alton knew that the rest of Karen's support team would have gone into hiding after the shooting. He would need to coax them back into the open. And get them away from Egypt.

He pressed the phone again.

"Doug, it's Richard. We have a problem; I will need some help. And someone TL4 Arab speaking. I'm thinking Muhammad? Can we meet? This will be ears only."

"Lambeth Walk?" suggested Doug, "Give me ten minutes to find Muhammad Mubarain and we'll be along, 11:30, by the snack bar."

Gerald

Most people who saw Gerald for the first time would avert their eyes.

He lived in a squat near the Balls Pond Road area of London. Gerald wryly called the area part of the up-and-coming Hoxton, but he lived by deserted warehouses and a Saturday ad-hoc marketplace where middle Europeans would attempt to sell dubious goods from cardboard cartons.

Gerald lived by his wits and scrounged a living from small errands and some petty crime.

Gerald walked around in a grey raincoat, with a knotted scarf and a trilby hat. In a clean and well-fitted version this could have made Gerald look respectable, but with the uncared-for styling that Gerald displayed, the overall impression was that of a scruffy down-and-out.

A grey, drizzling rain had persisted all day. It flattened the landscape and blurred detail. Car lights smeared and sound deadened. This was not a good rain, just a persistent one.

Gerald was shuffling back to where he lived. He looked as grey as the surroundings and blended into the general misery.

Things had not always been this way, and Gerald had gone through a good education until the point where drugs had seen him expelled from multiple schools.

The last time he just ran away and travelled south to London as a missing person. He didn't have any serious money and nowhere to live and no plans. He had been picked up at the station by a do-gooder who had helped him into a temporary hostel. There he had made contacts and become better versed in the art of street life, which was now his main means of survival.

He'd met Lucy near to the hostel, and they'd turned tricks around the back of the north London train stations to buy drug money. One cold night, for the second time, Luce had OD'd and been taken away in the ambulance. They had taken Gerald too. He later had to identify her after she had passed away. The hospital staff had a care worker present who had offered Gerald rehab.

Gerald decided he owed it to Luce to get straight and went away to a turnaround place for several weeks to break the habit.

It had worked, and they initially moved Gerald to a small hostel to get started on his climb back to civilisation.

The Square

It wasn't an easy climb, and he'd been robbed on the first night and then blamed for another robbery, which he didn't commit.

He'd decided it was better to get out and so with little clothing but with a stash of items in a Tescos supermarket trolley he had struck out to find a squat. Gerald now lived in an unheated and semi-derelict house due for demolition with several others of similar circumstance. He was now stable, if not happy, in his lot and with his life.

There was a delicate balance amongst the squatters. Most lived off the land, begging, dealing and some petty crime. There were a couple with dogs, and the rest kept their individual areas in the house. They looked after one another to keep a balance.

That was until two new people moved in. There was something incongruous about their demeanour. By rights, as squatters, they would be poor and have only their feet to walk around. These two guys had their own van, which had a recent number plate.

Gerald knew that most people like him would not have transport -or if they did it would have not be as clearly modern as this van.

Gerald monitored his recent neighbours. They seemed more purposeful than most of the people in the area. Anyone in the squat would hide their belongings or be sleeping or chilling out from cider or drug-related abuse.

Gerald knew these guys were different, and the level of their apparent industriousness combined with their relative wealth meant they were probably involved in some higher form of mischief.

They appeared to be well fed, seemed to have supplies of snack-food whenever he had seen them and seemed to be able use normal pubs whenever they wanted. Gerald thought of them as 'the geezers'.

It seemed strange that they would use the squat at all. They had a van and took it when they left to go away, often for several days at a time. Gerald could tell when they were around because the van was pretty much their only mode of transport, unless they walked to the nearby pub.

The van was parked outside on the road, but twice it had been backed gingerly across the rubble at the front of the premises right up to the main doors. The back doors of the van had been opened and something thrown inside. The first time it happened, Gerald was further away and unable to see what was happening, but this time Gerald was close enough, shielded by a low wall.

The geezers were collecting something else, unaware of Gerald's presence.

Gerald took a look in the van. Not to steal - it was too close to his doorstep, just to know more about the two guys. Maybe it was cigarettes, booze or maybe even drugs?

He climbed over the low wall and edged to the back of the van; whose doors were still open. He felt the adrenalin as he peered around the rear doors and spotted two aluminium briefcases in the whole rear compartment.

Next, he slipped onto the back flooring of the van. He reached towards the nearest case and flicked the lock. To his surprise, the little silver clasp pinged upward. Then he tried the second clasp. The same thing happened. He could open the case.

Gerald looked around and listened. He could hear his breathing sounded loud in the back of the van. Gerald was used to the area around the squat and the noises of people moving.

He could tell if anyone was close by. No sounds. He stood a little further back from the case - now at arm's length and then, carefully, he raised its lid.

Envelopes - the case contained envelopes. Not slim white ones, but thick orange-brown padded bags. He estimated there were about ten in the case. So he slipped one into his raincoat, hurriedly closed the case and made his way back to his own side of the wall.

He could hear his blood pumping in his head as he squatted down. He had taken a risk with these two guys. They were better fed and fitter than him. If they wanted to hurt him, it would be easy for them.

Gerald decided he would go further away before he opened the envelope. He did not want to be caught red-handed. Instead, he would go to another spot, just along the road. Not good as the squat, but a great hide-away. He crept out of his part of the squat and started walking along the road. He knew he was a well-known sighting in the area, so if he behaved then no-one would think anything of it.

Ten minutes later he was in his other hideaway. He pulled the envelope from his pocket. It was about the size of a half sheet of office paper. He fingered the top where it was sealed. There was nothing special about the way it had been closed.

He opened it in a way that would allow him to re-seal it if needed. This took a couple of minutes, and at the end he could pull the flap open with no tears or creases in the envelope.

He peered inside. There was a small metal container inside. It looked like it was made of machined steel, and had a rather unusual clasp at the top, which looked as if it needed a special machine to open it. He felt the weight in his hand. For its size, it was heavy, and he assumed the metal was thick. There was a small glass bulge at the top, like an indicator light, although it was not switched on. He wondered what would happen if he pressed it like a button but thought better of it.

He noticed some small writing. A serial number and the inscription "вольфрам" on the bottom of the container. He decided it was Russian but was too difficult to decipher.

Then, on the side of the container, he noticed another small inscription. It was a symbol and a number 4. He recognised the symbol from back when he played school-time computer games. It was just like the logo for a game called Bioshock.

Gerald lost his nerve to delve any further with the container. It looked expensive, well-machined and indestructible. He wondered if the glass button was a control. Would it unlock the container, or worse, would it arm it?

Whatever it was, it looked as if they designed it to protect something expensive and to avert prying eyes.

The apparent warning logo made him think it contained something dangerous. Aside from the word and the symbol, there were no other markings on the cylinder. There was nothing else in the padded envelope. He decided the container was full of something, but it was not like any drugs he had ever seen. The guys who had been handling it were planning to deliver it and the rest of the contents to a buyer somewhere.

He would hide it somewhere safe for now and await developments. No-one had seen him at the squat while the van was there, and now he had successfully moved the envelope away.

He found a special corner and wedged the envelope and its contents behind, then replacing a couple of broken boards so that the area looked undisturbed. He thought the location was especially useful because it was so totally random.

Gerald decided to take a long walk before returning to the squat. It would put distance and an apparent alibi between him and the people with the van.

Back at the squat, the loading of the van was complete. In total, six cases, no bigger than briefcases had been placed in the van. The driver was getting ready to close the doors when he noticed another member of the squat returning.

The newcomer swayed towards them, apparently looking for some cider money from the driver or his passenger. He noticed the open doors, and the pile of aluminium cases in the back and staggered towards them. The driver and his passenger looked briefly at one another and then at the man. With a sudden movement, the passenger swung his arm towards the drunk and chopped him across the neck, crumpling him to the ground.

"Let's go," said the passenger and he and the driver ambled to the cab of the van and pulled away. The drunk lay where he had fallen, in the mud of the yard behind the van.

An hour later, when Gerald returned, the drunk was still laying there, in the same position. Gerald noticed the body, and walked cautiously forward, listening for any other sounds. He could see the van tracks and boot marks where the driver and passenger had been standing and knew what had happened.

Gerald recognised fallen person as Ben and shook his shoulder. It wasn't that unusual to see Ben slumped somewhere. He had something of an alcohol problem. Gerald and Ben shared the adjacent property but usually gave each other a lot of space. Ben was breathing and slightly choking, as well as reeking of cider and something that smelled like garden compost.

Gerald gave Ben a couple more shakes until he started to groan. Whether it was alcohol or violence related was hard to tell, although it was clear that Ben was in a bad way.

"Ben?" shouted Gerald as he shook Ben's shoulder. Ben opened his eyes and spluttered, "They hit me!"

"Yeah" said Gerald, still not completely convinced, "Who?"

"I just got back," explained Ben, "I'd been drinking and when I got back here there were those two guys with their van. I was just asking them if they had some spare change for me when they hit me!"

"Are you sure that's all?" persisted Gerald.

"Oh Yeah," continued Ben, "Their van had a lot of silver cases in the back. It looked like something expensive - maybe jewellery?"

Muhammad

Muhammad Mubarain was contacted by his team boss Doug. He was being asked to meet Robert Alton off-site, although close to the main SI6 headquarters building. This was unusual, even for Robert.

Muhammad had become part of SI6 via Robert Alton, who he had first met several years ago, when they shared a train ride across Turkey. Alton had helped Muhammad and got Muhammed's papers straightened and provided initial work, largely because of Muhammad's good English mixed with knowledge of local Arabic dialects in an area of strategic military interest.

Muhammad knew his entry into SI6 was improbable, and that was quite an asset in some of the situations over the last few years.

Muhammad's family were all from Iraq but killed as part of Saddam Hussein's purges during the 1980s.

It had started when a green army truck arrived in young Mohammad's village with five or six men in the back of it.

The men walked around and used their radio to call their base. Muhammad's father had taken Muhammad to one side.

"Go now from the village," his father had said, "Don't come back. Go on your bicycle, and leave the village along the low road, the road which runs downhill. Take this bag and take this money. It is your ticket to another life. Son, however difficult this is, you must never come back here. Do you understand?"

Muhammad was a tough youth, very fit from running and climbing in the area around the village. He had strong desert craft and knew how to stay out of trouble in the scorching sun and how to find water in the cooler evenings. He knew how to drive a car, but he would not admit this to his father, because it would cause a serious amount of disciplining.

"Something bad will happen?" he asked his father, knowing the stories from other parts of his region. "Yes, son, something terrible will happen. I don't want you to be here when the rest of the troops arrive".

Muhammad nodded. He would do as his father requested, although he hated the thought, he would be alone without his family and friends. He picked up his bicycle and made his way to the edge of the village, so that the noisy troops would not notice. Then he slithered down a bank onto the low and overgrown road leading from the village, down a long sloping hill which ran for several kilometres.

On his bicycle, the gradient gave him distance without much effort and within an hour he was many kilometres from the village, now the other side of some mountain ridges. He stopped to look back. The air was silent. The heat was intense. He could see some wisps of black cloud from behind the ridges. The black clouds were coming from about where his village was located. He blinked back a tear, turned and cycled on.

Muhammad spent three weeks alone in the open. He had to break some of his religious laws along the way, neglecting prayer and stealing food to eat as he headed eventually to the north of the country and across the border into Syria, where he could pick up a freight railway line which headed into Turkey.

He had stayed on a long and very slow freight train through Nusaybin and Senyurt and then on a long slow journey across Cappadocia to Narli, which was the nearest thing he had seen to civilisation in weeks.

Narli was also a modest vacation destination, with a famous lake and some resort hotels. Muhammad had money and identity documents from the package that his father had given him, but he knew he would need to use them with great care.

In Narli, he found a hotel laundry and instead of buying clothes, he borrowed a few from the laundry bags, converting himself into a western-looking youth.

Muhammad had been awestruck with the gargantuan landscapes of the area, the enormity of the skies and the sheer awe-inspiring natural beauty of the area sculpted by volcanoes.

Like those before him, Muhammad saw this as an area through which he was fleeing from something terrible. Before him, early Christians fleeing persecution from Rome settled here and created frescoe-rich churches and monasteries throughout the valleys.

He was on the Silk Road and it could lead him to the fresh life his father had described. Muhammad was also streetwise enough to know that drugs smugglers nowadays used this same route. Seljuk Turks had built respites for camel caravans travelling the route. These and the caves were chiselled into the tufa rock creating the underground settlements once used to escape the attentions of invaders.

Muhammad knew that he should use some of his money to take a train for rest of his journey across Turkey to Istanbul, which he perceived as one of the big cities of the West. His father had always encouraged him to speak English and he was able to buy the ticket from a hotel ticketing source. The concierge was used to handling strange requests and didn't seem at all phased that a 16-year-old Iraqi was travelling the length of Turkey unaccompanied.

There was only a train every two days, but fortune on his part meant that Muhammad could catch a train later the same day. It was a two-part journey and Muhammad was travelling in unreserved seating in the lowest class on the train. He didn't care. His main objective now was to get to somewhere large and anonymous. Istanbul was his steppingstone for this. In the area around Narli, although two countries away from his native Iraq, he could still understand the language surprisingly well. A part of the old Ottoman Empire and the dialects had survived.

Muhammad moved to the station and looked for where the train would appear. To his surprise, it was already in place at the platform, some two hours before departure. It was being stocked with water, drinks and snacks for the journey. He decided to see if he could get on board and found that they locked the doors, except by the area where items were being placed on board. He snuck on and found a seat. There were no warnings it was reserved, and he sat comfortably, using the small bag as a pillow for his head.

An hour later he was disturbed and awoken by another three people moving in this area of the train. They were foreigners talking in English, though he did not know where they were from. They were talking fast, but he could understand most of what they were saying. He noticed their short haircuts and wondered if they were military. One of them looked at him now he appeared awake.

"Isalaam Aleekum," said one of the British to Muhammad.

"Wa aleekum isalaam," replied Muhammad, automatically.

Muhammad realised from the look of the three travellers, that their language was limited to hello and welcome, so he switched into English.

"I go to Istanbul, this part of the train is correct, Yes?".

The three travellers smiled, "Yes, this is the right part of the train. We are also going to Istanbul, then flying back to England".

They smiled. Muhammad smiled back. These looked as if they would be trouble free companions. Muhammad noticed they had high technology phones and music equipment, expensive looking backpacks and stylish clothing. He decided they were wealthy and that the money and goods which he had would not be of much interest to people as wealthy as these three.

One of them offered him a can of drink - Coca Cola. He took it with some ceremony and watched as the three of them all took cans, clicked them open and began drinking. He had been sparing with water for the last three weeks and this was some contrast.

Another half an hour and the train lurched out of the station. There had been a lot of commotion with items being loaded and last-minute retail opportunities for bottled water, Turkish coffee in small paper cups served through the windows of the train and even some large cases being fed in through the windows instead of via the doors. Muhammad sat with the British people and wondered if he would get to Istanbul with nothing being stolen.

"What's your name?" asked one of the Brits. "My name is Robert, and here are Adam and Richard," he continued. "We have been seeing the beautiful countryside around Narli."

"I've been in the desert for the last three weeks," replied Muhammad, "It has been a long journey for me."

Muhammad described the village he had left and the long trip across difficult terrain to get to Syria and then across into Turkey. The area he had crossed was the western tip of Syria and also where the freight train line ran, and so he had taken an optimal route.

Robert looked at the other two Brits. "We know about that village. It has been in the news here." He asked, softly, "Did you know other people in the village?"

The Square

"My family were there, and many of my relatives and friends. I think I know someone murdered them," said Muhammad, "I could see smoke and hear noises like gunshots as I left. I was already a long way from the village, but you are confirming something that I already knew."

Robert looked Muhammad in the eyes, "I'm sorry to be the one to tell you this."

"I'd known and have already had three weeks to grieve. Now I know I am alone and must make my own way. My father told me to find a fresh life."

Muhammad had just heard the news he had expected ever since he left the village. The first truck of soldiers was a vanguard for a larger group, and they were there to destroy what they saw as an oppositional force, based upon a different interpretation of religion. Muhammad's father had given Muhammad everything that the family possessed in order to help him make his escape. Almost certainly, his whole family were now slaughtered in the village and Muhammad was alone in the world.

"You are Kurdish?" asked Robert. Muhammad nodded, "Yes, it's where I live". As an Arab, Muhammad didn't see land borders in the same way as politicians. The land was for everyone. People should be able to live anywhere they wanted. He had just proved that by moving from Iraq, through Syria and into Turkey.

"Okay," said Robert, "I think it's better now that you keep your origins quiet unless an official asks you; you have some papers?"

Muhammad nodded, he knew his rucksack contained papers prepared many months earlier by his father. They were papers that should allow him to travel to many countries, as long as he had money.

"...So can you help me at all?", asked Muhammad, who at this stage didn't think he had anything to lose.

The three travellers looked at one another again. A local person well versed in desert-craft and with an understanding of the terrain and local dialects. This was a strong find for the travellers, as Muhammad spoke good English and did not have any other ties.

"We might be able to help," said Robert, as the train rattled onward through the orange landscape of Cappadocia. It would be another 750 kilometres before they reached Istanbul.

During his time in the desert, Muhammad had decided that Istanbul would be the start of his new life.

Istanbul, a real edge city, between East and West, spanning many different cultures. Part European and part in Asia, where it crosses the Bosphorus. The only metropolis in the world on two continents.

Istanbul, capital to three empires, the Romans, the Byzantine and the Ottomans. Then, after the establishment of the Republic of Turkey, the capital moved to Ankara although most Turks would still see Istanbul as the capital for all but government bureaucratic reasons.

It would be easy to get lost in Istanbul. Easy to find something to do. A way to make some money. Muhammad didn't mind starting low. He thought he had enough cash to get started, although the money from his father seemed to be American money. He would need to be careful so that people did not think he had stolen it.

But now, on the train, Muhammad had been given a new proposition by the three people on the train. Employment in return for a place to stay and some proper paperwork.

The work involved him travelling with them back into desert areas, providing translation, cultural references and access to locals. For Muhammad, the thought of a safe place, some cash and proper papers made a very compelling option for Muhammad. In this terrible situation he had found a good route.

"A bird in the hand is worth ten in the tree," he thought, remembering the Arab proverb.

So right there on the train, Muhammad had agreed to work with these three British military people and would accompany them to the British Embassy in Istanbul.

Muhammad knew that he was getting involved with something that may make him take sides, but there had been such terror in his own country that siding with people opposed to what had happened made sense.

At the embassy, the three travellers showed passes. Robert spent several minutes explaining the purpose of bringing Muhammad along. Muhammad could see that Robert wielded considerable influence. Muhammad was admitted to the embassy but taken to a separate area, where he was told they would question him before they would allow him regain contact with the others.

The room was pleasant enough, upstairs, in a separate block from the main buildings. There were guard dogs on the ground floor and armed militia inside and in most of the corridors.

Muhammad was offered fruit and drink and then after about twenty minutes someone came to ask him questions. he noticed that Robert, from the journey was also present, although now in fresh clothing and looked somewhat smarter than he had done on the train.

"It will be fine," said Robert, "Just tell them what you told us."

Muhammad thought for a minute in case this was some kind of trick but decided that it was safer to follow the instructions. He again explained his story and the route he had taken. His description was easy and unlaboured, because everything in it was very real and true. His questioners could see that too.

It did not take long for Muhammad to be provided with temporary accommodation in Istanbul and a small allowance, provided by Her Majesty's Government.

Muhammad had then been introduced to the work of Robert, Douglas and others. From the embassy, they were all trained for other more specialized duties and needed ways into and out of Syria, Iraq and Iran.

Muhammad became a guide and a translator for them and helped with missions which had a semi-military nature. Muhammad was happy to co-operate and considered the work of the UK Government to be a way that he could get back at the people who had destroyed his village.

The Square

Over the next few years his bitterness dulled, and in the same period the loyalty to his UK friends increased. Robert Alton, the first person he had met on that train rose through the ranks within the Government group and was soon a senior player, with Muhammad as a loyal supporter.

Lambeth Walk

Robert Alton was standing by Lambeth Bridge as Muhammad and Douglas approached.

"Coffee?" asked Robert Alton.

"Water, maybe," smiled Muhammad.

Doug nodded. "You too, Robert? I'll get them, let's find a quiet spot." He walked towards the small coffee shop perched on the edge of a jetty by the Thames.

"It's odd, even the television spy series use this stretch of the river," said Muhammad.

"I know," said Robert Alton, "I think it's also because they can get the Houses of Parliament into the background."

"So why aren't there lots of microphones and surveillance cameras around here?"

"Oh, there are. And not just ours. Even the juice bar over there is wired up. But we'll walk along the road over there in a minute. It's out of any practical range. And, after all, we are only talking about the next all-Department meeting."

Doug returned with three bottles of water.

"Okay, let's go."

They turned from the walk alongside the Thames back onto a busy main road.

"I wanted this to be away from normal recording because I think we may have a loose tongue somewhere inside the Department," said Robert. "I need people I can trust on this."

He turned to face Doug and Muhammad. "Look, Karen has been killed. It looks like she was run down on a package exchange mission. I've checked through her files. She'd insulated the mission using a stringer to do the exchange. There's no name on file."

"What was the mission about?" asked Doug.

"It's linked to a threat we received about some terrorist movements in London and Frankfurt. The package that was being moved was linked in some way. I'm going to go 'upstairs' to try to get more information."

"What was in the package?" asked Muhammad.

"We don't know. We just know that it was supposed to be of a size that a single operative could collect and move in the back of a car."

"Could it have been a bomb?" asked Muhammad.

"Bomb, money, drugs; we just don't know. The truck carrying the package was destroyed. Blown up by a missile from a helicopter."

"What?" said Doug, "This isn't in mission reports. All it said something about Karen in a road traffic accident in Cairo."

"I know," said Alton, "It has been given a cover story. It was all very messy. Karen was shot down in a cafe. Before that, the helicopter that destroyed the truck was blown up by a surface to air. The stringer guy running pickup has disappeared. It's a mess. The whole trail is dead."

"That's where you come in," said Alton. "We need to get on top of this. Find the stringer. Bring him in."

"What about the people operating with Karen?" asked Muhammad, "She would have a team with her."

"She did, but it's no good," said Alton, "After the shooting, they went into hiding. There were two of them. One's now back here in London, the other is still in Cairo. They are good people. The one in Cairo says that there is a rumour that the helicopter was Israeli."

"Shit," said Doug. "That would put the cat among the pigeons".

"Yes, and now we must seek a white dove of peace," continued Alton. "This could already be a major incident if the word gets out that the Israelis were flying missions into Egypt."

"Not one for us though?" questioned Doug.

"Not directly," answered Alton, "Although if the U.K. involvement is discovered it would change things. More importantly, there's what this all means, linked back to the terror threat. I think Karen stumbled into something much bigger than we expected."

"And it does create a useful trail for us?" said Muhammad. "If the Israelis were prepared to send an unauthorised gunship chopper into Egypt, then they must know something about the truck or it's package?"

"My thoughts, too," said Alton. "We will need a small team that can operate away from base for this. There seems to be a leak. And it seems to be cross border too. If it's as sloppy as it appears then the smugglers, terrorists or whatever they are know what is going on too."

Robert Alton looked at Muhammad and Doug carefully, "You know this needs total discretion. This situation is a Category One threat".

Muhammad and Doug nodded.

"We'll go external," said Doug. "It will be easier if you can give us another cover investigation. That way we can be off-grid but with a reason."

"Use something that won't involve too many other people. How about that gas fracking security probe up north?" suggested Alton.

"Perfect," said Doug, "Miles of fields and hills to investigate based upon a security rumour."

"I'll up its security level too, so that access to what is happening becomes more limited," said Alton, "…And Muhammad, your cover story is because we suspect parallels with something that has happened in the middle east."

They had arrived in an area close to another busy south London traffic intersection.

"There's someone else I'm going to meet about this later this afternoon. Someone I shouldn't really be talking to. I'll let you know how I get on.

"We should split up here; Gentlemen, a pleasure," said Alton, "Oh, and remember - only communicate to me in person on this and all meetings off site."

TWO WEEKS EARLIER

Ed Adams

The Pentagon

*I think it makes people in the Pentagon kind of nervous
to know that chemical agents and environmental factors
could cause so much damage
in terms of what may happen in the future.*

Bernie Sanders

Washington Alert

When the first news of the terrorist plans reached the National Security Agency in Washington and GCHQ in the United Kingdom, they conducted a trawl to find senior ranking experts who could interpret what was happening.

They had called Robert Alton for this reason. He had also asked to involve Muhammad. There had been ripples of dissent from command office, but Robert was by now very senior and vouched for Muhammad's integrity.

Muhammad had spent ten years in loyal service, initially overseas in Turkey, but then since he was 26, spending time in the UK in some of the more sensitive control and command centres related to understanding Middle Eastern motives. Muhammad knew his way around now and at 28 years old was fit and self-confident. He had shown unwavering support for Robert since they had met and had been involved in exercises which spanned the continents and countries around the middle east.

The news from GCHQ gave Karen and Muhammad a lot to work on. They had a sense that there was a serious attempt being made to do something on a large scale to cripple London and other UK centres.

"Why don't we announce something?" asked Muhammad, already aware of the protocol.

"We can't," replied Karen, "Two main reasons; it would create widespread panic, and this can create further problems of its own and second, it is better that the terrorist doesn't know we are on to them as we close in."

The plan was now to determine and triangulate the sources and reliability of the information about the plot. Muhammad would send out probes via the internet and through the cellular network, to see if there was further information.

Muhammad also now had a strong network, so he was sure that if there was news, he would stand a good chance to find it.

Muhammad's problem with the briefing from Karen and Robert was that he had no idea what he was looking for. It was some kind of plot, involved London (or maybe Frankfurt) and was terrorist led, by people from the Middle East. Next stop was Government Communication Head Quarters (GCHQ-Cheltenham), to see whether there was any more concrete intelligence to help him in his task.

Muhammad didn't have the top-level security clearance and needed someone who could help him with this part of the activity. Because of Muhammad's background, he was still regarded as an outsider by some parts of the British security fraternity and so full clearance was all but impossible.

He called Karen and asked for her help. She agreed and together they called GCHQ to ask about other intercepts and links with other significant events.

They were patched through to a Commander Simpson from GCHQ, who asked a series of detailed security clearance questions before he was prepared to proceed any further. They were on a top secured line between their headquarters and GCHQ and Karen had Level 1 clearance. Commander Simpson was satisfied with this and relaxed as he prepared to answer questions.

"Here's what we have," he began. "some intercepts from Iran and Pakistan suggested that there was an increase of information flow related to the geography of parts of Central London around Parliament Square and Whitehall and also around the Western part of Frankfurt in the financial district."

"We have been tracing the calls and some of the calls have been to call boxes in West London, mainly around the Paddington area". Then we picked up satellite phone calls, also from West London, which seemed to link to the same thing."

"We think there is a cell operating in London and that they have acquired some nuclear or chemical/biological agents which they intend to use in an attack. For the last couple of weeks, we have been trying to identify if there has been any major theft of loss of materials. That's when we discovered a cover-up that has been operating at CTL."

"CTL?" queried Karen, "what is that?"

"CTL is Chemical Testing Labs, it is part of Porton Down," continued Commander Simpson, "They test new and specialised chemical and biological agents, whether UK, US or originated from other areas. Two weeks ago, a consignment of tubes containing a new compound going by the name Crylo-37 was diverted en route to a testing suite and has not been recovered. It is believed to still be inside the complex but has not been located. This is very irregular, and we are holding a full investigation. Crylo-37A is a neuro toxin antidote for one of the deadliest nerve toxins identified. The test tubes are not normal glass ones. They are special titanium containers with injection capabilities. The antidote is to be used against a severe form of nerve agent."

"So, we have a terrorist alert and a mysterious disappearance of nerve agent antidote? both within a two week timeframe?", queried Karen, "This is rather a large co-incidence?"

"Precisely", said Commander Simpson, "That's why we have alerted your organisation as well as a few other Agencies, but we are still keeping this Strictly Confidential. We have not told press or public and even kept this from all except the Defence Secretary, Bernard Driscoll. It's the same intel with the US and Germany at the moment, and with Germany, they know about the terrorist alert but not the nerve agent. We had to tell the Americans because the original nerve agent compound was American, and they would wonder what had happened to it."

"I know we are not supposed to make assumptions", said Karen, "but this is too much of a co-incidence. Is there any chance that the tubes will still be found inside CTL?"

"It's unlikely", replied Commander Simpson, "The individual tubes have activated RFID within the facility, which means every cylinder can be pin-pointed by radio waves to within a few centimetres. Away from the facility, the RFID needs specialised equipment to track it, because of its short range.

"The more dangerous compounds (like the actual nerve agents) also have an outer container which includes satellite tracking. They are set up as binary too, which means they have to be activated and mixed together by a digital code, before they become lethal.

"The tracker transmitter used in the container for the toxin tubes has to be switched on. It uses composite technologies. A radio transmission and a special circuit which made it appear as an internet node similar to a web site. This precaution means that it, like any other highly valuable cargo could be traced without giving away that it was special.

To start the signalling a special code sequence is needed which is a hardware address wired into the tracker.

These gadgets are a fairly new technology and only used in two main areas : specialised weaponry and for extremely high-risk items such as nuclear and highly toxic chemical components that were on the move.

The hardware address was kept under secure access control. You'll have to get the address codes from the Defence Secretary.

"Do you have a picture of one of the canisters and one of the antidote tubes?", asked Karen, A screen flicked on in the room and a back projection appeared showing a couple of pictures. One looked like a bomb or missile and the other a machined metallic cylinder with a complex top mechanism.

"Wow", said Muhammad, "That's some cylinder and some test tube".

"Yes", said Commander Simpson, "We don't want them to be breakable or for just anyone to be able to hack into what is a massively secret payload".

"You are talking about these as if they are bombs", responded Karen.

"The nerve agent canisters are", replied Commander Simpson.

"A single canister, diffused into the air, could have a devastating effect upon a population of 50 to 100 thousand, depending on wind conditions. The effective life of the agent compound is around 24 hours - a so called 'short spike' - and that is why it is supposed to be such an effective but deadly compound. Normal troops can re-enter an area where it has been deployed soon after its use."

"But this is totally illegal and breaks every rule of warfare," said Karen.

"Correct," replied Simpson, "Unfortunately, it cannot be un-invented and that is why it is being examined at present, to understand its weaknesses and to provide emergency procedures should it ever be deployed. The nerve agent canisters are truly Weapon of Mass Destruction."

"And part of the reason it is being examined at Porton Down is to check the weapon's footprint and frailties. We need to be able to tell when it has been used, like the detection of the way that Saddam Hussein deployed chemicals.

"Is this after the fact?" asked Karen.

"It kind of is," replied Simpson, "But we have little choice in these troubled times, and failing to have any response whatsoever would be criticised just as heavily."

"So, we now have a lethal nerve toxin, probably in the hands of terrorists and possible threats on London and Frankfurt," continued Karen.

"And enough toxin in circulation to damage all of the major population centres of the United Kingdom," added Commander Simpson, "Although they seem to have stolen the antidote as well."

Muhammad and Karen made their way to Robert Alston's office to provide him a full update. He listened to their news and realised they now had a dead-end, since the containers had gone invisible.

"Muhammad, do you think you have enough to make some enquiries?"

Muhammad nodded. He was well-connected. Since spending time in the United Kingdom he had learnt a lot and acted well. He had access to local Mosque communities and through his attendance at varied group meetings, he had a strong access to what was happening in the London area. He admitted to himself that there was no word about the current situation anywhere in the community. No-one had talked about chemical plots, or the arrival of any special activists from overseas.

Muhammad would spend time searching for information and try to seed some rumours which could cause something to surface. He decided that an announcement about a suspected terrorist cell in Central London would be a good way to shake some information from the trees. He knew a few contacts where the word could be put out and would create a desired amount of gossip.

"I'm on to it," said Muhammad as he walked towards the door of the room.

Hoxton

Jake was just leaving the offices of 'The Triangle' for the evening. It was in the trendy part of Hoxton, not far from the well-known Hoxton Square, which had its own bustle every evening.

When Jake had stated the company with Clare and Bigsy, they had decided it needed a base in London. They had come into some serious money as a result of a previous escapade and the advice they received made them think it wise to create a proper base for whatever they decided to do next.

Hoxton emerged as the first choice for a couple of reasons.

Firstly, it was near enough to the centre of London and in an area generally considered to be quite cutting edge.

Secondly, they had been told by Richard their estate agent friend, that Hoxton was one of the areas where property prices were moving up the fastest. Richard had been right and despite the general economic conditions, almost from the time that they acquired the property they had seen its value soar.

The Triangle had come about after a grisly set of events where one of Jake's friends had been murdered. They had been caught up in the aftermath, befriended a solitary American known as Chuck Manners and through lengthy series of events had eventually collected a sizeable amount of cash.

They all knew that the origins of the original funds were dubious, but that there was no practical way to declare or hand in the money without putting themselves in danger.

Instead, they had walked away with enough funds to do what they wanted and had set up the Triangle business as a convincing front for whatever they decided to do next.

The company was a media organisation with a small investigatory business on the side. It fitted well with Jake's interest in journalism, Bigsy's clever ways of working with technology and Clare's grasp of media and photography. They had skills for certain types of activity, although there was little way to publicise the more fringe aspects of their existence.

Jake had been pleased to get the call from Clare about their mutual friend Christina.

"Hi Clare, where are you right now?"

"Doing fine, Jake, and I was on my way over to meet Christina, I thought I'd call you about that little meeting Christina and I had with the promoters. Looks like there may be a gig."

"Sounds great" said Jake,

"Yes, there's a series of concerts in the summer and they are keen to get Christina as the support act. We're just back from the meeting and headed across to the South Bank, do you fancy a drink?"

Jake nodded as he spoke into his phone. "Sure thing, where?"

"How about the Cafe at the BFI? We can watch the world while we chat?" Clare smiled to Christina - they would share their story with Jake over a bottle of wine.

Jake finished his call, just as another message appeared on the phone. A text message.

A blast from the past, after 18 months, it was a message from Chuck Manners. Jake tensed. It wouldn't be a call to see how he was doing. There must be more to it.

The message was characteristically short and obtuse.

"Hi Jake, I'll need to meet you, will call later. Chuck."

Jake tapped in two letters and replied.

"OK," he said.

Whatever it was that Chuck wanted, Jake knew this would be no idle request.

Ed Adams

Politician

*Hey now, baby
Get into my big black car
I want to just show you
What my politics are*

Jack Bruce / Pete Brown

Defence Secretary

Robert Alton was in his office at SI6. He had been unsuccessful at speaking to the Bernard Driscoll, the blustery Defence Secretary.

Given the current situation, he was surprised by the lack of contact. It could only mean that the Defence Secretary already knew something about the situation and maybe had another team working on it.

Alton decided that a personal appearance would be the next stage and he would need to get some answers to serious questions.

Robert Alton made a direct visit to the Defence Secretary. The Defence Secretary had potent powers within the United Kingdom reaching into policing, crime reduction, counter-terrorism, immigration, asylum and citizenship as well as the related topics of identity cards and passports.

A situation involving terrorism within the United Kingdom using nerve agent weapons should be high on his priority list, yet Alton seemed to sense that there was a muting of interest in the topic.

"Hello Robert," began Defence Secretary Bernard Driscoll, "To what do I owe this pleasure?" His eyes sparkled with interest but if he knew about the terrorist incident, he was not giving much away.

"It's about the alert," explained Robert, "We think this one is real."

"Ah, the terrorist alert in London… and / or Frankfurt?" replied Driscoll, "We have been watching this one, but don't think it is serious. We have between ten and thirty alerts active on average and most of them are rather feeble-minded and some are even pranks which do just waste our resources."

"A couple of months ago we had a Channel Tunnel alert which was extremely plausible but turned out to be animal rights activists on some kind of crusade about foxes."

"We think this is being covered up from inside", said Alton, "that people even from your areas are involved and are hiding their tracks.

"I've already been looking into it, let's say that there's some vested interests in this one" replied Driscoll, waving his hands in front of Alton.

"What do you mean?" asked Alton.

"Another government or two could be very embarrassed"

"What, the Germans?"

"…No, not the Germans." His hands continued to have a life of their own, " Look, this is very delicate. There are some international relations at stake. It overstates the threat, although we do wish to get back a certain consignment."

"Do you want us to stop what we are doing?" asked Alton, "Things could get out of hand." Alton was amused to see that his last phrase had temporarily halted the wilder flourishes from Driscoll.

"No, continue to do what you do. It will arouse the least suspicion. I don't think you will find anything though," answered Driscoll.

"Look, Defence Secretary, if I find anything, I will inform you. I will also need some freedom to act on this one."

"Robert, take all the freedom you need," smiled Driscoll, "but be careful not to upset any of our big friends."

Alton shook Driscoll's hand, and patted him on the right shoulder. Then Alton took his leave.

It had been a very short meeting but Robert had achieved his primary objective. He had attached a small bug with a short-range transmitter. Now he could hear what Driscoll was doing. He walked back to the outer lobby of the building, where he could pick up his mobile phone, which he had been asked to hand in before visiting the Defence Secretary. Some would think this unusual, but there were so many ways to infiltrate using cell-phones that he was not at all surprised at the tightening of security.

Back outside, he flipped his phone on and dialled a special number. Sure enough, he could hear some sounds from Driscoll's office and then he heard Driscoll making a call on a secure link to someone else.

"Avi," he heard, "There have been people around to check what has been happening. Someone is creating a leak. You need to block it".

Robert could not hear the other end of the call. "Yes, yes...I told them that there was nothing unusual and that this alert was commonplace...You need to locate the missing pieces and have them destroyed...We have set up tracking...The trackers for the nerve agent and the antidotes have both been activated...This is still need to know...I cannot stay on this connection any longer."

Robert had listened intently during the call and left the listening device open now. He wondered if Driscoll would make further calls but instead, he heard Driscoll getting ready to leave the office. The type of listening device used by Robert had two major drawbacks. The first was because of its small size it only had a very short battery life. The second was that its range was limited to 500 metres and through walls and metal the range was even more limited. If Driscoll went out now, the device would have no further use. The design of the unit was small pin that looked like a piece from lady's jewellery, It would not stand close scrutiny, but had a high chance that if discovered would be assumed to be a lost item rather than a bug.

In the meantime, Robert now had a name. Not much to go on, but the name was Avi.

Robert called Dorothy, "I've some more investigation for you," he continued, "I'm looking for someone named Avi?"

"Do you mean Avi Abner?", replied Dorothy immediately, "Head of the Israeli Intelligence Agency here in London?"

Robert nearly kicked himself that he had not thought of this. "Dorothy, thank you!" he continued. In a moment Dorothy had short-circuited something which could have been a long and protracted search, to probably the right answer based upon her own encyclopaedic knowledge.

"In that case, Dorothy, Please can you help me create a reason for a short term meeting with Mr Abner?"

"How about lapsed renewal of diplomatic passes, leading to ejection of two or three of his people if not dealt with immediately? We can claim it was an error after the meeting!"

"Perfect!" replied Robert. He knew he was getting into something very clandestine now. The Israeli Intelligence Agency was the polite name for the organisation usually referred to as Mossad. They were involved with counter terrorism and covert activities and had been linked with many rumours including forged British passports found in grocery bags, letter bombings, several allegations about assassinations including of the Canadian involved with the Iraqi super-gun and failed attempts such as a poison attempt on a senior Jordanian official.

Robert prepared himself for what he knew would be a tough session and he knew that Mossad would see straight through any renewed diplomatic passes ruse and realise that they were being approached about something else. Dorothy called back within ten minutes.

"You have a meeting," she said, "It's going to be on Westminster Bridge, in two hours, at four pm". Robert was impressed. Dorothy knew a lot of people and there was another layer of 'fixing' involved in getting meetings. Robert was a senior official and so his own 'label' got a few doors opened, but Dorothy needed to know how to play the game to get things set up as fast as this. It suggested that there was something big in play and that the Israelis were willing to assist.

Westminster Bridge

Robert Alton stayed away from his office until his next meeting. He would take a taxi, then double back on the tube. His next meeting was very close, but he would take a circuitous route.

At the appointed time he was walking across Westminster Bridge.

"Oh, how the seasons change," said a deep and friendly voice behind him. He turned to see an over-coated, bearded short man with a dark hat. He was smiling and caught up to walk alongside Robert.

"Avi! It has been a while! Too long, probably."

"Robert - Too long, yes. And the last time was when we were talking about those bus bombs in Tel Aviv. We should find reasons to get together that are pleasant. To talk about times in Oxford."

Avi Abner shook hands and then patted Robert on the back.

"No Avi, I'm not wired up, I'm alone and this is off grid," said Alton.

"Desperate times," answered Avi.

"Desperate measures," replied Alton. He paused and looked Avi in the eye. He was pleased to see Avi, despite the vicious power that he wielded.

"Avi, We know about the truck. The one crossing the desert."

"There are a lot of deserts," said Avi, "…and a lot of trucks, come to that."

They had walked south across Westminster Bridge. Ahead was a large hotel.

Avi continued, "Let's go inside, we can get a coffee or something. And if I knew what was being targeted, what reason would I have to tell you? We could both find ourselves in a lot of trouble."

"I think we are already both in a lot of possible trouble over this one," replied Alton.

"Assurances," said Avi, "Assurances. If I tell you more about this, you'll be implicated and there's no easy way back. I need your assurance that you will play this close. And that you'll limit any damage to Israel and me."

"I'm already off-grid for this," said Alton, "I'm running this covertly. You have my assurance this is between the two of us."

They were on an escalator to the first floor, where there was a coffee area. They sat in a quiet area, with a large plate-glass window view back across the bridge towards the Big Ben clock tower.

"Frankly, I think we have a leak," said Alton, "That's why I'm running this quietly."

"I know you have a leak. That's what caused this situation in the first place," said Avi.

"Okay, you'd better explain."

Avi started, "Let's hypothesize that there is a threat. A threat to the UK and maybe to Germany. And let's say it is terrorist inspired. Maybe the British don't know enough to stop them. Perhaps someone else knows more. Perhaps someone else can stop them in a way that doesn't implicate the British."

"Now why would anyone want to do that?" asked Robert.

"Let's consider; you might think there are some people that don't see eye to eye with what might be an Arab terrorist. But, and here's the very sensitive part, perhaps the terrorists would use something that they gained from another country, and perhaps they had got it illegally."

Robert's mind raced. "What? I still don't know what we are dealing with here. Is it something that Israel produced?"

Avi continued, "It's good that you work this out rather than me telling you. Let's assume that a friendly power wanted to show the United Kingdom some materials it had constructed. Let's say that the materials were an inconvenience to the friendly power, and they wanted know the best and most permanent methods of destruction."

"Perhaps the United Kingdom was more specialised in the ways to handle such troublesome substances. But maybe somehow the substance was intercepted in transit."

"What, it was stolen?" asked Alton.

"Fortunately, the cylinder included a tracking device which was activated to determine that the substance had been moved."

Alton responded, "I see. This would create something of a predicament for the British Government and for the other friendly power. I assume they expected the consignment to get to the United Kingdom without explicit paperwork?"

Avi nodded, "You still have excellent powers of deduction."

Alton interrupted, "Avi, you will need to be more specific with me if you expect me to help with this. I've already lost a good agent in the field, and our other trails are dead. We don't know what we are looking for."

The coffee arrived, and Avi immediately paid the waitress. He waited until she had walked away before continuing.

"Okay. You seem to have worked out part of this, anyway. The truck contains toxins. They were supposed to be taken to

The Square

Porton Down in the UK for disposal. Someone intercepted their route and stole the cylinders. We think the route was leaked from the UK, but can't prove it."

"Why take the toxin all the way from Israel to the UK to destroy it?" asked Alton.

"You know how these things work. It would all be destroyed except for a 'file sample' which Porton Down would keep for a rainy day.

"But why ship so much?"

"It's regenerative and the only way to be sure is with the technology that they have in Porton Down. Look - it was a weaponised tertiary toxin."

"Tertiary?" asked Alton. "I know about binaries, what's a tertiary?"

"Like a binary, there's two parts to activate it. The third part is an antidote. It can neutralise the toxin but also stop its effects. The part in the desert was the bulk half of the binary. A small reactive agent is added to make it live. Another different agent can neutralise it."

Avi looked at Alton. "I can make this all go away, if I have the precision tracker codes. I'll arrange a strike, and then only the antidote will be out there. That's no use without the main toxin."

Avi continued, "This is also time critical. At the moment the cylinders are still in the middle east, although they have already moved from the original holding location. Another day and they will have worked out how to move it to somewhere that may be much harder to strike."

"Okay, so suppose I can get the code. How would this work?" asked Alton.

"Detached. I can arrange everything. Swift, clinical. No British implications."

"What about Israel?"

"No, no Israeli implications either. It will look like mercenaries.

"Give me a little while to find out about this," said Alton. "And is there a secure private way that I can reach you?"

"Take this," said Avi. He handed Alton a cellphone. It looked well-used.

"Old school. Sometimes it's still the best way. It's from a secondhand shop and has been re-chipped. It's got a full charge. These old phones stay charged for days. Don't use it for anything else and throw it away when we are done," said Avi.

"Avi - it's been interesting," said Alton.

"Don't forget, this is urgent," replied Avi, "and afterwards we really should have a proper lunch together, maybe in Oxford?"

Robert Alton shook Avi's hand and turned to leave the hotel's coffee bar. He would pick up a taxi from the front of the hotel, back to SI6. He had a busy afternoon ahead briefing Karen on her visit to Egypt.

Thames House

Robert Alton arrived back at Thames House. The journey by taxi had taken about fifteen minutes, which was a consequence of the amount of traffic in Central London. He re-entered the secure area and made his way to his office. His assistant, Dorothy, was waiting.

"I have the codes," Dorothy said, "from an excellent source - the Defence Secretary."

"Codes?" repeated Robert, "I was expecting one."

Alton considered. Defence Secretary Bernard Driscoll must be rattled to have sent the codes through in this way. Maybe he was looking for a scapegoat.

"There are two sets", said Dorothy, "And they were requested together- One set comprises an arm and a disarm protocol. The other set starts a precision tracker. They are both listed as munitions.

Alton thought again, why would Driscoll send two sets of codes across, when he'd only asked for one? Driscoll knew more about this situation than he was letting on.

Dorothy continued, "I will hand them to you, you must then re-encrypt them and we must then destroy the paper where I have written the information."

Robert knew this protocol and retrieved a paperback from his pocket. This ancient process was to be the source of his encryption.

Digital security had superseded arcane processes with books and cyphers, yet Alton knew the real story.

The digital codes were easier to break. Not by any normal person, but by the Americans.

They had persuaded everyone that digital was stronger, but what it did was ensure that encrypted codes were more visible on the internet.

As for cracking the codes, the irony of the American system was that it forbade the use of certain types of cryptography. In effect, the codes had to be crackable.

Alton knew that his use of a paperback book and a sequence of randomised letters would be a stronger code than anything using regular digital encryption. It was so strong that even a different imprint of the book would give a different result.

He looked at the code and wrote a different sequence onto a fresh piece of paper, referring all the time to the paperback.

The Square

"These codes have never been stored anywhere electronic?" asked Robert.

"Correct" said Dorothy, "Nor been discussed on any phone line. This is absolute Level 5 material now."

They both smiled at the rather odd title for Level Five Security - Beyond Top Secret it was referred to as 'Cosmic Top Secret' - someone in NATO had decided to have a little joke the day that term was invented.

He was using the paperback as a long cipher encryption key for his work.

"Dorothy, thank you again," he said as he finished the sequence and the two of them tore the original paper into insignificant pieces and then set fire to it in a small container designed for this purpose. At the end Dorothy added a small container of chemical to the remnants which were, by this time, unrecognisable.

"You now have the only copy of the codes, except for the Defence Realm Registry and your version is encrypted using a one time code." Robert knew the protocol. He now had to decide whether to give the information to Avi.

"Let me make the call to my associate," he said to Dorothy. There was no point in telling Dorothy more than she needed to know. If this came out, Dorothy would be questioned. She understood the advantages of 'need to know' basis in such circumstances.

Robert left the building again. He didn't want more than necessary to be captured in the unremitting cameras of Thames House. He phoned Avi on the special phone Avi had provided.

"I will be on a 452 bus south of Chelsea Bridge in one hour," he said.

"See you", said Avi.

Robert made his way to Sloane Square in west London, around ten minutes by foot from Chelsea Bridge. He would wait here until the allotted time and then catch the bus to the bridge. The bus service was frequent, more than one every ten minutes. He waited until around five minutes to six, hopped onto a bus and climbed upstairs. Here he had a suitable vantage point from the front windows.

A few minutes later the bus was crossing the bridge over the Thames with the tall chimneys of Battersea Power Station off to the left-hand side. Sure enough, as the bus stopped over the bridge, Avi climbed on board and made his way to the seat behind Robert.

"It's here," said Robert, and pointed to an envelope, which contained the encrypted codes.

"Thank you", said Avi. You will need something else, replied Robert.

"Aha, the key", responded Avi, "When?"

"Once I am away from this bus," replied Robert.

"Of course," said Avi.

Robert smiled and stood to exit the bus.

The Square

"I'll call you in a minute, stay on the bus," said Robert.

He exited and as the bus drove away he called Avi to explain where he had hidden the paperback on the bus.

It was behind a seat at the other end of the upper deck. With the encrypted code and the book as a key, Avi would be able to translate the code back for his purposes.

 Avi smiled as he located the book. It was a simple substitution cipher to get the code. Easy to decode with the book, impossible to crack without. He now had not just one code, but to his surprise he now had two codes.

Ed Adams

Walk like an Egyptian

All the bazaar men by the Nile
They got the money on a bet
Gold crocodiles (oh way oh)
They snap their teeth on your cigarette

Foreign types with the hookah pipes say
Way oh way oh, way oh way oh
Walk like an Egyptian

Bangles/ Liam Hillard Sternberg

Coded binary

Karen Martin was already waiting in Robert Alton's office. She had taken the call from Dorothy and, realising its importance, come straight across.

"Karen, you know the Egyptian situation," said Alton.

Karen nodded, "What is this about?" she asked.

"We've some stolen equipment to neutralise," explained Alton.

"It's a neurotoxin. Multiple containers. They are worth a lot to bad people. We've got to disable them."

Alton was taking no chances. He knew Avi Abner was on to the case, but he would also run a mission of his own, to create a similar outcome, which would at least be the neutralisation of the nerve agent.

"Disable them? And how do we do that?" asked Karen.

"The neurotoxin is a coded binary. We can use shutdown codes to neutralise it. That will render it useless. The neurotoxin will self-clean."

Alton decided he would keep Avi's role and the Israeli part out of his explanation.

" Take a stringer and use the stringer to intercept a truck, which will cross the desert. We can give you the co-ordinates of the truck because its cargo will be sending out a tracker signal.

"Your stringer has two jobs.

"He needs to hand over codes held in an electronically locked briefcase. In return, the stringer should also receive a bag back."

"What happens then?" asked Karen.

"We'll need to set the codes on the devices, and they will disarm."

"What about the codes to re-arm them?"

Karen realised that there would be a second set of codes to override the actions of the first set. In effect an Arm and Disarm set, with the material in transit in the disarmed state.

"Agreed, there are some codes, but we don't need them for this exercise. Once we've disarmed the consignments, they can't be restarted in any case. Disarm is a polite word for 'destroy'"

"That sound simple enough," said Karen, "What is the problem with it? Is it 'hot' or something?"

"Very hot," answered Alton, "They are likely to be pursued. Your job is to wait in Cairo for the return of the stringer."

"Will the stringer be at risk from the destruction codes?" asked Karen.

"No, the cylinders contain internal chemicals which are released to do their work," Answered Alton.

"When your stringer returns, we know that we have passed the disarm codes to the truck. Then they will need to be actioned by the driver."

"So, the driver is one of ours too?" asked Karen.

"I hope so," answered Alton.

Firepower

Avi was an experienced operative, and the code provided by Robert Alton was easy to decipher once he had the paperback book.

The code was the sequence needed to enable and locate the transmitters for the two consignments.

He had everything he needed to activate a plan to get the consignment destroyed. He would use military firepower for this and particularly large conventional weaponry to create such a fireball that nothing would survive.

There was a slight risk of toxic escape, but with a large enough warhead he could be sure that the toxins with their short half-life would be annihilated.

Avi decided that this mission was so delicate that he would supervise in person, from Israel. The people involved needed to be as few as possible and everyone needed to have it made clear just how secret this mission would be.

The Square

Avi decided to catch the plane that evening across to Tel Aviv. He could fly on El-Al and this would be a direct overnight to Ben Gurion Airport in Tel Aviv.

He headed first to his office, prepared some paperwork to speed his transit through the airport security systems ,and then arranged for a taxi to take him to London's Heathrow Airport. His use of his diplomatic status gave him a slightly faster and more pleasant route through the airport, when compared with many of the other travellers planning to fly to Israel.

It was a five-and-a-half-hour flight across most of Europe and then along the coast of the Mediterranean and down to the strife-torn area of Israel and its surrounding desert. Many years ago, a small group of Jewish families had moved from the overcrowded, insanitary and hostile Arab town of Jaffa to a selected desert spot which became Tel Aviv.

Avi could see lights of the city on the Mediterranean coast which had developed at great speed and brought with it some characteristics of an American city. Residents sometimes compared Tel Aviv to New York and in a short time, Tel Aviv had absorbed tens of thousands of refugees from Europe, Asia, Africa and South America and turned them into free citizens in their own homeland.

Above all, Tel Aviv appeared as a beach city; a broad expanse of fine sand extending over 6 miles along the seashore. City residents poured onto the beach for air, space and relaxation every weekend and at any opportunity during the day. The wide promenade runs for miles all the way from the port in north Tel Aviv to the old quarter of Jaffa which had become a popular waterside dining and leisure district of Tel Aviv.

Although mentioned several times in the Bible and developed as Jerusalem's principal seaport, Jaffa gives little sense of its long history.

Only a small section of Old Jaffa remains today, its lanes and stairways cleaned up and restored beyond recognition and the squalid centre replaced by a park. Most of the town was built after Napoleon's destructive raid in 1799. Thus, the oldest port in the world (with all its trade long ago moved to Tel Aviv or Haifa) has become a mere district of a modern city.

Here, in the mid-morning, Avi Abner met with two members of the Israeli Air Force to discuss the interception of the trucks. The two men arrived in their civilian clothes, although both had military haircuts and wore dark aviator sunglasses. It was not so unusual to see military anywhere in Israel. Most people had completed compulsory military service, and guns on the street were commonplace.

"Shalom," began Avi, "Let me explain the situation. We have a security risk and need to take down a truck which will be in the desert. We need speed but also an ability to cope with a very rough terrain," he added.

"The contents of the trucks are lethal, and we must use a large amount of explosive to ensure that nothing survives," he added.

"We will have satellite tracking to help us locate the targets. We have co-ordinates and a real time feed. There is one thing though", he added.

"The desert in question is in Egypt".

The Square

The two members of the Israeli Air Force looked at each other and then back at Avi.

"Commander Abner", one started, "What you are describing is illegal. We could be shot down by the Egyptians or the Americans or anyone from a peace keeping force."

"This mission will be highly covert," continued Avi, "You will use an unmarked helicopter for the mission and because you have the exact co-ordinates and will be operating in the desert, the whole mission inside Egyptian airspace will be a matter of minutes".

"F15s can scramble in minutes " came the comment.

"You will have enough time and you will fly the helicopter as close to ground as possible. There will be a route which will protect you from radar and border controls. There will be a time window for you to operate. Let's just say the Egyptians owe us for something."

"When?" asked one of the pilots.

"Tomorrow, " answered Avi.

At 14:00 the next day, the two pilots were flying an electronically cloaked unmarked black Apache helicopter along the Egyptian border before encroaching into Egyptian military airspace at an altitude of 30 feet. The helicopter tracked terrain but showed no signs of being followed.

They locked on to a signal beacon ,which was moving slowly along a road. As they approached the target and their target acquisition system switched in, they elevated the helicopter to a safe firing height and then let loose a single high -powered missile towards the target. As it left the helicopter, they felt the recoil, but it was immediately interrupted by the sound from the targeting alert.

"We're lit up," said the pilot, "something has acquired us, I'm taking evasive action." At that moment their own missile hit the truck and the sky rocked with an explosion out of all expected proportion. They didn't have time to wonder what had happened because they were in the midst of their own programmed evasion.

The helicopter banked, jettisoned hot strips of metal to decoy the missile, but they could see on their radar that it was on a collision course. One second later the helicopter was struck and with a huge explosion the helicopter's world stopped and the simple physics of gravity took over. No survivors from the helicopter or the truck.

Driscoll

Defence Secretary Bernard Driscoll was worried.

He needed to handle the missing toxin situation from within the UK. It needed to be kept secret on account of the way the chemical agent was in the UK in the first place.

"I have some codes which may need to be intercepted," Driscoll had called the US operations room in the American Embassy in London. He was using the priority phone.

"Sure thing," said Colonel O'Malley, waving to others in his own facility to listen in, "How can we expedite this?"

O'Malley was an intermediary. He didn't really know the significance of the codes or the situation. But he could get them wired back to the NSA in Maryland and there would be fast action. Depending upon where the codes referenced would affect how the US processed them.

The codes were wired on a secure system to the USA, where the trackers were shown as deactivated, and the static markers were showing in an area of desert near to Riyadh, at a US Air Force base.

This was a fairly ideal situation, because it meant the consignments were currently being stored in an isolated area of desert. If a removal was to take place, then this would be a great location, away from built-up centres and limiting collateral damage.

.... .. -.. . / .. -. / .--. .-.. .- .. -. / ... .. --. .... –

The code of the transmitter sequences was passed from the contact office in Washington direct to Fort Meade in Maryland to the ECHELON headquarters which had technology for tracking and satellite intercepts.

Here, the simple code for the two consignments passed for verification to a duty desk and then authorised such that a transmitter could be started in each consignment.

This would give a third party with the right permissions access to the consignment location and could allow a special group to be dispatched to locate the items.

The first surprise was that the two beacons were co-located, not as expected in Riyadh, but that they had moved to the White Desert just outside Cairo. Using advanced telemetry, a satellite-based sweep of the desert was planned on a high-resolution setting. Because of satellite positioning, it took three hours before the right satellites were in a good position to run surveillance.

The Square

"Live and hot!", shouted the duty sergeant who had loaded the code and co-ordinates as the first images came in. The desert showed some small buildings, but also a clear image of a single truck, parked.

General Simpson was heading the American part of the operation. "Who do we have in the area?", he asked. "Overt or covert?" came the reply.

"This is very covert," said Simpson, "We need to blow up a couple of US manufactured consignments which were stored in Saudi Arabia and are now illegally in Egypt. The consignments are a high technology design which could be part of a terrorist plot. We need to act with maximum focus to neutralise this."

"We have some operatives in the area fit for this purpose ," came the reply, "I'm looking through the files and in country we have a small base, and some regular soldiers who could be asked to work 'native'," suggested O'Malley.

"No, I want a top person for this, we must fly someone in-black-op style. Normal airlines, under cover, provisioned with non-American weaponry in country."

The trail was now leading towards a delta force person and before very long the name Chuck Manners had surfaced. He had many awards for bravery in the field.

He was tracked down to an American military base in Germany area and called in for a briefing.

"You'll be at Stuttgart, Echterdingen airport tonight on the first plane to Cairo. You'll be provisioned with civilian transport and undesignated non-American armaments to get to a spot in the desert where you will be asked to destroy two consignments."

Chuck paused and then nodded. "This is an illegal operation?" he queried.

"Yes, it is, but there are very high stakes involved."

"If I do this and get captured, what happens?"

"You won't. You have perfect co-ordinates for the consignments and will have enough personal fire - power if anyone pays you a visit. No-one even knows the consignments have been stolen, let alone their new whereabouts. We have just diverted satellites to get this information. The consignments are currently parked, but we expect them to be moved again later today.

Chuck Manners nodded. He was used to these types of operations. He had no qualms about driving a hard position to get things done. He would work alone. He could be very fast and nimble. When involved in this type of operation, the trick was to get in and get out fast before anyone noticed.

One hour later Manners was at the airport for the flight to Cairo

Ed Adams

NOW

Ed Adams

Park Lane

*Park Lane is the second most valuable property
in the London edition of the board game
Monopoly.*

*The street still has a prestigious social status similar to
when the British version of the Monopoly board
was first produced, in 1936.*

*On the board, Park Lane forms a pair with Mayfair,
the most expensive property in the game.*

From Wikipedia, the free encyclopaedia

Car chase victims

Muhammad Mubarain knew the points where he could gather information and made personal calls. Despite the reputation of terrorist cells being very secure, there were many ways that gossip travelled and the people he would speak to would know if there was anything unusual.

Muhammad made his first call with Firas Belhassen, a leading Imam in the local community. He changed the story enough to avoid direct traceability, but with enough of a ring of truth to attract corrections and further confirmation.

Firas Belhassen listened and after a long pause said, "You know, I think something is happening. A few days ago we heard that Ghali Yassim would visit the UK and sure enough he arrived with his brother and a close associate named Mehdi Akren.

"Initially, they seemed to spend their time doing tourist things, spending money, gambling and behaving in a fairly non-Muslim way.

"Besides their time in Central London, they seem to have been out for several long drives to other parts of the country and instead of flying out of the UK, they have left by car into Europe. This is unusual transport for Ghali Yassim, for whom speed is the essence.

Muhammad understood the significance of this information. A senior, royal and diplomatically secure person had arrived in the UK, with supporters. He was suspected of terrorist involvement, yet had moved around freely, finally leaving the country, by car, through to France.

"Do we know when Yassim left?", Muhammad asked.

"I'm not sure, but it was in the last few days", replied Firas Belhassen. Muhammad knew that Firas wanted to lead a straightforward life, to be involved with the local community and that he deplored efforts of extremists to undermine the community and relationships within the country.

Muhammad knew it was still a tough decision for Firas to make these disclosures, because Yassim was a fellow Muslim, whereas Muhammad would provide the information to non-Muslim authorities in the United Kingdom.

Muhammad knew that he needed to get the information relayed back to Karen and the primary investigation team. They now had three names and a location and probable cargo. It was possible that the cargo had left the country with the three suspects and that it was travelling by car to France.

While Muhammad was investigating, Karen was busy too. She received notification of another incident involving Arabs in

The Square

Central London. There had been a car chase involving a Mercedes and a BMW through the centre of London. Along Park Lane, the Mercedes has run into a set of railings and the people in the BMW had stopped behind the car, calmly got out, walked to the Mercedes appearing to be carrying handguns.

The commotion of the chase had created a general alert in the area and several Police motorcycles on embassy and royal duties had been able to reach the scene more or less as the car crash occurred. They had also radioed to an armed response unit which was also on its way from around a less than a mile away. The incident was close to many embassies and there was plenty of police cover.

The pursuing occupants of the BMW had seen that they were about to be out manoeuvred and had driven into a nearby underground car park. They had abandoned their car and then used a pedestrian exit to leave the car park, before anyone realized what was happening. Then they boarded a taxi from an adjacent hotel and moved quietly out of the area.

The police had created a cordon around the crashed car and had also radioed for a paramedic. The three Arabs in the car had been heavily shaken by the crash but were fundamentally uninjured compared with the heavy damage sustained by the car.

Karen had been among the first on the scene and her initial instincts were to be suspicious of what was happening. She approached the Arabs, who were trying to make excuses and to leave the scene.

"No", she instructed the Police, "We need to question these about another matter". She radioed for SI6 backup and another Paramedic ambulance arrived, driven by her own staff.

The Arabs were instructed to get into the ambulance and then it moved away followed by Karen. They would take them to a hospital ward, with the small difference that it would be within an SI6 complex. The wards were fully camera and sound enabled, which would mean if there was anything to learn from the Arabs, then they would hear it.

The ambulance cut through London traffic; Karen followed in her car. She did not understand what had been happening, why they were being chased or who the assailants were.

The hospital looked very realistic. Karen watched the three Arabs being escorted in and then being moved to individual rooms, close together. The cameras and sound were already running and within minutes they had started to talk to one another about what they needed to do. They spoke Arabic to one another, but the SI6 facility had already provided translators.

"This is not good", said one of the three. He was wearing a suit and looked very smart. "I agree", said the second, "I think they were Mossad. We need to get out of here fast."

The third Arab spoke. "We still have the rendezvous in Ashford, tomorrow".

The first Arab spoke again. "We must just leave here. Because of the car chase, we will be detained for questions, but because we are the victims, we should be able to negotiate our way out fast. My preference is to tell them we are shaken up and that we would rather answer questions tomorrow. That gives us a chance to completely leave the country."

The Square

Karen was pleased with how this was going. Without so much as a word of interrogation, they were telling her a lot about their plans. Karen's team had been running checks on the Mercedes too, and discovered that it was a recently purchased new vehicle, from a Central London garage. It included all the extras, and this included a built-in phone, which was still in the car when the police were getting ready to tow it away. Karen had requested an immediate phone trace, both of calls and of their originating location. This had shown that there was a long string of calls to many numbers, both in London but also to the middle east. In among the series were several calls from the M2 and A2, leading out of East London, through Kent and towards Dover. There were also a series of calls from a location near to Ashford.

"We have a fix on a location, and we know there will be a meeting tomorrow", thought Karen, "Now we need to know what they are expecting". She decided it was time to speak directly to the Arabs. She had already radioed to Muhammad, who was also on his way to the special facility.

Karen decided that they may get more information by using Muhammad, particularly if he could befriend them in some way. To stall until his arrival, she had a doctor visit them, say that they each needed an x-ray and that after this they would be free to go, but until this had been completed, he could not release them because of liability.

The Arabs talked amongst themselves. Then the one in the suit shrugged, "Please try to hurry, we have other appointments this evening". The Arabs had decided it would be easier to leave after the procedure had finished and with no fuss and not raising any further suspicions. At this time Muhammad arrived. Karen explained what was happening and that Muhammad could probably intervene in a way that would get further information. They decided to send him in as a medic, and he donned some hospital clothing to look the part.

 He walked into the holding area where the three men were kept.

"Hello", he said, then overtly noticing they were Arabs he added *"as-salām 'alaykum"*.

The three Arabs all turned together as they heard this.

"wa 'alaykum as-salām", one of them replied. "It looks as if you could be here overnight", continued Muhammad, in English.

"They have just told me they want to do some further tests before they will let you go, in case of concussion. You won't be able to leave without the paperwork."

He continued. He was trying to create more of a feeling of being trapped and the Arabs seemed to respond to this.

"What do you mean?" asked one.

"You are to be fully examined before you can move, in case there is concussion or internal bleeding from the accident. The Arabs again consulted one another, this time in English. Then the one with the suit said, "Perhaps you can help us?"

"Sure " said Mohammed, switching back to Arabic, "what do you need?".

The Square

"We have to be at a meeting tomorrow afternoon by 16:00 and need to leave here tonight to prepare for it", said the suited Arab, "Can you help us get processed this evening?"

"I should be able to," continued Muhammad, "I am duty medic this evening, can you give me a little more information so I can complete a form to get you processed?"

He smiled to the three of them and continued to speak in Arabic. "What is the nature of your visit to UK?", he asked.

The Arabs again looked towards one another, "Business - We need to attend a meeting tomorrow afternoon, where we are to receive some goods".

"Business - that's all I need", said Muhammad, looking officious and studiously writing something onto his note pad. "I will go away now to get the paperwork produced so that you can be processed quickly".

Before he turned, he said *"ma'a as-salāmah"*, and the three Arabs replied with the same greeting.

Muhammad walked slowly to the door and then into the corridor. He had enough to go on. The three Arabs were expecting to pick up something at 16:00 tomorrow from somewhere in Ashford and they had located the pickup point from the car's mobile phone.

Muhammad relayed the information to Karen Martin. "This is great," replied Karen, "Now we have what we need to be at the pickup in Kent tomorrow".

So that is how Muhammad found himself on the Honda approaching the truck lay-by.

Mossad

The Arabs knew exactly who had been chasing them in central London.

Ghali Yassim was speaking, "They were the Israeli Intelligence Services and the reason we were being chased was because someone has made the connection between the missing nerve agent and Al Aktar. I guess the original theft has been planned for so long that someone has let it slip."

"But why would Israel be so interested?" asked Mehdi Akran.

Ghali Yassim responded, "Israel has long been on the cutting edge of research and development in advanced technologies. It may be a country of very limited natural and financial resources, and not at peace with some of its neighbours. However, Israel's scientists and engineers have faced the challenge of devising new and innovative solutions, which has led to research for military technologies, both for defence and as part of offensive border enforcement."

"Inevitably, having fought three major wars in the first two decades of its existence, the Israeli government reached the conclusion in the late 1960s that it would have to develop as much of its own defence capabilities as possible and it is through that time that we can see the closer affiliations with the USA.

"It was this combination of biotechnology research and prior warfare related research that had led to the establishment of special facilities such as the Ron Hebron Research Park where the advanced research had taken place and finally led to an accident.

"A nerve agent had been tested but then leaked with disastrous consequences. A complete lab was sealed and the remaining nerve agent packaged, ready for destruction. The tough deal for Israel was that the nerve agent would be destroyed by another country, ironically because their own capability had been sealed off because of the accident.

"The nerve agent produced had surpassed the Israeli's own expectation of strength and virulence. To destroy it required a highly specialised capability, of which there were only a few in the world. The UK's Porton Down had been selected after pressure from the United States. Although the USA could also handle the chemical agent, it had been agreed that a low-key process through the UK would attract less attention.

"We know that Avi Abner had negotiated the transfer of the canisters to the UK, via diplomatic channels
"Careless Americans," said Mehdi Akran, "Creating a deadly toxin, then leaving it in Saudi Arabia, before dumping a deadly quantity in Tel Aviv. Then leaving diplomatic channels to clear up the mess."

Ghali Yassim spoke, "It makes Al Aktar's decision simple. Steal it from Israel. That's why we ship it through various countries like regular freight. It also insulates the theft and transaction from Al Aktar."

Ghali Yassim continued, "Avi Abner's counter-intelligence services are good. Very good. But they have gambled on finding the links back to Al Aktar. Now they have tracked Al Aktar representatives to London, but they have given away their cover by the car chase involving the Mercedes and BMW. I suspect Avi Abner had wanted to act unilaterally to gather intelligence and took our arrival in London as a sign that the containers had arrived."

New York bed

After the horrific incidents in Egypt, James had a simple plan to create distance and to monitor his sources for any reports of what had happened.

The helicopter strike on the truck in the desert and the cold-blooded gunning down of Karen Martin would make normal news feeds unless the authorities were trying to pull a security curtain over what had happened.

James had left Cairo rapidly and knew that by the time he reached New York he could easily be ahead of the news, even in an internet world, particularly because of the lower interest in 'foreign' news in the USA, unless Americans were directly involved.

James had a simple plan when he arrived in New York. He would go to Léa's. He and Léa had been close for two years, but when Léa moved away from London to New York, they had both agreed to part as friends.

It wasn't one of those said but not meant things. James and Léa had always been clear about their relationship and their different worlds but had seen the time together as a sensible collision and a lot of fun.

Léa was a designer for an advertising agency and a smart highflyer. James had a role seemingly as a management consultant, but he found it difficult to manage the dual-role deception with Léa , especially when they lived together in the same apartment.

Léa also has a busy and itinerant lifestyle. The work and her contracts took her to several major centres, principally New York, Frankfurt and a fair amount of work in London too. Léa also enjoyed skiing and water-sports, so there were parts of the year when she would head to Klosters or the Mediterranean for extended breaks.

Neither James nor Léa had any shortage of money and could easily move around a wide circle of friends and a broad range of locations. James preferred that Léa did not meet too many of his ex-military or special forces friends because that would give the game away. James soon found out that although Léa was very sporting, she detested soccer and that had given him a cliched alibi to meet some of his more specialised acquaintances. It was similar with Léa and her yoga and meditation, which James could appreciate but which was an area of Léa's life that he stayed away from.

They had been together for around two years until the end of last year. There had been a great opportunity for Léa in Manhattan and she had really wanted to make the move. It was great money in a vibrant city. James had initially accompanied her, but they had both known that this was probably the beginning of the end of their full-time relationship.

They had both been very good about it. Neither of them had anyone else in mind when they said final farewells and Léa had said to James that, anywhere, she would be there for him.

She had given him a key to her apartment in lower Manhattan. It was really a gesture, but at the time it made James feel good.

James took a taxi from JFK and asked for the address in SoHo where Léa lived. He had another mobile phone with him and had called the number but only picked up the answer phone. He thought it would be good to see Léa but wondered what he would find when he approached her building.

The taxi driver knew the way to the general area but was slightly confused with the street names in this unstructured part of Manhattan. James directed the last couple of turns, which had caused the driver making the equivalent of an extended U turn around a block because he had missed the turn the first time around. James paid the driver and stepped onto the sidewalk.

He looked at the building, and a strange sense of emotion washed over him. Léa had represented comfort for him when he was involved in some other tough situations and now he was standing outside her apartment some three and a half thousand miles from where he lived and he was about to say hello again for the first time, when he was in some kind of trouble.

He climbed the steps to the entrance to the apartment building and wondered whether to let himself in or whether to ring the bell. He knew the bell was the right answer and tried it twice,

with   no   response.
"OK", he thought, "I shall check things out."

He opened the main door and took the elevator to Léa's floor. The hallway was immaculate in this well-heeled and gentrified block. He approached the door and opened the lock. There was an alarm too, and he disabled this with Léa's birthday date, American-formatted, a little joke they had had when back in London.

The whole apartment looked very similar to the last time he had visited. He called out loudly in case anyone else was around, but Léa was out and that she was living there alone. He snuck a look in the wardrobes and the coat closet, but apart from a pair of his old boots, useful in snow, there was nothing else to show anyone other than Léa was living in the apartment.

Next, he checked if Léa's laptop Apple mac was around; this was a good sign that Léa was working; she always carried the machine if she was on business. A desk and a charger looked forlorn, and he knew that Léa was out somewhere on business. That could be local, but could equally be anywhere.

He flipped the telephone answering machine. Just one message from a Fed-Ex delivery, but nothing else. In the old days that could have meant she was only out for a short time, but now, with voicemail, it was less of an indication. James decided he would leave a prominent message and then return later in the evening.

If Léa was around, she would pick up the message and be able to call him. He knew she would not hesitate for a second to contact him but if she was prepared to tolerate his proximity for a few days, it could help the overall situation whilst he needed to stay under cover and not traceable.

James had used a false passport when he arrived in New York. He had dual nationality, with a right to a Canadian and a British passport and with a small amount of adaptation, his Canadian passport which had him as "Jamie" also gave a reasonable level of subterfuge to his whereabouts. He hoped that his traceability from Egypt was low and that no-one would expect him to travel to the United States.

There was, however, a drawback to his plan. The passport he was using from Canada had an embedded chip. As soon as he had handed it to the custom and immigration person in JFK, it had been activated on the passport scanner and had sent a digital stream into the main NSA tracking systems. This linked him with his slightly changed name, with Egypt, and the route he had taken was immediately detected.

Two homeland security guards had noticed when the passport had been scanned. There had been some strange developments in Egypt over the last few days, and some key individuals were being singled out for further investigation. His own Canadian passport had been the basis to trip the tracking of him and the two men were right now positioned one at the entrance to the apartment block and the second on the very floor where Léa's apartment was located.

James decided he would take a more detailed look around Léa's apartment. He was actually somewhat fuzzy from the flight and thought he would make himself some coffee to shake away the cobwebs. He knew that Léa would be fine about him making himself at home, but he also didn't want to surprise her with his entrance to her apartment.

"All in its time", he thought as he filled the coffee machine with fresh ground coffee and water and then looked in the refrigerator for some milk. None there, in fact the refrigerator was empty. Interesting, it looked as if Léa was away. He looked around for other evidence while the coffee brewed. He considered this to be good fortune if he wanted to lie low for a few days. With Léa away, he could use her apartment, and this would almost guarantee he was off of the grid and undetectable.

James had not allowed for the passport and his detection. He watched as the coffee finished filling the glass flask and then selected a mug with "I love NY" and poured in the coffee. He normally drank coffee with a dash of milk, but this would do until he could visit a nearby store. He sipped the liquid and felt an almost immediate jolt from the caffeine. Like himself, Léa liked robust coffee, and this Java was doing the trick.

He walked around for a few more minutes while looking at the rest of the apartment. Very tidy, lived in, but neat. He went out to a nearby store. He could buy provisions and also some flowers as a peace offering for Léa, based upon his breaking and entering her apartment.

James took the elevator back to ground level and was emerging back to the street, when a man in front of him called out, "Hey Bud, do you know where 3rd Street is?" He looked up, tensing in case this was a trap. He knew he was operating below his normal reflexes and realised about half a second before the move that a second man was standing just behind him. The two men neatly scooped James into a nearby car and locked the doors.

The Square

"Mr Goodwin," started the first man, "Welcome to New York, there are a few people we would like you to meet."

"Who are you?" questioned James, "And what do you want?"

"Relax," said the first man, "You will come to no harm and all we require is some limited information."

The car, a large square looking Ford, a Crown Victoria, waddled along the bumpy streets of Manhattan, James couldn't get used to the sea-sick feeling of American suspension, even in this challenging situation.

"Look, I don't know who you are or what you want, but I'm in Manhattan to see a friend," he continued.

"We know you were in Cairo," said one of the Americans, "We know you were in the desert and that the truck pick up went wrong. We have photos of the damage, both the truck and the Israeli helicopter," he continued.

James didn't know that the helicopter was Israeli and had no idea who had fired the missile that blasted the helicopter from the sky.

"Who are you?", asked James. He didn't feel in direct danger, because if the men had intended something terrible, they would have started on him by now.

They looked American, had American accents, east coast. He could see them, there was no bag over his head and they had not stabbed him with a hypodermic syringe or anything worse. There were no visible guns, although he suspected that his abductors would have easy access to firepower.

He would give them something, but not much. He knew there was no point in denying this, and that all he was doing was prolonging the inevitable.

"So, if I was in Cairo, what links me to whatever you are talking about?"

"Let's just say we had a very experienced operative in the area, and he followed you back to Cairo. He was also nearby when the woman was shot by a high-powered rifle. We are trying to join some pieces together and we need to know what you were expecting in the pickup. Your transport was a regular car, so I don't think you were expecting the actual cargo of the truck."

It mystified James. He knew that the desert exchange that had gone wrong was supposed to be a swap of some holdall or case, but he had not been told its contents.

"I was expecting a small delivery," he replied, "Something I could carry, but I have no idea what the consignment comprised. I expected it to be papers or film or maybe DVDs or similar."

"So, the rather larger contents of the truck were not of interest?" continued the first American.

"I don't think I know what you mean", replied James, thinking there was something that he had not been told. "What was in the truck?"

"The truck contained a missile", replied the second American, speaking for the first time since they had been together in the car.

The Square

"A serious piece of weaponry, so serious that it had built in trackers which were activated when it started to move around. It was from the Saudi Arabian Air Force."

"So, what was it doing in Egypt, in a truck?", asked James, genuinely confused and thinking these Americans couldn't know much about what was happening. Unreliable witnesses, he decided.

"We thought you might tell us," said the second American. "Look we know all about you, that you freelance, have been in a few scrapes but don't really do violent things."

"Just dangerous things." added the first American.

"Look, I'm co-operating," said James, "Just who are you?"

"We're from the NSA - the National Security Agency," explained the first American. "We are local agents sent out to talk to you. I don't think you know how serious this is."

"I'm getting the picture," said James, "If you've been that speedy following me, then there has to be something big occurring. Show me some identity, please."

The first American showed a metal badge and an identity card. It all looked genuine, but James realized he wouldn't really know if the papers he was being shown were real. But the identity card had a hologram and looked fairly high-technology.

"I'll co-operate," said James, "I'll tell you what I know."
The car pulled over at a small cafe on the edge of Central Park. The two Americans stepped out and beckoned to James. "Let's

have coffee," said the first American, "No funny business, though," added the second.

"We're cool," said James as they sat down at a small table. "Three Americanos," said the second American to the waiter.

"Okay, so I'm Scott and he's Nick," the first American started to explain, "So James, tell us what you know,"

James was certain now that these two were low-level operatives. They didn't seem to know much about the situation and were cross-examining him in a coffee-shop.

James started to describe the situation he'd been in. He changed as little as possible, in case he was asked the same things again, which was a frequent interrogation technique. He decided that he would be prepared to disclose everything except Karen's name and the amount they paid him. But he needed to say another sum, which seemed low enough to make him seem small-time. He settled on £10,000.

"So, I was already known to the UK authorities. I do some driving for them when they want to be anonymous. I'm reliable. On this occasion I was instructed by a woman. I don't know here name, not her real one anyway. Just that she was called Mrs Clinton. I knew that was a code name.

"The drop was to take place in the desert. I was given GPS co-ordinates and a time. I took a car and waited. Then I saw the truck and then the helicopter. The chopper fired on the truck. Just one missile. Then a surface-to-air from about a mile away took out the helicopter.

"The helicopter had locked on my car before it was destroyed. I think I would have been next. I drove away fast after the helicopter fell, before the guy with the SAM could get creative."

"So what was the pickup?" asked Nick.

"It was supposed to be small, a holdall or a case. That was all. It was something I could carry. I didn't ever see it."

The two Americans looked at one another. "So you were not expecting the truck to contain a missile?"

"Absolutely not," said James, "And my instructions were to swap the goods, not to take over the truck."

Scott said to Nick, "This seems plausible. The consignment was small, and that is consistent with what we've been told from the site in Egypt. You can go back to the apartment. Stay in the vicinity for the next few days, we will make some further investigations, but your story is consistent from one we have from another source."

The other source was another freelancer, ex American military named Chuck Manners. Since he'd been sent to Cairo, he had also been told that the consignment was small and that it was easy to locate via a tracker beacon. That is how he had been tracking it until the appearance of the helicopter. He was certain that the unit destroyed was the source of the beacon. Now Scott, Nick, Chuck and James were all reaching the same conclusion. That they had been following the wrong GPS beacon.

"Okay," said James, "I'll go back to the apartment. I'll stay a few days, but I'm expecting you to be watching. And looking out for me."

James was back at Léa's apartment. As he opened the door, he noticed that there were some differences. Where he had picked up the pile of travel documents and moved them to the desk, they were now back on the table. He called out for Léa. Maybe she had returned during his rather unexpected absence. There was no reply, and he wondered how the papers could have moved, or whether he had somehow imagined it.

He flicked through the stack and noticed some documentation related to a trip by Léa to Cannes, France.
She was away right now and not expected back for several days. He thought about calling her, but decided, given the other circumstances, that it would be better to stay as dark as possible. Léa's absence gave him a chance to lie low with the minimum of people knowing his whereabouts.

Downstairs, the two members of Mossad were already relaying the information about Léa to their contact in Nice, France. Mossad, the Israeli secret service had also followed James to the apartment. It had been easy, they'd tracked James' departure from Cairo to New York, spotted the two men that were following James, placed a small radio beacon on both of them in the airport and then followed them across Manhattan to Léa's apartment.

Once James had entered it, they waited for him to go out, in order to do some breaking and entering and to find the papers about Léa. They would use this to gain some leverage over James.

Unwind

James decided to lay low in Léa's apartment. He still could not contact her because of the threat of being followed or traced. He could see the date she was due to return from her vacation and he was looking forward to seeing her. He was not contacted again by the Americans and had been treating his time as a kind of vacation in New York.

The last few days had been both tiring and shocking and time to unwind seemed like the perfect antidote. He suspected that he was being observed, but didn't let that deter him from moving around Manhattan. He did nothing related to the events in Cairo. He had checked the news including the Cable feed from Al Jazeera, but there was no mention of the truck or helicopter incident.

James still had the case from the desert. It was the one he was supposed to exchange with the truck driver.

Now, he decided, was the time to open it. To find out what the fuss was about. He would need assistance for this. The case might be rigged. He would need to contact Karen's handler back in the UK. To arrange a meeting and a hand-over.

James checked the phone that Karen had given him. It included a second number. SERVICE DESK. He knew what it meant. The standard protocol for expedited calls to Karen's Handler.

He dialled it.

"Karen's florists. Jane speaking, how may I direct your call?"

"I need to speak to the owner."

" What Karen? - I'm afraid she is out."

"No, Karen's boss. Karen says we need more petals."

"One moment please, please hold."

There was silence on the line. A click.

"Hello, who is that speaking?"

"I'm an associate of Karen Martin. I was in the desert. My name is James,"

"Hello James, I am sorry for your loss."

"I have something of interest to the company. I would like to bring it along and get it opened, Karen gave it to me."

"Ah yes, we know about that item, can you describe it for me?"

"Yes, it is a case. A briefcase."

"Yes, it is tamper-proof. Can you look at the front lock? There should be a small number stamped underneath the catch, next to a USB port."

"Yes, there is, TRQ73845. And a small USB port next to it."

"That's the right number. We would like to arrange collection."

"Okay, please let me give the collectors something for identification."

"Of course, what would you like?"

"A lampshade," said James, looking for inspiration around the room.

"I will make sure that the collector can tell you that."

"Now, we need an address for a pickup."

"Tomorrow evening - 19:00 Molly's - 3rd and East 22nd - I'll have the case in a Macy's white star tote."

"That's very clear. Someone will see you tomorrow evening."

Chuck goes to MI6

Robert Alton was informed of the arrangements made with James. He was considering whether to send someone from the embassy for the pickup. He'd requested a USB stick coded with the unlock logic for the case, which he had collected in person from the technical department.

As Robert Alton re-entered SI6, there was a message waiting for him at the front reception.

"You have a visitor Mr.Alton; a Mr. Manners. He is sitting over there. He says the appointment was made at the last minute."

Alton looked towards Chuck Manners. He didn't recognise him. Suntanned in a suit, he looked like a military man.

"Er, Mr Manners. I don't think we have a meeting booked. Perhaps there is some mistake?" asked Alton. He looked towards Manners, who stood and walked towards him.

"Good morning, Mr Alton, I think you'll want to talk to me," said Manners. "I'm just back from the desert. I think you know where. It would be useful to talk."

"In my office?" asked Alton, "Or maybe it's better to go outside?"

"I'd prefer outside too," said Manners.

Manners removed his visitor pass, handed it to the reception and walked through the revolving doors to leave the building.

"You're not from the Agency?" said Alton.

"Correct. I've just come back from Cairo. Look, I was involved in the op. Don't pretend you don't know. Karen was there. You Brits were set up."

Alton looked at Manners carefully. "Who are you? The stringer? You worked for Karen?"

"No," said Manners, "I didn't find out about Karen, or her stringer buddy James until after the mission. I thought I was working alone, and that it was for the Americans."

"Why would you be telling me this, now?" asked Alton, "If you are working for the Americans, then I'd expect them to pass the information through normal channels."

"Ordinarily, so would I. Except there are no normal channels for this. There's something wrong. The people who paid me to go to Egypt have disappeared. My field contact in Cairo has disappeared. The only person I've found was one of your people, still in Cairo. I told him to get out."

Alton looked again at Manners. "What were you doing in Cairo? Were you part of what happened to Karen?"

"Not at all. I was there to prevent the truck in the desert from being destroyed. I was under orders from DoD to bring down the helicopter. I was told that the truck contained something of National Security to the United States."

"So, the Americans sent you to bring down the helicopter? Why would they do that? It would certainly antagonise a lot of people."

"Not as many as you might think. I was told that the truck contained something important to America. Something whose delivery was being intercepted by a hostile force. To be honest, I'd no idea that the Brits were also involved in this.

"I know it wasn't one of your helicopters - even in the stealth paint. An Apache, but it was one of the Longbows, really jazzed engines, swept rotor tips and the extra radar bubble for target acquisition. Top specification. It was playing for a fast kill and exit. We Americans have them, but I don't know if anyone else has these high spec versions."

Manners continued, "To be honest, what started out as a clean mission has become very dirty. The truck was destroyed by a very purposeful hunter platform, and then the Brits were chased back to Cairo. Originally, I didn't think anyone wanted this to leak out. I've changed my mind now, though. That's why I've brought this to SI6. There's something deeply wrong with the American intel around this."

Alton looked at Manners, " You need to tell me, but first, how did you link this to SI6 and trace it back to me here?"

"Cairo is a small city if you are involved with our kind of work. It didn't take me long to follow the link to Karen's local help. Think about it. I also needed local support. SAMs are not that easy to walk through as hand luggage.

"My local guy put two and two together and worked out who would have been helping the woman that was shot. Curiously enough, he thought the sniper was another woman - a mercenary named Katarina Voronin.

"I followed the trail and although one of your guys had skipped the country, the other was still lying low. Waiting for payment. 'Follow the money' still works.

"It was lucky for me, because if he had skipped then there would be no links left. After I met him, I told him to lose himself, or he'd be next on the hit list.

"He told me about your mission to collect something from the truck. That there was supposed to be a hook-up in the desert. I don't believe it would have happened, even without the helicopter being present. I think the Brits were there to witness what happened - no more and no less."

Alton interrupted, "Why would that be? What is the point of setting up such an elaborate scheme?"

"I think this was a demonstration. Ahead of something else. There's going to be some kind of downstream threat. Or maybe there has already?"

Alton shook his head, "Frankly, if this was true, then you'd know far more about what is happening than we do. I agree it looks as if they set us up. The fact you have shown up here is pretty rich considering the trouble you are in."

Manners responded, "Sure - and that's why you need me on the outside. I'm more use to you in the field than locked away in some suite in SI6. My self-interest is running this down so I get out in one piece. Whoever ended Karen probably has a long list that includes me - and your other Cairo buddies."

Manners continued, "Believe me, I wouldn't have brought this to you unless I thought something terrible is going down. You guys seem set up as the 'validators'. People who have witnessed what might happen. My guess is the hostile playbook will say, 'contact you, show they know all about Cairo and then start making new demands against a bigger threat.'"

Alton nodded, "You could be right. I'll be honest with you. You have already filled in some gaps. I have one other piece you haven't picked up. The helicopter. It wasn't American, it was Israeli."

Manners pretended to look startled. He had already seen the black overpainted markings on the crashed 'copter. He decided it was better to play along, "An Israeli helicopter on a stealth assault in Egyptian airspace. You have got to be kidding me."

"My reaction too. They dressed it to look like mercenaries and will deny everything, but this was one well-funded and high-tech mission."

"Okay," said Manners, "I'm staying involved in this for two reasons. One: America seems to be handling this as a black op. Two: It's turning into a threat against me too.

"That's why I've come to you. I've already given you a lot of information. I'll ask you to provide me some cover as this plays out. I may need to disappear by the end of this."

Alton looked at Manners, "I respect you coming to see me like this, Mr Manners."

"Ordinarily I could not agree to work with you, though. Understand my position on this. A blown operation, casualties, new threats and then an unknown American turns up out of the blue offering assistance. Furthermore, he knows more than the intelligence agencies about what happened in Cairo 48 hours ago."

"Now here is the thing. I have Karen's stringer making contact with us. His name is James, and he is British. He still has the briefcase, which he was supposed to exchange with the truck driver in the desert. It's a booby-trapped device which will destroy its contents if opened without a special electronic key.

The case contains a series of decommission codes for the canisters in transit. I am arranging for our embassy in New York to pick them up. We will then have the codes, which I think can disable the canisters.

"These are the canisters in transit across the desert from Saudi Arabia?" asked Chuck.

"That's right," answered Alton.

"Well, the explosion of the first canister was a regular fireball," answered Chuck.

"It looked as if they were trying to incinerate something."

"What was it?" asked Chuck, "A further weapon of some kind - I don't think it was a missile, despite what has been put out there?"

"Yes," answered Alton, "We think the truck was carrying a binary neurotoxin. The case also contains the codes to disable the neurotoxin."

"You said it is a binary. Does that mean there are codes to enable it as well?" asked Chuck, "I've worked at Los Alamos and know about some of these chemical weapons, from a distance."

"You are right," answered Alton. "There's one set of codes to arm the toxin and a different set to destroy it. The codes are all in that case which James holds.

"So, some bad people want the case now?" asked Chuck.

"That's what we think, the toxin was on its way to being destroyed but now it has been intercepted."

"But if it has been destroyed, then surely the codes are worthless?" asked Chuck.

"Normally I'd agree, but there is a second truck with a further 10 canisters of neurotoxin."

"… And where is that?" asked Chuck.

"We've no idea, " answered Alton, "The trace on the second truck has gone cold."

The Square

"I think James might need some help," said Chuck, "Can I visit him?"

"I thought you were working for the US on this?" asked Alton.

"I was, but things just got more complex," answered Chuck, "Where is James now?"

"New York," answered Alton, "We've arranged to pick up the case from a meeting with him, in a bar."

"Next flight tonight, then," answered Chuck,"BA around 1900 if I remember correctly, from T5 - I can just make it. You'd better get me the unlock code for the briefcase and tell me the rendezvous."

"Use this," said Alton handing over the small USB stick he had collected earlier that morning,

"Just plug it in and then the case should open. That flight should get you in by midnight. You'll have most of tomorrow to locate James and meet him at the bar, Molly's bar," Alton handed Manners the address and contact details to meet James.

Ed Adams

Manhattan

*"Steel, glass, tile, concrete
will be the materials of the
skyscraper.
Crammed on the narrow island the
millionwindowed buildings
will be just glittering,*

pyramid on pyramid

*like the white cloudhead
above a thunderstorm"*

— John Dos Passos, Manhattan Transfer

Molly's

Evening in New York. James was in the Irish bar. He'd already bought a glass of black beer and was sipping it, waiting for someone to arrive. Prominently on the chair next to him was a Macy's tote. Bright red, with a white star on it, and inside it a metal briefcase.

"Good evening," said a voice. James looked towards a tall figure, slightly tanned and with a clipped American accent.

"Do you mind if I sit here? I've been shopping for lighting. Someone asked me to get a lampshade,"

"And you are?" asked James.

"I'm Chuck Manners," came the reply, "I think we met once before briefly. In the desert. I was pre-occupied, and I think you drove away."

"Mr Manners," answered James, "I assume we both know some of the same people,"

"It's Colonel, but you can call me Chuck," smiled Chuck back towards James.

"It has been an intense couple of days, for both of us I'm sure."

Chuck replied, "They have asked me to retrieve the case; I think I might assist defuse it too."

"Okay, but I think you should know that there is someone following me. They have come across to New York from Egypt. They were in my girlfriend's apartment."

"Okay, we will need to resolve that," answered Chuck, "Do you know who they were or what they want?"

"Not exactly, although they seem to be after some codes."

"I think I know what that is about," answered Chuck, They are codes to disable the content of the truck that was blown up by the helicopter."

"So, they must know that, why do they still want the codes?" asked James.

"There were two; two trucks and two consignments. I think they have lost the other consignment at the moment. If they can find it, they will want to arm it."

"That was a pretty powerful warhead," said James, "Even at three clicks it was devastating."

"I agree," said Chuck, "So we can be sure they are up to no good."

"Okay," said James, "I'll hand over the case, but I might need your help if they continue to pursue me."

"You have my word," said Chuck, looking James in the eye, " One casualty from this already, we don't want any more."

"Look, I'm staying at the W just off Times Square. Room 5111. 51st floor. I'm taking the case there now. I'll open it and then we can get back together, if you like. I'll be flying out tomorrow, back to the UK. I assume you will want to get lost, so that whoever had been tracking you can't locate you any longer. Just make sure to give me a way to stay in contact at least until we both leave New York."

James nodded and wrote something down.

"We should exchange contact details," he said.

Chuck nodded then rose, picked up the Macy's bag and raised his glass of beer, "Slàinte Mhath!" he said.

"Cheers;" said James.

Léa

Léa had first met James in London when he was sitting in a cafe drinking a latte and there was no other table spare.

She'd been in a hurry and had left a bag behind - a genuine accident.

James had called after her, and then left the cafe to pass the bag back to her. In a moment of impulse, he had invited Léa for a supper any time in the same week.

Léa had, to her slight surprise, agreed, and they had met later the same evening and over a short time developed a strong relationship.

They had made a good couple and although Léa still didn't know fully what James did as a consultant; it gave her some surprise vacation breaks as she could sometimes follow him around during his assignments.

The Square

She wasn't at all phased to receive the ticketing for Cannes, from James, with its clandestine romantic message, "Not a word until we meet."

The current situation was great and after two years apart a chance to re-acquaint.

James had contacted her to offer her a visit to Cannes for a water sport break until he could join her there on his way back from Turkey. He had sent her the ticket and hotel information, and it was a great surprise.

So now Léa was enjoying every minute. Sea-spray, bumping, solid power. Cannes has been a stroke of genius.

Now she was in a smart hotel, with a private beach and enjoying as much water sports as she could handle. The complementary hotel upgrade had been a bonus on top. The powerboat lesson had been great, and she was really getting the hang of the water-skis. In the distance she could see another fast powerboat, but apart from that, she seemed to have the immediate bay to herself.

The other boat was similarly practicing water-ski manoeuvres but didn't seem to have a skier in tow. Léa assumed it was someone out to try the boat's manoeuvrability, although it was now getting closer to the area where she was practicing.

Then suddenly, it spun towards their boat and manoeuvred itself in parallel, but with a closing gap. It slowed, so that instead of being in line with her boat, it was now in line with her.

A blur of something dark. It was a net like the kind used to land a large fish. It had been fired somehow from the other boat and landed just in front of her. She was in it. The safety line to her powerboat had disconnected. She was now in the sea, in her wetsuit, floating on her buoyancy device and in a net.

She struggled to get free but could feel the net being pulled. She was being reeled in, like some captured exotic fish. The other powerboat was not visible, it was somewhere to the left of the boat that was pulling her in and she could only hear noises of engine and shouted instruction from the boat which was now her capturer.

She was hauled up the side of the boat, banging her body and then her legs and shins against the edge of the craft, then flopping with a thud to the deck surface of the boat. Without removing the net, two men had slipped a white plastic loop around her legs and her arms. She felt immense fear, what on earth was this about? She tried to scream, but nothing came out. Then darkness as she was pushed down some steps in the boat into a darkened room.

She heard the engine rev and the boat took up a quick speed away from the area, the floor of her temporary cell sloping and bumping with the progress of the boat.

Less than an hour later they stopped. The boat was being docked, and Léa guessed they were not so far from Cannes, where she had been staying, but that they had taken her to a different location for whatever purpose.

Then she heard footsteps approach and saw one of her captors descend the ships stairs towards her. "Don't worry', he said, "If you co-operate, and your friend co-operates, then no-one will get hurt. We don't want you, but you are a way to get to James and in turn to something he has which belongs to us."

Léa was mystified by this, as well as scared, "I don't know what you are talking about she said,"...and how do you know James. I think you have the wrong people. Neither of us is mixed up in anything, so I don't think holding me will get you anywhere. Just let me go!"

"I can't do that, we need to get to James, and you will help us," continued the captor. He motioned towards a video camera.

"You will make a small video now and we will use it to attract James. You must say you are in captivity, and that you want to be set free. Ask James to come here and we will arrange for your freedom. It's really that simple."

He positioned the camera on a small tripod and switched it on. "No" said Léa, "I won't ask James to help me. You must just let me go. This is illegal and you will be in a lot of trouble." Léa stared towards her captor, who kept the camera running.

"To be honest, it doesn't matter what you say," he continued, "As long as you show James you are with us. I can then add a message to the video recording."

Anonymity

After James had returned to Léa's Manhattan apartment and seen the disturbed papers, his thought was of how comprehensively he had been rumbled. His original plan to depart from Cairo and to select a pseudo-random destination had been well and truly intercepted. Not only did he have local US spooks onto him, he also believed that he was being followed by a second team or ironically that the second team had been watching the Americans who had visited him.

Either way, "Team 2" has somehow tracked him down and also broken into the apartment and found enough material to be able to track down Léa.

Even he had only just figured out that she was in France, but his main concern was that she would now be part of a trade for the information that he held about his recent aborted project.

It didn't take a genius to work out that 'Team 2' and possibly also 'Team 1' would be looking for the means to get information from James. And it would be via Léa.

He looked around the apartment. He switched on the television; he flicked on a few more lights. There. That would make the place look busy if anyone were to check his whereabouts.

He exited via the elevator but then through a back exit to the building. It brought him to a short lane which led onto another busy thoroughfare. At the end of the lane he could see yellow cabs.

He thought about the need to phone Léa. He hadn't wanted to do so from her apartment and he'd deliberately not kept a cell phone with him from the time he had started the live part of the mission.

He would head directly to the airport and phone her from the anonymity of the airport.

Take the AirTrain

James sat in the airport lounge. He'd been able to use his traveller card to gain access despite a lowly economy ticket. New York JFK was quiet for a Friday, as had been the entire drive from midtown.

The route from 42nd Street had been along to the midtown tunnel and then out across to Long Island. The long streets were lit with afternoon sun, which glinted from the skyscrapers as he looked down towards Lower Manhattan. Long Island traffic was almost at a standstill, although the cab driver wove a complicated route, dodging the worst of the clogged streets.

Instead of going directly to the terminal at JFK, he had asked the cab to drop him at the Hertz car rental depot.

He had used the AirTrain back to the terminal and the long way around to Terminal Seven via all the intermediate stops. This gave him a chance to see if he was being directly followed. No-one in their right mind would use his route so any co-incidence would probably be more than that.

The Square

It didn't take long to get around to the check-in area. Then through self-check-in, the enhanced security which involved removing shoes and into the area with the streams of water and the mini escalators rising half floor height before following the signs to the haven of the lounge.

He could tell it was a Friday in the lounge, however. There were plenty of executive types sitting around, but instead of the usual bleeps of mobile phone tunes and the murmur of business conversations, there was much more of a hush. The bluetooths had been retired for the weekend. Much of Europe was already out for a Friday evening and so the usual source of much of the conversation had already subsided.

Time's arrow was working, and the weekend was already underway in the places that many of the people in this particular lounge were travelling to. Sport pages were being read, people were reclining on beach loungers (an improbable feature of this airport lounge). It was time to power down for the next couple of days.

Sleek brown tee shirt

James knew he was still on duty. He was expecting to be contacted before he left New York. As the minutes were reducing, he wondered how this would happen. He only had the time between now and the walk to Gate Nine to board his plane. The relaxed businessman nearby was reading a book about Caesar. Maybe he was the contact?

James looked at him cautiously. He seemed engrossed in his book, and then a flight was called to Madrid and he rose and left, to be replaced almost immediately by a French mother with two children.

James noticed her commandeering the space and spreading her bags and the childrens' belongings around, then removing a chunky woollen cardigan revealing a sleek brown tee-shirt. James looked away before the woman noticed and continued to read his newspaper.

The Square

One of the children, around ten years old, was by his side and counting a few dollars conspicuously to his right. James glanced up and at the same moment met the woman's gaze.

"The bag is for you," she said, glancing towards a white carrier bag by the side of the child. It looked like a newsagent carrier bag, similar to the one he had been given when he purchased his own newspaper on the way to the lounge. The mother called something to the boy in French and he jumped up taking his younger brother by the hand walking across to the display of cookies and potato chips.

"Take the bag, now", spoke the woman softly, "and make your way to Gate Nine. The content is papers, but it includes what you are looking for," she continued softly.
"Don't try to follow us - we are travelling to Paris but know nothing further of your plans. They tricked me into making this contact - I want nothing further to do with it and I'm scared that if you don't follow my instructions then something will happen to me or the boys," she added.

James nodded, swept up the carrier and then moved towards the exit from the lounge. He knew he would examine the contents when he was away from the area but realised that he was putting the woman in some danger if he didn't do what was requested.

Calling Chuck

From the airport, James called Chuck.

"Wow, that was quick," exclaimed Chuck, "Is everything all right?"

"Not really," answered James, "They've kidnapped my girlfriend, Léa, and are asking for codes, like we talked about yesterday."

"Where is she?"

"Yeah, and where am I? I'm at JFK about to leave New York for London, then Cannes, France to find her. I don't really know what I'm up against, but I might have to pick up a small toolkit on the way."

"I thought I'd best let you know, seeing as you followed me across to New York."

"Okay," said Chuck, "I'll be thinking about this and how best to deploy."

"Thanks, Chuck."

Ed Adams

La Côte d'Azur

*"Dark Sunglasses: You may want to pick up a pair of
especially dark glasses (to be more discreet when
appreciating the beautiful people of Aix-en-Provence)."*

— Rick Steves (Provence & the French Riviera)

Croisette

James had not really slept since New York. He had fitful bursts in the economy section of the BA plane, and then while waiting in London. Now he was in Cannes. He knew he should sleep to be sharp for the next day, but a combination of adrenaline and anxiety had kept him awake. The hotel room was in a side street on the fourth floor. He had a small balcony and had wanted to keep the room unlocked to improve ventilation on what had been a warm night. But he had spooked himself and was worried about intruders. His logic was that anyone serious about finding him would not let a small hotel window deter them, but on the other hand, the glass looked thick troublesome to break and there were extra security devices on both the hotel room door and the sliding patio window.

So, after interrupted sleep, James had awoken and freshened up for the day. He could feel a dull edge in his head, which he knew was the effect of too little sleep, and he worried that this could reduce his reactions during the day's events.

At around this time, a noise from roadworks outside the hotel disturbed him and he looked down to see a series of road markers and two men drilling the road surface. He wondered if this was linked to his presence, but assumed it was coincidence. It was directly outside his hotel and meant a small village of workman's huts had been erected during the night. His vantage point meant that he could see what was involved and as well as the paraphernalia of the roadworks, there appeared to be a satellite dish and some sort of communications station.

Maybe he was paranoid now, but this did not look normal to him. He looked through the belongings he had brought with him. A small holdall and a separate, tiny rucksack. He weighed up his possessions and moved a few into the rucksack. A tee-shirt, a camera, phone, cash and credit cards and a few other small items. The rest he left in the other holdall. He looked behind him as he reversed out of the room. Goodbye room 425. He left the hotel without checking out. He was still booked for another day which gave himself longer to escape detection.

It was still only just after nine in the morning, and James decided to scope out the area designated for the meeting. His small hotel was near to the old town and the harbour. He could lose himself in this part of town until the time arrived to meet with the dangerous people who had abducted Léa. He knew why and would need to play the whole situation carefully.

Eventually he found a small area of wall, by the harbour, away from the bustle of people and with a good view towards a large clock on the hillside overlooking the old town. A perfect vantage point in the sunshine whilst he waited for the due hour to arrive. He had picked up a newspaper from a table as he left the hotel and now read this quietly.

The Square

At ten minutes to eleven, he stirred to begin his trial walk to rehearse the meeting with the abductors. He calculated it would take five or six minutes to get back to the Palais de Congress and then he could walk slowly towards the Western end of the Croisette, It would take him at least twenty minutes to walk along at a moderate speed.

A warm blue sky and just the trail of aircraft crossing Europe and the tiniest wisps of cloud. He had been told to walk the length of the Croisette promenade at 11.00 on Thursday morning and that he would be contacted. The situation seemed strangely ironic as he walked past billboards advertising the latest spy movie, along with pictures of playboys and the silhouettes of shapely women.

Cannes seemed geared for pleasure, with its combination of languid cafes, meticulously expensive shops and sunshine, even here in November. It was Wednesday, and he had time to make a survey of the area, both anxious to understand what would unfold within the next twenty-four hours but also inquisitive of the mainly relaxed lifestyle of the local inhabitants. It was clearly the end of the season. Businessmen mingled with suntanned locals, the darker tanned types who looked as if they either lived in Cannes all year and the cosmetically enriched tans of the jet setters with their expensive wrap-around sunglasses.

James was aware that he may already be under observation, but even as he pivoted and took a slightly erratic path along the promenade there was no discernible reaction from anyone except an old lady walking a very small dog which itself had been alarmed at one if his sudden movements.

James also recognized that there was a chance that he was observed from a car or even maybe a rooftop, but then, maybe the people he was dealing with were just confident enough to not consider it worth the effort .

The start of his walk had been near to the old town, where there was a harbour, many small boats moored and some small but presumably expensive seafood restaurants. He knew the area was not the primary one he had been asked to walk and in the near distance he could see the large concrete slab of the Palais de Congress, which marked the start of his route. He skirted the harbour, noticing a small and moderately camouflaged MacDonald's on his way to the start of the route. Passing the Palais, there were various business folk standing outside chatting in small groups. There was some kind of exposition in progress and these suited and sombre looking people were the overspill. Mainly smoking, they stood in small knots chatting together and across in a corner a TV crew was filming an interview with someone who James presumed to be a conference presenter.

Then he walked along the expanse of the curving Croisette. James had even noticed this from the air on his flight into Nice. The bay was a great shape for a sunny view towards the Mediterranean and the mainly low-rise hotels had a grandeur and sense of belonging. The road was wide with twin carriageways and a central median of palm trees so the whole effect was exactly what one would want for the South of France.

James continued, checking the terrain, which was flat, although at intervals with ramps from the promenade down to the beach, some 10 metres lower. Despite being November, there were bathers on the beach and several bikini clad women soaking the last rays of the year's summer-like sunshine.

The Square

As James walked, he noticed the varied transport around him. In addition to walkers, there were motor scooters, in-line skaters and cyclists. The road was often separated from the promenade by between two and twenty metres, so there was a high probability that whoever was to meet him would be on foot or aided by a bike or similar.

A couple of times James simply stopped and sat down on blue chairs which had been placed along the edge of the pavement. It gave him a chance to look around and really to see if there was anything unusual about the people around him. But his fellow walkers were of many types, with no obvious pattern. There were no para-military types or anyone looking furtive or surprised by his sudden movements. He concluded that he was not being followed and that the group would first appear the next day.

At the end of the main route, he turned, crossed the entirety of the promenade and started the walk back. He eyed the large hotels and their opulent entrances. The mainly black-clothed inhabitants of the hotels, the well-coutured women with sleek hair, tans, immaculate lip gloss and inevitable sunglasses, The clusters of sleek Mercedes and the street parked Bentley, Maserati and a row of three Ferraris. This was no ordinary town and there was clear wealth around.

He selected a café ahead. It had a slight stairway leading into it and a row of concrete garden pots along the roadside. The height gave it a slight advantage and he was able to select a small corner table which gave a great vantage of the road. His interest was two-fold. To observe the type of traffic at this time of the day and to see whether there was now any overt sign that he was being observed. Jake knew this was irrational, but alone, in an unknown place and with a situation tomorrow which could be dangerous, he felt the need to cross-examine the situation from every possible angle.

"Café au lait" he requested to the waiter, who appeared surprisingly quickly and was very attentive. James paused now with the coffee to contemplate the next 24 hours.

Then, from his cafe position, James saw a large, tanned and thickset man on roller blades moving towards him.

"Surely not?" he thought, but yes, as the man approached James, he held out an envelope and thrust it to James. James looked around. The man was already 30 metres away and still moving fast. James opened the envelope.

Inside were two items. First, a picture of Léa, in a wet suit and tied up. She looked petrified. Then a sheet of A4 paper, typed with the message, " Go down the slip to Café L'Ondine".

James looked around and realised it was one of the cafes along the beach. He had not been paying attention to their names but assumed that the one in question would be close to his current location. He looked at the next one, which was named after a hotel, as was the next one. Then one small private one and then the one he had been directed to.

From the top of the slope he could see five or six people sitting at a table and chatting, laughing, in fact. He moved down the slope and as they saw him, their demeanour became very serious, very fast.

One of them stood. "Mr Goodwin," he started, "Welcome to our dejeuner, would you care for some wine?" he offered.

James declined. "Where is Léa?" he began. "She has nothing to do with anything."

"I'm afraid she does," continued the same voice, "You implicated her by your very friendship—now we want to do a simple trade. You have something of ours, and we have something of yours. At the moment, I trust that both items are in very good condition."

"What do you need?" asked James.

"Simple, we need the code sequences for the canisters. I know your government intends to disarm them. We will want to prime them."

"And if I get them for you?" asked James.

"We'll return Léa and you can walk away. You won't be able to stop us in any case. Our interest is just in the codes and their consequences. You and Léa are just a cost of doing business."

"So how do I get the codes?" asked James.

"We thought you'd know. We both know you are well-connected. You'll either have to ask for them or steal them. And don't think about giving us the wrong information. We'll test them before we return Léa. You have until Friday - I assume you will do this by phone, not by travelling."

"Yes," said James, "That would be my method."

James thought to himself. He knew the codes would be a two-signature process, so the chances to get the information other than formally would be very unlikely to succeed.

"Okay," said James, "Give me three days. I will get the information."

"No," said the smiling voice, "You have two days - no, 1 day, 23 hours and 50 minutes. And we will end this when the clock runs out. That's *en plein midi* midday, French time, on Friday."

James nodded. He would get the codes.

He left the cafe. He wanted to check that he wasn't being followed. Then he called Chuck Manners once again.

"James?" said Chuck, "This is becoming a habit!"

"Hi Chuck, thank you for picking up, I met with Léa's captors. They have asked me for the codes. They don't know that I had them, nor that I gave them to you, but now they want them in exchange for Léa."

There was a pause, "Okay," said Chuck, "I have the codes. I could send them to you. You'd get Léa, but the captors would have access to the weapons. It also assumes they don't try to double cross. I think we need a better play than me sending the codes and you handing them over. I need to talk to Robert Alton again. "

James considered, "Okay, but I need you to promise that you'll send the codes to me by 11:50 French time Friday. It's my last chance to get Léa back."

"Here's what I'll do. It's Wednesday. I can get across to Cannes by tomorrow around midday, if I leave quickly. We can meet up and by then I'll have a plan for what to do on Friday."

Trip to London

Chuck checked the flights to get to Cannes. He'd have to fly from New York to London, or Paris, and then take a flight to Nice. It was about 30 minutes by taxi from Nice to Cannes. He worked out he could be there by Wednesday afternoon.

Chuck remembered that he'd texted Jake and now decided to call Jake, in London.

" Jake, It's Chuck, I'm on my way to Cannes, France, via Nice."

"I'd like to meet you in London on the way. Heathrow, Terminal 5, airside. Jake, can you arrange to get a ticket also same flight BA348 ? 17:10 London time tomorrow, arrives Cannes at 20:10 French time."

"Whoa, Chuck, Sure, Are you all right? where can we meet?"

"Doing fine, but life is somewhat hectic. How about the pub in the terminal? You know, the nice one, airside?"

"Huxleys? That's the less crowded one."

"Great. I'll see you there tomorrow. I'm in New York right now, so I'll be flying in during the day, on BA and then I'll make my way to the bar."

"Okay - I'll see you there, complete with a ticket!"

Huxley's

Chuck had flown back to London. He was in Heathrow Terminal 5, looking for the bar where he would meet Jake. Huxley's was busy. It was a replica pub, built into the 21st century fabric of the air terminal. It attempted to recreate a version of a gentrified London boozer.

"Jake!" called Chuck from across the bar. Jake noticed that Chuck was wearing one of his slightly green looking suits. Now was not the time to say anything.

"It's been a long time!" greeted Jake, "And I assume there's something 'unusual' involved?"

"Yes," said Chuck.

"What are you having?" asked Jake as he reached the bar and caught the eye of the bartender. She smiled at him with a twinkle in her eye.

"A water, please," said Chuck.

"Still or sparkling?" asked the bartender.

"Still," responded Chuck.

Jake looked across to Chuck.

"I need some help," said Chuck, "From people that are unknown. I seem to have got myself into a spot of trouble. There's been an incident and I am trying to put things right."

"Okay," said Jake, "I assume it's dangerous too, given that you are involved?"

"Yes," replied Chuck, "Some people have already been killed - but I don't want you to do anything dangerous, although your help could be a great game-changer in the current situation."

Chuck looked at Jake.

"Look, I'm going to trust you with this. I think you know me well enough to know I'm not making this up, although it might sound a little far-fetched."

"We'd better get a table then," smiled Jake. "And some pork scratchings".

Chuck began his story, "A few days ago I was sent to Egypt by the US Army. I know, I'm not officially anything to do with them now. I was contacted by the U.S. Army's 1st Special Forces Operational Detachment-Delta (SFOD-D). It's a special unit of the U.S. government tasked with counterterrorist operations outside the United States."

"Sounds rather elite?" ventured Jake.

"Elite, deniable and deadly," answered Chuck, smiling.

"No clichés here, eh? I'm going to trust you with this information. I wouldn't usually tell anyone about this stuff, but I am going to need your help with something where I just can't go to the normal sources."

"Why is that?" asked Jake.

"Leaks," responded Chuck, "A major leak that makes me think some very senior people are involved in something that can create a global catastrophe."

"I hardly think that Bigsy, Clare and I can somehow fix this then?" smiled Jake.

"You are right, Jake. The point of getting you involved is to help me find some information that can then lead to unlocking what we need to do."

"My mission in Egypt was supposed to be fairly simple. The country has an inherent instability and I was to use the unrest to cover up my actual mission, which was to blow up a helicopter."

"Whoa," said Jake, "This is already getting dark."

"Literally. I'd been tasked with this as a black-op against terrorists. I was told that the truck carried something valuable to the U.S. but would be under attack from terrorists or mercenaries. They gave me co-ordinates to hit the helicopter before it could take out the truck."

Ed Adams

"I'd been told that there were two parallel missions to take out two different trucks on different routes. I assumed they were carrying missiles, but I was wrong."

"They said they could give me the exact co-ordinates of the helicopter strike. I assumed that they obtained the intel from some kind of counterintelligence probe.

"I was to operate alone as a civilian, except I'd be a surprisingly well armed civilian. I was to have a selection of surface to air missiles at my disposal."

" I was given the intercept co-ordinates and told the truck would look like a petrol tanker. I was to use the weaponry at my disposal but explicitly it was non-American. I had to spend some time learning the controls on the Russian SAM launcher and on a Korean surface missile."

"I got this job on a 'non-refusal' basis. Uncle Sam has a few other facts about me that made this difficult to refuse. As an ex-Delta Force person I had the right credentials."

"Of course, if you are in the regular US Army you think that Delta Force has all the latest weaponry and equipment.

"The reality is that often, when someone like me is called in to action, the last thing required was a sophisticated American technology gloss on the operation. It's too much of a fingerprint when we need stealth. That is why I had to familiarise with foreign ordnance for this mission."

"I arrived in the locale for the operation in a 4 wheel Drive. A Nissan Patrol - the kind that everyone from the suburbs through to local gangsters and drug smugglers use.

"The vehicle I used looked slightly beaten up and in town would not be noticed. In the desert it was a typical vehicle too, and had plenty of space for the weaponry it currently carried.

"I never did find out who the other shooter was supposed to be, or even where the second convoy was heading. It's fairly standard in a black-op to know as little as possible."

"But you're telling me this now?" interrupted Jake,

"Yes, that mission is dead, but it is useful for you to have the context for what is about to happen next," Manners took another sip of his water.

"I guessed that the truck contained ordnance in transit. My guess was a very long-range missile. The popular theory is that any one of the Iraqis, Iranians, Libyans and Afganistanis would be seeking mischief with this sort of technology. It could be against a variety of nations, including the Americans, and all of Europe."

"How would the surveillance know about this?" asked Jake, "If major nation states can't find weapons of mass destruction then finding a single missile seems somewhat more far fetched?"

Manners nodded, "That's what I thought initially. A needle in a haystack. Unless there had been a tip-off. That's where this gets suspicious. If it really was a dangerous weapon, then in effect the Americans were helping it get to its destination.

Except it didn't because it was destroyed by the helicopter before I took the helicopter down.

"It turned out that whoever was shipping the consignment had tried to initialise it. Unsuccessfully."

"It had sent out a beacon pulse to say it was being tampered with. Like a silent alarm message which had found its way onto the internet and then been picked up at Langley."

"I'd speculated that this was no ordinary missile. The Pentagon showed a direct interest in this which made me think it was a 'bus-MIRV' which basically means long range nuclear capability."

"Bus doesn't sound very fast," queried Jake.

"These missiles are very fast. Ten times the speed of the fastest plane. They are launched into space and then triggered. The 'bus' means that one missile can contain multiple independent re-entry vehicles - that's warheads in plain English."

"That's why they are well scrutinised and tracked then?" commented Jake.

"Yes - the Pentagon can't keep up with all the smaller stuff nowadays. In Libya alone there's about 20,000 unaccounted surface-to-air missiles. They found an unguarded complex with 100,000 anti-tank mines as well. So, it's really the big stuff that gets their attention."

"My job was to shoot something at the missile to bring it to a halt. It could then be noisily recovered and put out of harm's way."

"Er - wouldn't your own missile cause it to explode or something?" asked Jake.

"Not a chance," answered Chuck, "Without the code sequences and arming commands, the whole missile is effectively made neutral. Don't get me wrong, there's very nasty stuff inside but the weapon is considered 'safe' until primed. They have to think of these things when they design the weapons or else it could all get very messy," explained Chuck.

"I was sitting in the Nissan, in the desert, pretty well concealed. I had some long-range digital binoculars and was scanning the area for other signs of people. All I could see was a single small car, but it was so far away that even with image enhancement I couldn't work out what it was doing."

"The next thing I heard was a high-pitched engine sound from the diesel truck. The sound reminded me of an American Army M923 transporter, but this was definitely a civilian rig.

Chuck continued, "I could also hear a low frequency sound which was getting closer. It was a helicopter"

"I looked up and could see the large attack helicopter. An Apache. Fully loaded. The chopper was following the truck and I noticed that the markings on the chopper had been painted out. I wondered initially if the helicopter was some sort of defence for the truck but realised that it had locked on to make an assault on the truck.

"The Apache fired one missile and the truck was obliterated. My orders were to take out anything associated with the truck and this now included the helicopter. I used a SAM to bring it down. I'd already got a laser and range lock from the digital binoculars.

"Two seconds and both the truck and the chopper were gone. The explosion from the truck had been huge, but non-nuclear. I was actually quite deaf at this point. In the far distance I could still see the other vehicle, which was now moving away, but it was out of any practical range for me to do more.

"So, did you leg it at this point?" asked Jake.

Chuck continued, "Strictly I could have left at this point. I was supposed to confirm that I'd taken out the truck, but it was plainly obvious even from around 3 clicks away.

"But I wanted to take a look because the helicopter wasn't playing by any normal rules.

"I had to look around the sky first, in case there was a backup plane, but if there had been it would have gone through very soon after the explosions. There was nothing, so I decided to edge the Nissan along the road towards the craters.

"I needed to move fast because even on this desert road there was traffic every 15-20 minutes.

"As I approached the helicopter I could see the extent of the damage. The SAM had destroyed the whole left side of the helicopter as well as the entire cockpit area. The remains of the rear part were clear and even its two remaining missiles were still attached but unexploded.

"The helicopter had been an AH64 Apache and this one was painted all over black and did not have normal markings except what looked like painted over squadron marking on the tail fin.

The Square

"I examined the remains of the intact side and then saw a painted over star. At "first I was thinking 'American' but the star was not in the right rotation - It looked Israeli.

"I scraped the paint. Under the black, the star was blue. I could see the surrounding circle which had also been painted out. I knew it would be white. It was.

"This was as Israeli helicopter, operating in Egypt. This broke all kinds of conventions and could only be assumed to be a covert operation."

"This is one twisted operation," said Jake, "No wonder you need someone with no background."

"I couldn't work out why an Israeli helicopter would be on fundamentally the same mission that I had been set. I also couldn't work out why they would take such extreme risks to attack in a stealth helicopter across an international border.

"I know I was doing this as a Delta Force gig, but only the Israeli equivalent Sayeret Matkal would be likely to do this.

"The difference was that the Americans had covered their tracks by using deniable resource, foreign weapons and local transport.

"The Israelis had just flown a repainted helicopter into the area. They must have expected to get away with their plan and to be able to escape quickly back to an international zone.

"I decided to fire another missile into the helicopter. Mainly to destroy the remains of the identification. I also thought it useful to mix in another type of armament to really mess things up, so I used the Korean surface missile. It was just a pop compared with the original explosions, but the tail section with the identity was pretty well obliterated.

"I also needed to check the minor remains of the truck, but was fairly sure they would provide very little information based upon the scale of destruction when the helicopter's own missile had been fired into the tanker.

"It took me another few minutes to get from the helicopter crash to the tanker's crater. There wasn't much to see. It had been a huge explosion, but still sub-nuclear. I looked around the site for evidence of the what had caused it, but there was nothing. I don't see how it could have been on board, but there was some kind of explosive being carried. Otherwise it doesn't add up. The missile from the Apache couldn't create as much devastation as it did, so my theory is that the truck included something to help things along."

"You're saying it was staged?" asked Jake.

"Staged isn't the word I would use, but it looks to me as if the intended result was to give the impression that something very big and powerful had been blown up."

"So they knew that someone was on to them?"

"I don't think the driver of the truck would have known, but someone must have leaked the information - and in more than one direction too. The destruction also was not consistent with a large missile being blown up. It makes me think that truck was carrying something else."

"So, they wanted everyone to think that the truck had been blown up?"

"Yes - and the fact that they'd got the Americans and the Israelis onto it suggests that they didn't want to take any chances."

"So, then what?" asked Jake.

"I had to get out of the area. The road where it happened was pretty out of the way. It ran parallel to another busier road but was about 10 miles to the south. The amount of noise and smoke would attract attention and only give a few minutes before others would come for a look. And then the police and military.

"As it happens, for me it was 'Mission Accomplished' - the truck was gone, it's just that there was a spare helicopter downed as well. My Nissan was completely unscathed in all of this, so I headed along the roadway from Cairo and then turned down another small road back towards the main highway and across to the other highway."

"Wouldn't someone want additional support in the area?" asked Jake.

"Too risky," answered Chuck, "If you think about it, the truck was supposed to be travelling under cover. No-one was supposed to know about it. The Americans could hardly appear in the area unless everyone pointed a finger towards them and as for the Israelis, forget it. One disguised helicopter was the absolute limit."

"Yes," said Jake, nodding, "showing up just after a massive missile fight wouldn't be the brightest move."

"And as it was, I didn't see anyone approaching the crash by road, as I headed back to the main route. But I guess they would have come from the Cairo direction. Any normal civilian would probably want to give it a wide berth - either because it was insurgents of some kind, or simply because they were in a hurry and didn't want to get stuck in a traffic hold-up."

Jake nodded.

"So, what do you want me or us to do?" he asked again

Diversion

"It's something you are very good at," Chuck replied, "A diversion, while I do something else. I am trying to recover something for our Governments. To be honest, I am trying to recover something despite our governments."

Jake smiled. A diversion would be fun.

"What kind of diversion?" he asked. "And why is it despite the government?"

"It's best you don't know too much about what I will be doing, but whilst I'm doing it, it would be great if you can help the people we are working with look the other way."

"I'll level with you. My colleague James has had his partner kidnapped. They are after some codes and want to arrange a trade."

"The captors could play nice or could act up rough. The intention is to show them that I have back-up with me."

"We need to go to a bar in Cannes, hand over the codes and walk out with James' partner Léa."

"You'll be my driver. We'll also have someone from the Embassy to add colour and texture inside the handover."

"How will they know the codes are genuine?"

I guess they will have a boffin along," answered Chuck, "someone that can test the codes somehow."

Will anyone get hurt during this?" asked Jake.

"No, they shouldn't. If we do this right, then no-one should even know what has happened until it is too late to do anything at all."

"Chuck, why won't you use the normal security services for this?" asked Jake.

"It's delicate," said Chuck, "This is one situation where I need to ensure there are no leaks of information and frankly that no-one else knows what I'm doing. I know I can trust you for this."

Chuck looked Jake in the eye, "But I do need to know that you'll be prepared to do this."

"Chuck, you've assured us that we won't be in danger. Of course we will help you."

Jake nodded. It wasn't so different from the last time he'd been with Chuck. Nothing was really what it seemed, and this was a typical extension.

"Don't you ever get confused with all of these parallel realities?" asked Jake.

Chuck smiled, "We both know how it is," he replied, "if it was too simple then everyone would do it."

"I've set up a fake conference number to control the operation. Like a dial-in conference call. We are going to leak the number to the people at the meeting. We will need some voices on the line to sound like it is a major operation. They need to think that you've got the phone for that purpose and are under orders."

"Okay, so that's where Bigsy and Clare come in? Making air chatter?"

"Precisely," said Chuck. "To bulk out the operation with voices on the line. We'll want them to think they had better play nice with us."

"Okay, I'd better get on to Bigsy; get him to come up with some sound effects,"

- .... . / .... .- -. -.. --- ...- . .-.

Léa's handover had been arranged. James made his way to the Carlton Beach Club along the Croisette. He could see Chuck Manners and someone else already there, sitting at the bar.

"Hi James," called Chuck, "This is Jake, he'll be joining us for the occasion."

Jake nodded; the sleek setting of the jet-set exclusive club seemed an incongruous place to meet for the handover.

"And over there is Oliver, from the British Consulate," he gestured to another table where Oliver sat, flamboyantly listening to a radio communication on an earpiece.

James also noticed a small group of the people he had met in New York and that had then seen him at Café L'Ondine a day or so ago in Cannes.

Oliver's earpiece was quite loud and he could hear sound leakage from it as it changed modes.

James adjusted his own earpiece, which also had the running commentary from further voices which sounded as if a full stake-out was in progress.

At that moment, he noticed a sleek powerboat curving its way across the bay. He realised it was planning to dock on the jetty and he realised that this was where Léa was held.

Ever so slowly he moved forward towards the end of the jetty, holding a machined briefcase in his right hand. He knew it contained the codes which Chuck had painstakingly retrieved with the assistance of Robert Alton. The difference was that the case was now a regular one, without a special electronic lock incorporated.

Someone stepped from the launch. It was a bespectacled man, in a grey tee-shirt and shorts. He was carrying a small laptop and gestured to James to hand over the case.

Chuck stood at that moment and James could hear the sound in his earpiece get louder.

"Okay, here's the case, now hand over Léa," he said.

"I need to validate the codes first," said the man. He flipped open the case and took a sheet of paper from it. He opened the laptop and started to type in something. James could not see what he was doing.

"I'm using the validation suite to check the codes are correct," said the man. There was a pause as he continued typing.

"Yes," he said eventually, " These codes all pass the validation tests."

He signalled to back to the launch and Léa appeared on deck, held by two men in suits.

"You can release her now," said James. Chuck looked across to the man with the laptop.

"That way we can let your scientist friend go," said Chuck, grasping the arm of the man with the laptop.

"Okay, Okay," said one of the men holding Léa, "We are releasing her now."

The boat rocked against the jetty as Léa walked towards its exit. Chuck moved his arm into his jacket. The radio chatter in James' ear continued.

Léa was now close to the bar in the Beach Club and James put his arm around her, moving her towards the exit. Jake was sitting in a car on the Croisette as the two of them approached. Chuck moved towards the boat with the man with the laptop.

"He can go now," said Chuck, "This should be an end of it."

The man on the powerboat nodded, "Yes, your team can go now."

Chuck walked backwards towards the exit from the Beach Club. Oliver stood and took a couple of photographs. The radio chatter continued. Chuck could hear Jake revving the engine of the rental car as he made his way along the Croisette.

"Mission accomplished," he said to Oliver. He gestured to a second car parked on the Croisette opposite the Beach Club. "That's ours, " he said, "We are off to the heliport and then flying to Marseille. Hit it, Oliver."

Oliver looked over to the black Mercedes E-Class and jumped into the driver's seat.

"You've done well," said Chuck, "The least we could do is give you a fast route back to Marseilles."

At the heliport, they regrouped. Chuck could see that James and Léa were delighted. Chuck announced, "We are going to head for Marseilles. It is harder to follow us there. And I've arranged in the UK for Léa and James to be put up in a somewhat secure location, until the dust from all of this subsides."

"Good," said Jake, "Now we have everyone back together,"

"Yes," said Chuck, "but the bad guys have the priming codes for the toxins."

Chuck could see Oliver taking rapidly to someone on the earpiece.

Oliver soon announced," That was Robert Alton. He confirms if we bring James and Léa in he will provide them with secure cover.

Truck One

Ghali Yassim was thinking back to the first news of the destroyed truck. Most of the conversation was recorded and he was playing it back for the fifth time, trying to find any new meaning in it.

"Something has happened," said Ghali Yassim. "We have lost contact with the first truck."

The destruction of the truck had been fast. It had created a lot of noise, even more because of the subsequent explosion in mid-air of the attack helicopter.

Al Aktar had used their normal procedures to send the two trucks out by different routes.

In practice, Al Aktar had no idea about what had been happening or that they were down to one consignment. This would change in the next couple of hours, when the truck missed its call-in time.

The Square

The other truck containing the second consignment was still on its longer journey, to London, England.

Al Aktar's control centre was in the desert along a trail that branched from Egypt 75, which led to Abu Simbel. The makeshift centre included a neglected airstrip. They could land a medium sized plane, had a helicopter port and also several tin sheds which could be used to store trucks and other vehicles and armaments. They were also within easy reach of the main Abu Simbel Airport, which gave them access to main routes.

Al Aktar devised a safety protocol for the trucks, to call in at two-hour intervals to allow an update of their position to be tracked. The next checkpoint time arrived, and the London-bound truck called in and noted that all was okay.

There was no message from the other truck and there was then an attempt to call it directly from the radio-masted control system. They left it another thirty minutes and then tried to call the truck direct.

There was no response.

They would do these another three times and at the end of that period they would assume that something had happened to the consignment.

Their control centre was already checking the television channels for any reports of trucks being stopped, unusual road conditions or worse, but there was nothing.

"Send up the helicopter, along the route; we need to know", and a few minutes later the helicopter departed, creating a small swirl of sand as it moved skyward. It covered the first part of the route in a few minutes, and soon radioed back with the news of the wreckage of the truck but also of an adjacent helicopter wreck and some new air traffic approaching the wreck.

"They may think they have stopped us,"said Mehdi

THE SQUARE

PART TWO

Ed Adams

THREE WEEKS AGO

Kent

"The hop gardens turn gracefully towards me presenting regular avenues of hops in rapid flight, then whirl away."

Charles Dickens, rail journey through Kent

Ashford

Ashford, Kent, Channel Tunnel train station: It was the stopping point for the white van containing the cases being driven from the dilapidated houses in Hoxton, London. The driver of the van and his passenger had been hired to convey the cases to Ashford, where they would be swapped into a large truck for the rest of their journey.

The October rain from London seemed to have swept across the whole of the south of England. As Alan drove and Dave sat in the passenger seat, they talked to begin with, but then fell silent as they each were caught in their own thoughts before the drop-off. This was an expensive piece of ferrying for their clients, but there was always a chance that something would cut up rough when they got to the drop-off point. They'd been warned not to bring anyone else along and had decided that they had little choice but to obey. They had worked for the same Arabs before on a couple of smaller deals and had found them to be reliable and to always pay without asking questions.

The Square

Alan, the driver, and Dave, his passenger, knew that they were moving the cases to another vehicle and drove to the appointed rendezvous. They were punctual and noted a huge Scania articulated truck already parked in the lay-by behind a black Mercedes with blacked out back windows. Two men with middle eastern looks and beards were standing by the cab of the truck. One wore a black tee shirt, the other was in a green jacket. A third man was sitting in the truck's cab, which had Polish number plates on the cab and what looked like Dutch plates on the trailer.

Dave jumped from the van onto a slightly crunchy road surface in the lay-by. As he looked around, he realized that he didn't know the men who he was being asked to meet.

"Guys, we're here", called out Dave, "Who is in charge?" as he looked around. With a whirring sound, a back window in the Merc ran down and a third Arabic looking face peered out. "Do you have the cases?" he asked.

"Six cases," answered Dave. "Everything's here!"

"Let's check," responded the guy in the black tee shirt, as he pulled the door of the van open and pulled the first case forward. The second man pulled open a large holdall, like a military kitbag. As the first man opened the cases, he handed the envelopes individually to the second man, and they counted them into the holdall.

Despite the rain, the envelopes were counted as they were transferred. Six cases with ten envelopes in each. "There's only 59", called the Arab with the black tee shirt.

"Are you sure?", said the man in the green jacket, "Count them again".

The van driver and his passenger looked at each other.

They had worked together a long time, and neither of them would double cross the other.

"We don't have any other envelopes", said the driver. The three Arabs briefly conferred.

"There is an envelope missing", repeated the Arab with the black tee shirt. The Arab in the black Mercedes called out something else. The driver and passenger looked at one another, worried now that something bad was about to happen.

"You have two days," said the black tee shirt, "We don't care what has happened, but you will find the missing package - it is essential that we retrieve it. As good faith we will still give you your money, minus fifty percent. You will get the rest minus ten per cent when you provide the missing package. Please do not fail, it will be very unpleasant for you and your families. You have forty-eight hours. We meet again here at the same time. Do not fail and do not think you can walk away from this commitment."

The Arab in the green jacket moved to the trunk of the Mercedes and lifted a briefcase, which he carried to Dave. He briefly flicked it open.

"You'll find half of the money here," he said and flipped the two catches of the case to reveal the money. There seemed to be a lot of cash in the briefcase and Dave briefly flicked through a couple of the stacks and noticed that they all looked like used notes too.

"Thank you for this first payment," he said and scooped the case so that he and Alan could move back to their van. He nodded to Alan, who swung back onto the passenger seat. They started the engine and pulled back out onto the busy road.

Dave and Alan had just received £300,000, which was exactly half of the £600,000 they had expected. It was still a considerable sum, and they knew it would get very nasty if they tried to argue about the rest. They were really small-time criminals, and the job they had been given was essentially the delivery of the six cases. They had considered this easy money but were now concerned that things were getting complicated.

"Dave, do you think that the drunk could have taken an envelope?", Alan asked, as they thought over what had happened.

They had been professional about counting the envelopes when they had been given them in the first place and had kept the six cases under watch at all times except briefly when they were transferring them from the hide-out to the current van.

"The only time we didn't have the full set in sight was when we were clearing up at the lock-up," said Dave. "The envelope is either there, or one of those squatters has it," he said referring to the drunken guy who had been loitering at the squat.

"Okay," said Dave, "We'll go back to the lockup, check that we've not done something stupid and find the guy that probably has!"

Back to the lock-up

Dave and Alan drove straight from Ashford back to central London. They were both furious about what had happened. The original deal had seemed sweet. All they had been expected to do was collect some cases and move them.

They had checked the cases when they collected them and somehow had lost one of the packages along the way. The only clue that anything was wrong was when they had met the drunk during the loading of the cases into the van. Neither Dave nor Alan believed that they were being double crossed and they both believed it was an accident. Either they had really misplaced a package (unlikely) or the drunken tramp had somehow stolen one. If it was the tramp, they would find him and ask him where the package had now been taken.

The next morning, at seven o'clock, they pulled the van onto a pavement around two blocks from the squat. They would walk the last part of the way to the lock-up garage and the deserted houses, to find the tramp who would probably still be asleep.

The Square

First they checked back to the original yard where they had parked the van.

"There's nothing here," said Dave, "although you can see where the tramp was laying on the ground".

Alan nodded. He had brought a small holdall with him. It only contained a few workman's tools, but his intention was to get the information from the tramp under any circumstances. The Arabs now had half of the money he was owed but had also threatened him and his family if they did not return the envelope. And the irony was, he still didn't know what the goods actually were.

They climbed a small wall into the area behind the yard and looked around for the tramp. Ben had a normal sleeping area, and it was in a different house from Gerald, so they kept some distance and some slight security because of this.

The two men had first spotted Ben's house and lifted the broken door inwards to enter the house. There was a crash of timber as they did this. Both Ben and Gerald had learnt that causal intruders usually walked in through the doors and so had piled some noisy items against the door ready to fall, as a form of primitive burglar alarm. Ben was in deep sleep, an after effect of cheap cider, when Dave and Alan found him. They woke him and he groggily asked who they were, then recognising them as the men who he had startled the previous day by the van.

"What do you want?", coughed Ben, as the first man started to hold him to the wall.

"You know what we want", answered Alan glaring at Ben, "You took something from us yesterday - we want it back".

Ben looked confused, "You hit me yesterday, but I had not taken anything", he replied, "I don't know what you want!"

Dave and Alan looked at one another. "This will get very painful for you if you don't tell us the truth!" responded Dave, as Alan opened the zipper on the holdall revealing a few tools including a plumber's wrench. Ben looked at the bag, and its contents, and could see also some knives and a hacksaw.

"I promise you," said Ben, "I don't know what you are talking about!"

The noise had created a commotion in the house, but Gerald, in the next house, had been alerted even by the first crash when the men had entered through the front door of the house. He had slipped quietly in through a window and could now see what was happening. He quickly realised that the two men were trying to find the missing envelope which he had stolen from one of the cases. He could see that Ben was in a lot of trouble.

Gerald decided to find the envelope and try to return it to the two men. He crept out of the house via the same window and then stealthily moved to his hiding place. He considered substituting the strange metal container for something else from his collection, but then realised that he would not want another visit from the same men, looking for him. He just wanted this visit to be over.

He slipped back to the window and could see one of the men placing the plumber's wrench around Ben's left hand as if to crush it. Ben was screaming, but still seemed relatively unscathed. Gerald decided to take a gamble. No-one had seen him, and the two men did not know his appearance. He would throw the envelope into the room and run away and hide. If that was all the men wanted, this could be the end of it.

He took a corner of the envelope, briefly stood, threw the envelope which flew directly towards the cluster of three men in the room and then turned and ran. Gerald was thinking to himself that this was the opposite of brave, but at least it gave Ben a chance and whatever was in the bag was untraceable to him.

Dave and Alan turned as the brown padded envelope slid across the floor. They couldn't make out where it had come from but assumed it had been thrown from one of the windows. "Is this the envelope?" Dave asked. "If it is, we are out of here!"

Alan looked at the package. "It's been opened," he said.

"I'm going to check what is inside". He slid the small cylinder into his hand. "Is this what we have been carrying?" he asked Dave.

"It looks special enough." replied Dave, realising that neither of them knew the original contents so this was a gamble.

Then looking back to Ben, "You are very lucky," he said to Ben, then punching him in the stomach, causing him to arch double and slide to the floor.

"C'mon," said Dave, "Let's go".

They walked out through the front door and then nonchalantly along the road back to their parked van. They would lay low until their second meeting with the Arabs.

Gerald saw the two men leave the house, he watched them as they walked back to their van. He noted the number. He would know if this van was back in the neighbourhood. Then he walked back to check on Ben.

Ben was still on the floor when he reached him. He was the worse for wear, but not a lot worse than he had been some nights when he had drunk too much cider.

"You were very lucky!", said Gerald, "They seem to have got what they needed!".

Ben nodded. "Have you got any cider?" he asked.

Containment

This time, Alan and Dave took a small car back to Ashford. It would be less conspicuous than the van and also gave them an element of surprise if they needed to make a reconnaissance of the area before meeting the Arabs. They arrived an hour early by the lay-by but kept driving as if they were heading somewhere else.

There were several large trucks parked and a couple of cars, but nothing as conspicuous as the black Mercedes from the last visit. They tried to guess the type of vehicle which would be waiting, but there was nothing obvious, like a large SUV. The trucks themselves had mainly foreign registrations, but this was perfectly normal for an area very close to the Channel Tunnel Europort.

They continued to another lay-by, a smaller one with a small snack-bar and here they simply waited until close to the appointed time. Then, with Alan driving, they crossed the road and headed back to the meeting point.

As they arrived, they could see a couple of long articulated lorries and a couple of vans. They pulled in and Dave stood up out of the car. No-one looked towards him and he decided to walk up and down the lay-by, ostentatiously banging his arms around his body, as if he was cold. This would attract oblique attention and should make it easy for the people he was to exchange with to make contact.

There was a noise behind him, and he looked around. A motorcyclist on a powerful Honda had just pulled in behind him.

The guy on the motorcycle called out, "Follow me", and revved his engine.

Dave ran slowly back to the car and exchanged a few words with Alan. They looked at each other; if this was the meeting, no-one had said anything about it being elsewhere. They decided they had really no option but to follow the biker. They didn't think anyone else could have known about the meeting.

The biker pulled out onto the road and headed back towards London, the direction they had originally come from. At the first major junction, the bike pulled off and then headed along a road to the left. They followed him and soon found themselves in a small industrial estate. In the distance they could see a couple of cars, including a Mercedes like the one that had met them the first time.

With some relief they pulled up at a small Portakabin adjacent to where the Mercedes was parked. The motor cyclist dismounted and gestured.

The Square

"Bring it with you", he said.

They looked at each other again, and Alan nodded. He had the envelope in a large concealed poacher's pocket of the Barbour waxed jacket he was wearing. They stepped from the car and followed the motor cyclist into the Portakabin. The biker had removed his helmet as he walked towards the Portakabin and Alan and Dave could see he was middle eastern, but not any of the people he had met before. They walked into the Portakabin, which was essentially one large room with some sort of annex.

Inside there were two other people, both seated. "Welcome", said the biker, "Hand over the item and you are free to go". "So why did you bring us here?", asked Dave.

"Containment," said one of the seated men. "If you have co-operated, then there will be no problem, if you have not, then we have some privacy".

Alan called out, "I am going to reach into my coat to get it".

One of the two men seated stood up as Alan said this.

"Slowly", he said.

Alan obeyed and gently took the item from his pocket and placed it on the desk in front of the still seated man. The biker reached over and picked up the envelope and very gently shook the contents onto the desk. The metallic tube rolled momentarily and then stopped. The three strangers all looked at one another. The biker said, "Okay, you can go".

Alan said, "Our money? you still owe us half...".

The biker responded, "You have your lives, go now, before we change our minds".

Alan and Dave decided this was probably their safest option and moved towards the door. They had still made £300,000 for a relatively small amount of delivery work. They hurried for the door, and then jumped back in their car to make their exit.

"I think we have just been very lucky," said Dave.

Back inside the Portakabin, the three occupants watched as Dave and Alan drove away.

"Well done, Mohammed," said Robert Alton, "That was excellent, now what have we actually retrieved?".

Muhammad smiled. If it had not been for Karen's discovery the previous day, they would not be this far along with their investigation. And now the extra SI6 men outside of the Portakabin had a tracker bug on Dave and Alan's car, so they could track them and pull them in at any time, if they needed more information.

. . .

There was a moment of silence in the Portakabin after Dave and Alan had left. Then Robert Alton emerged from the back office.

"So, we have a chemical vial full of Lord knows what," he started, "and a consignment bound from the Eurolink by truck to the Middle East. We will need to intercept the truck and retrieve the contents."

"In the meantime, we need to get the current sample analysed by a safe chemical facility. I suspect we need to send this to Porton Down, it could have anything inside."

At this time Alton suspected it was something very unpleasant but didn't know for sure. He could tell by the container that this was not something to be idly opened.

"We should pull in Andy and Dave," he said, looking at the evidence in front of him.

Andy and Dave were barely two miles from the Portakabin when they ran into the roadblock. It was a full military situation, and they knew better than to to try to drive past it. A single soldier was asking them to stop, but they could see other firepower immediately to the side and behind him.

"What seems to be the problem?" asked Alan. "Please just step out of the vehicle", came the reply, "and put your hands on your head."

Both Dave and Alan exited the car. They were frightened now and not sure if the soldiers were real or another part of some kind of deception. But the guns looked real enough so now was not the time to argue.

"Please step into the van," instructed one of the soldiers, "We will need to ask you a few questions."

Dave and Alan were transported to the large secure SI6 facility where the Arabs were under detention. They were taken to a different area for cross examination.

The key information required was a description of the vehicle used to transport the other vials. Alan was able to be very helpful here, because he had written down the number of the first truck when they had met.

"Here's the information." he said, handing over a small notebook. He had taken several notes during the job, more as insurance in case anything was to go wrong, but he had not expected things to develop the way the last few hours had been progressing.

"We do have a truck registration", he said, "Its Polish and the number is STO 792" he added. "I wrote it down when we transferred the first set of envelopes to the Arabs."

"And when was that?" asked his interrogator, smiling.

"Er, look, we are just drivers. This was a well-paid van delivery, that's all," continued Dave, "The original job was to get some packets from London to Ashford in the van. Somehow one went missing and we had to go back for it. The first exchange was yesterday. We were given 24 hours to put it right, so we just drove back to London, found the missing package and returned."

Dave looked earnestly at his interrogator. "Really, that's all I know."

The interrogator looked at Dave. The room was wired for sound and vision. He said to Dave and the cameras, "Okay, I'm going outside for a few minutes. Is there anything we can get you?"

"What, like a coffee or something," asked Dave, "Am I going to be here much longer?"

"I'm afraid so," answered the interrogator, "Actually, I don't think you'd last very long outside at the moment."

Dave looked concerned, "And what about Alan?" he asked, "When can I see him?"

The interrogator looked at Dave. "I'll see if I can get you some coffee," he replied.

Outside, Robert Alton and Mohammed had already compared the stories from Dave and Alan. They were almost word perfect, except that Alan didn't know the truck registration.

"Small time." said Alton, "And they seem to be telling the truth."

Mohammed nodded, "The truck registration is a lucky breakthrough."

"Yes, we are on to it," replied Alton, "Although, they will have done a switch by now, either in the tunnel or as soon as they got to France."

Ed Adams

RIGHT NOW

Strong women

Take this pink ribbon off my eyes
I'm exposed
And it's no big surprise
Don't you think I know
Exactly where I stand
This world is forcing me
To hold your hand

'Cause I'm just a girl, little ol' me
Well don't let me out of your sight
Oh, I'm just a girl, all pretty and petite
So don't let me have any rights
Oh, I've had it up to here!

Gwen Stefani

Elisa Solomons

Jake had decided to take Clare and Bigsy along to the next meeting with Chuck. He knew Chuck would expect this and it would anyway be easier to remember the complexities of the next stage of what they were being tasked to do.

"Why on earth has Chuck picked such a busy bar to meet?" said Bigsy. They were on a corner of Sloane Square in a bar heaving with an early evening crowd.
"It was my idea actually," said Jake, "I thought we could meet here and then immediately go to somewhere else. It reduces the chance we are being followed."

"That's not such a bad plan," said Clare, "I'm having flashbacks to our scrapes in Zurich."

"Yes - we just need to find Chuck and then we are on our way,"

At that moment, Chuck appeared leaving the doorway of an adjacent building. He was with someone else, a slim, attractive woman in a neat dark business suit. She was carrying a small bag and also a laptop case. Chuck appeared to be carrying a bulky camouflage coloured rucksack.

The Square

"Hi Chuck," called Jake. "Great to meet again and punctual as ever, you remember Clare and Bigsy?"
"Indeed, I do and hello everyone, let me introduce my colleague Elisa to you all".

They each shook hands and were about to find a way into the busy bar when Jake said, "Let's move. I know a great pastry shop nearby."

Bigsy smiled. He was already thinking about whether to have Black Forest Gateau or Double Chocolate Dream Gateau.

"I thought we could be more - er - alone - in the cafe."

Chuck nodded.

"Lead on."

"It's less than five minutes walk from here, across the Square."

Bigsy led the way, and the others fell into step. Clare chatted to Elisa about the area, and the fairly fancy shops close by. Bigsy and Chuck chatted about Stuttgart, which was where Chuck had been staying just before the call from London.

Jake looked behind as they walked, and then to left and right. There didn't appear to be anyone following. He noticed Chuck doing something similar.

Within a few minutes they had arrived at the patisserie.
"Not your most likely meeting place to hatch a plot?" said Jake.

"There's no place out of bounds," smiled Chuck.

They pulled two small four-person tables together, ordered some coffees and talked.

"Everyone, this is Elisa, or should I say Doctor Elisa Solomons. We have known one another for many years. When the recent situation that I've described to Jake came up, I thought I'd ask Elisa if she had any insights."

Elisa smiled, "I have known Chuck since a time almost ten years ago when he helped me with a big problem. I worked in a chemical facility in North Carolina. Unknown to me, I was being targeted for some retribution based upon another scientist that had died. It is crazy, but there's another kind of brain drain based around eliminating some scientists considered being working on things that could be classed as advanced weaponry. Someone had blown up an Iranian nuclear scientist with a car bomb. He wasn't the first to be killed. Maybe the fourth. The response each time was to look for a victim. I didn't realise it, but I had become a target."

"Why?" asked Clare, "What do you do?"

"What I did wasn't in any way dangerous. I was trying to find stabilisers for some forms of viral disease. It was mis-communicated that I was working on neuro-toxins. Then I met Chuck. It was at an airport actually, in a line waiting for a delayed plane. He started chatting politely to me and as we both had time to kill, I didn't initially think much of it."

Chuck looked serious faced as Elisa explained her story.
"Then he took me to one side and explained who he was. That he worked for the US Government and that he had been tasked with protecting me. I didn't believe it at first - thought he was some kind of crank," she smiled across the table to him and he

smiled back, "but he had a dossier of information about me and also a set of intelligence reports about the other scientists that had been assassinated."

"I was pretty freaked out by the whole thing, but then he said he would make the problem go away. I thought there's no way he can stop a determined set of assassins from targeting me and I couldn't face long-term protection."

She paused and looked across to Chuck again. "Chuck's plan was simple."

"Let me guess," interrupted Clare, "He would have you killed, anyway?"

Elisa nodded, "I can see you all know Chuck. That was his plan. He had located a cell supposed to be tracking me and would let them think they had blown me up."

"Wasn't that kind of 'elaborate' to achieve?" asked Jake.

"It was," interrupted Chuck, "But Elisa is a precious asset."

"Melodrama aside, Chuck is right," said Elisa, "the research I do is for the right and ethical reasons. It also means I am one of a few people who understand some man-made neurotoxins created in the era of the Cold War and beyond. Most of it is illegal now, but the USA and a few other countries like to have people around that can fast path the route to antidotes."

"Elisa is one of those people," said Chuck, "So, although she was being targeted for the wrong reasons, she was still someone we would very much want to protect."

"Cutting a long story short," continued Elisa, "I was then blown up in a very messy car bomb explosion whilst travelling through Nigeria."

"It was a perfect cover story," said Chuck, "and removed Elisa from circulation."

"You weren't called Elisa then?" asked Clare.

"No," answered Elisa. "The problem with all of this is that I had to get a complete new identity and move to another country. I chose U.K. And I don't think anyone else knows what you've just been told."

Chuck nodded, "I was the only person permitted to know Elisa's ongoing identity and also became the link should there ever be a need to call on Elisa's services to support a toxin related problem."

"So why now?" asked Jake.

"There's been some developments," replied Chuck. "The missile I was hunting wasn't a missile."

"No, it was some form of neuro-toxin being carried in a truck," replied Elisa.

"How so?" asked Clare.

"For the first time since my demise in the car bombing, someone has asked to speak to me via Chuck. It can only mean one thing. There's a neuro toxin agent on the loose."
"This is all sounding too Science Fiction!" said Jake.

The Square

"This is what I've put together so far," said Chuck.

"Firstly, I'm asked to visit the desert. To destroy a missile. I try, but someone gets there first."

"Secondly, When I look at the transport, the explosion is way too large to be from a dormant missile."

"Third, the people that blow up the truck are from Israel."

"Fourth, the whole thing is ultra-sensitive."

"Fifth, I get asked to restart a link to Elisa."

"This is what we think has happened," continued Elisa.

"Someone created a toxin; it's too dangerous to keep. It gets destroyed, except, someone keeps a small quantity on file for the records."

"The toxin gets stolen or released and everyone sees how dangerous it is. It gets passed along to be destroyed, but somehow gets stolen in the process. They call me to help them figure out how to contain and destroy it."

"So did the truck in the desert have a missile on it?" asked Jake.

"I was told it did when I was out there. The truck was carrying a set of disabled neurotoxin canisters."

"So why not just let the various government agencies clean this up?" asked Jake.

"That's what I thought initially," answered Chuck, "but then I realised that there was a power play in all of this. My guess is that some of the people involved in this see the toxin as a form of leverage. Someone I was speaking to from SI6 said that the toxin can be deployed from a MIRV."

"Eh?" asked Clare.

"Yes, a Multiple Independently-targetable Reentry Vehicle or MIRV - that's exactly what we are dealing with, and what I originally thought was on the transport." answered Chuck.

"They were originally developed in the early '60s to permit a missile to deliver multiple nuclear warheads to different targets. We used to test them in the desert, around Nevada. Not just our own ones, we also had some captured Russian ones.

"For instance, a Russian MIRV missile could carry up to 16 warheads, each in a separate re-entry vehicle. Warheads on MIRV missiles can be released from the missile at different speeds and in different directions. Some MIRV missiles can hit targets as far as 1,500 kilometres apart.

Then we had some land-based ones too, they were particularly destabilizing, because it was a game of cat and mouse to find them.

The common consensus was that development of MIRV technology was difficult. A combination of large missiles, small warheads, accurate guidance, and a complex mechanism for releasing warheads sequentially during flight.

That's why it is likely that the truck would have both the missile and some warheads on board. It would also explain the absolute intensity of the strike by the helicopter, to destroy absolutely everything.

"I'm afraid that points to one thing, said Elisa, "That the warheads were not conventional, not even fissile. It points to them being biological."

"What?" said Bigsy, "So the truck was pulling a set of biological warheads across the desert, the sort that can be used in a MIRV?"

"Yes, " answered Elisa, "And the individual warheads will be deadly by themselves. It becomes a case of using a different delivery mechanism."

"That's right," said Chuck, "We used to test both long range delivery and asymmetric delivery, using something like a truck-bomb."

"The truck bomb was supposed to be a poor man's cruise missile, but trust me, it was effective."

"If we envisage one of these small units in a truck and then it driven to a specific location, then anything could happen?" asked Clare.

"Yes," said Elisa, "But for one safety mechanism. Usually these weapons are digitally encoded, to fail safe. That means that inside them is a safety component. If the canister is tampered, the safety explodes and destroyed the payload. Similarly, without priming, these warheads can't be detonated. The same safety mechanisms cut in to destroy the warhead content."

"Yes, ever since the 1960s, Failsafe has been a big deal with the more advanced weapons," added Chuck, "Remember the dead-man's handle on trains or the cut-off on lawnmowers? It's the same idea."

"Yes," although one of these would mow an awful lot of grass if in the wrong hands," added Jake.

"So what is this about now?" asked Bigsy, "Leverage?"

"Yes, I can see that," answered Clare. "He who controls the missing weapon has a lot of power."

"Yes, the ability to make all kinds of demands," answered Chuck, "Now I don't want to be all self-righteous about this but I'm fearful if we don't put an end to this then there could some serious power brokering from unpredictable sources."

"Do you think the US and UK governments are mixed up with this?" asked Clare.

"Almost certainly, and for their own ends," answered Chuck, "Hence the need for stealth."

"So, here's my supposition," continued Elisa.

"When I lived in Tel-Aviv, I used to work with the Israeli government on virus research. The funding provided by the government to this was exceptional and it was a great place to work."

"My own research was purely medical-related and was looking for advances in immunology. I knew many of the other scientists and although we didn't talk directly about the classified material, it was obvious that there was another group working on munitions style virus product. - A reverse take on scientists that build and those that destroy. This was science to kill and science looking for an antidote."

"At some point one of the labs was closed down completely. We were told it was electrical problems, but everyone knew it was a toxin related closedown. The whole lab system had to be sealed off. I wasn't directly involved in any of it but several people I knew were and they looked pretty scared about what had taken place."

"And then I noticed that the team were all transferred away. It was overnight, and they just disappeared. I have not heard from any of them since."

"So how did this link to the threat to you?" asked Clare.

"It didn't," answered Elisa.

"But I did spend some time thinking about what seemed to have happened."

"They were making something nasty and then disappeared?" asked Clare, glancing towards Chuck.

Elisa continued, "Clare's right. They were working on a type of biological weapon. Using some form of airborne viral carrier - which is actually more difficult than it sounds. Let me explain."

"A virus is a piece of genetic information a bit like the way DNA works. It is packaged in an envelope of proteins or lipids sometimes including sugars. Viruses cannot live by themselves but must be able to quickly get into a plant or animal cells to survive."

"These viruses use the energy metabolism and the biosynthetic machinery of the host cell to replicate themselves. It is like they harness the existing biological machinery of their host"

Jake interjected, "Like a sort of parasite?"

Elisa nodded, "It's similar, during the phase of replication inside the host cell - we scientists call it a eukaryotic cell - a virus makes a copy of its RNA or DNA and from that copy duplicates itself."

"It's quite a clever process, because it also makes extra enzymes so that it can build a protective envelope while it is working."

"I know about DNA, what's RNA?", asked Clare.

"If you know about DNA, you'll remember it has a special structure - the 'double helix' - RNA, which stands for Ribonucleic acid is a similar type of molecule, but without the double helix structure. It's used by living things to make more protein and to keep DNA structures called ribosomes regulated."

"Whoa - here comes the science part!" joked Jake.

"Jake!", Clare jabbed Jake in the ribs and looked towards Elisa to continue.

"Yes, there is some more science," said Elisa,

"The three-dimensional structures of RNA molecules show architectural motifs exploited for the design of artificial RNA nanomaterials.

"Put simply, at present , scientists can only create RNA objects in certain shapes. One of these at a tiny size of 2.2 Ångstrom is a square-shaped nanoobject made entirely of double-stranded RNA.

The RNA square is comprised of 100 residues and self-assembles from four copies each of two oligonucleotides of 10 and 15 bases length.

You have to imagine the programmed self-assembly of RNA squares from complex mixtures of corner units to build the RNA square as a combinatorial platform. It's that square shape that can regulate the nerve agent.

In other words, the same biological machine that can replicate nerve agent can also hold it in check?" asked Bigsy.

"Yes, that's why they call the agents tertiaries. A base agent. A reactant and then a suppressant."

Bigsy nodded. Elisa continued, "There's been a lot of speculation around forms of virus that can be airborne but also managed. Most people have heard of the Ebola virus in parts of Africa. It's been in movies as well, but actually even that virus really needs contact with living matter in order to spread. It's usually through the contamination of cuts or similar that create the spread and airborne spread is quite unusual because the virus can't survive."

"But what had been secretly happening in the labs was a series of defence-based investigations of ways to create airborne payloads of virus. This wasn't just being run by the Israelis, but also actually by a consortium of interests. The reason had been stated as defensive. To determine the virus effectiveness as a threat - and just as importantly, what techniques can be used as a way to stop it."

"...And the answer?", asked Clare, "How do you stop it?"

"That's the point," continued Elisa,

"There isn't a good answer. So far nature has been fairly kind to humanity on all of this."

"The really nasty viruses affecting humans won't travel by air alone. Ones that mutate heavily and are quite infectious - like influenza - will travel for a short time by air and exceptionally can kill but are generally less lethal.

"A combination of an airborne toxin with lethal characteristics has only happened a couple of times."

"Once was Anthrax - which was strictly a spore based biological weapon - and that had erratic, but deadly contagion characteristics. There were also a few US Chemical Corps attempts with fleas and mosquitoes as delivery mechanisms back in the 1950s."

"I see," said Clare, "The virus was actually hosted on something else, like the spore or the bug? So, it had some cells to keep it working whilst it travelled?"

"Exactly," said Elisa, "The spores and mosquitos were the delivery mechanism, and in each case, they were unpredictable to the extent that the whole process had to be stopped."

"Yes, and that Scottish Island with Anthrax is still off limits all these years later?" replied Clare.

"Let's say I don't think there's a line of people waiting to explore the island…" said Elisa.

"What evolved though from the various experiences, was a different delivery mechanism. It had to be fast acting over a small area and limited in terms of its long-term effect."

"They evolved a 'glass bomb' full of a compressed toxin protected by its surrounding enzyme. The virus had to be created just before use, because without its host it had a very short shelf life."

"The bomb could be broken and then spread toxicity at up to 50% for maybe a few square miles. Contagion would need to be within the first hour for it to be effective. Anyone affected would die but continue to be a host, creating a chain reaction in the area surrounding the release of the substance."

"A second timed capsule would release an antidote, which worked by breaking down the enzyme envelope that kept the virus protected as a way to limit the spread."
"It sounds awful, but entirely imaginable," said Clare.

"Is this work still taking place?" asked Bigsy.

"Not officially, actually it was Richard Nixon who ended the research in the late sixties."

"A long time ago. Surely there's not anything left?", queried Jake.

"Actually, there were a lot of people involved and they were effectively stopped from their main lines of research. Some of them may well have drifted off the rails since." added Elisa.

"Officially, there's been a virtual ban on this type of research since the nineteen-seventies, so that a sequel to atomic bombs was effectively stopped."

"Yeah, right", said Jake, "but how would anyone know?"

"Exactly," continued Elisa, "The Soviets and then the Iraqis continued with programmes. A Russian defector named their Biopreparat programme and then later its deputy director also defected to the USA."

"It's much harder to know what the Iraqis were doing, although they did admit to the U.N. that they had produced concentrated botulinum toxin during the first Persian Gulf War. The amount they produced was enough to wipe out the planet, except for the same distribution problem I mentioned with the viruses."

"So, what are we looking at here?", interrupted Clare. "It looks as if there's someone making a weapon which is some sort of virus. It can't survive for long in the air, but if it can be carried, then it could do a great deal of harm."

"Exactly," said Elisa, "It's the scenario we were simulating for years. A virus, effective airborne for short times and capable of being carried over other distances by a host such as an insect, without destroying its host in the process. It also needs to be stable and not modify itself, or else it becomes the new God of the planet."

They looked at one another.

"This is kind of doomsday," said Jake.

"Correct", added Elisa, "When we ran our scenarios, the only fully effective defence was to destroy it within the first hour, using the enzyme cracker. "

"Won't the people producing it have the same concerns about using it?", asked Clare.

"It's difficult to comment. Extremists, lunatics, mercenaries, criminals, people with nothing to lose. They may all take a different world view on such matters. We don't know what we are dealing with."

Elisa absently stirred the coffee cup and looked at the pattern on the surface.

"So how does it get used?" asked Bigsy. "It sounds almost too powerful to release?"

Chuck leaned forward. "There are three main scenarios. Sell it on, use it as threat or monetize it"

"I can understand the 'sell it on' scenario," said Clare, "but if it's such an unpredictable threat then who would actually use it?"

"That's where dealing with terrorists and criminals is so unpredictable," answered Chuck, "Sometimes ordinary logic doesn't work, plus there will be 'spin' from whoever holds the toxin. They will make it all sound safe and containable."

"Yes," continued Elisa, "the advanced work I was involved with in Israel before I was targeted was looking into the types of deterrent for this class of weapon. It was often a case of scientists trying to copy nature - something I thought was massively dangerous."

"Nowadays I look closely at news of new influenza strains or sudden crop devastation. That 2019-nCoV 'bat-bug' from Wuhan, China was a case in point. Did it display any of the characteristics of something engineered? Is it a cover-up because something has broken out of a lab somewhere?"

"What did you think?" asked Bigsy

"Well, it looks natural rather than machined. By using the Chinese virus as an example, we can see that nature is ingenious and has evolved the coronaviruses as large, enveloped, positive-sense, single-stranded RNA viruses that can infect both animals and humans. It's not been in the news, but there's four kinds, Alpha-, Beta-, Gamma-, and Delta-coronavirus. But all the CoVs that can infect humans belong to the first two types. The trick is to be able to store them somewhere and that's where the bat's DNA comes along as an ideal storage container. Let's remember that the bat has been around for 50 million years."

"Wow, plenty of time to get robust!" said Jake.

"Yes, don't get me started on spiders. They've been around for 380 million years," replied Elisa.

Chuck interrupted, "So I suppose what will have happened with the scientist development is the development of some kind of science-based storage container for the weaponised virus?"

"That's right," said Elisa, "Probably non organic, to keep the virus stable rather than see it further adapt,"

She continued, "We classify bioweapons by type. Toxins just kill everything in the radius. Herbicides like 'wheat blast' just take out the food stock in the fields. Neither of these are the type we are describing here"

"The one we are dealing with here is more sophisticated. It can be used selectively, targeted, do huge damage, but there can be an immunity vaccine. This one can be used to hold a planet to ransom."

"When I was at Ben Gurion University we developed and trialled something called the BioPen. It was originally a field diagnostic for many classes of chemo and bio attack - to help identify the type of weapon being used.

"The original pen used a technology called multiwells. They are microscopically small holes like mini test-tubes used to scan and detect the enzymes used in a biohazard. I think they are called microplates now, after some copyright fracas."

"The BioPen with these diagnostics could tell you what you were up against but it wasn't a cure."

"Then we worked out that if we knew the make-up of a viral hazard, we could use the same technology to deliver antibody enzymes. Basically, the BioPen could be modified to detect and immunise. It could be turned from a diagnostic into a field defence."

"So, as Chuck says, if someone wants to deploy the virus or to 'monetize' it then the modified BioPen becomes part of the process. It's either to provide immunity to the people deploying the virus, or to sell the antidote to the population being affected. The BioPen technology is what keeps it in balance."

"Is that like you see in the movies?" asked Clare. "The magic syringe that fixes everything?"

"I wish it were that simple," continued Elisa.

"We can't predict side effects. When it is viral, just like the flu bug or HIV, there's a type of modification which can occur. It's the natural mutation of the virus. Those that built this bioweapon know they have a tiger by the tail. It can be used as they intend it, or it could start to behave differently."

"The point with viruses is that they modify and unless you know enough about them you could spend years trying to figure a cure."

"That's why weapon-grade virus research was originally stopped. They could create the toxin, but no antidote. Except for the enzyme work linked to the pen. But the pen also relies upon knowing how the original virus had been constructed. Basically, you have a window to deploy and destroy."

Chuck interrupted "Exactly as Elisa describes it, there's a short time when you know what you are dealing with and can stop it."

Elisa nodded, "Yes, that's where mankind can't be as clever as nature. In a natural virus, it will self-modify but then stop once it has found a way to inhabit its host but keeo the host alive. The payoff for the virus is that it can persist for longer. A man-made virus won't have this check and balance. Just the BioPen to stop it."

"So, destruction at source is the only answer."

Elisa added, "Strictly there are still some other checks and balances:

One: Don't let the toxin get primed - hence the binary transport. Two: Use of the BioPen as an antidote. Three" The decay period of the toxin being short - like one hour.
They are all equally effective safeguards against the latest neuro-toxin."

Chuck stirred his coffee for the fourth time.

"Look, I'll be accompanying Elisa back to her home, "She's not implicated in this at all but I wanted to get a sense of the situation from her. Elisa, I'm sure you'll be wanting to help us further?"

"Sure, Chuck, I just hope the scientists knew enough about what they were doing to build the virus in a way that keeps it stable. It's the best chance we have to destroy it."

A moment of silence and then Jake spoke.

"Er, so just what is it you want us to do again? This has got a lot wilder as each day passes."

He looked towards Chuck, who was working out what to say.

" Jake, it's the same deal. I just need you to run a diversion for me. I'll be meeting the main people involved with this and you'll be creating some separate theatre for the Secret Service to watch. When I get the information about the placement of the real toxin, I'll be bringing it in to be destroyed using the BioPen method that Elisa has described.

"The thing is, I'll want to know that every container has been neutralised so that we don't get back into the same situation. I don't want this to go through the normal channels because I'm afraid of the interceptions that could take place, whether it is US, Brit, Arab or Israeli, government or terrorist. Everyone's combined motive is to get to the material as a source of power and leverage. I just want it destroyed."

"There's a lot of American history around these neurotoxins actually," said Elisa.

"There were a couple of strains developed by the Americans at the time of the second Gulf War. They were called C1 and C2 (Yes, there is also a C3) and they were built to attempt to simulate the type of product that Saddam Hussain would be using.

Chuck said, "I remember that; gossip had it that they could even be used as a plant for WMD if things got really embarrassing. Morality prevailed and they were never shipped into Iraq, although the product was moved as far as Saudi Arabia, where they were stored on a USAF base near to Riyadh. I was still in the desert then, in the USA, and we had some contact with these so-called chemical and biological weapons."

Chuck added, "If I remember rightly, the Saudis were never informed. All comms related to this was at the highest and most secure level.

"Urban myth says the information leak was originally via a secret project called Room 641A. This was a splitter closet in San Francisco used for covert monitoring of signal intelligence.

"It's a fairly crude form of digital wiretap, to split the signal in half and send half to its proper destination and the rest to the NSA."

"Incredible," said Bigsy, "But I suppose the most blatant things can win out. Like those guys who built the trading intercepts for the flash trading on stock markets."

 Elisa continued, "So a stream of discussion about C1 and C2 (also known as BK238) was initiated and tracked. There's another one, by the way, the well-known Novichok, which is categorised as A234."

"Ah yes, the Russian Wikipedia-loving assassins in Salisbury!" said Jake.

Elisa continued, "Right, and then the person monitoring the source used the ageing NIS (Narus Intercept Suite) to track down the calls and their purpose under the auspices of CALEA (Communications Intercept for Law Enforcement). It's old enough to have been something that Clinton's administration had originally set up for wiretapping but had extended to many matters of national security.

"In today's digital world, these all seem to be lightweight ways to provide the intelligence, so I'm assuming that there's better stuff available that hasn't leaked into the public domain.

"Anyway, on this occasion, the person had discovered what looked like a covert shipment of toxins to Saudi Arabia, without realising it was US DoD that was actioning the request.

"Ahah, said Bigsy, "So it is not just the US who use splitter programs and intercepts?"

"No, Bigsy, I don't think it would be a technical intercept. More likely to have been a human one this time," answered Elisa.

"The person had forwarded an alert under the PRISM surveillance program (SIGAD US-984XN) to the NSA but used his own grade level for the initial communication. The message had contained the phrase 'BK238' and its location in clear text.

"So a clear communication was intercepted? No wonder the US are sheepish about this!" said Bigsy.

"Yes, it was all that Al Aktar had needed to mobilise from within Saudi Arabia. A barracks was targeted with a conventional truck bomb as a diversion and a regular US Army vehicle with American mercenaries was dispatched to collect the cylinders from their safe store.

"The base had been pre-occupied with the bombing. The cylinder transit looked routine and the trucks had been able to drive from the base unchallenged. This all happened about three weeks ago."

"Yes," said Chuck, "But Al Aktar have done more than steal the neurotoxin." They have also stolen the smaller vials containing the antidote."

"Antidote?" asked Clare.

"Yes, the antidote can be used in a combat situation to neutralise the effect of the neurotoxin," answered Elisa, "It's not a perfect science, but it allows troops to be dropped into the kill-zone before the toxin has decayed."

"Ew," said Clare, "It's disgusting, like spraying people with fly killer and then going in to watch the effects."

"Yes, that is why we scientists were working to eradicate these kinds of terrible weapons," answered Elisa.

"Not to mention the small matter of them being illegal in just about every country," said Chuck, "You can see why a few superpowers are trying to make the whole situation go away."

"Yes, and why a few countries are now desperate to hide the fact that they have continued to work on this kind of weapon," added Clare.

Mesopotamian Heritage?

"Tell me about Al Aktar," asked Clare to Chuck, "You must know more about their origins?"

"Yes, it's deeper than Al Aktar, and goes back to the Iraqi mindset," replied Chuck, "The Al Aktar people had thoughts which went back much further than the war driven by George Bush.

"This group believed themselves to be part of the Iraqi Mesopotamian heritage, which was home to the Sumerian culture, dating back to 5000 BC. So, these should be smart people, with some of the first sciences and mathematics originating from the cradle of civilization.

"Wow, that's going back a long way," added Bigsy.

Chuck continued, "Later came Islam, with the prophet Mohammed's cousin and son-in-law moving his capital to Kufa "fi al-Iraq" when he became the fourth caliph.

The Square

"That's the start of the rise of Baghdad?" questioned Clare.

Chuck answered, "Yes, This led to Baghdad being the leading city of the Arab and Muslim world for five centuries but then, as early as the mid thirteenth century, Baghdad was devastated by the Mongols and later occupied by the Ottoman Turks.

"Such conflict would become a facet of this area, but the Ottoman Empire lasted right the way through until World War I when the Ottomans sided with Germany and were later driven from the area by the United Kingdom.

"For true Ottomans, this was only a short time to remember and British control of Mesopotamia with a United nations mandate created a lasting sense of colonial rule.

"Yes, that's the period I know more about," said Bigsy, "Iran under British rule,"

Chuck continued, "Occupation would be a better word. During the British occupation, the country was ruled by British administrators who used British armed forces to put down rebellions against the government. They selected the Hashemite king, Faisal, who had been forced out of Syria by the French, to be their client ruler.

"Between World War I and II, Iraq was granted independence, though the British retained military bases and transit rights for their forces in the country.

"King Ghazi of Iraq ruled as a figurehead after King Faisal died in 1932, while Iraq suffered from military coups until he died in 1939.

"This was all about the oil?" Asked Clare.

"Yes," said Chuck, "This led to the start of the fears of oil cutbacks and Iraq was again invaded by the United Kingdom in 1941, for fears that the government of Rashid Ali might cut oil supplies to Western nations and because of his strong leanings to Nazi Germany."

"Hmm, tricky," said Bigsy.

Chuck continued, "You could say that - A military occupation followed after the restoration of the Hashemite monarchy and this lasted until 1947. This reinstalled monarchy lasted until 1958, when it was once again overthrown through a coup d'état by the Iraqi Army, known as the 14 July Revolution."

"The coup brought Brigadier General Abdul Karim Qassim to power. He withdrew from the Baghdad Pact and established friendly relations with the Soviet Union but his government lasted only until 1963, when it was overthrown by Colonel Abdul Salam Arif."

"I think we must be nearly up to the Saddam Hussein era?" asked Clare.

Elisa nodded.

Chuck continued, "Yes, that's right. After Salam Arif's death his brother, Abdul Rahman Arif, assumed the presidency but was soon overthrown by the Arab Socialist Ba'ath Party. This movement gradually came under the control of Saddam Hussein al-Majid al Tikriti who acceded to the presidency and control of the Revolutionary Command Council (RCC), then Iraq's supreme executive body, in July 1979, killing off many of his opponents in the process."

The Square

"Saddam Hussein's rule lasted throughout the Iran-Iraq War (1980-1988) (in which the United States, Soviet Union, and France backed Saddam Hussein after 1982, at least in the open), a war that ended in stalemate.

"That backing of Hussein was because of oil?" asked Clare.

"Yes, strategic importance of the region," answered Chuck.

"In the late 1980s, Saddam Hussein's regime launched the so-called al-Anfal campaign (it means Spoils of War), which led to the disappearance of tens of thousands of Kurds (182,000 is the number given by Kurdish authorities for the year 1988 alone) in northern Iraq when the military razed thousands of villages, launched poison gas attacks and rounded up men, women and children before shooting them or burying them alive in mass graves."

"Note the poison gas, used this time," said Chuck, "It was instrumental in firing up new research by other countries."

"Yes, said Elisa, "Although there's a couple of aspects. There were some countries that had buried their research in deep cover. Other countries thought they would need some kind of R and D capacity for purely defensive measures."

Chuck continued, "Then, in 1990 Iraq invaded Kuwait resulting in the Gulf War and United Nations economic sanctions imposed at the urging of the U.S.

It left the U.S. In something of a quandary, having backed Hussein previously but now forced to turn against him.

The economic sanctions were designed to compel Saddam to dispose of weapons of mass destruction.

By that we mean the chemical and nerve agent weapons. Critics estimate that between 400,000 and 800,000 Iraqi children died as a result of the sanctions."

"The U.S. and the U.K. declared no-fly zones over Kurdish northern and Shiite southern Iraq to oversee the Kurds and southern Shiites."

"Iraq was invaded in March 2003 by a US-organised coalition with the stated reasons that Iraq had not abandoned its nuclear and chemical weapons development program according to United Nations resolutions."

"The justifications given for invasion included purported Iraqi government links to Al Qaeda, claims that Iraq had Weapons of Mass Destruction, the opportunity to remove an oppressive dictator from power, and the bringing of democracy to Iraq."

"That was all over the media, of course," said Clare, "But many people suspected that it was misleading."

"Yes," said Chuck, "A range of other possible motives include control over Iraqi oil fields, a desire to make amends for failing to overthrow Saddam during the Gulf war, revenge for Saddam's effort to assassinate former President George Bush, and creating a counterbalance to a nuclear-armed Iranian theocracy."

"There was even a theory that the war generated business for the U.S. based reconstruction contractors," added Bigsy.

Chuck nodded and then continued, "Subsequent post-invasion investigation did not uncover any evidence that the WMD programs were active; although some chemical shells were found that were left over from the Iran-Iraq War. Likewise, al-Qaeda had no presence in Iraq, where it had been suppressed by the secular Iraqi government, until after the invasion, when it exploited the insurgency to establish its organisation in the country.

"What about the rumours that America had WMDs stashed in Saudi Arabia and was going to plant them in Iraq?" asked Bigsy.

"Well, there's no evidence of that either," said Chuck, "Although these recent neuro-toxin findings make me begin to wonder."

Chuck continued, "The US established the Coalition Provisional Authority to govern Iraq. Government authority was transferred to an Iraqi Interim Government in 2004 and a permanent government was elected in January 2006.

"By 2006, over 140,000 Coalition troops remained in Iraq in order to assist the government in countering a Sunni-led insurgency, frequent terrorist attacks, and sectarian violence, which plagued the country.

"Then, in 2006, Foreign Policy Magazine named Iraq as the fourth most unstable nation in the world. I guess that is around when Al Aktar decided it was time to make their statements and to recover what they considered to be the state of Mesopotamia."

Chuck's involvement

"Chuck," asked Jake, "How come you're fighting the good fight alone on this one? You are usually tasked by a government."

"I have a history with this program," answered Chuck.

"I didn't realise it until Elisa's name came up again, but then I realised that the reason they had originally got me to protect Elisa was because of the biological work they were doing.

"Elisa isn't the only one, but the fact is, there's a set of scientists that have been kept on retention alongside the continuation of the bioweapon research. I hadn't realised it, but by helping Elisa I was also helping preserve this bioweapon threat. This is my way to settle things and clear up a mess."

"Are you acting independently?" asked Clare.

"Yes, well that is, I'm acting with you if you will support me."

The Square

"So not for a government or paymaster? And the end result is that the biohazard is destroyed?" asked Clare.

"Correct. This is one of my few completely self-run missions. And for the record, Chuck's Mission Guide 101 says 'Don't do self-run missions."

"That's why I need to keep it close. No-one will know any of you. Apart from the original 'Triangle' connection we have never been in contact."

"And we are not in danger?" added Bigsy.

"You should be okay. I will be in danger," said Chuck, "And the end result will be the removal of the threat. Completely."

"What are we supposed to do?" Asked Jake.

Chuck continued, "There will be a meeting. A sort of trade show where the owners of the weapon state their terms. It will be set up to look like an innocuous event. Just that the people there will be special."

"I'd like you to go along and to listen out for what is happening. It shouldn't be too difficult. They'll have some entertainment and that will make it easy for us to get some electronics in."

"We could provide the entertainment," said Clare, "we have the media contacts and I could pull some strings to get to the front of the line."

"It'd be with Christina Nott - who is a singer in any case. If you can help us find out how they intend to run this, then we can hook into the event management."

Chuck looked confused. Jake had never seen this before.

"It's not really my area," said Manners.

"No, but it is ours," answered Clare. "Let me get on to it."

"Do you need time to consider this?" asked Manners.

"We should, we need to know that Christina Nott is prepared to be in on it."

"Give us until tomorrow," said Clare, "Does Jake no how to contact you?"

"Put an entry on your website," said Chuck. Mention the word "Square" if it's a go or "Circle" if it's a no-go."

"I can do that," said Bigsy. "It'll be in the top article on the home page."

"By tomorrow, please," said Chuck, and then we will follow the process I've described to Jake."

"Basically, that I'll get a phone call with some instructions," answered Jake.

"Correct," said Chuck, "The coffees and pastries are on me." He stepped to the cash till, paid and waved to them, still seated.

They returned the gesture, slightly surprised at Chuck's sudden speedy exit.

"Man of action, even when eating cakes!" quipped Jake.

The Square

Bigsy grinned as he finished the last mouthful of Clare's chocolate dream cake.

"I told you this was large," said Bigsy.

"The cake? I got it for you," said Clare.

Jake turned to Clare and Bigsy, "Well, what do you think? This one seems crazier than ever."

"Yes, Chuck doesn't lead dull life, does he?" answered Bigsy.

"But he does have a twinkle in his eye when he asks us for help. I think he likes us," said Clare as she left the cafe.

"Oh, that's good to know, what could possibly go wrong?" answered Jake, walking briskly towards the bustling main road.

Jake hailed a taxi on the King's Road and the three of them climbed in.

"Altogether, that wasn't quite what I was expecting," said Jake.

"Chuck Manners doesn't lead a very normal life," added Clare.

"Are we going to do this thing or walk away?" asked Bigsy.

"Chuck hasn't mentioned it, but we do sort of owe him," said Jake.

"Two levels - one he helped us when we were in deep with that Lucien thing. Two, when the excess money came our way, he knew about it but has never mentioned it or hassled us."

"Jake's right," said Clare, " we do owe him, and he is saying that our role is peripheral."

"Yeah, I think Chuck will want to keep us out of any rumpus," said Bigsy, "He must know plenty of people who could help him with a fight."

They looked at one another. The taxi lurched over a speed bump and they all jumped slightly in the air.

"You know what," said Bigsy, "I have a great new story for the front of our web-site. About Squares…"

They nodded.

They were in.

Still in the taxi, Clare put in a call to Christina.

"Christina, I think I might have a gig for you, "she said, "Although it's not what it seems. Call me back."

Two minutes later Christina was returning the call. "I was on the tube. I just picked up your message."

"Not by phone. Let's meet" said Clare.

Clare met Christina to explain the proposition. They would need to provide facilities for an upcoming event.

Clare could pull strings so that they were asked to do the work and Christina would have to perform. It was all short notice, but it would be quite a coup for the organisers to get Christina Nott along.

Planning a gig

"Now I know what happens at a gig, I will be ready for it, next time--I will come in just a T-shirt and shorts and books, and fight my way to the front, like a quietly determined soldier, and then let the band take my head off.

I want to walk into rooms like that every night, with a sense of something happening."

— Caitlin Moran

Ed Adams

Birmingham Mailbox District

Christina's meeting was scheduled to take place close to one of the Birmingham canals in the proximity of the area called the Mailbox. This up-and-coming area of Birmingham comprised some modern developments along the edge of the major canal infrastructure which cuts through the city.

The venue for the meeting was an attractive wine and champagne bar called Epernay and Christina had arrived early and decided to order a cocktail. Christina chose a comfortable seat close to the window which would make it easy for the people she was to meet to spot her when they entered the bar. In the opposite corner and close to the bar was a piano player who was dawdling out some jazzy tunes, languorously to the

The Square

Sunday punters who were sitting drinking exotic cocktails and eating fancy canapes.

Christina had arrived alone for the meeting and had busied herself with some email on a notebook PC whilst she awaited the arrival of her contacts. In a slightly irritating way, she had been hit on by two men whilst she sat waiting, but they were good natured as she politely explained she was busy and waiting for someone. The piano player had noticed this too and looked across at one point as if to enquire whether Christina had wanted any help.

Eventually, the music contacts arrived and looked briefly around the bar before spotting Christina and making their way to where she was seated. There were three people, a tall slender woman with a knee-length leather coat, a flamboyantly dressed blonde haired guy with a dark suit jacket, purple shirt and red waistcoat and a dark haired rugged looking guy who looked as it he'd just come back from somewhere with unremitting sun.

They introduced themselves as Annalisa, Sacha and Douglas and made small talk about the weather in Birmingham and the accessibility of their current location.

"Whether you drive, take a taxi or bus, the only way to here for the last piece is on foot with a good view of everyone else who may be approaching the restaurant", said Sacha.

"This all sounds like a spy movie", smiled Christina, as she prepared to talk about the plans for the gig.

"Actually, Christina", stated Annalisa, "We are looking for some other help from you". Christina was intrigued with this and asked what they were talking about.

"The show we want you to do will be to a fairly large group", continued Annalisa. "and on this occasion, we will take care of all the ticketing. You'll still get a healthy split of the box-office. This is, in effect, a private concert".

"I thought it was a public concert?" queried Christina. "I'd expect to advertise and get some publicity as a result."

"We know it is a prestigious venue", replied Annalisa," We have a large group who wish to get together and your concert provides an ideal backdrop for their meeting. We can use the event to ensure that they all meet and transact a small amount of business with no one noticing that the group also has another interest."

Christina fiddled with her glass. She had only had one cocktail because she had wanted to keep a clear head for the meeting. Now she was glad she had, because the discussion had the chance to start going a little weird.

"What are you suggesting?", asked Christina. "I take it this is legal?"

Annalisa smiled. "Totally legal; we have the challenge to bring a large group together, allow them to swap some information and just to not create any ripples by being together. Your gig creates a perfect environment for this group of people to meet in a relaxed and entertaining setting.

"It's very simple", Sacha said, "We are creating an event in effect, a fully sold out concert. It will be in a prestige venue and the majority of the people there will have tickets.

"So, is there any risk to me or anything odd going on at this event?" asked Christina. "If it's drugs or anything then I'm not going to do it. I can walk away now, and it will be as if we have never met."

"There's nothing illegal or even slightly shady," said Annalisa. "We will, though, be using the event as a type of cover for a quite innocent meeting on another topic. I think you have already noticed that the fees are quite interesting."

Christina had noticed the fees for this event and that is what had attracted her to the meeting. It was significantly more than she had received for other appearances and could be the start of raising her profile. The deal included a well-above-average performance fee, a box split and even a bar split. Christina was beginning to wish that Clare had been able to attend.

Christina said, "I'm still interested. Let's talk about the date and the venue as well. I'll need to get my agent Clare to tidy up the details." This was definitely a situation where two heads would be better than one.

"Here's the plan", said Douglas, flipping open a small computer bag and extracting a couple of sheets of paper stapled together. "You'll find the details including the staging and the attendance numbers", he continued.

"We will give you an up-front payment, but if you still need to talk this over with your agent, then we will give you 24 hours to confirm your interest. We can't leave it longer than that and will need to find an alternative if you decline."

Christina was weighing this up. She liked the idea of the exclusive concert but had expected to be able to advertise and spread the word. If everyone was being invited to the session, then it may not get advertised or reviewed by the press, which was not ideal.

"Will there be press at the gig?" she asked, expecting that she already knew the answer.

"It's not very likely", answered Douglas, "We will want to keep the event very select - I think you consider it more like a large but private party. We'll also want to vet any production shots or crowd shots. Confidentiality is paramount."

"Okay", said Christina, "You'll get an answer from my agent tomorrow."

"And what is it likely to be?" asked Annalisa.

"It will probably be yes", replied Christina, already thinking about how to reach Clare quickly.

The three who had met Christina then started to make to leave the wine-bar. Sacha graciously paid the bill and the four of them left together. As Annalisa, Sacha and Douglas made to turn right from the entrance to the wine-bar, Christina walked in the opposite direction, over a short bridge and along a short piece of busy canal towpath back towards the city centre. She knew there was something unusual about what she was being asked, but the money being suggested for the gig seemed considerably better than other gigs she had performed and with her current unstable finances, the money would come in very useful.

A few minutes later, Christina was on the phone to Clare and recounting the story. Clare agreed it all sounded quite intriguing. "When do you get back to London?" she asked, "We can meet and decide what you want to do. I think you should do it, but maybe ensure that one of us is included in your back-up team. Even better if they can sing or play some tunes!"

Christina hailed a cab from the town centre back to the train station. She would be back in London in a couple of hours. It had been a strange day.

Clare had flipped off her mobile after the call from Christina and then called Jake.

"Hi, Jake, Christina's got the gig, but they don't want to advertise it. It sounds as if there is something else happening in the venue and that whoever is running it doesn't want to draw real attention to the situation. This could be something for us to have a look at!"

"Okay, " said Jake, "Team meeting at the 'Porter."

Ed Adams

The Market Porter

Jake arrived first at the pub in London's Borough Market. He had grabbed a cab from outside the office and it had only taken about fifteen minutes to thread through the traffic to just south of the river.

Around him, there were many other Londoners standing, chatting animatedly and occasionally returning to the bar for more drinks. Jake wasn't a fan of the plastic beakers used when standing outside the pub, but still preferred this lively view to sitting inside with a proper glass but a less interesting vista.

Jake had also realised that he'd spent the whole day without eating anything and now noticed the sausage shop next door to the pub and was mulling over whether to spend the equivalent of a pint on a gourmet bap filled with the posh sausages on offer.

It was at this moment that Christina and Clare arrived together. Jake had known Clare longer than Christina and had originally met Christina when Clare used to want to support Christina at various small gigs sprinkled around London. Originally Christina had been a well-travelled singer with an acoustic guitar but had later adapted to a more commercial dance style of music, which had also been the basis of her modestly successful CDs and iTunes track downloads.

Christina was also adept at creating appearances which could range from stunningly eye-catching to being able to blend into the scenery to avoid attracting attention. Today, Christina was out with her friend Clare and the two of them were dressed to a matching level and would certainly turn heads but not attract the wrong kind of attention whilst they walked through the market.

"Would you like a drink?", asked Jake, "or shall we find somewhere we can sit down?" The venue was a great place to wait for one another but wasn't the best location for a private conversation about what had been happening. "Let's go around the corner," suggested Clare. There was a nearby exit from the market area, and this led onto a busy main road. Just around the corner was a doorway and some stairs leading down into a subterranean wine bar.

"This will do fine," said Christina. "It's a quiet enough place for me to be able to tell you what has happened and ask for your advice".

They traversed the stairs into the wine bar. It looked as if it had been constructed in a cellar and there was a neat looking bar area with a couple of people standing waiting to serve them. "Shall we have a bottle?" asked Clare. The others both nodded and Clare requested a bottle of white wine and three glasses. They selected a table and Jake started to pour the wine.

"Tell all," said Jake to Christina, "Just what are you getting yourself into?"

Christina explained about the possibility of the gig, the meeting with the Italians, and the slightly strange way that the venue and conditions had been specified.

"Perhaps it's the Mafia!" said Jake. There was a pause and then he could see that his joke was slightly backfiring. "Er, I'm joking, you know."

Christina looked at Clare and they both smiled. Jake realised he had just been out-manoeuvred.

"I forgot", said Jake, "When you two are together, I don't stand a chance if I want to 'wind you both up'."

"Right," said Clare laughing, "You know when you are outclassed!"

Christina also smiled. "I did, initially start to wonder things like that myself", she admitted.

"The original arrangements for us to meet were straightforward enough, and the plan was for Clare to also be at the meeting. It was only a last-minute thing that meant I had to go alone. I'm sure my imagination has just been working overtime."

Jake agreed. Christina had been asked to perform a music concert at an attractive venue. The guests were to be personally invited by the Italian organisers and there would not be any public admission. Disappointed, Jake didn't think there was anything suspicious after all.

"So where is the gig and how much do you get?" he asked as a prelude to changing the subject. Christina's reply made him change his mind.

"What?" he exclaimed, "That is a lot of money for a private show and to such a large group, too. They must really like you a lot!"

"Precisely", replied Christina, "Now do you see my point!"

Jake, Christina and Clare had continued to work their way through the bottle of wine.

Clare and Christina had pretty much decided to accept the deal with Annalisa and the Italians, and Clare was to call them first thing in the morning. If needed, Clare would dispatch paperwork and contracts for the gig by Christina.

The three of them could not decide if there was really something suspicious about the requested performance. The money on offer for Christina to perform was probably three times as much as Christina's wildest expectation to the point where Christina and Clare somehow wondered if the whole thing had been a hoax.

Jake knew, however, from his journalism work that there were plenty of examples of people from the pop industry being offered everything from advanced copies of new materials, through to petty theft by musicians of tunes and riffs to unusual methods to hype a record or group to the top of the charts. He supposed that the angle on Christina was something like this, although he couldn't quite work out how the scam was operating.

"Don't sign anything without reading it properly first," he offered as rather obvious advice.

Christina and Clare stifled grins, both aware that there was still something unusual about the gig planned for Birmingham.

Ed Adams

Fake News

"You are fake news."

— Donald J. Trump

Carson's meetings

Colonel Carson was being given an ultimatum. He wanted to stay in his senior role and was now being told that the situation was a matter of Homeland Security. Carson was loyal, so it was inconceivable that he would not follow the order, or in this case the request.

"We need to top and tail the travel arrangement. Terrorists can gain an upper hand in the United States if we don't do something about it. Our citizens are becoming disaffected with the ever-increasing level of threats to the United States. We are now squeezing the various air travel trips because of the heightened security, plus eco-concerns.

Carson had been involved with some tough and some covert situations, but he wondered here what he was being asked to do,

The Square

"We want you to help us turn the opinion around," continued another suited man. He had not seen him before and considered that it was probably a civilian advisor to the government.

"What are you asking?" quizzed Carson.

"We need to create a change of focus," continued the advisor. "It involves moving the emphasis from North America. We are seen by most of the middle east as the enemy and there is little sympathy for anything we do to try to support or improve anything in any of the middle eastern counties.

" We need the next wave of terror attacks to be elsewhere; somewhere in Europe is the preferred location. This will give the USA a chance to clear its portfolio and for any next round of counter measures to be led from another base. America First, remember.

"The United States is having too many problems at the moment. Most of our electorate want our people back home, not stuck in a desert somewhere. At home there's major paranoia associated with possible further terrorist attacks and there is a real risk that another big thing could happen.

"Even when The White House opens its mouth or tweets something, there's a risk of ripples from around the globe. We are getting too much of the wrong kind of attention."

"That's why we need for something bad, originated from an identifiable hot-spot, but deployed in say London or Paris. There will be a forced acceleration of their involvement in retaliation and the focus will inevitably shift to those areas where the most damage had occurred."

Carson was taken aback. He'd been asked to do some pretty covert missions in the past, but usually involving unstable regimes that just needed small push to tip them into some form of junta or major change. This was different; he was being asked to devise a way to shift terrorist activity away from the United States by creating activities in another country. He was also being, in effect, asked to incite a declaration of war from those other countries against the Middle East. This was like starting a World War Three.

"I'm not sure about this," ventured Carson, "I've had to do some pretty big things in my time, but this is huge".

"We thought that might be your reaction," said the suited advisor. "We have worked out the main plan and let me assure you that your part in this will be strongly acknowledged. I don't mean gallantry medals or anything that leads back to you in a dangerous way, but let's just say we have a very large budget for this assignment and its leader will be rewarded in a way that means they won't need employment after this and can live very well indeed.

Carson considered. If he said no, but already knew what this was about, then he would be in some danger anyway. If he said yes, he would need to take his chances during the mission and needed to find a way to disappear with whatever was on offer at the end of the mission.

"Count me in," he said decisively, "But you will need to explain to me in more detail what we are supposed to do."

The Advisor introduced himself more fully, "I am Deputy chief of staff Brendan Cullane, advisor to the US Armed Forces and to the President. There are several people like me, who operate in a special capacity in times of extreme difficulty. We are always around but the nature of our office is kept rather quiet."

Carson was aware of this from a similar experience on a more minor scale when he had been asked to do something in Sudan a few years ago. He had been involved with an operation which required a silent entry and exit from the country along with the extraction of one key individual. The circumstances were that the whole mission had to be accomplished without any media or military attention. He'd worked with a small team of free-lancers for that and the whole mission had run very smoothly.

He had been given a briefing by the advisor on that occasion and was somewhat amazed at the diplomatic and clandestine tricks which were smoothly pulled in order to make the whole operation successful.

This would be another situation like Sudan, only on a much larger scale and potentially disadvantaging some of the European Superpowers. He was still somewhat shocked by this but knew that total commitment to the plan was his only real option.

"So, explain the mission," asked Carson.

Cullane continued, "We intend to divert attention from the USA as a consequence of a major terrorist attack in mainland Europe. Rest assured that the terrorists are planning to do this anyway. The effect will be to galvanise the countries affected to strong and decisive action to put down the attackers and to take control of the country harbouring the terrorists.

"The impact on the USA will be to deflect much of the current attention away. Both in terms of terrorism and also in terms of our contribution to the war efforts in the Middle East.

"Our current action is becoming unpopular with the citizen electorate and also our military support is extremely expensive, far beyond our original estimates. The other economic support industries are still working well, so a reduction in our level of arms will help redress the overall balance well.

"If the British and Germans take a stronger interest in the region, then they would help this economic re-balance.

"Your role is to ensure that a plot already in progress is deflected from US shores. We have picked up intelligence that the Al Aktar organisation have been busy recently and have gained access to some nerve agent which originated from Israeli testing.

"Al Aktar are stealing the nerve agent and are intending to use it in some attacks dependent upon the highest bidder.

"There will be some kind of decoy attack and we believe this will be some sort of rocket attack into an airport or similar, and that this will create a diversion whilst their main attack was run.

"We can ensure that the resultant news coverage is suitably pointed. And that it will deflect away from the United States.

"What?" asked Carson, "Manipulation? Of the News?"

"We want you to ensure that Al Aktar are discouraged from thoughts of using this in any of the Homeland territories. If anything is going to happen it needs to be elsewhere. We think they will also have a decoy operation. Both need to be managed.

"But what about the nerve gas? Won't it be so lethal that it breaks all of the conventions of war?", asked Carson.

"Yes, the nerve gas is very strong, but there are some aspects of the way it will be deployed which keep us in control.

"We don't know why they are doing this at the moment. It could be ideology, but it seems to be being driven by some other financing, which we've not managed to unscramble. This looks like a case of giving a weapon to someone prepared to use it indiscriminately - except they can't afford it, but someone else is paying the bills."

"Shouldn't we just alert everyone and try to stop it?

"Yes, we could do that, but the likelihood is that the terrorists would simply turn attention back to the United States. At the moment, we have a confidence that we can run faster than anyone else from the pursuing wild animal.

Carson nodded. He knew the old story with the punchline 'I just have to be faster than you' when escaping from a tiger.

"Who else knows about this?" Asked Carson.

"Just us - and the President," answered Cullane.

Ed Adams

Weight throwing

Robert Alton was back at his SI6 office. Dorothy came through on the phone, "There's a US Colonel on the phone for you. A Colonel Carson."

Alton grimaced, "Thank you Dorothy, you'd better put him through," Alton knew that Dwight Carson was one to throw his weight around and quite capable of small-time blackmail and threats to get his own way.

"Dwight, to what do I owe this pleasure?" he began.
"Hello Robert, I think you might be in some kind of trouble at the moment. We are aware of an explosion near Cairo. Word has it that some of your people were involved."

"What is that to which you are referring?" asked Alton.

"Don't play dumb with me, we both know you had Karen Martin along for a rendezvous... That she was managing the Egyptian situation on the ground, from Cairo... That she commissioned a stringer to go out to exchange data with the truck driver. I'm keeping it out of the media here, as we speak."

"You know that we'll have to deny it all?" answered Alton, "It's easier now with so much Fake News around."

"It's luck then that we've got a photograph of Karen waiting at the cafe, for her stringer, and then another one of him walking past the spot, just before she was murdered. James, I think that was his name."

Alton looked dismayed, "Even if what you say was true, why would you be calling me about it now? Why not two days ago?"

"Two days ago, we didn't need anything. Now we want something from you. Something that I guarantee will make this go away."

"Go on," said Alton.

"We know that James has made contact with an American. We think the contact is ex-military. We just need a name. We have, shall we say, some interest in him and his association with James."

Alton was thinking quickly. Now he'd met Chuck Manners and seen that he was a professional and something of a slippery character. He decided that Chuck could handle himself.

"And if I could provide this information?"

"Then we'll lose the evidence about your UK involvement in the recent helicopter crash and truck destruction."

"I want something else," asked Alton, "The name of your parallel operative. - An eye for an eye, after all." He wanted to see if he could push Carson, to find out how desperate he was.

"So, we have a deal?" asked Carson.

"If you provide us with the information. It also gives me something to show as collateral from the trade." Alton smiled. Carson was desperate.

Carson paused, "Okay. We'll forgo escrow protocol, you give me the name now, and I'll give you the name in return."

Alton thought - Carson is really desperate.

Alton said, "Colonel Chuck Manners."

Carson paused again, Alton could hear some noise in the background.

"And your field agent was?"

"A stringer also - US citizen, Steve Ruben."

Alton was aware that Carson had just thrown the US stringer to the wolves. He hoped that he had not done the same for Chuck Manners.

"Okay, thank you for that, I'll see you at the next NATO session, probably," said Carson, "Over and Out"

The Square

Alton felt suitably trampled over by Carson. He was the proverbial bull in a china shop and simply didn't care how he obtained his information. In a few minutes Alton had been threatened, and then seen a US asset thrown away to get what Carson wanted.

Tracker lock

Carson's mood escalated when he heard the news from Alton. That Colonel Chuck Manners was deployed alongside the UK stringer "James" raised the game.

Carson was aware of Manners from varied black-ops dotted around the world. He had a staggering success rate and yet he seemed able to disappear from view between operations.

Now he alerted his own operations centre. They were to track James, whose cell-phone ID they had already captured and Chuck Manners, whose cell-phone could be tracked back via his stay in Cairo. They needed his hotel room and then they would have a fix on the unique identifier of the American-issue cell phone, which legally had to carry its own tracking device.

Carson was familiar enough with the Fourth Amendment to know that he could break it to find Manners and used the US5519760A Cellular network-based location system as the basis for a tracker alert.

From this, his operations centre could see that Chuck had been close to James in Egypt, even in the same sector of desert as the truck. They had then split up and travelled separately to New York. That James had then travelled to Nice and Cannes in France, and that Chuck had followed a day or so later.

They were currently co-located in Cannes, France.

-.-. . .-.. .-.. - .-. .- -.-. -.- / .. ... / .-.. . .- .-..

Chuck picked up his cell phone.

"Hi Chuck, it's Robert Alton,"

"Hi Robert, this is unexpected?"

"Yes, the worst news I'm afraid. A Colonel Carson in the US DoD has requested your name and we've had to supply it. I guess he will be looking out for you now. Please consider this a heads up."

Chuck looked around, "How long ago?" he asked.

"Less than an hour, but I expect you are being tracked."

"Okay," said Chuck, he looked at his phone, "I'll do a reverse lookup to see who is tracking me, and thanks for letting me know. I'll go dark now. Expect a text with my new phone."

Chuck looked at his phone, he accessed an App called Celltrack. He pressed a special key combination and sure enough it revealed that there was a tracker lock on the phone. He wrote down the codes for it. Then he ejected the SIMM.

He knew that was not enough now that the trackers had got his phone's device identity.

He walked outside to the busy street. A builder's truck from Newcastle-Upon-Tyne was stuck in the traffic. He gently tipped the still switched on phone onto the truck's open rear platform.

"Bye bye," he said, "Happy trails."

Bad America

Major Garcia Ramirez reported to Colonel Dwight Carson in the Special Operations Unit, based in the Pentagon.

Ramirez himself was a career military person and had distinguished himself in the first Gulf war. He was now involved in senior and special work, and Carson was his normal direct reporting officer.

Colonel Carson operated in a shadow world. He was involved with politics to a greater degree than anyone else that Ramirez knew, but it had normally served his department well, because it was usually easy to get funding for new projects or special operations. In that respect, Carson took care of his team.

But Ramirez wondered what else there was to know about Carson. He seemed to be out of the office a lot, had various secret high-powered meetings and treated a lot of information on a strict need to know basis.

This created an image of mystique around Carson and Ramirez was one of the people who sometimes wondered what Carson's full agenda entailed.

The reality was very complex. Carson had direct access to the President of the United States and access into the major areas of the CIA, FBI and NSA. Carson was also well connected and senior in military terms and so could get his own way on many matters.

As a result, they often sought his opinion from high levels within the US government and Ramirez suspected that some of this opinion giving was off the record.

Examples included opinions about the second gulf war, including some kind of direct involvement in the discussions about the Weapons of Mass Destruction. But Ramirez also knew that Carson had been operating long before the Iraq war started officially.

Carson had been involved in the planning of a series of air raids in an air corridor which started several months before the formal war started. The plans driven covertly by the Americans were to start to destroy certain kinds of border environments and logistic support points well before a war really kicked off. This gave the US military some early advantages because they both knew some terrain but as importantly had already destroyed most of the military hardware used by the Iraqis.

Ramirez had been sent into the area at this time, into Saudi Arabia, to act as a nearby observer and to provide logistical support if required during the period that the bombings were intensifying. The most difficult press reports to suppress at the

time were the Al Jazeera television reports. This was
interesting to Ramirez, because although the main language of
the television station was Arabic, there were an increasing
number of English language reports being produced which
described in some detail the missions which were underway.

Ramirez had been situated in Saudi Arabia's capital city of
Riyadh for the majority of his time in the country. He had been
posing as a civilian worker and was based at a Sheraton Hotel
not far from the downtown area. It was a short drive to the
military camps, but he preferred to stay close to the hotel and
to have people visit him, suitably dressed down and definitely
not in uniform.

Ramirez had found the operation to be fairly predictable,
involving some spin of the things that were taking place and
some reasonable bribes to be placed to prevent certain stories
from surfacing. During this time, Ramirez had seen Carson at
work close hand for the first time. It was obvious that he knew
his way around the people, but also the customs and what could
and could not be done and said.

And at present, it was obvious to Ramirez that Carson was
involved in some special agendas. Ramirez tried to speculate
what Carson knew or was doing, but it was not so very obvious.
Carson had been to several meetings with Chiefs of Staff and
direct advisors to the President. It was obvious that there was
something happening, but Ramirez had no idea what it might
be.

Brief Ramirez

Major Garcia Ramirez was sitting with Colonel Dwight Carson.

"This situation…There's something wrong with it isn't there?" asked Ramirez.

"Yes, I'm stuck between a rock and a hard place," answered Carson.

"If you are, does that mean I am as well?" asked Ramirez.

"Let's just say the President is involved."

"You'd better explain."

"You know that black-ops chopper that was downed in Egypt?"

Ramirez nodded.

"It was Israeli, operating across the Border."

"That's like an act of war, isn't it?" asked Ramirez.

"Unless it has been condoned, and I suspect the US put on pressure to let it take place."

"What was it doing, blowing up some road traffic or something, wasn't it?" asked Ramirez.

"Correct," said Carson, "In fact, it was blowing up a missile transport."

"That's why the reported explosion was so large?" asked Ramirez.

"Not exactly; the truck was transporting something else. Not missiles. Neurotoxins."

"What? They are outlawed. Had the Egyptians been making them? We are in WMD territory here."

"No, the toxins were originally manufactured in the USA. Then they were shipped to Israel for testing."

"Something went wrong during the tests and they had to close the lab."

"Fatalities, or what?"

"Yes, everyone. Everyone in the lab was killed. The neurotoxin has around a one-hour life, unless re-hosted."

"So, what was it doing on a truck?"

"We'd done a deal with the UK. To ship it to Porton Down for destruction. Except for a very small amount which would be held in their sample bank."

"I see, instead of holding the dangerous materials in Nevada, we're outsourcing it now. Very smart."

"Yes, the Brits think it is a sweet arrangement."

"What were they doing in Egypt?"

"The route was road and sea. Egypt, Libya, Tunisia, Algeria, Spain, Santander and then sea to the UK. It was intended to be low profile, compared with going across the whole of mainland Europe."

"Libya though? Surely that is a hornets' nest?"

"Yes, but since the UN 'unity' Government, there's a hint of American control. And it should have been one Arab-plated truck, looking like an oil truck."

"But the truck didn't make it?"

"No, the Israeli helicopter blew it up, with extra powerful munitions to destroy the toxins. Then the chopper was downed as well. We think that was by an American freelancer - Colonel Chuck Manners."

"But doesn't that mean the mission is finished?" asked Ramirez.

"Ordinarily, yes, but on this occasion there's something else. A second truck. Another set of neurotoxin warheads."

"Where are they now?"

"No-one knows. The trackers have been demobilised and we don't know who is controlling the operation."

"Who knows about this?"

"Almost no-one. A few advisors and the President. I doubt if the truck drivers even know what they are carrying."

Unstoppable

I'm unstoppable
I'm a Porsche with no brakes
I'm invincible
Yeah, I win every single game

I'm so powerful
I don't need batteries to play
I'm so confident, yeah, I'm unstoppable today
Unstoppable today, unstoppable today

Sia Furler

Al Aktar

Al Aktar was a trading company shell with Iraqi-based owners. They had never claimed their Iraqi origins in the UK and instead pretended to be Lebanese.

Their view was that Lebanese were generally accepted to the point that Lebanese restaurants and food were a very acceptable part of British culture, whereas Iraqi connotations immediately created ripples leading towards the George Bush war and even echoes back to the events of September 11.

The headquarters of Al Aktar Trading was a small depot in a factory estate near to the A4 main road to London. It was in an area sandwiched between railway tracks and arches.

Nearby, an elevated section of the M4 motorway leading between London and the London Heathrow Airport created continuous noise. The entrance to the trading estate advertised van rental and shot blasting, along with a mobile phone number. This was a fairly rough part of town.

The environment was a low-rise series of buildings where double-glazing depots, carpet warehouses and a small company who installed car alarms were grouped together. There was a steady traffic of cars, vans and small trucks, which was a combination of private customers and low-end tradesman.

This was the area where the middle eastern traders were able to run a bland-looking business in a way which pretty much escaped detection.

There was always some bustle from the premises and occasionally people engaged in prayers at certain key times of the Islamic day. But the people kept themselves to themselves. They wore mainly simple western clothes, although sometimes there would be visitors in more overt Arabic clothing. But the location and the type of visitors did not seem unusual or special.

The reality was very different, because this trading company held a cell of a terrorist unit with plans to destroy key parts of the London infrastructure.

"We can control via asymmetric warfare", explained Ali Al Mansour.

"The power we bring can crush opposition and make strong our view."

In the corner sat another western-looking man, in his late forties, but tanned and fit, looking like a soldier or ex-soldier and certainly someone who could handle himself.

"Correct," he commented, "We have some extensive plans for the next two weeks". He looked around the room meaningfully, "Is everyone clear that they want to help?".

Ali Al Mansour repeated the question in Arabic and there were a few yelps of support from those in the room. Al Aktar was forming its army of destruction and had the first block of recruits ready for action.

"Let's go through the plan", continued Al Mansour.

"Not now", responded the European, looking down to the floor, "When we have a clearer plan, I will want to brief people in groups. I don't want everyone to know all aspects in case someone is captured."

Al Mansour nodded his agreement. "Then tonight we send people away, and then meet again in smaller groups, maybe at the mosques."

The European nodded again and walked towards the door. As he did so, a black car pulled up outside the office. He stepped into the back seat and waved the car away.

-... . .-- .- .-. .

Al Aktar had created their base camp in Egypt. It was far enough from Cairo to be inaccessible to casual travellers, yet close enough to benefit from the transport infrastructure. It was also outside of the usual zone of spy planes and satellite surveillance which would attract attention in any of the "-istans".

The White Desert is a large area of remote desert yet the four strategic oases of Bahariya, Farafra, Dakhla and Kharga provided water, accommodation and ready transport together with a traffic of tourists which provided good cover for the terrorist cells as they moved people into and out of their training and briefing centres.

Khalid Al Sharif was the head of the cell and had run several briefings to recent groups about the plans for ways to destabilise the western economy.

To achieve this, they needed significant weapons, and had decided to infiltrate the DoD to achieve this. They would need to know where significant weapons were stored and when they were due to be transported.

A contact high in the US military had been identified who could be leveraged to provide the basic information. The contact had asked for money, both for himself and to pay another person, from the UK security services.

Al Attar's plan was to hit two major financial centres in Europe, in a way that would create mass outward movements of money. This would have a devastating effect upon the Western economy of Europe, as money was moved to other parts of the world.

There would be a combination of civilian casualty from the acts of terrorism, but there would also be a great levelling of the conditions between Europe and the Middle East as a consequence of the outflow of money and the collapse of companies.

The level of this required major impacts in the areas to be affected, and in London there were features such as the transit system which could help the effective spread of a chemical agent.

In Frankfurt it was slightly harder because there was no equivalent of the London Underground, but the major intention was to get two major exclusion zones created for the city centres of London and Frankfurt. The plan required careful co-ordination such that the two planned attacks would happen within a short time of one another.

Al Aktar was using the desert base as a briefing and training centre for the people to be involved in the attacks and because the training camp was close to a tourist route through the desert it had the advantage of ease of access without undue suspicion.

There were several companies which conducted tours in the area, and Al Aktar had created its own company for the same purpose, with the exception that guests were all part of the terror cells. It was a bold plan but worked well and created little suspicion.

Another camp in Pakistan was used for firearms and general fitness training and it was only the elite who passed through into the Cairo desert base on their way to full deployment.

Khalid Al Sharif was in a meeting with several of the key operatives. "Most people will not know the full plan", he said," You are a few privileged to know what we plan to do. We will take the nerve agents and deploy them in two city centres. We will also create diversions at nearby major airports as a way to distract large amounts of military from our primary purpose."

"There will be a couple of random attacks on civilian planes as the start of the plan. We will detonate planes on the ground. This is symbolic and will create huge flows of police and emergency services to the respective airports. Whilst this occurs, we will launch our primary attacks in the two major city centres. This will involve the release of nerve agents, simultaneously from several key locations in each city centre. The diversion of the airport attacks will create confusion which allows our primary purpose to be achieved."

"There are a lot of questions," said one of the people being briefed.

He was a 25-year-old, with a dark beard and wore desert clothing and dark glasses.

"How do we attack the airport and what happens when we release the nerve gas?"

"First there will be an attack on airports using Saudi Air Force Missiles which we have acquired via a series of contacts.

"We are incorporating them into the design of a couple of trucks for shipment to the respective countries

"The nerve agent is very compact and can be handheld by our followers up to the moment of deployment. They will be martyrs as a consequence of freeing the chemicals into the air. The chemical agent is of a power that each cylinder will affect 50,000 people. Once in the system, such as the railway system, it will have devastating reach."

The group receiving the briefing talked briefly amongst themselves. "Will we be martyrs as part of this?", one of them asked. "No, your job is to find the believers who will take the chemical to the places where it needs to be deployed. You will ensure that trusted men carry forward this mission", replied Khalid Al Sharif.

"And how will the airport part be handled?" asked another.

"We have already selected a driver to take the payload across Europe and we have two locations where the commissioning can take place. We have been planning this for a long time, we are well bankrolled and have access to the necessary people," continued Khalid Al Sharif.

Unstable

Back at the Al Akram industrial site in London, Mehdi Akram was shaking his head.

"Those delivery drivers Alan and Dave were duped by UK government forces. The last BioPen vial was handed over to the UK instead of to us."

"Do you want us to fix them?" asked Ghali Yessim.

Mahdi Akram replied, "Ordinarily I would say yes, but I don't want to draw any unnecessary attention to ourselves. We should put the missing vial down to a cost of war and let the two drivers go. Let's face it, they have only made half their money and we have nearly all of the BioPen vials."

The BioPens each had a small glass window at the top, which had started a clear green colour. On a few of the containers it was beginning to change to a yellow/green colour.

The Square

"It is the start of the decay process for the BioPen content, said Mehdi Akram, "Normally these pens should last for several years. It can only mean that the handling has been compromised. "

Ghali Yessim asked, "Does that affect their usefulness?"

"There's a significant safety margin built into the warning display. They should be good for several months beyond their decay point."

"Even so, it will be harder to shift them if they look defective," said Firas Belhassan, "Maybe I can rig the warning lights?" Said Firas Belhassan, "Let me have a try."

He opened it cautiously.

Ghali said, "Just don't be pressing the release mechanism. The pen should only be used against the neurotoxin. In concentration it is also virulent."

Firas gingerly did things to the BioPen vial and made the light reset to green, "See. I can short the detection circuit. Let's do it on the rest,"

He worked his way through the first box. Successfully. Then he move along to the second box, about to start the same process again.

"Ach!" he announced, "I've tripped the mechanism on this one." It had accidentally released some of the antidote onto his skin.

He wiped it off with his hand and continued and he continued the process with the second box of BioPens. As he finished, he looked back towards his hand. A large blister was forming where the antidote had struck. He could see it was tracing the arteries in his arm.

Mehdi Akram looked over. "Firas Belhassan, my friend, I think you have been infected. Infected with the antidote. Without anything to work against, I fear it is unstoppable.

Truck Two

Major Garcia Ramirez was thinking about Truck Two. For the Israelis to have tracked the first truck they must have known its whereabouts. The strike was cleanly executed and precise.

It implied that there was either excellent intelligence about the trucks' movements, or more likely that there was a tracker of some kind on the vehicle.

If so, then who would place it there.

The Americans? Unlikely, or he'd already know about the device.

The British? Possibly; they were taking control of the toxin at its destination.

The Egyptians? Unlikely, and they would also be unable to keep the information secure.

The Israelis? They would need the transmitter to be able to locate the truck from the helicopter.

In all probability, the British had supplied the Israelis with the tracker code.

Ramirez would need to be onto his contacts in both UK and Israel. They would certainly deny it, but he had something that he thought they would need. His silence over the first mission.

He put through a call to London. He could be blatant, it would be a shorter route to the people who knew anything.

Dorothy entered Robert Alford's office. "I've a Major Ramirez on the phone for you," she said, "It seems to be about something that happened in Cairo. It's come through on a diplomatic line."

"You'd best put him through," answered Robert Alton.

"Robert Alton?" queried Ramirez, "I think we need to talk."

"On what matter?" asked Alton.

"The stealth Israeli helicopter for which the Brits gave a precision tracker code and which blew up a tanker in transit across the desert," bluffed Ramirez, "I have pictures," he lied.

"Just supposing that were true, why take so long to come through to us?" asked Alton unrattled, "I assume you want something?"

"Correct," said Ramirez, "You will know that there are two trucks on the loose. One has been found and dealt with, the other one is still out there."

"And why would I be interested in that?" asked Alton.

"You'd want to know that the neurotoxin was safe on its transit from Tel-Aviv to Porton Down," bluffed Ramirez.

"Ah, yes, I see what you are speculating," said Alton, "I don't suppose it has occurred to you that the original munition was developed in the United States? At the Edgewood Chemical Biological Center."

Ramirez was taken aback. He had heard of Edgewood, in Maryland, but didn't know it was capable of nerve agent development. Maybe Alton was also bluffing?

"Full disclosure?" asked Alton.

"Okay," said Ramirez.

"What you said has a semblance of truth about it," answered Alton.

"You did provide the codes to the Israelis?" asked Ramirez.

"Let's understand how we got to this position. America developed the neurotoxin - against international agreements, and then shipped some of it to the Saudi desert, where you put it into storage at an Air Force base. Then, you sent some more to Tel-Aviv, for further refinement. The Tel-Aviv samples went rogue and wiped out a lab. You asked for the toxin to be destroyed, as well as for a small sample to be kept, and started the movement towards Porton Down, UK."

"That's consistent with what I know," bluffed Ramirez.

"Did you know that Al Aktar found out about the shipment and were planning to intercept and steal it?" asked Alford.

"They have already stolen the BioPens which contain an antidote for the nerve agent."

"If they get the container with the second batch, they will have a complete neurotoxin kit. Except for one thing. They also need to code to arm the neurotoxin."

Ramirez said, "You'll have to explain that last part to me?"

"Well the neurotoxin can't be shipped in a primed state. Instead there's a two-part container, with the bulk of the reactant in one compartment, but a smaller internal container which has to be digitally activated by a code."

"Okay," said Ramirez, "I'll level with you. We are only interested in the truck at the moment. The one with the containers. We want to destroy it and the containers of nerve gas. Much like the Israelis did with the first truck."

"Yes, well that's the challenge," said Alton, "The trackers have gone dark."

"Since when?"

"Since about two hours after the first truck was destroyed."

"Okay, so you must know the other truck's approximate route?"

"Yes, it was heading across mainland Europe. It was in Turkey when we last had access."

"I'll guess the route then," said Ramirez, "Ankara, Istanbul, Sofia, Belgrade, Vienna, Frankfurt, Cologne, Brussels, Calais."

"How can you know that?" asked Alton.

"Sat-Nav," replied Ramirez, "Think about it, a truck driver wants to take the shortest or speediest route to the UK. He'll dial it up on Google or Sat-Nav. It's effective too, because we'd need a roadblock to stop it, rather than a missile strike on those busy roads."

Alton paused, Ramirez had made a good point.

"But we don't know where the truck is, nor do we have its tracker co-ordinates."

"Agreed, but we know when it stopped and where. The NSA has a great little phone signal tracker RTLS - Real Time Locating System - We should be able to tie down the phone at the last point of contact and then see where it pops up again along the route."

"Aren't those things illegal?" asked Alton.

"Only if you get caught, replied Ramirez, "And let's face it, this is for the greater good."

"Now, I still need those codes from you," asked Ramirez.

"Okay, but we must work together on this one," said Alton.

Ramirez had a plan.

He called NSA and they traced the phone signal from the driver of the second truck. To Alton's surprise, it had traversed Europe in the last couple of days and had made its way into the UK, via the Channel Tunnel.

Along the way, the truck had stopped near Ashford and from other phone signals, it looked as if there had been several extra people involved.

Ramirez looked at the additional identities which his NSA system had picked up. He had several additional numbers which he decided to share with Richard Alton.

"You are good," said Alton, "You've found a couple of SI6 phones in among all of the numbers."

He looked more carefully, realising his own phone was listed but then he noticed something odd. One of the phones listed was the contact number for Karen Martin.

Alton decided to keep this information to himself.

"That's incredible," thought Alton, "Just over two days by road from Israel to the UK. Intercepted and let go by us yet now the truck is parked somewhere around Birmingham."

PART THREE

Ed Adams

Event Management

To achieve great things, two things are needed:
a plan and not quite enough time.

-Leonard Bernstein

The gig

Bigsy drove the van to Christina's private party gig. They'd brought their musical equipment but the whole sound system had been prepared by the venue. It was one of the concert halls around Birmingham. The kind that was re-purposed for trade events.

It was a clever premise. The various key individuals had been invited but there was a kind of 'padding' of other people around the event, which had been billed as a kind of international trade congress, with evening entertainment.

Bigsy thought it was quite an elaborate method to get the various people into the country without raising particular suspicions. Sure enough, there were representatives from many nations, Europeans, Africans, Chinese and Americans. Bigsy had heard Russian being spoken and worked out quite quickly that many delegates were using English as a sort of international translation language.

Bigsy's team role was twofold. There was the main event to set up but also the small matter of ensuring that the various other rooms were also 'adjusted' for the meeting. This needed to be a fairly basic form of monitoring that would somehow get past the suspicions of anyone brought in to handle counter surveillance. Bigsy decided that it would be easiest to simply 'flaunt it' and hide his gadgets in plain sight. He did this by simply bringing small mixer desks with lots of lights into each room and securing them to the fixtures and fixings. They could be obviously 'on' with twinkling lights but also could easily and very obviously switched off. He had signs for them with 'do not switch off' which he suspected wouldn't buy him much but was worth a try.

'Do not switch off - dial 94 on the house phone for an engineer' - he hoped this would work.

Inside the devices he had arranged a small extra battery circuit. It would last around 9 hours once initiated and could digitally record sound without sending out radio signals. No radio signal meant it was virtually undetectable. It also meant it couldn't be used for live monitoring but did mean it could keep a record of whatever happened in the session.

He hoped this would work and that he would be able to gather suitable intelligence from the session.

The format of the day setup was fairly straightforward. There were a range of daytime sessions for 'the teams' from the various organisations present and then some evening entertainment. A few breakouts had been scheduled for the time between the day sessions and the evening's entertainment.

The Square

Bigsy was pretty sure that this would be the time when the discussion about the weapon would take place - that it would be on-site and in one of the break-out rooms. He had no-idea which one and had needed half a dozen of the mixer desks to cover the whole area.

He did notice that one other rooms seemed to be a little more well-appointed than the others and assumed that this would be the most likely one. He resisted the temptation to put additional equipment into it, on the basis that it also increased the chances of discovery.

The conference kicked off - with several well-known and quite controversial speakers. There were press present and they also seemed to have their own small room as part of the arrangements. There was also a special understanding about what could be put on the record and the participants seemed to be keeping the bargain around this.

Christina prepared for her gig. Bigsy noticed that Clare was going to be on stage as well, but he wasn't sure what she'd be doing there.

Then the bass kicked in and Christina was singing:

"I want to feel your body all over mine"
"I wanna get right to it, loving you…"

Bigsy blinked under the power output from the blaster lights but couldn't help but admire the way Christina had the audience in the palm of her hand.

Bigsy couldn't help but also notice that several of the representatives seemed to have particular teams of suited bodyguards around them. And that they seemed captivated by the music. He was not going to try to find out if they were effective, but they certainly looked like they enjoyed Christina's set.

The various breakout rooms were getting used. Most people just ignored the extra sound system available and were happy to sit around the table with its supply of coffee, fruit and pastries.

Bigsy made sure he was evident around the area as a part of the technical support for the event so that he did not suddenly appear at the time of the special assembly convening.

Sure enough, at around an hour before the close of the main day-time event, there was a meeting convened in the well-appointed room. Bigsy introduced himself and asked if they needed any special facilities.

"Actually, no, we have brought our own equipment for the next session. In fact, we would prefer that you switch off the projectors and other equipment."

Bigsy walked around powering everything down except the mixing desk. He would do this at a later stage. He left the room and could hear the people inside checking for electronics and microphones. They seemed amused that the room had so many obvious microphones present and were disconnecting them by hand.

Then Bigsy's phone rang.

"Hello, we would like you to return to the room, please."
Bigsy agreed but deliberately waited around 10 minutes. He arrived holding his phone and looking busy.

"Please disable the mixer desk, we prefer no electronics except our own for the next session."

Bigsy nodded ostensibly still on the phone and moved towards the desk. He flipped a couple of switches and pressed a series of buttons in a very deliberate looking sequence, as if there needed to be a special disabling sequence. The desk lights went out and then Bigsy unplugged the cord from the back of it.

"There," he said, "Completely off. It's cabled into this position so I cannot physically remove it.".

The security people in the room looked at one another and thought that they now had a suitably disabled piece of equipment.

"That's fine," said one of them, "Now we'd appreciate it not to be disturbed for the next hour."

"OK - but you have my number if you need to call me," said Bigsy, pointing to the number displayed on the card.

Bigsy left and took up a position in an adjacent room. He left the door ajar enough to be able to see the comings and goings related to the other room. Sure enough, a short time later a group of people started to arrive. There were several groups in total and they seemed to comprise a mix of main players and some clearly heavy set support staff. Then the door closed and Bigsy could hear it locking.

Bigsy knew that his audio was working but would not dare to monitor it directly for fear of being caught. It was much better to check the recording later and away from the venue.

Now it was working, Bigsy had decided it was better to be further away and moved to a different room. He would have someone from the venue administration inform him when the meeting was finished.

Three hours later, his phone rang. It was the signal that the room was ready to be cleared. There would be no more meetings into the evening, when things would turn towards a mix of dining and entertainment. Bigsy suspected that the key people he had seen would be long gone by this time.

He collected the kit from the various rooms and moved it back to his van. It would be another hour before he could play it back, and that would be from another location completely. He manoeuvred the van through the dark streets of Birmingham and on his way to the meeting place outside of Birmingham.

Listening in

Bigsy had arrived at the hotel on the main toll road bypassing Birmingham.

There would be no reason to stay at this location except for people 'in transit' and the nearest facilities were the motorway services, a short walk from the hotel room.

Bigsy manoeuvred the small white van next to another one parked at the far corner of the car park. It was one he'd parked there earlier before picking up the one he'd driven into Birmingham. He swiftly moved the content of his current one to the new one and then re-parked the one he'd arrived in back in the main area of the car park. Both vans were on hire and he'd be paying a penalty to have the one that had gone into Birmingham picked up from the car park. The van switch was designed to reduce his chance of being followed based upon advice from Chuck.

Bigsy smiled as he thought back over the extra efforts to get new pay-as-you-go phones and the need for the van substitutions. Like a proper spy movie.

The whole exit from Birmingham had taken less than an hour and Bigsy now flipped the small memory card containing the recording into his hand. He'd go into his room in the hotel to listen to the playback, where Chuck and Clare would also join him.

Bigsy's small MacBook flicked into life and he plugged the card into its side and copied the recordings onto the computer. He swiftly copied them into another program and hit 'Play'.

Then he looked at the sound wave. There was a long period of relatively low activity, which sure, enough, was people arriving and settling down. He slid the recording forward to a more continuous series of activity and sure enough there was the start of a more formal meeting.

"One two."

"Gentlemen, thank you for taking the time to visit Birmingham today and I must apologise for the elaborate subterfuge. We wanted to ensure that all of the right parties had an opportunity to be part of this discussion and to be able to opt into what should be a highly profitable situation.

"You will all understand that we can't issue a prospectus for this, but we are looking for - 'Stakeholders' to be part of our plans. This is a little unconventional, and I'm sure that will appeal to the nature of many of your businesses.

The Square

"Put simply, we have acquired a weapon. Some would call it a 'Weapon of Mass Destruction'. I think we will call it a 'safeguard'.

"We intend to deploy it once to demonstrate that we are serious and to use it in a way that will provide gains to the interested parties within this room.

"The weapon contains a biohazard, one for which we have an antidote. It can remove populations quickly but once the antidote is applied, within a very short time a normal environment can be resumed.

"We intend to deploy this in a way that will be disruptive to a major city in a major economy. We intend to use it to drive economic chaos that can be advantageous to all of us that sign up to the programme.

"You have some decisions to make.

"Firstly, will you wish to be in on the process?

"Secondly, you have a vote about where we deploy the weapon based upon a nominated series of locations.

"Thirdly, we will be driving a particular currency to become stable and destroying two or three other ones based upon the outcome of this. You may nominate the preferred strong currency.

In case you wonder about any parts of this - we have arranged a small demonstration of the toxin. We also have an example of the antidote with us at this meeting. We will use another technique to create a diversion before we deploy the main toxin and we already have a countdown schedule arranged.

"You each have the option to join us and take a part in the decisions, then in the knowledge that you will be protected from the outcomes, both in terms of health and wealth.

"Or, you can choose to leave now, in which case you may know about this, you may even decide to tell others, but it will do you no good and, I can assure you, there will be suffering which will affect you directly as a consequence.

"It is regrettable if this sounds like a ransom request, it's better to think of it as an attractive offer for you and your various consortia, and that this is quite literally a 'once in a lifetime' situation.

"I shall give each of you thirty minutes now to consider. At the end of that time, anyone who does not wish to participate will be asked to leave. In this thirty minute period you will be asked to stay in the room. After those that decline have left, we will run our small 'product demonstration'.

"There was a clattering sound on the recording. Bigsy worked out it was the doors being secured in the room.

The crunch

Bigsy listened to the recording. It had quietened down and he could hear the mixed conversations of the groups in the room.

He fast forwarded the recording to when the volume raised again. It was around 30 minutes later.

"Hello, ladies, gentlemen," came the announcement.

"Let's see who wants to be in on this? I have arranged for the doors at the end of the room to be opened. If anyone needs to leave, now is the time."

Bigsy could hear some scraping of chairs and a few footsteps.

"There, it seems around ten people have decided that this opportunity is too rich for them, we can see each of them on the television screens. We set up a video link to that next room."

Next, you must each sample the BioPen. This is the antidote to the neurotoxin and a great form of defence.

Bigsy could hear the clink as what he imagined were the syringes of antidote being handed out.

"This is how you use the syringe, explained the voice. Hold it to your arm and press the small button. It should leave a small impression on your arm. A square of four dots where the needles fire.

"It is almost painless.

Bigsy heard a noise like a vacuum tube which repeated around a dozen times.

"That's great, you are now all inoculated from the nerve agent."

"Let's see what it does. Watch the television monitors."

There was a silence and then a muffled scream. Bigsy worked out it was coming from the TV monitor relayed from the next room.

He listened for several minutes and was aware that the people in the room with the recording had gone quiet.

"There, you can see just how effective this agent is. No-one survived. Now we will open the doors to this room," There were cries of "No, Stop!"

"You are all forgetting that you are immune to the agent. The injection has rendered the nerve agent useless against each of you."

Bigsy could hear the doors being unbolted. There was movement as if of feet running.

"See," said the voice, "You are all unharmed.
Furthermore, in a half hour the neurotoxin will have been rendered harmless. Until that time, no-one unprotected should go into either of these rooms. That is why we are keeping the outer perimeter doors locked."

"Now we need to talk about the price of continued admission to this very select club."

Bigsy realised what had happened. The nerve agent had been demonstrated, the antidote had been shown to work and now the representatives were being asked for money.

"I think we will set the admission price in US dollars. Let us say 10 million."

Bigsy could hear the hubbub as people discussed this and he realised they had all worked out that there would be a higher price to pay if they didn't accept. This was no auction. It was simply holding the players to ransom.

"Think you should appoint a spokesperson and then let us know your response within the hour. It is 15:30 now, we will return at 16:30. Some of you will pay and others may wish to visit another of our rooms."

Bigsy called through to Chuck.

"Chuck, I have the recording; it was not an auction. It was a ransom. Pay $10 million for a piece of the action or become a lab experiment for the toxin. They just killed the people who opted out and have threatened the rest. My guess is that they will make around $100 million from this one deal."

Chuck replied, "Do we know if the rest of the toxin is here? Or was it just enough for the demonstration?"

"I don't know, they asked where people would like it to be used - for example in a major city - and which currency they would like to affect. This takes terrorism to a whole new level."

Chuck relayed the information on to Jake and Clare and then called Richard Alton.

"Richard, they have the toxin here in Birmingham. We are also concerned that they have another supply of it somewhere else and are getting ready to deploy it."

"Okay, my source, a Major Ramirez, in Washington, tells me that the threat is planned for London. He has been asked by Colonel Carson to come over to London to co-ordinate American involvement. Carson is heading for Frankfurt, where there is another large US control station."

"Ramirez says he thinks the second truck came across mainland Europe, through a significant number of major cities. Look, I've some other news. James wants to come back to support you in the next stage."

"James? I'd have thought he was well out of it now?"

"No, we've agreed to keep Léa safe, but James says he considers the mission as unfinished business. He's asked to meet up with you again in Birmingham."

"Sure," said Chuck, "He knows his own mind. Send him along. We're at the Hyatt Regency Birmingham. We'll see him tomorrow."

Ed Adams

Under Pressure

*He who cannot stand the heat
should stay out of the kitchen.*

Harry S. Trueman

Ramirez thoughts

Ramirez was still thinking about Truck 2. It had traversed Europe. It could have delivered some of the containers to an intermediate city on its way through.

He placed a call to Alford.

"Hi Robert,"

"Hi Ramirez, the truck has finally arrived in Birmingham. At least that is what my people are saying. I've also got a recording from one of Chuck Manner's friends."

"I'm slightly surprised that your own NSA hasn't picked up on this. Why didn't Carson know this? He'd have expected to have received the intel from the NSA faster than from the Brits."

It made Ramirez wonder whether there was any form of delay being introduced.

Ramirez also considered the BioPens. It seemed that the BioPens had found their way to the Birmingham venue, at least according to the information that he had received from Alton.

Once again, nothing from Carson. Ramirez began to wonder whether there was some kind of mute switch being applied to the information about these consignments.

He took a closer look at the delay around Ashford, on the way between Dover and London. There had been intense activity around this point, although the toxin transfer had continued.

It looked as if some of the people at this rendezvous had moved back towards London, but that others had continued on the way to Birmingham.

The challenge was, which items had gone to which location?

Fortunately, now that Alton had phoned, Ramirez could do some hunting. He knew that both the toxin and at least several of the BioPens were in Birmingham.

"Look Robert, I'm going to need to be able to talk directly to your contact in Birmingham. That's Colonel Chuck Connors, isn't it?"

"Yes, I'll send you his phone details. I'll also let him now that he should expect a call from you."

Unexpected guest

Chuck was in the bar at the hotel when James arrived.

"You must be crazy!" greeted Chuck.

"I sometimes wonder," said James.

"You've met Jake, I'll have to introduce you to the creators of sound effects during Léa's rescue," said Chuck.

He gestured across to another table. Bigsy, Jake and Clare turned and waved.

"I thought I'd introduce you in stages!" said Chuck, as the others walked across.

"Hey again," said Jake, "I guess they found somewhere to squirrel you away, in London?"

"I'm under great pains to not disclose locations," said James, "You know how it is."

"Not really," said Bigsy, "Hi I'm Bigsy and helped manufacture that soundscape for the extraction!" I used some CSI banter and a couple of comedy cop movies to create the frantic mission effect."

"Well it did the trick," said James, "And you must be Clare!"

Clare grinned, "Yes and I'm pleased you all got through that tricky extraction. I'd expect no less if you get mixed up with Chuck Manners though."

James replied, "I'm not surprised you are in this rather spiffy hotel, either. It is typical of a well-off freelancer or a high-end government official."

"And in case you are wondering, I think I owe it to all of you to try to see this thing through now," said James.

"It's interesting for a freelancer to think like that," said Chuck.

"Yes, but if you think about it, I'll still want more work from the UK government, so it's better that I get a gold star, rather than a question mark in my report."

The bar was filling. A trade convention of salesmen had arrived and were busy slapping one another on the back. Adjacent to the bar, James could see a dining area. It looked positively peaceful.

Then he noticed something.

"My god!" he whispered, "Don't look now, but that's Karen," he gestured to a woman sitting alone in the restaurant.

"But Karen was murdered with a sniper rifle?" asked Chuck.

"I'm telling you, that is Karen. I need to get away from here, she doesn't know any of you."

James moved across the bar, past the salesmen and towards the exit from the area. Chuck could see he was by the elevators, and then gone.

"We need to check this out," said Clare, "I'll go in and check," she walked away pressing buttons on her phone. They could see Clare reading the menu outside of the restaurant area. Then they saw her take a photograph of the menu, turn around and walk across to the bar.

"She's trying to separate herself from us," said Chuck, "Let's go to that other lounge area over there, the one without the bar."

Jake and Bigsy stood and the three of them strolled nonchalantly towards a seating area away from the bar. Clare moved across to re-join them.

"I've got her photo, here," she said, "I'll share it with you all."

Chuck reached for his phone and took an AirDrop copy of the photograph.

"I'm going to send this on to Robert Alton for positive confirmation," he said.

He sent a short message to Alton and they all waited, slightly unsure of their next move.

A text came back to Chuck's phone.

"Confirmed, it is Karen Martin."

"Very interesting," said Chuck, "It can only mean that Karen is involved in the biggest plan."

"This has to be money motivated," said Jake. "Or else why would she do it. Ideological reasons? I don't think so. Pressure applied? Maybe."

"The sort of money they were talking about for the pre-funding was huge, in any case," said Bigsy, "Several partners-in-crime, each putting up $10 million. I guess Karen might only get small slice, but it is still a lot of cash."

"Okay," said Chuck, "We have a couple of options. To observe her or to reel her in?"

"Well she is very close at the moment, I presume she could easily hide from us if she realised we were on to her."

"I agree," said Chuck. I think we must corral her and find out what is happening. I'm going to contact Robert Alton again and clear this with him."

He picked up his phone and walked away into a corner of the room.

Bigsy and Clare thought of a plan.

"I'll go to the restaurant. I can get an adjacent table," said Clare.

"I can get a table by the exit," said Bigsy.

"And Chuck can cover us from the back. We can't use James for this, because she will recognise him."

Chuck returned. "I've spoken to Robert Alton. He is quite relaxed about us pulling Karen but would like an opportunity to talk to her himself."

"We are going into the restaurant, once we have her, we can take her to your room in the hotel."

"I'll engage her in conversation first," said Clare, "We need to stop her from running away."

"I'm going to explain this to the restaurant staff," said Chuck, "It's time to flash a badge."

He walked towards the restaurant to seek the manager.

Then Clare wandered towards a table and asked to be seated at one very close to Karen. Bigsy followed and then Chuck took a seat much further away at the other end of the restaurant.

Karen briefly looked up, but then continued to read her phone. She was waiting for a next course to arrive.

"Excuse me," said Clare, "I hope you don't mind me asking this, but I've been chatted up by several of the men in the sales conference. Could you keep an eye out for me in case anyone tries to follow me in here?"

Karen smiled, "Yes, I'll keep a lookout, but I think the staff here are very good and they will ensure that you are not the source of unwanted attention."

Clare smiled, "That's the thing. We think you might also be the source of something. Is your name Karen?"

Karen tensed, "No, I think you have made a mistake?"

Bigsy moved from his table and Chuck stood. Karen looked around. She could assess the odds at three declared to her one.

"Look, what is the about?" she asked.

"I think you had better come with us," said Chuck, "I think we know something you will want to hear."

Karen looked around; she realised that escape would be difficult. The staff in the restaurant appeared to be taking the scene in their stride and she realised that they had been badged or briefed in some way.

"Okay, I'll come along," she said, "I don't know who you are or what you want, but you have the wrong person."

They all moved towards the elevators. Chuck used his special access key to the executive floors. Clare and Bigsy looked at one another, they just knew that Chuck would have a suite.

In a few moments they were entering the room. Karen remained very calm and unruffled by this strange behaviour. Chuck was on the phone to James and a few moments later he arrived at the door of Chuck's room.

"Hello Karen," said James, "I was expecting to see you in Cairo."

The Square

Karen looked towards James; they could all see that her last opportunity to bluff through this situation had just evaporated.

"James," she said, "This is most unexpected."

"You will need to tell us, to tell us all, what is happening and what is your part?"

Unbelievable

Karen began, "Okay, you know I've been a loyal member of SI6 for many years. I've been put under pressure in the middle east on numerous occasions. I was working with a guy called Fredericksson in Istanbul. He was supposedly from American intelligence but didn't have the moves that I'd expect. I thought all along that he had been wildcatted into the mission.

"We were to extract a small cell of American undercover agents. They were Muslim and had been able to work across the borders into Iraq and Iran, mainly intelligence gathering. Something had gone wrong and they had been discovered. One of them was killed in Iraq. A most bloody turn of events conducted under the ISIL penal code.

"A beheading?" asked James.

"That's right," said Karen, "A televised beheading. To keep everyone else in their place."

Clare shuddered, "How awful."

The Square

"Yes, I felt responsible for the whole cell. It had been my job to place them in Iraq and now it was my duty to get them freed again."

"It's brutal in some of these countries," said Chuck, "I've seen the hangings and beheadings in Riyadh too. They even push westerners to the front in so-called Chop-Chop Square, to show them what happens if we misbehave; it runs at something like 150 executions per year. That's three a week. It's where the phrase 'blood money' comes from. In a murder, the family of the murderer can pay the victim family blood money to atone for the crime. "

"Yes," said James, "and the Testament that those to be executed utter, it brings us back neatly to Karen."

"No, I'm not going along the Shahadah route," said Karen, "Or before I know it my head will be rolling several metres from my body."

Clare grimaced at this, "Can we get back to Karen's explanation?"

"Well, I was threatened, by, of all people, my own bosses - or, I should say, one boss in particular - Carson."

"He told me that I should take personal responsibility for the exfiltration of the agents. That they needed to be brought back intact and that they were valuable assets. To my eyes, they were burned assets. We could never send them back into such a scenario again."

"I arranged for an extraction, from Istanbul. It was supposed to be very low key. I took the team of them through the commercial airport on regular passenger tickets. We all arrived at İstanbul Havalimanı - which is the main airport and were checked in to a flight to Washington. Nothing suspicious, regular amounts of luggage and no tools of the trade.

"Tools of the trade?" asked Clare.

"Weapons or suspicious items in our baggage," replied Karen, "Three of the guys were greeted at the airport by hospitality people. They said they had been upgraded and would be able to fly in the front of the plane. First Class. I was wary of this, but let it go ahead. The others were escorted to the business lounge at the airport. They were told that they had not made the upgrade but that the lounge was the least they could do. That was another four, plus me, left to go in economy."

"It has all the hallmarks of a trap," stated James. Chuck nodded agreement.

Karen continued, "Of course, the other four were delighted to spend some time in the lounge and followed the hospitality people. That left just me - the woman. It was over an hour to the flight, so I went to sit in the cafe area downstairs in the terminal.

"Then I noticed a black military truck outside the glass windows. All seven of the men were being loaded onto it.

Karen continued, "A man approached me. I was adrenalined out at this point and worried that this could be my grim reaper. He was softly spoken. Said his name was Fredericksson. Told me that the seven would disappear, but that I was to be left to go about my business. That the story of their disappearance would be of a lurid rounding up, well before I got to the airport. In effect the men had not disappeared in my care.

"In return he said he didn't want anything at this time, but that he would be back at some point for a favour. He didn't say what it was, or who he worked for."

Chuck and James looked at one another. It was clear that they couldn't work out where Fredericksson had come from.

Karen continued, "Years have gone past since that event, but I still think of it every day. How seven men in my care were loaded onto a truck and taken away to be executed.

"Then, around a couple of months ago, I was contacted by Fredericksson again. He said he remembered me and the touching scene at the airport. He now had something he wanted me to do. He explained that a Colonel Carson would be in contact. It was about a truck carrying - he said - missiles from Israel across Egypt. I was to do what I was asked by Carson and should expect to disappear at the end of the mission. He put it that if I did it well, then I would survive and simply disappear. If I did it badly, then it would be curtains.

"That's when I was asked to exchange the briefcase in the desert, via a stringer- you James. I didn't think it could be that complex, so I agreed.

"Did they offer to pay you anything for any of this?" asked Chuck.

"No, the only payment was their silence, my guilt and my life, including anonymity," answered Karen.

"I think Ramirez works for someone called Carson," said Chuck, "we had better be very careful with this information."

"Couldn't you have told someone, somewhere?" asked Clare looking at Karen.

"I suppose I could have right at the beginning, but I was so scared then, having seen several good people put onto a truck. - It would have destroyed my service career too, I suppose that doesn't seem important to most of you, but it is a very complicated life that we all lead in this line of work."

Clare shuddered again.

Jake looked at Bigsy, "Don't you feel any remorse?" asked Jake, "For those men or what you have got into now?"

"It completely ran away from me," said Karen. "Just think about it, I'm asked to pass a case to a lorry driver via a stringer - no big deal. The next thing I know I'm caught up in some death threat to wipe out half of London."

"So, do you know the plans of Al Aktar?" asked Jake.

"Spell it?" asked Karen.

"A-L space A-K-T-A-R," responded Jake.

"Al Aktar - That's surely a bit of badge engineering?" said Karen, "You know in Arabic it means "the most", but its only a letter away from a Pakistani outfit called Al Akhtar, which have been mujahideen supporters, providing quarter-mastering under the guise of humanitarian aid."

"No, I don't know their plans, but I suspect they have been produced as scapegoats for whatever threat has been laid down."

"So, what do you know then?" asked Chuck. "You must have been told something, to make you come back here?"

"They told me that there were two consignments to be dispatched to London. A cylinder, which contains a toxin and a set of smaller units which are antidotes - mini-syringes if you will. They told me that the codes to activate were originally in the case which James was to hand over to the truck driver."

"So, we have a perfect storm?" asked Jake," The cylinders, carrying toxins, the arm codes and the antidotes all bound for London?"

"That's right," said Karen, "and I've seen each of the item be dispatched during today."

"What have we got?" asked Chuck, "Number plates, types of vehicle, endpoints?"

"Nothing," said Karen, "I've got nothing. I could see the dispatch from here in the hotel. On a tv monitor wired into my room in the hotel. I couldn't even swear that the dispatch was from Birmingham."

"At least we have got London, " said Chuck.

"And we know that the antidotes are individually RFID'd" said Bigsy, "That should make them easier to track down."

Carson and Ramirez

Chuck's phone rang. It was Robert Alton.

"Hey, Chuck, I wanted to let you know the latest. I've a contact in the Pentagon, a Colonel Ramirez. He has been following your situation and trying to trace the trucks. I have told him about you, and he is likely to call you sometime soon."

Chuck commented, "We need to find out whose side he is on. He receives direct orders from Carson but may not be aware of Carson's role in all of this."

"Meaning what?" asked Alton.

Chuck continued, "We've been with Karen."

"Karen?" Alton sounded surprised, "Karen's phone turned up at one of the truck rendezvous points. It made me wonder if she was still around. How is she?"

"She seems fine - the shooter was working for her and the hit was staged. She has told us about the situation as well as how she became implicated. Part of it has been to tell us that Colonel Carson is not what he seems. Karen has him pegged as an opportunist, working for a guy called Fredericksson."

"It also casts a shadow over Ramirez. He appears to work directly for Carson."

Alton continued, "Many people have been wary of Carson for a long time. He acts with political will and keeps much of what he is doing secret. A lot of people in Washington don't trust him, although I don't think they'd expect him to be working for another state actor.

"I don't think Ramirez is aware of the depth on this situation, Carson was talking about sending Ramirez to London, to supervise the operation more closely. I doubt whether Ramirez would go if he knew what was planned for London? Additionally, Ramirez has told me that Carson is planning to go to Frankfurt. Strangely co-incidental?

Alton added, "Something else, I was out on a mission yesterday. We caught some local lads moving BioPens around. We detained them just outside of Ashford. They were handing the devices over to a group of Arabs."

Chuck said, "This is very useful. I think we can assume that London is being targeted, and that perhaps Frankfurt will be the centre for financial trading during the disruption. Look - we'll be in London soon. It would be best to meet with you there. How about Westminster?"

"Certainly," replied Alton, "You couldn't get much closer!"

Ed Adams

564

Triangulation stations

"The only people who can see the whole picture," he murmured, "are the ones who step out of the frame."

— Salman Rushdie

Showdown mechanics

Karen asked, "What about those BioPens you mentioned. What are they?"

"Don't you know?" asked James. Karen shook her head.

"They are antidotes to the cylinders of nerve agent. They were smuggled in ahead of the main cylinders of nerve agent that were on the two trucks"

Karen looked confused, "What two trucks? Not the one I sent James to intercept? I was told this truck carried a missile."

"Yes, but that was yet another layer of deception, the truck was carrying the nerve agent. James had the unlock codes for the nerve agent, which was a binary."

"And the BioPens?"

"They provide the antidote to the nerve agent."

Chuck could see that the situation was registering with Karen. She realised she had been told something different and was having to re-piece the story together now.

"Wagons roll," Chuck declared, "We are all going to London, right now."

Two and a half hours later they were in Central London and driving into a car park underneath College Green, adjacent to the Houses of Parliament.

"We could hardly be more central," said Chuck. Jake nodded agreement.

He had driven the silver BMW hire car and Bigsy drove the black one. Now they were conveniently parked and ready to meet Alton.

Karen was in Bigsy's car, with James who had told her in no uncertain terms not to attempt to escape.

Chuck was already on the phone to Alton, "We're here, in Westminster - can we meet along Millbank?"

"Sure thing, How about Ravello's coffee bar - it's on Horseferry Road, just up from MI5."

Chuck said out loud, "Ravello's."

"I know it," said Jake, "Up from Lambeth Bridge. Less than ten minutes by foot."

The Square

"We'll see you there, in around ten minutes," said Chuck.

They walked to the small coffee bar, past the entrance to MI5, which Jake pointed out for everyone else. As they entered, Bigsy spotted a large group of tables and pulled two together.

Clare went to the counter to order some drinks. As she returned to sit down, the whole group were sat around the two tables, with a couple of spaces, which she assumed were for her and for Alton.

"We are suddenly quite a large group," she said.

At that moment Chuck stood, "Robert," he called.

Robert Alton smiled and looked over. He saw Karen in the group and his face hardened.

"Hello Chuck," he said, "Hello Karen, we all thought you were dead - not involved in some terrorist plot."

"Chuck, I brought a couple of friends who are waiting outside," Alton looked pointedly towards Karen.

"So what do we know?" he asked, "A terrorist plot to unleash US nerve gas modifications in central London. Financial manipulations. Carson involved. The binary to be mobilised with the codes from the briefcase. But we don't know where."

"That's about the shape of it," said Chuck.

"One thing," said Bigsy, "We know the BioPens were tracker enabled, with active RFID encoding."

"That's not enough to mean that GCHQ or anyone could track them down, but with a blast of radar at the right frequency, we should be able to spot a whole cluster of the pens."

"How would we achieve that?" asked Alton, "It sounds like mad science."

Bigsy grinned, "not really, your Typhoons have advanced radar on them, usually used for targeting. It's called Paveway, I think. If several Typhoons flew over London and used their targeting systems, we could possibly triangulate the RFIDs from the BioPens.

"Hmm, I'm not sure of this as a plan," said Alton, "nor am I certain that I could whistle up several Typhoon fighters."

"They have flown jet fighters along the Thames in the past," said Clare, "For big celebrations, like Royal Anniversaries."

"Wait," said Jake, "There's a meeting in London today. Some kind of government financial forum - the World Financial Forum - Could the planes be a useful added feature?"

"That might also be a clue," said Clare, "Disrupt finance whilst the WFF are meeting in London?"

"Okay," said Alton, "This could be my career defining moment. I'm patching through to Operations Centre, to see where we can rustle up some planes. Bigsy, I'll need you on the call to help explain all of this to the centre."

Bigsy nodded, "It's simple really, instead of the planes having their targets 'lit' by a beam, they will be looking for the beam generated by the RFIDs on each of the BioPen vials.. Those antibodies used active tags. That means they will be in the 433 MHz frequency range. I just hope that the Typhoon sensors can go that low. We are almost into shopping cart territory."

Alton could see that Bigsy was rapidly scrolling through what appeared to be a car brochure, but was actually a brochure for the $35m Eurofighter Typhoon.

"We ideally need two sweeps, he added, One along the river and another north London to south. That way we can triangulate the findings."

Alton grimaced,"It's not going to be that simple. I've been told we can have three planes and that they can pass once along the Thames. North to south isn't possible though, it cuts right across the Heathrow flight path."

"Go with it," said Chuck, "we'll see where we are after the first pass."

Alton said, "No wait, the RAF have come back with a counter offer. It's a Sentinel R1, which is already airborne and could be over London in about ten minutes. It can fly high and across London."

"The Sentinel?" asked Chuck, "They were used in Afghanistan against pop-up targets. I didn't know there were still any out there."

Bigsy was scrolling through more pages on the internet. "I see," he said, "They have a sensor bulge to track for targets. The radar it uses is quite an old system, but I suppose the active RFID is also quite old technology."

"Right," said Alton, "We'll have one pass over with the Sentinel north to south and then the scrambled Typhoons flying up the Thames. It's our best shot at this. It'll all be over in about 20 minutes."

They scrutinised a map of London and the intended course of the two sets of planes. Trying to guess where the sensors might be located.

Alton's phone rang.

"It's the feedback from the Sentinel. It has flown over London and says it seems to be acquiring active RFIDs from 51.51,-0.08 That's over the City of London."

They scrutinised the map. Bigsy typed the co-ordinates into his laptop.

"It seems to be St Mary Axe," he said, "that's the Gherkin tower."

"It is also where the WFF Conference is taking place," added Jake.

"How accurate are these sweeps?" asked Chuck.

"Without triangulation, they claim to be only to within a couple of street blocks," answered Alton.

"Listen," said Clare, "She ran to the door of the cafe and looked along the street.

"That was the Typhoons! I saw them fly past the end of the road. They were low!"

The Square

As she spoke, Alton's phone rang again.

"We just got the Typhoons' readings, 51.513929, -0.0883573. They say it is a sample of the three. It comes out at the Bank of England.

Jake looked at the map, "Yes, that makes sense. The latitude of the Gherkin and the Bank of England are almost identical."

Chuck stared at the map. "So, this road - Threadneedle Street - runs between the two areas? I'm going to take a look."

To everyone's surprise, Chuck walked out of the cafe and hailed a London black cab.

"Well, I suppose it is the fastest way to get there," said Jake.

"And pollution free, now they are electric," added Clare.

Right, now I think, Karen, it is time for you to say goodbye to these people and to come with my colleagues. You'll recognise the building we are taking you to."

Karen nodded. She knew she had run out of road.

Alton stayed behind

Bank

Chuck arrived at the busy road junction in London known as Bank. The taxi driver dropped him off on the triangle of land adjacent to the Duke of Wellington statue. Ahead were the steps leading up to The Royal Exchange.

"The Bank of England is across the road there," said the cabby, pointing towards the front entrance.

Chuck paid with his card and climbed out. There was an amount of disruption on the pavement. He could see that a new art installation was being installed on the concourse of the Royal Exchange.

He looked again, there were several bearded workmen around in high visibility jackets. He noticed they were of middle eastern origin. He could see the cylindrical artwork and realised that it was the missing canister, which had been hastily sprayed with a dull metallic finish.

Chuck called Alton,"It's here, the canister. I think the antidotes will be in the truck that is parked in the sidewalk outside the Royal Exchange."

Chuck looked towards the Bank of England. The canister was placed to be directly outside. If it was allowed to release the nerve agent, there would be a huge disaster in this part of the City.

There was a news feed on an adjacent building. It was scrolling that an airstrike had been attempted on Heathrow. Chuck thought that it signified the start of the terrorist distraction plan.

Ravello's cafe had BBC News channel scrolling across it. The latest updates were about the attempted attack on Heathrow. But that three RAF fighter planes had intercepted the missiles and then located the original attackers. No-one explained why the three Typhoon planes were flying across that part of London at the right time.

.--- ..- -- .--. / -.-. ..- - / - --- / ..-. .-. . - . -.- ..-. ..- .-. —

In Frankfurt, Carson was sitting in the control room, waiting to start running the trader scripts. He could see that the plan was unravelling. The diversion had been intercepted. He didn't know whether the nerve gas would work. He decided he would need to take over control of the London site.

The London truck had been wired for a conventional bomb as well as the nerve gas. Carson had a phone number to trigger the bomb. He dialled it.

Chuck heard a phone ringing in the truck and ran towards the Tube's subway entrance. There was an almighty explosion and the truck was lifted several feet into the air. The men who had been installing the artwork didn't live to tell the tale.

The cylinder had been fractured and now a green fluid was leaking onto the ground from where it soon evaporated. Emergency sirens moved towards the area and a rapid response team dressed in Hazardous Material suits from the City of London started to cordon the area.

... --- ...

Clare, Bigsy, James and Alton could see events unfolding from the television in Ravello's. As TV crews arrived, they noticed the fractured cylinder and wondered why it had not created more havoc.

Alton was on the phone. "Yes, good, clear. Thank you."

He turned to the group.

"We had to keep it quiet, but we'd swapped the codes to the cylinders when Chuck brought in the case from James."

"We swapped the 'arm' codes for 'disarm' codes. They still looked right and registered on the device, but they had the effect to neutralise rather than excite the cylinders."

"Do you mean Chuck raced all across London for nothing?"

"Not quite. Chuck knew about the exchange of the codes. He also knew how much we wanted to get these terrorists brought in."

Alton continued, "I have just had it confirmed that we have also found Carson in Frankfurt. He was sitting in a financial trading desk waiting for the shares and financial position to go crazy. We can link him directly to the phone call which exploded the truck bomb."

"What about Fredericksson?" asked Clare.

"No, we still don't know who he is, or who he works for. Maybe when we have Carson, we can find out some more. Don't forget we also have Karen Martin now."

"And Chuck? How is Chuck after the explosions around Bank?" asked Jake.

Alton looked stony faced, "Chuck would prefer to be gone," he replied, "Later on today we will find Chuck's green suit as the remnants from the explosion."

"Okay, I hear you," said Bigsy, "Chuck has disappeared on us again."

"I think he would like it to be thought that he had been blown up by the truck bomb," said Alton.

James looked at Clare, who looked quite tearful.

"I get the impression that you all liked Chuck?"

"A lot," answered Clare.

Jake and Bigsy nodded.

The Anchor

Jake, Clare and Bigsy were sitting around a raised table in the Anchor pub. It looked out onto the River Thames, close to the city and central London.

"Tom Cruise made a movie that included this pub," said Bigsy.

"Well, it is kind of scenic," said Clare, "with that view of St Paul's Cathedral."

"I doubt whether his impossible mission was as complex as ours," said Jake.

"But I'll bet our mission is just as secret as anything that MI5 would run," added Bigsy.

"And we'll still be waiting to hear from out mysterious disappearing Colonel Manners again," said Jake.

The Square

"Or that Robert Alton, maybe, or even James." Said Bigsy, "Hey, look, here comes Christina, we'll have to tell her all about this one."

"She'll never believe us," said Clare.

Ed Adams

THE CIRCLE

Ed Adams

a firstelement production

Ed Adams

First published in Great Britain in 2020 by firstelement
Copyright © 2020 Ed Adams
Directed by thesixtwenty

A CIP catalogue record for this book is available from the British Library.

ISBN 13 : 978-1-9163383-6-4
Ebook ISBN : 978-1-9163383-7-1

Printed and bound in Great Britain by Ingram Spark

Ed Adams
an imprint of firstelement.co.uk
ed.adams@Ed-Adams.net
rashbre@mac.com

Mailing list: https://mailchi.mp/9f0b30712620/ed_adams

THANKS

A big thank you for the tolerance and bemused support from all of those around me, especially Julie who has to make up the excuses. To the readers of my prior novels and to the requests for further frolics from Bigsy, Clare and Jake.

Sometimes one has to get out into the wild, and this trip around Route 66 and out into the deserts is a case in point.

Aficionados will realise that I didn't mention the Grand Canyon once, although I do still have the extensive video.

And, of course, thanks to the extensive support via the scribbles of rashbre via http://rashbre2.blogspot.com and its cast of amazing and varied readers whether human, twittery, smoky, cool kats, photographic, dramatic, musical, anagrammed, globalized or simply maxed-out.

So, let's fly like eagles and let our spirits carry us into the wilds.

And thanks also to the cast of characters involved in producing this, whether real or imaginary

And of course, to you, dear reader, for at least 'giving it a go'.

Ed Adams

Contents

THE CIRCLE   587

PART ONE   587

Starting Out   588

Arizona   589
London   592
Sedona   596
How did we get away?   602
Sleepers and Ties   607
Campfire   611
Crossed Arrows   615
Esther   618

The Desert   631

Scottsdale, AZ   632
Mount Ord Trailhead   635
Elemental   638
Gas station   643
Missed calls   647
The I-17   651
Phoenix Airport   654

Navajo Nation   659

Dangerous bends   660
Saddle up   668
Esther's end   671
Homing in on the range   677
Starting a fire   685
How the people caught the sun   688
As above, so below.   694
Albuquerque   698
Hotel Parq Central   700
Legal document   711

Chucking it down 714

Ministry Moments **718**

Penny for the Guy 719
The four winds 724
War Chalk 728
Vauxhall Cross 731
Amanda Miller 733
Route SI6 737
Cold Stone Creamery Jelly Belly jelly beans [TM] 741
Los Alamos 748
Tonto (Jay Silverheels) 753

THE CIRCLE **759**

PART TWO **759**

Route 66 **760**

La Fonda 761
Cache 765
Loreto Chapel 769
Breakfast in Santa Fe 772
Quickcode 776
Shortcut to the museum 779
Galaxy Defenders 782
Leaving 788
Delta Seven loses it 791

Wagons roll **793**

Interstate 794
Private Security 797
Frosting 799
Get your kicks on Route 66. 808
Taxi swap 812
Quesadilla and meatloaf 814
Durango 817
Kirtland 820

Bagels, Guns, Shacks and Oilfields — **824**

Einstein bagels for breakfast — 825
Tonto One — 830
Jake sifts — 836
Safe shack — 840
Second Amendment, 1789 — 845
Texan oilfields — 849
Two hours west — 854

Mormons came thru' a hole in the rocks — **857**

Bluff, Utah — 858
Leaving, on a prop plan — 863
Regular Jeeps from the carpool — 871
Footsteps — 875
The Groove — 877
On the radio — 880
Jake update — 883
Predator — 885
ScanEagle — 893

THE CIRCLE — **896**

PART THREE — **896**

Don't Mess with Texas — **897**

Houston — 898
Refundable — 903
Cowboy boots from Sheplers — 906
SI6 — 923
Liaison — 925
Joint Terrorism Task Force — 933

You can't touch this — **946**

Trap — 947
Conference Call — 950
Tony Capaldi — 958
AVGAS 110LL (blue) — 963
All together now — 965

International call 967
EnergyChina 970

Pressing the wrong buttons **972**

Bunker 973
DEFCON 976
Amber Alert 979
Tom 982
Monumental 984
A quicker scramble 987

Know a pistol shot's effective range **989**

UAV 990
DFW 994
Free to go 997

THE CIRCLE
PART ONE

Ed Adams

Starting Out

There's talk on the street
It's there to remind you
It doesn't really matter which side you're on
You're walking away
And they're talking behind you
They will never forget you 'til somebody new comes along

Glenn Lewis Frey, Don Henley

Arizona

Bigsy was bent into an unusual shape. He draped over the front seat of a car at a diagonal angle to the dashboard. Everything looked blurry, and he knew the car was moving fast. Intense heat as his head angled back towards the sky.

He tried to remember how he got here. His head pain and lack of limb control made it challenging to focus on anything. He made out a driver shape and the bumpiness of the route. He heard a pulsing sound, like a deep bass note mixed with a metallic edge.

Then a sharp bang which fired some adrenaline into his system. He tried to fix his eyes on the driver, wearing sunglasses and a baseball cap. Bigsy tried to speak. Still nothing from his mouth. The car lurched again with strong forces as it made a sharp turn. His eyes moved back to a central position, and he saw the sky again and a cactus branch. He realised that his vision was returning and tried to speak again.

Another voice behind him said, "Don't speak right now. They have drugged us. It was pretty effective. Someone doesn't like us."

Bigsy remembered the previous evening. Then his body jumped involuntarily.

A loud explosion and a scraping sound of big metal from close to their car. They still seemed to be moving forward. Bigsy still did not know what was happening, but it was something furious.

"Okay, they're gone. Now we need to find somewhere to hide." The voice behind him. Bigsy recognised the voice. American. Clearly spoken, clipped and precise. Chuck. Oh, yes, he had met Chuck Manners the previous evening.

"Yeah, and what are we going to do with him?" said the other voice.

"No, he stays with us. Bigsy is a friend. I asked him to be here," came the reply.

Bigsy sensed the car edge forward and saw sparse cactus bushes replaced with a canopy of overhead cover. Then some stunning orange rocks. He realised that his senses were returning, but he still couldn't move his arms.

 The driver continued driving, although without the urgency of the chase. Bigsy knew that he was drifting in and out of consciousness.

"We'll get into this shelter and wait for both of you to get your senses back." said the driver. "Chuck, you seem to be recovered, but the other guy's got a way to go."

"Yes, Mike," replied Chuck, "They have been quick to make us. Almost like an insider told them."

"We should be okay here for a while," replied Mike. "And there are provisions in the car's trunk."

"A regular tourist, huh?"

They had stopped in an area set back from the main roads. An area surrounded by desert, but with a range of distinctive red rocks rising on all sides. The driver had manoeuvred the large, blue, softly sprung slab of a convertible car into an area giving shelter from the sunlight and an almost garage-like cave with a high overhead roof and on a downward incline back towards the nearest track.

"This is a good spot," said Chuck, "Mike, you haven't lost your field-craft."

"Look, you take it easy for a while, Chuck. Get recovered. I'll keep watch first; then we can have a chat, and then maybe you'll want to check the area. I think your buddy will take longer to recover from this."

Chuck's eyes flickered, "Yes, whatever they gave us was slow-acting but powerful."

Ed Adams

London

Jake was away for the whole weekend. Family business and somewhat stressful. Not just the travelling, but some of the entertaining and conversations of the weekend proved difficult.

Since Jake and his two friends had set up their business called 'The Triangle' there were a lot of questions asked around the family about what they all did.

Jake, Bigsy and Clare produced a good front story, but behind it all, they sometimes mixed up in quite complicated situations.

The Circle

The creation of The Triangle led back to a time when one of their friends was murdered, and it dragged them into a complex web which led to them receiving a significant financial windfall. At the time there were no strings attached, but it meant they also became involved in another somewhat political situation. Jake couldn't explain any of this to his family and made up a bland story that they were advertising and media consultants.

Now, when Jake visited his family, they would ask questions about his life and fortunes, and he would make up answers which didn't always tally. It created a shifty impression of what Jake did for a living. Jake was convinced they thought he was selling drugs or doing something equally unsavoury.

Jake's prior background as a journalist didn't always help, because he would sometimes over-elaborate a story, which was then difficult to keep consistent if he was asked about it later. As a case in point, he had rented a family compatible practical hatchback for the weekend instead of his fancy Italian sports car. But then, he'd forgotten the colour of the hire car and neatly described something different when someone had asked, "What are you driving, these days?"

Now he was back in London at The Triangle's small offices in Hoxton. A weight had lifted from his whole being. It wasn't that he didn't like his family - far from it - it was much more to do with his need to keep them away from his business affairs.

Monday morning, and Jake flicked on the screen of his PC and waited for it to come to life. As it burbled through the start-up processes, he straightaway noticed a virtual sticky label attached to his desktop wallpaper. It was classic Bigsy. A note from Bigsy to Jake not sent by email or text or any of the standard methods.

Bigsy's computing background had devised a straightforward but secure way to send messages between the principal members of the office, but in a way that was not detectable by the usual snoopers. Bigsy had made the point to Jake that snoopers trying to hack into their system looked at the typical email and social media traffic and cookies. By having a completely separate system, they would be one step further ahead of anyone trying to pry.

Most of the time, they used it for shopping lists, but sometimes there would be something more significant. Now was one of those times. Bigsy's note said that he and Clare were contacted at the weekend and asked to go to Arizona.

Jake's eyebrows lifted as he read this. It was not a typical request, and he was slightly surprised that they did not phone him about this during the weekend.

Jake also realised that this must be a sensitive topic, which was why Bigsy and Clare were not making phone calls or emails about what was happening.

Bigsy's note continued that they had been contacted by a special friend who had disappeared. Jake knew immediately that this reference was to Chuck Manners. Colonel Manners was a contact that they knew from a couple of previous situations when they had got involved with the police and the military and some criminal types.

Chuck Manners was also elusive, and the strong rumours were that he had been killed after their last exploit together. Jake,

Bigsy and Clare had never believed that Chuck had been killed, but they had been sure he had wanted to get away from anyone that might be looking for him.

Jake reached for his phone. "Ping me," he typed and then sent a message to both Clare and Bigsy. He was only signalling that he had read Bigsy's message and would now wait for them to make contact

Sedona

Bigsy awoke with a start. He still felt woozy. He noticed it was dark and that he appeared to still be in the car. Earlier the roof of the car had been open, but now he seemed to be more enclosed. He attempted to move his arm, and to his relief, it appeared to be obeying him.

"Hello," he ventured. "Is there anyone here?"

He looked around and could see that he was alone in the car, parked in a small enclosed area surrounded by rocks. He worked out that they were still in the desert. He remembered that they were in Arizona. Then he noticed the driver of the car standing a few metres away.

Bigsy clicked down the door handle and eased himself out. He swivelled in the car seat and put his feet on the ground and gently pulled himself upright.

"Great, you can stand again!" said the driver. "Chuck has been able to walk around for a couple of hours. Can you talk yet?" he asked.

"Yes," replied Bigsy, slightly surprising himself that the words were coming out of his mouth. "What happened?"

"I guess you met with your buddy Chuck and have got sucked into something," answered the driver. "My name is Mike, by the way. I have known Chuck for many years. Let's say we shared a few moments."

"That was you driving a while ago?" questioned Bigsy.

"Yes, things were getting a little hot," answered Mike.

Bigsy took a closer look at Mike now. A wiry, slim build, deep tanned face that was still partly concealed by the baseball cap. Bigsy could tell that Mike was probably from a similar background to Chuck. Another ex-military type, American forces - no doubt - and perhaps some kind of special unit. There was a hardness to his face that Bigsy could see. The look of someone who has been in many fights and could stand his ground. Bigsy was glad that they were on the same side.

"We will wait for Chuck to get back." said Mike," He has gone for a scout around our location. I think you'll understand that I won't be saying too much about what has been happening until all three of us are together."

"In the meantime, you might like something to eat. Or at least something to drink? The trunk of this car has quite a few supplies."

Bigsy nodded, "Mike, thank you, that would be great. Water is my priority right now."

Bigsy made his way around to the trunk of the car. He was a little unsteady on his feet and realised that he had not recovered from whatever had affected him. Mike smiled and walked over and helped Bigsy open the back of the car.

Bigsy smiled. He could see that someone with a military mind had arranged the contents. There were several camouflaged bags arranged in the back.

"Yes, we have food, water and other items that might come in useful," answered Mike.

Bigsy lifted one of the bags. It was very heavy and seemed filled with some kind of mechanical equipment. Bigsy thought of guns.

"Not that one," said Mike, smiling. "The two on the left are the food and drink compartments."

Bigsy put his hand onto one of the other camouflage bags and could feel the outline of water bottles. He unzipped the top of the bag and pulled two bottles from it.

"Let's share one for now," said Mike, "I'm not sure how long we will be out here."

There was a small noise. A clink of a pebble hitting the edge of one of the large boulders.

"That's Chuck," said Mike, "He's sending us a message he is nearly back. We've worked together a lot, and that's a typical way to warn one another when we're approaching the base camp. We'll tell you more in a moment, but we both worked together for quite a long time out here in the desert."

"Chuck recovered his senses a lot earlier than you. We had a chance for a good chat while you were still out of it. You seemed oblivious even when we were laughing. He's told me a fair bit about you, Clare and your friend Jake in England."

There was another sound; the crack of a stick being broken.

"Now he's just having a laugh," said Mike. "He can hear us already."

 Bigsy looked around just as Chuck emerged from behind the rocks.

 "Hi, Bigsy," said Chuck, smiling, "How's Rapunzel? Do you remember anything at all from yesterday? We were both given some kind of drug while we were in the bar."

"Hi, Chuck, I gather you recovered ages before me. I don't think I can remember as much as I should," said Bigsy. "I can remember flying here from Heathrow to Phoenix with Clare and then driving to the hotel with the fire pits in Scottsdale. I remember splitting up from Clare and even remember meeting you in the bar at the hotel. I think we also had something to eat?"

 "Yes," said Chuck, "It was the dinner when things went wrong. Someone had intercepted us even before I explained what has been happening."

"But wait a minute," said Bigsy. "Where's Clare? She flew out with me but was too jet lagged to meet again last night. She went straight to bed."

"Yes - although you called her room and told her you had run into me when we first met in the bar. And that we would eat something."

"Okay - so Clare knows that we met, but not much about whatever happened after that?" asked Bigsy.

"Correct, and we were in such a hurry to leave the place that we didn't have time to explain the circumstances."

"I presume Clare will be concerned?" asked Chuck, "Because we will need to extract her, but it may not be so easy to return to that hotel right now.

Chuck continued, "She wasn't seen with me, and I think I'm the person who's attracting the trouble right now. If Clare stays in the hotel, she should be all right."

"Clare won't move for a couple of days even if I appear to have gone." said Bigsy. "She already knows that we have met. She will think you have taken me somewhere related to your initial contact with us." said Bigsy. "But look - what about last night - I don't know what happened. I have a vague recollection of being in a car - this car? - and that some people were chasing us?"

"Someone was out to get us, or more specifically to get me, and you've got caught up in it," answered Chuck.

The Circle

"I knew you wouldn't have contacted us again unless it was important," said Bigsy. "You know that most people thought you were dead after that trouble with the vaccine last year?"

"Yes," said Chuck," and I'm sure you'll understand it was best to leave it that way with most people. I'd always assumed that you would have suspected the truth - that I was still around."

"We worked out that you had escaped and changed your identity or something," said Bigsy.

"But it was obvious when you contacted us at the Triangle it was you. I left a secure note for Jake about your contact but have sent no emails or texts or used the phone about you," said Bigsy.

"As I said yesterday evening," said Chuck, "Thank you both for coming straight over here to assist me."

"You're welcome," said Bigsy, "and I'm reminded that there's never a dull moment!"

How did we get away?

"So, look," said Bigsy, "I still don't know how we got away from whatever was happening at the hotel?"

Mike explained.

"There were several of us on the way to the meeting place at the hotel. I don't know who called us there. I wondered if it was Chuck, but he told me he hadn't requested the meeting. What I know is that it was one of the original team of us that worked together out here a few years ago. Anyway, I was the first to arrive. You and Chuck showed up soon after me, and I could tell you knew one another well."

"I didn't want to show my hand the first evening because Chuck and I arranged to meet the next day. It looked as if you guys were catching up. I could see you both talking fast in the bar before you got something to eat."

"I didn't spot you there," said Chuck, "And usually, I'd be good at this."

"It takes one to know one," said Mike. "But you said there was another person with you; Clare? I didn't see you arrive, Bigsy, and I wasn't aware that you were with someone else. I think it would be the same for anyone else checking out what was happening. I guess they will only look for you two, Chuck and Bigsy, because you sat together.

 Bigsy commented, "Yes, and that was an accident. I didn't expect to see Chuck until the next evening. I only visited the bar because I couldn't get adjusted to the time difference and needed something before I went to bed. Clare had gone to her room. We'd arranged to see Chuck in the evening and Clare was going to check out the spa during the day.

 Mike looked at Bigsy. "I couldn't work out what happened. Partway through your conversation, I could see you both looking tired, and I noticed that after this you both left the bar for your rooms."

"Bigsy, you mentioned your room number to Chuck when you were still sitting down, and then Chuck signed the bill for the meal, so I knew the room numbers for both of you."

"Old habits," smiled Chuck.

Mike continued, "I was suspicious that something was wrong but didn't know what had happened. I checked that you got back to your rooms safely, and that you were not followed. I could only follow Chuck because I thought if anything was likely to happen, it would be to Chuck, the trouble magnet.

Bigsy grinned.

Mike continued, "Sure enough, there were two guys on Chuck's floor, standing a few doors along from his room when he returned. I watched Chuck go in, but then saw the two other guys getting ready to break in. I knew that Chuck's drink or food had probably been spiked, so there would be very little resistance from him if they got through the door."

"Just as I was thinking this, I saw them use a small electronic key to enter Chuck's room. I had no choice but to pursue and, er, what's the word? 'neutralise' the two guys.

"Chuck was in no fit state to help, but he was still standing. I called him towards the elevator and then selected your floor, which was only one floor down because of the low-rise shape of the hotel. I didn't have the luxury of a special key and had to damage your door to get into the room. You were also in your room but looked as if you had passed out on the bed. I woke you again and got you standing. You were both the worse for wear, and I thought it was the tranquilliser drug effect, which had kept you both functioning but only just able to move. It was like talking to slow-witted zombies as we all got into the elevator and went down to the ground floor."

Mike continued, "An advantage of that Scottsdale hotel is we knew our way around its back-doubles because of earlier times spent there. It meant I could cut through to the car park lot with no need to use the main exit. I got you both into my car and you both passed out almost at once."

Bigsy watched as Mike paused. He had run through this story with Chuck, who also seemed to have little recollection of what had happened. Chuck seemed to be listening to the story, as if trying to remember more of the situation first-hand.

Mike continued, "My main aim was to get us all clear of the hotel as fast as possible. Unfortunately, my car wasn't low profile enough, and the guys I had left in Chuck's room had their buddies waiting in another car at the front of the hotel. I thought I got away from them and onto the main route towards the north and decided it was better to stop somewhere off the road in the dark. With you guys both needing to sleep it off, I had little choice but to wait until the morning for us to regroup and decide on a further move."

"My hiding tactic worked because they could not find us. Both of you were completely out of it in any case. I worked out they had spiked you both with slow-release sedative - something potent but non-deadly and I would need to let you both sleep it off."

"Then, at around dawn, I set off along the main road towards the north, and everything looked as if we were in the clear. not. After about an hour of driving, I noticed a fast car behind us and realised that we were being followed. I think this when Chuck came to and it could have been my erratic pursuit driving that helped shake him back into life. The guys behind were angry and trying to force us off the road or worse."

"I had to take serious evasive action, and this caused their car to turn over soon after we left the Interstate."

"I think that's when I first woke up," said Bigsy. "I remember being violently shaken."

"Yes, that would be us being chased," said Mike. "I don't think they built this car to go over the country routes at such a speed." He patted the side of the blue car, and Bigsy noticed there were a couple of added bends in the metalworks as well as light red flecking of mud from the rear wheels, sprayed onto the rear part of the vehicle.

Bigsy asked, "So the guys in the car that chased us…Who were they and what were they doing?

"That's what we were trying to work out while you were still out of it," said Chuck. "Mike and I were discussing this earlier. We've got a general sense of what is happening, but we don't know who is behind it."

"The fact they are at the hotel in Scottsdale suggests that they are now like bees around a honeypot looking for other people from our old team. I think it puts anyone else from the old gang invited to the hotel in danger."

Sleepers and Ties

"What I can't understand," said Bigsy, "Is how Chuck keeps coming back to us when there's a problem? A year ago, we had trouble with the vaccines, and now again? Surely there are other people he could call on?"

Mike looked at Chuck, and they both smiled.

"Go on, tell him," said Mike.

"Well, Bigsy, it's like this. Have you heard of sleepers?"

"What the things that keep railway lines apart?" replied Bigsy.

"Er no - and we call those things ties here in America - I meant sleepers like you see in spy movies."

"Oh, the people that take up life in a foreign country and then get activated?"

"Yes, that's the type of thing," replied Chuck.

"Only the way they show them in movies isn't the only way that it works. When you are an agent like me or Mike, part of the training and fieldcraft is to get some people that are entirely 'off the grid' that can be relied upon under challenging circumstances."

"You mean like Clare, Jake and me?" asked Bigsy.

"Yes, and you are a classic and, dare I say, excellent implementation. We are supposed to find people and also to make them a little grateful for their contact with us. In your case, it was easy because we had that large lump sum windfall from the first situation."

Bigsy nodded. He knew that the first time he'd met Chuck the result had created a lot of money for himself, Clare and Jake. He knew that the money they had received was 'no questions asked' because of the basis by which they had received it. The only person who knew anything more detailed about it was Chuck Manners.

"In the movies, the sleepers learn all about the culture of the place they are planted and then get activated for ideological reasons or because someone has planted a chip in their head," said Bigsy, "You know that Manchurian Candidate that was programmed to kill the President. Or terrorist cells that are awoken to go bombing."

"Yes, you are right, but the way we are trained is to find a small group of people we can rely upon. They should have a good degree of trust with us but are going about their routine business. You, Bigsy, Clare and Jake are like this, but as you you've shown, you would all come to my aid if I needed it.

And you have plenty of access to cash, so you have the wherewithal to do it."

"Yes," Mike agreed, "I had a similar small team, in my case recruited via a sports network where I'd helped them win a large donation."

"The point isn't to use them all the time but to rely on them in a difficult situation. They are like sleepers because they are in effect activated, but the difference is that they still have the free will to decline."

"So, if Clare and I hadn't agreed to meet you, then you'd have been stuck?" asked Bigsy.

"Or I would have had to try my other group of friends in Canada," answered Chuck. "In fact, I contacted them, but you agreed to come along first. I'm glad it was you, actually," added Chuck.

"Good plan, except, of the three of us, one is still in the UK, I'm being chased, and Clare has gone missing," said Bigsy.

"Yes, we need to put that right as quickly as possible."

"And Mike, what about you? Have you also been working with 'sleepers'?" asked Bigsy.

"The difference for me this time was that I didn't realise how bad things had got until I saw what was happening to you and Chuck," answered Mike. "I haven't had the time or an opportunity to contact anyone. The message was signed by Esther to meet in Scottsdale, like Chuck. I knew it related to the work we'd done together and also that 'Esther' was a made-up name."

"Made up, but designed to ensure it would get our attention," added Chuck.

"So, what did you want us for?" asked Bigsy, "When you assumed that we thought you were dead?"

"Not at all. I didn't underestimate your thinking on this," answered Chuck, "I realised that you'd at least maintain doubt after what happened and that therefore if I made contact again, you wouldn't be surprised. Come on - you thought I blew up in a car. That would be shoddy."

"You are right," said Bigsy, "None of us thought you'd been blown-up, and that car explosion was a little too -er - big and isolated for us to believe in it. You were driving all that way to the marshes in a car filled with a big bomb. A crater the size of a tennis court. No remains. You averted a major London catastrophe, but it also gave you a perfect chance to disappear. It's annoying that you didn't tell us you were okay. In our hearts, we knew it anyway, though."

"I would not take any chances, nor create any new links to you so soon after that last little scrape," said Chuck.

"So, when your message arrived, we were pleased to hear that you were okay, although we were also sure that your contact with us would be because of some problem!" continued Bigsy.

"Correct," said Chuck, "Although neither Mike nor I have worked out what has been happening. Except that it to do with our old project out here in the deserts."

Campfire

"So, what would be the reason?" asked Bigsy, "Why are they after you? What was 'The Old Team' doing?"

"Okay," said Chuck, "let us check our logistics and then we can tell you more. I started to explain this last night, but I think both of us have a hazy recollection of what we said."

"First things first, we should check logistics," said Chuck. Mike nodded.

"We must use the backroads to get to somewhere where we can swap the car." Mike looked over to the parked vehicle, and Bigsy had a first chance to notice that it was quite a sleek and retro-looking convertible.

"Why have we got something that looks as if it should be in a movie?" asked Bigsy, "It is the most discreet form of transport?"

"It's mine," said Mike, "Or at least it is for this journey. I thought I'd hide in plain sight. It would have been almost more noticeable if I'd turned up in a black van or an F150. Like I was working undercover. This makes me look far more like a tourist."

"It worked well to get me from L.A. to Scottsdale, I'm sure I wasn't followed, but that means that they've picked up on us when Chuck arrived."

"Or Bigsy?" asked Chuck.

"I don't think so," replied Mike, "I'm certain that Bigsy wasn't expected or known about. He's hardly part of our structure," said Mike," Oh, no offence, Bigsy"

"None taken," said Bigsy. He looked into the small fire. He wasn't sure of anything now. A day in Arizona and he was already under some form of attack, holed up in the desert, with a Machiavellian ex-marine and a new guy who looked like an outlaw.

Bigsy smiled to himself. The pain and dullness were beginning to wear off. The food that Mike had prepared out of a can had been good. A cowboy supper as Bigsy thought of it. Beans and sausages from a can. A much bigger can than he'd ever seen from the stores back in England.

"So, it looks as if they spiked our food?" mused Chuck.

"The symptoms you both showed were like a slow-acting tranq," said Mike. "You were both zoned out and tripping. But it wasn't just some magic mushrooms or peyote mixed in the food, it must've been a far more refined version of whatever."

"Yes, enough to knock us out, but after a delayed period rather than immediately," said Chuck.

"Yes," said Mike. "It meant you could eat, get to feel drowsy and then get back to your rooms before the full effect kicked in. Then as you drifted off to sleep, you would in effect be out for the count."

"Long enough to be extracted from our rooms with no resistance."

"Yes, although I don't think they were interested in Bigsy. Just in you, Chuck," said Mike.

"So how come I'm here as well?" asked Bigsy,

"That was because of me," replied Mike. "I'd seen you together in the hotel and had you both under observation since you met. I didn't want to show up too soon, and it is lucky that I didn't," continued Mike.

"All this adds emphasis that there's something significant going down," said Bigsy.

Chuck nodded. "Yes. Bigsy, that's why I'd asked you and Clare to come here, I needed to tell you I think I'm under some threat, although I don't know its source."

"So why to call Clare and me?" asked Bigsy.

"The same reason as last time. You are unknown and have no records leading back into the military or the secret services. I'd wanted someone who could make some enquiries for me but drawing no attention. It needed to be face-to-face because I don't trust using email or phone calls for this kind of thing. You know I'd disappeared too."

Bigsy nodded. He and Clare both knew they'd help right from the first moment they received the call from Chuck.

Mike looked across to Chuck. "I'll go get the SIMMs then," he said, "We're in burner country around here, so it shouldn't be too difficult."

"Burner country?" asked Bigsy.

"Yeah, ever since that TV show about a schoolteacher making MDMA out in the desert, we've an extra traffic across the desert of camper vans and beat-up looking cars. Some are doing it like a travel route, others might well be cooking."

"Welcome to the land of opportunity," said Chuck.

Mike strolled towards the car. "I'll be back in the morning; I'll find a gas station with a store. May just stay in a motel tonight. You two will be fine."

Bigsy wondered why they all didn't move to the motel.

Crossed Arrows

Bigsy awoke. He could hear something around the camp. A crack of a twig. The merest hint of pebbles skittering down towards a gully.

Then he noticed a light. Within it he could see a shadow. A silhouette of someone. Slim, with a hair bun.

He turned to shake Chuck but realised he had gone. No, the shape wasn't Chuck.

Then a hand appeared around the tent fastening. Bigsy felt queasy until a voice said, "Hey Bigsy, I'd like you to meet Tom!"

Bigsy felt the relief wash over him. Instead of being stabbed by a spirit, he was about to meet one of Chuck's friends.

"Hello, Bigsy," said the second voice, "My name is Atsa Tahoma - but most people call me Tom."

Bigsy flicked his iPhone, and its torch lit the scene. Bigsy could see a tall, athletic man, with dark hair, pulled back into a bun at the back of his head.

"Hello," said Bigsy, " I won't lie, I heard you moving about, saw the outline of a face and thought we were being overrun."

"No, I'm alone. Chuck called me up when he arrived in Phoenix. He's been devilishly difficult to track down. He texted me last night with your current position."

"So, where do you know Chuck from?" asked Bigsy.

"I used to do some work with him," said Tom, evasively.

"I see," said Bigsy determined to get more information," What kind of things and was it here?"

"Yes, it was," said a voice from behind Bigsy, "Tom was one of the greatest guides to the desert, he taught me about desert craft, showed me where people had gone and showed me the spirits of his people. The Navajo", it was Chuck who took a couple of strides towards Tom. They embraced heartily.

"Man, it's great to see you," said Chuck, "You too, my friend," said Tom laughing and tapping Chuck's belly. "Not quite as wiry as before? Too many American treats?"

Chuck smiled, "I wish. And this version of me is with a morning jog every day."

Bigsy smiled while breathing in; he wondered whether Tom would wish to remark upon his shape next.

"Okay, I think we can relax now, Bigsy," he beamed towards Bigsy, who looked a little rattled, "I'm pleased to make your acquaintance." Tom looked towards the breaking dawn.

'Before me peaceful, behind me peaceful, under me peaceful, over me peaceful, all around me peaceful.'

There, I've said it." He looked towards Chuck, who grinned back.

"Tom's people are quite spiritual," Chuck explained," They know things about the Desert, its Spirits and the ways to live within it."

"And how to follow a set of map co-ordinates!" laughed Tom.

Esther

Chuck, Bigsy and Tom sat on rocks a few yards from the car. The shelter of the rocks around the cave worked well to provide efficient cooling. Bigsy realised that Mike had an excellent desert craft to find this spot but couldn't help wondering if there was any undesirable wildlife in the neighbourhood.

"Okay," said Chuck, "I ran through this yesterday with Mike, who seems to know less than me about what has been happening. He'll be back anytime now, I guess. I doubt if he'd spend much time at the motel.

As if on cue, they could hear a car approaching. It did a complicated manoeuvre, so it was facing back along the track.

"Hey Mike," called Chuck, "Look who is here!"

Mike looked up and then bounded towards Tom," Atsa Tahoma - Tom - It's been a long time!"

They hugged, slapping each other on the backs.

"So, are you still tracking out here?" asked Mike, "Working for the military?"

The Circle

"Yes," said Tom, "They seem to need a lot of help."

"Well, it's brilliant to see you," said Mike," But hey, I don't want to interrupt. I could hear Chuck spinning some kind of yarn."

Chuck smiled. "Yes, it's what I was telling you yesterday, Mike. I'm bringing Tom and Bigsy, up to date."

Chuck continued with his story.

"Ben Leitzmann, an associate of mine and Mike's from project Esther, was killed in a boating accident. I knew about this, although Mike didn't. And Bigsy, I know what you are thinking, a boating accident by itself may not be suspicious."

"And I'd agree. A tragedy, but there is a reason for my apparent paranoia about it though."

"Ben had tried to contact me just before this happened. It was indirect, in that he had notified me via a postcard from his hometown. It wasn't sent to me either; he didn't know how to get to me except via an ancient post box number."

Chuck added, "Ben's approach was a perfect tradecraft way to tell that something was out of the ordinary. Just a card, out of the blue, but with a way to contact Ben. It would be a classic 'Call me' type message."

"Although, because of my circumstances, it took two weeks to reach me."

"Not just the US Postal system then?" said Bigsy, "And why you? and did he tell anyone else?" He noticed a small lizard flick across a boulder. Chuck smiled.

"Completely safe here," he said, "except for the scorpions."

Bigsy flinched.

"It's okay in the daytime. They are night creatures looking for spiders and bugs. And don't expect ones like you see in the movies six inches long. These little critters are more likely to be a couple of inches at most. My advice is just don't be looking under any rocks."

Mike was nodding his head. "Yes. There's only one critter that's bad called the Bark. It looks kind of transparent straw coloured and packs a punch. But we should be fine here. If you see any big ones like four inches or more, then they are the hairy desert kind. They also have a darker coloured body.

Chuck said, "Now you know why I had that black light last night. It wasn't to show up your dandruff, just to look out for the critters."

Bigsy could feel his toes curling inward as he heard about these unexpected co-residents of the area.

Mike continued, "And no, I got nothing from Ben or anyone else. Just the request to come to Scottsdale, which I thought was from Chuck. That's also why I was scouting before I made contact. In case there was another dimension to this. Looks as if I was right and that someone is out to get us."

"Yes - there's a group of us," said Chuck. "You know something Bigsy, what I'm about to tell you is sensitive. Tom knows too, because of the work he did with us when we were at the base. I'll only tell you enough to give you context, but I don't want to put you in more danger by knowing more than you need."

Bigsy nodded. Chuck looked at Mike. "Are you okay with this, Mike?" asked Chuck.

"Sure," said Mike, "Bigsy is your contact, and if you've hauled him from the UK then I guess he must be all right." Mike was reaching into his jacket for something.

"Okay," continued Chuck, glancing towards Mike's jacket pocket," Here's the situation."

"The reason I asked you and Clare to come to Scottsdale is also no coincidence. Mike can confirm that this location, or should I say the hotel we were in, used to be a bolt-hole that some of us know about from work we did together a few years ago."

Mike was lighting a cigarette. Bigsy noticed as Mike replaced the shiny Marlboro package inside his jacket.

"How come?" said Chuck. "That's new?"

"I used to, then I stopped. Then I fell into some bad company, I guess," said Mike. The smoke drifted, and Bigsy wondered why it was trailing towards him.

Chuck continued, "It's like this. We're just over the state line here from New Mexico, and you may know that's where some of the big deserts provide space to try out new US military ideas."

"Mike and Ben and I and another few of us were part of a project a few years ago which was testing some new defence technology."

"There are some big ranges in New Mexico that can be used for missile testing and it provided perfect cover for some of the things we were doing."

Bigsy asked, "So was what you were doing legitimate? Was it part of something you were doing for the US government?"

"Bigsy, yes it was legit and for the DoD. US Army Intelligence employed Mike and me. Tom was employed too, in manner of speaking. It was an offshoot of a special unit called IARPA which stands for Intelligence Advanced Research Projects Agency. We both had special assignments to look after some of the more specialised and secret projects."

Bigsy nodded. He noticed that Mike was now stubbing out his cigarette with his boot.

Bigsy said, "So what were you doing there? Were you guarding the area or something else?"

Mike chuckled. He was already rummaging for another cigarette.

"Not exactly," said Chuck, "We were there to try out the technology."

"I think you know that I've been involved with several missions inside and on the edges of what the US government does. This time, we were trying out some new weaponry supposed to be for use by some of our elite forces.

"Mike, Ben and I were all part of a team that was involved in the testing. In effect, we were the users of this equipment."

"So, what did it do?" asked Bigsy.

"The project was called Esther. I think the simplest way to describe it is that it was a kind of guided rocket system."

"The jargon name we used for this was spot rockets. They are a kind of guided missile that can be fired with remarkable accuracy. It works by putting an identifying homing beacon onto the target."

"Most targets don't take to being identified in that way, so there's another aspect. They make the homing signal to be a tiny unit which can be hidden. It works by pre-locating the homing beacon well ahead of the deployment of the missile."

"But surely the homing device needs to create quite a big signal?" asked Bigsy, "Just the battery packs alone, plus the transmitter would make it large?"

"That was what made this clever," said Chuck," The technology used leveraged other technology to make itself work. It used a device like a SIMM card from a phone and a tiny aerial to hook itself into either a cellular network or a wifi environment. In effect, it was piggybacking on someone else's communications infrastructure."

"I see," said Bigsy. "It could use the effect of wide cellular and wifi coverage to transmit. It still doesn't explain how it could work for a long time without a big battery. Sending out a signal would still use a fair amount of power."

"That was a clever part," said Chuck," They had made the homing identifiers the same size as paperback books. There was quite a lot of technology in a tiny space. First, there was a little computer. Then there was a little battery pack. And third there was a wire-wrapped aerial that looped around the inside edges of the unit, . Like a square shape."

"At the time we all thought this was a cool technology," said Mike.

Chuck added, "What I remember is that the units produced sent out a very slow pulse. They designed it for something like four pulses per day - to conserve battery. It was only trying to find out if it had been woken up."

"I see," said Bigsy, "Low battery use running a timer like on a watch and then an occasional big pulse to see if they had woken it?"

"Yes, Bigsy, I can see you are still the computer geek I remember," said Chuck, "The pulses were to find WIFI or a cellular network and to see if the device was polled. Every device had a unique identifier and only if it was called upon would it then power up into its targeting state."

"Brilliant," said Bigsy, "It would mean the battery could last, what one to two years, and still be able to run at full strength for maybe an hour or two?"

"Exactly," said Chuck," It was a way to deploy very stealthy targeting devices which could be powered up when needed."

"And what could they be used for?" asked Bigsy.

"There are more moving parts than I can describe," continued Chuck, "For example, the payload that can be delivered is configurable by this system. It's used to drive targeting of anything from a small tactical rocket launcher right through to firing armaments from something like an F-15 fighter plane."

Mike nodded," Yes, we got to test some cool things out in the desert. Although we were only allowed to make tiny bangs."

"It's much the same here nowadays, just the names of things change," added Tom.

Mike and Chuck grinned.

Mike added, "The delivery system missile or rocket needs to have the guidance capability to work with this device. That's what we were testing out in the Mojave Desert a few years ago."

"Yes," said Chuck," The transponder technology worked pretty well, and it relied upon being able to upload the co-ordinates of the small device to the guidance system. The cool part was that we could also use for moving targets once we had activated it. That's another reason why the devices are only activated just before use. It helps avoid detection."

Bigsy asked, "So did these devices get made?"

"Only the prototypes. There were still problems ironing out the linkages between the missile systems and the small transponders. It worked well with a reasonably sophisticated system like the payload you'd get on an F-15 or a big drone but was sketchy with smaller weapons like the field launchers.

"There was the main problem with the speed of response of the targeting over short distances. If you fire something from close by, there isn't time to change its direction. It is basic physics that you need some distance and a reaction time. It is like trying to make a bullet turn through 90 degrees."

"So, the DoD viewed it as a problem. The people sponsoring the research for this system wanted to use it for battlefield systems rather than long-range systems. They already have all kinds of satellite technology is to do the same things for the long-range."

Bigsy looked at Chuck. "But isn't this a Pandora's box? Once the transponder technology has been developed it could define targets anywhere? They could lay dormant for a long time and then be activated?"

"That's true, but without the payload part working properly, it wouldn't be viable," answered Chuck, "And that was the area still being developed when the program got canned."

"That's right," added Mike, "One minute everything was being tested and then everything just stopped. I think other technologies had overtaken this one and made it irrelevant."

"Yes, it was a budget cut decision," said Chuck. "In typical Government style, they were running multiple programs with similar aims. It was a bunch of advisors that came in, and the result was a cut. DoD decided this was a dead-end technology and had been superseded by more rapid response targeting. The long delays before the targeting system could be activated, the erratic nature of cellular coverage and so on killed the whole idea. Project Esther was shut down over a weekend."

Mike chipped in, "Yes, so Project Esther was quietly terminated, and we were all released with the usual heavy-duty secrecy agreements."

"And how many of you did you say there were involved with this?" asked Bigsy.

"There was only an internal team of six of us working on the user and testing aspects, and that included Mike, Ben and myself. But altogether there were probably around 35
 people involved including the technicians and the scientists who were putting all of this together.:

 Bigsy asked, "So is someone trying to get at you now because of this project?"

Chuck and Mike nodded.

Mike was on his next cigarette. He replied, "We're guessing that that is the least part of the reason. But some of it doesn't make complete sense because we are the people testing the weapons rather than the people inventing them."

Bigsy watched as Mike fiddled with a few small branches that he had made into a small pyramid shape. Then Mike took his cigarette lighter from his pocket. Bigsy noticed that it seemed to have a high setting, more like a minor blowtorch. In seconds the wood was on fire.

"It's not to keep us warm," said Mike," It's time for some proper coffee."

He walked to the back of the car and returned with a small coffee pot.

"You have to have some creature comforts out here," he said.

"I know that pot," smiled Chuck.

"You know one that looked very similar," said Mike.

"We don't look like a very obvious target, and, we are also harder to eliminate than a few scientists. I suppose we are the ones who used the stuff, but that's less interesting than the people who designed it?"

"My thinking too," said Chuck, "I'd have thought the people who know how to build it would be of greater interest than the people who have handled the systems. Although ironically, I suppose the individual scientists and designers wouldn't be as easy to round up as we seem to have been."

Mike nodded," Yes, the scientists and designers will have dispersed. Some went to Seattle, others to Washington, some to Chicago. Maybe a few to Houston. They will all have been reassigned to other projects."

"So how did you first get involved with this?" asked Bigsy.

"It was routine for me," said Chuck. "…And I guess so for you too, Mike? The military needed a group of professionals who could operate a wide range of weapons and didn't mind sleeping in the middle of the desert for weeks on end. We even had a cover story that we were just testing a new short-range missile in the desert. In that part of the country it is no big deal. They even set up a company as a spin-off of Lockheed, and gave the missile a name - ADONIL"

"Sounds like a headache tablet," said Bigsy.

"Oh, it's a headache for someone, all right," said Chuck.

Mike added," …and that's why I guessed we were using Scottsdale as our meeting point."

Mike had been making the coffee. The pot had a traditional percolator which he had arranged over the fire. Bigsy noticed it was like a little ceremony. First, Mike had taken the coffee and pressed it into the metal container in the pot. Then he had rigged the pot so that it could brew the coffee. And finally, he had poured the coffee into three metal mugs.

"I know this is the Starbuck generation," said Mike," but you, Mr Englishman, need to try some proper cowboy coffee too.{"

Mike smiled as he passed the mugs around.

"When we all worked on the project, we would sometimes have some downtime. Then we'd get away from the base and out of the desert. It was better for us to do this under some kind of cover and we would usually go to Scottsdale to that rather nice hotel as a nearby base where we could let off some steam."

"We used to call it the convention centre. It was where we had our 'quotes' Sales Meetings." He moved his hands to make the symbol of quotation marks in the air.

"We would use the time to play golf and mess around but needed some cover and for it to be far enough away from the missile ranges not to cause suspicion. It's only about two- or three-hours' drive, but it's amazing that just crossing a state line somehow changes everyone's perspective about who we are and what we were doing."

"I see," said Bigsy, "So you'd go to Scottsdale or Phoenix, but you wouldn't go to say Albuquerque?"

"Way too near to the base," said Mike, "Albuquerque would be filled with other people involved in the business that would be conducted at the ranges. It was also just next to Kirtland, which has a huge Air Force base and the nearby Albuquerque International airport.

"I get it," chuckled Bigsy. "It's like not going to the nearest pub to the office when you are in London. But the distances are so much greater in America."

He looked at Chuck and Mike and laughed.

"You Brits have such a strange sense of humour," said Mike. He smiled and winked towards Chuck, "You know something. We were talking about the scorpions earlier. Did I mention the spiders? We have some cool spiders here too."

The Desert

There's a man who sends her medals
He is bleeding from the war
There's a jouster and a jester
And a man who owns a store
There's a drummer and a dreamer
And you know there may be more
She will love them when she sees them
They will lose her if they follow
And she only means to please them
And her heart is full and hollow
Like a cactus tree
While she's so busy being free

Joni Mitchell (23) - Cactus Tree –
October 12, 1967

Scottsdale, AZ

Clare had slept through until what she thought was late. She had woken up once at around 7 am UK time, which was still only midnight in Scottsdale. Then she had slept for another 7 hours. Her watch was still on UK time and said 2 pm.

She looked towards the large television in the room. She flipped it on with the remote control and waited for the menu system to start up. 7 am. It was still only 7 am. She was convinced it would be later. It felt a lot later. And she was hungry.

Maybe it wasn't such a good idea to go straight to bed after they arrived. Perhaps she should have joined Bigsy downstairs in the bar.

Clare remembered that she and Bigsy had made no specific plans for breakfast time. She'd told him she would try the spa and he'd said they could meet again in the evening. She knew his room number, and they had even swapped spare keys. Clare spared Bigsy the early morning wake-up call and instead arranged for her breakfast.

She pulled the curtains and looked at the bright light of the view. She could tell it was already hot outside. Hot and sunny. She was on the second floor of what looked like a low-rise block with a great view from its balcony.

Problem solved. Clare would take breakfast on the balcony. She wouldn't be meeting Chuck until the evening and that gave both her and Bigsy a chance to try the facilities of the rather luxurious hotel.

Clare reflected that it was always easier to fly from the UK to America because the time zones worked in favour of being able to get up late. The days before her flight had included time on the road with her musician friend Christina. The music business was all late and later nights. So, this excuse for a lay-in had been most welcome, and she could still feel semi-righteous that she was starting the new Arizona day early. She picked up the phone and ordered breakfast, being sure to include strawberries and maple syrup.

Then she showered and prepared for the day, ahead of the breakfast in her room. Maybe she would call Bigsy after all. If he was awake, they could share the breakfast on the balcony. She knew there would be too much for her to eat alone - this was America - and they could easily order extra coffee.

 She called Bigsy on the hotel system. Clare knew that it was better to avoid using cell phones until they had contacted Chuck and understood what they were getting into.

Clare dialled Bigsy's room but could hear the standard hotel voicemail message. Either Bigsy is still asleep, or maybe he too had got an early breakfast and was out somewhere. No big deal and no need to order extra coffee.

Clare spent the day until at least mid-afternoon lounging in the hotel. Bigsy would make contact at some point no doubt with an update from Chuck.

The hotel spa treatments looked good. There was an excellent half-day special. The spa and the pool would be fine until she had to meet Bigsy and then Chuck.

Mount Ord Trailhead

"Guys, I need to contact Clare," said Bigsy, " Otherwise we don't know what she will do. She knew we'd treat the first day as decompression and had already said she'd go to the spa in the hotel. She won't be looking for Chuck or me until early evening. But we don't want my apparent disappearance to alarm her."

"At the moment I don't think there will be any link back to Chuck," said Mike,", I was monitoring you last night, and I didn't work out you'd travelled with someone else. I very much doubt if anyone else will be able to. The main thing will be to stop Clare from creating a trail that links you three together, at least until she is away from the hotel."

Chuck nodded. "I think you are right, Mike. Although, I'd have expected to pick up on you being at the hotel early."

"Whatever," said Bigsy, "We must make contact and also pick up Clare. My hire car is also still at the hotel. Valet parked."

"I think I should call Clare. on her mobile phone number from a pay phone. I suppose I could use your phones, but I don't want to create any more links than we need to."

"You are right," said Chuck, "We must find somewhere to hide for another night and then to pick up Clare in the morning. It would be best if she can get your car too. We should check the maps for a good position for a meeting place."

"How about the airport?" said Mike. It is busy. It gives access to other vehicles - like a replacement hire-car. You can select a random incoming flight as the rendezvous?"

"I agree," said Chuck, "It's close to us here too, but big enough to make tracking us difficult."

"We'll get back to the road now," said Mike," We have left a very long gap here. We can find a different gas station from the one I used last night and Bigsy; you can make the call."

"Yes, said Tom, I can direct you to one; it is operated by Navajo, and I can ask there if anyone has been looking for you."

"What about cameras?" asked Bigsy. Mike and Chuck smiled. "Just smile," said Chuck, "We'll lend you a baseball cap and some big sunglasses."

"No need to worry about cameras," answered Tom, "Let me go into the gas station first. I can ask for a short-term blackout."

Mike had been packing the small number of items he had retrieved, back into the car.

"Ready to roll?" he asked.

Chuck took the second front seat, and Bigsy and Tom climbed into the back. Mike gently revved the engine, and they picked their way through rocks back onto a track and back towards the main road.

"Bye-bye scorpions," said Bigsy.

"Don't get your hopes up too soon," said Chuck, "There's a lot of desert out there."

Elemental

Clare had visited the elemental spa. There was a willow stream that ran through the area which the brochure said was inspired by a place called Havasupai, an oasis deep in the Grand Canyon where energy unites and restores.

The spa had a mesa rooftop pool under the deep blue Arizona sky. Clare enjoyed a private cabana and could look out towards the McDowell Mountains.

It had said 'take a half-day' on the brochure, and Clare had followed the advice trying the Desert Oasis, the open-air reflection atrium and also dawdled at the waterfall. To her surprise, the treatment room also had a private outdoor patio,

Now she felt pleasant and relaxed, but thought it was probably time to find Bigsy again. And anyway, if they stayed a few more days, then maybe she could have another go.

She returned to her room.

Clare looked towards the room phone but saw that the red message light was not flashing. No messages. Bigsy hadn't called. He couldn't still be asleep. It was inconceivable that he would wait this long to make contact, and anyway she had called him at breakfast time.

It was now 2 pm, which would be around 9 pm in the UK. Clare also checked her mobile phone. She didn't expect messages from Bigsy there, aside from the text he had sent when he had found Chuck the preceding night.

Clare decided she would check in Bigsy's room and made her way to his floor. The door had a 'do not disturb' sign on it.

She felt into her jeans for the key to Bigsy's room. First, she tapped on the door. No reply. Again, a little louder. No reply and no sounds from within,

She opened the door, noticing the damage around the lock, and tapped again, this time on the open door to the side bathroom.

No-one.

Then inside the main room. It was just like hers, only a floor lower. Curtains were open. She had the best view.

Bigsy's case was on the bed. A few items scattered around, which showed Bigsy had been in the room, but didn't look as if he had unpacked.

The bed looked as if it had received turndown service, but no occupant. There was a small chocolate in a wrapper. Bigsy's red backpack on the bed looked as if it had only been placed there before Bigsy headed for the bar. Bigsy could only have spent a few minutes in the room.

Clare realised Bigsy must have met Chuck. She wondered if they had gone somewhere that evening. It was unusual for Bigsy not to leave any message though. Clare would need to resort to using her phone to contact him, even if they had preferred not to use this form of communication.
She clicked her phone, ready to text. Then she noticed it. Bigsy's phone was one of the loose items in the room.

Highly unusual. Bigsy wouldn't go without his phone unless he was in a big hurry.

Clare would lay low in the hotel until Bigsy contacted her. She was sure that she would be contacted by the evening in any case. She chose not to contact Jake in this period, but in the evening to check the bar in case Chuck showed up.

Clare picked up the most important of Bigsy's belongings and put them into the small canvas laundry bag in the wardrobe. She would take them back to her room for safekeeping.

Then she left the 'Do Not Disturb' sign and headed back to her room.

No sign of Bigsy, no messages, but he had been with Chuck. That would be the explanation. The enigmatic Chuck had taken Bigsy somewhere as part of the reason they had been called to Scottsdale.

Clare would need to sit tight until Bigsy, and Chuck returned.

Clare looked through the items she had picked up from Bigsy's room. A small bag containing a laptop computer, the phone, two spare SIMMs, some connector cables, two different sets of keys, a small empty notepad, a few pens.

She moved the various items to the small safe in the cupboard in her room. She noticed it had a charging socket inside and charged Bigsy's computer while it was inside. She placed the other items inside the safe, except for one set of keys.

The set which said 'Hertz'. She would check out the car to see if there were any further clues. She smiled at the thought they referred to it as a car. When they had arrived at the car counter, they had expected the vehicle to be ready to drive away.

It hadn't been ready, and when they did eventually get it, the original one was enormous, like some van. They had made a fuss and had it 'downsized', which seemed highly amusing to the people working in the booth. They were much more used to people asking for something larger.

It was still a big vehicle and looked very capable of going off-road. Clare and Bigsy were both relieved to see the large-sized parking bays in America and could understand why everyone 'front parked'.

Clare walked to the parking area. They had valet parked the car, so it was fortunate that Bigsy had only handed over one of the two keys supplied. The car was still there. Clare thought that even this downsized car looked enormous. Clare peered inside. There was nothing to indicate that Bigsy had moved it. It looked as if he had gone wherever with Chuck in Chuck's car.

Gas station

Bigsy looked out of the car windows as they drove along the highway. It wasn't a fast road, but one with long curves and undulations. Both sides Bigsy could see prominent red rock outcrops. Quite striking.

"Many people say this area is mystical," said Chuck.

"I can see why," said Bigsy. "The scenery is most impressive."

Tom nodded, "Around this part of the desert there is much of four colours," he said.

"You'll see the shadows of black, whites from the rocks, blue from the sky and yellow from the sands. When the conditions are like this, we sometimes call it the Ni'hodilhil First World."

"Ni'hodilhil First World," said Bigsy, "I must practice that one."

"On a spiritual day, you will see the four cloud columns. They are white dawn on the east, blue daylight to the south, yellow twilight to the west and black night to the north. It is said that only First Man and First Woman lived here, far apart on opposite sides of the plain."

"Like Adam and Eve?" asked Bigsy.

"These Mist People had no definite form but were to change to men, beasts, birds, and reptiles of this world," continued Tom.

"Okay, not like Adam and Eve then," said Bigsy.

"Once they found one another through the use of their fires and crystals, they were tricked by coyotes — one coyote who was formed in the water and the angry coyote who wore a hairy coat.

"This group attracted more to their number and the wasps, bees, and stinging ants arrived.

"Then more insects arrived in this primordial land, and all became chaotic with fighting. The man brought a big reed, which he planted in the east. It grew fast so that when the gods became angry with the first world and destroyed it, most creatures could escape to the Second World.

"Wow, that's quite a story," said Bigsy.

"Remember that's only one of four worlds," answered Tom.

"No wonder so many crystal gazers have migrated to the desert," mused Mike," Take Sedona as an example."

"The residential areas around here are well-heeled nowadays," said Chuck,"… not exactly where hippies that have made it come to, but you'll find a fair share of crystal gazers."

"It's mighty impressive," said Bigsy.

"But a long way from the ocean," added Mike, "Look, Tom, is this the one? This will do fine." He gestured towards a filling station ahead of them. There were already several other cars and camper vans filling up.

Tom nodded, "See the dreamcatcher outside of the door? That's not just for tourists, you know."

"I'll fill, you make the call Bigsy," said Chuck, handing Bigsy a pile of small coins.

Bigsy walked towards the payphone. He could see that the phone had a card slot but also a small coin slot. He realised he could fill it with small coins to make the call to the hotel. Chuck had given him several dollars' worth of quarters; he just hoped it would be enough.

He dialled and was connected. He asked for Clare's room and was put through efficiently. He hadn't needed to top up the call yet. Clare's voicemail.

"Hello, this greeting recorded at 3.30 pm. Please leave a message."

She had gone to the trouble to put her voice on instead of the standard message. Bigsy worked out that it would be for his benefit so he would know he was calling the right room and that she was all right.

"Hi, it's me. I'm with him. Meet this evening at the airport as if for the return flight. Park. Leave the bags in the car and meet me at the gate as if we are going back. Don't check-in. Don't call me. All Okay."

Bigsy was pleased; it was a short message. He knew Clare would understand it and he also knew that she was okay, based upon the message she had left. His meeting was a little improvised but gave enough for Clare but not a huge amount for anyone else who was trying to figure it out.

He still had a lot of Chuck's change as he made his way back to the car.

Bigsy also knew that Clare would not try to make any other contact with him. There was nothing more he could do until the next day when they would meet.

Bigsy knew that Clare would get to the check-in area around 2 hours before the flight time as if they were going back to London. This limited the amount of time they would need to spend there and also kept their options open about what they would do next.

"All good," he said to Mike and Chuck, "Clare will be meeting us later at the airport."

Missed calls

Clare couldn't believe it. She'd headed downstairs to check with the front desk in case Bigsy had left a message.

That was precisely when he called her room. She had missed him.

In a way, she was still relieved. He'd got into a scrape already with Chuck but at least was in communication and making a plan for what they needed to do next.

Unfortunately, it blew a hole in the repeat spa treatment idea.

The message from Bigsy was very short. Clare knew this meant he was trying not to give too much away. She assumed it was a payphone. The message was clear enough, though. Get back to the airport with the car and meet Bigsy and Chuck at the departure check-in.

It was very short, and she knew that Bigsy was trying to avoid giving too much information away.

Clare looked at her watch, which was now on American time. She had about six hours. Include an hour to get to the airport. Two hours to wait. Maximum.

She hurriedly packed her own items and carried her bag to Bigsy's room. Then she scooped the few items of Bigsy's into his bag and using her bag as a support wheeled both bags to the elevator.

She wondered whether to check out but decided it might be better to leave the option to return to the hotel open. Also, if she was being watched, it would help keep any followers off guard.

At the valet area she explained that she was with Bigsy from room 317 and that she was getting the car brought around. No, she didn't have his ticket, but she had the other car key as proof. Bigsy "Mr Carter" was out, and she was going to pick him up.

The valet hurried away to get the car, and a few minutes later the luggage was loaded, and she was on the road. It was only about 35 minutes to the airport, but she'd allowed more time because of the chances of getting lost on the way. Although she had navigated for Bigsy when they had driven to the hotel, she had expected it to be tougher going back. It was simpler because she soon picked up the road signs towards the airport and then towards the terminal car parks.

She moved the vehicle into a short stay bay in the pickup area close to the terminal and crossed to the arrivals level in the terminal. She looked around as she did this, but then crossed via the escalators to the departure level check-in.

It was busy with people, and a few security people in uniforms. Nothing out of the ordinary. She spotted a small coffee shop in a corner and, after buying a newspaper, headed to the area and sat with a tall latte waiting for Bigsy to show.

She was sure that he would arrive around two hours before the flight time, so she probably had less than an hour to wait. She sipped at the latte.

Clare felt somewhat cut off from the action but decided it would be even worse for Jake. She called him to bring him up to date. Jake's mobile was ringing.

"Hi, Jake," began Clare.

"Clare," he answered, "It's about time I heard from you. Are you still in the US?"

"You bet; How did your weekend go, with the family?

"Don't ask, they were keen to hear what I was doing. I'm sure they think I'm selling drugs or something. How did you get on?"

"Well, we arrived at the hotel, both of us tired from the flight. I went to bed. Bigsy had a drink. I think he ran into Chuck. They've gone somewhere now. I don't know what has been happening during today, but I'm sure that Bigsy will try to make contact this evening.

"We'd agreed to have a day to chill before we met Chuck, I can only guess that Bigsy ran into Chuck in the bar yesterday or something."

"Aren't you concerned?" asked Jake.

"Not yet," said Clare, "But monitor the comms. I'm certain that Bigsy won't want to use too many phone calls or ways to trace or link us all together. Look, I'll call you as soon as anything develops. Meanwhile, I'll keep you updated via that stickies App that Bigsy has put onto all of our phones and laptops."

The I-17

Mike had driven the blue car back onto the I-17.

They were heading south again, back along the road that Bigsy assumed was the same one they had driven in the other direction the day before. The road was busy with traffic, and Bigsy assumed this would this give them an element of cover.

"A little further and you can drop us off," said Chuck. "There's a big shopping mall, which will give us somewhere to be lost until it's time to get to the airport."

Mike nodded. The mall would be an easy place for a drop-off, provide anonymity and also give easy access to taxis to get to the airport later.

"Will you be all right with this car?" asked Chuck, "I think they know it now, so I wouldn't stick with it for very much longer".

'That's fine," said Mike, "It's on my list too. I don't want to jack something though, because that will add the cops into the equation. I need to move the gear in the trunk to something else but will probably head to a rental to get a replacement. As a matter of fact, I'm planning to go to the rentals at the airport after I've dropped you off."

Chuck nodded. He also knew it was better for them to split up and that it was not sensible to wait at the airport longer than necessary. The shopping mall was a better location because it was both random and also had plenty of hiding places.

They drew up to the entrance to mall and Bigsy looked at Chuck.

"Er- is this the right place?" asked Bigsy. It was a large mainstream mall just to the side of the I-17.

"Right now, there is no right place," said Chuck. "We need somewhere to stop until we get to the airport."

"I guess it is then," said Bigsy.

His eyes searched along the signage, and he spotted the words 'Food Mall'.

"Okay - I can lead us from here," he said, grinning, "There's a food mall and also restrooms to freshen up."

"Hey Mike - Thank you for everything - it's been a strange 24 hours," said Bigsy, shaking Mike's hand vigorously, "You take care now."

Chuck looked at Mike, "We'll need to stay in contact until this has played out." said Chuck. Mike nodded. "Yes. What will it be?"

"We'll use gunfight at the OK Corral," said Chuck, "It seems kind of appropriate."

Mike nodded, "Que te cuides, Chuck. You take care now."

"Hasta luego, Mike," said Chuck, "See you later!"

Mike tapped the gas, and the car eased away.

"What was all that about?" asked Bigsy. "The OK Corral? Very cowboy."

"It's if we need to get in contact, we'll use Amazon and add comments in the sale of that DVD. It'll only be for the next week, but it is a quick way to communicate without it being very obvious what we are doing."

Bigsy nodded. Another piece of field craft in Chuck's trade.

But now it was time to check out the Food Court.

Phoenix Airport

Chuck's plan to get a taxi from the shopping mall to the airport worked effortlessly. There was a full cab rank outside the mall, and the journey to the airport was only about 25 minutes.

The three of them, Chuck, Bigsy and Tom, had arrived with about two hours to the departure time for the British Airways flight to London and made their way to the area by the check-in desks. Bigsy looked for Clare while Chuck and Tom looked for anyone that may watch them.

They had agreed that they would separate when they were in the airport and would only meet up again once Bigsy had met Clare and they were walking back to the car.

Soon enough Clare spotted Bigsy and left the cafe to walk directly towards him. She could see that he had seen Clare, but only signalled with his eyes to follow her outside and back to where their rental car was parked.

Clare understood immediately and without showing recognition, made her way quite slowly back towards the short stay car park. Bigsy couldn't see Chuck anywhere but was sure he would be following.

Clare found the payment machine, paid for the parking ticket with several dollar bills and then walked towards the car. Bigsy held back until Clare had opened the car and then stepped forward to sit in the back seats of the car.

Before they even started talking, Chuck appeared and climbed into the front seat next to Clare. Tom slid into the rear seat, next to Bigsy.

"Just drive," said Chuck, "We can do the proper greetings later."

"He's right," said Bigsy, "We need to be away from here."

"You know what," said Chuck, "it's probably better if I drive for the moment."

Clare climbed out of the car while Chuck shimmied across into the driver's seat. Tom climbed into the back next to Bigsy.

"You don't give a girl much time to catch up," said Clare.

"All in good time. This should only be precautionary," said Chuck, "And me driving is only in case we are being followed and need to take some evasive action. I know these roads… And say hello to Tom, he is a great friend of mine and a wonderful person to have assisted us here in the desert."

"Well, hello Tom," said Clare, "Hey and good to see you all. I was just starting to get worried!"

Chuck gently moved the car towards the exit from the car park and then out into the confusing ramps and exits from the airport. He soon took them back onto the I-17 and was heading north towards Flagstaff.

"I'm starting to know this area's roads," said Bigsy.

"When we are out of this area we can stop, swap drivers and have a proper conversation to bring Clare up to speed," said Chuck," I'm sorry it has started like this. At the moment I'm keeping a lookout to make sure we are not followed."

"Did you get our bags?" asked Bigsy, "There were quite a few important things in my room."

"All taken care of. They are in the back of this huge, so-called car. I took everything loose from your room and put it in your backpack, then had all the luggage transferred to the vehicle by the concierge," said Clare, "Although I've left us checked in at the moment."

"That's good," said Chuck," If anyone is checking for us, it will take another day to realise we have gone."

"Yes, I'll check out by phone tomorrow," said Clare.

"We have quite a few tales to tell already," said Bigsy, "It's not been dull. How about you?"

The Circle

"Spa treatment," said Clare, "I didn't realise anything serious was happening until I got your voicemail. I thought you were with Chuck and had probably gone to pick up something."

Chuck smiled, "You know guys, I'm very grateful that you have come along to assist me with this. I still don't fully know what is happening, but I'm getting more of an idea."

"So where are we heading right now?" asked Clare.

"Mainly north," said Chuck, "and then, Tom, I think we'll be heading east into the desert. I think I will need to visit the area around which I worked a few years ago if we are to get to the bottom of this."

Tom nodded agreement," Yes, we must head for the bases. Don't worry though; there will be plenty of opportunities for concealment."

"Concealment, chases, mystery; Chuck, it's fun, as always, being around you," beamed Clare.

Chuck answered, "Originally I'd hoped to keep it very simple with you running some anonymous interference for me. But whoever is after me has already seen us together. Well, they have seen Bigsy and me together. Oh, and they have also seen Mike, who you haven't met, Clare."

"Okay, you must slow down and explain properly," said Clare," I can tell you've been living it fast. We also must update Jake with what is happening,"

Clare noticed that as they drove further north, the scenery changed from the suburbs of Phoenix to a more arid landscape. They could tell that they were on the edge of the desert. The fast road was mainly straight, but every so often there would be a split between the northbound and southbound carriageway is which would sometimes appear to be a good quarter of a mile apart.

Bigsy looked from the back seats of the so-called car that the rental company had given them. Even this scaled-down one was more like a small van. Huge by British standards with sliding doors for the back section. It also had a brilliant air-conditioning system which kept everyone cool.

"I can see why this size 'car' is so useful now," he remarked, stretching his legs out in the back.

Navajo Nation

She heard about a place people were smilin',
They spoke about the red man's way, how they loved the land
And they came from everywhere to the Great Divide
Seeking a place to stand or a place to hide

Down in the crowded bars out for a good time,
Can't wait to tell you all what it's like up there
And they called it paradise, I don't know why
Somebody laid the mountains low while the town got high

The Last Resort - Glenn Frey / Don Henley

Dangerous bends

Clare watched the scenery as Chuck continued to drive north at a steady speed for two hours and then turned east onto the I-40. She could tell that both Chuck and Bigsy were tired and that this drive was their first chance to unwind, maybe since they had left the hotel back in Scottsdale.

"We will keep going along this road for about a couple of hours," Chuck said, "By then we will be around 250 miles from the Scottsdale hotel. It is far enough away for us to be harder to trace. And it's also in the right direction for us heading towards the ranges. It will be good to take a break then."

"I think you and Bigsy are way ahead of me about what's happening," said Clare. She considered asking Chuck if he would prefer her to take over the driving, but he seemed engaged with the task on these smooth roads.

The Circle

Chuck signalled and pulled off of the main road and into what looked like a 1950s motel. Clare thought it looked like a classic design and would have made a good venue for a television series.

"This will be a great spot for us this evening," said Chuck.

By now the sun was setting, and there was an orange glow across the scene. They climbed out of the car and Chuck led the way into the small reception of the motel. As they walked across, it amused Clare and Bigsy to see a dozen Prairie dogs lined up along the roadside, like so many inquisitive meerkats. Chuck asked for four rooms and after a short discussion paid with cash.

"It's for overnight," he said," And we will leave here early tomorrow morning." Then he turned to Bigsy, "Meantime, we should find somewhere to eat, and we can try to explain what has been happening, to update Clare."

Across from the motel was a small diner, and they walked across to the entrance. They ordered some burgers and coffees and talked about the last couple of days events.

In the room's corner, a television was playing the local news. A traffic incident showed up. A blue convertible had crashed off a bridge and into a river. Bigsy noticed it first.

"Chuck you'd better look. Is that Mike's car?" he whispered. Chuck stood up and walked closer to hear the sound better.

"Bigsy, it's happened again. That was Mike. He's gone like Ben. The news report shows his car crashed clean off the bridge and into the river. It was a 100-foot fall. They have not found the body yet, but there's no way that Mike could have survived that. Remember, this was the second attempt to get Mike. I thought he should have changed that car. It was too distinctive. Although, strangely enough, they are not mentioning anything about the car's content. Mike's trunk was 'fully loaded'."

"If they think there was something suspicious about the car, then they may hold the information back on purpose?" suggested Bigsy. "…And I presume there's no link back to us?"

"Nothing," said Chuck. "I was very careful when we left the car to check for lost belongings. There will be fingerprints and so on, but not anything more obvious to create a fast and direct link to us."

"I wondered about those other bags in the back," said Bigsy, "They felt kind of heavy."

"Yes, weapons," said Chuck, "Mike had a one-man army provisioned into the trunk of that car."

"That news means they won't give up looking for me," said Chuck.

", I think we could give them the slip after we stopped at that shopping mall and then switched to this car. They would need to be very on the ball to keep up with that switch. I think we were also very careful around the airport, so I don't think they have followed us. I think we have an advantage as long as we don't do the things they will predict."

"But what about going to the military ranges?" asked Clare, "Surely, they will expect that?"

"Maybe," said Chuck, "But it is a huge area to monitor."

"But what about phones and other things they could use to track us?" asked Clare.

"They don't have my cell phone identity, nor either of yours. I didn't give that information to Mike either," said Chuck, "At the moment we are clean."

"They don't know about me, either," said Tom, "That could also be useful later on."

"It's a pity that Bigsy has already been linked to me," said Chuck," Although I don't think they could link Clare at the moment. When I asked you guys to come over to join me, it was to help me find information without it being detected. Look, Clare, I think we need to bring you up to date."

Chuck recounted the previous events to Clare, and Bigsy and Tom added what information they could remember.

"Well we still have one advantage that neither me nor Jake is known to your pursuers, Chuck," said Clare, "As Bigsy has been seen with you, it could compromise him being involved in the next stage."

"So, here's what I think is happening from the way you describe it. You, Chuck, and some of your ex-colleagues have been called back to this base where you used to work. We know it's something to do with this special missile guidance but that the project was cancelled." Clare twisted the top of her coffee mug around through a quarter turn.

"I'm guessing that this guidance technology has resurfaced even if it is defunct and superseded. For some reason the people that know of its existence are being eliminated. Although it's strange because you guys were users of the technology and different people were its inventors." She moved her coffee cup another quarter turn.

"Agreed," said Chuck. "I was thinking the same thing. We were also the people that knew where the individual scientists had gone after they finished their work on this assignment."

"We were each responsible for the re-allocation of between one and three of the lead scientists. I had to take one to Seattle and another one to Washington. Mike had a couple in Portland, Oregon and I think he had another one somewhere in New York."

"That part was more-or-less babysitting them until they got to their new roles. Kind of breaking the trail back to New Mexico."

"So," said Clare, "Maybe they are trying to track down the originators of the technology?"

"That's a good point," said Bigsy," But why would they tried to restart this after all of that time?"

"I'm not sure," said Clare," But I wonder if it's because some of the ideas were in the original design were perhaps ahead of their time?"

"That's a good point," said Bigsy, "If some of the systems worked too slow or were maybe too large then the technology will have moved on."

"That's it," said Clare," Maybe with a modern design they can make everything smaller and faster?"

Chuck said, "Yes, I think you're right. The idea was to get the little transponder devices to the size of a credit card. Then to male them about as thin as a credit card too. The early ones we used were about the size of a paperback book, so they were hardly discreet."

"Chuck, you know I spend quite a lot of time working with technology. Computers and the like?" said Bigsy.

"I expect nowadays they could shrink that device down to the size you say. It's like the credit cards that can be used for remote payment. There's a little computer inside the credit card and also a large aerial that runs around the edge of the card. I expect for these devices they would also need a small battery, but it will also need to last for I'm guessing several years."

Bigsy picked up a piece of paper and drew a small sketch. It was a credit card with a microchip on it and an aerial around the edge. He added a small circle about the size of a coin that was the battery.

"There," said Bigsy, "My back of an envelope design for the transponder using today's technology."

Clare looked at the picture and then at Bigsy. "I think you've just drawn something like a transit card?"

"Yes, it's like the Oyster card used in London, but with a self-contained battery," said Bigsy, "all stuff that is readily available nowadays. Which reminds me, I've always wanted to take one of those Oyster cards apart."

"If you are right, then this introduces a whole new small form of targeting device. Such a small targeting device could be planted pretty much anywhere and could remain undetected for a very long time," said Chuck.

"Although, for regular military use nowadays, they still would not be much good. The speed of activation was a bigger problem. The slow pulses sent out to preserve battery. The reliance on phone carrier signals or Wi-Fi. I can understand why the system was scrapped."

Chuck continued, "By comparison, we already have pretty sophisticated laser targeting devices which can be used to light up a target from the ground for detonation by either a military plane or even by a drone aircraft. It's much more usable in a field situation."

"So maybe this is not something for the military?" questioned Clare.

"Maybe for others. I think you are right," said Chuck, "Maybe this could be something very interesting to terrorists or assassins."

"I can see what you're thinking," said Bigsy, "It would be possible to set up a target for future use."

Clare nodded, "but I suppose that even Google maps could be used for some of that nowadays. For example, to type in the coordinates using the GPS grid?"

"Yes," said Chuck, "That's pretty much how it works in a battlefield nowadays, although the grid can be inaccurate on purpose within a war zone area. These little devices could be used to set up a target which could be very refined such as a person or a vehicle, and it could be used even when GPS is switched off, such as in a war zone."

"But what about the other parts?" asked Bigsy," You know, the part that goes into the warhead or another device?"

Chuck said," Yes, that was a big problem with the work that was going on. The response time of the system was both technical and physical. I mentioned this when we were together in the desert Bigsy. It wasn't easy to make the missiles change direction, and every device needed a different setup of connections. It was a big problem. No standardisation."

"But, of course, if you are a terrorist you don't need all the kinds of weapons to work. You just need one or two," said Bigsy.

"Correct and also scary. I'd partly forgotten what it was like working with you two, "said Chuck," But now it's all coming back."

He smiled.

Saddle up

Bigsy remembered that Chuck had suggested they made an early start the next morning. He realised for Clare this was easy. She'd relaxed in the previous hotel with the added benefit of being pampered in a spa.

Bigsy considered his condition by comparison. He had been drugged, hauled around the countryside, slept rough, been in hiding plus the worry of finding Clare again. It had taken its toll, so the current bed felt soft and welcoming.

There was a loud knock at the door of his room. He looked at the clock. 6:30am. The time that Chuck had suggested for them to leave.

He looked through the spyhole. It was Chuck holding two cups of coffee.

He opened the door.

The Circle

"Here you go Bigsy. A cup of Joe to set you up for the morning. I'd rather we moved from here like we said and took breakfast on the road. Can you be ready quickly?

"'Saddle Up,' as Tom might say. I suggest we go for about half an hour and then find some breakfast by the roadside."

Bigsy nodded. "Thanks, Chuck. Give me a few minutes. Have you checked that Clare is also ready?"

"Clare is already in the car," said Chuck, "We gave you the extra beauty sleep."

"Okay, give me 15 minutes, and I'll be ready to go," said Bigsy.

A few minutes later, as he walked outside, Bigsy noticed how hot it already was, even on the short walk to the car. He hadn't been convinced about the air conditioning in the room, but now he was outside he realised it had been doing its job.

Tom was sitting in the front passenger seat, looking alert and ready for the day. They exchanged greetings as Bigsy grunted and climbed into the back seat, next to Clare who was dozing. Then Chuck pulled away into the light early morning traffic. Bigsy noticed there was more traffic heading the opposite way to their direction.

Bigsy noticed as they moved away from the motel and scattering of other small buildings, they were soon back in the desert. A flat and arid area, with distant hills to the left-hand side of their direction of travel.

"So how far are we travelling today?" Asked Bigsy.

"It's about 2 hours for us to get into the right area, but we will then need to take some care," said Chuck. "I will also want to stop somewhere to pick up a few extra supplies before we head towards the ranges."

Esther's end

The noise of them chatting woke Clare.

"Good morning, Clare," said Bigsy," I see you were up bright and early."

"Yes," replied Clare, "I set the alarm and then Chuck brought me a coffee."

"It didn't work too well," said Bigsy.

"I think yesterday's spa worked a bit too well," replied Clare.

"So, Chuck, you'd better tell us some more about your experiments in the desert. I've had a chance to think about it now, and I can't imagine why anyone would want to restart something that has been superseded.

Surely all the technology is pretty well understood nowadays?"

Chuck continued, "I'll explain a little more of the history. The testing was handling a range of ship defence systems, before the new transponders for the Project Esther came along. We were not involved then, and the systems were routine. They were important but routine."

"It all started with traditional stuff. The scientists were looking at ship-based weapons as part of a defence shield.

 This was big guns, vertical-launch missiles and variations of cruise missiles like the Tomahawk."

"The ship defence systems needed to stop smart missiles being fired at the ships. You may have seen it when a ship fires a whole bank of missiles to take down something incoming. It's a kind of brute force system, but it stops the incoming missile from destroying the ship."

"They often refer to them as layered systems, with both missile defence and large calibre guns to stop the incoming."

"Since the work on those naval systems, they have become common as land defence systems too. They are sometimes referred to as 'Air shield' systems and have been used to protect country borders from incoming short-range missiles."

"I've seen that," said Bigsy, "I've seen the Israelis using that defence shield."

"That's right," said Mike," An early system was the one the Israelis call Iron Dome. They designed to it intercept and destroy short-range rockets and artillery shells fired from distances of 2.5 miles to around 50 miles away when the trajectory would take them to an Israeli populated area. They used it a few years ago, but now it claims to have intercepted over 1,500 incoming rockets.

"Israel are not the only ones, the technology has been sold to many countries as part of land-based layer systems, I think it is also called SkyHunter nowadays," said Chuck

"That's right," said Tom, "We had some big half-track systems with boxes of rockets delivered to the base. They were called SkyHunter. Among the Navajo it created quite a wave, because of our Sky hunter legends. I don't know why the American DoD want to name its craft and weapons after Native American Indian Tribes. Cherokee, Apache, Iroquois, Chinook, Kiowa, Tomahawk"

"There was even the experimental SM-64 Cruise, which was called the Navaho with an 'H' - notice the spelling," added Mike.

Chuck continued, "But that's only a part of the story. As is often the way, it was the discovery of a spin-off that caused me and the rest of our small team to be called in."

"So, did you work with the ship and land systems?" asked Clare.

"No, not directly," said Chuck, "We were only called in when the systems were flipped from defensive systems to ones that could be used offensively."

"Where you attack rather than defend?" this gets a lot more sensitive," said Bigsy.

"Yes and No," said Chuck, "It's inevitable with these systems that the research and the results get repurposed. Some of it gets very sensitive, when certain sets of components are linked, and it makes a whole new type of delivery system."

"By delivery system I take it you mean weapon?" asked Clare.

"Er - Yes," said Chuck, "Excuse my jargon."

"They had been solving a problem because incoming anti-ship cruise missiles were becoming increasingly sophisticated."

"They were trying to devise new transponders or waves to confuse the incoming missile so it would think the image of the ship was somewhere else. In effect, the incoming missile would be tricked to think an electronic shadow was the actual ship. So, the clever incoming missile would aim itself at a virtual ship instead of the real one."

"That's where the original transmitters were designed, as kind of cloaking devices to protect the ships."

"Basically, they didn't work because they needed such a powerful signal to be sent to ensure that the incoming missile caught it early enough"

"They were trying to make it harder for the extremely fast and agile missiles to lock on. Remember these things are flying at up to 5 times the speed of sound, so there is a very short reaction time. Which is why the transponders need such high power, because they needed to send their false image far enough out for the missile to have a chance to react.

"I see - like a many mile range or something?" said Clare, "so that they could trick the fast-moving missile?"

"Yes," said Chuck, much like a 75-mile protective bubble around the ship. A dome above the water, if you like," said Chuck.

"Yes, remember that 75 miles is only just over a minute travel time at Mach 5," said Mike.

"So, the smart guys moved to a different technology to protect ships, called field-effect lasers. They disrupt the missiles with particles of light. Photon beams."

"Woah," said Bigsy, "This is starting to sound like science fiction."

"No, it's all out there," said Chuck, "Sailing the seven seas."

"Meantime, the scientists flipped the logic of the original transponders. From units requiring a massive bubble of energy to defend, they could turn it on its head and use it with a tiny amount of energy to drive a highly targeted attack."

"That's when we were called in. They wanted a small team try out a selection of weapon systems with the prototypes of the new technology."

"That's when your paperback book-sized units were in use?" asked Bigsy,

"Yes," said Chuck, "With the idea that they could be made smaller and faster. We were using them with a range of weapons, from small rockets, jet plane and eventually through to drone-based delivery."

"I personally worked with the initial field-based weapons, the short-range missiles and so on. There were others in the team beginning to use the jets and drones around the time this attack-based part of the project was cancelled."

"And again, why was it cancelled?" asked Clare.

"Simply put, it was funding," answered Chuck, "but I think there were probably a couple of underlying reasons,

"Firstly, as an approach, it was already superseded for use in the battlefield because of other laser and GPS targeting."

"Secondly, and I think sensitively, and this is my personal opinion because there were political reasons for discouraging the use of this on drones. The US had positioned drones as surveillance devices rather than as weapons. This pushed it into a whole other area and one that had a lot of political ramifications."

"Anyway, the project was stopped, and everything was bunkered away like you see the old warplanes waiting to be scrapped."

"Like a deadly car park of old technology?" said Bigsy.

"More like a large pile of freshly manufactured scrap metal," said Chuck.

Homing in on the range

"I should probably tell you something about the ranges as well, "said Chuck. "I expect you have heard of Los Alamos?"

"Yes," said Clare, "It was used for designing the original atomic bombs."

"It was," said Chuck," but it is still used as a major weapons development environment. The leading site is tucked away around a town, but there are several locations outside of Los Alamos in the desert where we used to run tests. We also used an area to the south-east of Albuquerque. There's a massive airbase in Albuquerque and it's also a big storage facility run by the DoD."

Clare asked, "So these were your test areas?"

"Yes," said Chuck, "And don't misunderstand the scale. We are talking about some vast areas. Some parts are public access, even tourist spots. The Native Americans mainly use some, and some fenced off as military spaces. There's a lot of space out in these deserts."

"But wouldn't somebody notice if you are doing this kind of thing?" asked Clare.

"The environments and areas around Los Alamos are a kind of open secret," said Chuck.

"Quite a few people in the area work at one of the bases and they are used to planes and rockets as part of the testing. By the way, we don't need big explosions to test things. We just need to know that the armament has reached its target."

"But before we go to Los Alamos, I'm going to make a diversion," said Chuck, "I'm going to go to visit one of Tom's buddies who can help us with some, let's say, precautionary measures."

Bigsy had been looking out of the windows of the car and could see that at intervals along the road were various signs for Indian jewellery and other artefacts. Soon Chuck took a turning to the left following one of the signs towards the jewellery. Clare and Bigsy looked a little surprised.

"Are we being tourists and buying souvenirs?" asked Bigsy.

"You can if you like while I visit my contact," said Chuck.

He pulled up in a car park by two slightly makeshift shacks. They were both selling jewellery and other native American Indian paraphernalia.

A brown dog was sniffing around at the site, and a couple of other tourists were climbing back into another SUV.

"A chance for us all to stretch our legs," said Chuck.

"I might just have a look at that jewellery," said Clare.

"This is part of the plan?" asked Bigsy.

"Yes, we'll be seeking a particular person who can help us now," said Chuck. He and Tom climbed from the car and moved over to start talking to a woman selling pictures. They spoke for around 10 minutes, and Bigsy could see that the woman was giving some kind of instructions to Chuck.

Chuck also bought three small crystals which he brought back to the car.

They waited patiently for Clare to finish looking at the jewellery items and noticed that she also returned clutching a small bag.

"Successful?" He asked

"Yes, I have got a little necklace which has a depiction of Kokopelli on it. It's a great souvenir of this area," said Clare.

Chuck and Bigsy both looked at the necklace and agreed.

Tom smiled, "Yes, Kokopelli is a special deity. Kokopelli is the humpbacked flute player. A God of harvest and plenty. It is thought that his sack was made of clouds full of rainbows or seeds. Kokopelli is said to be a wandering minstrel with a sack of songs on his back who trades old songs for new.

"Kinda' like Aladdin, except with songs instead of lamps!" said Bigsy.

Tom smiled again, "I think you'd find that Kokopelli was somewhat raunchier than Aladdin. Not everything is modelled in the tasteful jewellery that Clare has obtained."

Clare asked," Is this where I'm supposed to blush?"

"OK," said Chuck - "We need to continue now we've just found the location of the person we need to visit. It's about another 7 miles from here across the back roads through part of the desert."

They drove on, and in the distance, Bigsy could see several rocky outcrops quite high and the route that Chuck was taking seemed to lead into them.

They soon arrived at a small house. There were a couple of old vans parked in the front area and a couple of dogs sitting tied with ropes by a small broken-down fence.

Despite the scorching temperatures, there was smoke coming from the chimney of the house.

"Wait here," said Tom. "I'm going to see my friend alone."

He climbed out of the car and walked across to the stoop of the house. He tapped on the glass and waited. A tall, dark-skinned man appeared with shoulder-length hair. He smiled as soon as he saw Tom and stretched out both arms. They slapped one another on the back, and it was clear that they knew each other quite well.

The Circle

Clare looked at Bigsy," What you think is happening?"

"My guess." said Bigsy, "Tom is getting some kind of weapons. This guy can help supply them. They are probably buried in the back garden."

"I think both Tom and Red are more sophisticated than that," said Chuck.

 They waited a few more minutes and then Tom came out.

"Guys," he said, "I'd like you to meet Kilchii Bidziil – 'Red'. He already knows Chuck and when we all worked together, he was also assigned to help up when we were out in the desert. He knows it like the back of his hand."

"Hi," said Kilchii Bidziil, "You can call me Red - and welcome to my home. I am alone here at the moment, but my family will return in a couple of days. They have been visiting Santa Fe for a festival. I had to stay around here for a couple of reasons. I didn't expect to add to them that I'd be seeing Tom."

"Red can help us in a couple of ways," said Tom. "First, I think he will be able to provide us with some additional ironware in case we need it."

"Guns?" asked Bigsy, "You know that is not Clare's or my thing."

"Yes," said Chuck, "but it is purely precautionary. I don't want to find ourselves in the middle of something and not have any form of defence."

"The second thing that Red can help us with is to get into the complex and the ranges undetected."

"Er- isn't that kind of thing impossible nowadays?" asked Bigsy. I thought there would be so much security around anything related to defence systems and the US Government?"

"Correct," said Chuck," but that's why Red can help. He and others from his tribe have ways to walk through walls."

"But for that to work, I'll have to invite you to my hogan," said Red.

"Is that the local secret society?" asked Clare.

"No," said Red, "it's my real house in the desert. Come. We will go immediately."

"So, will we walk?" asked Bigsy." What? When we have your Dodge?" Asked Red. "Let's go."

Chuck took the driving wheel again, and Red sat in the front. Bigsy and Clare discovered that there was a third row of seats in this so-called car. They headed off further along a trail, which soon became a single track and dusty. Then they took a sharp right and drove very slowly for another 20 minutes.

In the distance, Bigsy could make out a small conical structure. It appeared to be made from logs.

"That's my hogan," said Red," and it's where we will be spending the night.'"

"Wow," said Clare," this is amazing."

The Circle

"It is my proper home," said Red, "Nowadays we have houses like the one where you met me, but the tradition of the Navajo is still of a nomadic people."

Chuck added, "Red is a shaman from his tribe. Tonight, we are in his place and will follow his ways."

"Thanks," said Red," although it is strange nowadays because I also get called up on email about being a medicine man. You can imagine that I do a lot of that from the house by the roadside. Coming here is a bit more of the real deal."

"I hadn't thought of it like that," said Bigsy, "but I suppose the world moves on."

"Yes, you'll have seen along the road that we sell jewellery, run casinos and do other things to keep current and make a living.," answered Red.

"Most of us are used to living in two worlds, aren't we, Tom? There is the modern world where we use mobile phones and the Internet and satellite TV of course, and then there's the old world where the commune with the spirits."

"So, if I emailed you and asked to see a shaman, would you be able to do that?" asked Bigsy.

Red smiled, "You know something, quite a few people do exactly that, and you know something else, they get what they have asked for, and they pay a fee."

"Some would say it is entertainment in the same way that the casinos are entertainment," said Red.

Ed Adams

"But that's not why you're here, and we have two things to do. One is to find the instruments that Chuck has requested and the other is to spend a night with the spirits."

Starting a fire

Red started to prepare a fire. He stacked logs in a pyramid shape and outside of this created further logs in a circle. Then he retreated into the hogan and brought out some smaller twigs.

"These are very dry. They will start the fire," he explained, "We need to light it but one of you should do this. He gestured towards Clare. "Clare, I think you should have the honour to start this fire."

 Clare looked worried, "I don't think I've ever started a fire from scratch."

Red laughed," Don't worry, we will use the white man's world to start the fire. Here is my zippo lighter."

They all laughed. Red demonstrated how to flick the lighter. He handed it to Clare. He kneeled close to Clare.

"Look," he said, "Put the flame there."

He guided Clare's wrist.

There was a crackle. The small twigs caught fire. Clare stepped back. They all watched, and in a few moments, the fire had taken. It was still light, and they could see black smoke curling along with the orange flames.

"That's perfect," said Red.

"We will let the fire take hold and then we will begin the ceremony."

"Chuck come with me. I will get you the equipment."

Chuck and Tom followed Red into the hogan. Clare and Bigsy could hear clanks and sounds from inside the structure. After about 10 minutes Chuck reappeared carrying a cylindrical camouflage bag. It looked heavy, and he moved it towards the car. Then Tom emerged carrying another similar sized bag. It also looked heavy.

"It's probably best that you don't know what is in this bag," he said, "Some of it might have been borrowed from the US government."

Red returned and sat and sat by the fire.

The darkness was already descending. It was possible to see a few stars already in the dwindling light.

"Now it is time for your alibi," said Red.

But first, you must say goodbye to Tom. Chuck has asked Tom to go back to the desert, to keep an eye on what is happening, and to tell you if there is anything strange."

Ed Adams

How the people caught the sun

"Now it is time for your story," said Red. "But first, you must say goodbye to Tom.

Chuck has asked Tom to go back to the desert, to keep an eye on what is happening, and to tell you if there is anything strange."

Tom walked around the circle, looked each of them in the eyes, hugged them and said, "Walk with beauty"

Bigsy could see Clare looking slightly tearful.

"Walk tall," said Bigsy to Tom.

Tom smiled, "Yeah, and walk straight; I know that one!"

He laughed as he walked back towards his 4x4. I'll be seeing you guys!" and with that he took off is a cloud of desert dust.

Red continued, "The reason you visited me was to sample my hogan and hear one of my stories. Remember this well in case you are asked about the encounter by anyone."

He looked up towards the dark night sky. A red spark from the fire cracked and spiralled upwards. He began.

"Saynday's world was dark, and he kept falling over things. He began to get angry because the darkness made him clumsy.

Then, just when he was losing his temper he crashed into his friends, Fox, Deer, and Magpie.

Magpie flew straight up in the air, but Fox and Deer were hurt when Saynday tripped over them and did not try to move.

"Look where you're going, can't you?" Fox demanded.

'It seems to me you could do better than that," said Deer.

"Well you try it and see how you make out," Saynday snapped, sitting down by a prairie dog hole.

All of them were fed up with the darkness.

"What we really need is some light," Deer said, "I can't tell if I'm eating grass or weeds. Sometimes the weeds taste disgusting and make me feel sick."

"Well, at least you can find something to eat," said Fox.

"How would you like it if you had to run after your food and catch it in the dark? Something I thought was a rabbit turned out to be a bear, and nearly ate me."

"What about you?" Saynday asked Magpie.

"Well," answered Magpie, "I can fly up in the air. When I get extremely high, I can see a little rim of light over in the east."   '

'There is light, then," said Saynday. "What we have to do is figure out a way to get to it, so we can find our way around and be sure of what we are eating."   '

'Well, you work it out," remarked Deer. "You're the one who's supposed to be smart."

The little prairie dog, by whose hole they were sitting, burrowed deeper in the earth. She was afraid that if Fox could see her, Fox would eat her instead of a rabbit.

"Now, then," said Saynday, "if the light is so far away that Magpie can see only a little rim of it in the east, it will be too difficult for one person to get it alone.

We will have to line ourselves up like a relay race. Fox, you can run hard and far. Go to the east and get into the sun people's village.

When you get to know them and they trust you, grab the sun and run. Deer can carry it next, and then Magpie. I'll put myself last, because you're all better runners than I am."

Fox started his journey to the east. At first, he stumbled around in blackness, but finally he began to see the little rim of light on the edge of the world that Magpie had talked about.

The Circle

The light grew ahead of Fox, and sometimes he had to stop and put his paws over his eyes, for fear it might blind him. When he did that he rested, too, to get ready for the big race.

Eventually Fox came to the sun people's camp, and he saw that they were playing a game. The men were lined up on two sides, and each side had four spears.

First the leader on one side would roll the sun along the ground then the opposite leader would.

While the sun was rolling like a big ball, the men took turns with the spears trying to hit it. Fox watched very quietly.

One side was ahead, and when the losing side took their turns with the spears, Fox said, under his breath, so only their leader could hear him: "Good luck to the losers."

That time the losing side scored more points than the other, and again Fox wished them luck, and a third time when the score was even.

When his side won, the leader came over to Fox, and asked, "Who are y
"Never heard of him " said the sun camp man. "What are you doing here?"

"Just going along," said Fox, "trying to see the world."

But he had to shut his eyes then, because the sun was so bright. Remember, a fox always sees well at night, and the sun is reflected in his eyes in the darkness.

"Why don't you stay here a while?" asked the man.

"You are pretty lucky. We can teach you to play our game if you promise to play on our side."

"All right," said Fox. "I'd like to learn the game."

Fox stayed in the sun camp for four months, and though he never did get used to the brightness, he did learn to play the spear game. When he got good at it, and the game was going fast, Fox stabbed his spear into the sun, put it over his shoulder, and ran. He ran as hard and fast as he could, with the sun people right behind him.

Just as Fox was about to drop from running, he met Deer. Deer grabbed the sun from Fox and ran as fast as he could, with the light growing and glowing all around him.

The sun people were not used to the darkness they were running into, and they began to slow down, but Deer didn't. He just tore along, and as he began to lose his breath, Magpie dived down out of the sky and grabbed the sun away from him.

Now the other side of the world was getting darker and darker, was becoming bright.   When Magpie dropped down to the earth and gave the sun to Saynday, they had all the light there was in the world, but the sun was so hot it had burned black streaks on Magpie's feathers, which had been all white before. Now the sun became a problem.

Nobody knew what to do with it, and there was so much light all the time nobody could sleep except Fox, who was used to it.

"Maybe we'd better put it in the tipi," Saynday decided, "that way, it might not be so bright."

But the tipi didn't seem to darken the sun enough.

"Put it on top of the tipi, so we don't have to look right at it," suggested Fox. But that was no good, because the sun set fire to the tipi and burned it right to the ground.   "Oh, throw it away," said Magpie. 'it's just getting to be a nuisance."   "All right," Saynday agreed.

"Now stay there and travel around the world," Saynday ordered the sun.

"Spend part of your time with the people on the other side, and part of it here with us."

And he pushed the sun to the west to start it going around the world.   And that's the way it was, and that's the way it is, to this good day.

As above, so below.

"Tonight, our ceremony is being one of protection for each of you," said Red

"We should link hands. Clare should sit opposite me."

Bigsy and Chuck looked at one another and then at Clare, but Bigsy noticed that Chuck had already linked hands with Tom.

They all linked hands around the fire. By now the flames had subsided, and there was a gentle glow from the centre. The sky had turned black and was speckled with stars.

Red began.

"We sit around the fire; the fire that is the sun within the Earth.

"We form a circle. The circle that has another edge outside of us.

The Circle

"We use the fire and the Earth and the stars to absorb their beneficent power and strength into our minds and bodies hearts and songs just as the plants, animals and other beings are now drawing power and strength during this time.

"We ask for the circle to be filled with the light and enlightenment needed to grow.

"And we ask for the circle and the outer circle to extend to those we need to protect.

"We do this in the relationship of Earth, Sun and Moon bringing this unity with the larger web of being and becoming.

"Within you and without you. As above so below. As without so within.

"Allow us to shine to the greater Pattern."

Bigsy looked up. The sky was clear. There were no stars. It was dawn. He looked towards Clare. She was also sitting cross-legged, looking at the sky. Red and Chuck were nowhere to be seen.

Then Tom appeared. He was carrying two 2 cups of coffee. He handed one to Bigsy and the other to Clare.

"What happened?" asked Clare.

"One minute we were having a ceremony and the next minute it was morning."

"Yes, Red is good with the spells. I only woke myself a few moments ago," said Tom.

Red emerged from the hogan, "Good morning everyone," he said, "it is still very early, but it is a great time to see the desert and where the eagle flies."

"Red," said Bigsy," I don't think I knew what happened last night. I remember the ceremony and a sitting around the fire but then nothing until this morning."

"That is part of the magic," said Red, "As you commune with the spirits of the desert and ask for their protection you can be sure that there are powerful forces at work."

"Sometimes it is easier for a two legged to take on these powers while they are sleeping. I think that is what the desert wanted. I don't think you will feel any different, but you will start to notice some things change as you go about your quest," said Red.

Bigsy looked around him. There were marks on the ground behind him where the others had slept around the campfire. Bigsy assumed they were symbols that represented animal spirits.

"What are they?" asked Bigsy, to Red.

Red looked, "They are some clues for you as you go forward. They are symbols from the spirits. Each one has a meaning. The Elk, the Lynx, The Caribou and the Hawk."

"These will be spirits that will guide you in your mission with Chuck."

"And what do they each mean?" Asked Clare.

The Circle

Red looked. If you see these symbols, as you would on a totem pole, they have particular meanings. The meanings are representative of the animal.

The elk shows strength and agility, pride, majestic independence, purification and nobility

The lynx is a keeper of secrets; a guardian listener and guide
The huge Caribou is a symbol of travel; of mobility, and nomadic adaptability to adversity

And finally, the hawk is a messenger bringing great intuition, victory, healing ability, recollection, cleansing, visionary power and guardianship.

"I think if we have these spirits to help us, we would be in good shape," said Bigsy, smiling towards Red.

Red replied, "but now I think you will need to be on your way."

"Red, these are from us," said Chuck he extended his hand and placed something into Red's palm.

It was the three crystals that Chuck had bought at the shack by the roadside in the desert earlier the previous day.

Albuquerque

Chuck slowly drove them back towards the main road. It took about 30 minutes to get onto a normal road surface and then another 20 minutes before they were back on the highway.

"What's just happened back there?" said Bigsy, "One minute I was watching the flames around the fire and the next minute it was dawn."

"I know," said Chuck," There are some powerful forces here in the desert. I've experienced this kind of thing before with Red and although you don't have to believe it, don't be surprised when something returns from the evening later.

Clare asked, " What's in the back, Chuck? It is something we can all get into trouble for, if the police stopped us, for example?"

"Not necessarily," said Chuck," but it's still better that you don't know."

The Circle

Today before we make any plans to go into the missile ranges, I'd rather check some things. We are close to Albuquerque now, so I suggest we stop there for the rest of the day. Find a hotel and use the Internet to check a few things.

Tom suggested a hotel in the centre of Albuquerque. Bigsy smiled at this idea. The chance of a decent night in a hotel, not in the car or a wooden shack or a ramshackle motel would be excellent.

"Good Plan," said Bigsy.

They could already see the sights of Albuquerque appearing, and Chuck headed for the middle. There was a very central hotel with an adjacent parking lot. He pulled the car in, and they walked the short distance to the hotel. It was a pleasant environment with a huge atrium and an expensive look about it.

"This looks fine," said Clare smiling. She noticed that Chuck was carrying a small camouflage bag, which she assumed had been inside the larger one.

"And I will get this," said Chuck as they checked in. He asked the receptionist if they could pay cash for what would be an overnight stay. Chuck rummaged into the camo bag and pulled out some hundred-dollar bills. He counted them out and handed them over for the rooms.

"I suggest we all freshen up then meet in the bar to discuss our next plans. Bigsy, I may need your help with some of the internet things."

Hotel Parq Central

As well as the main bar there was a row of booths along one side of the hotel atrium. Each one was different and featured some kind of unique ambience.

They picked one which seems to have a Japanese theme and sat down with a couple of laptops. One was Bigsy's and the other was a rather military-grade device carried by Chuck.

"Okay," said Chuck. "Tomorrow will be when the fun starts. We will visit the base and try to find out what has been happening to my colleagues. Tom will guide us in. I expect there's more to it than the old experiments from eight years ago. Some of that equipment that Red's people provided will help us get into the base. "

"Is it guns," said Clare.

"Not exactly," said Chuck, "It contains uniforms and badges. Red talked about walking through walls. I think we need to walk through checkpoints then the easiest way is to look as if we belong on the inside.

"So how have Red's people come by this equipment?" asked Bigsy,

"Simple really," replied Tom, "Red still sells a few items to people on the inside of the base and to assist this it is helpful if he has some ways of getting in and out easily."

"Is that not a major security flaw?" asked Clare.

"Kind of yes, and kind of no," said Tom. "The Navajo guards that work at the base have excellent field craft and great fighting skills. They also still speak the Navajo language. This provides a ready-made code for communication. You may have heard about this being used back in the Second World War?"

"It means if we get into the base using the material supplied by Red, then the base guards will know that we are friends of Red."

"I just hope this works," said Bigsy.

"Do not forget that you'll have me along too," said Tom. "I don't traffic material into the base like Red, but plenty of the people across the security control will still know me."

"But this evening we must check the status of my colleagues," said Chuck, "I know that Ben and Mike were both killed. That leaves three others. We need to find out if they were contacted. Bigsy, this is where you can help me."

Chuck started up his computer and logged in to an email system.

"These emails are not stored on this computer, they are installed in a secure site," said Chuck.

"You can see this the message sent to me that first told me that the project Esther links would be re-established."

"And you can see the message that asked me to come to the hotel in Scottsdale. It doesn't mention the hotel by name but uses the slang that we all used for when we worked at the base."

"The convention centre?" asked Bigsy

"Yes, that's what we called it. And it was an accurate description often," said Chuck.

"Okay but the location is vague enough to mean that if you didn't know the slang, then you wouldn't even have a clue about which country to visit."

"Exactly," said Chuck, "It either means somebody has been leaky with their email communications or that somebody from our team has let it be known where we would meet."

Clare asked, "So the other three people. Have we checked on their whereabouts?"

"Not yet," said Chuck, "I didn't have time to piece this together when I first arrived and then after the hurried exit from the hotel this is the first chance I've had to carry out any research."

"So, what are the names? ... Klaus Wegener, Barbara Somerville and Tony Capaldi"

"Let's start with Wegener," said Bigsy. "It's the most unique sounding and the easiest to track down on the Internet."

He typed it into a search engine on his computer and a recent news item from Vancouver came up as the first result.

"Man dies in lake," it said. Bigsy scanned the article.
"It says that Klaus died trying to rescue a dog in a lake," said Bigsy.
"Two weeks ago," said Chuck.
"There is a clear pattern here," said Clare.

Bigsy searched for Barbara Somerville and Tony Capaldi. Barbara Somerville's name was too common and there were many hits.

"I don't think we can tell whether Barbara Somerville is the same one," said Chuck, "And anyway there doesn't seem to be any mysterious accidents listed in the recent past for that name."

They looked for Tony Capaldi. Again, there were some mentions, and it looked as if it was several different people.

"Tony also had a nickname," said Tom, "Try again and add in 'Buckeye'."

"Huh?"" Said Bigsy.

"Buckeye, well done for remembering that, Tom" said Chuck, "He was from Ohio."

"I'm none the wiser," said Bigsy.

"Buckeye is a nickname for someone from Ohio," explained Chuck, "it is named after the buckeye tree."
"I've never heard of it," said Bigsy.
"Me neither," said Clare.

"OK - but let's try it."

Bigsy typed the name again and added 'Buckeye'.

To his surprise, a name now rose to the top of the list. It even had a picture.

"That's him," said Chuck, "although the picture is probably quite old."

They read the entry, and it described him as a lecturer now based in Columbus, Ohio and working at the Ohio State University.

"That's great," said Chuck, "we should be able to trace him easily from that."

Bigsy was already typing in the web site address for the university.

"Let's try the Employee self service area," he said.
"I will not hack into it, but I think we can use it to get some information."
He flicked through a few screens and made some notes.

Okay. I have a plan. Here's what we need to do.

The Circle

Bigsy explained how they would call the University about a personal package that needed to be delivered to Tony Capaldi.

"I don't need to know more than whether he is there. We'll need to do this tomorrow morning when there are some admin staff on the faculty."

"We also need to get some up to date satellite images and maps of where we are going tomorrow," said Chuck.

They used the mapping functions to produce area maps, which Bigsy saved to a memory stick.

"Now to go to the hotel offices services to get four copies of everything printed," Chuck grinned.

"That story of Red's" asked Clare, "It was quite haunting."

"I know, said Tom," He's a medicine man, some say shaman, so he should be good at telling it."

"You know there's a next part? We all learn it. It is passed down from generation to generation."

"Remember you were in a hogan? The wooden shack construction? That's a woman's hogan.

"First Man and First Woman wanted a hogan. They wondered where to build it.

"The Talking God helped to build the first hogan. This was a male hogan. lot was like the forked stick hogan we have today. It had a doorway facing east. This let in the early morning light.

"The Talking God explained that the male hogan was only for ceremonies.

"What, like a church?" asked Bigsy,

" Yes, kind of like a church," continued Tom

"First Man and First Woman still needed a home where they could live. With the help of other beings, next, they built a female hogan.

"This hogan was made of mud and logs. It was shaped like a circle. This was the place where the people lived and worked.

"That's like the one we were inside," said Clare, "with a hole in the roof to let out smoke."

"That's right, said Tom, "Hogans are energy efficient, timber structured with doors pointing to the sunrise.

"By now, First Man and First Woman had become human. They were like us. For food, they ate wild plants and animals. The Holy People sang songs and gave prayers to let plants grow. Then the people planted their own food.

"Then came the four seasons. In the spring, the plants came up from the ground. In the winter, the plants died and were hidden under the snow. The plants grew into crops like corn, beans and squash.

"But all was not well.

"There were monsters who hurt people. Horned Monster chased people and killed them with his horns. There was a monster that kicked people off the edge of a cliff. Another monster killed people by staring at them until they were under his spell. Then he ate them.

"First Man and First Woman could not stop the monsters. They did not know what to do. Then one day they looked up. They saw a cloud over a bluff. First Man went to the top to see what the cloud was. In the cloud was a baby girl.

"First Man lifted the baby into his arms and carried her down to First Woman.

"The Holy People helped First Man and First Woman raise the baby girl. They named her Changing Woman. In time, Changing Woman grew to be an adult. She had twin sons. One was named Child Born of Water. The other was called Monster Slayer. The twins grew to be tall and strong. One day they went hunting. They looked down and saw a hole in the ground.

Smoke was coming out of the hole.

"Hmm, that's usually a bad sign," said Bigsy.

Tom continued, "They looked closer and heard a voice say, 'Come in.'

"They climbed down into the hole. At the bottom, they found Spider Woman.

"The Twins always wondered who their father was. They asked Spider Woman about this. 'The Sun is your father,' she told them. The Twins decided to meet their father. They left Spider Woman and went toward the Sun.

"It was long, hard trip. Many things tried to keep the boys from their father. Finally, they reached the Sun. They told him about the monsters that were hurting people. The Sun promised to help get rid of the monsters.

"Before the Twins left, their father gave them weapons and knowledge. "Use these to kill the monsters," the Sun said.

"So, the Twins left. Monster Slayer used his new weapons to kill many monsters. His brother helped.

"It included killing the giant, and Monster Slayer stripped off his helmet and coat-of-mail and put them in his two big baskets, to carry home to their mother. Then the younger brother, Child-of-the-Water, cut off the giant's scalp, whence he got his other name, the Cutter.

"When the twins got back, they found their mother making baby-tracks of corn-pollen, as a prayer for the return of her sons. She also had a long piece of turquoise, which she held up to the Sun. When smoke arose from the upper end, it was a sign that the boys were in danger. When drops of blood appeared at the lower end, it was a sign they had killed their enemies.

"The next morning the Slayer went out alone and killed the great one-horned Monster which had tried to eat him up. The next day he went to Winged Rock, where the harpy which had pursued him dwelt; and so on each day he went out until the last of the monsters was dead.

"But just when he thought the land was freed of all evil, he spied four ugly strangers. They were Cold and Hunger, Poverty and Death, and straightway he went to destroy them.

The Circle

"Cold was an old woman, freezing and shivering.
'You may kill me if you wish,' she said. 'But if you do, it will always be hot. There will be no snow, and no water in the summer. You will do better to let me live.'

"'You speak wisely, my grandmother,' he answered; and so we still have the cold.

"'If you kill me,' said Hunger, 'the people will all lose their appetites. There will be no more pleasure in feasting and eating.' So, the Slayer let him live.

"Poverty was an old man in filthy garments.
'Kill me,' he said, 'and put me out of my misery. But if you do your old clothes will never wear out, the people will never make new ones. You will all be ragged and dirty, like me.' So, the Slayer spared his life.

"Death was old and bent and wrinkled, and the Slayer was determined to kill her.

"'If you slay me,' she said, 'your people will never increase. The worthless old men will not die and give up their places to the young. Let me live and your young men will marry and have children. I am your friend, though you know it not.'

"'I will let you live, my grandmother,' he said. And so we still have Death."

Tom had been leaning forward while he told the story. Now, he leaned back on his chair.

"Wow, great story," said Clare, "The sun providing weapons, the four old women of death, poverty, Hunger and cold. The roaming badass monsters. The twins Child-of-water and Monster-slayer!"

"It's more than a story," said Tom, "It's a belief in our culture."

"Yes, and it differs from, say, the four horsemen," said Bigsy.

Tom agreed, "Yes, and it is a well-repeated tale among Navajo and other Native Americans."

"Thank you," said Clare, "Thank you for sharing it with us."

Legal document

The next morning Bigsy could hardly contain himself. They had breakfast and then waited until after 9 o'clock when they will be sure that there would be people present in the administration block in the University in Columbus, Ohio.

They decided that it would be best if Clare made the call which she did with a straightforward message. It was to explain that Tony Capaldi was to receive an important legal document that had to be signed for personally. It would be delivered later that day, and could we be sure that Mr Capaldi would be available to receive it.

The admin staff confirmed that although Capaldi worked at the University at they could not get out more specific address information. They noted that he was away for a few days but would be back the following week.

Clare thanked them for this information and hung up.

"Well, he works at the Uni," said Clare, "But is not there at the moment."

"I'm sure all thinking the same thing. Capaldi is already in Scottsdale or on the way unless something has already happened to him," said Bigsy.

"Unfortunately, I agree," said Chuck, "But this is where we need some of that behaviour that Red was talking about. The need to know whether Somerville and Capaldi are being chased or whether they are the chasers?"

"Yes, but it has given me an idea," said Bigsy. "If Capaldi is on his way to Scottsdale, we can page him there at the hotel, maybe try Somerville too."

"Good idea," said Clare, "But we must distance ourselves from this. What about Jake? He can call the hotel and then advise us of the outcome."

"That's great," said Chuck, and it should still preserve the gap between us via communications monitoring. I'm sure that those following Mike, Bigsy and I won't know anything about Clare, Tom, nor the link to Jake."

"So, what's the message for Barbara Somerville and Tony Capaldi?" asked Bigsy.

"That this is a courier and we are trying to get their papers for the conference delivered," answered Clare.

"They won't know whether this is something they have shipped or whether it is something from the organiser of the conference. We should say that there has been a mix up with addressing and they are now to be shipped to the hotel in Scottsdale, but would they confirm that this is correct."

"Perfect," said Chuck. We should be able to find out whether they are in the hotel in Scottsdale.

Chucking it down

Clare rang Jake again. This time it was from Chuck's room and on the hotel phone system.

"Hey Jake," said Clare

"Hey - I've been wondering, you know," replied Jake, "so what has been happening?"

"Plenty - Bigsy ran into Chuck. Chuck was about to be inconvenienced by two gangster types, but then Chuck's colleague from their desert days showed up in the hotel. His name is Mike. All three of Mike, Chuck and Bigsy high-tailed it out of the hotel pursued by the two gangsters. Mike's driving appears to have thrown them off the trail, but we are still worried that they might follow us.

"They went into hiding in the desert, where they met another ex-colleague, a guy called Tom, who is Navajo Indian."

"What?" said Jake, "This is sounding a little far-fetched?"

"Nope," said Clare, "Then we drove off into the desert and met one of Tom's buddies, a trader named Red who got us some new hardware for the mission. I know it included military uniforms, but I think there might also be guns."

Jake interrupted, "America, Land of the Free."

"Land of the NRA more like," said Clare, "Well Red is a shaman and took us to his hut - which is called a hogan, by the way, where we were treated to a night under stars and spells. It was all very mystic. Now we are in Albuquerque in a nice hotel, where I've just come back from sipping cocktails."

"Wow," said Jake. "That's an impressive 36 hours. You certainly know how to pack in adventures."

"You know what," said Clare, "I don't think we've even scratched the surface yet."

"Do you want me to come out there?" said Jake.

"Jake no. I think it is better that you stay in the UK. I think you can be very useful to us by helping us to track down some of the information about what is happening."

"Okay, but you will have to tell me more about the direct situation for me to help you."

"Sure," said Clare, "It appears that Chuck and another few military types were involved in protecting some scientists back about seven or eight years ago. They were working on guidance systems for weapons and targeting systems that could guide in a rocket. It was like a souped-up homing device that could be planted on the target.

"The project was called Esther. The scientists were based in Los Alamos although the testing was done in deserts all over Arizona and New Mexico. We are only less than 100 miles from the area now.

"Anyway, the people that Chuck worked with seem to have been picked off over the last few weeks. The latest casualty was Mike, who we were with until yesterday, when his distinctive blue car crashed off a bridge and fell 100 feet. Another guy died in a fishing incident. Another one drowned rescuing a dog.

"Then some men came for Chuck, but he managed to wriggle free, with the help of Mike. Chuck reckons that only two of the original team he belonged to are left now."

"So how can I help?" asked Jake.

""We've set up a little test to find out whether the others have been invited to the same hotel as the rest. Chuck and some of his buddies were invited to a reunion of some kind associated with the original project - Esther it was called. Now we want to find out whether two of the are present.

"Their names are - get your pen ready - Barbara Somerville and Tony Capaldi - both part of the old Esther project and both known to Chuck."

"We'd like you to call the hotel and to ask for each of them. Say you are a courier company and want to know whether to deliver the conference papers to the hotel or to another address. It should be enough to flush them out.

"Then ring me back to let me know what has happened."

"Got it, said Jake, "It sounds as if you are having a great, if somewhat dangerous, adventure out there."

"Adventure? It is one of the scariest things I've done in a while, " answered Clare.

"Hey, how's the weather?"

"Scorching hot sunshine 42 Degrees" answered Clare.

"It's been chucking it down here in London," said Jake, "I was out drinking with my buddies yesterday afternoon - you remember David and John - it was hilarious. They were soaked through and looked like two drowned hipsters - they even made a walk-along iPhone video around Canary Wharf. We all stopped at a bar for some light refreshment."

"I must explain 'chucking it down' to Chuck," said Clare.

The Circle

Ministry Moments

"Power is in tearing human minds to pieces and putting them together again in new shapes of your own choosing."

\-   George Orwell 1984

Penny for the Guy

Jake saw whether he could piece together anything from what he had been told. He started by checking out the names they had given him. He found the same contact in Columbus University. Also, some papers by him related to electronic surveillance systems.

He tried typing in Esther. But found nothing related to the project. Then he tried the leading Los Cabos site and soon found quite a range of topics related to shooting things at one another.

But the emphasis seemed to be more around nuclear research and around guidance systems. Jake tried a more comprehensive search and found some other sites which described similar technologies to the ones that Clare had mentioned.

But it was also clear that newer space-age technologies had superseded most of these systems with laser beams and photon guns. Jake thought it was all getting a bit Star Trek.

He went out for a walk around the streets of London. It was a shopping expedition for some milk and coffee, but he decided it would also be a way to clear his mind.

It was early November. The trees had turned golden, and there was a covering of further leaves on the ground. He also noticed curious obstacles where the council had already begun sweeping the leaves away into bulbous plastic bags.

Jake approached the garden area in the centre of Hoxton and noticed some kids with a Guy Fawkes on a small trolley. He thought for a moment. This wasn't a common sight anymore. Maybe the thought of a terrorist set to blow up Parliament had become a little too realistic.

'Penny for the guy' had very much disappeared from the streets. Then he noticed the kids behind the brightly coloured Papier-mâché masks were older than he had first thought. Students with some kind of enactment of the childhood scene. He walked closer and could see they were advertising a show at a nearby theatre.

They had cleared part of the path and had that old trick where they had put a couple of pound coins on the ground and were watching passers-by attempting to pick them up.

As someone spotted the coin, they would pull it with a nylon fishing line, and it would jump towards the Guy.

The Circle

Jake stood at a distance and watched them doing this. They were being remarkably successful and about every two or three minutes someone else was being caught.

A girl from the group spotted that he was watching and walked over with a leaflet about the show. "It's simple," she said, "very low budget marketing to the right audience for the show. We use something small to attract attention. Everyone we catch takes the leaflet. It sure gets attention."

Jake smiled and took the leaflet. He continued around the square. What he had just heard had given him an idea about what was happening in New Mexico.

He stopped at a small shop to pick up some groceries and then headed back to the office.

…

Clare's phone rang. It was early evening. The number showed as Jake's mobile.

"Hi Jake," she said.

"Hi Clare, I've been thinking about your situation with Chuck. Suppose that technology isn't used anymore because of all this new stuff. Suppose the military has decided it's a dead end. That doesn't mean it isn't something that somebody else could use. I think sometimes a simpler technology could still be very useful."

"What do you mean?" asked Clare.

"There are still many people who couldn't use fancy laser guns but would find a simple technology that could deliver something to a target very interesting."

"What like terrorists?" asked Clare.

"Exactly," said Jake, "Or any hired guns that need to create disruption without the expense of a full army. What's the word, Asymmetric warfare?"

"But I thought the homing devices that Chuck described didn't work?" said Clare.

"I agree," said Jake," but we shouldn't forget that this was designed several years ago. There's been enough progress with most technologies to mean that this could work now."

"We should ask Bigsy," said Clare, "I'm sure you are right, Jake, and I am confident that Bigsy will know what is possible regarding the way such a transponder could be designed now. He almost implied that the technology could be scaled down to the size of a credit card - he said an Oyster card - with an extra battery added to it.

Jake said "Yes, and that's one thing I can't figure in all of this. If someone like Bigsy can figure out how to build the transponder - even at a general level - then what is it about this that means it is so sensitive?"

"I think I need to take your news to Chuck," said Clare, "But first, did you find out anything more specific about the project Esther and those two people?"

"I rang the hotel. They knew about both of the guests, although they said that Barbara Somerville had cancelled. They said they were sorry for the loss. Someone has died, but they were not saying who."

"For Capaldi, they seemed to think he was booked in but uncontactable. I must try again."

"I'll keep looking. Let's sign off now and pick up when one of us has more news. And, hey, Clare. You take care now and take care of the others!"

Ed Adams

The four winds

It was 7 pm, and they were all sitting together in one of the small booths in the hotel. This time the booth looked middle eastern.

"It's more like something out of Scheherazade or Aladdin than something that I'd expect to see in the middle east nowadays," said Chuck.

Bigsy nodded. He'd been on an assignment to Turkey once to fix a bank's computer systems. It didn't look like the booth — not one little bit.

Tom looked around, "Some of the symbols are quite like Navajo," he said, "Look. The four winds, spirits in the sky, water, the elements."

"But no magpies, foxes or deer?" asked Clare.

"So, you were paying attention!" laughed Tom, "Don't forget to tell the story to a friend. Pass it along in the Navajo way!"

724

Chuck smiled, "I brought us together this evening so we can explain more about the military situation around the Albuquerque area."

"As well as Los Alamos, there is another facility in the same area. It's called Kirtland Air Force Base. It's linked to the Albuquerque main airport called Sunport.

"Okay," said Clare, "I guess you were based there as well then Chuck? - And you too, Tom?"

Chuck replied, "Not exactly although we were all very aware of its presence."

"If Los Alamos researches then Kirtland handles implementation. The base is called a material command base. In practice, that means it's the nuclear weapons centre for North America."

"You'll have heard of the original Manhattan project when the first nuclear bombs were being constructed and tested? That was all done around this area, and back in those days they flew the scientists in and out via the old Kirtland base."

"I guess you might say 'welcome to nuclear central'" said Chuck.

"I'll tell you more about the base. The NWC is the center of expertise for nuclear weapon systems, ensuring safe, secure and reliable nuclear weapons are available to support the National Command Structure and Air Force.

Ed Adams

"The NWC's responsibilities include acquisition, modernisation and sustainment of nuclear system programs for both the Department of Defense and Department of Energy.

"There are two main wings to the NWC - the 377th Air Base Wing and the 498th Armament System Wing.

"Wow - not the easiest numbers to remember," said Clare.
Bigsy smiled, "But these things sound heavy duty."
Chuck continued, "Oh yes, they are:

"The 377 ABW provides munitions maintenance, readiness and training, and base operating support to many Federal government and private sector tenants.

"Among these is the Defense Threat Reduction Agency's Defense Nuclear Weapons School, the mission of which is to provide nuclear weapons core competencies and chemical, biological, radiological, nuclear, and high explosive (CBRNE) response training to DoD, other Federal and State Agencies, and National Laboratory personnel.

"The Defense Threat Reduction Agency was the part that we were working for when we were involved in the tests, although we didn't operate at the air force base. We were further out into the desert,

"The other one is the 498th NSW is responsible for the sustainment of nuclear munitions and cruise missiles, including operation of two munitions maintenance and storage complexes (at Kirtland AFB and Nellis AFB, Nevada) and the 498th Missile Sustainment Group at Tinker AFB, Oklahoma. It encompasses the entire scope of nuclear weapon system support functions to include sustainment, modernisation and acquisition support activities for both the Department of Defense and Department of Energy.

"So, you were working close to some big explosives then," said Bigsy.

"Yes. Most of them are within 100 miles of us."

"I can see why they have been put in the desert," said Clare.

"To put it in context, there's over 20,000 people working at the Air Force Base; we are going to a different site, to a low-key admin building.", said Chuck.

War Chalk

They arrived at the Los Alamos site and followed the plan with Chuck changing into the uniform and then using the access pass to gain entry to the building. It worked well, and it surprised both Bigsy and Clare that there had been so little effort required to gain access.

Chuck looked the part wearing the uniform and knew the best things to say at the entrance. He'd arrived by taxi and used the pretence of meeting a particular person to get through to the cafe area within the building. Because he had an access pass, there was no problem for him to do this and he was not treated as someone that needed to be escorted around the site.

Chuck bought a coffee and sat down for around ten minutes, by which time he looked part of the establishment. Then he made his way to the restrooms adjoining the cafeteria and after a short time, moved towards the back of the building. He could see that the cafe area had back doors and that they led towards the area he had seen on the map.

He noted this and retraced his steps towards the admin block. It would be easy enough to get to the right area, but he was not sure how he could gain access to the files he wanted.

He approached the area and asked one of the administrators about the project. He said he was only looking for the year of the record- nothing more and could he borrow the file.

The administrator said she would need to check whether it was still restricted but came back a few minutes later with a folder.

"There's no restriction on the basic file," she said, "but there's also nothing in it. Here - you can take a look," She handed him a manila folder which contained a couple of typed sheets. It provided a two-line description of the program and a summary of its status as 'Closed - No further action - Technology superseded'

He looked at the folder again, and at the sheets. Nothing untoward.

This had been very easy but had given no information. As he was handing the sheets back to the administrator, he noticed something on the cover. It was two halves of a circle with the word Esther2022 written above it.

Chuck recognised the symbol immediately. It was a warchalk. Something he had not seen for several years but was once a way to communicate about access to private networks. They had started in the days before wi-fi and internet signals were pervasive and were a way that hackers signalled to one another about networks they had found.

This was clearly a pointer to such a network, which Chuck suspected would give further information about the project. He realised there could be a problem though; that the signal was only available from within the facility.

He returned to the cafeteria and to see if it was possible to gain access. He had his phone and could try with that.

A few minutes later, he had a second coffee and was accessing his phone, very much as if he was reading emails or doing any of the normal corporate things people did while they were waiting.

He tried the node, and to his surprise, he found it immediately. It was not broadcasting its presence, but once he had typed in the identity, it let him in without asking any security questions. He looked at what it provided. It was a code GC1G655. That was all it said. He wrote it down and flipped off his phone. He would leave now and based on what he had found, he could exit through the front door rather than climbing through the cafeteria and over the bins. Much tidier.

He was sure the combination of the warchalk and code was what he needed but he didn't know what the code referred to at all.

Vauxhall Cross

In London, Jake continued to review the various web sites and contact names they had given him. The work related to what he assumed was Project Esther was available. The technology had moved along and that the Esther project had been parked.

He had also tried further searches for Tony Capaldi and found him listed for both his work at the University but also some other work related to radiofrequency spectrum.

This was consistent with him being involved with the transponders, but his work seemed to have veered towards educational systems including ways to provide peer communication amongst devices.

This all looked mainstream to Jake and not suspicious although it provided the tie in with the earlier other work.

He decided also to look at other related papers and content that might shed some further light on what had taken place. Everything pointed the same way that Chuck had described it. The technology was superseded, and the more space-age sounding laser guns and something called a dazzler, which was about as close as it got to making ray guns for real.

The other names Chuck had provided him didn't feature.

Jake noticed that there were many references to GOT (which he realised wasn't the TV show). It referred to Go Onto Target systems and semi-active homing used to send a signal from the target to the incoming device.

These systems were using variations of SSKP Single Shot Kill Probability enhancement, and this gave Jake a few more ways to search around for information. It comprised systems to light up a target with laser beams and then fire a missile. Jake decided it was a variation of the homing system that Chuck had tested.

None of what he discovered was helping Jake to find out the reasons for the interest in Chuck and the others. Jake had been working on this for several hours and could feel his eyes gazing over.

Amanda Miller

There was a sudden noise as the office security phone bleeped. Jake flickered back from his reverie. A visitor to the office? He looked at the entry phone picture.

A dark-haired smart-looking woman dressed for business looked into the camera. Jake thought she had piercing eyes.

He answered the door via the speakerphone.
"Mr Lambers?" Asked the woman.
"Er yes" answered Jake, "How can I help you."
"May I come in?" she asked.
"Who are you?" asked Jake.

"I'm from security services. We are aware of your little excursion to America and the items you are uncovering," she said. "We need to ask you a few questions."

"Can you show me some proof?" Asked Jake and the woman produced a very official-looking badge and also a smaller pass card which had SI6 written large on it.

"You'd better come in," said Jake and buzzed her in.

"I've brought a couple of colleagues," she said. She gestured behind, and Jake could see two policemen standing wearing bullet-proof vests.

"I'm not expecting any trouble because we want to help you," said the woman.

"You've been creating quite some interest with your use of search terms: Esther, SSKP and even Go Onto Target were the technological equivalent of looking for 'how to make a bomb' on the internet.

Your internet location was intercepted and monitored. Not just by the British, but by at least a couple of other agencies."

"Am I under arrest?" asked Jake.

"And why would that be?" replied the woman.

"Precisely, "Said Jake, "What if I were to say 'No, I won't come along'?"

"It would be better for you and also for your friends with Colonel Manners in Arizona," said the man.

"How do you know this?" asked Jake. He was sure they had been careful.

"Your activity with your computer led us to realise that something was happening. We have been monitoring you for the last 24 hours."

"I'm not sure that is legal," said Jake.

"I'm not sure that some of the things you have been doing would be classed as legal if we want to get particular about it," said the woman.

"Okay," said Jake, "Just give me a minute."

He looked into the office, picked up his keys, his phone and a small memory stick.

He would go with them but wasn't sure if this was his brightest move.

They walked outside to a waiting black Jaguar car.

"Please get in," said the woman.

Jake sat in the back on one side; the woman sat in the back on the other side. One of the policemen sat in the front passenger seat, and the other sat in the remaining empty seat in a second car.

As they pulled away, Jake noticed that there were also two motorcycles with police officers which now moved to the front of his car, then another vehicle dropped into a gap in front. He was now in the middle of a three-car convoy, led by two motorcycles.

"Thank you for co-operating", said the woman, "I think you can see it was a lot simpler that you've agreed to come along voluntarily. My name is Amanda Miller. I work for SI6. You seem to be tripping a lot of wires with your recent investigations. I hope you've only tripped wires that we can see."

"You must tell me more than this," said Jake, "I won't deny accessing the sites, but I've not done anything wrong, and everything I've looked at has been in the public domain."

"Agreed," said Miller, "but you and your friends have stirred a hornets' nest. I think all of you are now in danger."

Route SI6

Jake recognised the route from Hoxton down towards the Embankment and then along to Vauxhall Bridge, where they turned left. He assumed they were heading for the SI6 building on the south side of the Thames and, sure enough, they took another left and then down a slope into an underground area.

Jake noticed that the route had been continuously moving which implied he had received some priority treatment based on being part of a cavalcade of police cars. He thought this was a new record to cross this area of London.

He looked across the back seat to the woman, "Okay, Ms Miller."

"Call me Amanda."

"Okay, Ms Amanda Miller, why are you so insistent on bringing me here?"

"I think you and your friends have got caught up in something which has international dimensions. Not that you are in the USA, but that there are other forces at play."

"Okay, and the reason you need to bring me here?"

"In the short term, it is for your protection. We will want to ask you some questions, and I notice that so far you have been very cooperative. It would be better if it stayed that way. We want to protect you and your colleagues while getting access to the information that you uncover."

They led Jake from the car and into a reception area. There were conventional office security systems in use. Glass barriers and swipe cards. There didn't seem to be anything robust about the entry security,

He followed Ms Miller through the barrier and into another room.

"I must ask you to leave your phone, keys and other personal belongings here," said Miller. "The people over there will look after them for you and give you a small token that you can use to release them later."

"And if I say No?" Asked Jake.

"Please, Mr Lambers, please continue to co-operate. We have your interests at heart."

Jake noticed that other people were entering the room and going through a similar process. He remembered doing Jury Service once and that there had been a similar process to stop mobile phones from being used in the courtroom.

"As you can see," said Miller, "This is a routine procedure. We need to know you are not photographing or recording things inside the building."

Jake emptied his pockets, keys, phone, the memory stick.

"What about my money?" asked Jake.

"You can keep that," said Amanda, "Although I'll be buying the coffee."

The woman behind the counter scanned Jake's wallet with a small device. There was a beep. "It'll be your Oyster card," she said. "They have aerials inside them."

Jake opened the wallet and flicked through the cards. The Oyster card was in there. He removed it, and the security woman tried scanning the wallet again.

This time it was clear. "I'll add the Oyster card to your stored items," she said.

Jake nodded. A significant security risk - his Oyster card.

"That's fine," said Amanda. We still have to go through the metal detector, which is just like the ones at airports. Jake walked forward and to his slight surprise could pass through this with no beeps.

"Good," said Amanda, "You are on the inside now. Let's go to somewhere where we can talk."

Jake thought about this. He was now cut off from everyone he knew, and after speeding across London in a matter of minutes, he was now inside the centre of the UK security machine.

"Here," said Miller, "I have a room for us."

Jake expected to enter a grim grey walled room with a table screwed to the floor and some mirror glass. Instead, he was now in a small conference room. There was a coffee pot, some cookies, a picture of a field and an oval table surrounded with about a dozen chairs.

At the front was a screen and a whiteboard, also on the wall was a sliding flipchart.

"I'm sorry - I couldn't get a smaller room at short notice," said Amanda," but I hope this will do. And won't be off-putting. A couple of others will join us and want to ask you a few questions."

Cold Stone Creamery Jelly Belly jelly beans ^(TM)

Jake watched as two other people entered the room.

A blonde man, early thirties, well-tailored, carrying a slim computer. A woman, similar age, bright coloured outfit and Jake guessed she was of a Caribbean origin.

 "Hello, my name is Richard, Richard Brookfield and this is my associate Harriett **Delancey**. We both work for the The National **Counter Terrorism** Security Office."

"Look, I'm not a terrorist," said Jake - "I still don't know what this is about,"

"No, we know you are not a terrorist, and that your two associates in the USA aren't either. Colonel Manners has some interesting attributes, but we wouldn't class him as one either."

"So why have you brought me here?" asked Jake.

"It's for your protection," answered Broomfield. He looked across the table to Miller.

"Amanda, have you explained what we think is happening?"

"No," answered Amanda, "I thought we'd wait until we are all together."

"Harriett, can you start this for us?"

Harriett leaned forward and pressed the remote-control unit stood in the middle of the table. There was a whirr and then an overhead projector flickered into life.

'Tony Capaldi
Mike Chambers
Ben Leitzmann
[Redacted]
Chuck Manners
Barbara Somerville
Klaus Wegener '

Harriett pointed to the list of names displayed.
"Colonel Manners and his sub-team comprising Mike, Ben and Klaus were assigned to Project Esther a few years ago. There were two specific scientists who were at the heart of this process. Their names were Barbara Somerville and Tony Capaldi

"They worked on the guidance systems that we can see you have been researching on the internet. After they cancelled the project, the scientists were re-assigned, Barbara stayed in the service, but Tony left and took a role in the University of Columbia.

Although the technology wasn't much further use to the military, it became apparent to the two scientists that it could be used as an element in asymmetric warfare, if the size of the targeting devices could be reduced.

"Is that when they devised the credit card-sized units?" Asked Jake, "we found out about them and Bigsy could even describe how they would be set up to work."

"Yes," said Harriett. She looked towards Jake, "The clever part of the design was more about the way it could hook itself into a nearby network. This also meant they could pick its coordinates up by a remote sensing system."

"Because the units also have on-board batteries, we could leave them for a long time. Up to 5 years, they could broadcast a signal back to any adjacent Wi-Fi or mobile telephony mast."

Jake asked, "but they have superseded the technology, why would someone still want it?"

"That's the point, no one is very interested – no one until it became apparent that the transponders were being produced in bulk."

"We intercepted some signals from China where a manufacturing plant was producing batches of these transponders to the size of a credit card. Think about it for a minute. Mail order missile attacks. Send the unfortunate target a card. Then set loose a UAV-launched rocket.

It took us a while, but we intercepted a sample of these which was being couriered to somebody in Beijing. Our trail went cold, but it's also around the time that some upcoming Colonel

Manners associates were being chased and some of them eliminated."

Jake asked, "but if you knew all this, why didn't you do something about it to intervene to stop people from being killed?'

"Firstly, this was out of our jurisdiction," said Richard, "and secondly we think this could be part of some major conspiracy."

Jake smiled despite being in a difficult situation, "Yes, I can understand that if it involves Chuck Manners then there's something big in the background."

Harriett continued, "We need some help now, and because it already involves Chuck Manners and your little team, and we think this may be the fastest way to find out what is happening."

Jake asked, "You just said that this was outside your jurisdiction. If that's the case, how can you help us when part of this is happening in America, and it sounds as if the rest of this happening in China?"

Richard answered, "Things have moved on fast since we uncovered what was happening here, you'll have noticed how we moved you from your offices to our building and that we seemed to be able to clear most of London's traffic to do this. That wasn't for effect. We are treating this as a very high priority item, not just here in the UK but also in the US. You won't know yet, but the Department of Defence are also involved, and we have a direct link with them for this."

There was a crackle and Jake knew the phone system on the middle of the desk was live. It had the regular little tell-tale lights on it, but they were all switched off.

"Hello Mr Lambers, my name is Captain Garcia and I have been listening in on this call. As the man says, I am from the United States military and based in our counter-terrorism unit in Washington."

Jake looked startled, "Can you just do that?", he asked, "Just listen in on the conversation like that without telling anyone?"

He realised what he just said was a little bit naive in the circumstances, but it just blurted out. After all, he'd just been transported across London in a police convoy and was now, he wasn't sure, captive inside MI6 or SI6 or whatever they called it nowadays.

"I guess I got to get used to all of this," he said, "Things are moving fast. How much of this can I tell Chuck and the others?"

Amanda answered, "We want them to know what is happening, but we want to tell them without it being a phone call from you."

"The reason is simple. At this stage, we think it is very likely that whoever is chasing Chuck will have started to make the connections with Bigsy and Clare as well and that this will inevitably lead back to you Jake."

"But we are also sure that they have no idea that we are tracking them from MI6 or from the US antiterrorism group."

"We don't want to give the game away I'm sure you understand, so this means they could be a small gap before we can somehow advise Chuck and the others about our presence."

"So how you do it?" asked Jake, "Will you send somebody to meet Chuck."

"Yes," said Amanda, "But we'll need something from you to help him believe that we are genuine and not another trick being played."

"I see," said Jake, "You'll need something that only I know that you can pass on to the others as a form verification?"

"Yes," said Amanda, "and something recent, not something that could have been looked up on the Internet or from some pub conversation."

Jake thought for a while. He tried to single something that only Bigsy and Clare would know about. Something recent and probably trivial but something that they would remember. There were a few possibilities, like his support for Fulham F.C., but he thought too many other people would know his team.

Then he remembered the thing he asked Clare to bring back from the USA. Daft, but also very memorable. Jellybeans. Not any jellybeans, the Cold Stone ice cream flavoured jellybeans that you can't get in England.

Jake spoke, "I'm not sure if I should say this. At least not say this out loud. I think the password you need will be 'Cold Stone ice cream jellybeans '!"

The Circle

Amanda looked at Harriett. Harriett held her expression for about half a second and then laughed.

Amanda said, "Perfect. But please tell me this is something recent!"

Jake said, "Oh yes, I asked Clare to bring some back from this trip. You don't think I'd be telling too many people about this do you?"

Harriett asked, "Are they delicious then?"

"The best," replied Jake.

Los Alamos

Bigsy looked out on the morning. It surprised him to see it had been raining overnight. There were still some puddles on the ground by the car park at the side of the hotel. There were early signs that this would be another sunny day. Bigsy wondered what it would be like to live in an area that was an arid desert.

He prepared for the day and repacked is a few items into his small bag.

Bigsy left his room and headed for the breakfast area. Clare and Chuck are already seated. "We need to plan the day," said Chuck.

"But first, you must say goodbye to Tom; It is too risky for him around the base with us. He's still known, and it would be more than embarrassing for him and his people to be caught with a group of interlopers. I've suggested to Tom that he go back to the desert, to monitor what is happening, and to tell us if there is anything strange."

The Circle

Tom walked around the circle, looked each of them in the eyes, hugged them and said, "Walk with beauty."

Bigsy could see Clare looking slightly tearful.

"Walk tall," said Bigsy to Tom.

Tom smiled, "Yeah, and walk straight; I know that one!" He laughed as he walked back towards his 4x4. I'll be seeing you guys!" and with that, he took off in a cloud of desert dust.

Chuck continued, "We are going to the base this morning. I have worked out that only one of us needs to go inside. That will be me. I know my way around and if someone challenges me, I have the right language to be able to get out of most situations without drama."

"I assume that means you won't need too much of the heavy stuff from that camouflage bag?" asked Clare.

"That's right," said Chuck, "I'll be using a uniform and the ID card to get into the base. Once inside I can walk around easily. I know where I'm going and can keep my time on-site as short as possible.

"What will I do?" asked Bigsy.

"You'll be my getaway car," said Chuck, "although I hope I won't need it."

"I assume from that you will not be taking the car into the site?" said Bigsy.

"That's right," said Chuck, "I'll take a taxi to the base. It will look less suspicious if I show up in a taxi."

"So, I assume we will park somewhere close by?" said Clare. "That's right," said Chuck, "Look at this map."

He showed them an extract from the Google maps they had made the previous evening. It showed an aerial view of the site and several main office complexes.

"It would appear," said Chuck, "we will not be going to their most secure environment. The project was stopped and is off of the radar now. They are far more interested in the new laser guns and photon systems."

Chuck pointed to the map. "See. This area has a setup for testing rail guns and other high energy devices. All we need is a little office block over to the west of all of this. That's where anything we need would be stored. "

They looked at the map. It was a small complex considering the work that took place.

"Of course," said Chuck, "You can't see most of the site because there is quite a large underground complex. We need not go anywhere near that for this little excursion."

"The main extra thing I need is to find a spot where I can be met later," said Chuck, "I don't want to rely on a taxi to take me back out again."

He scanned the perimeter area and pointed to a small area to the north of the office block he would be entering.

"There," he said. "That's our best opportunity. I'm using the low-security area of the site where deliveries or the catering or made. It has still got fences, but look. There are all kinds of carts and general rubbish behind this area. I'll be using one of the carts to help me get over the fence. As long as you are there, we can be away in a few minutes."

"To be honest, I don't think they'll even notice. I expect this site has been sleepy for years. I wouldn't fancy my chances across the way at the main accelerator site though."

Clare and Bigsy looked at one another, "Do you think we will be safe driving this automobile to where you have showed?"

"Look," said Chuck, "There is a regular car park about 200 yards away. I think you need to park there and drive towards me when I am leaving the site. I can be in the car in a moment."

"I don't want to be in the site for over one hour. I want them to think I am at a meeting and for us to be away before they expect me to check out again."

"By then, we will have what we need. They may have a good photo of me, but they know me anyway. Frankly, if I am recognised it could also be a signal to both the good guys and the bad guys that we are on to something."

Clare asked," So do you think this is part of a bigger conspiracy?"

"Undoubtedly," said Chuck, "I think Jake is right that this is some small breakaway team that is picking up this outdated technology."

Bigsy nodded, "Yes, it's hardly ancient if it's only been around for a few years and could still be dangerous in the wrong hands."

"It's almost showtime," said Chuck, "But I don't want to be seen in the uniform until we are almost at the site. We should leave here in civvies. I'll get changed when we are very close to the base. It'll take us about an hour from here. I'll drive."

Tonto (Jay Silverheels)

Bigsy looked out of the front windscreen of the car. He'd moved forward when Chuck had left. Clare was seated next to him. They had been watching the time, wondering when the moment would be to go to the side of the Los Alamos establishment which Chuck had described.

Then, to Bigsy's surprise, he saw Chuck walking towards him. No-one following, no dramatic chases, just Chuck in the uniform.

Chuck smiled and walked around to the rear door on Clare's side and climbed in.

"Let's go," he said.
Clare turned backwards as Bigsy manoeuvred the car away.

"So how did it go?" She asked," That all seemed undramatic,"

"It was," said Chuck, "The admin area was pretty much unsecured as part of public information, and I almost think we could have got the same information from the internet. The Public Access to Information Bill can explain a lot of things," he added.

"But if we'd gone to the internet, we would not have discovered the additional information that I got by turning up in person," he added.

"What was it?", asked Clare. "There was a marking on the folder containing the information. It was quite 'old school' but effective. A symbol that told me there was a hidden wi-fi network in the vicinity. I went back to the cafeteria, logged on, found it and it took me to a home page with a code reference on it."

"What kind of code reference?" asked Bigsy. He was driving.

"Not anything I've seen before," said Chuck, "Here it was an alpha-numeric string 'GC172NM' It looks like a plane marking or something," said Chuck, "I think G is Great Britain." "So, it could be G-C," said Bigsy?

"I think 172 is a type of plane too," said Chuck, "The Cessna is one of the most common civilian plane types - it would be a needle in a haystack to look a British Cessna with G-C markings."

"I don't think we are on the right track at all," said Clare, "although I suppose there is that big air force base to the south of here."

"Not the place to find Cessna though," said Chuck. "Tank busters maybe and F-15s, but not little civilian pop-pops."

"Okay," said Bigsy, "We should find somewhere to regroup. I think we'll need some internet time to make more sense of this."

Bigsy had been driving out of Los Alamos, and now they were on a long strip of road with a ribbon development of modern shops and stores.

"There will be somewhere along here where we can stop, have a drink and score some internet," he said.

Sure enough, within another mile, they were at the approach to a sprawl of individual stores.

"This is fine," said Chuck. He gestured to the Coffee House Cafe. "Look Burritos," said Bigsy. "This is fine."

"They pulled off of the main road and into the parking lot. As they climbed from the car the temperature of the day startled Bigsy and Clare. "Whoa, it is hot," said Bigsy.

"Welcome to the land of air conditioners," said Chuck. They walked into the cafe. Clare ordered three coffees, and Bigsy added some orders for Burritos and a side of nachos.

Bigsy fired up his computer.

"Okay, let's start by doing the obvious thing," he said, "He typed the code from Chuck into the computer's search engine."

To his surprise, there was an immediate hit. "Wow," said Bigsy, "I think we are on to something. The code appears to be like a map reference."

"It is not GPS," said Chuck

"No, it is a 'Geocache'," said Bigsy, "People use geocaches to set trails for hikers. This is a reference to a particular cache."

"This seems more likely than the Cessna idea," said Clare, "Where is the Geocache located?"

"I don't know yet," said Bigsy," but it's got a name. Er - a slightly crazy name. 'Tonto Number 2' according to the search."

"Let me find a geocache site."

He typed in Geocaching Maps, and to his surprise, a map of the west coast of the United States appeared covered in little symbols.

"Hmm," said Bigsy," This could take some while."

 The map covered the area around San Francisco and was covered with little symbols which Bigsy took to be Geocache locations.

He zoomed in, and there were even more locations shown.

"This could be like looking for a needle in a haystack," he said.

Clare pointed to the top of the map. "Look," she said," it says 'Search'. Let's type in the code."

The Circle

Bigsy typed in the letters, and the map swirled to a different location. It was difficult to tell where it was because the symbols more or less obliterated the place names. Zoom Out, said Clare let's see if we can find something we recognise.

Bigsy zoomed out, and they could make out that the area of the map was in the locality where they were travelling and seemed to be centred on Santa Fe.

Okay, now let's zoom right in, said Chuck, to see where this cache is located. Bigsy pressed the button a few times. The map got more crowded, but then it started to clear. They could make out an aerial grid of streets, still with a surprisingly large number of locations shown.

Then it started to clear as they got to a level which began to separate the individual markers. They could make out the city and an airport. It was Santa Fe. They were looking at a map of the very centre of Santa Fe inside a hotel called La Fonda.

"Look," said Clare, there's another cache close by as well. GC272NM. At that Chapel.

"Yes, we have found the location," said Chuck." That's the place where something has been left which will tell us what to do next."

"Isn't this becoming like a treasure hunt?" asked Clare, "Why doesn't the person just put the information in one place."

"It's very deliberate," said Chuck," This is to create a chain which needs to be followed and also to ensure one person only holds that information. Like a cell. I'm sure you've heard of that idea before?"

Chuck and Bigsy nodded. Something was being hidden and there was a difficult process to uncover it.

Bigsy was busily typing in another reference 'Tonto Number 1'.

"I've been chaining along these Geocaches. This seems to be the last one in the series. It's at a hotel in Santa Fe." He dialled up the hotel on his computer.

"That looks nice," said Clare, "Another winning combination! Let's go check it out. It's only around 35 miles from here."

THE CIRCLE
PART TWO

Route 66

You'll see Amarillo, a-Gallup, New Mexico
Flagstaff, Arizona, don't forget Winona
Kingman, Barstow, San Bernardino

Would you get hip to this kindly tip
And take that California trip?
Get your kicks on Route 66

--Bobby Troup

La Fonda

It took around forty minutes to drive to Santa Fe. The route headed to the east and then in a curve around towards Santa Fe.

Both Clare and Bigsy were taking in the scenery while Chuck was driving. There was plenty to look at; this was a rugged country. A mix of mountains, valleys, and desert scenery. All baking under 35°C temperatures.

They arrived in Santa Fe. Both Bigsy and Clare were expecting it to look like a typical American city with a skyline of skyscrapers as they approached. Instead, they were surprised to see it was quite a low-rise environment and that the central area comprised Pueblo like structures.

As they drove into the centre, they could see many people walking around the varied shops and cafes. There was a square near the centre, and Chuck looked around for somewhere to park. Then Clare pointed, "Look, 'La Fonda', that's our hotel."

It was just to the edge of the central grassy square. It had a small entrance, but there was a valet parking spot outside. Chuck manoeuvred the car to the entrance.

The valet asked if they needed any help with their bags, but Chuck refused," We'll take the bags. Thank you, but please park the car for me." He gave the valet banknote.

"I think this place would be difficult for us to park in if we were not staying at this hotel," said Chuck. "This means we can be very central but may slow us down when we need to leave."

"I hope we won't need to be leaving in that much of a hurry," said Clare.

Bigsy looked around and could see that Santa Fe was geared up as a tourist destination. It seemed very Spanish but along one edge of the green square was a kind of Native American market. He was too far away to look at it closely, but could see that they were selling jewellery, clothing and other first nation artefacts.

it reminded him of his time only a day ago with Tom and Red.

"Let's get in here," said Chuck, "And then we will need to find the treasure chest," he joked.

Clare also looked around as they walked into the hotel. It was deceptive; the inside somehow seemed much larger than the outside. It was because they had set up some shops along the outer facade of the hotel. Inside it appeared to cover most of a block.

"Wow," said Clare, "We are getting to some fascinating places! I feel like we are on vacation while we are being chased."

"Don't get too comfortable," said Chuck, "Once we have found the cache, we will need to be on our way again."

"Maybe it will take us a while to find it," said Clare, smiling.

Chuck arranged the check-in and once again paid with cash.

He looked at Clare and Bigsy, "You know I'm paying for all of this with cash to reduce our electronic trail?" he said.

"I'm guessing I know what some of the contents of your big bag is then," said Clare.

Chuck nodded, "Yes, set aside for a rainy day; yours is not the only stash of money that I know about."

They walked through the busy corridors of the hotel towards their rooms. There were various side rooms and a cafe and a restaurant together with a central atrium area.

"If we are looking for something here, it could take some while," said Clare. Bigsy nodded.

"You know what," said Chuck," I think whoever has hidden it here will have found somewhere obvious to protect it. No one will look here unless they know about the cache.

"When I get to the room," said Bigsy, "I will look at the Internet again and see whether I can get a more precise positioning for this cache,"

"Great," said Chuck," but I think we all owe ourselves time some downtime now. We should rest this evening and be fresh for an early start tomorrow."

Clare looked at Chuck, for the first time she could see that he looked tired.

"Good plan," she said, "We can meet in the restaurant this evening for something to eat and then take an early night."

Cache

Bigsy unpacked when he got to his room, he didn't have much by way clothes because they'd only expected to be in Arizona for a couple of days. He visited the small market to pick up a couple of tee-shirts to add to his available options for the next few days.

Before that, he checked the information about the geocache. He found a website he used and once again zeroed in on the area, this time going directly to the hotel. To his surprise, the geocache he had found on the search didn't show up when he attempted to look for it directly. As a comparison, he looked at another nearby geocache. He remembered that there was a chapel shown on the map almost next to the hotel.

Loretto Chapel. He zoomed into the map to find the chapel, and sure enough, there was a geocache shown at this spot.

Then he tried the name he remembered from searching for the geocache inside the hotel. He typed in the code again, and this time the geocache appeared. It looked as if it was almost central within the hotel. Pretty much in the area of the atrium where the restaurant was situated.

Bigsy decided that he would look at the restaurant on the way to the stalls selling tee-shirts in case he could see anything. It would impress the others if he'd already located the geocache.

The restaurant was busy, and he skirted the edges looking for anything obvious that might be a hiding place. Bigsy realised that this location was bustling and that it was unlikely that anything would remain hidden for long because of the sheer volume of traffic of people through the room.

He also considered that it would be unlikely that a lot of treasure hunters would be allowed to wander through the restaurant area unchallenged.

He left further investigations of this type until he met with the others, but he could at least tell them it was the restaurant area that they needed to examine.

Instead, he walked out of the hotel and across to the area selling the tee-shirts.

He'd taken his backpack for shopping and his small laptop computer.

One tee-shirt with an iguana looked good and another which said Santa Fe also looked good. He decided not to become distracted with all of the other things on offer and was about to head back to the hotel when he spotted the Loretto Chapel. As this was another spot with a geocache, he thought he would look inside in case it was easier to find the geocache at this location. It might give him some ideas about how these things were concealed.

First, he looked at the inside of the chapel as if he were as a tourist. He considered he was here working at the moment. The featured aspect of the chapel appeared to be a unique wooden staircase that had constructed without the use of nails and which had the same number of steps as Jesus' age.

He looked around inside, and similar to the hotel realised that there were many hiding places but also very large foot traffic which should make concealing and keeping a geocache tricky.

Bigsy decided to go back outside the chapel and found a small cafe where he could sit with his laptop and a cold drink and examine the way that the caching worked. He typed in the code for the geocache at the chapel again and this time found a site which had more information. It appeared that there were two caches at the chapel: the virtual cache and another physical one.

For the physical cache, there was a further clue in the information. It was written in code, but also included the key to the code on the same page. Bigsy worked out that this was so that people travelling a long way to find the cache had a way to locate it if they were stuck.

He sat for a few minutes, decoding the instructions about the geocache in the chapel. It turned out that the instructions were for a location in the car park of the chapel and that the hidden information was on a magnetic sign for a reserved parking area.

Bigsy realised this was a whole world it had never involved him had never with. But he could learn fast.

 He headed for the car park at the chapel. It was really for staff members and quite small. He found the reserved sign and although there were quite a few people around, he could see a small box attached to the back of the sign magnetically. Inside the box was a small logbook that people had signed. There was also a code to verify that people had genuinely found the cache.

"Great," thought Bigsy, "Now I know how this works it should make it a little easier when we are trying to find the geocache in the hotel."

 Armed with this new information, he made his way back across to the hotel and straight for the restaurant where Clare and Chuck were already sitting eating something that looked Mexican.

Loreto Chapel

"Bigsy!" said Clare, "You were gone a long time. I thought you were getting a couple of tee-shirts?"

"I did, said Bigsy, "but I also had a look at the geocache in the Loreto Chapel next door."

"Wow," said Clare, "was it easy to find?"

"Not especially, "said Bigsy," I had to use a clue. The one in this hotel doesn't have an entry like the one for the Loretta."

"The entry for the chapel included a kind of code which explained where to find the geocache. It was very precise and explained that it was in the car park magnetically attached to a sign on a fence post.

"The actual chapel was very busy, and it would have been difficult to hide something in it, and I am not sure that the people running the chapel would have taken too kindly to a lot of treasure hunters running through their building looking for hidden items.

"So, do you think that will be the same problem here?" asked Clare.

"I do," said Bigsy, "and unless we can find something like the clue at the Loretto Chapel, then I think it could take us a long time to find this."

"I suppose the other thing we can do is ask someone?" said Clare.

"Good point," said Chuck, "If they have a regular traffic of people looking for this thing, then maybe the staff will know about it?"

"We should ask," said Bigsy, "but I doubt whether this item is as known as the one across the way at the chapel because it seems to have been concealed from the geocache maps. I only found it because I knew its reference number. When I searched the maps, it doesn't show up."

"That's a neat system," said Clare," It means anyone could hide anything on a map but unless you know the reference you won't be able to find it."

"Yes," said Chuck, "this is good fieldwork by whoever has hidden this item. Tonight, I think we should study this room but then tomorrow only one of us should ask about the geocache. Ideally alone so that we don't draw attention to our full group."

 "That's great," said Bigsy," and tonight, I will continue to check on the Internet in case I can find any other ways to locate this geocache."

Ed Adams

Breakfast in Santa Fe

Bigsy returned to his room. He tried a few more ways to access the information about the geocache. There was nothing just the two references to the geocache in Santa Fe and the other one at Kirtland airfield near Albuquerque.

He decided he'd had enough for one evening and that it was time to get some sleep.

Next morning, he woke early. 6:30 AM. He realised it was still an effect of the jetlag because of the time zone differences between the UK and the US. He had still only been in the country for about four days but had almost no proper sleep during that time and he was quite shaken up with the various sleeping arrangements.

Chuck and Clare had agreed that they would all meet in the morning at 9 o'clock. Bigsy decided he would go downstairs to the restaurant and take an early breakfast in any case.

The Circle

When he needed to meet the others later, he could drink coffee while they ate. He knew that the restaurant would have great breakfasts and was in the mood for something with lots of American styled peppered potatoes and lashings of bacon maybe also a fried egg on top and some strawberries. That would make a good starter. Then perhaps some of those pancakes piled high and dribbled with maple syrup.

He took a quick shower and then headed to the breakfast room. It was quiet, and they showed him to a large size table in the middle. As he had hoped, there was a good buffet, and his dreams of a fry up could even be improved upon with some of the other things on offer. Although he wasn't sure about what looked like apple crumble being served for breakfast even if it was coated in cinnamon.

And the deep-fried bread with eggs yet more cinnamon also looked a little too much after the sugar frosting had been applied.

Maybe his appetite wasn't quite as large as he thought.

He'd picked up a copy of USA Today from outside his hotel room and brought it along to read during his solitary breakfast. He could see the other early folk tucking into their food. There were individual people on business and small groups that were vacationing.

The room was interesting too and the wall had many small squares with what looked like small motifs from native American Indians, maybe with a Spanish twist. He had seen some similar signs before and recognised the similarities with the symbols that shown him after the night around the campfire.

But then he noticed something unusual. One of the small panels looked different from the rest. Instead of having an ethnic motif inside it; the five-inch square seemed to contain something else. Bigsy the realised it was a quick code. The thing used for guerrilla advertising in the UK. One of those little squares that comprises binary dots that somehow make a website address when you point a camera at them and have the right software.

Bigsy realised that maybe this was the hidden geocache. He felt in his pocket for his camera phone and decided he would get close enough to take a picture of the square. It was at a low level in a corner. He decided that it would be simplest to walk across to the corner and take the picture without attempting to hide what he was doing. Fortunately, that part of the group had not yet been filled by the waitresses allocating tables.

He walked across to the square, took the picture and continued on his way towards the metal containers with the hot food.

He'd noticed that there was also writing on the bottom of the code. "Santa Fe Electric," it said. This was probably just a sticker related to the electricity contractor.

He put his phone back into his pocket and picked up some food. It would be better to check what he had got when he was back in his room. He didn't want to draw too much attention to what he had been doing.

Bigsy settled into his breakfast, reading a newspaper for around 15 minutes before leaving the breakfast room and returning to his room in the hotel.

Now he could see what was on the quick code. Maybe he would have information for Clare and Chuck, or perhaps he would be just be able to read the local power meters.

Quickcode

"The problem with technology," thought Bigsy, "is that it's never as simple as it makes out."

Bigsy had got the photographs he took from his camera displayed in front of him. He looked on his camera for the software that reads quick codes and realised he didn't have it. He would now need to download it from the Internet.

The problem was that the special program would not capture the picture he'd already taken. He would need to make a copy of the quick code and then take another picture of it after he downloaded software.

This was all turning into something of a nightmare. He persisted, downloading the special phone App so he could read the quick code. Then he transferred the picture to his PC and displayed it as large as possible. Then using the special software on his phone, he took another snapshot of the code, this time using the special software.

"If this turns out to be a meter reading point or an advert for a CD then I'll be annoyed," Bigsy thought.

Moments later, the quick code revealed a website, he read it on his phone but decided it would be easier to type it back into his PC. He re-entered the web address, and sure enough, his PC displayed the site.

At the top the text looked to Bigsy like an advertisement for a weight loss program using tablets. Instead of abandoning this, Bigsy took it as a good sign. It was what would put most people off browsing further through the site. Clearly an advertorial.

He scrolled through around three pages of unconvincing photographs and text about how these tablets were the most fabulous way to lose weight and came to a section which seemed to break away from the main topic.

"Bingo!" Said Bigsy.

It was a block of text which was related to the project Esther. He read through what it said…

"Project Esther was cancelled because the technology wasn't was not fast enough to be deployed. Everyone involved knew that within a few years, processing speeds would increase, and a dangerous form of missile homing could be created.

"Someone involved with the project has reactivated it within the last few months. They are brokering a deal to sell three components. First, the transponder units which can now be manufactured to the size of a credit card. Second, a new and crucial component which allows the credit card transponders to hook onto a nearby Wi-Fi or cell phone link to transmit their information. Third, the device that is required within a missile or other guided device that can lock onto the transponder.

"My investigations show that the reason for the relaunch is financial. Someone is trying to cash in by selling the design. A small terrorist unit is buying it. They are planning to target key individuals and some locations in both the USA and mainland Europe.

" I have had to go to ground now so they cannot trace me. This is my way to pass the information along to whoever finds this from the original project Esther team. I think it involves someone from that team in this conspiracy."

The message was unsigned and after this block of text went back into more advertisements for weight loss products.

"Brilliant," thought Bigsy." We are a step closer to understanding what is happening. Someone is trying to sell the design that the labs came up with a few years ago. And it is to terrorists."

Bigsy looked at the clock. It had taken him some time to fiddle around with the various software and crack what they said on the website. It was now a few minutes before 9 o'clock when he was due to meet Clare and Chuck for breakfast.

 Carefully Bigsy selected the text that described the project and saved it into another folder on his computer. He decided to put the laptop into the safe in his room and tell the others the story over breakfast.

Shortcut to the museum

Chuck was alone in the breakfast area when Bigsy arrived.

"Hungry?" asked Chuck.

"I've already had breakfast, thank you," said Bigsy. "I've been busy this morning. I think I have found the geocache and also decoded it."

"I don't think we should talk about this here," said Chuck.

" You will want to hear this," said Bigsy, "I won't describe the detail, but someone is trying to sell your old project to another group. They want to use it for bad things."

"Okay," said Chuck, "I think we need to move on from here then. We may have inadvertently led people to the information."

"Right," said Bigsy, "We can talk further in the car once we are on the road. I'll get Clare."

Bigsy made his way to Clare's room and tapped the door. There was no reply. He wondered if Clare had overslept or like him had gone out early.

He opened the door using Clare's spare key. Their original arrangement to swap keys was proving invaluable. Inside the room, he was surprised to notice that all of Clare's belongings had gone. It looked as if she had moved out. There was no message or other sign.

Bigsy was concerned by this and retraced his steps to the reception area of the hotel. He asked if Clare had checked out.

"Yes, Clare Richardson checked out about 7 AM," said the receptionist.

Bigsy went to his room, picked up his belongings and headed for Chuck's room. "We need to go," said Bigsy, "Clare has gone missing."

"What?" said Chuck, "Are you sure she has not just gone for a walk?"
"No, she has checked out from the hotel," said Bigsy, "I have already been to reception and also to her room. There is no sign of her."

"Okay, we must find her then," said Chuck, "We should check out and meet somewhere near here. I will arrange for the valet to bring the car to us. We'll meet across the way at the New Mexico Museum of Art. It is just far enough away to create a problem for anyone following."

 Bigsy nodded. The museum was diagonally across the grass square. It was only about three- or four-minutes' walk but would be inconvenient for anyone following them by car.

 Bigsy was anxious about Clare. He and Chuck could leave, but they had no idea where Clare was at this time.

 From a distance, he could see Chuck asking the valet to bring the car across to the museum. He saw Chuck slip the valet a small selection of dollar notes and was sure that Chuck had made it favourable for the valet to do this.

 Bigsy then checked out and made his way across the square.

Galaxy Defenders

Clare had woken early at the hotel in Santa Fe around 6:30 AM. She thought it was the time zone difference that had caused her to wake early but then realised that someone was knocking at the door. She went to look through the security keyhole and could see that it was someone delivering room service breakfast.

Using the security chain, she slightly opened the door.

"Good morning, room service," said the waitress, "with the compliments of Chuck Manners."

Clare thought she had arranged to meet Chuck and Bigsy for breakfast at 9 o'clock? Maybe there was a change of plan and that everything had been brought forward. It wasn't unusual given the circumstances of the last few days.

"Okay," she said, "Please bring it in. Do I need to sign something?"

The Circle

The maid brought the breakfast in and set it down on the table by the side of the bed.

"I have been asked to give you a message," she said, "The message is from Jake."

Clare stiffened, "How do you know Jake?" she asked.

The maid continued, "This is the message…He said I should tell you that it is important you bring some jellybeans, not any jellybeans but especially Cold Mountain ice cream jellybeans."

"You have to be kidding me," said Clare.

"No," said the maid, "I am from British intelligence, and I have been asked to make contact with you and to tell you about what has been happening to Chuck and more recently to Bigsy. All three of you are in danger, but at the moment they do not know that you are connected with Chuck although they do know that Bigsy is connected."

"Please come with me now, and I will explain what is happening. The plan is for you to be told so that in turn you can update Bigsy and Chuck about all of this. We cannot go directly to Bigsy or Chuck in case we are detected. You are still independent of this and can pass on the message without suspicion. It will mean we need to take you away for a couple of hours and then arrange for you to be reunited with the others. By then, you will know what is happening and can tell them without suspicion."

"And if I say no?" asked Clare.

"You could say no," said the maid, "But I think it will leave you all in great danger. Additionally, the information we wish to give you should help you and us as well to resolve all of this.”

 “Can I speak to Jake, please,” said Clare. “I need to know that this is genuine. I prefer to do this now in my room.”

 “Okay,” said the maid, “Let me introduce myself; my name is Jennifer Burns and I work for MI6. Here is my identity card. She produced a card and showed it to Clare.”

“This looks fine, but it could be anything,” said Clare,“ I need to speak to Jake if I am to believe you. Jennifer flicked on her walkie talkie and asked for a line to Jake.

“There have been other people listening into this conversation,” said Jennifer,” They are arranging a line to Jake as we speak.”

 “Hello,” came a voice from the radio “it’s Jake.”

 Clare listened, and it did sound like Jake’s voice. “Hi, Jake, where are you?” asked Clare.

“Clare, you won’t believe this I am with MI6 in London. I didn’t know they would go after you - I only told them the bonkers story about the jellybeans - as identification - about two hours ago. They took me from our office to their building on the South Bank at Vauxhall. I am still in it. I think I am in some kind of bunker but it’s pleasant. Not a steel wall in sight.”

 Clare knew by now that this was Jake talking to her.

“They have asked me not to tell you about the situation - secret squirrel and all that - but someone, where you are, will explain it to you. I think they want you to go with them for two hours while they do this. The plan is to link you back to Bigsy and Chuck afterwards so you can pass on the message. It's big stuff that is happening."

"Okay, Jake I will do as they say. Look, are you all right?"

"Clare, I'm fine. I think we are now doing more to help Chuck than he could have imagined. Of course, he hasn't got a clue that any of this is going on at the moment."

Another voice cut in on the speaker.

"Thank you, Jake," said the voice, "my name is Amanda, Amanda Miller, I am with Jake, and we will take good care of him until they finish this. We don't want any of you to be hurt, but there is a very high stakes game in play at the moment."

" We are trying to get to the source and isolate it so we can shut everything down."

"And thank you for your co-operation with this Ms Clare Richardson we will look after you and we will do the same with the others."

Jennifer looked at Clare, "I'm going to switch off this speaker now," she said.

"Goodbye Jake, "said Clare
"'bye Clare," said Jake.

There was a click, and there was now alone again in the room with Jennifer.

"Look, Clare, I must ask you to give me your cell phone while you get ready, we can't have you calling Chuck and Bigsy about this. We must keep the isolation of you from then until after we have briefed you. We don't want them to react in a way that tips off the people are following Chuck. I'm sorry to have had to do this, but I hope you will understand we cannot take any chances."

Clare nodded, "I guess so. I am, at the moment, the messenger between you and Chuck and Bigsy. You're about to tell me some things that could save them from something unfortunate. I would be crazy not to cooperate with you. You have my support. Please, give me a few minutes to get my things together and then I will join you. She was already drinking the coffee and looking at the pastries in the breakfast tray.

"That's fine," said Jennifer, "I will wait outside for you for 15 minutes, then we must leave."

Clare readied herself to leave. She left a short note for Bigsy, thinking he'd try the room when she didn't show. Then she opened the door of her room and saw Jennifer patiently waiting along with two other men.

"We will go out through a side exit from the hotel," said Jennifer, "There is a car already waiting. We have already checked you out you need not go to the front exit at all."

They took some stairs from Clare's floor to the ground level and then exited through a fire door towards the rear of the building. A large black SUV was waiting for them there. A further black SUV was parked behind it. They were clearly a convoy.

"Er, isn't this conspicuous?" asked Clare, "Surely a beige Honda would have been better?"

 "Yes, they are cars from our local carpool. I thought the same. Nothing says 'Men in Black Spy Movies' more than black SUVs. But don't worry," said Jennifer, "We are only going a short way across town to a location where we can explain more what has been happening."

"We have also arranged for one of our teams to follow Colonel Manners and Bigsy so that at the right time we can we reunite you all with one another."

 Clare looked wistfully towards the hotel spa sign as they pulled away.

Leaving

Bigsy exited the hotel first. He was carrying his backpack which now had a small extra content of tee shirts.

 He made his way across the square through a garden area with a small bandstand and tourists who were taking photographs and sitting on the grass and various chairs surrounding the square. A guitarist was busking for small change from the passers-by.

"In London, he'd have a contactless system, not an upturned baseball cap." thought Bigsy.

 Everything looked very pleasant and like the place that to take a short vacation.

Bigsy arrived at the entrance to the museum and could see his car already waiting with the valet standing by its side. He showed the driver his ticket and fished in his pocket for some change to give the valet another tip. Bigsy looked back across the square but couldn't see Chuck yet. He loaded his bag into the car and sit in it, waiting for Chuck to arrive.

A few minutes later, Chuck appeared but from a completely unexpected direction.

He threw his heavy bag into the back seat and jumped into the front seat of the car.

"Let's go," he said, "I think I'm being followed."

Bigsy manoeuvred the car away from the square. He drove cautiously, and there were many people around. Tourists ambled across the streets as if they were not intended for vehicles. Then Bigsy reached a set of traffic lights.

"Swap over here," said Chuck, "Let me take the wheel. I don't know who is following us, but I want to shake them off."

Bigsy jumped out of the car and walked around to the passenger side. As he climbed back in, he could see that Chuck was already in the driving seat.

"Fasten your belt," said Chuck, "I am going to lose these guys."

Bigsy looked back and could see another dark-coloured SUV about 10 cars behind. It had four occupants who looked suitably business-like.

"It could be that SUV," said Chuck, "but I think it's the guys in that taxi over there."
d out towards the ring road," said Chuck. "I will drive around like I'm lost on the way and see whether they continue to follow us. If they do, then I will find a way to lose them."

Chuck accelerated hard from the lights and changed into the same lane as the taxi. He was now around eight cars ahead. At the next right turn, he cut into the side road and then took a further right. He was now heading back in the direction he had been driving.

"This will help us eliminate anyone that is not following us," he said, "Not many people double back on themselves when they are going to a destination with a taxi."

"Have you been to London recently?" said Bigsy.

Chuck looked behind in the mirror and could see that the taxi was still following. A disadvantage of his change of direction was that the car was now much closer. There was another set of traffic lights about to change to red and Chuck accelerated through "That will inconvenience them, " said Chuck, "They can't jump those them, then took a left.

lights."

Bigsy noticed that there was now just one truck behind them.

Chuck continued to drive fast, beyond the speed limits for the side roads in Santa Fe.

"In a moment I will head towards the freeway," said Chuck, "Then we can throw some distance."

Bigsy nodded. Chuck seemed to know what he was doing.

Delta Seven loses it

Clare's journey across town was sedate. On the way, there was a call from the radio in the front of the car. It was a call for Jennifer.

"Hi, this is Delta Seven. We have been following the Firefly. They have identified us and our starting to move out of our range. Damn, they just jumped a red light. We have had to stop. Now I can see them turning down another street. Don't think we should put on any lights around here.

 Clare saw Jennifer's expression change. Jennifer looked troubled.

Then Jennifer spoke, "I think Manners is good. He has identified the people were following him. The problem about this, Clare, is that we were using the people following him to help us link you back together after we have debriefed you."

Clare said, "so does that mean they have given you the slip?"

Jennifer said "Yes, I don't think we can catch up with them using just one vehicle and we have had to take two vehicles with us to make sure you are safe.

"We are sharing this mission with the Americans, and you can

He pointed to another car in a different lane at the lights. It was also several cars back in the traffic.

"I'm going to try to imagine that this was short notice to get everybody together. Speed was of the essence, and we got a good team with nine people and three cars.

"That's two cars for you and one for Chuck and Bigsy. They will have to look after themselves, which I guess will be easy with Chuck Manners there.

Clare said, "Okay, but this whole thing falls apart if we can't figure out how to get me back to Chuck and Bigsy."

"I agree," said Jennifer.

Wagons roll

They say I'm crazy but I have a good time
I'm just looking for clues at the scene of the crime
Life's been good to me so far

My Maserati does 185
I lost my license, now I don't drive
I have a limo, ride in the back
I lock the doors in case I'm attacked

Joe Walsh

Interstate

Chuck led the vehicle back onto the I-25 out of Santa Fe. He was now heading south-west in the general direction of Albuquerque.

"Look," said Bigsy, "I don't want to leave here without figuring out where Clare is. I know she left us that message in the hotel room about not worrying but: come on, we need to find out where she is."

"My guess," said Chuck, "She has been picked up by someone from intelligence services."

"The room and Clare's message are typical of the way they would work."

"If it was the bad guys, I think we would have found Clare already and I don't think it would have been very nice."

"To be honest I think the people following us were also from the intelligence services."

"If it was a hit team, for example, they wouldn't have been put off by a little red light.

"Frankly they would also have had someone on a motorcycle pith a shooter. This smacks of something that has been put together in a hurry by the local field intelligence team.

"So do you think we have just run away from some people that could help us?" asked Bigsy?

"It's possible," said Chuck but I don't think it was the right thing to do to wait around to find out just now, especially after Clare's disappearance."

"This way it gives us a chance to figure things out," said Chuck

"… and also, to figure out the best way to find Clare again, " added Bigsy.

"One advantage that I have in all of this is that I've seen a lot of these things before and know the way the moves work. If you think about it although you and I have been seen together by whoever is chasing us so far claimed has been separate most of the time," said Chuck.

"We have also not used our cell phones between one another so if someone has some surveillance, they still can't make the links. Also, the amount we have travelled has helped because it would require some determination to follow us around as much as we have been travelling."

Bigsy nodded, "I hope you're right Chuck, you seem to know what you're doing, I just will make sure we don't have any problems with Clare and that we remain safe."

"Absolutely," said Chuck, "The point that I brought you into this was not to put you into direct danger but for you to help me without drawing attention to yourselves."

"We've blown that, then haven't we?" said Bigsy.

Private Security

After about 20 minutes, Clare's car pulled up outside an office block. It was a central hub and two wings diagonally at 90° to one another across a paved area.

 Some flags were flying in front of the building, but Clare didn't recognise any of the logos.

 "Welcome to our out-of-town office," said Jennifer.

 "This doesn't look like a government building," said Clare.
"No, it isn't," said Jennifer, "It's a private security firm that is based here, but we have some facilities. It doesn't draw too much attention, and there's a reasonable selection of SUV's and cars with flashing lights pulling up as part of regular business here."

 They walked towards the building, and Clare noticed that the guys from the other car were also looking and that she seemed to be surrounded by the others. It was not very obvious, but she knew that they appeared to be shielding her.

 She looked towards Jennifer, who recognised it in Clare's eyes.

"Yes, that's right," said Jennifer," but this is so you don't get recognised."

 "We're pretty sure we have not been followed here."

They entered the building and passed through a security screen. It was a full length 'air-lock' kind of device which Clare thought looked efficient at its job. She also realised that she was now effectively a prisoner on the inside of this building.

"Look," said Jennifer, "You are free to go at any time. We have brought you here so we can brief you about what we know. We will want you to brief Chuck and Bigsy and also Jake."

"We will want you to do it discreetly though so that anyone conducting surveillance is unaware."

Frosting

Jennifer accompanied Clare into a briefing room. It had frosted glass walls and a central table, complete with a telephone system. One wall had flip charts, and there was a full projection system built into the ceiling.

"Is this being recorded?" asked Clare.

"Yes," said Jennifer, "and filmed. The record stays here though. They won't be removed unless there is an emergency."

"Okay," said Clare, "You'd better explain what is happening."

"We know that someone from Chuck's original team on Project Esther has leaked information about the project. We don't know who, although some of the original team members have started to turn up dead.

"From what we can see, Chuck is also on the hit list.

"We think he realised and that is when he asked you to get involved in helping him find out who was behind it.

"If this was a small team then Chuck and his associates could handle this alone, and we would never even know that it had happened," said Jennifer.

"In practice, this seems to be a much bigger conspiracy. We think someone is selling the technology from Project Esther to the Chinese. We believe the Chinese are ready to go into production. They would make clones of western armaments technologies.

"It would have several effects. It could undermine the pricing structures and bring down some of the well-established companies. They may not be as picky about who they sell it to. And they can make a tidy sum for whoever is behind this.

"It could be money motivated or ideological. We don't know that because the link to the people behind it isn't clear. They seem to be operating through a web of other people, from western countries. UK, USA, Switzerland and Holland.

"There are three parts to the Esther solution, and we've already briefed Jake about these. Chuck will know about this, although his knowledge could be a little out-of-date. One part is the transponder; the second is the guidance system and the piece in the middle is the unique communication link-up to make this all work.

"I don't understand why this would be so useful?" said Clare, "Surely a mobile phone would also make a homing device?"

The Circle

"The difference with these units is we can set them up as passive units. They are small and don't give off any radio signals until we deploy them," answered Jennifer.

Jennifer continued, "They are also addressable uniquely, but unless you know the code for a specific unit then you can't turn it on. To start up a unit can take two days because they can be set to have a very slow poll rate. That is a deliberate part of the design.

"If they are to be used in an active war setting, they can have a much faster polling interval, but when they are to be used clandestinely, the rate can be set to be so slow as to make them almost undetectable."

"I see," said Clare, "so the transponders can be placed on things and left dormant for ages. Then they can be switched on and effectively light up a target."

"Yes," said Jennifer, "Imagine a scene where several politicians are gifted items which clandestinely contain the homing beacons. No need to trigger anything at that point, but one day in the future...Kaboom."

"That has to be illegal on so many levels," shuddered Clare.

"Exactly," said Jennifer. "And that's the problem now. If the design is refreshed and sold on to terrorists or state actors, it becomes, for them, an attractive way to create major disruptions."

"Wouldn't the people using it need the other two items as well? The special signal protocol and the guidance system?"

"Yes," said Jennifer, "and we think that is the deal being brokered at the moment."

"We think one person from Chuck's original team has gone rogue and is behind the trade. We think they invited everyone not already dead to Scottsdale so they could finish the job. That way only new allies know about this technology and its planned use."

"So, do you know what has happened to the members of Chuck's team," asked Clare. She could see now that a few pieces were falling into place.

We know that Ben and Mike were killed. We also know that Klaus Wegener died. Chuck has been attacked and Barbara Somerville and Tony Capaldi are unaccounted for. Capaldi we think was on his way to Scottsdale and Somerville's whereabouts are just unknown.

Clare told Jennifer about the signal that Chuck had found.

"Look, we also tracked down some information. We worked out that someone was trying to make contact and Chuck found a signal which gave us a code. I'm sorry but I don't have the code although I can try to remember it."

"Chuck found something written in Los Alamos - in an admin file - which pointed to a secret Wi-Fi system. He logged on and it gave him a code - we think it was a geocache code and that's the reason we were in Santa Fe. We checked the code on a map, and it seemed to be somewhere in the Fonda hotel in Santa Fe. That's where we were staying.

"We planned to look for the geocache today and try to figure out what was happening."

Clare looked at Jennifer, "Dis you know about the hidden code and the geocache already?" she asked,

"No, I can't say that we did."

"The thing was, when Bigsy tried to find the geocache on a map it didn't exist unless you already knew its reference… and the problem I have is that I can't remember the code. Bigsy has all of that information."

"It also had a name: 'Tonto' or something and I think there was another one like it with a similar name at Kirtland Airfield; the one at the airfield was on the map. Maybe you can use that to figure out the code?"

"There's a whole park and forest named Tonto outside of Phoenix. That's where the Lone Ranger companion's name came from," said Jennifer, "But can you remember any more?"

Clare thought back. She remembered they had talked about the code when they were trying to figure out what it might be.

"Oh yes, I can remember a part of it. When we were trying to work out what the code represented, Chuck said it sounded like an aircraft registration. It started with a G- like Great Britain. Oh, and they said it also had another connection with planes. It was like a Cessna plane type - a very common Cessna plane type, I think. But I can't remember the number."

"Okay," said Jennifer, "We can try to figure something out from that G, a plane type and Tonto, That's pretty good."

Her colleague was already typing Cessna into a search engine. Cessna - it says here Cessna Aircraft Company, wait the third entry is Cessna 172. It says it is the most prolific Cessna plane type 'in history'."

"I'm sorry." said Clare, "I think it was a three-digit number. That might have been it, but I honestly can't remember."

"Okay," said Jennifer, "So we have G maybe 172 and 'Tonto'. Spencer, can you get onto it?"

"Sure," said Spencer as he left the room.

 "What happens next?" asked Clare.

Jennifer said, "Look I think we've given you everything we know, and you have all of our information. What I want to do now is arrange that we have a way for you to communicate with us."

"We'll be giving you an additional cell phone the same as your one so you can charge it easily. This one will only have numbers to call me, and we have set it up so that is independent from your other phone."

"Okay," said Clare, "But I still need to get back to Chuck and Bigsy."

"I guess we can call them," said Clare, "I at least can call them using a landline to arrange a meeting point for me to hook up with them again."

"Sure," said Jennifer, "I think they will have left Santa Fe by now."

"Our guys thought they were probably heading towards Albuquerque."

"Okay," said Clare, "We stayed in a hotel in Albuquerque two days ago; maybe we could meet there?"

"Not a good idea," said Jennifer, "It would be standard for whoever has been following you to have asked the concierge or somebody in the hotel to keep an eye out for you in case you returned."

"You need to find somewhere different, but somewhere that's in that area is okay.

"There's a diner called Route 66 which is a tourist venue we could send them there and then arrange you to join them. We can get you to Albuquerque pretty, but you must take a taxi for the last part of the journey. We can arrange that as well and use one of our drivers to drop you off at the venue. That way if for any reason there is any trouble, we can still keep you with us."

Clare said, "In that case, we'd better get onto this then so I can make connect them."

Jennifer took Clare to another room.

"This is a special telephone," she said, "This is our special communications complex and we've it set up so that the call appears to come from a different location.

"We can change the area code to something like San Francisco."

Jennifer spoke to one people in the room.

Jennifer returned Clare's cell phone to Clare.

Clare said," I suppose you've copied all the numbers are on this already in a case? all my text messages as well?

Jennifer nodded, "Routine but it's still easier to ask you to give us Bigsy's number."

Clare read out Bigsy's number. Jennifer typed.

"Right you now have a direct connection to this cell phone as if you are in San Francisco."

The phone rang three times.

It was picked up.

It was Bigsy.

Hello?

"Hi Bigsy," said Clare.

"Hi Clare, are you all right?" asked Bigsy.

"Yes, Bigsy, it's a long story," said Clare. "I can't say anything on this call."

"I'm guessing you are heading back towards the town we were in two nights ago. The people I'm with had given me a suggested meeting place. They say don't go to that hotel again. The location is a diner called Route 66 and it is on the old Route 66 in the middle of town. I can be there in an hour.

"Hold on, I will just tell this to Chuck," said Bigsy.

Clare could hear the conversation.

"Chuck says it is 13:15 now. Allowing 90 minutes for you to get to here, we will be in the diner at 14:45 until 15:15. Chuck has suggested we stay away from the venue until that short window."

Clare looked across at Jennifer who nodded.

"That's fine," said Clare, "I'll be arriving by taxi. People are driving me to Albuquerque and then swapping me into a local taxi. They are also driving the taxi."

"If there is any problem, they will stay until we are back together."

"That all makes sense said Bigsy. I'm just relieved that you are all right."

"Listen Bigsy. You need to take care. I have additional information for you when we get back together."

"Okay, nice phone spoofing, by the way!"

"That's all," said Jennifer, "We need to go now."

"Okay," said Clare.

"See you soon," said Bigsy.

Get your kicks on Route 66.

"We're all okay again now?" said Chuck, looking at Bigsy.

"Yes," said Bigsy, "I think we've had a chance to cool off and I feel a whole lot better now that I know that Clare is safe and, on her way, to meet us again."

"I suggest we go to this diner, check it out its location and then find somewhere else to wait," said Chuck.

"Good plan," said Bigsy.

By now Bigsy was starting to recognise the roads around Albuquerque, and they were soon heading back towards the centre. Chuck was driving carefully and following the traffic at a normal speed.
The outskirts of Albuquerque were new housing estates and some low-rise malls by the side of the main route. Bigsy could see they were on the edge of the desert, and soon the landscape transitioned from arid to signs of trees and foliage.

Bigsy thought it looked as if man was sustaining most of this and that if the desert had its way it would soon overrun this area again.

As they approached the centre of Albuquerque again, Bigsy noticed that they were passing their prior hotel. Chuck soon took a left turn, and they were on a street which looked wide but had a selection of 1950s looking shops along it.

"Welcome to Route 66," said Chuck.

"Really," said Bigsy, "It does kind of look like Route 66."

"Although I'm not sure that we need any more kicks at the moment," said Chuck.

"The real Route 66 has been superseded by the Interstate," said Chuck," but because this is such a well-known route across America it used to be called the Main Street of the USA, so there are a lot of sections of it that have been preserved. It's like a tourist route now. This middle section in Albuquerque is an example where they have kept some look and feel of the old route. As long as there are enough tourists to sustain it, then I'm sure this will continue."

"But I guess you have to be determined to come here if you are in the US?" said Bigsy, "We seem to be right in the middle of the desert in New Mexico."

"Yes," said Chuck," That's what many people do, they will either travel from the East Coast or even from Chicago which is where Route 66 starts or they will start somewhere along the road and head across to the West Coast at Santa Monica which is the other end of the route. I reckon from the middle to the coast is the most interesting part."

"So, I suppose there's quite a few Route 66 diners along this road?" said Bigsy.

"Sure," said Chuck," but luckily, there's only one of them in Albuquerque." He gestured to the left as they drove slowly past a grey low-slung building which prominently displayed the logo Route 66 diner.

"I tell you what, Bigsy," said Chuck, "I'll buy you a milkshake there in about 45 minutes.

"What, a five-dollar shake?" asked Bigsy.

"I think they even do six-dollar shakes there," answered Chuck.

"Meantime I think we should get some gasoline and find somewhere quiet to wait."

Chuck drove on until they reached a Texaco gas station. Chuck stayed in the car while Bigsy filled the gas and paid with more cash.

"You know something else," said Chuck," We may need to think about whether we keep this car much longer. It's from the Hertz at Phoenix airport and as it's a hire car it will be fitted with a Lo-jack tracker device. So far, I don't think anyone has thought about this, but if they activate the tracker, it will make it very easy for anyone to find us."

"But so long as the car is going about its normal business, I guess we'll be okay," said Bigsy.

"Yes, it would be if the car was reported stolen or something like that, when the tracker would be switched on." said Chuck.

"You know something," said Bigsy, "That may even be useful to us later."

Chuck started the car again, and they hauled away from the Texaco. He turned it around and they started back towards the diner.

"Look," said Bigsy, "The thermometer in this car says it's 120°F outside at the moment. I can see an ice cream parlour on the left. I say we stop there until it's time to meet Clare."

Chuck smiled, "You know something, I don't think the people I usually work with would expect me to be in an ice cream parlour. We should do it. I'm buying."

Chuck drove the car into the parking by the side of the ice cream store. It was somewhere they could wait for 30 minutes until it was time to meet Clare.

Taxi swap

Clare's car had made its way back to Albuquerque. The driver had made good progress, and they were now close to the train station in Albuquerque.

"This is where we will make the switch into the taxi," said Jennifer.

"We've used a local car from here so that it looks more normal than somebody driving by taxi from Santa Fe."

"I'll be following in this backup vehicle just in case."

Clare picked up her bag from the back of the SUV.

"That's the car," said Jennifer and pointed to a lone taxi with its meter running.

"Look," said Jennifer, "The way we've done this means that no one should suspect anything. When you get back to Chuck and Bigsy, it will not be at all obvious that you have been with us.

Clare nodded, "I understand. We seem to have got ourselves into this deeply now. I will also need to contact Jake again to say that all is okay."

 "It's fine," said Jennifer, "I think you should contact Jake in a way to keep the separation between your communications and those from Chuck and Bigsy.

"Remember, you are the firewall between Jake and the others. You are also the firewall between Bigsy, Chuck and us."

"I'm not sure that I should say thank you exactly," said Clare, "but thank you, and I hope we can work this through successfully for all our sakes."

"I know what you mean," said Jennifer, "I don't think any of us could have planned for this."

 Clare was now in the taxi, and they moved away towards the main road. She could see that Jennifer was following in the SUV.

Quesadilla and meatloaf

Bigsy and Chuck were sitting in the diner. Bigsy was marvelling at the authentic 1950s look of the place. At least he imagined it was a 1950s look.

'Nothing could be finer' it said on the menu. And it featured blue plate specials, too.

There was a soda fountain and a jukebox that was playing old records.

"Chuck, if we weren't in so much trouble this place would be pretty cool," said Bigsy.

They were both a little unsure what to order having just beaten their way through two large ice creams at the store along the route. "Maybe a sandwich?" said Pixie.

"I'll have a quesadilla," said Chuck to the waitress.

"Er, and I'll have a meatloaf," said Bigsy.

Chuck looked impressed, "Seriously?"

"And coffee, please," said Chuck.

"That's two please," added Bigsy.

 Chuck had picked a table near to the back exit from the diner. It had a good view towards the front where people were shown to their tables.

 It would be easy to see Clare when she arrived.

 Chuck checked his watch it was 13:15. Precisely the time he had said. "We have given Clare a 30-minute window to get here," said Chuck, "if she is not here by the time, we said then we should leave."

 "I'm sure Clare will be here," said Bigsy, "We gave enough time for her to get from Santa Fe. Even if she was swapping into a taxi on the way."

Bigsy looked towards the entrance to the restaurant, and at that moment a taxi was pulling up outside. He saw Clare climbing out the car with her luggage and walking towards the diner.

 He also noticed the black SUV that was pulled up behind the taxi.

 "Clare's here on time," said Chuck, "and it looks as if she's with someone."

 "Will we stay here?" said Bigsy, looking panicked that he may not get his meatloaf.

"Yes," said Chuck, "We have to eat sometime, and we have at least two exits from this place."

Clare walked in and saw them immediately. Bigsy rose to greet her and they walked back to where Chuck was seated.

"There is a lot to talk about," she said, "Not here," said Chuck," Let's eat and then regroup somewhere."

"It's been quite a day," said Clare, "And I have somewhere for us to spend tonight."

Durango

"Jennifer has given me an address in a place called Durango," said Clare, " It's supposed to be like a safe house we can stay in, and there is another vehicle there for us to use. It's only supposed to be around two hours from here, but I think it's across part of the desert."

"Jennifer has also arranged that one of her team will pick up the car we leave behind after a few days and have it taken back to the car rental depot."

"Now why would Jennifer do all of this for us?" asked Chuck.

"When I tell you what I have discovered, I think you will understand," said Clare, "But I know you don't want to discuss this while we are in this restaurant."

They finished dinner and went back to the car. This was the first time that Clare had been with Chuck and Bigsy. She could see that Chuck was looking all around and as he edged away, he studied the cars on both sides of the road and looked in the mirror to check that he was not being followed.

"I think the road we take to Durango is cross country," said Chuck, "When we get to that road we can easily see if anyone else turns off to follow us.

"So far, I think we are okay."

Clare explained what she had heard from Jennifer. Then Bigsy added what he had discovered from the geocache in the hotel back in Santa Fe.

"It is all consistent," said Clare. "Someone, from Chuck's old team, is trying to sell technology secrets to another group who we think is Chinese. They are trying to eliminate the people that know anything about this.

"Chuck and the list of suspects is getting ever shorter. So far Ben, Mike and Klaus Wegener have been bumped off that leaves just Barbara Somerville and Tony Capaldi.

"And we think Capaldi is somewhere in this area now having travelled from Ohio," said Clare.

"Well," said Chuck, "If we are at this safe house, then we are still within range of most of the places where the action seems to be taking place. To the south-west there's Scottsdale to the south-east there's Albuquerque and Kirtland Air Force Base, and to the more or less direct east, there is Santa Fe.

"In the middle of a circle," said Bigsy.

"We should also check with Jake," said Clare, "Jennifer emphasised tome to be the only person to contact Jake. At the moment the security services think that you two have been seen together, but they have not made a direct connection with me. Jennifer described it as a firewall between us. So, I should be the one to phone Jake. I should be the only one to phone Jake."

Chuck drove off of the main interstate road and onto a north-facing country road which twisted and wove its way across the desert. In the distance, they could see hills, and as they approached Durango, they noticed that the land was changing from desert to a kind of low mountain slopes greenery.

It surprised Bigsy that in such a short area the terrain could change so much.

"We have been driving right along the edge of the continental divide," said Chuck, "When we were on that main highway the country to the left of us was on one continental plate, and the country to the right was on another. Yes, we have been in proper earthquake country."

Busy smiled, "That's just about all we need!"

Kirtland

Jennifer was driving herself back towards the Kirtland aerodrome airfield. The job she had just been on was not something she would typically do. They had asked her to step in because they needed somebody who could relate easily to a British woman, and they needed to make fast progress to make contact.

 Jennifer was originally British but had left the UK when she was twenty-one as part of a UK Civil Service deal. She had eventually settled down in America. Nowadays she was dual-citizen and worked around a mixture of the Air Force Base and the laboratories in the area. There was very sensitive work conducted and more routine subjects added to which the open-access programs had meant that there was high foot traffic of tourists looking at some of their facilities.

Jennifer's day job ensured that security was appropriate for the different environments. She was part of a government team but also worked with private sector subcontractors from time to time. They had used a private contractor's offices for the interviews with Clare.

Jennifer had needed to improvise some of the situation but had also reached out to her bosses in Washington, D.C.

It had been a long and somewhat stressful day, and she drove home and pulled the large SUV into the car park of her apartment block in Albuquerque.

Indoors, she called Spencer to see whether he had made anything of the geocache code. Spencer replied that he had been working on it and the best clue had been the codeword Tonto, which Clare had remembered.

Apart from the obvious references to the Lone Ranger and other trivia, it turned out that there was a bridge called Tonto bridge on the route between Albuquerque and Winslow, Arizona. But it also showed up as a geocache marker somewhere on the edge of the Kirtland airfield. Spencer had asked around in his office and discovered that Lucas Wilson was a keen hiker who also used the way markers and geocache treasure trails. If Jennifer agreed they would go to visit the geocache at the edge of the airfield.

"Okay," said Jennifer," But you know what it's getting dark, please can we do this in the morning?"

"That's fine," said Spencer," How about I meet you with Lucas tomorrow at yours and the three of us take off to have a look?"

"That will be great," said Jennifer.

"Hey," said Spencer," Did you hear the other news?"

"What's that?" asked Jennifer.

"There is another security alert running at the moment. It's all confidential at the moment. I only know because I'm still inside the building. It's not in our territory but it links to what you have been looking at. Someone has killed Senator Williams, from Texas.

"It's being kept out of the news at the moment because of the circumstances. Someone fired a big incendiary device at his car. The Senator was on his way to a meeting when it happened. It was out on the open road and although he was in a short convoy, there was a direct hit on his car. All the occupants of the car, including the Senator were killed.

It's being explained at the moment that it was a light aircraft that crashed onto the road. They cordoned the area either side and from what I can tell it's made quite a mess. Look, Jennifer, I was only in part of your interview with Clare Richardson, but it sounds a little bit like the weapon you described.

Jennifer reeled with this news. This was something more significant than the run-of-the-mill situations she was used to handling at the airbase. Smuggling, drugs, unconventional foods being imported, cash in suitcases. But nothing like the events of the last two days.

"Thank you, Spencer," said Jennifer, "I need to get some rest, but I suggest we meet at mine around eight tomorrow to follow up on this geocache. Meantime please keep your thoughts about the Senator to yourself. We should try to find out more before we make any hasty connections.

"Are you still at the office?" asked Jennifer.

"Yes," said Spencer," I was just about to leave."

"Maybe, please, you could pull some information about that Senator before you go," said Jennifer.

"Done already," chuckled Spencer.

Bagels, Guns, Shacks and Oilfields

I'm a picker
I'm a grinner
I'm a lover
And I'm a sinner
I play my music in the sun

Steve Miller – The Joker

Einstein bagels for breakfast

Jennifer was fixing some coffee when the doorbell rang. She flicked on the camera phone and could see Spencer at the main entrance. She buzzed him in, "Come on up Spencer."

A few minutes later Spencer arrived at her door, and she let him in.

"I'm just fixing some coffee," said Jennifer, "Would you like some?"

"Great," said Spencer, "But I've left Lewis downstairs in the car. Have you had some breakfast yet?"

"No," said Jennifer.

"It's lucky then," said Spencer, "That I brought this with me."

He held out his hand, and there was a bag containing two bagels.

"We got them from Einstein Bros," said Spencer, "We thought they would set us up for the hike. There's more in the car."

Jennifer smiled, "Did you find out any more about the Senator?"

"Yes," said Spencer," I brought that with me. They marked some of it restricted, but I thought you'd want to see it. I believe we have a connection with what is happening with our friends Clare and the others.

"Senator Williams was involved in quite a few things but the most notable was his connection with trade to China. He is part of an energy committee that oversees how energy is traded between the United States and other major countries. You can imagine that Texas has quite an axe to grind on this topic. Williams seems to be strongly opposed to the increased trading power of China. His argument was that they were ratcheting the pricing structures and the futures for most forms of fuel. He was about to make a speech on this topic at today's gathering in Dallas

"Some of that is in the newspapers and you see that there are reports now that he was killed in a plane crash. In other words, the story is being manipulated by people here in the USA.

"Another report says he was on his way back from Athens, Texas to Dallas. The thing is the road route he was on seemed to go around the other side of the big Cedar Falls reservoir. There is a much more direct route than the one he was taking. It was on this route that the accident occurred. I couldn't get any of the photographs of the accident without drawing more attention to myself. It was out of state, and there was a big security blanket over the whole thing.

"This smacks of a cover-up," said Spencer, "but it's been done professionally. It looks as if it's one of the agencies that have taken control. The best example is that there is a lack of press coverage. You'd expect some of the helicopters from the news gatherers in Dallas or Fort Worth to have been on this like a shot."

"Is this possible?" said Jennifer, "Surely the media would be onto something like this in a few minutes?"

"Normally, yes," said Spencer," But they seem to be taking particular care with this topic and protecting the story. It's hard for us to tell what has been happening from here and I didn't want to probe too deep in case someone picked up that we were interested.

"I thought the enquiries I ran were just those that would be typical of a nosy remote office looking at what was happening."

"You know something?" said Jennifer," I should have switched on the television this morning while I made the coffee. Sometimes I just like a few minutes silence before the day kicks in."

"Yes," said Spencer," Lucas and I drove over here, and it was one of the main stories on today's news, although the information still seemed sketchy.

"Spencer, that's great," said Jennifer, "I'm concerned that we may need to pass on what we know to others. I think we may be sitting on something significant. I'm wondering whether we should have let Clare go or should instead have rounded up Colonel Manners and the others.

"But that wasn't our instructions, was it?" said Spencer," I thought you had been told to let Clare go so she could continue to work with Colonel Manners and that this would draw out the people behind the attempt to steal the technology secrets?"

"You are correct," said Jennifer.

"So, do you think we are also now in danger?" said Spencer, "The very fact it involves us could mean that someone will look for us?"

"Yes," said Jennifer, "We shall need to tread carefully. I don't think we should put too much of our communications through normal channels until we are sure that they are secure."

"I also think we may wish to go to the safe house we sent Colonel Manners to? We said we would go there anyway to pick up their car and we know the one they have as a replacement. Unlike the hire car, this has one of our regular trackers on it, and it will be much easier for us to follow them in the new vehicle."

"We should assess after we have checked out this geocache," said Spencer, "I see you have your hiking boots."

"So how come you're not wearing a checked shirt?" said Jennifer.

"You should see Lucas sitting in the car downstairs," said Spencer, "He really looks the part."

Downstairs, at the car, Spencer introduced Jennifer to Lucas.

"Hi," said Jennifer, "I think I've seen you around the offices. I see you come prepared for a hike across the airbase."

"Hi, Miss Burns," said Lucas, shaking her hand, "I'm pleased to help with this, and Spencer has said we need to keep it quiet. Please rely on my discretion."

"That's right, Lucas," said Jennifer," Call me Jennifer, by the way, we don't know quite what we are facing here, but there is a chance that it is quite dangerous."

"I'm based in the office," said Lucas, "It's quite a change for me to get out like this."

They were in Spencer's truck. It was a 4x4 and had two rows of seats. Jennifer sat in the back seat and left Spencer sitting next to Lucas in the front.

"Okay, let's go," she said, "Hey, and these bagels are superb."

Tonto One

Lucas had been researching the geocache information before they got into the truck. He knew he was being brought along as a specialist and wanted to make sure that he could help.

"I've checked the code references for this location," he said," It looks like a regular geocache. There's quite a few on the airbase. I guess they use some of them for orienteering by troops during drills."

 "This one appears to be in a public area and is accessible by road, at least until we are close to it. They call this one Tonto one.

"The geocaches have a standardised structure - like a phone number has an area code. You were lucky to find the code reference from Chuck's base break-in. The one Bigsy saw at Loretta Chapel isn't anything to do with this trail, but the one that Bigsy found, with the 'Cessna' middle section and then the one that Chuck found from the base break-in are part of a little set."

The Circle

"We should find one now on the airfield. It would make sense that someone with a military background has put one of them on the airfield. And I checked the Cessna reference yesterday. The number must be 172 - the most common type of Cessna plane.

"Isn't this complicated?" said Jennifer.

"Not really," said Lucas, "There is a standard format for geocaching numbers, and they hide some of them to not show on maps. Remember the people who do this - like me - are in it for both the orienteering and also for the puzzle solving."

They were on the outskirts of the main passenger airport for Albuquerque, which had been extended for military use.

"We need to go around the perimeter road," said Lucas, "It's quite a long route but should save us a walk."

They drove for another 20 minutes as they negotiated the edge of the airfield and looked back across fields towards the runways and the terminal buildings. To their left was a large expanse of semi desert and to the right was the edge of the grass strips and the adjacent terminal buildings about a mile or a mile and a half away.

 Jennifer knew this area well because of her role at the airport. She also knew that the desert area was part of the military testing grounds and also housed some other secure facilities. This access road between the two was a very quiet and seldom-used route towards some storage sheds and other miscellaneous maintenance facilities.

 "We need to slow down here," said Lucas. He was looking at a small GPS device which he had removed from his belt. "

"The geocache will be about 200 yards away on the right-hand side. I think it is outside of the fence, but only just," he said.

They slowed the 4x4 and looked for anything that could be the basis for the hidden information. There was a small sign attached to the wire fence. It was one of the regularly placed signs that said, 'keep out' and gave other general instructions and warnings about not trying to enter the airfield.

"Look," said Spencer, "There's something else across from that sign." It was a small roadside box. The kind of thing that was used to provide improvised firefighting in the case of a small brush fire.

"Yes, I think that is likely to be where the cache is hidden," said Lucas. They stepped out of the truck and walked across to the roadside box. Lewis looked around it quickly.

"It won't be very well hidden," he said, "They don't want you to be dismantling the facilities here. It will be something simple like a tin box or maybe something smaller, such as a film canister.

"This is it," he said. It was a small tin box, the kind that could hold cookies, it had been nailed to the side of the roadside box such that the hinge was at the top and the box was placed vertically. He flipped it open. Inside was a sheet of paper in a polythene wrapper and also a small black notebook and a cheap pen attached via a piece of string to the metal box.

"This is a pretty basic geocache," said Lucas, "Sometimes there would be a small toy or something like that included in the box as well. The main deal is that whoever has located this geocaching will take notes from the paper and also add their name to the little book. Then take a photo of the artefact and big tick."

"That way they can prove that they have visited because they will know what the content of the cache was and also, they will have their name recorded for posterity. "Okay," said Jennifer, "Let's take a look."

The paper was a short poem:

'the detonation sites at Yucca Flat
Frenchman Flat, the subsidence craters, the playa:
50 times brighter than the sun, hell
burst from the skies torched ancient Joshua trees
their teddy bear & oven-mitted hands
Buster-Jangle, Tumbler-Snapper, Plumbob
Ranger, Latchkey, Sunbeam, Tinderbox
devastatingly beautiful some called it
a letter from home or a firm handshake
from someone you trust

i had blood running out of both ears
out of both nostrils
while on the diving platform at the Last Frontier
the man in a T-shirt, the man
with no shirt; the two men underneath playing ping-pong

-Extract from Desert View Overlook by Rose Hunter.'

They read the poem couple of times and looked for any obvious hidden messages. Spencer took a photograph of the box and its contents and the poem.

"We can look at this back at base to see if there is anything else hidden," he said.

"Should we take the whole box?" asked Jennifer.

Lewis looked a little distressed at this idea, "You don't do things like that with a geocache," he said, "It spoils the fun for everyone if the little gifts or the boxes get removed."

"Take it," said Jennifer, "We need this back at our office."

She opened the notepad and flipped through the pages. It reminded her of an autograph book most people had put one name and signature on the page and additionally added a code of some kind.

"Those codes are the names and reference numbers of the individuals involved in the geocaching fraternity," said Lucas.

"It is so that people can contact one another, although most people will do this online through the websites nowadays,"

Andy looked at the last few entries. Most people had taken the next page and simply added their name for this cache. There were only about two dozen names. Then she saw the last name. It was Chuck Manners.

"Look," she said to Spencer, "It's got Chuck's name here. Two things: firstly, I don't think he would have been here and secondly even if he had visited, I somehow don't think he would sign this."

"Not with a geocache collector number anyway," said Lucas, taking a look at the page.

Jennifer looked around. Busy trucks were moving around inside the airport perimeter fence, but there did not seem to be anyone expressly looking for them.

"We should get out of here," said Jennifer, "Back to the office."

Jake sifts

Jake was prepared for the lack of further information from Clare and Bigsy. He had decided he would monitor the Internet chatter that was related to their presence in New Mexico and Arizona.

When the news reports of the accident involving the senator in Texas started to come through, Jake noticed that the way it was being reported was surprisingly sparse even on the American newscasts.

He tried US-based Internet papers for the Dallas area and picked the Dallas Morning News and the New York Times and looked at each of them for coverage. More in the Dallas paper, but the reporting seemed to be about a freak accident involving a plane crash. No pictures, which he also thought was unusual.

There was more information about the senator himself. That Williams had been a Republican senator and very active in the energy lobby.

It said he was born in Calgary, Alberta in Canada and that his parents had been working in the petroleum industry. He'd got an impressive resume and had studied at both Princeton and Harvard.

After college he was working in the legal profession, starting in a practice that also specialised in petroleum law. This was a very specialised field and covered many topics related to territorial claims and the legality of certain types of energy-related trading instruments.

Because of some cases he had been involved with and the rulings made, the Senator had also been cited as a mover and shaker in the specialised legal areas related to energy matters.

Some of this had highlighted him to the extent he had become involved around ten years ago with politics. Nowadays he was regarded as a mover and shaker and had made fast progress in the Senate to his current position.

All of that stopped yesterday. Jake looked for any recent activities that involved Senator Williams which could be linked to what happened.

 The main news he found related to the Albuquerque area was things that he thought both Chuck and Clare knew already. They were related to the uses of the American base at Kirtland and the surrounding desert area.

Fundamentally it was now used for nuclear-related activities. There was both stockpiling of munitions and also further out in the desert there were various test areas.

Jake was sure that this was what Chuck had been involved with when he was working there. He also realised that Bigsy and Clare would know about this by now.

The question Jake was pondering was whether the various activities were linked and what had triggered the sudden interest in all of this.

Williams' recent speeches talked on reduction of energy sources in North America and ways this could challenge the economy.

He described a scenario where, in less than 15 years, there would be major energy shortages in both North America and many parts of Europe. This was unless specific steps were taken. The senator had outlined a three-stage plan which included the creation of new nuclear power generation sites but also extensions to windfarm and even more oil drilling.

The senator pointed out that it was possible to recover the situation for houses and industry based upon the use of nuclear power . For transportation systems, particularly the automobile, there would be substantial shortages starting to accumulate in around 15 years' time. Prior to that he forecasted massive increases in fuel costs out of all proportion to their current levels.

Jake read this and considered that some of it was making a political point rather than driven by accurate analysis. However, he thought there was a truth to the messaging. He noticed that the senator had not provided answers beyond how nuclear power would be affected and that there needed to be something to replace the current way that the automobile was powered.

 Jake thought to himself that this was nothing new and he was surprised that the Senator had made such a name from these types of speeches.

He looked more at the conference that Senator Williams had attended. It had been run by an Asian foundation called the Centre for Asian fuel studies.

Jake realise that this could be a connection with what Clare had been describing. Some kind of link with the Chinese. The question was whether Senator Williams was seeking help from the Chinese or making general points that were part of his day-to-day speechmaking.

Safe shack

The SUV bounced its last few yards towards the address that Jennifer had given Clare. There appeared to be a small house next to a huge wooden barn. Sure enough, as Jennifer had said, there was a red pickup truck parked outside the wooden barn.

"So that's our new car," said Bigsy, "Well, it looks just as shiny as this one."

"Two rows of seats again," said Clare, "I don't think you get that in England?"

"It'll be fine," said Chuck," although if I'm honest, the bright red colour is a little bit obvious."

"We'll be living the dream," answered Clare, "Well a girl, my Lord, in a flatbed Ford is slowing down to take a look at me!"

"Take it easy," said Chuck.

"But it means we'll be away from this car which somebody may have been able to track by now," said Bigsy.

"Yes," said Chuck," You can bet that the one provided by Uncle Sam will have its own tracker."

Clare nodded, "I think we should move our stuff into the new truck now. Then we should take a look inside the house and make a decision about whether we stay overnight night or move on immediately. I want to give Jake call soon as practicable so that we can compare notes about what's been happening."

They pulled up to the front of the house. "It's a shack!" said Bigsy. "A safe shack!"

"Hold on a minute," said Chuck, "We Americans enjoy making homes out of timber, particularly in the country."

"It looks very homely," said Clare.

Chuck said, "Let's get inside. We can see how homely it is by whether they've left us any provisions."

They made their way cautiously towards the front door. Chuck turned the handle, and the door opened immediately.

"I somehow don't think this is one of their most secure locations," he said,

"I'm more interested in it being safe," said Clare, "And ideally somewhere that nobody else knows about."

"Yes," said Chuck. He flipped the lights and walked towards the kitchen.

There was a small note on the table it said,

"Jennifer sends her regards.   There's easily enough here to cook a killer grilled cheese sandwich, love, bianca (shack keeper) "

"Okay, it looks as if we found the right place. Let's take a look in the fridge," said Bigsy.

"Wow," he said, "There are beers, pizzas, cheese, bread, salad, milk, Coke, and look some chocolate cookies in a jar. This may not be the healthiest place, but I'm not going to complain."

He passed the cookie jar around, and both Chuck and Clare took one.

"Monsters," said Clare, "These are big cookies! But first things first, I need to call Jake to update him. I'm wondering whether I should also call Jennifer now that we are here and also tell her what Bigsy had discovered when he was at the hotel back in Santa Fe."

"You know something," said Chuck," I'm pretty sure that they will have this place monitored. I don't think we could be in here without them knowing about it. Let's call Jake as the priority."

Clare reached into her bag and produced her regular cell phone, "I'll put it on speakerphone when we call Jake,"

There was a pause while she selected the number and then dialled it. They could hear it ringing — a proper British ring tone.

"Hi, Clare," said Jake, "How are you all?"

"We're doing okay," answered Clare, "but it's been eventful."

"I'm still with the guys in SI6," said Jake, "They've moved me to an adjacent building; it's more like a hotel room. "Good actually, but I don't really want to be spending much more time here."

Jake continued, "They told me about what they arranged for you, Clare. How you would meet with Chuck and Bigsy and all of you would move to a safe place outside of Albuquerque. I'm guessing that's where you are now?"

"That's right," said Clare, "There's some extra information too. Bigsy was able to find a note left by the geocache in the hotel in Santa Fe. It said that the main situation has been caused by someone selling out to, we think, the Chinese. We think they want to use that tracker thing as a terrorist weapon."

Jake replied, "Yes, I've been looking at that accident in Texas with Senator Williams. I guess you have seen that as well?'

"Yes, we did," said Clare, "and it looks suspicious the way it's being shown on television. It smacks of a cover-up. "

"That's what I thought too," said Jake," Although I don't think anyone unaware of our recent developments would think about it quite as suspiciously as us."

"When I checked Senator Williams records on the Internet, his profile said he was a highflyer that has been involved in the energy lobby. He has also been warning the Americans that they will run out of energy in around 15 years. There seems to be some deal with China in the background of all of this. You may have seen that he was speaking at a conference a couple of weeks ago where he made a speech about this.

"I passed this information onto the SI6 people already," said Jake, "I guess it will be with your security people there in America by now as well."

"We have not contacted them since I left them to meet Chuck and Bigsy," said Clare, "We are in a safe house at the moment, but we are alone. I say that, but we are probably being monitored," said Clare.

Chuck nodded.

"Jake," said Chuck, "Did you find out anything else ?"

"No," said Jake, "but I am wondering whether that 'accident' was the start of a broader campaign?"

"These people, whoever they are, don't seem to value human life very highly. In the last few days, there has been a mounting body count."

"We need to let Jennifer know what is happening," said Clare, "I think it may be better for you to do that, Jake. If Jennifer gets the information from you, it will be through secure channels rather than us calling her by phone and potentially giving away our location to anyone that is trying to trace us - Oh, Hi, Jennifer, in case you are monitoring this!"

Second Amendment, 1789

Spencer drove Jennifer and Lucas back to their office in Albuquerque.

"Well, this is a first," said Spencer, "I'm used to tracing a bit of drug trafficking or even people trafficking but this is a whole different dimension."

"Yes," said Jennifer, " That's why I'm not sure how much of this we should reveal to our bosses at the moment. Clare told us that Chuck has already been chased once and that his colleague Mike was killed. I think we may be stepping into a rather murky pool."

"I've rigged up this office as our control centre," said Spencer, "It's a bit improvised, but it means we can probably keep everything in one room. For example, I patched the monitoring of the safe house through to here."

"So, can we listen to a playback of what's been happening at the house?" asked Jennifer.

"Sure," said Spencer, "First of all, we can see that they all arrived."

He pointed towards some television monitoring. A single screen split four ways showed different views of the main room in the house. Spencer ran the pictures at high speed.

"Look," said Jennifer, "they are all sat down together now; let's slow this down and listen in."

It was Clare preparing to talk to Jake. The others were huddled around the small cell phone that she was using as a loudspeaker.

Jennifer listened as they talked to Jake. She also heard them say that they would not speak to Jennifer again at this time. She knew she could contact Clare at any time on the additional phone but thought it wise to wait until she needed to do that. She also heard them discuss that Jake would send information to Jennifer via the back channel through her departments.

"Spencer," she asked, "Has anything arrived from the UK?"

Spencer looked at his other screen and replied, "Nothing at the moment. I think that conversation was only about an hour ago. I don't know how long it will take for this kind of thing to be relayed."

Jennifer looked at Lucas.

"Look, Lucas, thank you for your help with this so far. You now know more than anyone else about what is happening here. I want to ask you if you can join us for a few more days.

I can square this with your department head, but it means that we can limit the number of people who are involved in all of this. I know you said you were mainly office-based, but I can also see that you spend time on the trails. This could all be useful for us over the next few days."

Lucas nodded, "Yes, I will be pleased to help. This makes a big change from my normal day job."

"Some of this might be dangerous," said Jennifer, "Both Spencer and I can carry pistols and have been trained for firearms. I think this will put you at a disadvantage if we are out in the field."

Lucas said, "Yes, I agree, I have not been through the training here for any of that. You should know though that I was in the Army for three years and when I go out on the trails, I sometimes go hunting. I'm used to using both small arms and a rifle."

"Okay," said Jennifer. "Let's not get carried away here but you do need to be prepared for some rough stuff as we go on."

Spencer asked Jennifer if she was going to tell her boss what was happening now.

"Yes," said Jennifer, "I think we need to give him the general outline, but I think we can keep it fairly simple. "

"We have met one American colonel and two stray Brits who have been attacked. We have given them some temporary shelter last week while we work out what has happened."

"We don't need to say anything about Senator Williams or the geocache at this stage. We can explain that the other guy in

Britain, Jake, is a good friend of the two Brits. The fact that the Brits had taken him into protective custody is nothing to do with us."

"Okay," said Spencer," I guess that would hold for about one day."

Spencer had switched on a television in the room that had been prepared. It was now showing some footage of the so-called crashed plane that had killed the Senator Williams.

"Honestly," said Spencer," This all looks a bit too neat. Somebody has gone in afterwards to make this scene."

He checked the local road summaries for the area around the reservoir in Texas. Sure enough, the road was still closed for several miles either side of the incident.

"My guess is that they have removed the site of the crash away from where it happened. I think there will be two sets of wreckage. The real set which will look as if it has been decimated by a missile and a second set which has been arranged to look like the plane crash.

"If this has been done by one of our agencies," said Jennifer, "Then it looks like there is a huge problem."

"We don't have any jurisdiction to go take a look at this," said Spencer, "But I'm not sure that we will get much from looking at this on the news feeds either. Someone is imposing a blackout on

Texan oilfields

Clare was brewing some fresh morning coffee. The television was chattering in the background.

 She could hear someone else moving about in the house, Chuck appeared.

 "You know I'm wondering about all of this," said Clare, "You ask us over here to help you, and we've come along."

 "But so far all that's happened is we are being chased around, found out a few things and are now in hiding. Not the greatest help."

 "I know," said Chuck," Don't think I'm not grateful, though, Clare. It was better when I was still hidden away. Unfortunately, because some of the guys that invited me to Scottsdale were my long-term colleagues I trusted, then I felt this would be safer than it's turned out."

Clare pushed a mug of fresh coffee to Chuck and then put her hands around the edges of her own coffee mug.

"So, what shall we do?" she asked.

"We seem to know quite a lot now, and we have got some backup from Jennifer and her team.

"But everyone seems to be running scared and we're still none the wiser about who it is that has somehow ratted you out. What about you, do you have any ideas?"

"I've been wracking my brains," said Chuck, "I think we are on the edge of something enormous. There's a link between the terrorism and what the Senator has been doing with the energy discussions. I don't know how we will get more information unless perhaps Jennifer can help us.

"The thing is," said Clare, "I think Jennifer was also out of her depth when we drove back to Albuquerque, and they were chatting in the car. I was of the distinct impression that Jennifer works with simpler situations than the one we have at the moment. I think she's involved with airport security and things like that."

"But don't you also have a link to Jake, who's now at SI6, said Chuck, "They are a much bigger source of influence in these matters. If we can get them more in the loop over what is happening, perhaps we can resolve this."

At that moment there was some breaking news on the TV station. It was showing a live picture from an oil refinery near Houston, Texas. There had been an explosion and was now a local state emergency as the flames and smoke from the refinery curled upward.

"I don't think this is a coincidence," said Chuck. They listened to the voice-over from the TV station. It was describing an unknown explosion which had wrecked the facility. Chuck looked at the aerial pictures, which were from a plane circling some miles from the site.

"Look, it's another one where they're not giving us the full picture," he said, "This one is so big they can't just hide it as with the Senator but even so they are not telling us what happened."

Clare moved closer to the television set to see the picture in more detail, "Yes I see what you mean, you can't tell an awful lot from this except something big is on fire."

"I want to find out the reason for the fire," said Chuck.

"You think it's those missile devices?" asked Clare.

"Let's say I'm not ruling it out," said Chuck," and it is a striking coincidence just after that Senator was killed."

Clare said, "Look, should we contact Jennifer about this and maybe try to get a link up with the people in London."

"It's a good idea," said Chuck, "The problem is whether the CIA will allow the British security services anywhere near this."

"But I thought Jennifer said that the agencies were cooperating on this?" asked Clare.

"Yes," said Chuck, "What they say and what they do are not always the same thing. I guess that's why they sent Jennifer from airport security to handle this instead of bringing in a bigger team."

"You know," said Chuck, "I doubt whether they have even linked what has been happening to us with what is going on with the Senator and the oil refinery."

At that moment, Bigsy appeared.

"Take a look at this Bigsy," said Clare and pointed towards the television. "An oil refinery has just blown up in Houston."

"You think it's linked with what happened to the Senator?" asked Bigsy.

"It didn't take you long to make that connection!" said Clare.

"We are going to need a bigger truck," said Bigsy.

"Ha," laughed Clare, then Chuck replied, "I'd think this was funny if it wasn't so serious."

"Look," said Chuck, "We can't work on this alone any longer. We need to link up with at least one of the other agencies."

"If that's the case, would they want to get rid of us," said Clare.

"Normally I would say yes," said Chuck, "but I think we are already in this up to our necks and I apologise for that. I'd hoped to get you to run some straightforward interference for me when I called the old gang back together. I didn't realise that I was being systematically hunted."

 "But is there a chance that there are people on the inside working this?" asked Bigsy, "For example, there seems to be a couple of big cover-ups about the two recent events."

 "I agree," said Chuck, "But I think this is something about cause and effect. What we're seeing is the US government pulling in the strings around both the Senator's assassination and the explosion at the oil refinery. Something else we can deduce from this is that at the moment the operations seem to be centred in Texas. It makes me think that whoever is involved is still local. This may be something that can be nipped in the bud before it spreads."

 "We should share the information with Jennifer about all of this," said Clare, "Although, I think Jennifer was already suspicious about telling too many people what was happening. SI6 in London are also involved anyway, and Jake is with that team."

 "So, although we don't know what they are going after," said Chuck, "we should have some advantage in having three disparate groups involved. And that's before 'we the people' are making the cover-ups for the two big emergencies in Texas.

"You are right, Clare; we need to put a call through to Jennifer."

Two hours west

Jennifer's phone rang. She could see it was Clare's special phone.

"Hello," said Jennifer.

"It's Clare, we need to talk. We put a few things together here," said Clare, "It would be best for us to meet together and again to pool our resources. Chuck's main motivation is to find out who is after him and make sure nothing can happen. We guess your motivation is on a much larger scale."

Jennifer considered for a moment,

"Okay," she said, "I'll meet you. We should not talk about this by telephone, not even using the phone I've provided for you. You are around 2 to 3 hours away now. I will find a place for us to meet, and I will text you the address on this phone. I'm assuming the two people you will bring are Chuck and Bigsy. I will also bring two others, that's Spencer who you met in the briefing room and another guy named Lucas who has some good hiking trail skills. He's ex-military."

"Are you going to tell your bosses about this?" asked Clare.

Jennifer replied," We have already told them an edited version of what is happening. We played it down. The link from the UK back to me is more likely to create ripples than anything."

Clare remembered she had told Jake to pass information to Jennifer when they had spoken by phone earlier.

"This is just to check," said Clare, "Have you received any of the information from Jake yet? That's the information I passed on earlier today?"

"No," said Jennifer," Not a word."

"Is this because the communication is slow or is someone checking what is happening before it is passed along?", asked Clare, exasperated that Jennifer had not been briefed by Jake.

"Honestly, I don't know," said Jennifer, "You have figured out I'm not particularly high up in the chain of command here? There's plenty of other people who could intercept and stop whatever is being passed through."

"But," said Jennifer, "On the other hand, I am part of the operations team here at the airport, and that does give me certain advantages. I'm going to suggest we meet at a covert location... It's an airfield about 2 hours west from you."

"Why is that?" asked Clare.

"I think I might go to get my hands on a plane which could save us in time if we need to move around quickly," said Jennifer, "By taking it to Bluff, it won't trip any suspicions. No one will be looking there.

Clare smiled, "Splendid, we could be in Texas quicker than we thought,"

857

Mormons came thru' a hole in the rocks

"If we have plenty of stickie-ta-tudy, we cannot fail."

-- Jens Nielson 1879

Bluff, Utah

Chuck looked around the house and across towards the red pickup truck they had swapped their belongings into.

They had parked the blue SUV in the wooden barn. Clare had told Jennifer its location, but Jennifer had said she would wait out a week before sending someone to collect it and to drive it back to Phoenix.

The airstrip they had been told to drive towards was about 2 hours away. It was on the Utah-Arizona border near to a place called Bluff.

"Why has Jennifer selected somewhere so far away?" asked Clare.

"Precautionary," said Chuck, "Two things - we'd see anyone following and we'll be able to see anyone waiting. It's a tiny airstrip."

The Circle

Bigsy offered to drive for this section and once again they were cutting across the desert, this time in a south-westerly direction. In the distance they could see various large red rock outcrops.

"We're driving along one of the routes that the Mormons took when they came down from the Chicago area," said Chuck, "Imagine having to drive across this terrain in a covered wagon. Imagine doing it when there weren't any roads. Literally through a hole in the rocks."

"It's easier to imagine than you might think!" said Bigsy. It's still desolate around here. Except when those massive trucks come honking over the horizon.

"I know what you mean when you say desolate," said Clare, "But I think I'd use another word like Majestic."

 They reached the small town of Bluff and continued to head west to its outskirts where they found the small airstrip. It was little more than a shed and a runway.

"Well this is utilitarian," said Bigsy, "Do we need to drive along the runway to make sure there aren't any wild horses or cattle on it?" he asked.

Someone moved out from the nearby tin shed. Bigsy could see that there were two small aircraft inside.

"Hello, neighbours" said the man, "Can I help you?"

"Hi there, we are waiting for a plane to land here in the next few minutes," said Bigsy.

"Okay, But I don't think it's on my schedule," said the man, "Are you sure you aren't looking for somewhere else like Cortez? That's a busier airstrip than here."

"No., we're sure we have the right one," said Beattie, "This is Bluff, isn't it?

Almost on cue, they could hear the distant growl from a small plane.

"Okay," said the man, "But I don't seem to have this in the log."

"I think the flight plan was only registered a short time ago," said Chuck, "This is an official plane, by the way."

"It's also quite a large plane for this airstrip," said the man, "We normally only handle single prop four seaters here. That looks like a twin turboprop. Beechcraft Super King 200, I'd guess."

Chuck looked impressed at the man's knowledge. The plane circled the entire air strip once and then made its way into a landing descent.

Bigsy noticed that it was a small twin propeller plane but had a row of windows along each side.

"I'd guess that it has flown down from Kirtland," said the man, "I think I recognise that plane. Ex-mil made to look civilian. See the loading hatch and the wingtip fuel tanks - dead giveaway."

Bigsy looked impressed, "Sure thing," he bluffed.

"Yes, we are about to hitch a lift from here," said Chuck. He realised that the man was ex-military himself.

 "Okay, we'd better do the right paperwork first then," said the man, My name's Aaron, by the way, Aaron McKarty."

The plane had landed and was now taxiing towards them. It stopped on a large tarmac apron area and a small row of steps was released from towards the back of the plane.

Bigsy saw people climb out of the plane. He noticed as Clare recognised Jennifer amongst the group.

They waited for the group to cross the tarmac area, and then Clare spoke to Jennifer.

"That was quick and quite an impressive entrance," she said. "I know," said Jennifer, "I know these guys who run this plane, and I have hitched us a lift to Texas. You met Spencer already, here's Lucas, and I also brought Davy who will drive the red pickup back to Durango. I guess you parked the SUV in the big barn?"

 "Yes," said Chuck, "we decided it was best to hide it."

"Okay, we will lose the red one too," said Jennifer.

 "We should leave our main discussion until we are inside the plane," said Jennifer, her eyes flicked towards the man in the hangar, "I shall go to explain our presence here today."

 Chuck nodded. He knew that Jennifer would tell a believable fiction about what they were doing.

Bigsy walked across to the red pickup with Davy and they swapped the luggage across to the plane.

Bigsy gave the keys to the truck to Davy, who climbed into the cabin, gave a wave and drove off.

"We need to get the next leg of our flight itineraries logged so there's a small amount of paperwork before we can turn this around and leave here. The pilot reckons about 40 minutes before we can be on our way again."

"It's not like driving a car," said Bigsy.

They walked into the shelter from the sun. Even in the shadows, it didn't seem much cooler. Jennifer showed the man her various passes and security information. He seemed satisfied that everything was in order and then started to chat about some people that they both knew in common back at Kirtland.

Leaving, on a prop plan

After a short while, the pilot beckoned for them to climb aboard. Bigsy noticed that the pilot had been around the outside of the plane, checking all the control surfaces. It intrigued him that the plane had only just flown in , but still everything was being checked before the next flight.

Chuck said, "Up in the air, a small glitch would be more problematic than on the road. No median, just a very hard ground."

It surprised Bigsy at the lack of formality for the luggage compared with his normal flights with all kinds of metal detectors and conveyor belts.

They climbed back into the plane through the rear door. Bigsy noticed that the fuselage roof curved, and that he had to stoop slightly as he walked towards the seat.

Unlike a commercial flight, they configured the seats in a small group of 4+4 with two seats in each group facing in opposite directions. It made the seating like a restaurant booth with a small gangway between the seats. Bigsy noticed that there was a pilot and also a co-pilot in the front of the plane. The co-pilot had another job to check that everyone was seated, belted and secure ready for the flight.

Engines on the plane started and Bigsy noticed that he was seated quite close to their exhausts, which were quite noisy. The pilot prepared for take-off and then after only a few moments they had sped along the runway and were up into the air.

As the plane banked following take-off, Bigsy could see that they were over a large area of red desert with spectacular rock outcrops.

"We are taking off in the direction towards Monument Valley," said Chuck, "I don't know if you know it by that name, but it's the famous rocks used in many of the well-known westerns. You know John Wayne, that kind of thing."

Bigsy looked and could see both the red rocks and also a long valley which he worked out was the continental divide that Chuck described when they were on the road a couple of days ago.

The plane levelled out into a steady cruising altitude, and as it did so the noise seemed to subside in the cabin.

"So, what's the plan?" said Chuck, looking towards Jennifer.

"I could only get this plane for the flight to Dallas," she said, "Then we will be on our own again. I thought it would get us near enough to where the initial incidents have occurred. We can look at both sites to see if we can gather any more information."

"We also need to share our information, I've heard most things from Clare, but I understand that Bigsy also found out something from the geocache in the hotel."

"Yesterday it was straightforward. There was a message which linked the intended transponder sale to some kind of Chinese business deal. I think they were being sold to a Chinese holding company to provide the power of the technology and potential to sell it on.

"It ties in with what we have seen happening over the last few days," said Chuck.

"What - the two incidents with the senator and the refinery?" said Jennifer.

"Exactly, and both of them were related to energy futures in some way."

"The two incidents also happened less than 100 miles apart," said Jennifer, "It makes me think whoever is responsible for this is still working from somewhere in the vicinity. Not some kind masterminded global plot."

"That also ties up with the initial attacks at the hotel," said Chuck, "It looks to me as if there is someone who has been moving from Scottsdale towards Houston."

"That's a direct route," said Jennifer.

Spencer and Lucas were sitting in the second block of four seats. They effectively had two seats each. Allen called across,

"Yes, that's about a thousand miles along the I-10, via El Paso and San Antonio.

 "I get it, they are using these transponders to provide targeting," said Bigsy, "but I can't work out what they'd be using to create the explosions. A missile being launched would look too obvious. And you'd need something with that kind of firepower to work on that refinery.

 Chuck look across towards Bigsy, "my guess is it something like drones that are being used."

Jennifer said, "No, I don't think so. I think they want to get to the drone technology and are using traditional weapons to simulate what a drone attack would look like. That's why everything is so localised. They are operating from a ground launcher."

Chuck looked impressed, "You seem to know a lot about this?"

"Yes, we run security drills over at Kirtland every so often. One of the scenarios is a ground launched rocket attack. We reckon with modern rockets; it can only be effective up to around 3 miles. That's for a precision hit, which is what seems to be happening with the Senator and the refinery."

Chuck replied, "It makes sense, and would also explain why the launch hasn't been spotted. A rocket attack rather than a missile, which would show up on radar and so on." Jennifer nodded, "That's until they get their hands on some of the drone technology available around the Kirtland military base," she said.

"I don't think people are aware of just how advanced a lot of this technology is nowadays."

Chuck nodded, "Yes when I was working on this program there were two types of assault drone in development."

"One kind was used for launching a payload, but the other kind was a kind of variation on the cruise missile and the actual drone was itself a weapon with its own built-in payload."

"If someone could launch a drone with a built-in payload, then it could be targeted and would have disappeared at the point of impact. Kind of Fire and Forget.

"Surely the people at the two sites will have figured this out?" asked Clare.

"Almost certainly," said Chuck, "Although they might not know the other part of this that we do. In other words, they may not know how these devices are being targeted so it will look like random shots in both cases."

"So, they may be looking for someone who can deploy a rocket launcher or something similar from close by whereas using a drone and the transponders the terrorists could be much further away?"

"That's right," said Chuck, "the US military uses these devices from a control centre in Nevada but can fly them into Iran. I don't think we are dealing with anything on quite that scale at the moment, but I do think the plans for the launch location could be many miles from where the targets have been bombed."

"Yes, and this is on US soil, too. US-launched against the US."

"But surely getting hold of USAF drones isn't going to be easy?" asked Clare.

"I agree," said Jennifer, and the way that bases like Kirtland are clamped down for such items is pretty impressive.

"So, there would be a supply of drones in Kirtland?" asked Clare.

"Yes," said Chuck, "Actually certain types of munitions are very closely monitored and only kept in a very small number of locations in the whole of the United States. The two main ones are in Nevada at Hawthorne and a much smaller one in Picatinny, New Jersey. There's also several chemical weapons storage locations, spread over the whole country."

"And forgive me for not understanding," said Bigsy. "Do these drones need to be launched by planes or are they something that can take off from the ground or all what?"

Chuck explained, "The one I worked with when I was on the base was something called the Predator. It was quite a large drone and could carry a couple of missiles."

"They are really UAVs which stands for unmanned aerial vehicles and the Predator is the most well-known.

Chuck described the predator and had a good working knowledge of it.

"Something you may be less aware of Chuck," said Jennifer, "Is that these Predators are used inside the US nowadays to control the Mexican border. So, within 5 to 100 miles of here all along the border there are uses of these drones for surveillance patrols."

"I guess these devices are the ones just fitted with cameras and no other payloads," said Chuck.

"Yes, Jennifer, and their numbers have been increasing over the last few years - Ever since that so-called president pushed for the wall."

"But something that might not be apparent from description is that these devices are large. When I've seen them at the Air Force Base, they are at least as big as a small single propeller plane. That's not the thing you can hide, and you still need a runway for it to take off.

"But once they are in the air, they can fly higher than normal jet planes," said Chuck.

"So, let's put this together," said Clare, "we think that perhaps somebody is using the transponder technology with some kind of drone to create the strikes that have taken place so far?"

Spencer said, "When we are back on the ground, I can take a more detailed look at this and see if I can find out from the USAF records."

To everyone's surprise, the pilot was getting ready to make his descent into Dallas airport.

"That was so quick," said Bigsy, "we've hardly taken off."

The pilot smiled and continue to make his preparations for their final descent. "We will be on the ground in around 20 minutes," he said, "And the air strip we have chosen should mean that you have a similarly smooth exit."

Spencer added, "I have arranged for a couple of SUVs' to be available for us at the landing strip. I asked for drivers so that we can get around more quickly than trying to figure it out for ourselves."

Jennifer and Chuck both nodded, "Yes, I think we should try to get to the location where the Senator was killed first," said Jennifer.

"It should be easier for us with local drivers that have all the right badges and passes. Just remember when we are in the vehicles that we should not talk about the specific details of what we are doing,"

"Yes ma'am," said Chuck, smiling.

Bigsy watched in fascination as the plane landed. Just like the take-off, he had a great view forward through the pilot's cockpit and could see the approaching ground and the white stripes of the runway.

He noted that this runway looked much larger than the one he had taken off from in Bluff.

"Everything is bigger in Texas," he said dryly.

Regular Jeeps from the carpool

"Hi," said Jennifer, "We need to be heading to the site of where Senator Williams was killed. You can see that I've got the right authority here. You also know that we are under strict radio silence on this, so I don't think I'd appreciate any of you tried radioing for confirmations."

 The two drivers nodded and waited for everyone to get into the vehicles.

 "It will take us about 45 minutes to get to the site where the aeroplane is supposed to have crashed," said Jennifer.

 They drove along sedately with a long gap between the two vehicles. Chuck noticed that the drivers were following a kind of military pattern that he'd seen in the Middle East. The kind of pattern where they might be expecting things to happen from the roadside.

 "Are these vehicles armoured?" he asked the driver.

"No, they are just regular Jeeps," said the driver, "We got them from the carpool."

They pulled onto another road. It was it a main route but there were diversion signs as they approached the area of the crash site. By now the crash site had been there for some time and the number of vehicles and the level of activity at the entrances was quite low key. The diversion around the area was extensive, and so most of the local traffic had decided either to avoid the journey or to take a different route.

As they arrived, the driver showed the guards at the checkpoint his pass and was waved through. The same thing happened with the second vehicle, so they were now on the inside of the cordon.

"Okay," said Jennifer, "I want us to look at the main crash site but also to continue past it. When I looked at it on the news cast everything looked somehow too neat."

Chuck nodded, "That was my impression too, like someone had sprinkled the wreckage after the event."

"Yes, it all looked very televisual," said Jennifer.

They were at the site of the wreckage now. It was harder to make out any patterns from the ground compared with the helicopter footage they had seen on the television news channel.

At the scene were more local police and a large flatbed trailer which was being loaded with the aircraft wreckage. A second vehicle had the remains of the car on it. Both had been parked inside a large tent.

Jennifer looked around the site and found the person in charge.

"Hi, I'm from the security services based out of Kirtland Air Force Base," said Jennifer, "They have asked me to come over here to take a quick look at the plane. She showed her pass and some other paperwork, which she pulled from a small bag.

"We were not expecting you," said the detective. "No matter," said Jennifer, "I only need a very brief look at the plane to see whether it is one of ours from the base." She could see the tail section and also the civilian N marking.

"It looks like a small light aircraft was in trouble and had crashed into the road," said the detective, "It's a one in a million chance that the Senator was driving along here at that time."

Clare busied herself with a camera and scribbled a few things into a notepad before walking back to Chuck.

"This doesn't look right," said Jennifer to them both, "It looks more like somebody has taken an old broken plane and sprinkled it around the area. I could go on to ask them about black boxes and other stuff, but I think we will be better off looking for other signs of what has happened."

She signalled to the detective. "Thanks, Detective. We will leave shortly but I'd like to just drive a little further along the road to check for anything else that may have dropped from the plane."

"You can't do that," said the detective. He stiffened. "I'm afraid that unless you have special clearance, we do not allow you go beyond the tape across the road over there. He pointed to a further set of barriers, and Jennifer could see that beyond them was a collection of military vehicles.

There didn't seem to be any activity at that point, but she was sure that it was a forward to station for something else.

Footsteps

"Okay, she said, "We will be on our way."

 They drove back along the road, past the roadblock that had been set up by the police cars. "We need to find somewhere to stop close to here," said Jennifer.

"This side lane looks promising," said Chuck.

There was a small turning to the left. Both vehicles drove in and stopped. Spencer was already on the computer and dialling up a map of the area.

"This lane leads through to a farmhouse which is back the way we have just driven," said Spencer, "If we follow the path from the farmhouse, it leads over those hills and past the military roadblock."

"Okay," said Jennifer, "which of us will go to check this out?"

Lucas stepped forward, "I think my hiking trails knowledge could be useful here."

"Good," said Jennifer, "Perhaps you, me and Chuck could make this journey. We still have several hours of daylight. We should travel light and only take the minimum with us. But that should include my camera," said Jennifer.

"What shall we do?" asked Bigsy. "I think we should take both cars to the farmhouse and use that as a temporary base."

"What if someone is there?" asked Clare.
"We should just explain that we will be on their property for a couple of hours whilst we are investigating something to do with the crash."

"Okay," said Chuck, that sounds like a good plan. They drove the two cars to the Farmhouse.

It appeared to be deserted.

"It looks as if they are out," said Chuck.

"Okay," said Jennifer, "Let's not waste time. Chuck you, me and Lucas should head off along that Trail. Bigsy - We should be back within three hours maximum."

The Groove

Jennifer, Lucas and Chuck walked fairly easily for the first mile or so along the track. It appeared to be a well-used path, but then at a gate the main path led off to the right. It looked as if it would be heavy going from then on. A combination of undergrowth and rocks. They would need to scramble across this to get to the point beyond the military roadblock.

"I think this natural hazard will mean that the troops are not being so fussy about blocking off this side of the access to the site," said Jennifer.

"Yes," said Chuck, "although we will need to be careful when we get closer; we don't want them to see us."

Lucas studied a small digital compass. "We are close now," he said, "I think we should drop down for the last part." They were approaching a rocky outcrop elevated above the road that they had driven along earlier. As they reached the top, they could see that they had bypassed the military roadblock and were now within the area that had been cordoned.

Jennifer looked to the right, "Oh my god," she said, "That is the real site of the crash."

Chuck looked across as well and could see a 100-yard-long gouge in the road surface, it had a kind of 'V' shape to it and at the end there was an upturned crater.

"That's the shape of a high-powered air-to-ground missile with a hard warhead," said Chuck. "Something like a Hellfire. That's an anti-armour missile and would be the thing to use against a car."

"They were not messing around, and that's not from a surface launch. I'd say it was from a helicopter," said Jennifer, "Something like an Apache or a Cobra. Kirtland has both." "Yes, and it's interesting that they have kept the road closed and preserved the situation instead of a complete cover-up," said Chuck.

"Agreed," said Jennifer, "If this was one of ours that had gone rogue, they would be rebuilding the road as fast as they could to support their cover-up statements. The fact they've left this means that they must still be trying to investigate what has happened.

"Yes," said Chuck, "It shows they don't know what happened, or who did it."

Jennifer took a few photographs using a telephoto lens.
"We should get out of here," said Chuck, "before we are noticed."

The Circle

Lucas turned around and led them back towards the farm track. From there, it was a fairly easy downhill walk back to the cars.

On the radio

The three hikers arrived back at the cars.

"What did you find out?" asked Bigsy.

"We saw the real sight of destruction," said Jennifer, "It was a missile hit. I have some pictures on my camera here. It looks like they fired it from a helicopter."

"Something else just happened," said Bigsy, "We've been listening to the radio and the conference that the senator was due to attend has been cancelled. They are saying it is because of the senator's death and that they are doing this out of respect. We are wondering if there is anything else behind it. For example, there were at least six other major speakers due to attend."

"Are you thinking the event itself could have been targeted?" asked Chuck.

"Yes, something like that," said Bigsy.

"That would be the third strike and all of them targeting this area," said Clare.

"Or someone's imagination getting the better of them?" added Bigsy.

"I know we are keeping this quiet," said Chuck, "but I think there must be some other people that know more about what is going on. Jennifer, do you think we should try to use your contacts to get more information?"

"It's a trade-off," said Jennifer, "At the moment we have freedom to act, and I think we have found out quite a lot of information. If we ask for formal help from the agencies, then they will take control of this. You can see that at the moment they don't appear to know what to do."

"We could try using the Jake angle," said Clare, "I'm sure the Brits can't help overtly but there may be some other channels through that?"

"That's a better idea," said Jennifer, "Although I am worried that nobody has contacted me to pass on the original messages from Jake."

Bigsy looked at Clare and then at Chuck, "You know something, we are now in this so deep that I think we are the best people to dig ourselves out. Jennifer, I know you've only just met all of us, but we have worked together successfully in the past. I think with your help we can get to the bottom of this."
Jennifer looked at Spencer and then Lucas.

"Okay, let's see whether this team can figure out the next steps."

Jake update

It was Jake's third day in the hotel-like rooms opposite SI6 in Vauxhall Cross. The accommodation was comfortable, and he could access the Internet and use the telephone and the television.

He'd been monitoring events in Texas and had seen the news down rated by the media; it was the same for both of the main items he was interested in. In the case of the Senator's air crash, it was now all-but-gone from the news. The oil refinery fire was still on the news, but the attention had already shifted to the possibility of legal actions, litigation and huge pay-outs for local disruption.

Jake hoped that it would not be too long before Clare would be in contact again. He had been instructed not to call her for fear that Clare's phone was now being monitored by someone in the US.

Jake's phone rang, and he saw it was Clare calling him.

"Hi Clare, I was getting worried," said Jake

"You wouldn't believe some of our stories," said Clare, "but now is not the time. We think it would be useful if you could help us link up with SI6 for some of our investigations."

"Well, as I'm in their building that shouldn't be too difficult," replied Jake.

"I'll need to contact Amanda Miller who is the person who moved me here. Do want to ask me what it is that you think you need, or would you rather wait until you can have her in a direct phone call?"

"I think we should put it to her we need a secure line to have the discussion... Ask Amanda to do that and also tell her you need to be in the call. We will have Chuck, Bigsy, Jennifer and me. Actually, it's better if we don't tell Jennifer's name to Amanda at the moment."

"I think Jennifer is concerned that she might be being traced herself. We don't want another hunt like the one for Chuck to be started up by accident."

"Okay," said Jake, "I'll see what we can arrange. I think I'm in some protective custody at the moment. Actually, for a few days it's not all that bad."

"Jake I will call you again in a couple of hours."

Predator

Chuck had found a manual about the Predator for Bigsy. Bigsy was reading extracts from it on-line.

"The USAF describes the Predator as a Tier II MALE UAS (medium-altitude, long-endurance unmanned aircraft system). The UAS comprises four aircraft or air vehicles with sensors, a ground control station (GCS), and a primary satellite link communication suite. Powered by a Rotax engine and driven by a propeller, the air vehicle can fly up to 400 nautical miles (740 km) to a target, loiter overhead for 14 hours, then return to its base."

"So, the original use of a Predator was for reconnaissance?" asked Bigsy,

"Yes, but don't be put off by those peaceful sounding words like 'loiter'", said Chuck.

"Nah, 'Loitering with intent' has a whole other meaning our side of the pond," said Bigsy.

He continued reading:

"Following 2001, the RQ-1 Predator became the primary unmanned aircraft used for offensive operations by the USAF and the CIA in Afghanistan and the Pakistani tribal areas; it has also been deployed elsewhere.

"Because offensive uses of the Predator are classified, U.S. military officials have reported an appreciation for the intelligence and reconnaissance-gathering abilities of UAVs but declined to discuss their offensive use.

"Isn't it being used along the Trumpwall nowadays?" asked Bigsy, "I'm sure they are using some big drones as part of the policing."

Chuck added, "Yeah, the U.S. Customs and Border Protection (CBP) agency has flown Predator drones at an altitude of 15,000 feet for policing immigration, drug smugglers and terrorists along the U.S.-Mexico border. They rebrand the Predator B as the MQ-9 Reaper, which can remain in flight for 30 hours. It has a characteristic Big Brother white blimp on the bottom that monitors illegal activity on the 2,000-mile border.

"The CBP wants to have a cluster of 24 Predators/Reapers that can be deployed anywhere in the continental U.S. within three hours."

Chuck sniggered. "Yes, but they are keeping quiet about the missile aspect of it. The thought a drone with a missile payload was on patrol along the border adds a whole extra level to the creepiness of the administration."

Bigsy continued, "I suppose the ideas of the Predator can just be, well, miniaturised nowadays?"

Chuck replied, "You'll know more about this than me. I know how to set them up, deploy them and so on, but I'm not sure what I'd do if you gave me some modern tech instead."

Bigsy read some more:

"Command and sensor systems
During the campaign in the former Yugoslavia, a Predator's pilot would sit with several payload specialists in a van near the runway of the drone's operating base. Direct radio signals controlled the drone's take-off and initial ascent. Then communications shifted to military satellite networks linked to the pilot's van. Pilots experienced a delay of several seconds between moving their joysticks and the drone's response.

"I suppose the latency, er, delays to the control's responses were because it was using satellite link ups? Like when people are on telly being interviewed live in different countries?" asked Bigsy.

"Yes, and that's what we were trying to fix with the new homing beacons. Instead of controlling them like some remote-controlled plane, we could set them to home onto the gadget at the target end. An altogether smoother way to blow things up," answered Chuck.

Bigsy continued, "It reminds me of the differentiation within scientists Type A: Make things Type B: Destroy things. A bit like a scientist take on Boyle's law. P1V1=P2V2."

"Anyway, by 2000, improvements in communications systems perhaps by use of the USAF's JSTARS system made it possible, at least in theory, to fly the drone from great distances. It was no longer necessary to use close-up radio signals during the Predator's take-off and ascent.

"Satellite could control the entire flight from any command center with the right equipment. The CIA proposed to attempt over Afghanistan the first remote Predator flight operations, piloted from the agency's headquarters at Langley.

"To be honest, this is so old-fashioned compared with what you were testing," said Bigsy,

"I can see two ways that you'd have seen improvements. First, the whole control system could be streamlined and made less complicated by the use of homing beacons. Second, and perhaps after your time, the miniaturisation of this could occur. Think of computer technology. Nowadays an old tower PC is more than matched by a modern smartphone. Even domestic photo drones have been made smaller. You can buy a pocketable drone with 4 propellers that can achieve stable hovering flight, with a camera, for about US$350.

"Yes, but it has a limited battery life, not the kind of thing that could fly 400 miles or more," said Chuck.

"But think about it, you're answering the question. Make a cylindrical drone with its length based on its battery or deployment requirement. Add an explosive nosecone and give it homing pigeon targeting. I could almost draw the plan for one. A super Dyson," said Bigsy, "The Predator is, like so many committee things, vastly over-engineered. Look at all the specs and pieces that need to work together on the Predator,"

Bigsy picked up reading the manual again:

"The Predator air vehicle and sensors are controlled from the ground station via a C-band line-of-sight data link or a Ku-band satellite data link for beyond-line-of-sight operations. During flight operations, the crew in the ground control station is a pilot and two sensor operators. The aircraft is equipped with the AN/AAS-52 Multi-spectral Targeting System, a color nose camera (generally used by the pilot for flight control), a variable aperture day-TV camera, and a variable aperture infrared camera (for low light/night).

"Ku-Band, that's something the US Navy uses. On their ships you see those white small aperture VSAT blimps. I guess the engineers designing this thing were from the Navy. Designing with what they could get their hands on?" said Bigsy, aware that Chuck couldn't respond any further.

Chuck said, "Bigsy, I'm guessing that things have moved on since they designed these devices. When they were new, they were like something out of Star Wars. They even came disassembled in a Star Wars container."

"Ah yes, I'm coming to that," said Bigsy, "Each Predator air vehicle can be disassembled into six main components and loaded into a container nicknamed the coffin. This enables all system components and support equipment to be rapidly deployed worldwide."

"The largest component is the ground control station, and it is designed to roll into a C-130 Hercules. It sounds more like Stanley Kubrick than George Lucas. 'Open the Pod Bay doors, HAL'"

Bigsy giggled, "So you need one of America's biggest transport planes - a Hercules C130 - to get the Predator into position? But that's not all…"

"The Predator primary satellite link consists of a 6.1-meter (20 ft) satellite dish and associated support equipment. The satellite link provides communications between the ground station and the aircraft when it is beyond line-of-sight and is a link to networks that disseminate secondary intelligence. The RQ-1A system needs 1,500 by 40 meters (5,000 by 125 ft) of hard surface runway with clear line-of-sight to each end from the ground control station to the air vehicles. Initially, all components needed to be located on the same airfield. This sounds more like something the Russians would invent."

Bigsy said, "It's some vast Lego kit and probably why people are interested in what happened to your secret missile project."

"Yeah, but don't diss the Herk. It was a monster of a plane that could take off on a handkerchief and could fly level with three of its four engines out. They've got me out of trouble in the most outlandish places," said Chuck.

 "Point well made, said Bigsy, "Designed in 1951. Kudos, Lockheed!"

Bigsy continued reading:

"Currently, the U.S. Air Force uses a concept called Remote-Split Operations where the satellite datalink is located in a different location and is connected to the GCS through fibre optic cabling.

 "This allows Predators to be launched and recovered by a small Launch and Recovery Element and then handed off to a Mission Control Element for the rest of the flight. This allows a smaller number of troops to be deployed to a forward location and consolidates control of the different flights in one location."

The Circle

"Aye, and there's the rub," said Bigsy," A single Predator costs $22m. That's a lot of wonga to have to recover from the desert."

"Yes, I agree, there's a money machine element to asymmetric warfare. It always sounds inexpensive to be using a drone, compared with, say, an F35, but we were always told it was 4 to 1 and then it went to 5 to 1. I think that was because the planes got more expensive, rather than the drones became better value," mused Chuck.

"So, we get up to the point where you were trialling these things," said Bigsy, "And nearly see the early demise of Osama bin Laden."

"Yeah, that was a covert period, indeed," said Chuck, " In the winter of 2000–2001, after seeing the results of Predator reconnaissance in Afghanistan, Cofer Black, head of the CIA's Counterterrorist Center (CTC), became a vocal advocate of arming the Predator with missiles to target Osama bin Laden.

"Black also believed that CIA pressure and practical interest was causing the USAF's Armed Predator program to be significantly accelerated. Black, and codename Richard, who was in charge of the CTC's Bin Laden Issue Station, continued to press during 2001 for a Predator armed with Hellfire missiles.

"Do you notice that turn of phrase too, 'Armed Predator' compared with the oxymoron of 'Unarmed Predator'?" asked Bigsy.

"Then more weapons tests occurred between May 22 and June 7, 2001, with mixed results. While missile accuracy was excellent, there were some problems with missile detonation.

No wonder! it was so blimming complicated," commented Bigsy.

"Then, in the first week of June, in the Nevada Desert, a Hellfire missile was successfully launched on a replica of bin Laden's Afghanistan Tarnak residence. A missile launched from a Predator exploded inside one of the replica's rooms; it was concluded that any people in the room would have been killed. However, the armed Predator did not go into action before the September 11 attacks. Instead, the CIA were batting around plans to capture ObL - Ouch!" said Bigsy.

"The USAF has also investigated using the Predator to drop battlefield ground sensors and to carry and deploy the Finder mini-UAV"

"Ahah," said Bigsy," so now we get to the Predator mini-me stage, where it can drop a miniaturised version of itself!"

Chuck commented, "When it's the War of the Worlds, that's exactly what will happen. Monster blimps spawning mini blimpette fighter units. We're all doomed!"

Clare had been quiet, sipping coffee in the corner of the room. "You've both had too much coffee and seen too many Will Smith movies."

ScanEagle

Here we are," said Bigsy, "The ScanEagle - An altogether more pragmatically engineered machine. Officially, this one's for fishing."

He had been flicking around the internet. And now read a page from another big manufacturer - Boeing.

"ScanEagle is a small, low-cost, long-endurance unmanned aerial vehicle (UAV) built by a subsidiary of Boeing. The ScanEagle was designed based on a commercial UAV that helped fishermen look for fish. The ScanEagle continues to be upgraded with improved technology and reliability."

"Sometimes you have to look at the most improbable advances", said Bigsy, "Now fisherman will be pretty single-minded about their need to find fish. They'll want stuff that can work efficiently and effectively. Think about their fish finding sonar, as an example. Deeper Fish Finder Pro+ is so simple now that it works on an iPhone and displays shoals and their depth.

"It means the whole crew can be in on the hunt for the fish and can set the nets effectively or whatever it is they do.

"So, let's go back to the Scan Eagle. It is a descendant of another UAV. The SeaScan, which was conceived of as a remote sensor for collecting weather data as well as helping commercial fishermen locate and track schools of tuna.

"The resulting technology has been successful as a portable Unmanned Aerial System (UAS) for autonomous surveillance in the battlefield and has been deployed since August 2004 when it was used in the Iraq War.

"ScanEagle carries a stabilized electro-optical and/or infrared camera on a light-weight inertial stabilized turret system integrated with communications range over 100 km, and flight endurance of 20+ hours. ScanEagle has a 10-foot (3 m) wingspan and can fly up to 75 knots (139 km/h), with an average cruising speed of 60 knots (111 km/h).

"Some modifications featured a higher resolution camera, an improved transponder and a new video system.

"ScanEagle needs no airfield for deployment. Instead, it is launched using a pneumatic launcher patented as the SuperWedge (snigger) launcher. Think of it as a catapult."

"It is recovered using the SkyHook retrieval system, which uses a hook on the end of the wingtip to catch a rope hanging from a 30 to 50-foot (15 m) pole. Yay, Heath Robinson rules!"

"Wait for it... This is made possible by a high-quality differential GPS unit mounted on the top of the pole and UAV.

The Circle

The rope is attached to a shock cord to reduce stress on the airframe imposed by the abrupt stop.

"There we have it - catapult launched and bungee cord retrieved. Bonkers? Or Genius?"

"I rest my case," said Bigsy, making his way towards the refrigerator

Chuck smiled, and Clare clapped.

"I think we are going stir crazy," said Clare.

Ed Adams

THE CIRCLE
PART THREE

897

Don't Mess with Texas

"So dry the birds are building their nests out of barbed wire."

-Texas Monthly

Houston

In Houston, it was only a few minutes after the phone call from Clare to Jake that the first news from Jake arrived with Jennifer, through official channels. She was contacted on her main cell phone and asked to take the call alone.

"Hello Ms Burns, they have asked us to contact you about certain topics related to a Jake Lambers, who is currently being held by the UK Security services.

"We'd like to ask you to come to our offices to discuss this."

"If you can tell us your current location, we will send around transport and will then ask you to accompany us to one of our main briefing center. I'm sure you understand this is a matter of National Security?'

"I do," said Jennifer, "but I'm also concerned for my own safety. I would rather tell you information from afar for the next few days and then return to base when things are a little clearer."

"Ms Burns we can't have you do that. We need you to come in now. Please tell us your address. We can be with you within the hour.

The Circle

Jennifer walked back towards the cars and to Chuck and Bigsy.

"I can't do that right now," she said. She gestured to them they needed to start the cars and move on. "I will call you again later," she said.

"We need to get away from here," she said to Chuck. "They are tracing me at the moment. I think they have responded to Clare's call to Jake. I'm impressed that the Brits and the US would co-operate on something like this"

"I guess they must be rattled by what is happening," said Bigsy.

"Yes, and I wonder if they now think we are part of the problem, rather than part of the solution," added Jennifer.

"We need to move away from this area," said Jennifer.

"And I think we should also lose these two government vehicles," said Chuck, "And their drivers, nicely, of course'"

"We should go to somewhere with a reasonable-sized car rental and pick another two new vehicles that we can use ourselves. I still have cash. Can we get the drivers to take us to somewhere for this?"

"Sure," said Jennifer, "We are still about 20 miles southeast of the main Dallas Fort Worth complex. There's the large international airport in the centre. We would have a big choice there and still be difficult to find."

"We could stay in a hotel near to the airport and leave a gap before we pick up the new hire cars,"

"I like that plan," said Bigsy, "Gaps are good. We provide a small gap between losing these drivers and picking up the new cars. And if we use cash for the hotel, we have another gap in our visibility."

Jennifer asked the drivers to take them to Dallas Fort Worth airport and to drop them at the International departures area.

She made a point of saying several times they were travelling to Seattle, hoping that this would register with the drivers.

"Lucas, I think so far you are not caught up in this and it would make more sense for us to let you go now. That way you can have helped us, but not yet implicated in a way that anyone else knows about. Can you please head back to Albuquerque?"

"Even better," said Chuck, "Is if Lucas gets tickets for all of us back to Albuquerque."

"Or even better, we get tickets to somewhere else!" said Clare. "Somewhere that sends them in the wrong direction. What about New York?"

"If this was coming from the agency's money, I'm not sure we could do this," said Jennifer.

"Don't worry," said Chuck, "It's taken care of. I will buy the tickets to the random destination and Lucas should buy his ticket separately. It will break us up in case anyone is looking at the ticketing. We've arrived at the American airlines desk. I will use American Airlines to put us some flights to somewhere a long way away. "

"How about Seattle?" said Jennifer. "It is consistent with what I told the drivers."

"Good plan," said Chuck, "And there are also various military connections in Seattle. It would be a good place to make them think we are heading. Boeing and all that."

"Okay and Lucas can get a flight back to Albuquerque. See, there are direct flights from here to Albuquerque."

They made their way to the ticketing areas.   Lucas booked his flight with American Airlines and remained separated from the rest of them.

"That's good," said Chuck to Jennifer, "He needs to be away from us now."

"You know something, I think I need to go to the cafe area and sit with the bags," said Chuck, "How can I put this; I don't want this bag to be too close to the airport security people?"

Jennifer smiled, "it's a bit heavy, is it?" she asked.

"It's a little unsuitable for flight," Chuck replied.

They located a small coffee bar and piled up their baggage.

Chuck said, "I will wait here. Bigsy, I think it's best that you buy the other tickets to our random destination. As long as its internal US we should not have too much trouble with getting the tickets. Look, here's some cash. We will give ourselves the best chance by not using credit cards. They will get our names, but they already know we are in the Dallas area. The best thing we can do is make them think we are leaving and give them somewhere to go to."

Bigsy smiled and picked up the pile of notes that Chuck had pushed across the table.

" Okay, we need to think about our next move," said Jennifer.

"First of all, I think we should stay here tonight," said Chuck, "Somewhere around the airport until we can figure out our next move. That still gives us the option to use planes or another car to move us along."

"Yes, and now there are five of us, it's easier for us to get a big single car, instead of two," said Lucas.

"Will your absence be noticed?" asked Chuck.

"I took care of that when we were last in the office," said Jennifer.

"I told them I was sick and that it could be two or three days before I was back."

Refundable

Bigsy returned with the tickets.

"I got refundables," he said, "They were more expensive, but we can change them if we need to."

 Chuck laughed, "So we have now got some refundable decoy tickets?"

  "I think we need to move from here now," said Chuck, "to find a base for the evening one of these airport hotels is best. At least it means we won't be where the drivers dropped us, and we have a trail of tickets that lead us to Seattle. That should all give us a breathing space."

 "Right," said Chuck, "Let's pick a hotel,"

 He noticed that Clare had already picked up some airport brochures.
"Pretty much all the main chains are here," she said.

"Marriot, Sheraton, Hyatt, Hilton, Holiday Inn, Embassy suites. You name it, they seem to be here."

"Okay, let's take one that's inside the perimeter if we can."

Clare smiled, "I like the Hyatt," she said, "It's got some cool facilities too."

"This isn't a holiday," said Bigsy.

 "I know," said Clare, "but heck we should make the most of any downtime."

She looked again at the leaflet. "We are in Terminal C country," she said, "International Departures."

"Yes," said Bigsy, "I think that is Gate 26 over there."

 "Then we are very well-positioned," said Clare," It says here that the entrance to the hotel is opposite gates 26 to 39."

Jennifer smiled, "You have no idea what it would be like to make this decision on agency money. We'd be staying somewhere across town in a motel."

"Excellent," said Chuck, "all the more reason to stay at the Hyatt. He patted the camouflage bag. I think the bank of Chuck will stand this, does anyone have some small change for one of those trolleys?"

"There's something else," said Clare, "we'd only expected to be here for two or three days to meet Chuck. I get the impression this will take a little longer. After we've checked into that hotel across the way, I will spend an hour going shopping. You have some clothes with you. I have almost nothing," she said.

Jennifer nodded, "Same with me,"

"Okay," said Chuck, "We should agree a time to meet somewhere in the hotel."

"How about the bar?" suggested Bigsy.

Chuck agreed, "Let's make it 7 o'clock this evening that we meet."

Ed Adams

Cowboy boots from Sheplers

Chuck had gone to the bar early; he had picked a corner table which had a commanding view of the room and was sipping on a Coca-Cola.

Clare was first to arrive, also early.

"Were you successful in your mission?" he asked

"What the shopping?" grinned Clare, "Oh, yes."

"And Jennifer too?"

"We sort of goaded each other on and it was quite fun using Bank of Chuck money. Thank you and I must repay you in simpler circumstances."

"No, it's my pleasure," said Chuck.

He noticed that Clare was wearing a new top and then noticed she was also wearing new skinny jeans.

Then he spotted the cowboy boots.

"Clare, it looks as if you've really gone to town with this."

"Yes, I found Sheplers. I also bought a couple of sunglasses would also be useful," she said, "A quick way to make a disguise. And the hats were unmissable. Quite a few people around here seem to be wearing them."

"Let's just hope we need to stay in Texas then," said Chuck.

"I've also got some news," said Clare, "I received a text from Jake about half an hour ago. He has asked for a meeting at 8 o'clock local time here. He says he will call my mobile phone number."

Jennifer arrived next; she was also wearing new clothes. Black trousers, black top and a grey jacket.

"Yeah," said Jennifer, "Don't mess with Texas."

"Very nice," said Chuck, "I see the two of you have been busy."

"At least we can both survive for a few more days on the road," said Jennifer. More than survive," said Chuck, "I think you will both do quite well."

"Something we need to get straight," said Jennifer, "I'm breaking all kinds of rules by using your money for this. I've kept the receipts and we should figure out how to rectify this later."

"Jennifer," said Chuck, "I think you will have worked out by now that our little group is fairly unconventional and trying to live off the radar. Let's say I have sufficient quotes supplies here for all of us and I don't want that to be an issue as we go forward."

"I'm very appreciative that you are helping me and, in your case, Jennifer, that you have taken some extra risks to break away from normal policies. I don't know how much you spent, and I don't care. Put it down to the cost of doing business."

At that moment Bigsy appeared with Spencer.

They were both carrying bags.

"That's a turn up," said Chuck. "The two ladies have bought their shopping, freshen up in their rooms, and come back on time. You looked as if you have only just returned from shopping!"

"I know," said Bigsy, "We were not as good at it. We were distracted. There was a great sports bar on the way into the shopping area. You know they had peanuts on the table to make us thirsty. We had to eat the peanuts and throw the shells on the floor."

"I've been into pubs in the UK with sawdust on the floor," said Chuck, "Over here its peanut shells."

Chuck waved a waitress over, and they ordered some drinks.

"Okay," said Jennifer," Let's talk. We need to figure out the next moves."

"Okay," said Clare, "Let's summarise."

"They invited us to Scottsdale via Chuck although we suspected that it would be more complicated once we got here."

"Chuck was invited for a mini-conference with a bunch of his old pals from the missile testing days."

"I guess that meant someone had broken Chuck's cover because he was missing after the last escapade."

"Yes, although, in fairness, we all thought Chuck had gone into hiding," added Bigsy.

"That is right," said Chuck, "and that's why I think it is one someone from the team I worked with that have called us together and is now systematically bumping us off.

"Right," said Clare, "**And** then as soon as we showed up you ran into Bigsy early and the pair of you got drugged."

"Yes," said Chuck, "But I think the only reason they drugged Bigsy was because he was with me. I think someone was trying to get me. I doubt that they even knew who Bigsy was."

"And then your friend Mike showed up and somehow extracted you both from your rooms and into the car. And then they chased you across the Arizona desert?"

"That's right," said Chuck.

"I don't really remember this," said Bigsy, "Whatever they had done seemed to affect me more than Chuck. I remember being in some kind of rocky area with Mike and Chuck when we waited until the next day to be on our way again."

"That's right, we were waiting for the effects to wear off. And remember, Mike said that there had been two people breaking into my room before that happened," said Chuck.

"And Mike took you back towards Albuquerque?" asked Clare.

"That's right; that's when you, Clare, were still at the hotel and around the time that Jennifer contacted you."

"Yes, we met Clare at that diner in Albuquerque, but Mike dropped us at that shopping mall where we waited until the right time to get a taxi to meet Clare.

"And Mike headed off by himself?" Asked Clare.

"The next day we heard that news broadcast that Mike had crashed the car into the river."

"Which repeats the pattern we've seen with Ben and Klaus, that they are being bumped off one by one."

"We also found out that Tony Capaldi had left the Colorado University and was travelling somewhere. Our suspicions are that he was also heading towards Scottsdale, but we don't have any way to cross check that.

"I can help with that," said Jennifer, "Using my contacts in the airport security network."

"But let's wind back a little," said Pixie, "Something I remember when we were being chased across the desert was that a plane pursued us. Maybe a helicopter. What was that about?"

Chuck replied, "No, I think you are probably suffering from the drugs. We were being chased, but it was a motorcycle. A hog. A mean looking Harley."

Clare giggled, "Ahah, so you were being chased by someone over 50?" she asked.

"What?" Asked Chuck.

"A middle-aged man who could afford a Harley-Davidson," she replied.

"I don't know who it was," said Chuck, "But we stopped the bike by me shooting out its tire."

"That would be the helicopter sound and explosion that I heard," said Bigsy.

"I think so," said Chuck, "That was the only thing following us."

"I'm already suspicious," said Clare.

"Some of this doesn't ring true. You go to the bar, get drugged and your long-lost buddy Mike conveniently finds you just before you are to be kidnapped?"

"Then he drives you away. Both of you actually. And someone chases you all on a motorcycle? Are you sure Mike couldn't have been involved in this?" asked Clare.

"I don't think so." said Chuck, "And anyway he's dead now."

"Not necessarily," said Jennifer, "Suppose the whole thing is a setup?"

"Maybe Mike is the one that has been hunting down the **old team?" said Jennifer.**

"And maybe he's also staged the car crash?"

"So, the guy on the bike could have been an accomplice of Mike?" said Clare.

"It is an interesting theory," said Chuck.

'It could also tie in with most of the action at the moment being between here and Albuquerque."

"I'm wondering if Mike was trying to find out something from one of you?" said Jennifer.

"This is something that one of you knew that would apply to the project?"

"Could it be where something was stored, on the base?" asked Jennifer.

"Some kind of secret or code or way something is hidden or something like that?" Asked Lucas.

"I think you might be right," said Chuck, "It was interesting when we were together in the desert that night. To start was I was waiting for the drug to wear off and at that point seem very sensible to stay hidden until the morning. As I came around, Mike started to chat about old times.

"Inevitably we talked about the work we've done together. But Mike knows that trying to talk to me wouldn't be a very good way to get information. I'm just wondering whether I said anything that he might have found useful related to the project."

Bigsy chipped in, "Yes, I was out of it pretty much all of this time."

"And Mike would have known that you couldn't have helped."

"But I seem to remember when I came to that you were somewhere away from Mike," said Bigsy.

"That's right, I'd gone for a walk. I'd told Mike I'd like to shake off the remaining effects of the drug. That was true but now you mention it I can remember thinking at the time, there was some kind of stabbing doubt in my head."

"I know that feeling," said Bigsy. It is the one you get when you've had enough to drink, and the next pint will send you over the edge.

"I'm not sure that's it," said Chuck, "but there's a kind of instinctive moment when I thought Mike was asking questions probably off-limits related to the project work."

"Can you remember what he was asking you about?" asked Jennifer.

"Launchers," said Chuck, "He was asking me about launchers."

I take it you mean that launchers for UAVs?" said Clare.

"Kind of," said Chuck, "but probably not the way you're thinking."

"He was asking me about catapult launchers. That's when I had the Bigsy drink effect moment."

"I started by saying I didn't know about this. There were two types of missile system we used to test. I guess you'd call them normal rockets the first type. And also, those Predator UAVs we talked about. There was another type - a smaller UAV. I didn't get involved but I knew they were being tested as well."

"So why if Mike has been bumping other people off would he have let you and Bigsy go?" asked Clare, "It makes little sense."

"Actually, I think it does," said Chuck. I knew that Tony Capaldi was the main person working with the smaller UAVs and that's what I said to Mike."

"It didn't occur to me that Mike was fishing for information and I gave him honest replies so he probably could see that I was not trying to hide anything."

"I still don't understand why he didn't finish you and Bigsy then?" said Jennifer.

"Mike is a pretty smart operator," said Chuck, "I think he worked out that it would be difficult to torture me to get the information if I knew it, but he could ask me gentle questions whilst we were waiting for Bigsy to recover. And if he left me alive, I could also help backup his disappearing trick when he drove the car off the bridge.

"I'd have been one of the last people to see him alive. I could pinpoint his location and also echo the story he was being chased like Ben and myself.

So is our guess that Mike is now trying to track down Tony Capaldi?" asked Jennifer.

"Yes," said Chuck, "I think that's highly likely. As is my suspicion that he is operating within this area."

"Although I very much doubt that he suspects we are on to him."

"So, are we running from shadows?" asked Clare.

"No, I don't think so, answered Chuck, but I think we can ask someone to take a look - Tom."

"Tom?" asked Jennifer,

"Yes, we let Tom go back to his homelands, which means he is well placed to look in the river, to follow any tracks left by Mike."

"How can we reach him?" asked Clare, "He's probably sitting in the middle of the desert somewhere. No phone signal…Please don't say smoke signals."

"No, Tom, is a very modern Navajo. I'll call him on his satellite phone."

"What?" asked Jennifer.

"We used to use them in the desert," said Chuck, "They were handy to have and so we just kept them, post inventory, I suppose you could call it."

"Tom has one, as do I, although if there's an ordinary cellular signal here then I can call his Iridium over cellular. Just add the 0088 prefix- then it's about five dollars a minute."

"Let's give to a go!"

Chuck looked up a number for Tom, "Here we go! - Hey Tom, I bet you didn't expect to hear from me this quickly? Say, you know that blue car that crashed off a bridge? What have you heard? Hmmm. Yeah. What did he look like? Who told you that? Did anyone else see? Where? What now? Who knows? Tom, I owe you. Until the next time!"

"Wow," said Chuck, "That was interesting. Tom says that the police version is of a crash. Tom says differently. He says they rigged it. Someone paid two guys from his reservation to stage it. They work in a garage and took two thousand each to do it."

"The usual story, they couldn't resist spending some of their new cash and one of them ended up in jail. They were rounded up by the Navajo Police, and we cut a deal with them in return for information. The guy who paid them fits Mike's description. He's stashed away in a Motel. Right on the Ten."

Bigsy asked, "The Ten, I assume you mean the I-10?"

"There's still something that doesn't make sense," said Jennifer.

" I can understand being chased by bad guys, but why would the US Army be running a cover-up? The plane crash and possibly the refinery?"

"It doesn't tie together."

"But I think we know that the two sets of events are connected," said Chuck.

"All right," said Clare, "Let's see if we can work this out. Suppose that Mike or whoever it is has been able to sell the missile technology to some power or other. Suppose it's linked in some way with energy futures. Would the American government be trying to hide that there was some sort of terrorist offensive in play? And if so, why would they be doing this?"

"Perhaps they are being threatened directly and so far are powerless to figure out what to do?" said Chuck.

"So, they try to make the two events look like accidents? Surely that can only work for a little while. Maybe it's just enough time to buy time for them to figure out what is happening?" said Chuck.

"I'm not sure I'm buying it," said Clare.

Spencer had remained quiet through most of this he had been flicking through screens on his laptop computer.

"This may be relevant," he said. He had found a report that had been due to be discussed at the energy summit that had just been cancelled in Houston. The title of the paper was 'Energy Futures the Next 15 Years.'

There was a précis of the document. It described some of the situations that could occur and that in particular North America would need to find new sources for fuel and other types of energy.

It also discussed the emerging power of the Chinese economy and the additional pressures it was creating on the energy infrastructure.

It went on to say that China were much less fussy about the way that they would site the new power stations and that they were quite capable of creating a surplus within a few years.

The Americans were taking a strong-arm position on this. They did not want to be seen to be reliant upon yet another foreign power. Having had to deal with the Middle East for energy particularly oil over the last 20 years they were now far more determined to make themselves self-sufficient.

A large Chinese conglomerate called ChinaEnergy had been formed to try to influence American policy on energy futures. So far it had been unsuccessful and there had been a number of challenges placed in its path.

Spencer pulled up a different article. This was from the Huffington Post and was more of an opinion piece. It commented that the Chinese power brokerage could be sufficient to change the whole dynamics of the trading position between America and the rest of the world.

It could have a significant effect upon the US dollar and raise the power of the Chinese currency as well as the yen and the euro. In effect the US would no longer have the dollar as one of the world's global strongest currencies.

Clare chipped in, "But this is an opinion piece - the writer is grinding a political axe on this. It's one of those things that could take years to play out and I think that the American government are stalling all of this in any case."

 "I think you're right," said Jennifer, "There's too many vested interests in the USA based around the energy business. Instead of doing deals, the Chinese were more likely to see a relaxation of our own standards to get to a similar position."

"What," said Bigsy, "the kind of thing where you find a piece of America to put power stations with no questions asked?"

 "Kind of," said Jennifer, "if you think about it that's not so dissimilar from storing lots of nuclear warheads in the desert near to Albuquerque."

 "So, are we dealing with terrorists or idealists or powerful corporations or what?" said Bigsy.

"I can see a picture beginning to emerge," said Clare. " There is some kind of big power interest in play and maybe they are using the terrorist angle to create a perfect storm. It could tip the negotiations towards the use of the Chinese power within the American economy."

 "So, kill an energy aware senator up and blow up a refinery? And not forgetting that they have successfully stopped the conference in Houston," said Jennifer.

 "And maybe the scale of this so-called terrorist attack is more limited than they imagine?" said Bigsy

 Yes, and this is with just a few rockets sent," said Chuck.

"It's still enough to be pretty lethal and could be enough to tip the whole economics around," said Bigsy.

Spencer was still using the computer.

"Take a look at this," he said, "it's the recent share prices of some of the American oil companies. Since the explosion at the oil refinery and the cancellation of the conference there has been a significant write-down of share prices for the whole energy sector. In North America it's affecting the rest of the market too."

He looked across to the European stock markets.

"It doesn't seem to have had the same impact in London or Frankfurt and actually in China the prices are rising."

"A lot of what we're working on is supposition," said Clare, "We may just be tying two things together without any real hard evidence."

"I agree, it may not be the sort of thing you could prove in a court of law," said Chuck," but there's an awful lot of circumstances that seem to link these things together.

"And I'm guessing that if Mike is involved and the current damage is limited to a radius of maybe 100 miles or so that he is not using the UAVs yet?"

"I think that's why he's trying to find out about these launchers. The idea of using something like a Predator as part of a private initiative is little far-fetched. It needs a proper runway to take off and at a fairly advanced subsystem around it. The smaller UAVs that can be launched using the catapult launchers are a much better bet. The trick is to figure out how to add a payload to them. If the work that was being done by Tony Capaldi and the rest of the team managed to solve weapon carrying, then I think we have the basis of a much bigger threat from whoever is running Mike and whoever he is else is involved with."

"So, Jennifer, is there any other way we can get help from the people that are holding Jake?"

"You mean SI6," said Jennifer.

"Yes, but what I mean is whether we can use them directly without getting involved in the local agencies here?"

"I think the local agencies here are trying to cover up the previous explosions rather than figure out the bigger picture. "

"That's why they are trying to get me to come in," said Jennifer, "Before I know it be in Plano in one of the agency facilities and that will take me off the grid."

"I think we have most of the pieces now," said Bigsy. "We also have a pretty strong team here plus Jake and SI6 people as backup. There must be something we can do that will flush this out. Jennifer my worry is that this will become dangerous again for one or more of us."

"I think we need to find a way to make contact with Tony Capaldi, " said Chuck. "If Mike has called him to a meeting, I expect it's also back in Scottsdale where he met me. We really need some sort of confirmation of that before we start moving around again."

"I think this is where I will need to call in a few more favours," says Lucas, "I can get information about flights and movements of passengers as part of my security role. This time it would be best if Spencer make the calls so that it dilutes attention. You have the full name of this person," said Jennifer, "We can call up to find out where and when he has travelled - he might even have declared his initial hotel in Arizona."

"This could be mechanical process, I don't like to say this," said Chuck, "but I think it might be too late to find Tony Capaldi now. If he travelled into Scottsdale, it could have been the day after me. When Mike left us, if he is still alive, I think he will have gone back to find this Capaldi before heading off to Texas."

"We should still check for flight information," said Jennifer, "Spencer could you get onto that?"

"I can't access this information from here," said Spencer, "it's all a secure link. I'll contact Lucas back at the office."

SI6

Jake had been in a further discussion with Amanda Miller from the SI6 group. "The team in the US have asked for a meeting. They wanted to be secure and limited to a few people. It's difficult because how people think the Americans are trying to hide what is happening."

Amanda Miller grinned, "That would not be the first time. I assume Chuck is still in danger then?"

"It is getting more complex," said Jake, "We will need the others to help explain it. They will then want some help from you."

"It's a judgement call," said Amanda, "We have to decide whether there is any UK national security at risk. We would cooperate with the Americans as well, but you can understand that some of this is out of our jurisdiction."

"Yes," said Jake, "But please can we keep this to the Brits for the next session."

"That's fine," said Amanda, "and it's part of the reason that you were here, anyway."

Ed Adams

"Can we set a time please, I'll text them," said Jake,

"Let's say two hours from now," said Amanda.

Liaison

Chuck looked at his watch, it was almost 8 o'clock.

"It's time for our call from London," said Chuck, "they must be staying up late."

"Should we stay here?" said Clare "Or maybe it's better to go to one of our rooms."

"Let's use mine," said Chuck, "As I've paid for everyone else, they seem to have given me quite a decent-sized room."

They followed him to the elevator, and he pressed for the top floor. It said executive floor.

"Get you," said Bigsy.

"I know," said Chuck, "there are a few perks to having the payroll."

 He led them to his room, which was a small suite. There was a separate room with a table, and six chairs separated from the bedroom.

 "This will do nicely," said Bigsy.

 They set up Clare's phone on the middle of the table.

At 8pm prompt, Amanda Miller called Clare's cell phone.

Clare introduced who was on the call and Amanda said 'hello' to everyone. She was with Jake and also Jim Cavendish.

"I think you should start by telling us what you know," said Amanda, "Jennifer, I know that both the CIA and the FBI are showing an interest in this, which seems to go beyond it being a matter affecting Colonel Manners and the inadvertent introduction of the three British Subjects.

Jennifer began, "Yes, I think the Agencies are also falling over one another," she said. "Let's start with a few of the things we've seen and the ways they link."

Jennifer explained:

"Colonel Manners and a few of his close colleagues from work at Los Alamos around seven years ago were all called to a hotel in Scottsdale. It is somewhere they all knew and had been a rest and recreation spot when they were on their mission.

"Some of their number died, in various unusual circumstances.

"Colonel Manners suspected something was amiss when he broke cover to come to Scottsdale."

"What do you mean, broke cover?" asked Amanda.

"To most people, Chuck Manners was dead, killed on a mission around a year ago. The people he contacted, Clare and Bigsy, were not surprised to be approached by the alleged missing Chuck Manners and came out to Scottsdale at his request."

"We'd never really believed he was dead," said Bigsy, "So when he asked for us to contact him, we were happy to do so. We moved pretty much straight away to link with him."

"So, the three of you meet together?" asked Amanda.

"Well, Bigsy met Chuck first, someone drugged them and then an ex colleague of Chuck's called Mike rescued them. He drove them to a safe place in the desert,"

"But we think it has implicated Mike in the disappearance of the others," chipped in Chuck. "We think he was trying to find out something about the old project."

"So, he rescued you, then what happened?"

"This is about when you, SI6, picked up Jake," said Bigsy, "Clare was still separated from us, but you sent Jennifer to find her and someone else to locate Jake."

"That's right," said Amanda, "We were trying to keep you safe because we thought you had stumbled into something important and sensitive.

"OK," said Jennifer," So next we arranged for Clare to meet with Chuck and Bigsy again. They located some information which we think is material to some recent events in Texas. The killing of the senator and the explosion at the oil refinery in Houston."

Chuck added, "It was a tortuous route to get that information but smacked of field skills of the kind that me and my colleagues would use. In other words, one of my buddies had left the messaging."

"The thing is, we don't know who sent the message to us, but it said that there is a conspiracy related to energy futures and the Chinese.

"So, the other piece we have," continued Jennifer, "is the weapon gadgets that Chuck was helping to support back seven years ago. It was a dead-end technology, but it sounds as if someone has resurrected it."

"Yes," said Chuck, "It provides a clandestine way to guide a missile into a target. The homing device is pretty much undetectable and can remain inert for up to, er, I'm guessing, five years."

"Okay," said Amanda, so you have put these events together…"

"Yes," said Chuck, "And we also think some of this is being covered up by the US Government. Both the death of Senator Williams and the Oil Refinery explosion are re-branded as 'accidents' by the media. We tried to get to the car crash spot and could see that there were two different locations. One shown to the press had a plane wreck sprinkled around it. A mile or so further along the same road there was a missile track that showed a major explosion from a missile had occurred."

"Yes, so our supposition is that they want to use transponders to send in missiles. The thing is, the range and radius of current operations isn't what you'd expect if they were targeting with a drone, which is the original design point of the transponder."

Jennifer added, " I think they are trying to simulate the effects of the transponder system now, but only have an airborne short-range missile rack at their disposal. They want the US to think they have something more, but they are still trying to acquire it."

Chuck said, "I think the original UAVs that we were trialling were fine for a military style operation. If you need to escape detection, you'd need something smaller I think the terrorists are using much smaller missiles - rockets even - which also have a much smaller range. I think this could get very messy if they got hold the small-scale UAVs. That would give a massive range and create a terror weapon that could operate over thousands of miles.

"I also think the reason Mike has been chasing people is to find the launchers for the smaller weapons. The most likely type is the Scan Eagle sized weapons, which launch from a small catapult. It's my guess that one of the team knew how to make this work and just as importantly, where to find these launchers."

"Okay," said Amanda, "but I can't understand why the US Government would keep this so quiet and why they would hide the aftermath of the various attacks."

"That is what we want you to help us find out," said Jennifer, "It looks to me as if the FBI have already been involved in both the Senator scene and the Oil Refinery," said Jennifer, "As it's become a cover-up, I doubt whether it is being treated as domestic terrorism."

"So, the CIA would also be involved?" Asked Amanda.

"Definitely," said Chuck, "This will be multiple agency. Some kind of Joint Terrorism Task Force."

"We need to find out if there is a new JTTF based around this situation," said Chuck, "I guess you already know that the original project seven years ago was Project Esther?"

"OK," said Amanda, "It's time I explained a little about what we know. Yes, we knew about Project Esther, but only recently. Someone from a JTTF called Alabaster called our team. They were looking into an old programme called Esther and were asking us a few routine questions. Like you say, they told us enough about the project such that we understood it was to do with guidance systems, but they also played down its significance and told us it was now defunct."

"They explained they were trying to track down the original members of the team because there were some missing components they wanted to track. They didn't say what or why, though."

"We treated it as routine and along the way they gave us a few names: Chuck, Mike, Ben and a few others. They said they were looking for these people and they could transit through the UK."

"A later update told us that two of them, Klaus and Ben, had recently died. They emphasised that if we could locate any of the others, then we should let them know.

The Circle

Within 24 hours it escalated because of a random call from Colonel Manners to the offices of 'The Triangle' which is the company run by Jake Lambers.

The call was to three of the principles of the company and, if genuine, it would show that Chuck Manners was still alive and not killed in an explosion as it said in his record.

The reason for the interest from the JTTF was that it could show that Chuck was acting subversively against the interests of the USA. Getting access to his contacts was one way to bring him in.

That's when we pulled Jake from the offices and across to SI6. We'd told the Americans we had Jake and that he might try to contact Chuck.

"That's also when I took a careful look at what was happening," said Amanda. "After the exchange between Clare and Jake, it became apparent that Chuck was being chased, but not so clear who was doing it."

Amanda added, "It made me wonder if there was a different agenda at play - one to neutralise the whole team that Chuck was a part of."

"I'm still acting with the CIA on this," said Amanda, "but I decided to take this call separately. I want to ascertain if there is a double agenda at play. "

Chuck commented, "There is something going on. The JTTF would tell you more than they have on this occasion. Also, you wouldn't get a JTTF if it is mainly a situation about the bumping off of half a dozen ex-military community."

"I have to agree," said Jennifer, "there must be a bigger situation in play."

Amanda paused. Jake could see he was thinking what to do.

"Hello, Hello," asked Jennifer, "Is the line still working?"

 "Yes." said Amanda, "I'm thinking. I'm trying to work out other angles."

Joint Terrorism Task Force

"The most obvious to me is a cover-up," said Chuck, "That could be because the US Government are up to something themselves."

"A more likely situation is that they don't know what to do," said Clare, "That would suggest they are trying to buy time by not letting too much information out."

"I like it," said Bigsy, "It's a fairly obvious explanation and fits the situation well. The JTTF has been charged to solve something big; the time is ticking, and they are already facing some early examples of a problem. They are trying to hide the current situation while they figure out how to solve the bigger problem."

"Yes," said Chuck, "I think it fits too. I'm guessing that the US Government have received a threat and are trying to decide their countermeasures. That's the role of the JTTF. In the meantime, they are being faced with the escalation of the threat that they are handling."

"Yes," said Jennifer, "and it is first one Senator, then a refinery and then something bigger. - But not the cancelled conference of energy executives."

"Is there a way we can find out about this?" asked Chuck, looking at Jennifer.

"I wonder if this is where SI6 can help us?" asked Jennifer, "If you could gain some kind of access to the JTTF, we might get more information."

"I can try," said Amanda, "but I wonder if it will have the right effect, or whether everything will just become more secure."

"That's what we need to find out," said Chuck, "But I wonder if we can also bait the question?"

"What do you mean?" asked Amanda.

"Well, if we can give them something that will intrigue them to let us know the background, it could help a lot."

"Do you have something in mind?" said Amanda.

"Yes," said Chuck, "I think we should tell them we think we know who is looking for the Project Esther components and that we think we know why."

"And who and what is that?" asked Amanda.

Chuck said, "You must trust me on this one, but I can answer both questions."

"He's right," said Jennifer, "I think he knows."

"But do you know too, Amanda?" asked Jennifer.

"I don't have the information that Chuck has about most of this," said Jennifer, "So No, I don't know."
She looked across to Chuck. She could see that Chuck recognised she had just lied to Amanda, but Amanda was only listening to the call and wouldn't be able to pick up on Jennifer's visual cue to Chuck.

"Okay," said Amanda, "I will make enquiries about this JTTF. As they gave me a code name for the JTTF at the beginning of their enquiries about Colonel Manners, I will use that as my route to get further information."

"When should we expect to hear something?" asked Jennifer.

"You must give me 24 hours," said Amanda, "On second thoughts, let's try to set the next call for a more civilised time for both of us. How about 10 am your time?, that will be 5 pm for me. That's about 32 hours away."

Chuck and Jennifer looked at one another. "Things here are moving fast," said Jennifer. I realise you'll need some time to get to people, well go with your plan; if anything untoward happens, we will use Clare's cell phone to communicate."

"Okay," said Amanda, "We'll use that as a plan. In the meantime, we will also be scanning our comms for any other signs of activity."

The line clicked off in the office where Amanda, Jake and Jim Cavendish sat.

"It's all sounding intense," said Jake. "Do you think you'll be able to get anything from the JTTF?"

Amanda spoke, "Our best chance is to do as Chuck suggests, to let them know that Chuck has some other information. The downside is that they will probably be picked up with half an hour of the call. I can't imagine that the CIA will leave Chuck and the others to run loose once they know they have information or may be implicated in some way."

"Will you be able to deal directly with the JTTF?" Asked Jake, "or do you think you must bring some other bosses into the situation?"

"I was wondering about this myself," said Amanda, "I should make an immediate report of all of this, but truthfully I'm concerned that if I do that, then we'll see everyone rounded up."

Frankly, we are better off leaving them in the field. They seem to get on and finding are finding out plenty, even if some of it is circumstantial.

"Welcome to our world," said Jake, "You'd be surprised how often the circumstantial stuff plays out as accurate."

"What will you do with me while this is going on? I can only watch so many box-sets." asked Jake.

"I will need to keep you here longer," said Amanda. "It's mainly for your own safety, no one can get to you here. If I'm truthful, it also means I'm certain that the comms to Clare and Bigsy will stay open."

"I trust that these temporary facilities are not too bad?"

Jake nodded. He would be comfortable enough here for another few days.

Amanda asked Jim to take Jake to the secure facility and to check if Jake needed anything. Amanda walked out of the room and into a corridor.

She decided she would approach the operations centre first about access to the JTTF. She already had the name of her contact and would use that to report to them as if on an operational matter.

Amanda returned to her office and composed a note to the JTTF leader. It was simple enough.

"My contact in Arizona has information about component placement from Project Esther. Wants to talk. Can we arrange?"

To Amanda's surprise, the reply came back in a matter of a few minutes. It was suitably terse, like her original email.

"We should meet," it said, "Come to the Duchess, at 11:00"

Amanda smiled, then groaned. The Duchess Belle was a known off-site venue. The CIA Station for London had a main office in the US Embassy buildings in South London. Before that, it had been in Grosvenor Square, where the Barley Mow had served a similar purpose.

Using the Duchess Belle was a way to signal Amanda that the meeting would be brief and informal. The pub was less than 10 minutes' walk from the American embassy, but for a visitor to the embassy, it was a welcome relief to go to the pub and miss all of the lovely US security.

Amanda knew that the pub was like another agency office, albeit with an easier access.

Amanda looked at her watch. She would need to leave soon to be there on time. The person she was meeting would not wait more than a few minutes past the appointed time.

In the pub, Amanda ordered a cafe latte and studied the room. It was still early, and there were only a few people in the bar. Two tourists in one corner. Two suited consultant types studying a laptop in another and a man at the bar sipping a pint of bitter.

It was five minutes to the due time, and she saw who she expected to be her contact walk in.

The man walked to the bar and ordered a coffee. He nodded towards Amanda, "let's get a seat," he said.

He acted as if he already knew Amanda, although she still didn't know exactly who she was meeting,

"I'm the person who received your request. My name is Spencer Brown." He shook hands with Amanda.

"Hello and I'm Amanda," she replied.

"So, what do you think you have?" asked Spencer.

"We have a strong lead from Colonel Manners," said Amanda, "He thinks he knows what they are looking for."

Amanda summarised the main facts to Spencer.

They both sipped quietly on their coffees. Amanda kept the explanations correct but sparse. The main point was to explain that Chuck had some further information which could be useful. But in return, the JTTF would have to give a little information too.

"Do you have your passport with you?" asked Spencer.

"Er, yes," said Amanda. She knew that to get in and out of some embassies she needed to carry her passport and security passes.

"Okay," said Spencer, "I suggest we take a short walk onto American soil."

He gestured towards the direction of the door. They would be going to the Embassy buildings situated in Nine Elms, just along the river from the pub.

"Okay, let's go," said Amanda, "You know I will need to be back to make a call to Manners in a few hours."

"That's fine," said Spencer, "we'll make sure you are back in time."

 They strolled the ten minutes back to the Embassy and on this occasion, Amanda could use a fast path route to gain access, sped on her way by Spencer's passes and authority.

"We'll be going to an underground part of the building," said Spencer, "I will need to ask you to leave phones and so forth behind in a secure locker."

Amanda knew the drill, which was very similar to the one at SI6. She wondered if they used the same contractors, although the US version of everything looked somehow more American.

They were soon in a secure area. "You have to be escorted here at all times," said Spencer, "I'll introduce you to someone else in a minute who will be your host for the time you are here."

They entered a room which was a mess of coffee cups and scraps of papers. Various laptops were switched on and a big screen at the end of the room said simply 'Thistle'.

"Okay everyone," said Spencer, "This is Amanda from our friends at SI6, she can help us locate Colonel Manners, one of The Six. The team we are trying to locate. I've brought her here for a cross briefing on what we know.

Another person in the room stood. It was a heavily tanned Colonel with the American Army, in a dress Uniform.

"I'll take it from here," said the Colonel. My name is Edgar Foster, I'm your local liaison point for this program which is being run from Washington."

"We think there's a significant threat to US Domestic security in play. That's why we have been watching the people we are referring to as 'The Six'. We think someone in this group has devised a weapon capable of creating extreme damage to the fabric of the US. Not by use as a massive weapon of mass destruction like a nuclear bomb or a chemical attack, but rather by structured precision hits on selected targets."

"That's what we think has happened with the Senator and the Refinery, but we have several other threats in current play.

These have all been notified to us before they happened, but unfortunately, they don't give a sequence or anything to help us take full countermeasures.

"When the first block came in, we didn't know whether to believe them. We have many spurious warnings, but with these, after the senator and the refinery, we knew that they were quoting the same code words . That's why we stopped the energy conference actually, we realised that it could be an obvious next target.

"The first few were all in Texas?" asked Amanda, "is that the same for the rest? In the current list there's a couple more within a 100-mile radius, but after that they start to become further afield."

"We'll tell you that in a moment," answered Colonel Foster.

"You said there was a code, does that mean there's other information too?" asked Amanda.

"Initially there wasn't anything else to go on," said the Colonel, "To be honest, initially we thought everything we had heard was a hoax. Students or something similar. The reason was that there were so many targets nominated all at once. We now find that the targets selected were not the first two on the list but randomly selected from the longer list."

"So that after they blew up the Senator, I assume you treated the rest of the list seriously?" asked Amanda.

"We had discovered the list again before the second event took place at the refinery but there wasn't time to move on all the different locations."

"At the moment we have another six targets within the United States. There are another six listed in other parts of the world."

"Why haven't you made a formal announcement about this on television, or the media? asked Amanda.

"For predictable reasons," said Colonel Foster, "We don't want the effect of the terrorist targeting to create the fear that they are hoping for."

"Is this being done in the name of something or for ideological reasons?" asked Amanda, "or is it connected with a demand?"

Amanda knew that the information she had received from Chuck and the others was that this was linked in some way to energy trading.

"We link this threat to something related to a deal with the Chinese", said Foster, "I haven't details of that here. The problem I see is that if we concede this based upon the threats, there's no reason the people doing this won't then ask for something else. We have to stop them at source, so it ends this whole thing."

"Our best lead on this is The Six. We think one of them is behind the terrorist threat and that they are trying to extend its effectiveness."

"When we looked at the two initial explosion sites both of them seem to use hot fix missiles. These are stand-alone missiles that can be targeted usually by laser beam. Based on what we have heard, it is possible that someone has changed the guidance systems for these missiles."

"If we are right, then these missiles have a fairly short range. They used on a battlefield and fired from a truck or similar. They are the weapons used by mercenary soldiers in places like Afghanistan."

"I don't think they have the sophistication to launch the attacks being described in the rest of the list."

"Can you tell me the other targets?" asked Amanda.

"I'm afraid it is highly classified," said the colonel, "I have not been told; I can only assume it is at the level that would affect national security."

"This smacks of an act of war," said Amanda, "For example is this the Chinese declaring war on the United States?"

"I think you are understanding why we are treating this so carefully," said the Foster. "That is also why we have two special units providing coverage of the sites of the initial explosions. We wanted to make them look like accidents so we could spin the news whilst we try to work out what is going on."

Amanda nodded. She could see that the suppositions from Chuck, Jennifer, and the rest of the team on the ground had been fairly close to what was happening. They just hadn't worked out the scale of what was going on."

Amanda spoke to the Colonel," You can't expect to keep hiding this for much longer. I'm amazed that the press is not already picking up on this."

"We have given the press a good story about the Senator, which doesn't impact what's been happening with the security aspects of this. It also makes the Senator look very good and I think at the moment everyone is focusing on that aspect."

"With the explosion at the refinery it's much more about the environment and pollution than those kinds of things we kept the story away from the true source of the explosion."

"But if one more of these things were to happen, then surely the media would piece it together?" said Amanda.

"What about the Chinese angle," asked Amanda, "Can't you bring that out into the open? I'm afraid that the politicians are all over that one," said the Foster, "At the moment there is a risk of economic downturn based upon the increasing power of the Chinese. What we're trying to do is avoid a situation where Chinese market entrants took over the American economy."

"I think it aims this terrorism at trying to chip the balance of power towards more Chinese takeovers. That would severely interfere with what we think of as the Western world and Western economies."

"Okay," said Amanda, "I appreciate your frankness on all of this. What I'd like to suggest is that we arrange another meeting which includes Colonel Manners, Jennifer and the rest of the team still based over in the USA."

I prefer that we do this at SI6 though and I'd like to reciprocate your kind offer to bring me here and instead that I would ask for you to bring maybe two people along with yourself, Colonel and Spencer. I should have a way to make a direct link to Colonel Manners and can also have one of his UK team here in my offices at SI6."

The Circle

Colonel Foster seemed impressed that Amanda had access to Manners and his team and even had one of them in SI6.

The colonel nodded , "Yes all right then, we will make the arrangements. What time do we need to be at Vauxhall Bridge?"

946

You can't touch this

"When you reach the end of what you should know,
you will be at the beginning of what you should sense."

–Kahlil Gibran

Trap

Spencer looked at the map.

"I think the most likely area for any kind of attack would be from the East," he said, "It's past the outskirts of Plano and turns back into deserts and mountainous areas. Can we think of some logic why we could explain Capaldi in this area."

"Yes, I think he needs to be visiting somebody to the west of Plano, may be across into Arkansas." said Spencer, "That would mean somewhere like Little Rock. I know it's amusing," said Spencer. "But if we pick Little Rock, then there's a direct route that runs from planar across to the east and then up into Arkansas state."

"Second, we find a location or a potential meeting."
Spencer studied the map, "There is an interesting place called Sulphur Springs on the way. The main advantage is that it has a range of motels on the main route."

Chuck had a look at the map that Spencer had pulled up, "Yes, this looks a good area. Now we need to track down Tony Capaldi and get him over to this part of Texas. We can be in Sulphur Springs in about three hours"

"Right now we do not know where Mike is, nor do we have any idea who is running him, "said Chuck.

"Look," said Colonel Foster, "The Chinese company in the trading arrangement is called EnergyChina. There are two possibilities; one would be that it is EnergyChina and another is that it would be a major shareholder. We have already run some investigations of this back in Langley.

Chuck asked, "Is there any way we can get more insight into what EnergyChina have been doing?"

"The US government has been watching energy China for some time. They have an interesting track record in their country. Because of their tight links with the militia and politicians and the freedom with which it pays backhanders, EnergyChina are doing what they like. The problem we've always seen with this company and others in China is their ability to upset the global economy for energy pricing."

"From the United States we've had a strong relationship with some middle eastern countries and have been able to keep a balance of pricing and futures for energy. Now that China has created such a new and powerful industrial drag on fuel reserves, there is a new force in play. Because China also has its own natural reserves and an endless ability to dig new pipelines and create new pieces of industrial infrastructure, it means that there is every chance that energy prices may get manipulated."

"We should also recognise that EnergyChina has seen a massive increase in its share price because of the injection of funding from the ChinaFin. ChinaFin is not a state-run organisation but has a major shareholding via Cheung Chau.

"I think we are on to something," said Chuck. "In some form or other, EnergyChina and ChinaFin are financing the plot that is running here in Texas."

Conference Call

The team had assembled back in Chuck's room for the call the next day. Clare had her iPhone set up, plugged in and ready to go. They sat around the table, waiting to hear any further news from Amanda.

 At the appointed hour Clare's phone rang, and she picked up.

 "Hello Clare, it's Amanda again. Things have moved on here since we spoke last. We are still in our SI6 headquarters and Jake is with us. There are some other people here this time. They are from the US government and our people based in London."

 "Please, could you introduce yourselves," asked Jennifer.

 Amanda asked the Colonel to introduce himself and his colleagues.

"Okay," said Chuck, "Before I say anything further, what else can you tell us about what is happening?"

The Colonel explained the same story that he had already described to Amanda. When he got to the part about there being several other targets, Chuck was very interested.

"Do we know where those other targets are?" asked Chuck. "Are there any further targets close to the ones we have already seen?"

Colonel Foster said, "I am under instructions that this is classified information."

"That may be so," said Chuck, "But at the moment we are the people closest to solving this and I need to know whether there are any targets in this vicinity?"

"Why is that?" asked the Colonel, "I think it is becoming evident that at the moment the person conducting these outrages is still using short-range missiles. I think the reason he has called upon all of us that were in the original team is to find out from one of us what happened when we use the drones with the much longer ranges."

"This is my new information," said Chuck, "We were testing two kinds of drone: The very large ones - The Predators which have massive wing spans and are not something you could carry in hand luggage. But Barbara Somerville and Tony Capaldi were also testing the smaller drones the kind that I used for naval reconnaissance. They are about the size of a large toy plane with a 4-foot wingspan. They don't need long runways to take off; we can launch them using special catapult launchers.

"That's what Mike was trying to find out from me when we were in the desert. Did I know where the catapult launches took place? I didn't but I think Somerville and Capaldi both knew about this. My guess is that Mike has called them to Scottsdale and is trying to link up with them and get the information about the catapult launchers. Then he could take a small van with a launcher and several of those UAVs and he would be a mobile arsenal.

"But where would he get the armaments?" said Amanda, "The UAVs are passive devices."

"That's the point," said Chuck, " I don't know, but I think Barbara Somerville or Tony Capaldi will know because of the work we all did. I think the equipment was stored somewhere in the desert, close to the Kirtland base. However, the area is so large, if you don't know where to look, you won't be able to find the equipment."

 "So, here's my scenario," said Chuck, "If there's another target close to the current ones I think they will try to take a shot at it with one of their rockets. That keeps the pressure on whilst they figure out how to get the UAVs and the launchers from wherever they are being held."

"In terms of threat it would work because it will become a point where the US government won't be able to contain the number of stories any longer. I think if there are three separate incidents within a single US state let alone anything further afield then the free press will make noises of its own about what is going on."

Amanda replied, "I think you are right, Colonel Manners. It is an ultimate form of leverage using a tiny unit to create such havoc. Of course, if they get access the homing control system and the real UAVs then it escalates this to another whole level."

Chuck replied, " Yes, that's why I need to know whether there are any other sites in the general area that could be targeted."

There was a long pause.

Bigsy and the others could hear murmuring from the London office. "I should get agreement to release the classified information," said Colonel Foster. "But I will tell you one thing. One of the other targets is, frankly, a lower priority target than the major ones on their list. It is the downtown area of Plano, around the Dart terminal."

"What's Dart?" asked Clare,

"That's like the main transit hub," said Jennifer. It's right in the middle of downtown Plano.

"I can see some logic to this," said Chuck, "If I only had access to rockets then something like that would be an interesting target. The reason is simple. I can choose an arc from that location where I fire upon the target. I only need to be 20 or 30 miles away, drive close enough, target and wham, preferably from an area that is isolated. Do you see what I mean?

"Okay," asked Bigsy," And the difference between rockets and missiles?"

Jennifer answered, "rockets just fire, missiles can be guided," "Ahhh," said Bigsy, "That makes sense."

"If I want disrupt everything, but I don't have the UAVs, I can simulate their effect within a small area, so long as I have some rockets."

If I am still trying to get access to the UAVs then firing a short-range rocket from a secluded site with very accurate targeting can keep the pressure on the US government until I can get the real weaponry from wherever it's currently stored."

"I concur," said Colonel Foster, "The question is whether we can work out where this would be fired from."

Spencer was sitting with the team in Chuck's room and was already looking on his computer. "There's a couple of areas that would fit that description," he said, "They are both some way out from Plano."

Chuck glanced at the map that Spencer had produced. "It's still problematic," he said, "This is too big an area."

"Or it's too big an area if we can't think of a way to attract the terrorists. I think we need to come up with a plan to make it easy for them to decide where they should take their missile."

"And how can we do that?" asked Clare.

"I think we need to use our other members of the team as incentive," said Chuck, "I still don't know whether we have found Tony Capaldi. If we can find him we could use him to help limit the area that Mike or whoever it is is operating within. We use Capaldi to attract Mike to a particular zone. And once we have him pinned down then we stand a better chance to stop him."

Jennifer asked Chuck, " It sounds good in theory but surely he is as professional as you are. Won't he work out you are trying to do something like this. He'll know it is a trap?"

"Not if we can get Capaldi directly involved in this process. At the moment Capaldi won't know that Mike has officially crashed his car into a river. We need to get Capaldi to call Mike direct, but ideally to have a cover story about why he is not in Scottsdale.

"You know we tracked down Capaldi," said Spencer. "He flew from Columbus to Phoenix, via Chicago."

"He arrived in Phoenix two days ago."

"I expect he has done the same as me," said Chuck, " and headed for that hotel in Scottsdale. Will he be there under his own name asked Spencer or will he have something else?"

"The difference between him and me seems to be that he's happy to use his real identity," said Chuck, "He was showing up as a university tutor in Columbus."

"Great," said Spencer, "That will make it much easier to find him."

Spencer got the name of the hotel from Chuck and was quickly onto the case to find the information.

"Right," said Chuck, "I think we have the basis of the plan. If we can contact Capaldi, we can ask him to meet Mike in a certain part of Texas. We should work out the areas from which he is most able to have a range on Plano and try in effect to force Mike's hand with where he is more likely to launch his attack on Plano.

"I think that means we need to make sure it is further out from Plano so that it stretches the line between Mike and Plano."

"I've worked out a plan," said Spencer.

"Capaldi likes golf. There's about a dozen courses to the north of the Dallas Fort Worth area, in a place called Fresno. It is less than 30 miles from Plano, has plenty of hotels and a secluded wildlife area. I'll just check the hotels and book Capaldi into one of the expensive ones around there. It looks as if the Omni Frisco Hotel is a good one. It's fancy, close to the golf, close to the Dallas Cowboys, you get my drift."

"It's also got controllable exits, if things cut up rough," said Chuck, looking at the hotel's location on the map.

"Yes, and if I wanted to fire a rocket, I could go over to the LLELA Nature Preserve, which is a few minutes away from the hotel. Line of sight to Plano or Fort Worth from there." added Chuck.

"Do you think Mike works alone?" said Bigsy,

Chuck replied, "No, he had the extra heavies that chased us. He will have some further help, but it is interesting how a tiny unit can create such a large amount of devastation."

"Guess that's what we were trained for," said Chuck.

"So if we can pin down Mike's unit, it would remove his leverage from the discussion about energy futures."

"We still need to find out who is driving the whole plan," said Jennifer.

"I agree," said Amanda from the speakerphone, "We will still need more help from you Colonel Foster,"

"This puts me in a difficult situation," said Colonel Foster, "I should communicate most of this back to my team in Langley."

"The problem is that Mike gets information from somewhere," said Jennifer,   "There seems to be a leak and also there seem to be people trying to stop us from tracking this down," said Jennifer.

"That's a big problem for me also," said Colonel Foster, "I think most of you seem to know one another but I'm afraid I have to continue to treat most of this with suspicion. For example, Colonel Manners you have been with most of The Six and know all of them. As we now think one of them is the suspect in all of this, it keeps you as someone under suspicion."

"I think we only have one shot at this," said Chuck, "At the moment we know that Capaldi has been called by Mike. We also know that Mike is likely to find out information from Capaldi about these launchers and possibly these UAVs. I'm guessing there is a mothballed stash of them somewhere in Kirtland. Right now, it is needle in a haystack, but with the right information, they could be gone in a few minutes.

Chuck said, "We can create a trap. If we don't do it then Mike will be through our fingers with access to a more extensive form of firepower."

Tony Capaldi

Spencer had tracked down another one of the invited guests. Tony Capaldi. Sure enough, he was in the Scottsdale hotel and staying under his own name.

"Okay, we need to contact Tony direct now," said Chuck, "I should do it, he will know who I am, and we can easily talk together about old times."

Bigsy commented, "You know, you may need to figure out whether he is working with Mike."

"I agree," said Chuck, "I shall need to listen out for any signs."

Chuck used the hotel telephone to call the number for Tony's hotel room. He dialled the switchboard number at the hotel, and he asked for Tony Capaldi. There was a few moments pause and then a ring tone.

"Hello," said a voice.

The Circle

"Tony?" Asked Chuck

"Yes, this is Tony, who is it?" asked the voice.

"Tony, it will surprise you to hear that this is Chuck Manners," said Chuck, "I think they called me just like you to visit Scottsdale."

"My God, Chuck Manners! It's been a long time. I assume you are still in scrapes? I've taken a more business-oriented route nowadays. To be honest, I thought it was you that was making the calls and sending the invitations. I'm told that Mike and Barbara will also be here. I'm guessing it wasn't you making the invitations, then."

"No, Tony, I think it's something to do with the work we did previously.

Tony continued, "I'm thinking it was Mike who called. He called me earlier and said that he would be in town in a couple of days. I guess you got the same message as me that this was important and that we need to be at all costs."

"Yes," said Chuck, "but Tony, I need you to do something for me now."

"Buddy, what is it?" asked Tony.

"There is something not right about all of this," said Chuck, "and I think you can help us to understand it. Did you know that Ben and Klaus have both been killed in the last two weeks?

"Wow. I'm shocked. I had no idea," said Tony, "to be honest I'm out of the community nowadays."

"Right," said Chuck, "But this is very important. We think it somehow involves Mike. He invited me to the same meeting, and I was in Scottsdale two days ago. I got chased by some bad guys and I'm lucky to still be alive."

"We think Mike is trying to get some information that only a couple of us will know. It's relates to the project, and it's the stuff that I think you and Barbara were working on. We shouldn't really talk about it by phone.

"Let's just say it is connected with the little things in the desert… "

"Okay," said Tony, "I understand - yes that was me that used to work with Barbara. But all of that was a long time ago."

"Yes," said Chuck, "However, we think Mike has gone renegade and is now working for another power. We think he is trying to find out about these small things and maybe where some of them are kept."

"I understand," said Tony, "And to be honest I'm not sure that I want to be mixed up in any of this. I came along because someone used the code. You know the emergency protocol."

"That's the same with me," said Chuck, "I had actually gone invisible before this and broke cover to be involved."

"So where is Mike now?" asked Tony.

"We think he's in Texas?" said Chuck, "actually we want you to come over here to help us track him down. We think he needs to be removed from play now."

"Removed from play… sounds a bit drastic… Are you working this alone?" asked Tony.

"No," said Chuck," and this whole thing has, let's say, escalated. "

 "Chuck, what if I just turned around and went back to Ohio?"

"I think you could do that," said Chuck, "but I'd be fearful that Mike or someone he's working with will be after you. I think you probably hold the key to this. To what it is that Mike wants."

" I thought the whole point with that program was that they deemed it redundant," said Tony.

 "Yes, it is to the military but not to someone involved in terrorism."

"Okay," said Tony, "I guess that Mike is doing this for money? And are you sure it's Mike and not somebody else?"

  "If I am honest, we are still working on theories for most of this," said Chuck.

 "Look, Tony, do you think you could get over here to us to meet us and we can give you more information? I think you can help us track down what is happening with Mike."

 "Where are you?" said Tony.

"We are close to Dallas," said Chuck, "in a fancy hotel, actually. Do you think you could get a flight across to us from Phoenix first thing tomorrow?"

 "Sure," said Tony. "I will check with the airport and try to be out on the first flight.

AVGAS 110LL (blue)

The next morning Chuck was awake early. He had packed all his belongings back into the camouflage bag and was ready to leave the hotel. He had instructed the others to be ready early and had said 7 o'clock was their departure time.

It was currently around 630AM in the morning and he was idly watching the television and looking out of the window of the hotel across towards the vista of the airport.

The daybreak news programme on the television switched to a story from a road in Arizona. There had been a major early morning crash. A truck carrying aviation fuel had crashed into a taxi and a fireball had ensued. The occupants of the taxi had been killed outright, although the truck driver was nowhere to be seen.

Chuck looked at the broadcast. It showed an aerial view of the tanker and large billowing clouds of smoke. There was still much traffic blocking both directions around the crash scene. Chuck was immediately suspicious of the coincidence of this situation. Also, that the avgas truck had so readily caught fire. Normally there would be sufficient emergency safeguards to prevent this from happening. Although this hadn't used any rockets it looked suspiciously like another incident created by Mike.

Chuck called Clare on the hotel phone. "Has Tony checked in by text as we agreed," he asked, "There's nothing," said Clare, " One message saying he left the hotel at about 05:30 this morning but nothing from the airport."

"Check out the news," said Chuck," Channel 9."

"I've already seen it," said Clare, "I thought momentarily it could be connected but decided it would be too much of a coincidence."

"I don't think so," said Chuck, "These many accidents following us around are almost certainly connected. Colonel Foster referred to The Six. There's Mike, me and Barbara left now."

All together now

Chuck move downstairs to the lobby of the hotel Clare and Bigsy were already waiting. Jennifer and Spencer arrived a few minutes later.

"Did everyone see that news broadcast?" asked Chuck, Spencer nodded but Jennifer shook her head.

"I didn't have the television on this morning at all," she said.

"There's been a massive road traffic accident in the Phoenix area," said Spencer, "A tanker carrying Avgas crashed into a taxi. There was a fireball and the taxi occupants were killed."

"No," said Jennifer, "are you saying you think it's Tony."

"We don't know," said Chuck, "he has left the hotel by now. Clare has a text from him, but he should have texted us again when he reached the airport - so far nothing."

"Are you saying you think they have killed him?" asked Jennifer., "If so then he will have also taken his knowledge about where those launchers and UAVs were stored with him?"

"If Mike has got access to the launchers then it could work to our advantage," said Clare, "I think I have an idea."

She turned to chat with Jennifer, "If my plan works, we will need more help from those guys in the UK."

Chuck nodded. "I know, that's what I thought, it makes me think Mike found out the information from Tony or that he has got the information by some other means. I can't imagine that he would lose his last link to the information about the UAVs and the launchers."

International call

Clare's phone rang.

"It's an international call," she said, "I'd better take it."

"Hello, this is Amanda Miller,"

"Amanda, I thought we'd only use this phone in an emergency?"

"That's right," said Amanda, "We have one right now."

Clare waved to the others and quickly said, "It's Amanda Miller and she says it's an emergency!"

Amanda heard Clare and then continued, "Since our last call, we have alerted our own systems and, via GCHQ, they have passed a wiretap requirement along to the NSA - that's the American Security services."

"Wiretap? of whom?" asked Clare.

"Of Mike Lee," answered Amanda, "We had to fib a little and say we thought he was smuggling drugs,"

Clare repeated, "They've been wiretapping Mike."

Amanda continued, "It turns out he called someone from MOFCOM - That's the Chinese Ministry of Trade and Commerce. He told them he thought someone was on to him and gave Chuck's name and last known location - which was the hotel in Scottsdale. I can only think the worst."

Clare replied, "That's all we need, I'll warn Chuck."

"Yes," said Amanda, "I thought Chuck might be even more in danger now, which is why I called."

Clare said, "Amanda, thank you, and now this phone line has been used, I may just keep you up-to-date on any further developments."

"Okay," said Amanda, "but be careful - signing off," The line chirruped, and Clare realised that Amanda had probably called her securely.

"Chuck, Bad news, I'm afraid, Mike has told the Chinese about you. Amanda thinks they may send out a search party for you."

"You should go to ground," said Jennifer, "Would you like me to help you with somewhere on the base?"

Chuck shook his head, "Normally I'd shrug off this kind of thing, but Mike is good. Look at his hit rate. He's knocked out nearly the entire team and improvised local facilities to make them look more like accidents. Jennifer, thank you, but No, I'll be better off alone. It will keep the nasties away from all of you, too. I will lose my cell phone and get a different car. I'll leave Clare with some of my carry-money too, it's in a separate small go-bag. This time I won't disappear long-term, just until we've seen the back of Mike. I'll text Clare with my revised cell phone number."

Chuck looked quickly around the circle of them all. "It's been a pleasure," he said.

They looked back at him and Clare stepped forward to give him a hug.

"Right, time to hit it," he said as he strode towards the air terminal.

EnergyChina

Bigsy read from his laptop,

"EnergyChina is best described as a giant corporation of China, a big oil company with an aggressive corporate swagger, tight political and military connections and a couldn't-care-less attitude about the views of others." Clare nodded, "A monster Corp!"

Bigsy continued, "Although EnergyChina is the most profitable company in Asia, this success may result from corporate management, but can also be attributed to the near duopoly on the wholesale and retail business of oil products it shares with EnergyChina in China."

Clare commented, "It's amazing that these mega corporations exist, yet we have hardly even heard of them!" Bigsy continued, "Or, in my case never heard of them...

Because of the EnergyChina link to Sudan through the parent company China Petroleum Products, several institutional investors such as Harvard and Yale decided, in 2008, to divest from EnergyChina. Sudan divestment efforts have continued to be concentrated on EnergyChina since then.

Fidelity Investments, after pressure from activist groups, also announced in a filing in the US, because it had sold 87 per cent of its American Depositary Receipts in EnergyChina in the first quarter of 2009."

"Wow, so some of the western smart-money has already pulled out," said Clare.

Bigsy read from his screen again,

"Another major controversial issue is EnergyChina's development in gas reserves in Tarim Basins, Xinjiang. It is now constructing a pipeline across Tibet to Gansu province in China, eventually leading to Shanghai.

"Some argue such a project might pose a threat to the environment, because the construction of the pipeline might affect wildlife in the regions where it runs. Also, the exiled Tibetan government argued that such a project is part of China's strategy to merge political control of the Western Region in China, including Tibet. However, no known environmental or social impact assessments have been conducted, as the environmental record of Tarim Basins is very poor."

Clare looked at Bigsy, "Wow, so they are a mega corporation, shunned by western smart money and building new politically sensitive pipelines, oblivious to eco-concerns. Big business, aye?"

Bigsy smiled back, "The trade-offs of modern civilisation?"

Ed Adams

Pressing the wrong buttons

A blackout is when you force all lights to go out, creating a completely black look.
There are multiple ways to achieve a blackout.
The two most common are via a cue and a Grandmaster/Blackout fader.

ETC High End Systems

Bunker

Barbara Somerville was surprised to receive instructions to go from the hotel in Scottsdale, to a smaller one in Gallup, on the route to Albuquerque. She had followed the instructions, drawn on by the code included with the messages. It was a special code only known to the members of Project Esther.

The Gallup hotel wasn't as pleasant as the ritzy one in Scottsdale.

There was a knock on her door; she looked through the viewer.

"Mike," she said, "Are we ready to go?"

"We are the only two left now," said Mike, "And the way I have set things up Colonel Chuck Manners is the one that will appear as prime suspect."

They walked towards the blue F150 pickup truck that Mike had hired. He started it up and they moved off to join the traffic on the I-40.

"I'm already dead officially," said Mike. "And you and I are the only people from Project Esther who know about the location of the UAVs."

"Yes," said Barbara, "And we can only be within a few miles of the storage bunker now."

"It's amazing how much stuff they store under the desert in this area," said Mike.

"I know," said Barbara, "although most of it is off-limits because it's classified as military ground."

"Or we have given it to the Navajo nation," added Mike.

They were still outside the perimeter fencing but could now see a range of corrugated huts and several bulges in the desert floor.

"There we are," said Barbara. "Those are the storage facilities. They don't look very well-fortified, but it's almost impossible to get from here to those bunkers."

"Normally I'd agree with you," said Mike, "But it's different if you've got one of these." He pointed to the skyline. They could see a black dot in the distance. It was moving rapidly towards them.

Barbara recognised the outline of an Apache attack helicopter. It approached their car close hugging the ground. It swung past the fence and turned ponderously towards the bunkers. There was a hiss and Barbara saw a small rocket fired into the bunker, which burst open in a hail of metal fragments and dust.

There was a huge amount of noise and dust as the helicopter settled down onto the ground and four men entirely in black ran forward towards the bunker.

Within a minute they were loading large square boxes into the helicopter and within three minutes returning to the helicopter which was ready to lift off again.

In the distance Barbara could see a dust trail as several armoured vehicles were moving towards the scene.

"Thank you for helping with this," said Mike to Barbara, "your part in this won't go unrecognised." He turned towards her, and there was a single shot. Barbara fell backward.

Mike carefully placed something on the floor next to Barbara's body.

Mike waved towards the helicopter which was circling overhead. A single man on a zip wire descended and clipped Mike onto a harness. The two of them swung away from the fence and as the helicopter started its ascent it winched them back on board.

"How many did we get?" asked Mike," as he looked to the people in the helicopter.

"A dozen," said the man who had just hauled him in on the winch. "Twelve NA-12 systems. Twelve Nathans."

"Hot-digitty-dog, that's more than enough," said Mike.

DEFCON

The news of the attack on the Kirtland airfield reached Jennifer quickly. There was a security blanket placed over what happened, but because it had taken place at Jennifer's own base, she was able to get inside information from Lucas, initially via Spencer.

Lucas had called Spencer and told him what had happened.

"It looks as if someone has broken into one of the storage bunkers at the back of Kirtland, out in the desert. It was a secured area but was unused nowadays. They used a helicopter to get in and took some containers."

"There was a truck outside the fence which I think was calling the helicopter in. Another one of the old team, The Six, was found in the truck but also there was a payphone which appears to belong to Chuck Manners. We only know this because the phone that the dead woman had included a number for Chuck which rang the phone in the car. The forensics guys have fast tracked the fingerprints on that phone, and they match with Chuck."

Jennifer had revealed this information to Bigsy and Clare.

"We still don't believe that Chuck is involved in this in any way other than as someone who is being hunted and framed," said Clare, "I think all this is being used to divert attention from the people who are really responsible."

"Will the security blanket continue on what is effectively the third attack?" asked Bigsy.

"Yes, it is," said Jennifer, "this has raised the whole DEFCON alert status of the US."

"I've heard of DEFCON" said Clare," but I don't really understand the different levels."

"We are normally functioning at DEFCON 5," said Jennifer, "This sequence of events has taken us all the way to DEFCON 3. That's the one where the Air Force has to be ready to mobilise in 15 minutes. You can see that the terrorists kept the helicopter attack very brief. By the time any land forces could reach the bunker they were long gone."

"With a faster mobilisation we stand a much better chance to intercept whatever's happening."

"Will those planes be able to stop the missiles now in the hands of the terrorists?" asked Bigsy.

"It kind of depends," said Jennifer. "If that Colonel Foster implies that they have a list of the planned targets then that would give military the best chance to deploy countermeasures."

"Isn't it kind of weird that they would raise the DEFCON level but still keep a secure blanket over what has been happening?" Asked Bigsy.

"Less unusual than you might think," replied Jennifer, "We sometimes get heightened security at the Air Force Base. Usually it only goes to DEFCON 4. When that happens, we are usually expecting it to be part of an exercise. However, everyone always takes it seriously."

"I guess a lot more of the senior people know what is happening, now," said Clare, "They can't keep a lid on this indefinitely."

"I think with the violence of the attacks now they will try to end this with extreme prejudice," said Jennifer.

"That puts Chuck in a very dangerous position too," said Jennifer, "As Mike has managed to make it look as if Chuck is involved then he will also be on the hit list."

Amber Alert

The DEFCON alert had also rippled through to London and Colonel Foster and the rest of his team were aware that things were escalating.

Jennifer had asked Clare to arrange for a follow-up call with the team in London. "We need to know those alternative targets now," asked Jennifer.

Colonel Foster paused to consider. "Amanda, this is the second visit I have made to your building. We are operating outside of protocol. Now that we are at US DEFCON 3, we should not really be giving you this kind of information."

"But I suppose you could have provided it at DEFCON 5?" asked Amanda.

"Let me just go to check that with the control room." said Foster, "it will only take me, say, five minutes," Foster pointedly looked towards his desk before exiting the room.

"Okay, I think that was a hint," said Amanda, "Lets copy that list," she flipped the sheet around on his desk and snapped a copy into her second cell phone.

Bigsy explained to Amanda," Now that they have taken those guidance systems and missiles, they are fully equipped to target any of those locations on Foster's list"

"I understand from Chuck that the basis of the targeting was to know the address of a particular transponder unit and use that to dial into the missile guidance system."

"My guess is that they will now take the captured equipment to somewhere remote and set up a base from which they can launch their next attack. We must move fast. I reckon they will go for a shorter distance target the first time to gain confidence in their approach."

"Yes, maybe Plano would be the next target, unless they have taken their helicopter on a very long flight."

"I think that's unlikely, said Jennifer, "the further they fly in the helicopter the more likely they are to be picked up by US defence radar."

"Exactly," said Bigsy, "So they probably drop somewhere in one of the desert areas in the general Albuquerque and Phoenix area."

"That's a large area anyway," said Jennifer, "It is," said Clare, "but there's also quite a lot of movement around some of those parts what with all the tourists and similar access."

The Circle

"It is also the access that the Native Americans have two large tracts of this land. It's the Navajo Nation. Quite a lot of it is still formally Indian Reservation territory. It's very unlikely that if they landed in one of those areas that they will go undetected for too long."

"This is useful, said Clare, "because it narrows down the areas."

"When we left Tom, he gave us his contact number. We've already called him once. I thought it was funny. Here was a native American Navajo, in the middle of the desert giving us his sat. phone number.

"Now is the second time that it becomes useful," said Bigsy. "I think it can help us in two ways. We can ask Tom about the helicopter, but also check whether he knows the whereabouts of Chuck.

Tom

Clare made the call to Tom.

"Hello," said Tom.

"Hello," said Clare, "It's Clare, who you met with your friend Chuck Manners a few days ago."

"But Clare, you are my friend now, also," said Tom, "I have been expecting your group to call."

"Tom, we have some difficult things happening here and our good friend Chuck is again in danger because of some of it."

"I know more about this than you think. Our friend has been with me since last night. He is safe until we can work out what to do."

"There was a helicopter attack in the desert yesterday," said Clare.

The Circle

"They have taken some very dangerous weapons from a hidden bunker near Kirtland. We think they have taken the helicopter into a base somewhere in the desert. It is likely to be somewhere isolated but that will have road access. I hoped that you and your friends can help us find where they would make their base."

"The desert talks to us," said Tom, "If someone is disrupting it, we, the Navajo, will know."

 "We have some other people looking into this," said Clare. "They are trying to do something clever with electronic surveillance to see whether they can find the base."

 "Maybe this will be an example where we all work together to find them," said Tom, "We can use this phone to communicate. If I go deep into the desert, I will plan for someone else to call you. They will say they are a friend of Tom and want to speak to you."

"Tom, we have noticed that Red's prophecy about the animal skills has been coming true as we have been on this quest," said Clare.

 "And I think there will be still one more to play out before the end of this," said Tom.

 Clare looked towards Jennifer and Bigsy. "I think we have the right people involved now. If anyone can find that place in the desert it will be Tom and his people."

Ed Adams

Monumental

Chuck could see Tom coming towards him. He had been staying in a small miner's shack deep in the desert to the south of the area known as Monument Valley.

Chuck knew the landscape from other visits, but still couldn't help but be blown away by it as one of the most majestic points on earth. This valley monuments were sandstone masterpieces towering at heights of 400 to 1,000 feet, framed by scenic clouds casting shadows that roamed the desert floor. Famous for many westerns, Chuck was rather sensitive to the thought he could be in a shoot-out from within it.

Instead, he marvelled at the angle of the sun accenting the graceful formations and providing spellbinding scenery. The landscape overwhelmed him, not just by its beauty but also by its size. Miles of mesas and buttes, shrubs and trees, and windblown sand surrounded the fragile pinnacles of rock comprising the magnificent colours of the valley.

The Circle

Chuck also realised it was like being on the inside of a natural fortress. The Navajo charged tourists admission and insisted that they drove on a set route around the spectacle.

The Navajo, and Chuck had an altogether freer licence. Tom had approached the last part of the journey on horseback. He had also used a horse to get Chuck to the location the first time.

"The advantage of here is that it is inaccessible by road and hidden from air," Tom had explained, "You are now in a sacred area and have protection of the gods."

"You also have good water and a plentiful supply of tinned food," Tom pointed towards the miner's shack.

"This will keep you off of the radar until we can work out the next moves. A shrew can catch a cobra."

"I have already put out word of what we seek," said Tom, "There is no way that a noisy helicopter can be in these lands without us knowing its whereabouts. I expect I will hear within another hour."

"Meantime I think we should sit and enjoy this special place." He sat atop a boulder and looked at the scene. Chuck became aware too of the smallest movements.

Tom was true to his word, and within the hour his walkie talkie radio crackled. The news was good. They had located a base in between the rocks. There was a small camp with several men, a military helicopter, two trucks and activity which seemed to be building something.

"It's got to be them," said Chuck. Tom nodded, "I know the place they describe. We should go there to check - it is about 15 miles from here."

"We will also need to let Clare know," said Chuck.

Tom led outside to the two horses he had brought. The one he had ridden and another one. They climbed onto the horses and Tom led Chuck carefully towards the track where he had parked his Jeep.

"I will make the calls to Clare from here." he said, "and another one to my friends to tell where we think these people are based."

"He spent a few minutes talking first to his friends and describing the area. Then he called Clare and gave a more basic description of the area. It is hard to find if you do not know the desert," he said. "We will be there in about one hour. I can send you GPS co-ordinates when we get there."

He signed off and they started their bumpy drive towards the helicopter base.

A quicker scramble

Jennifer had heard the call to Clare, and they decided that they needed to inform the people in London. Jennifer also said, "We should be careful that we don't start a major search mission across the desert."

"If the people hiding are wired in with radar, they will spot that we are sending reconnaissance waves around the area and either go to ground or move out.

"At the moment, with some stealth we should be able to catch them.

"It is ironic that the type of weapons we are hunting would usually be used for this search," said Bigsy.

"Yes, well, the not so big secret about those devices is that they are also offensive and not just for surveillance. You'll have worked that out by now," said Jennifer.

"So it's best for us to wait until Chuck and Tom get close to the location then, said Clare.

"Yes," said Jennifer," then we will have a fix that we can use quickly. DEFCON 3 should help us scramble quickly."

Know a pistol shot's effective range

Desperado, why don't you come to your senses?
You been out ridin' fences for so long now
Oh, you're a hard one
I know that you got your reasons
These things that are pleasin' you
Can hurt you somehow

- Donald Hugh Henley, Glenn Lewis Frey

UAV

Chuck and Tom made their way towards the location in the Jeep. For the last part of the journey, they had to leave the vehicle behind and move to foot. They both carried a small backpack and trod softly as they approached a scene with lights and several voices.

They worked out that it wasn't the main team, but the perimeter guards for the area where the helicopter was stored.

Tom called in a reference using his radio walkie talkie. "This isn't exactly GPS," he said, "but my friends will convert it and call Clare."

At that moment there was a noise behind them. A small crack from a twig.

"We need to move," said Tom. He pointed to the side walls of the canyon they had entered. "We need to be a little higher to gain some advantage."

The Circle

A shot hissed through the rocks. Then a burr sound from an automatic pistol. "They are close," said Chuck, "should we stand our ground?"

"No," said Tom, "we need to get higher. And they are at least 60 yards away. Their shooting is so wide."

He led Chuck through a small gully by the edge of the canyon walls. It led upwards. They crossed a small bowl of rock some 100 yards higher than the valley floor. The other side, the gully continued.

There was another crack. A sniper was getting a range on them. Then a rattle sound from a handheld machine gun.

They are gaining on us, said Chuck.

"Just a little higher," said Tom.

"Look we both have weapons, we could finish them," said Chuck.

"Keep going," said Tom, "my way is more certain."

With that, he looked back, and then so did Chuck. The well-armed team following them were gaining ground and had just entered the small bowl thorough which Chuck and Tom had passed a minute earlier.

Then Chuck saw the surrounding rocks move. There were at least a dozen Native Americans camouflaged in the rocks. They pounced upon the men following. There was a blur of metal through the air. And silence.

The entire team of pursuers had been dispatched by the group of Navajo.

"I know," said Tom, "That was the old way. But it is sometime still necessary."

They looked back further. Their elevation meant that they could now see across to the rest of the camp.

It was a small area and contained the helicopter, two ruggedized Jeeps and in the centre was a small catapult launcher. The men were placing the UAV into the launch system.

Chuck looked at how small it seemed, compared with the Predators he has seen during the tests seven years ago. Miniaturised warfare, he thought. Deadly Toys.

The people in the base were hurriedly preparing the launch. They had heard the gunshots and probably knew they were being followed.

A few minutes later there was a loud bang as the catapult launcher fired the small missile into the air. It surprised Chuck at how fast it accelerated when it was free of the launcher. It also gained altitude quickly as it headed away from them towards the east.

Then there was another explosion. Another two just behind. Chuck was aware that a dark shadow had just passed over his head. He looked towards Tom and realised that both he and Tom were now laying on the ground. He could feel a heat blast.

Then another bang and the sound of jet engines. He realised that a plane or a couple of planes had borne down on the site and destroyed pretty much everything in the area. He realised that he was shaking and could hardly move. The shock waves from the explosion had winded him badly and maybe broken some bones.

He gingerly felt his body and decided that all the main parts were still there. He looked towards Tom who was similarly in a kind of post explosion shock. He realised his hearing was damaged from the shock waves. Below him he could see that the Navajo people surrounding the bowl of the recent massacre were all similarly winded.

Then he saw more shadows. Dark profiles of men with guns. Desert-camo. They had appeared from the sky.

There had been a two-pronged attack on the area. Both bombers and then Para troops. He assumed they would be seals or similarly expert people. He moved his hands to above his head and gestured for Tom to do the same.

They waited and in a couple of minutes had been scooped into nets, like some deep-sea fish catch.

DFW

They were back at Dallas airport, sitting around a table in the hotel across the way from the International terminal.

"I hadn't expected to be in America for so long," said Clare. "Me neither," said Bigsy.

"It's been a blast," said Chuck.

"Yes," said Jennifer, "Literally a blast."

"And I can honestly say it's the first time I've been scooped like a fish," said Chuck.

"Just be pleased it was fishing nets rather than harpoons," said Jennifer.

"Yea, you can tell when it's the Navy on manoeuvres," said Bigsy, alluding to Chuck's rescuers, "Navy, in the middle of the desert."

"Technically we were not operating on US soil, either," said Jennifer, "It was the Navajo Nation's patch where we carried out the operation."

 Well the DEVCON status is back to Five," said Jennifer, "and I don't think most of the general public even know that this has occurred."

 "The news bulletins about ChinaEnergy were pretty mysterious," said Clare, "Seeing the board overthrown within 24 hours of the desert mission was a very suspicious coincidence."
 I think you'll find Foster had something to do with that," said Jennifer, "And the subsequent disappearance of those three board members . What is it you Brits say? 'I couldn't possibly comment.'"

 "So, are you heading back to London now?" asked Jennifer.

"And Chuck, I guess you are about to disappear again?"

"That's right," he said, "Did I ever mention my dual nationality?"

 "No," said Jennifer," and please wait until I've caught my plane out of here before you start waving alternative passports around."

"Look guys," said Chuck, "I know I got you all - including Jennifer and Tom - mixed up in more than you expected, and I don't think any of you will be able to brag about preventing 'the end of the world as we know it.'"

"But hey, thank you all." He shook hands and slapped the backs of each of them. He reserved a small kiss to the cheek for Jennifer and Clare.

"And Chuck," grinned Clare, "what's the other expression - 'don't call us, we'll call you?'"

Free to go

"As for those suspicions about EnergyChina being behind some of this, well the core three members of the board all stood down the next day and have been replaced."

"The new board is, how shall I say, kindly disposed towards the West.

"I don't know anything about that," answered Amanda, "Although I think maybe Colonel Foster would have some knowledge of what happened. He'll deny it; some baloney about being based here in the UK and too far away from the action."

"And there's something else. It's a small package that arrived here, addressed to you. It was couriered over from Arizona, actually. You'll understand that we've had to scan it before we could let it into the building."
He passed it over to Jake.

"I think you should open it when you are with the others back at your offices, but don't worry, I promise it is nothing unpleasant."

Back in London, Jake was back in one of the conference rooms in SI6.

"You'll be pleased to know you are free to go now," said Amanda. 'They have rounded up the miscreants and accounted for the missing UAVs. Unfortunately, the plans for the design was also destroyed in the fireball in the desert when the American planes bombed the terrorist camp.

"I saw something about the old board members not being seen since their last board meeting," said Jake.

"Free to Go."

"…And safe?"

"…And very safe. Good luck to you and the others."

Outside. Jake could taste the November air. Sharp and cold.

"Free to go?" he asked.

They shook hands, Jake picked up the small parcel.

"It's not the rolling credits music, is it?" he quipped.

"Here, let me show you out," said Amanda, as if they were in her home rather than a top-security establishment.

The Circle

The leaves had fallen, yet it was a blue-sky day. He'd walk across Vauxhall Bridge and maybe stroll back towards Parliament before deciding how to get back to Hoxton.

Clare and Bigsy would be back the next morning, when they would open the parcel from Arizona.

Ed Adams

1000

9 781838 014605